INK GIRLS

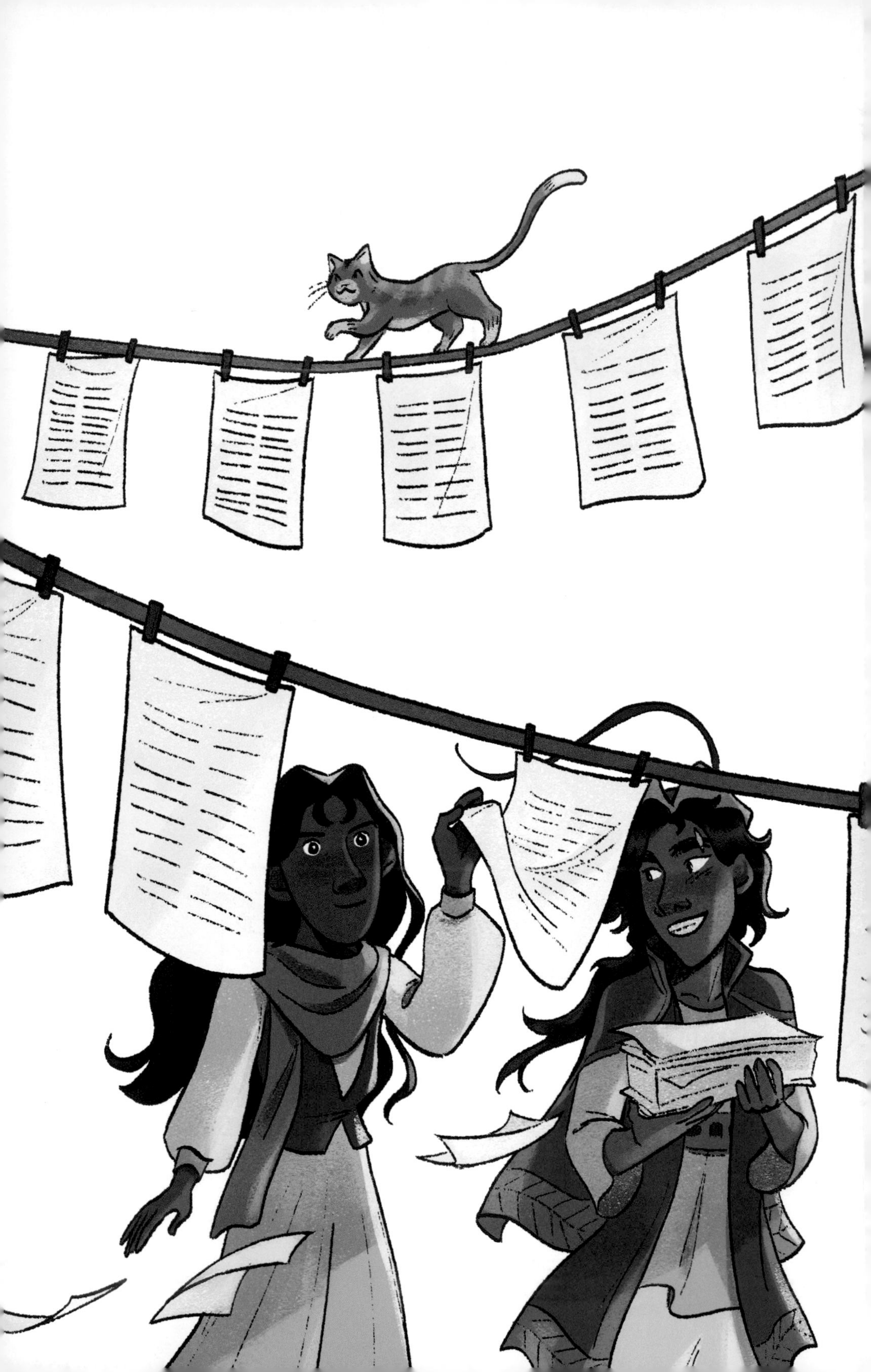

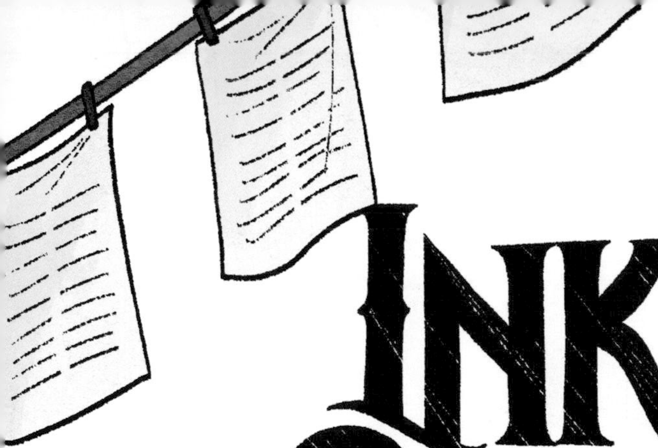

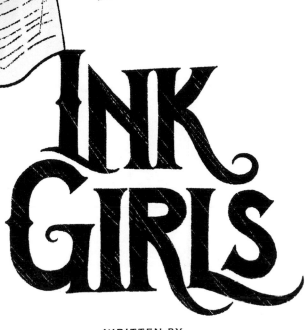

INK GIRLS

WRITTEN BY
MARIEKE NIJKAMP

ILLUSTRATED BY
SYLVIA BI

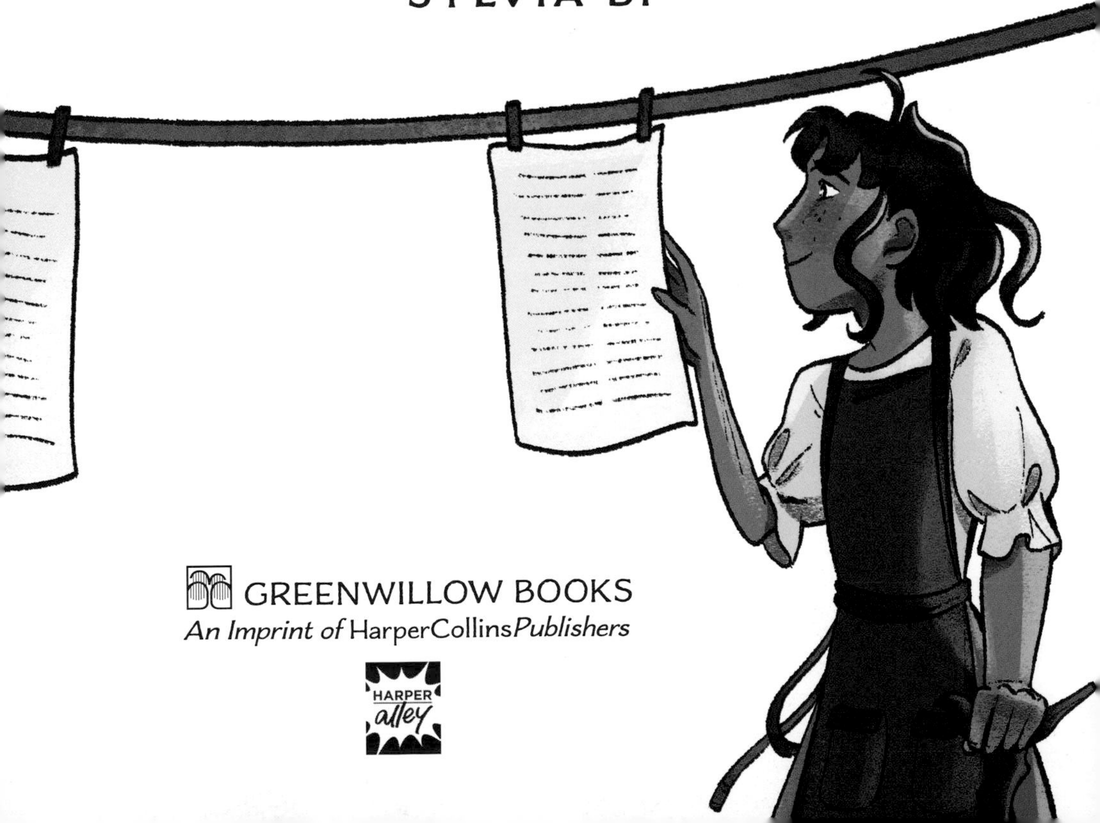

GREENWILLOW BOOKS
An Imprint of HarperCollins*Publishers*

HARPER alley

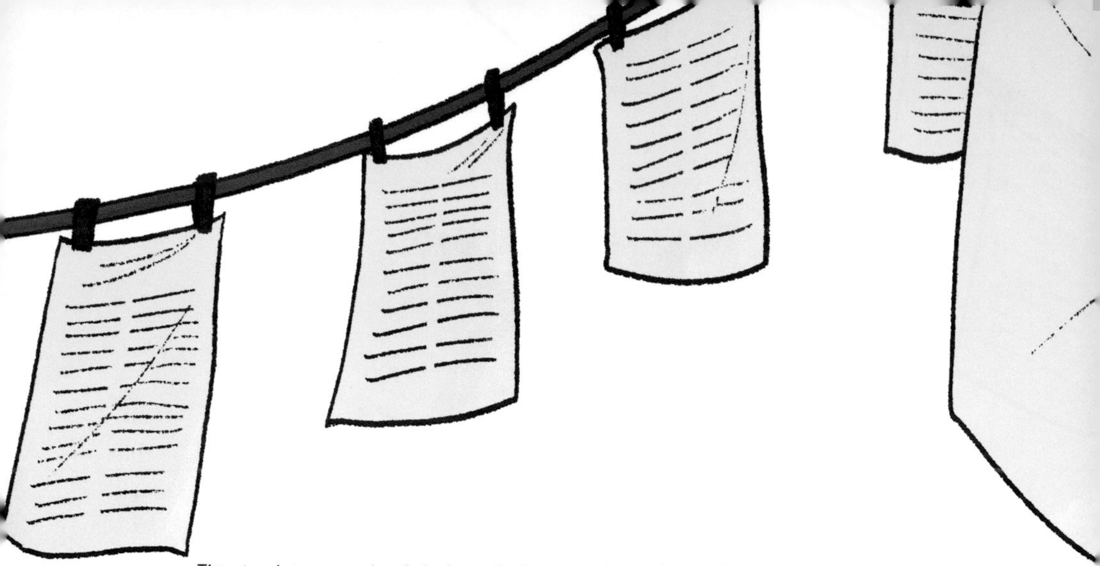

This book is a work of fiction. References to real people, events, establishments, organizations, or locales are intended only to provide a sense of authenticity, and are used to advance the fictional narrative. All other characters, and all incidents and dialogue, are drawn from the author's imagination and are not to be construed as real.

 Manufactured in Bosnia and Herzegovina. For information address HarperCollins Children's Books, a division of HarperCollins Publishers, 195 Broadway, New York, NY 10007.
www.harperalley.com

The text of this book is set in SS Pretzel. Book design by Sylvie Le Floc'h
Additional color assistance by Knack Whittle

Library of Congress Cataloging-in-Publication Data

Names: Nijkamp, Marieke, author. | Bi, Sylvia, illustrator.
Title: Ink girls / written by Marieke Nijkamp ; illustrated by Sylvia Bi.
Description: First edition. | New York : Greenwillow Books, [2023] | Audience: Ages 8-12 | Audience: Grades 4-6 | Summary: "In a vibrant city that thrives on trade and invention, two girls from very different walks of life join forces to fight censorship and protect the people they love"— Provided by publisher.
Identifiers: LCCN 2023011232 (print) | LCCN 2023011233 (ebook) | ISBN 9780063027114 (hardcover) | ISBN 9780063027107 (paperback) | ISBN 9780063027121 (ebook)
Subjects: CYAC: Graphic novels. I Friendship—Fiction. | Censorship—Fiction. | LCGFT: Social issue comics. | Graphic novels.
Classification: LCC PZ7.7.N54 In 2023 (print) | LCC PZ7.7.N54 (ebook) | DDC 741.5/973—dc23/eng/20230417
LC record available at https://lccn.loc.gov/2023011232
LC ebook record available at https://lccn.loc.gov/2023011233

23 24 25 26 27 GPS 10 9 8 7 6 5 4 3 2 1
First Edition

GREENWILLOW BOOKS
An Imprint of HarperCollins*Publishers*

HARPER alley

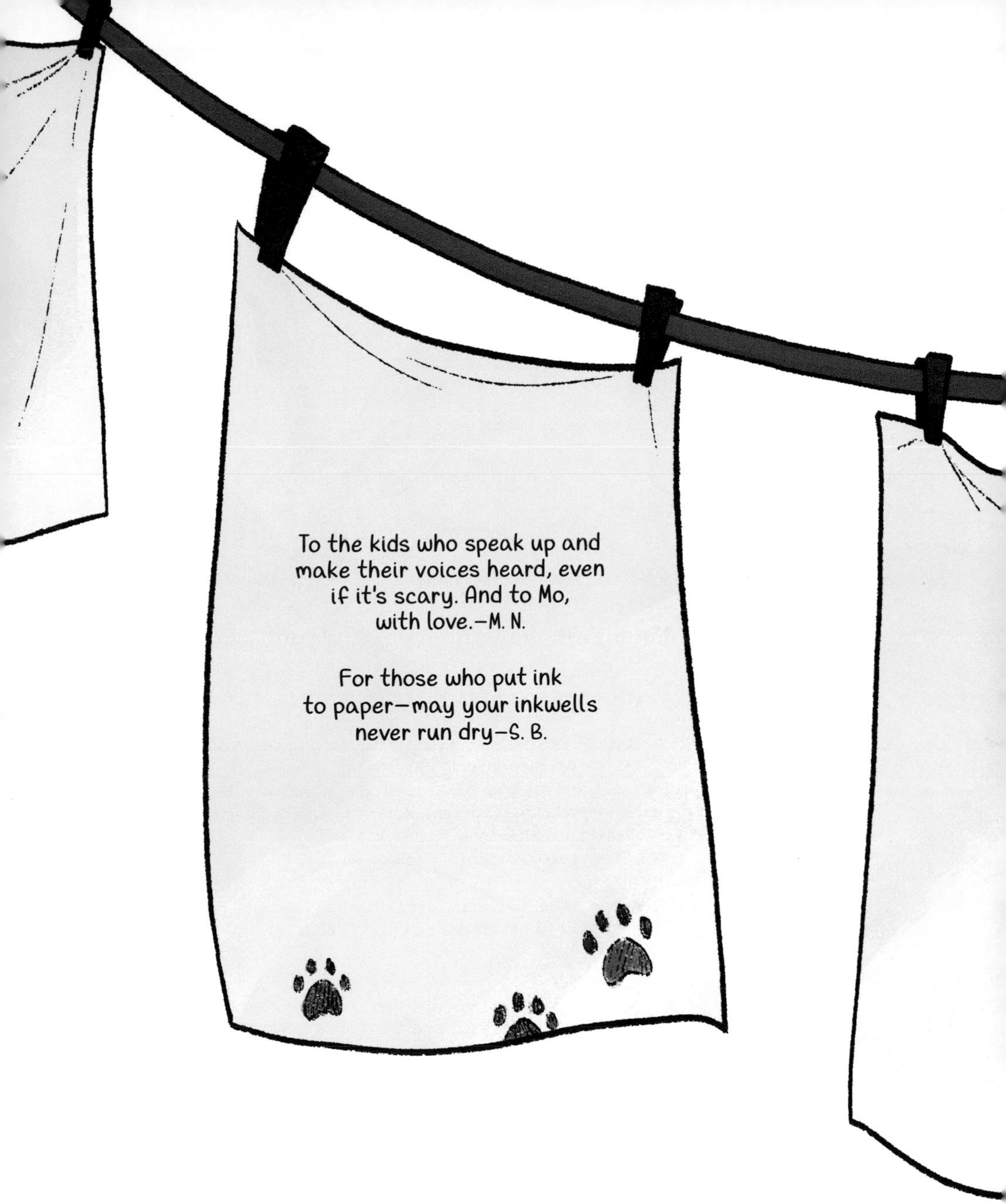

To the kids who speak up and make their voices heard, even if it's scary. And to Mo, with love.—M. N.

For those who put ink to paper—may your inkwells never run dry—S. B.

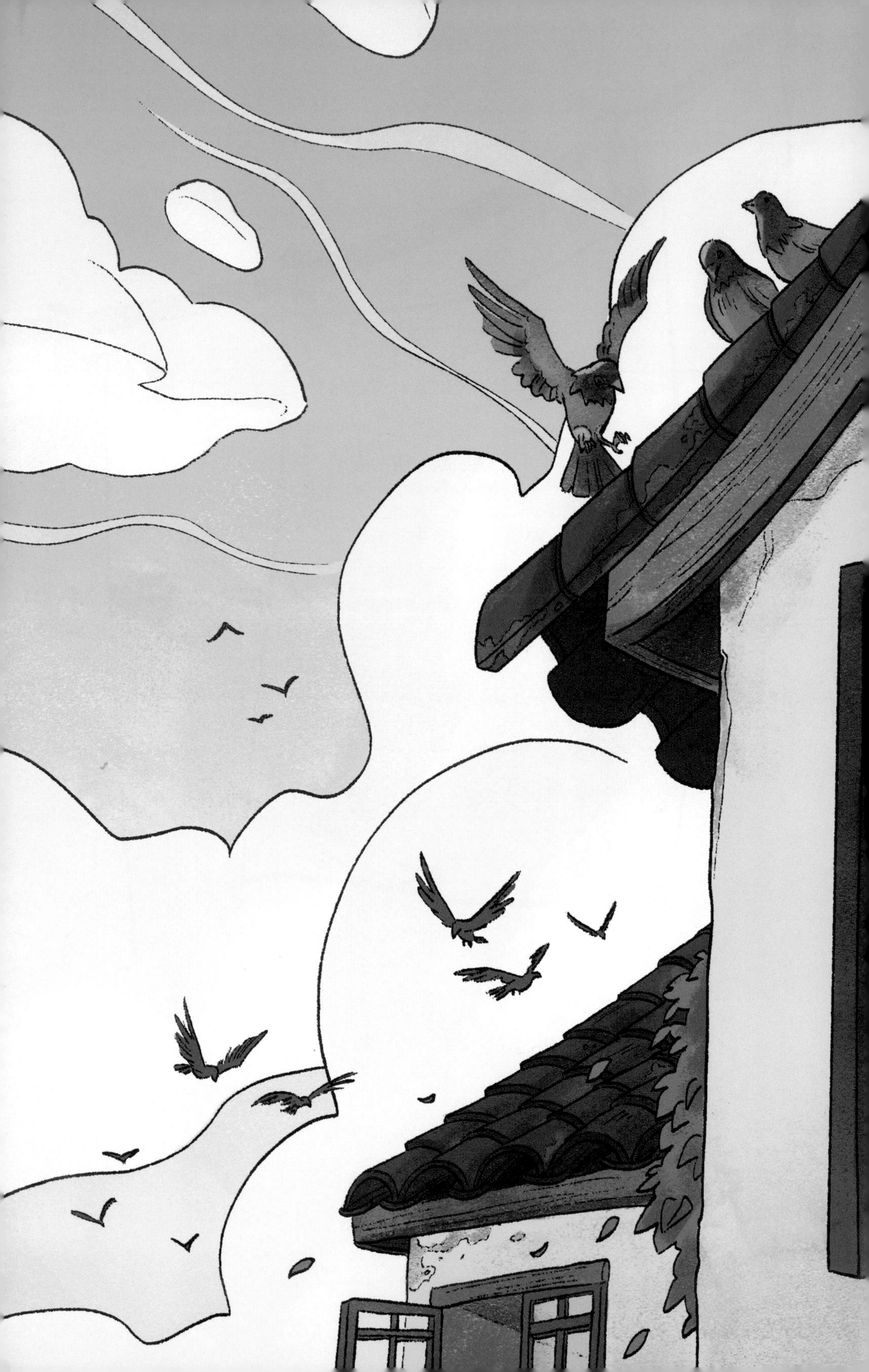

CHAPTER ONE

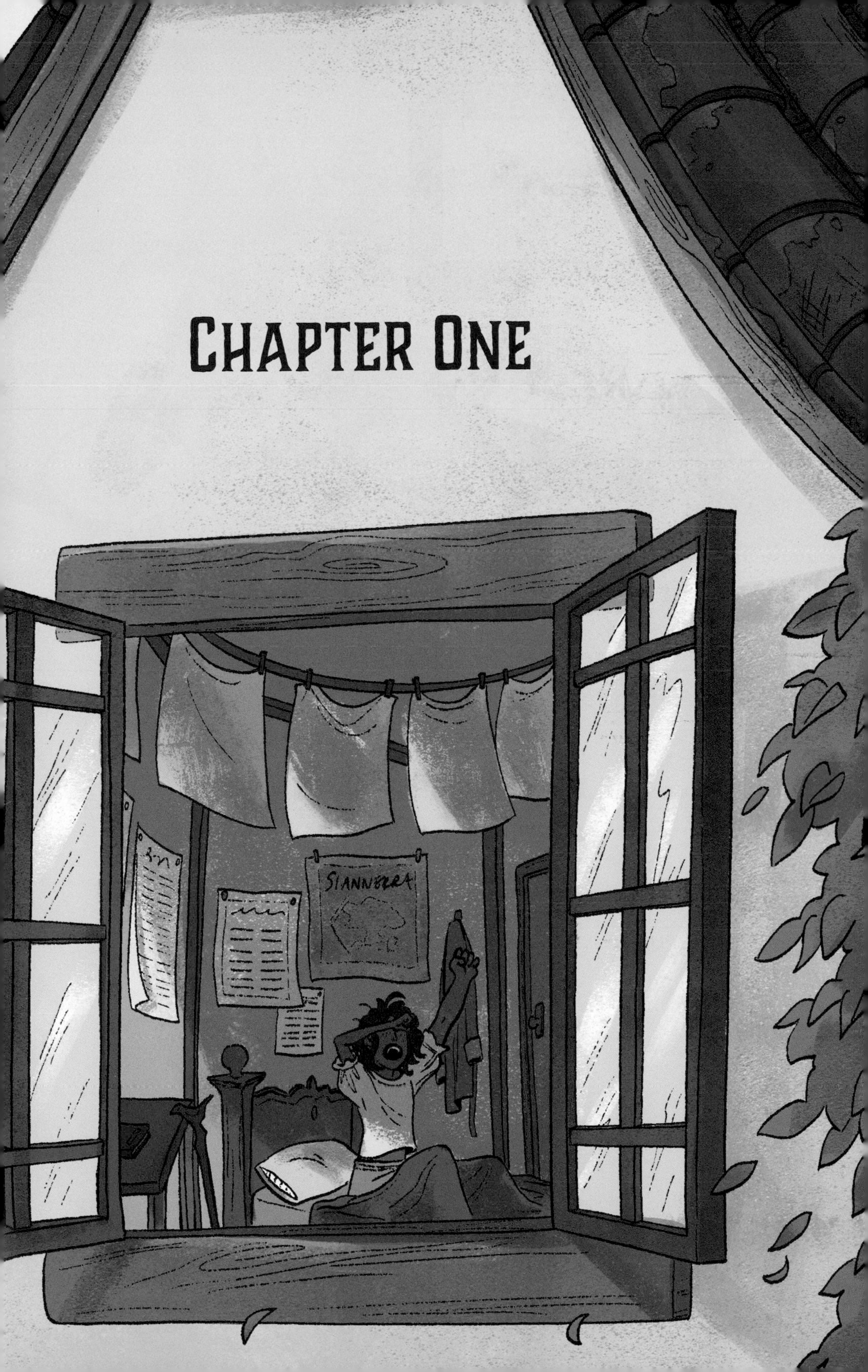
SIANNERRA

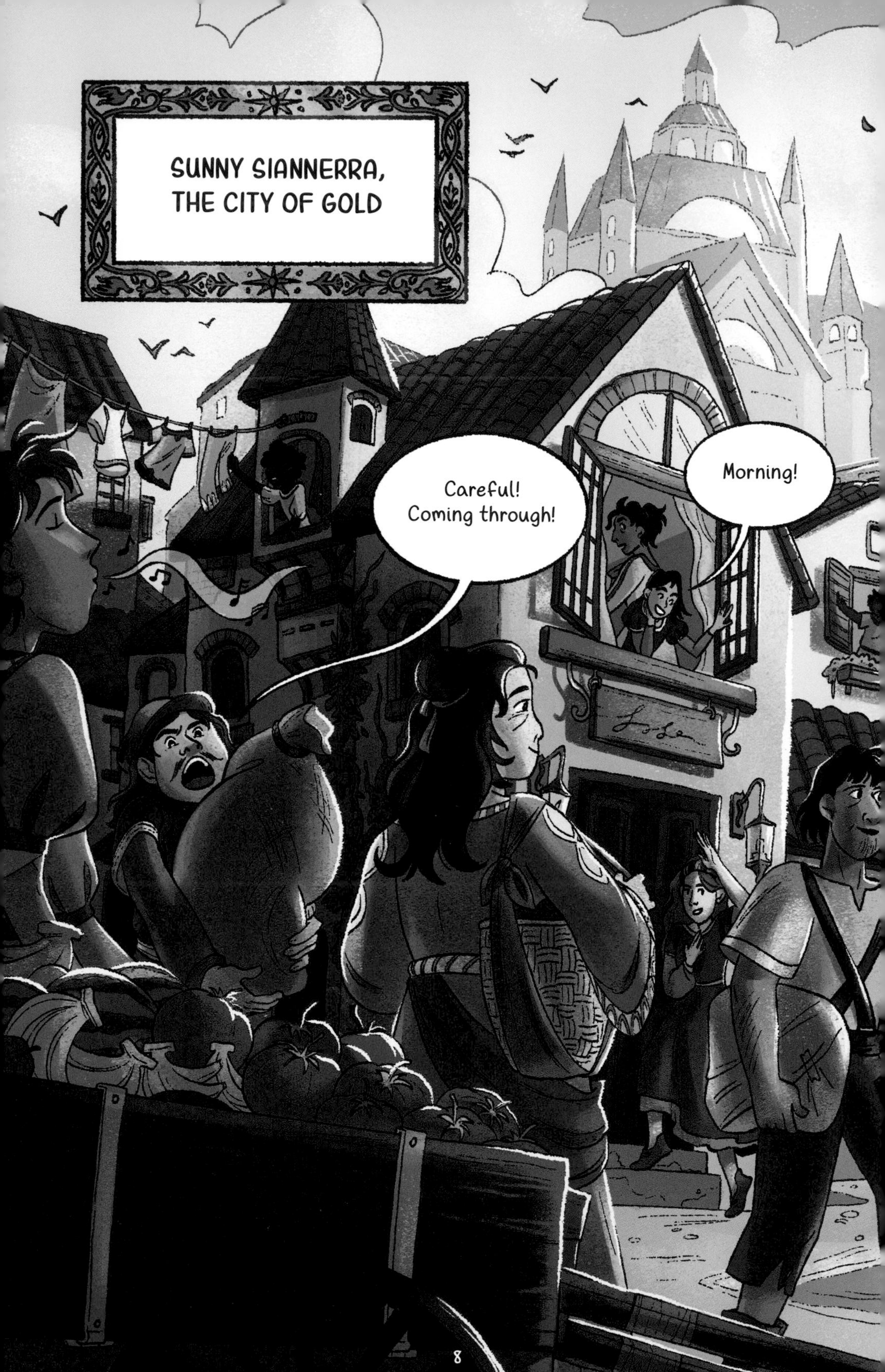
SUNNY SIANNERRA, THE CITY OF GOLD
Careful! Coming through!
Morning!

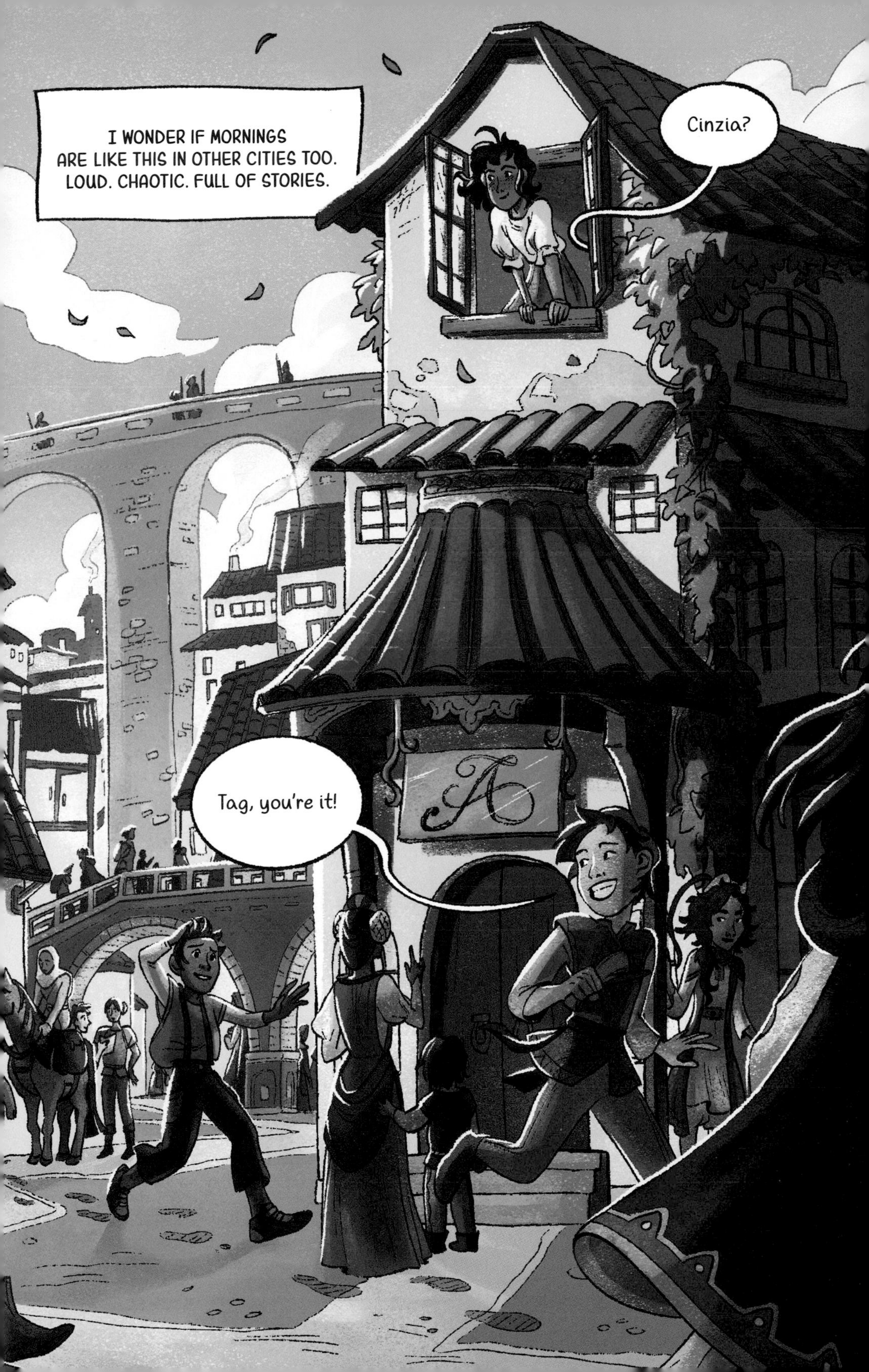
I WONDER IF MORNINGS ARE LIKE THIS IN OTHER CITIES TOO. LOUD. CHAOTIC. FULL OF STORIES.
Cinzia?
Tag, you're it!

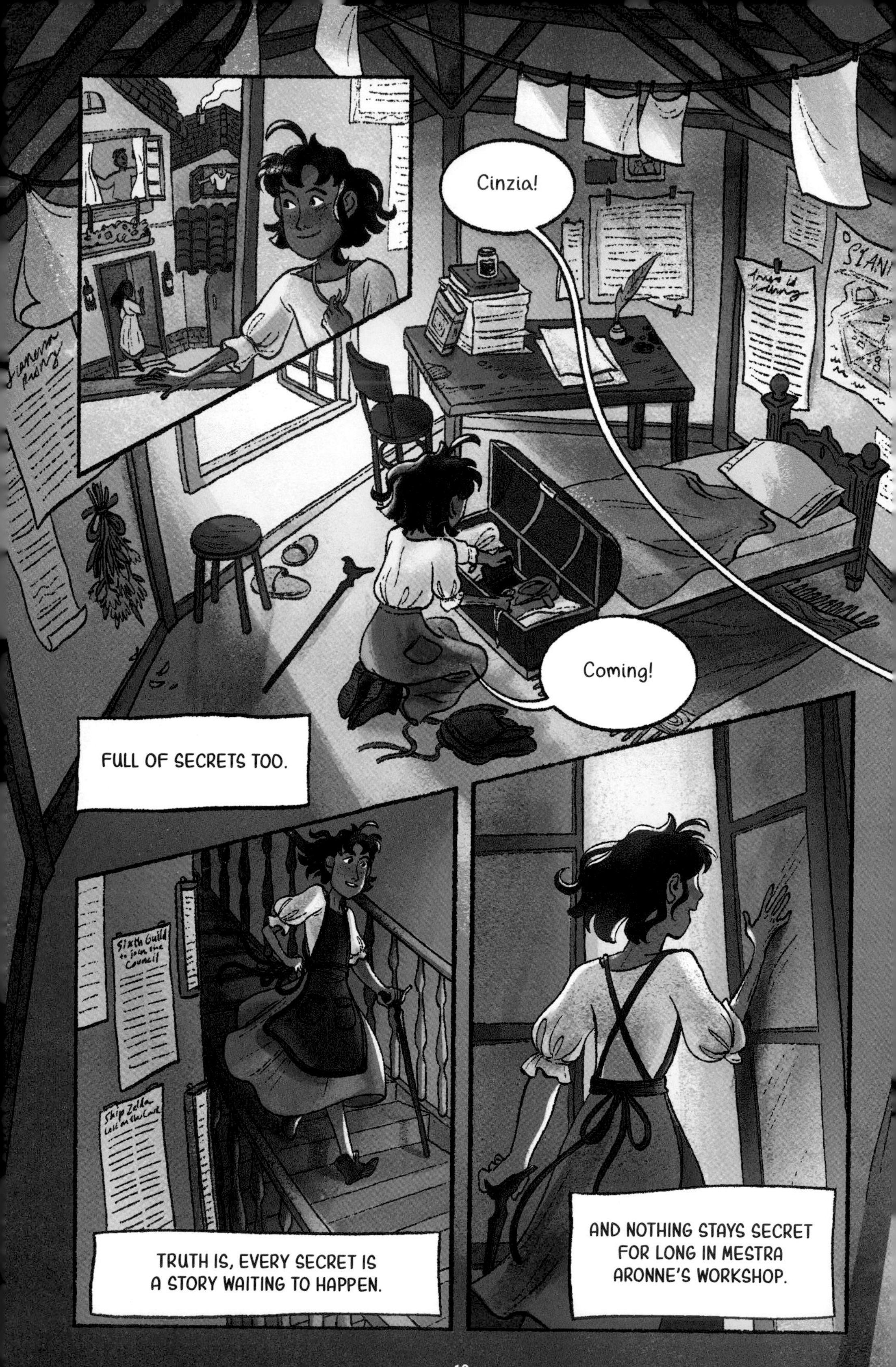
Cinzia!
Coming!
FULL OF SECRETS TOO.
Sixth Guild to join the Council
TRUTH IS, EVERY SECRET IS A STORY WAITING TO HAPPEN.
AND NOTHING STAYS SECRET FOR LONG IN MESTRA ARONNE'S WORKSHOP.

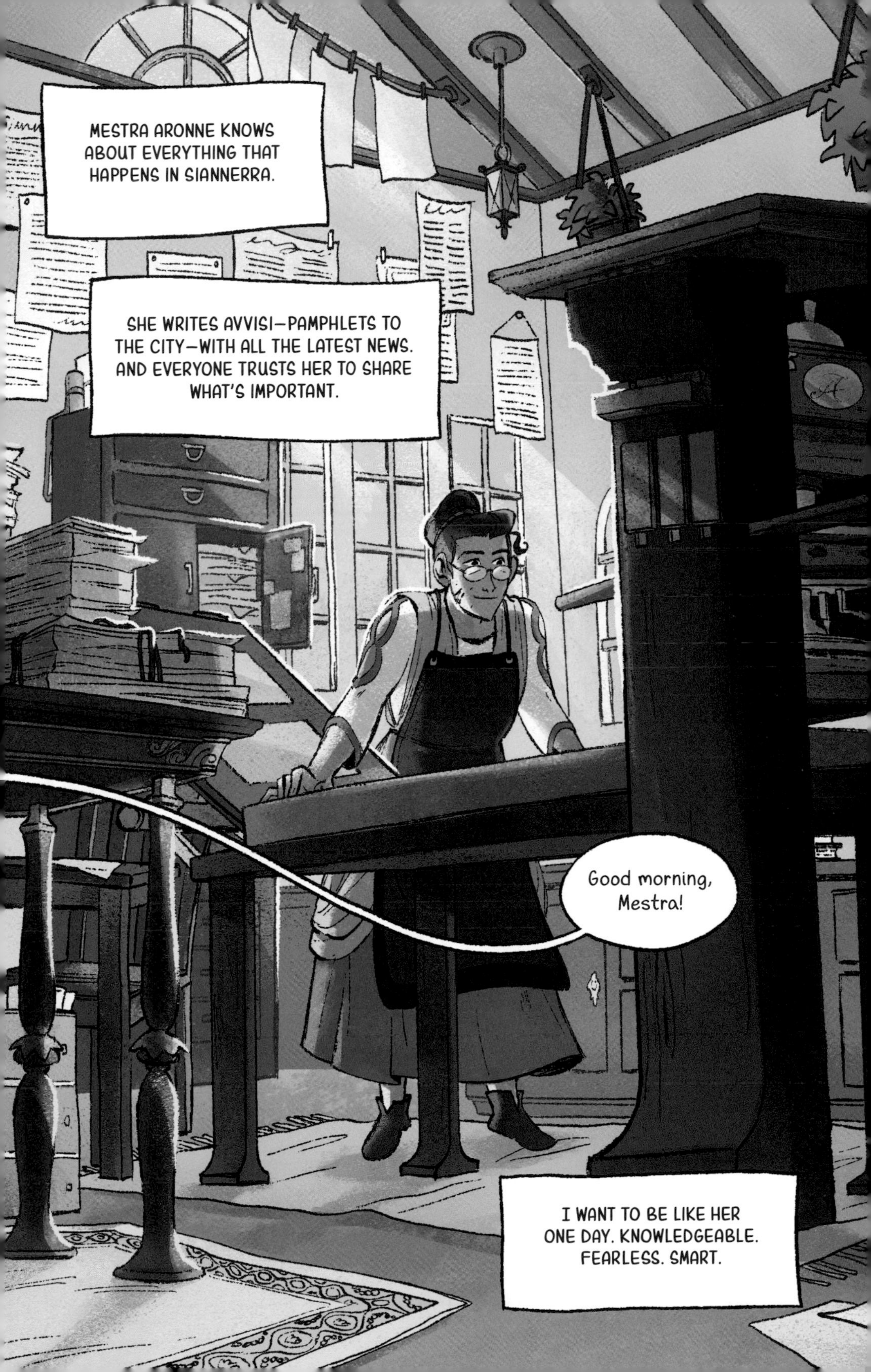
MESTRA ARONNE KNOWS ABOUT EVERYTHING THAT HAPPENS IN SIANNERRA.
SHE WRITES AVVISI—PAMPHLETS TO THE CITY—WITH ALL THE LATEST NEWS. AND EVERYONE TRUSTS HER TO SHARE WHAT'S IMPORTANT.
Good morning, Mestra!
I WANT TO BE LIKE HER ONE DAY. KNOWLEDGEABLE. FEARLESS. SMART.

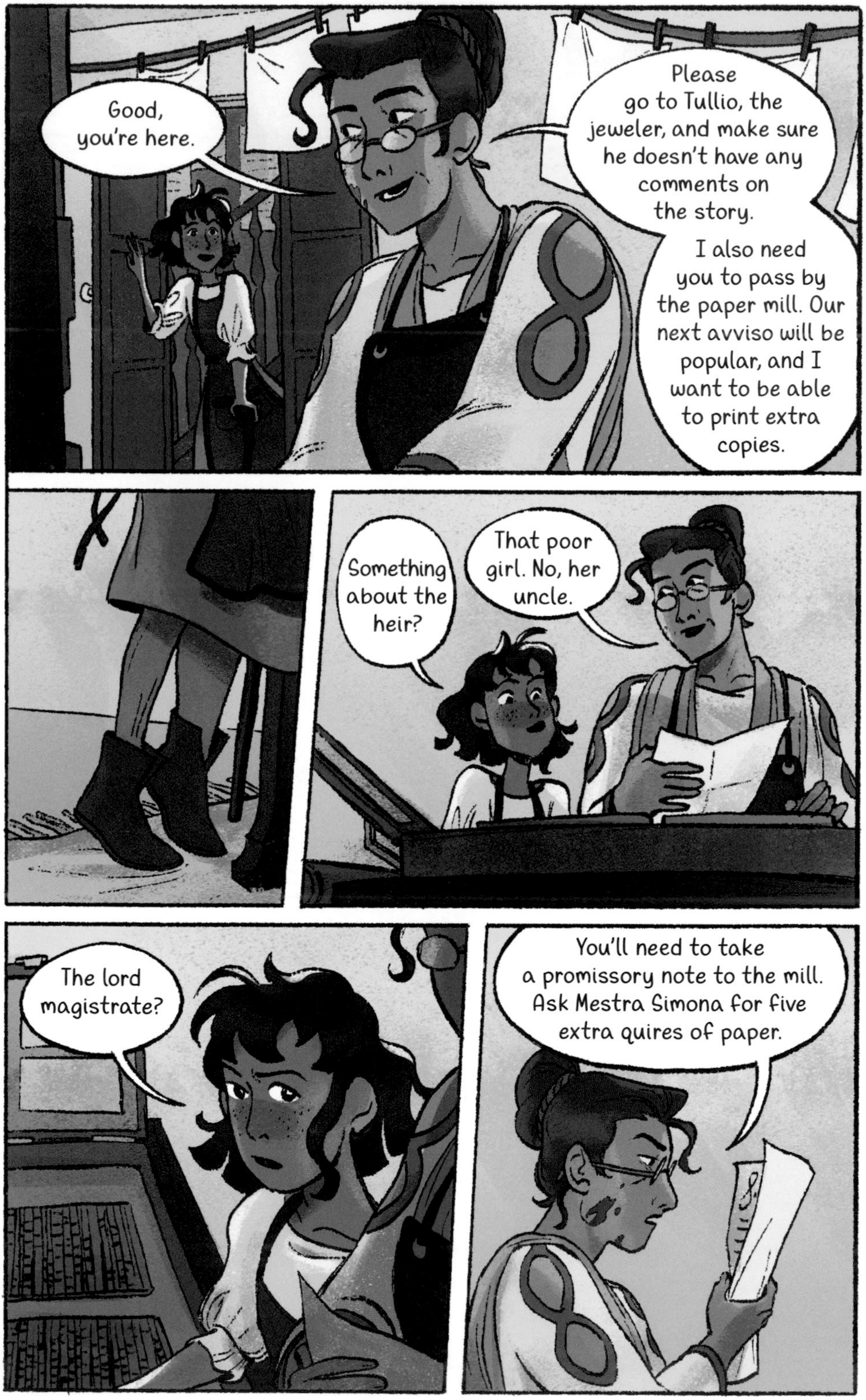
Good, you're here.
Please go to Tullio, the jeweler, and make sure he doesn't have any comments on the story.
I also need you to pass by the paper mill. Our next avviso will be popular, and I want to be able to print extra copies.
Something about the heir?
That poor girl. No, her uncle.
The lord magistrate?
You'll need to take a promissory note to the mill. Ask Mestra Simona for five extra quires of paper.

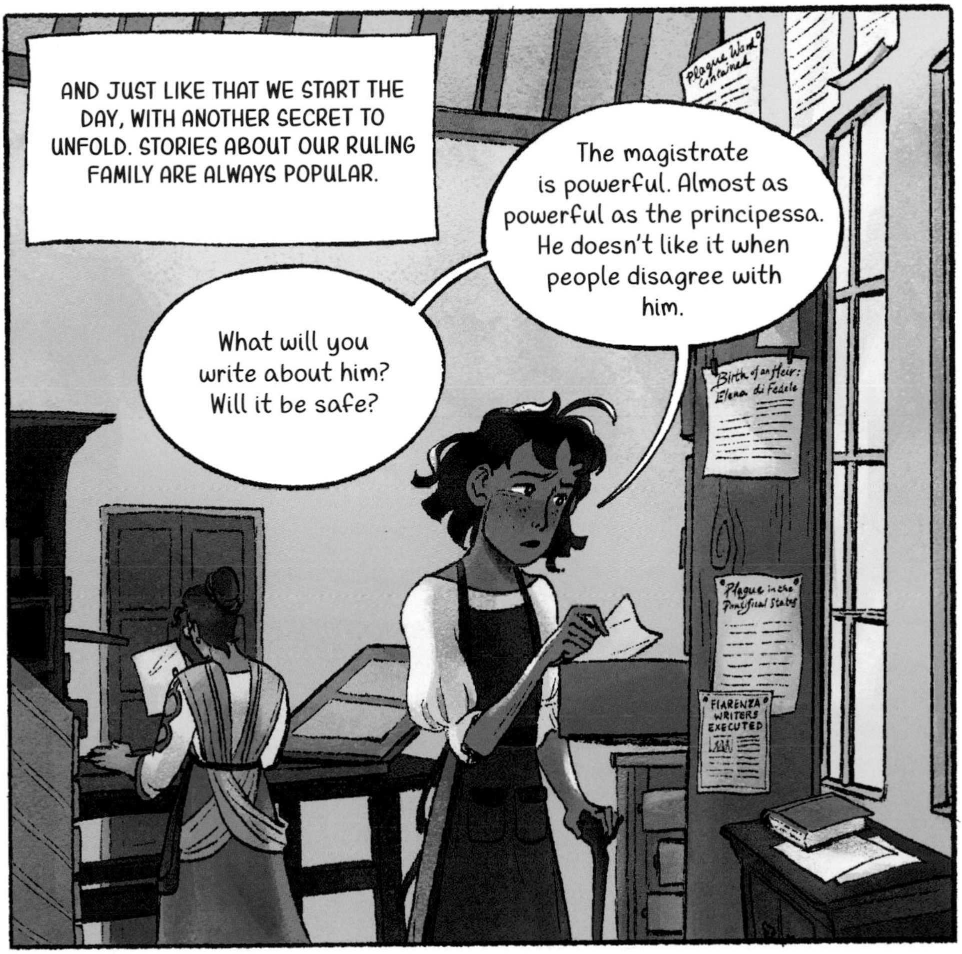
AND JUST LIKE THAT WE START THE DAY, WITH ANOTHER SECRET TO UNFOLD. STORIES ABOUT OUR RULING FAMILY ARE ALWAYS POPULAR.
The magistrate is powerful. Almost as powerful as the principessa. He doesn't like it when people disagree with him.
What will you write about him? Will it be safe?
Plague Ward Contained
Birth of an Heir: Elena di Fedele
Plague in the Pontifical States
FIARENZA WRITERS EXECUTED

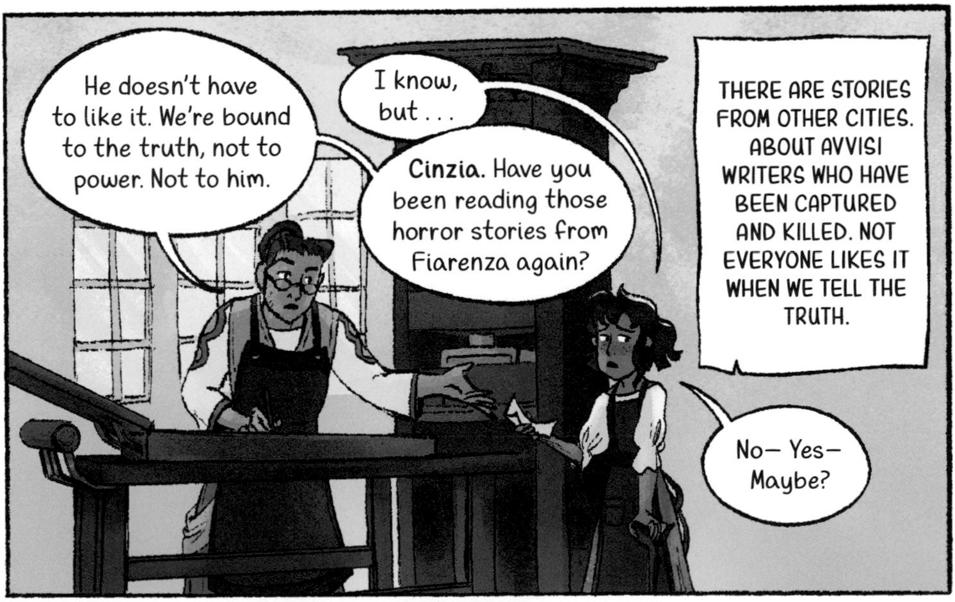
He doesn't have to like it. We're bound to the truth, not to power. Not to him.
I know, but . . .
Cinzia. Have you been reading those horror stories from Fiarenza again?
THERE ARE STORIES FROM OTHER CITIES. ABOUT AVVISI WRITERS WHO HAVE BEEN CAPTURED AND KILLED. NOT EVERYONE LIKES IT WHEN WE TELL THE TRUTH.
No— Yes— Maybe?

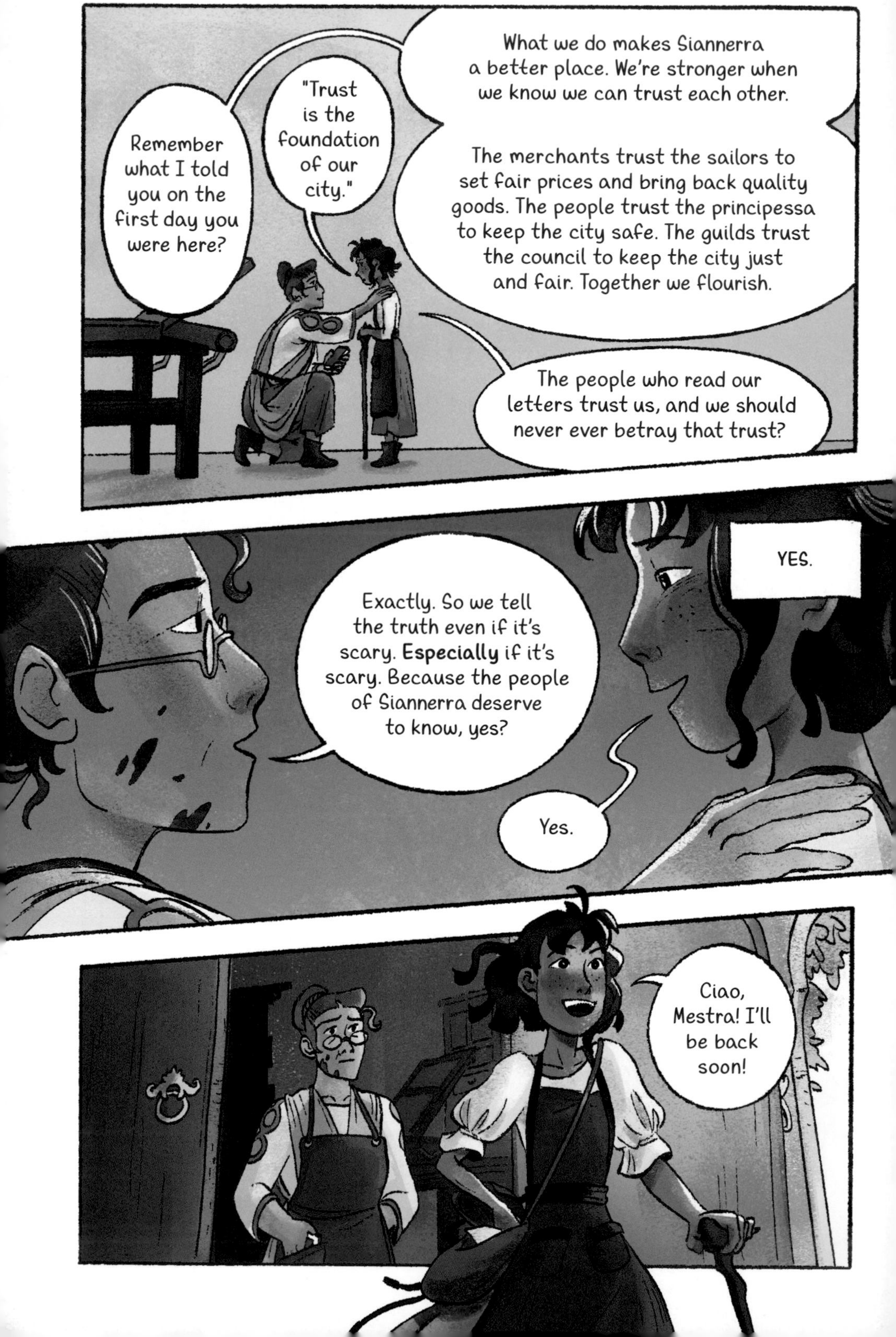
Remember what I told you on the first day you were here?
"Trust is the foundation of our city."
What we do makes Siannerra a better place. We're stronger when we know we can trust each other.
The merchants trust the sailors to set fair prices and bring back quality goods. The people trust the principessa to keep the city safe. The guilds trust the council to keep the city just and fair. Together we flourish.
The people who read our letters trust us, and we should never ever betray that trust?
YES.
Exactly. So we tell the truth even if it's scary. **Especially** if it's scary. Because the people of Siannerra deserve to know, yes?
Yes.
Ciao, Mestra! I'll be back soon!

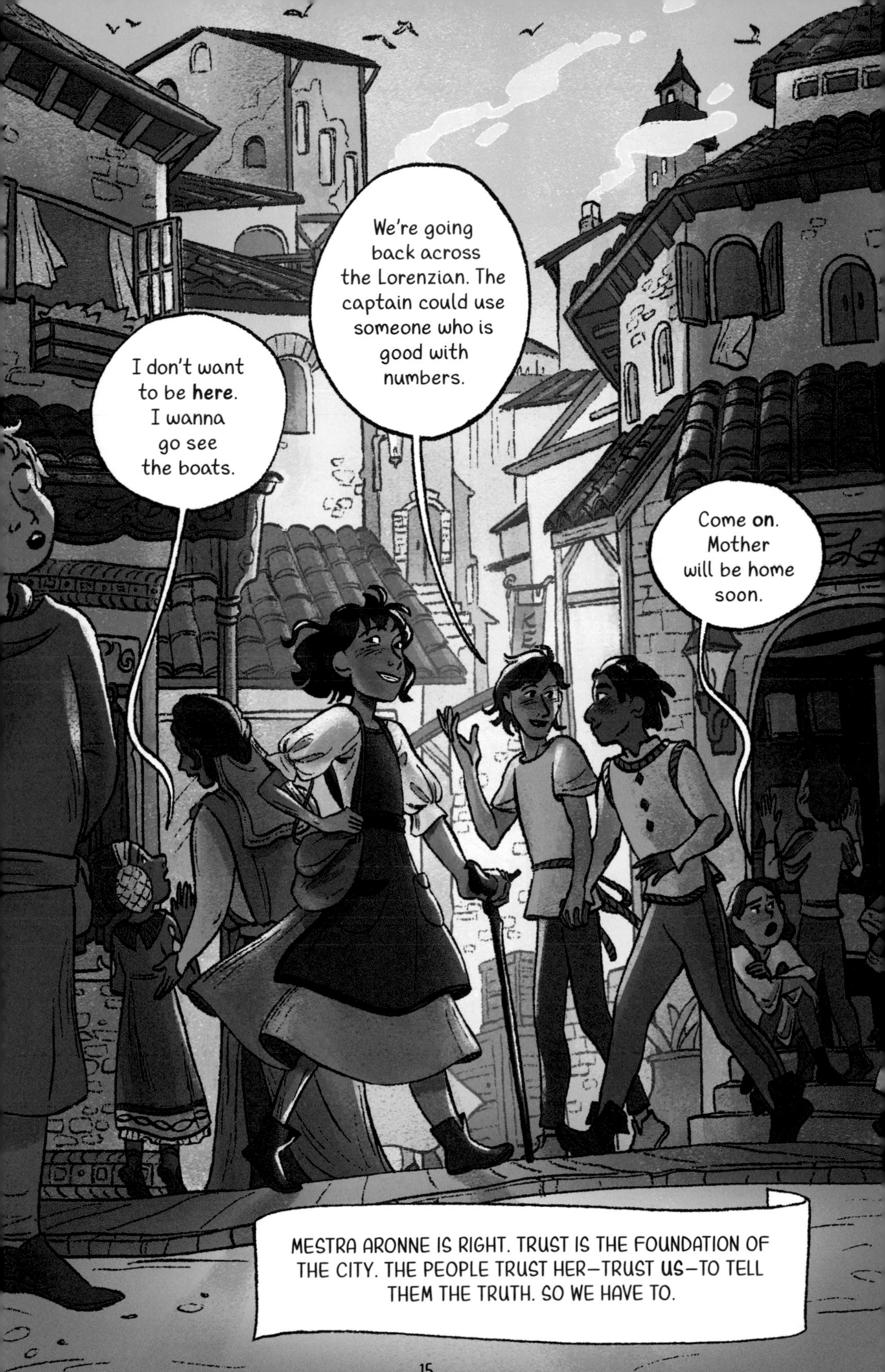

I don't want to be **here**. I wanna go see the boats.
We're going back across the Lorenzian. The captain could use someone who is good with numbers.
Come **on**. Mother will be home soon.
MESTRA ARONNE IS RIGHT. TRUST IS THE FOUNDATION OF THE CITY. THE PEOPLE TRUST HER—TRUST **US**—TO TELL THEM THE TRUTH. SO WE HAVE TO.

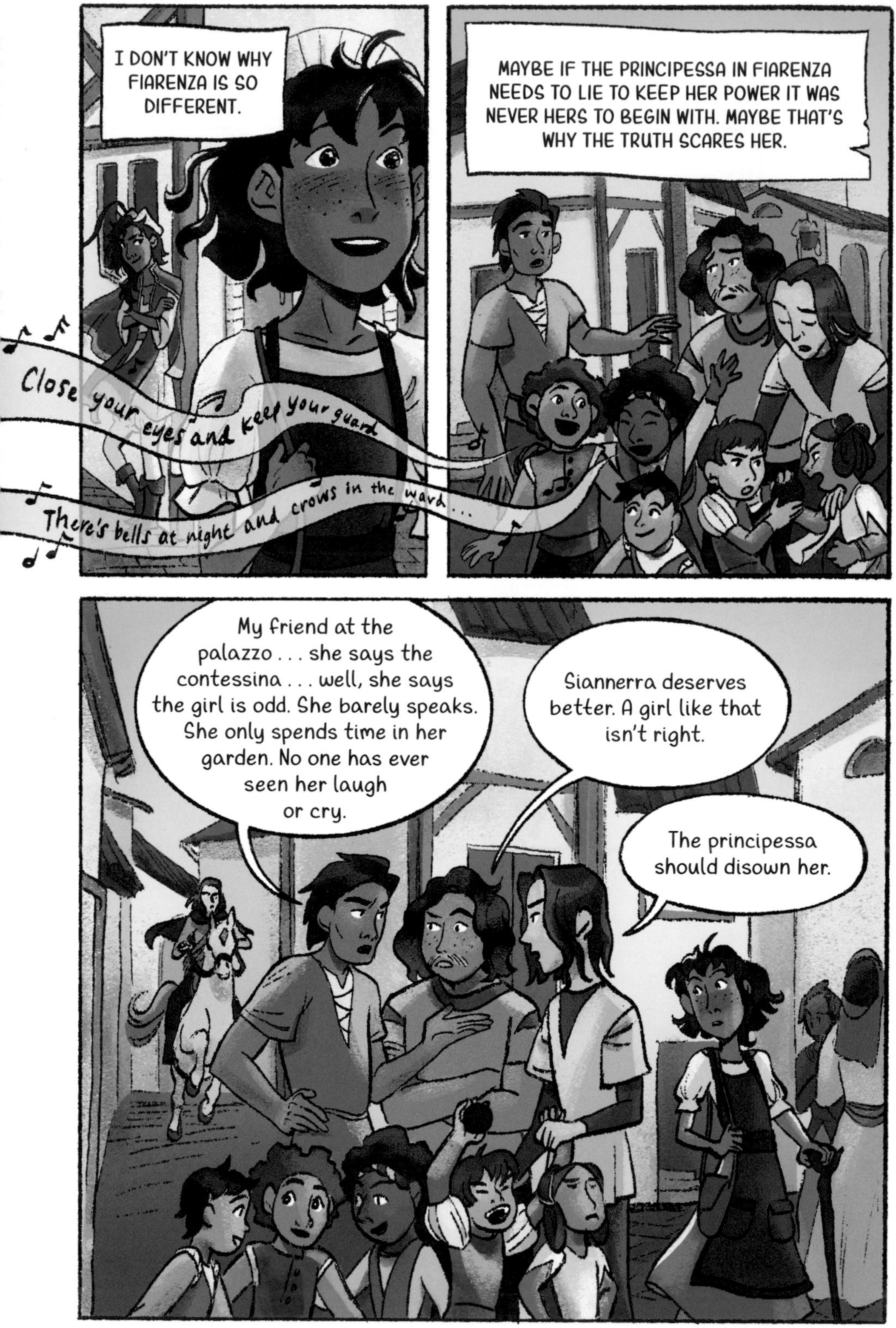
I DON'T KNOW WHY FIARENZA IS SO DIFFERENT.
Close your eyes and keep your guard
There's bells at night and crows in the ward...
MAYBE IF THE PRINCIPESSA IN FIARENZA NEEDS TO LIE TO KEEP HER POWER IT WAS NEVER HERS TO BEGIN WITH. MAYBE THAT'S WHY THE TRUTH SCARES HER.
My friend at the palazzo . . . she says the contessina . . . well, she says the girl is odd. She barely speaks. She only spends time in her garden. No one has ever seen her laugh or cry.
Siannerra deserves better. A girl like that isn't right.
The principessa should disown her.

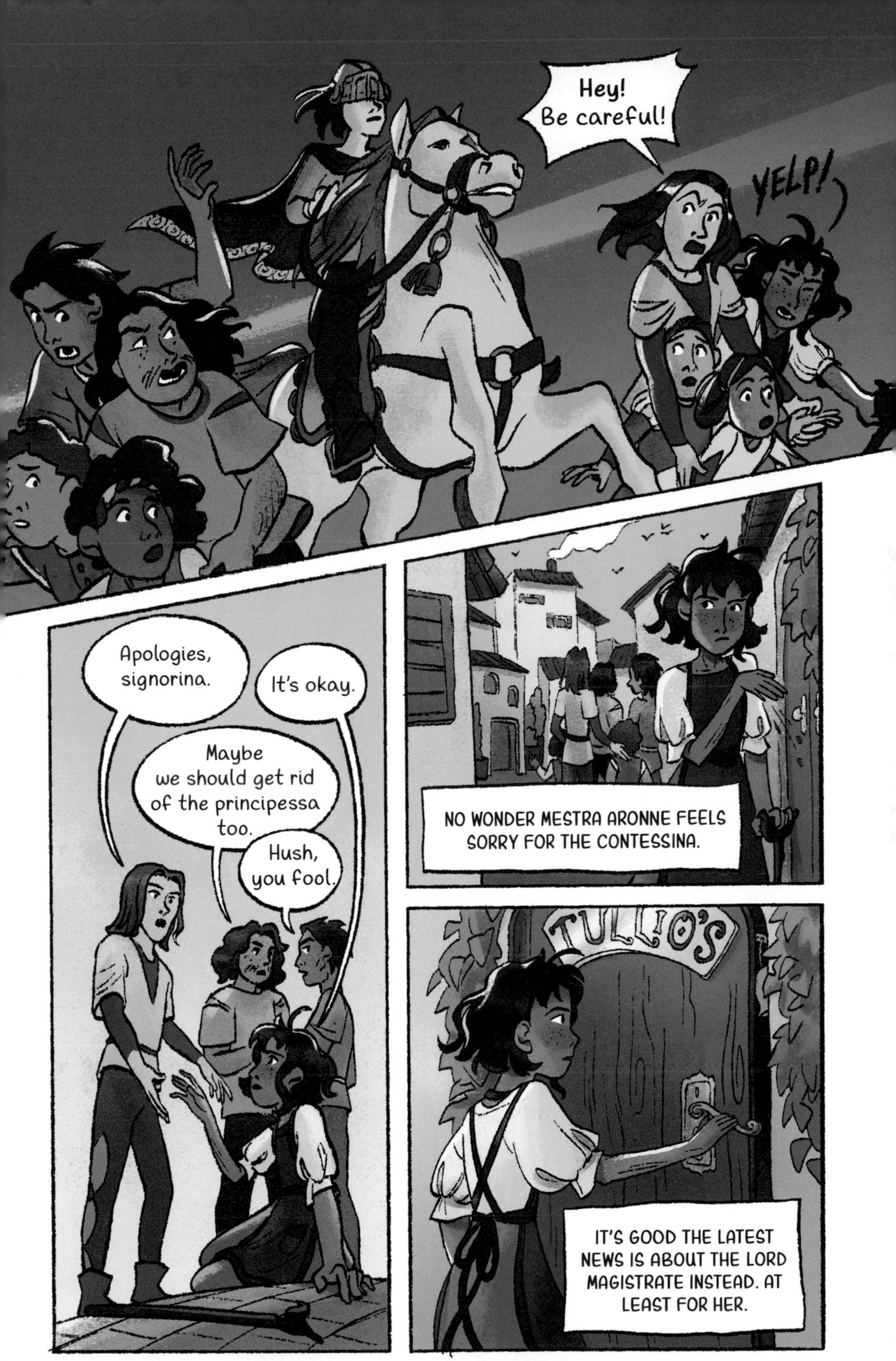
Hey!
Be careful!
YELP!
Apologies, signorina.
It's okay.
Maybe we should get rid of the principessa too.
Hush, you fool.
NO WONDER MESTRA ARONNE FEELS SORRY FOR THE CONTESSINA.
TULLIO'S
IT'S GOOD THE LATEST NEWS IS ABOUT THE LORD MAGISTRATE INSTEAD. AT LEAST FOR HER.

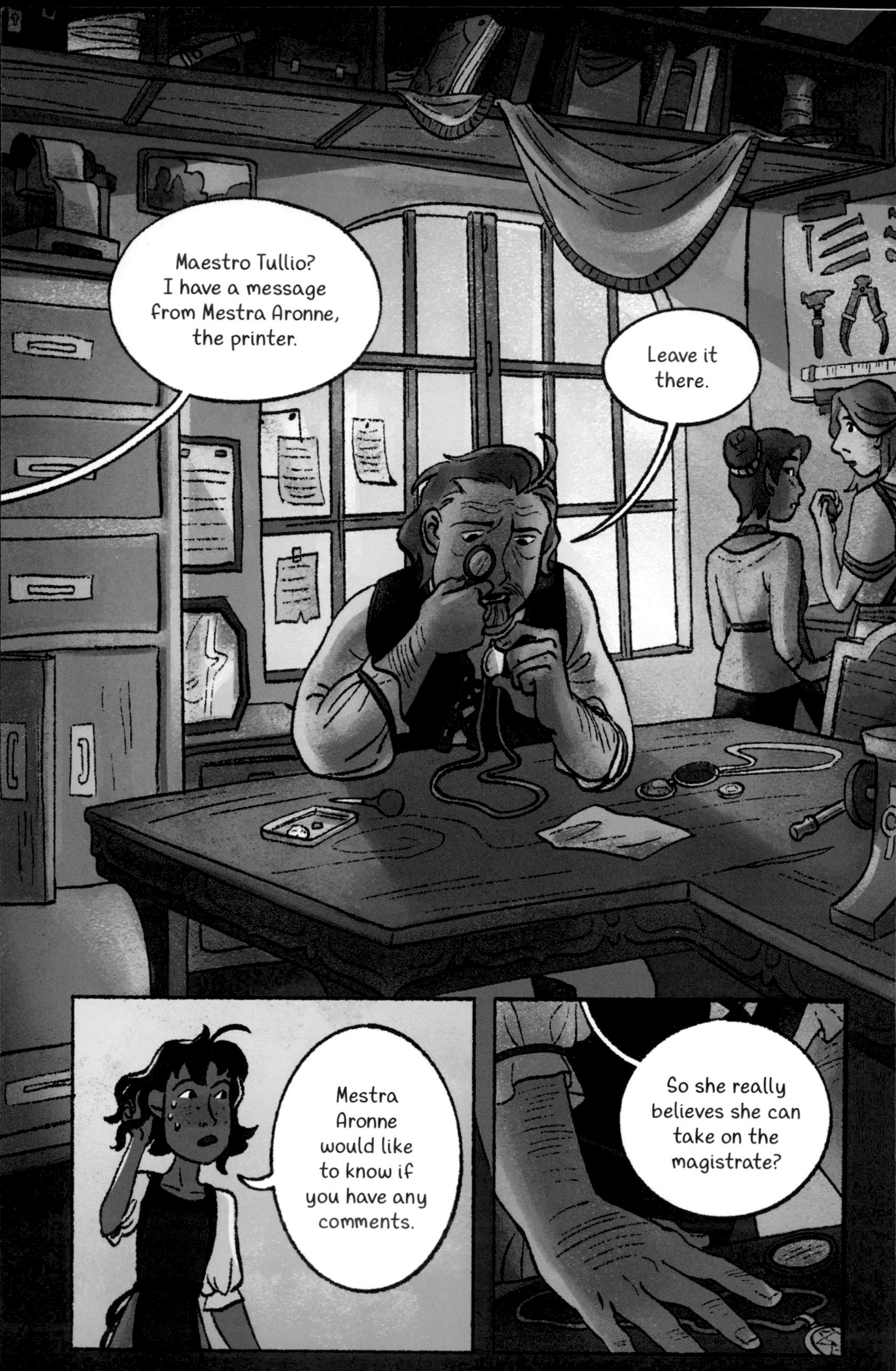
Maestro Tullio? I have a message from Mestra Aronne, the printer.
Leave it there.
Mestra Aronne would like to know if you have any comments.
So she really believes she can take on the magistrate?

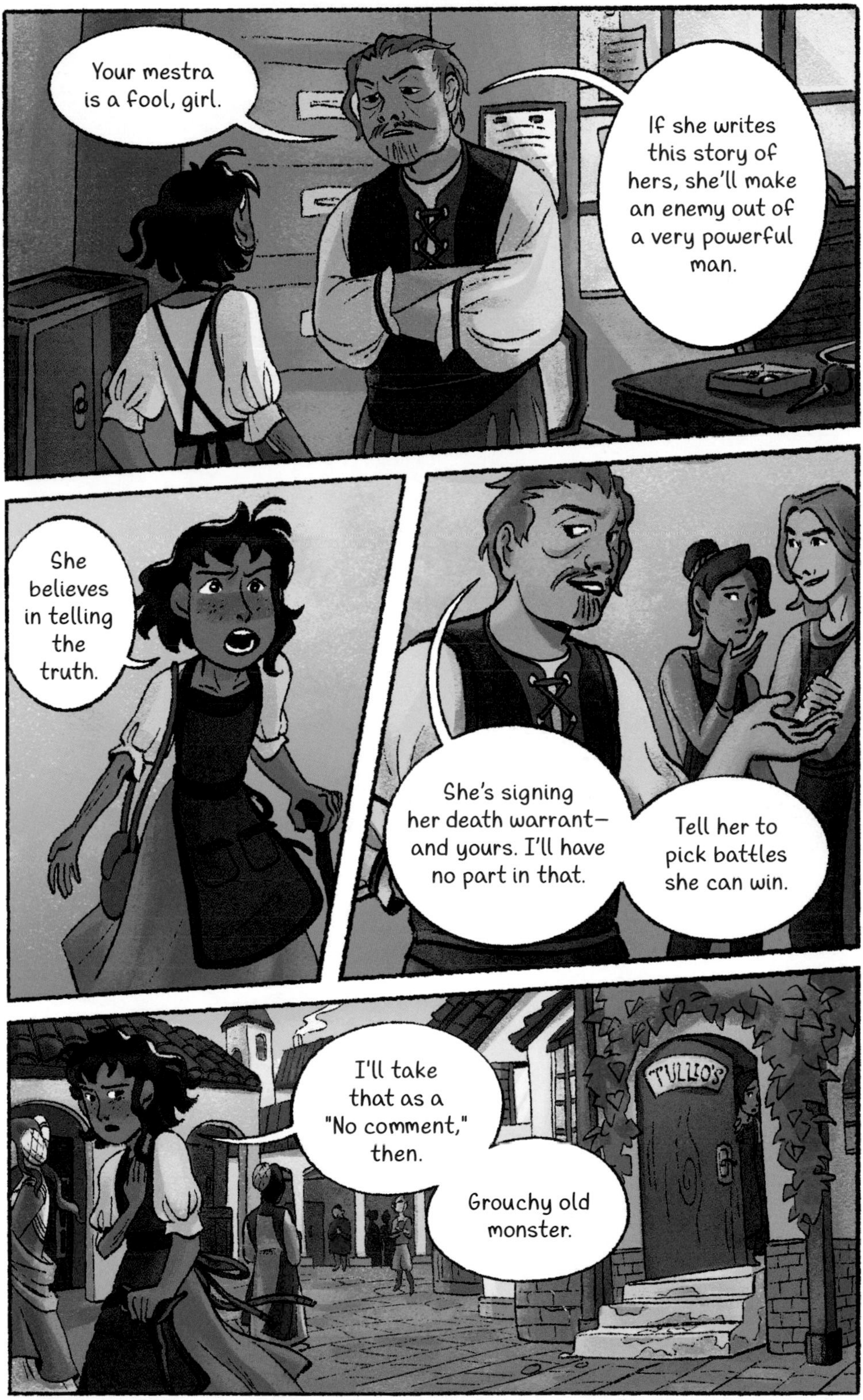
Your mestra is a fool, girl.
If she writes this story of hers, she'll make an enemy out of a very powerful man.
She believes in telling the truth.
She's signing her death warrant—and yours. I'll have no part in that.
Tell her to pick battles she can win.
TULLIO'S
I'll take that as a "No comment," then.
Grouchy old monster.

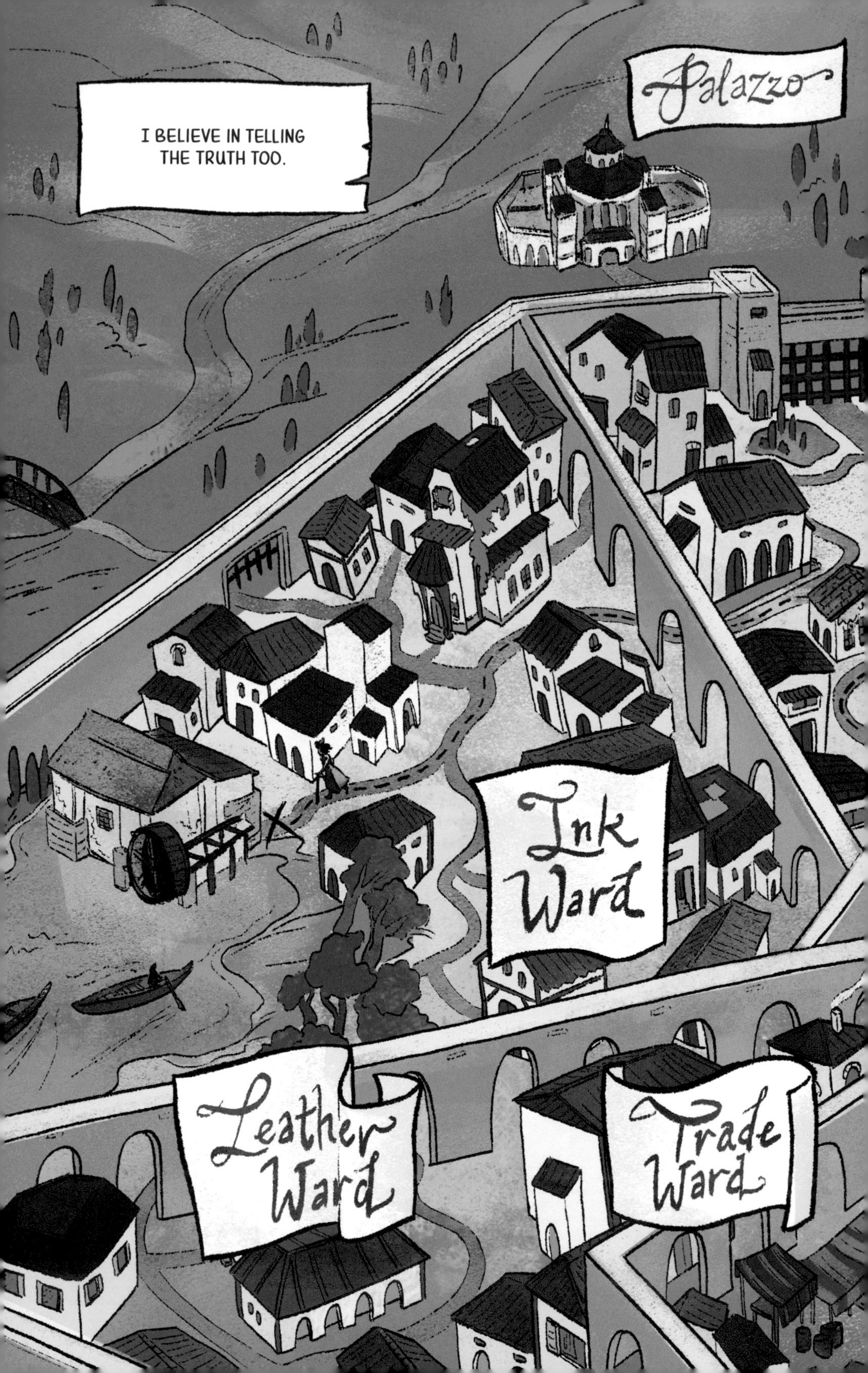
I BELIEVE IN TELLING THE TRUTH TOO.
Palazzo
Ink Ward
Leather Ward
Trade Ward

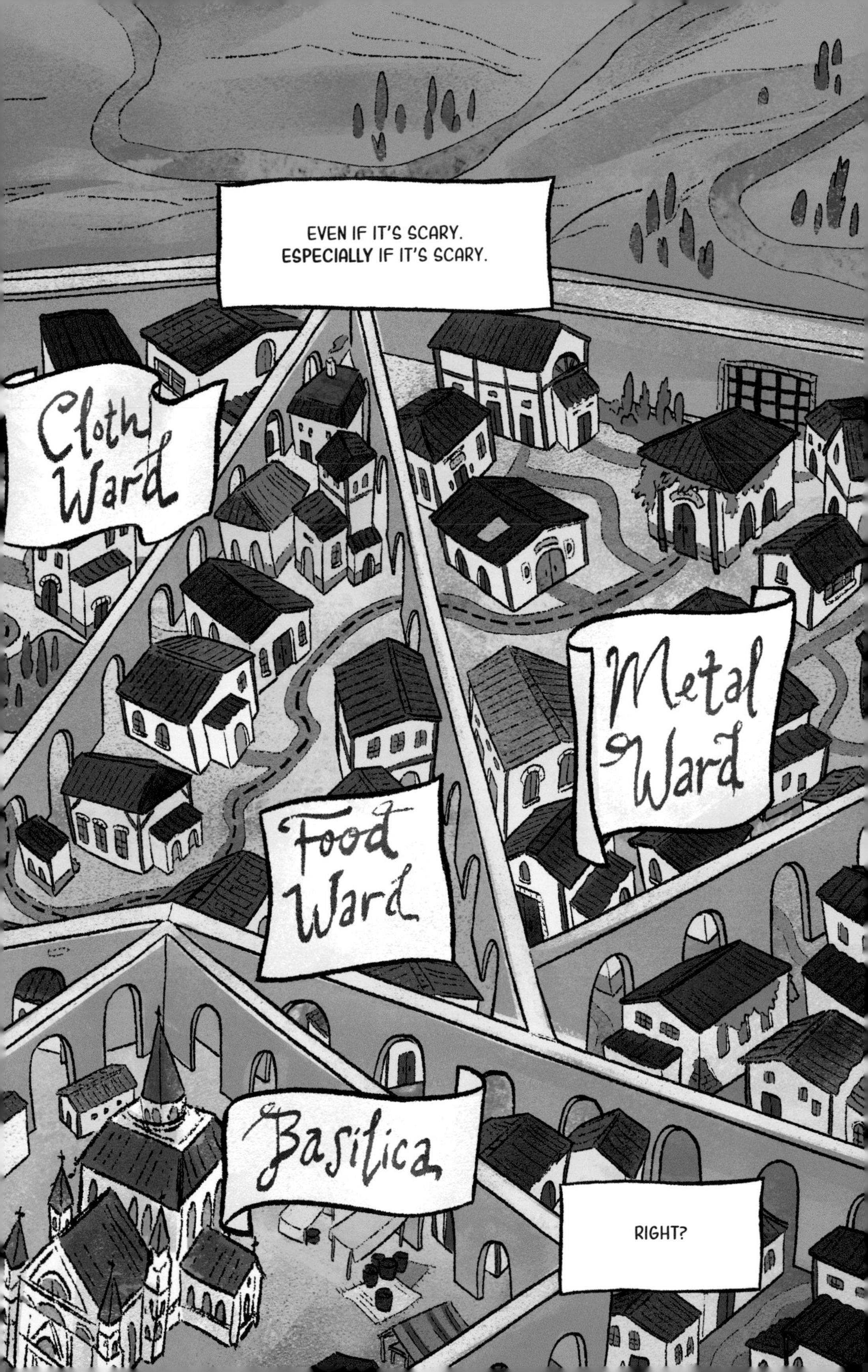
EVEN IF IT'S SCARY.
ESPECIALLY IF IT'S SCARY.
Cloth Ward
Metal Ward
Food Ward
Basilica
RIGHT?

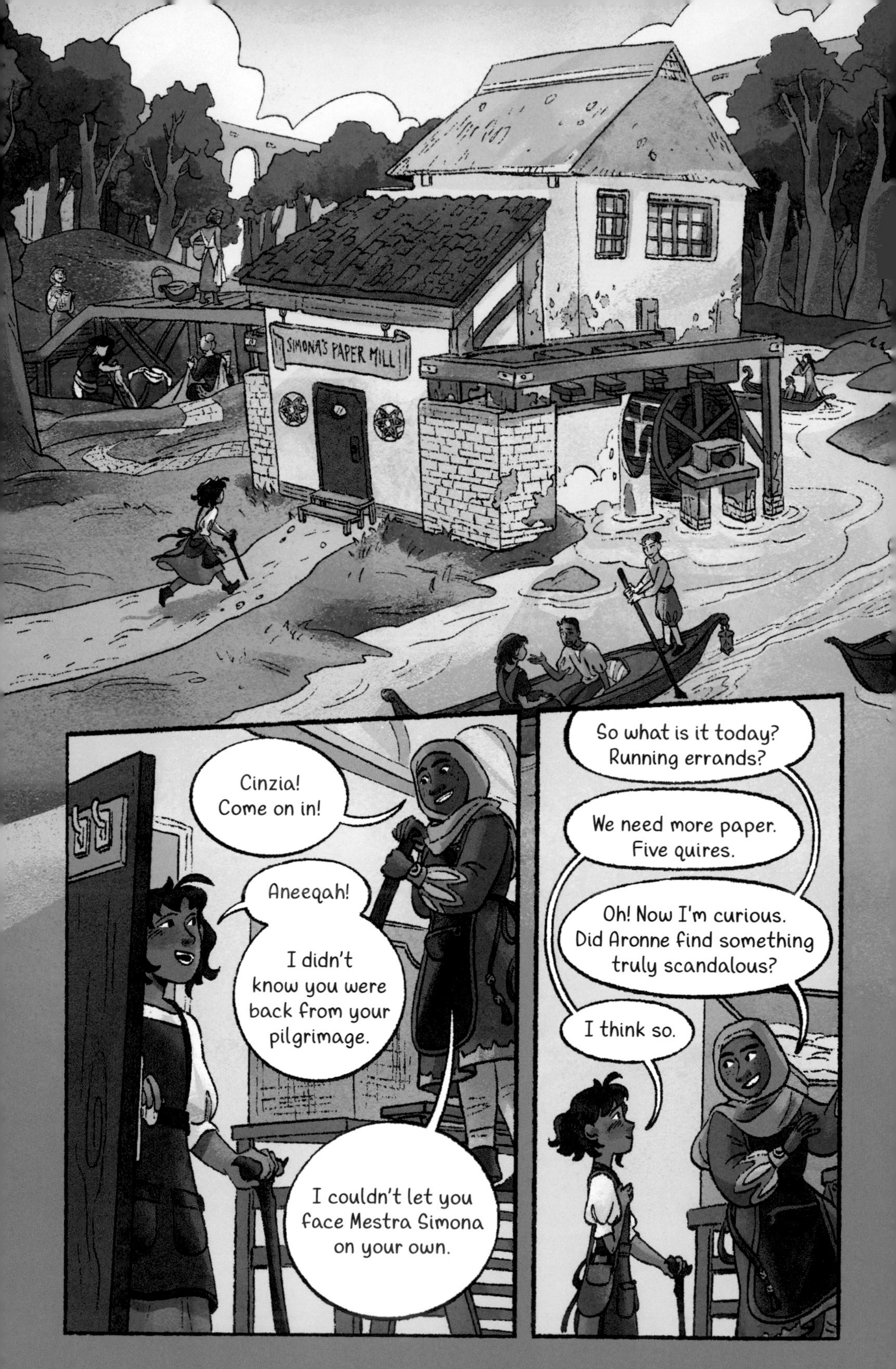
SIMONA'S PAPER MILL
Cinzia! Come on in!
Aneeqah!
I didn't know you were back from your pilgrimage.
I couldn't let you face Mestra Simona on your own.
So what is it today? Running errands?
We need more paper. Five quires.
Oh! Now I'm curious. Did Aronne find something truly scandalous?
I think so.

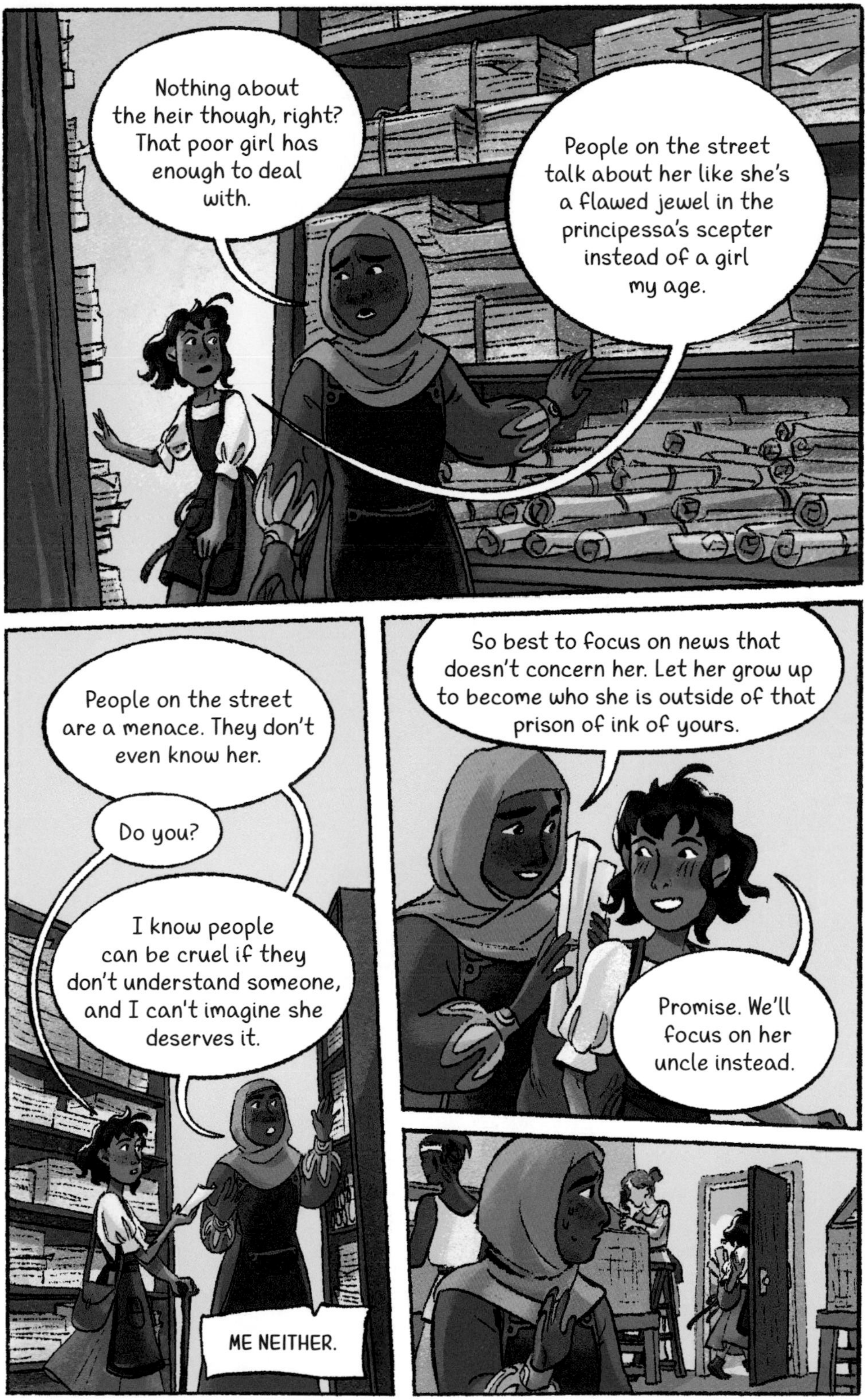
Nothing about the heir though, right? That poor girl has enough to deal with.
People on the street talk about her like she's a flawed jewel in the principessa's scepter instead of a girl my age.
People on the street are a menace. They don't even know her.
Do you?
I know people can be cruel if they don't understand someone, and I can't imagine she deserves it.
ME NEITHER.
So best to focus on news that doesn't concern her. Let her grow up to become who she is outside of that prison of ink of yours.
Promise. We'll focus on her uncle instead.

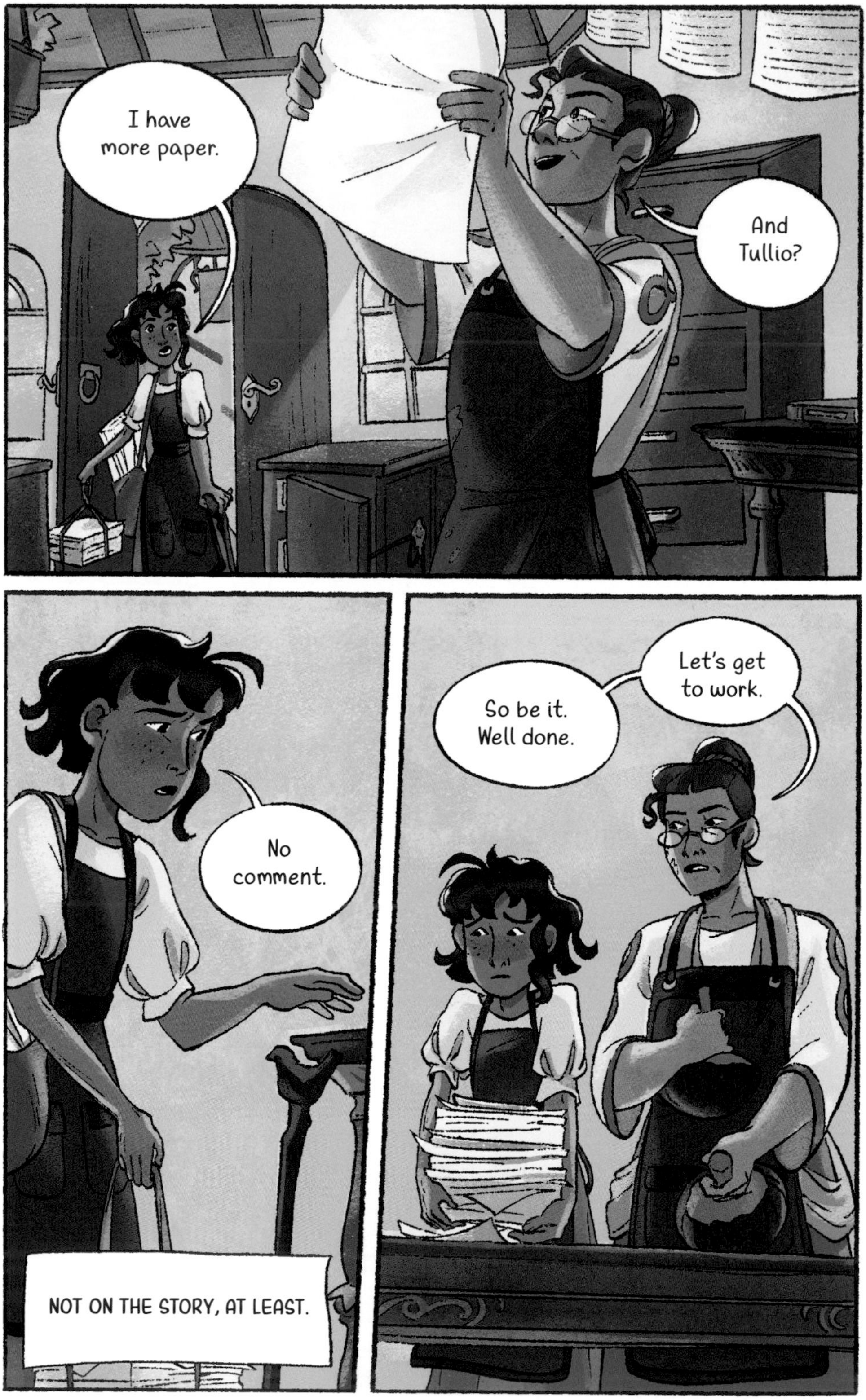
I have more paper.
And Tullio?
No comment.
NOT ON THE STORY, AT LEAST.
So be it. Well done.
Let's get to work.

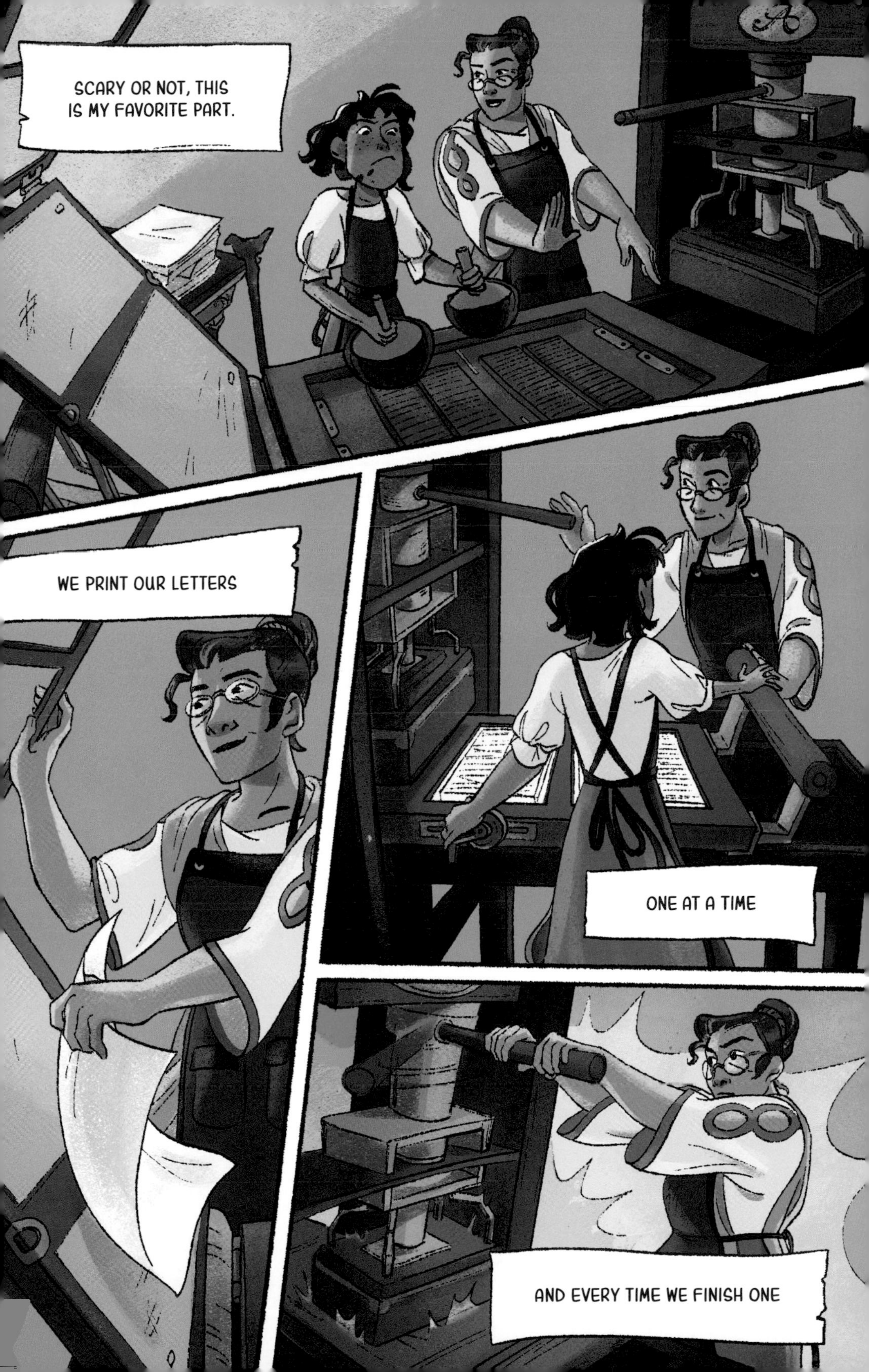
SCARY OR NOT, THIS IS MY FAVORITE PART.
WE PRINT OUR LETTERS
ONE AT A TIME
AND EVERY TIME WE FINISH ONE

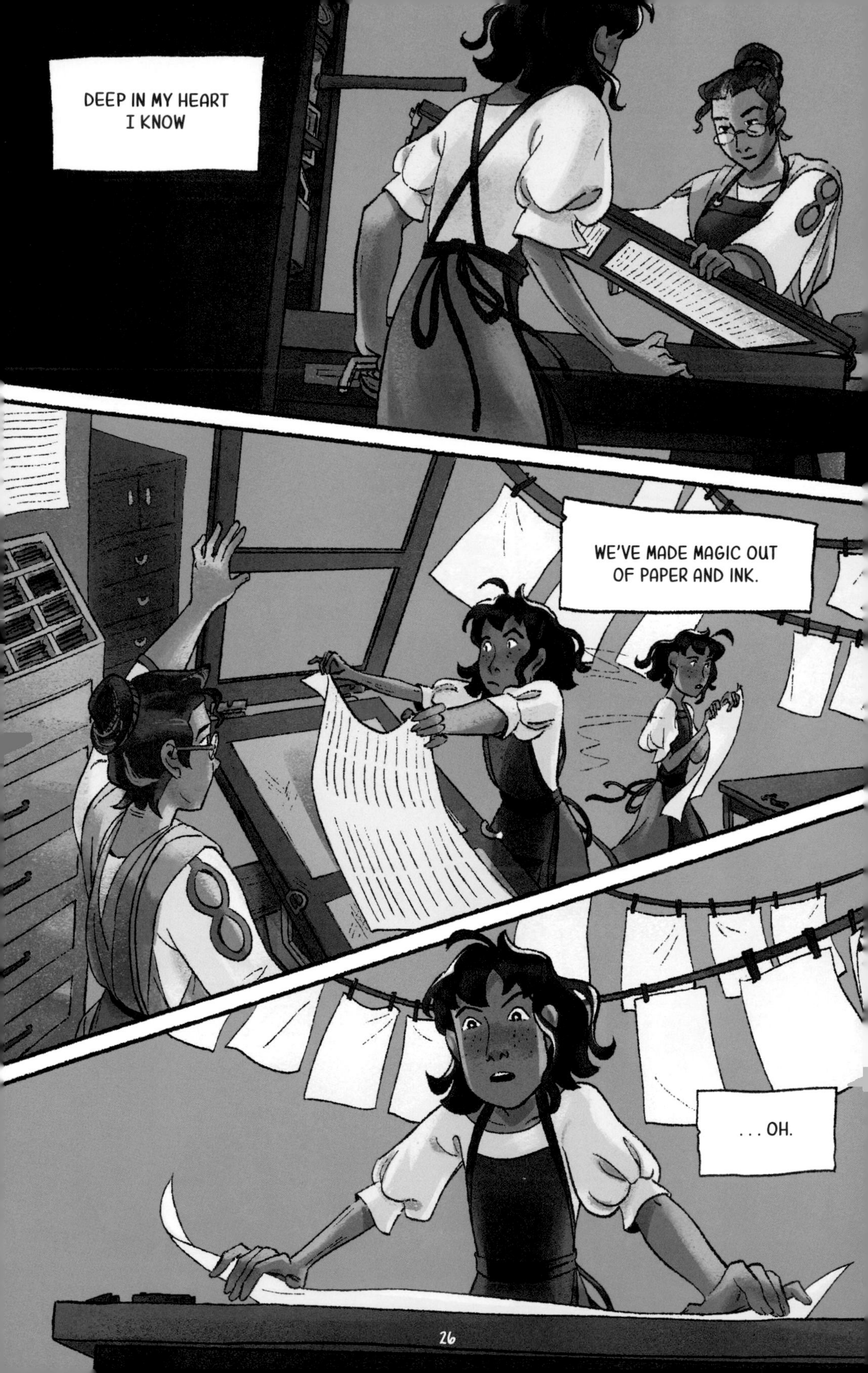
DEEP IN MY HEART
I KNOW
WE'VE MADE MAGIC OUT
OF PAPER AND INK.
. . . OH.

THE MAGISTRATE'S MONEY

As most of the citizens of Siannerra know, our beautiful city is ruled fairly by Celestina di Fedele and her family, while day-to-day matters in the city are presided over by her council. A council that exists of representatives of the six largest guilds, accademia, and the basilica. Its leader and lord magistrate is Lorenzo di Fedele, brother to our principessa.

It is the role of the council to ensure that our city is just, to ensure that our prices are fair, and to ensure that every merchant pays their share of taxes to make Siannerra brighter.

The lord magistrate seems to have misunderstood the purpose of the council. Over these past few months, credible reports have surfaced of Lorenzo di Fedele using his position to extort mone~~y~~ ~~from merch~~ants and members of the lower guild~~s, in defiance~~ ~~of the agreement~~s to the agreements and protection~~s they are owed~~ by right.

The Lor~~d magistrate has use~~d his position to coll~~ect~~ taxes f~~or his pe~~~~rsonal gain~~ and not the city's. And in ~~doing~~ ~~so~~ ~~he~~ ~~ha~~s be~~tr~~ayed the tr~~u~~st the people of Siannerra.

Mestra, we're accusing **the lord magistrate** of stealing.

We didn't say anything that isn't true.

I know, but . . . he'll hate it.

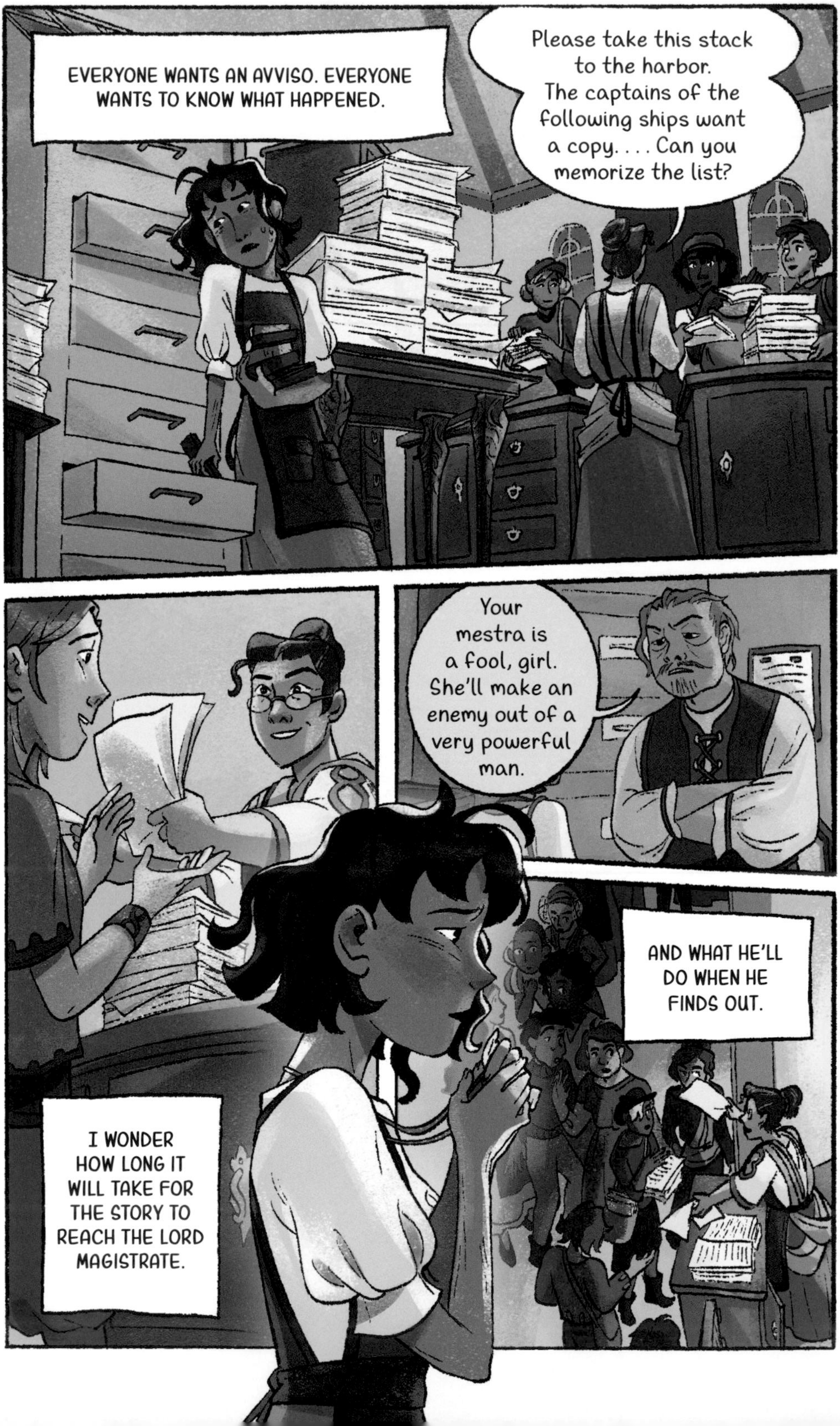
EVERYONE WANTS AN AVVISO. EVERYONE WANTS TO KNOW WHAT HAPPENED.
Please take this stack to the harbor. The captains of the following ships want a copy. . . . Can you memorize the list?
Your mestra is a fool, girl. She'll make an enemy out of a very powerful man.
AND WHAT HE'LL DO WHEN HE FINDS OUT.
I WONDER HOW LONG IT WILL TAKE FOR THE STORY TO REACH THE LORD MAGISTRATE.

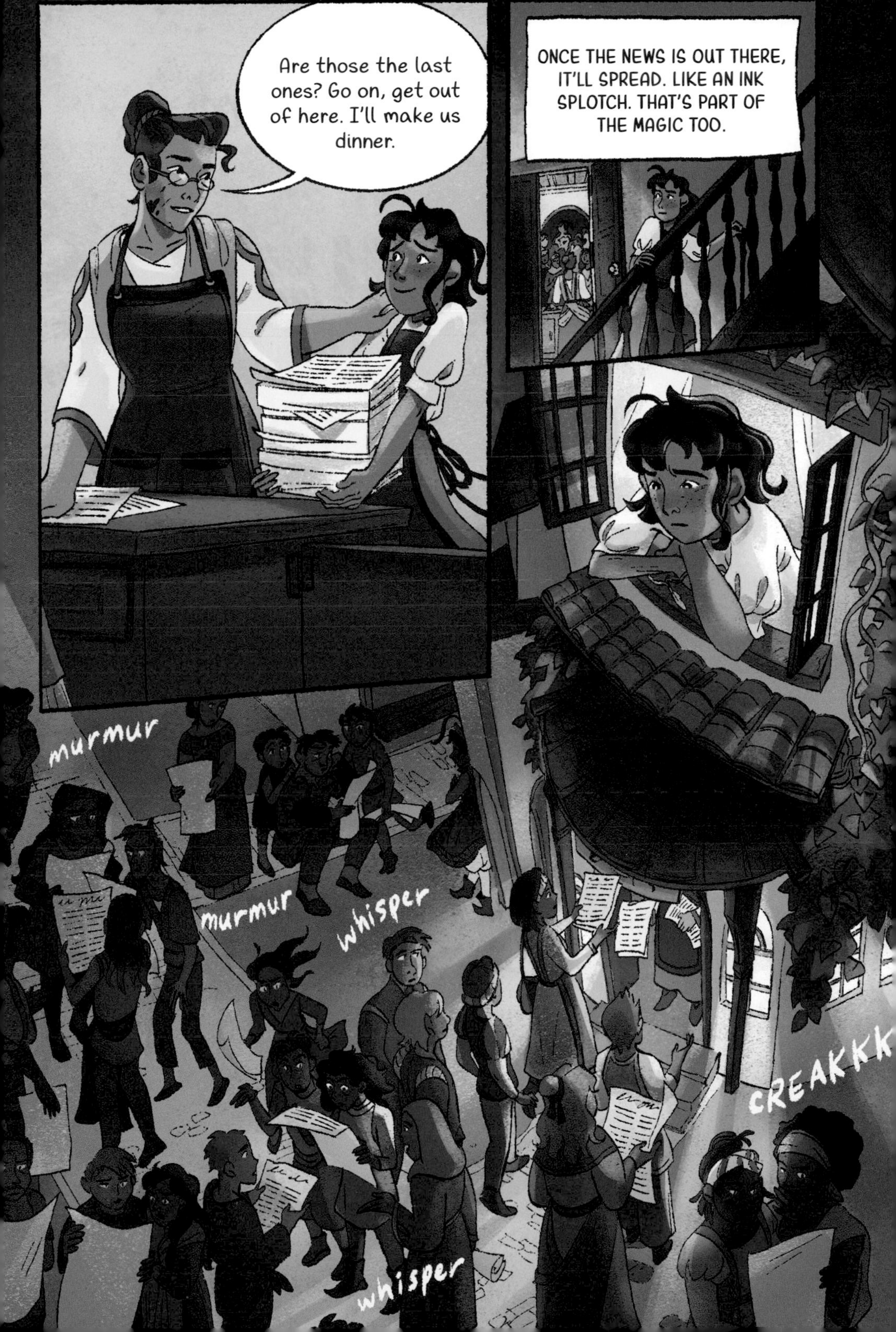
Are those the last ones? Go on, get out of here. I'll make us dinner.
ONCE THE NEWS IS OUT THERE, IT'LL SPREAD. LIKE AN INK SPLOTCH. THAT'S PART OF THE MAGIC TOO.
murmur
murmur
whisper
CREAKKK
whisper

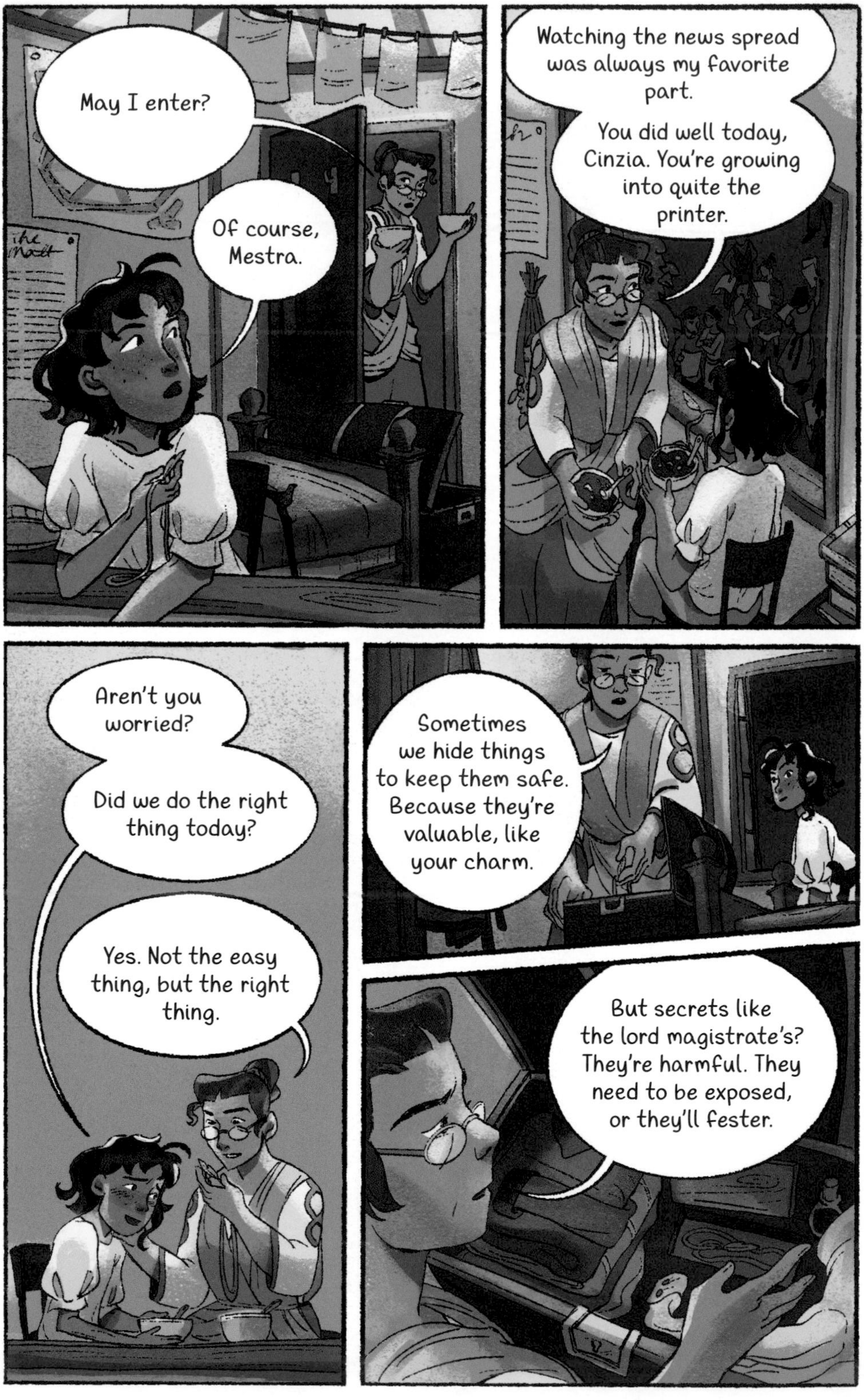
May I enter?
Of course, Mestra.
Watching the news spread was always my favorite part.
You did well today, Cinzia. You're growing into quite the printer.
Aren't you worried?
Did we do the right thing today?
Yes. Not the easy thing, but the right thing.
Sometimes we hide things to keep them safe. Because they're valuable, like your charm.
But secrets like the lord magistrate's? They're harmful. They need to be exposed, or they'll fester.

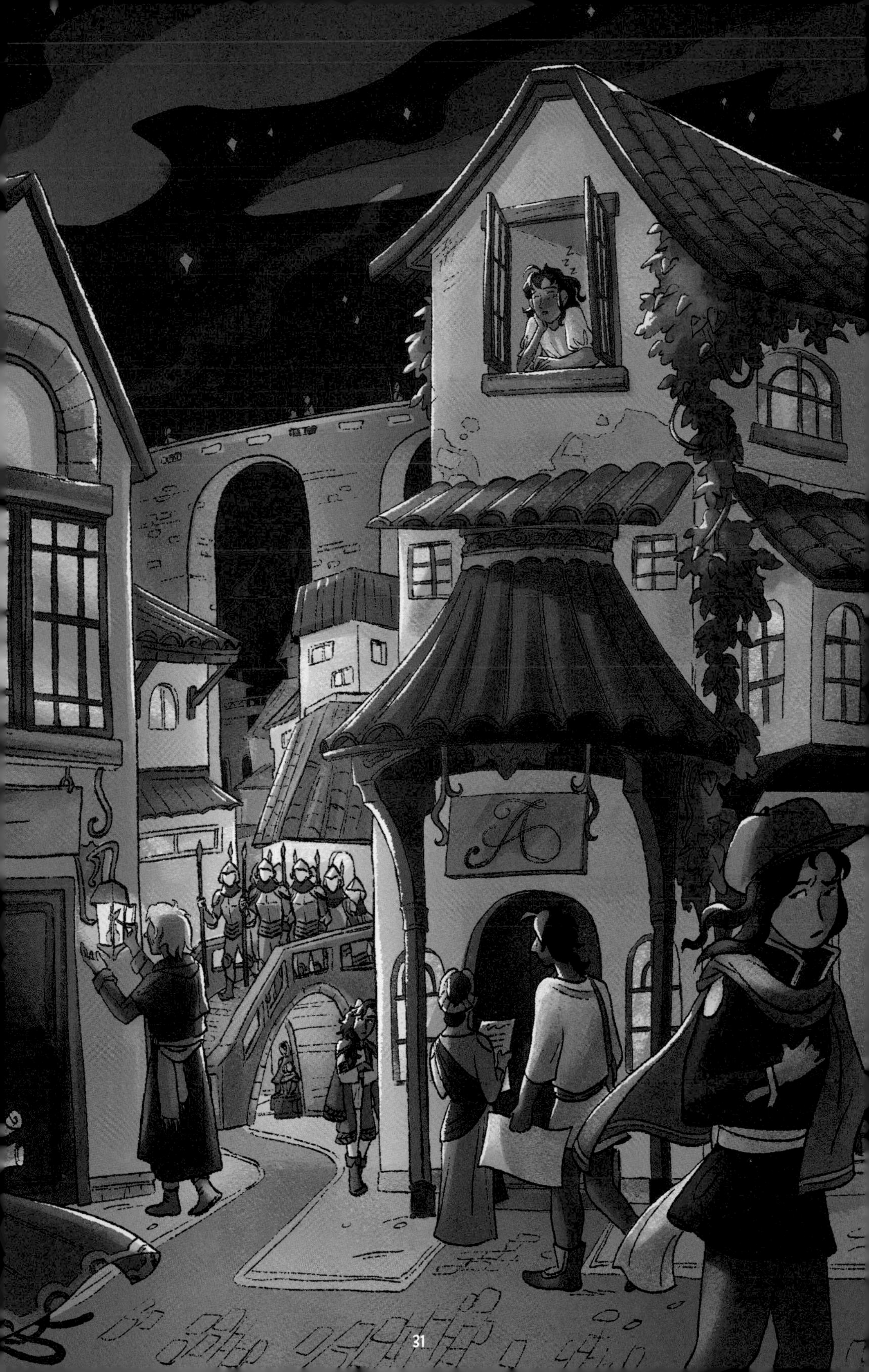

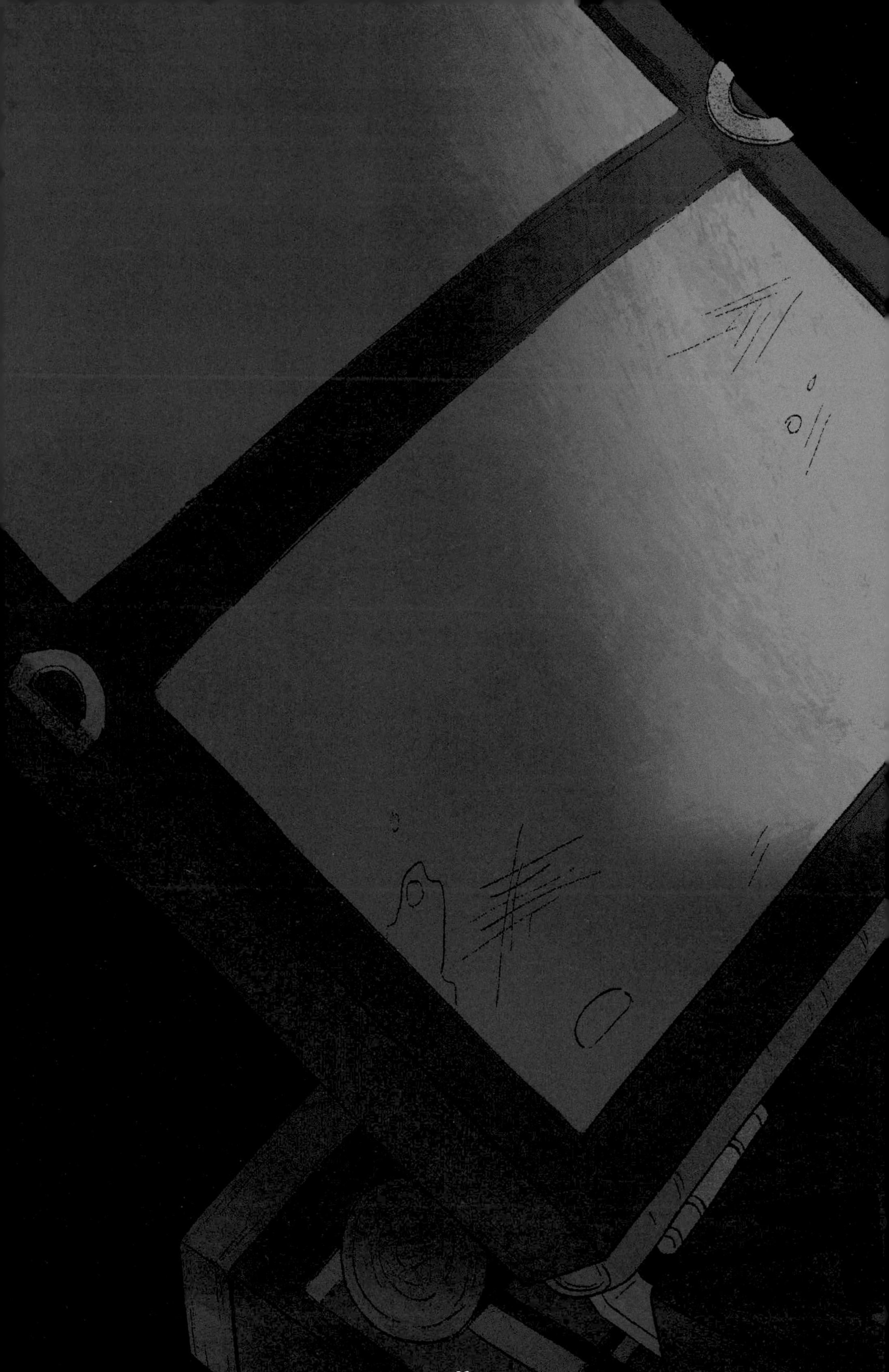

CHAPTER TWO

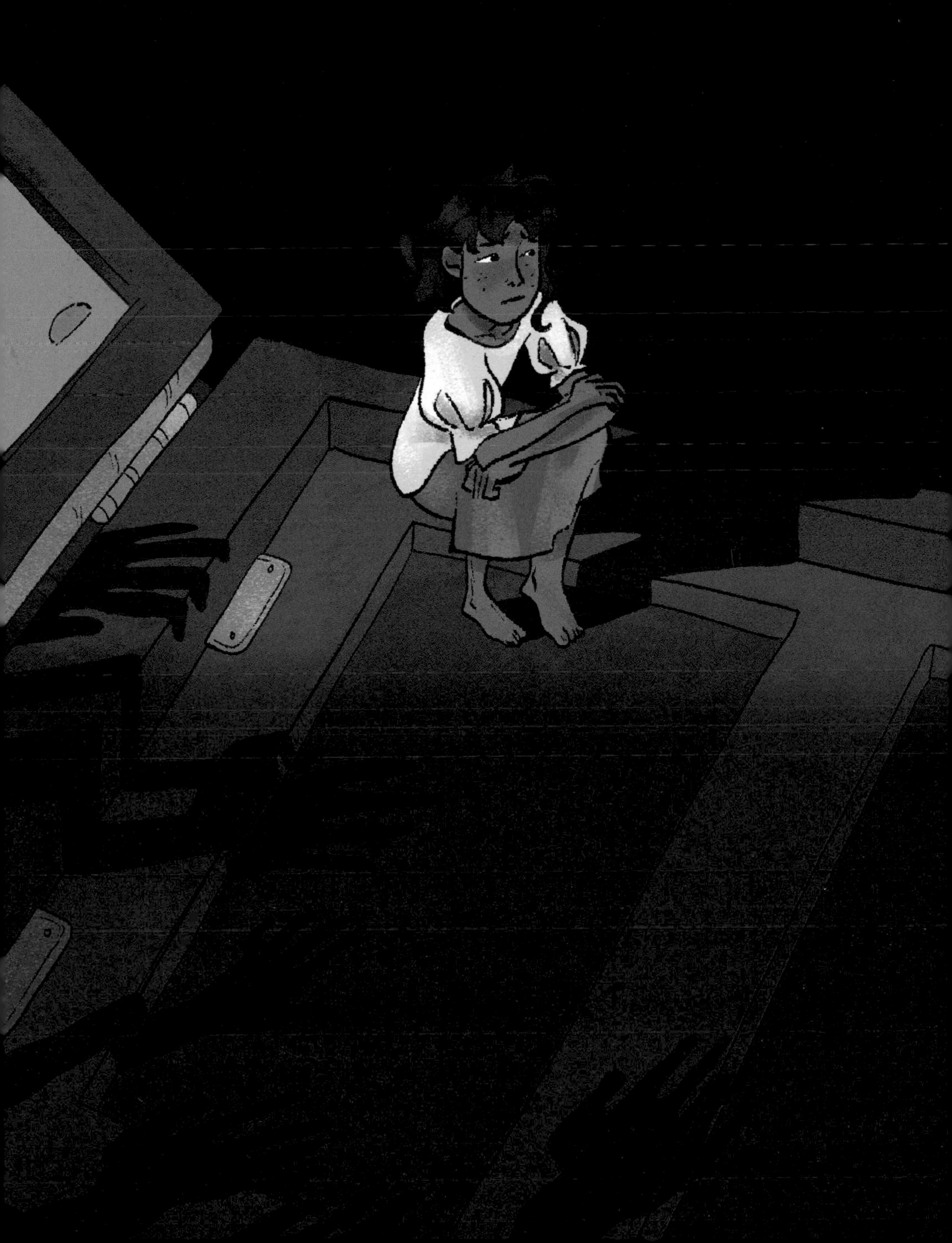

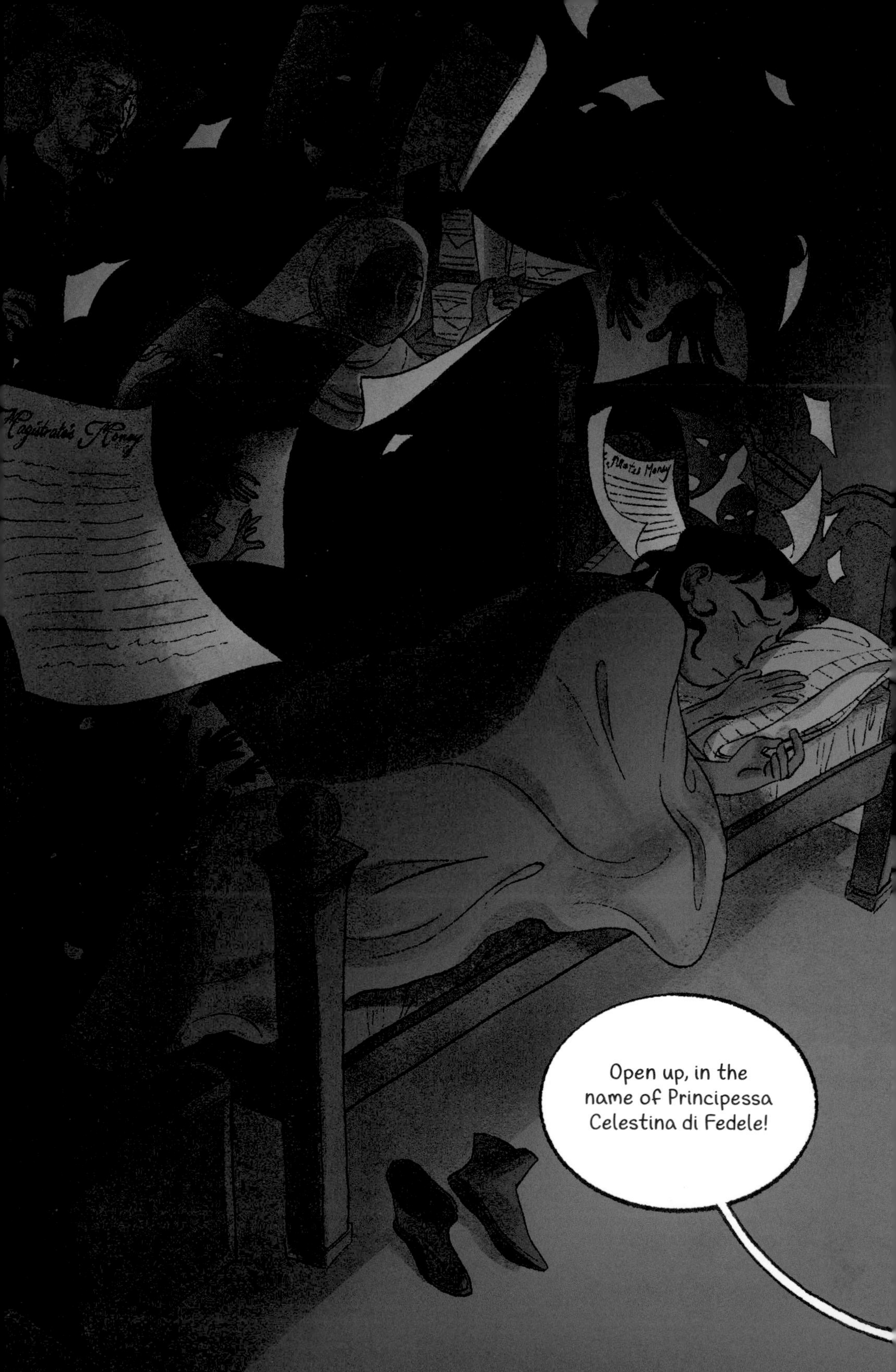
Magistrate's Money
Magistrate's Money
Open up, in the name of Principessa Celestina di Fedele!

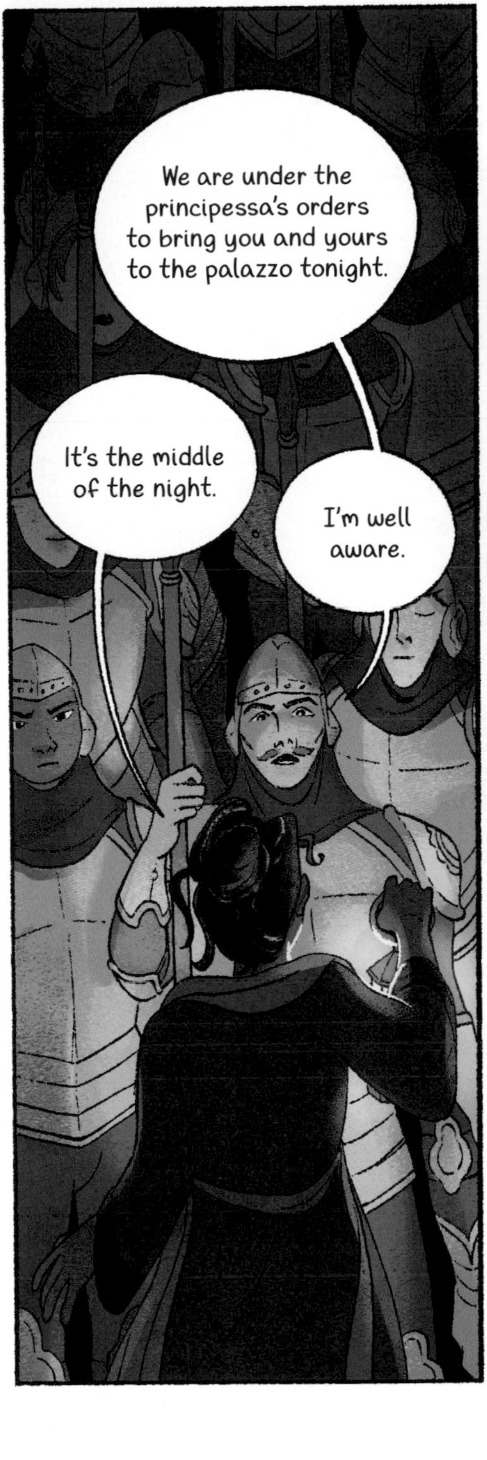
We are under the principessa's orders to bring you and yours to the palazzo tonight.
It's the middle of the night.
I'm well aware.

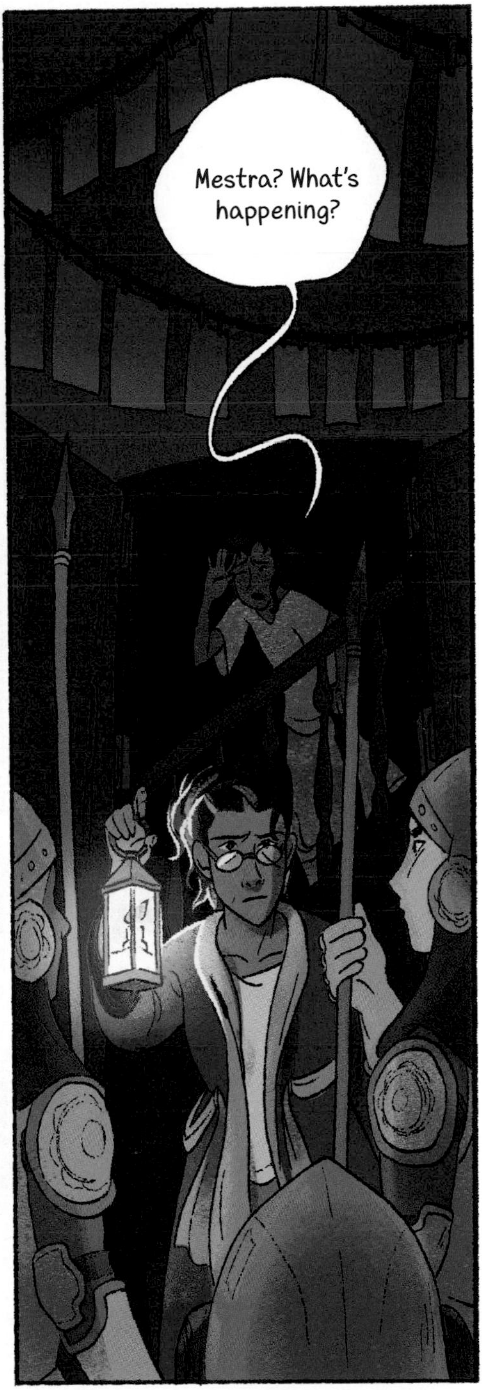
Mestra? What's happening?

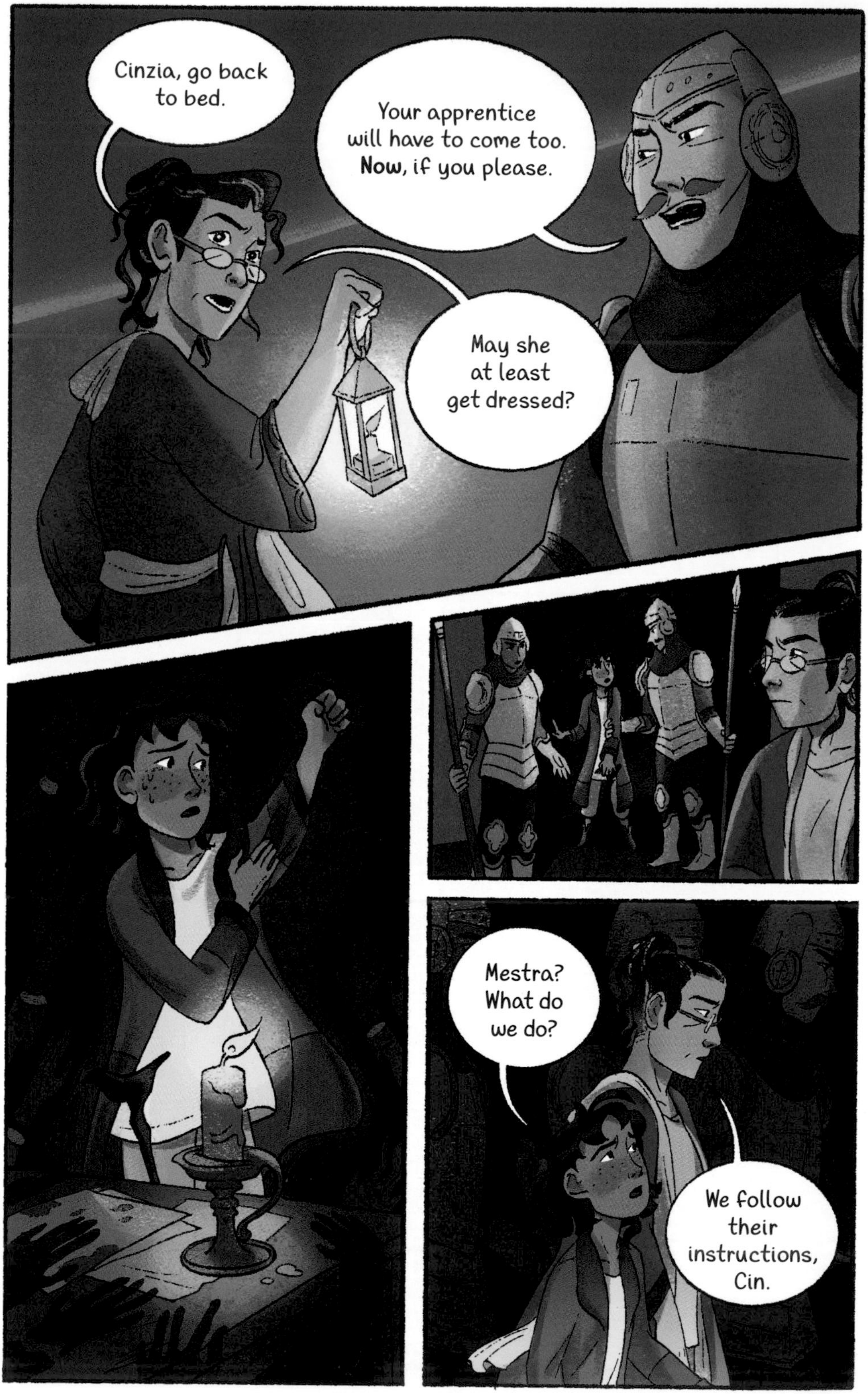
Cinzia, go back to bed.
Your apprentice will have to come too. **Now**, if you please.
May she at least get dressed?
Mestra? What do we do?
We follow their instructions, Cin.

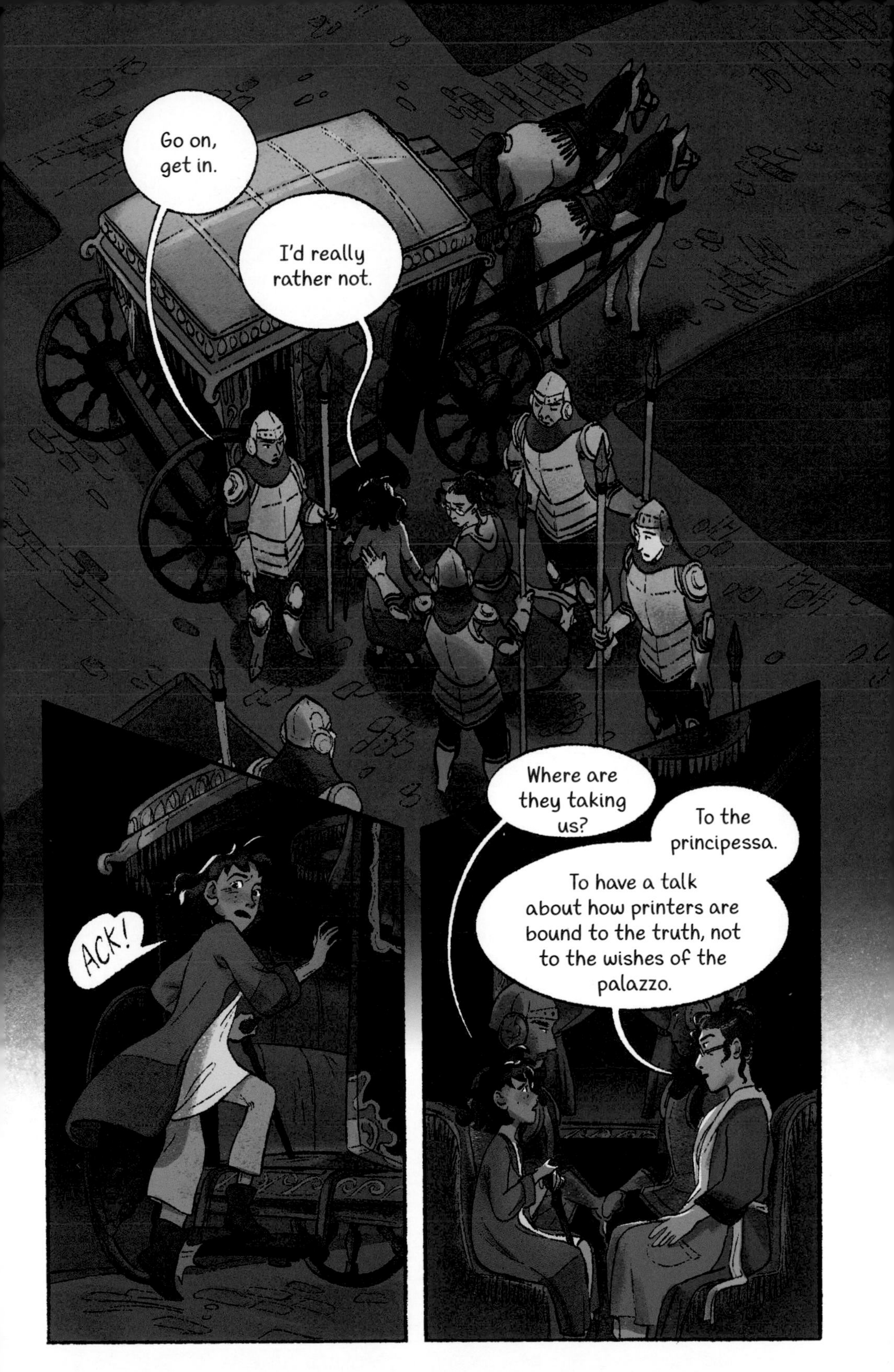
Go on, get in.
I'd really rather not.
ACK!
Where are they taking us?
To the principessa.
To have a talk about how printers are bound to the truth, not to the wishes of the palazzo.

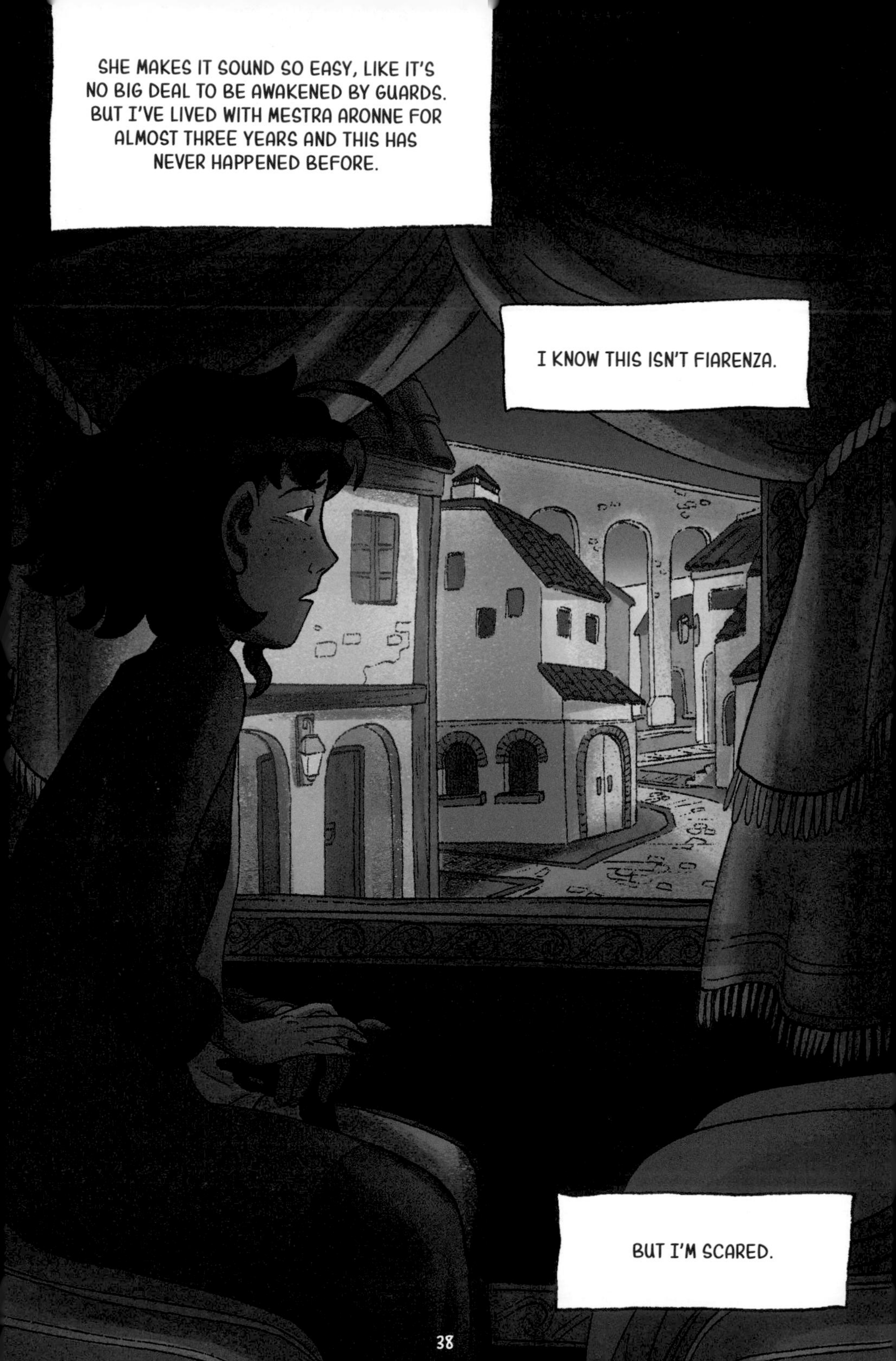
SHE MAKES IT SOUND SO EASY, LIKE IT'S NO BIG DEAL TO BE AWAKENED BY GUARDS. BUT I'VE LIVED WITH MESTRA ARONNE FOR ALMOST THREE YEARS AND THIS HAS NEVER HAPPENED BEFORE.
I KNOW THIS ISN'T FIARENZA.
BUT I'M SCARED.

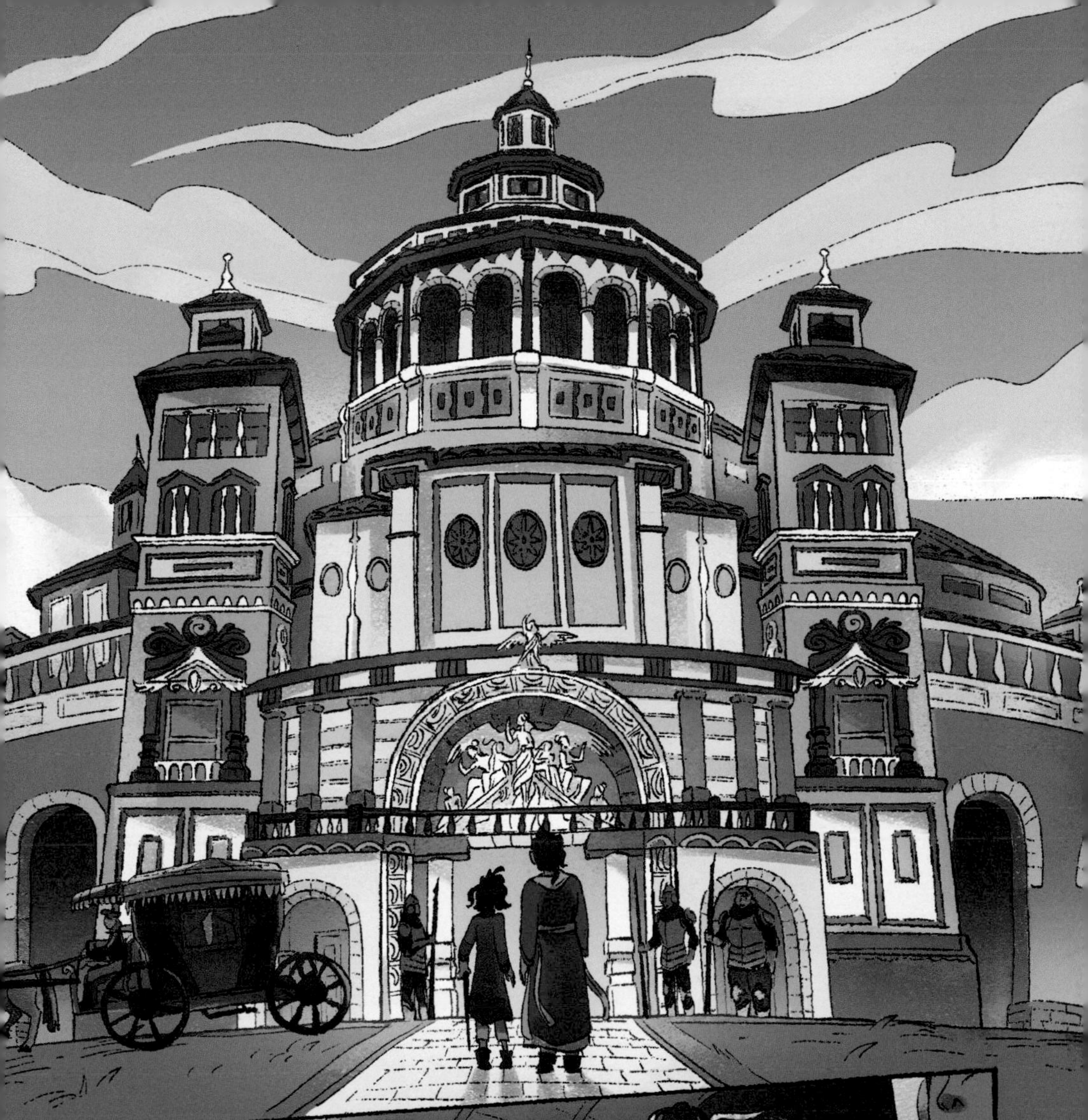

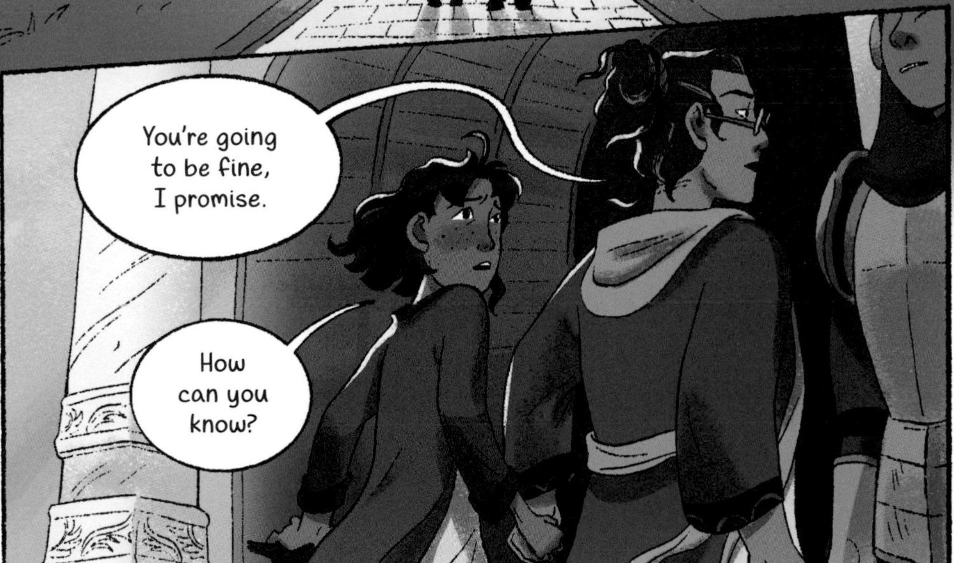
You're going to be fine, I promise.
How can you know?

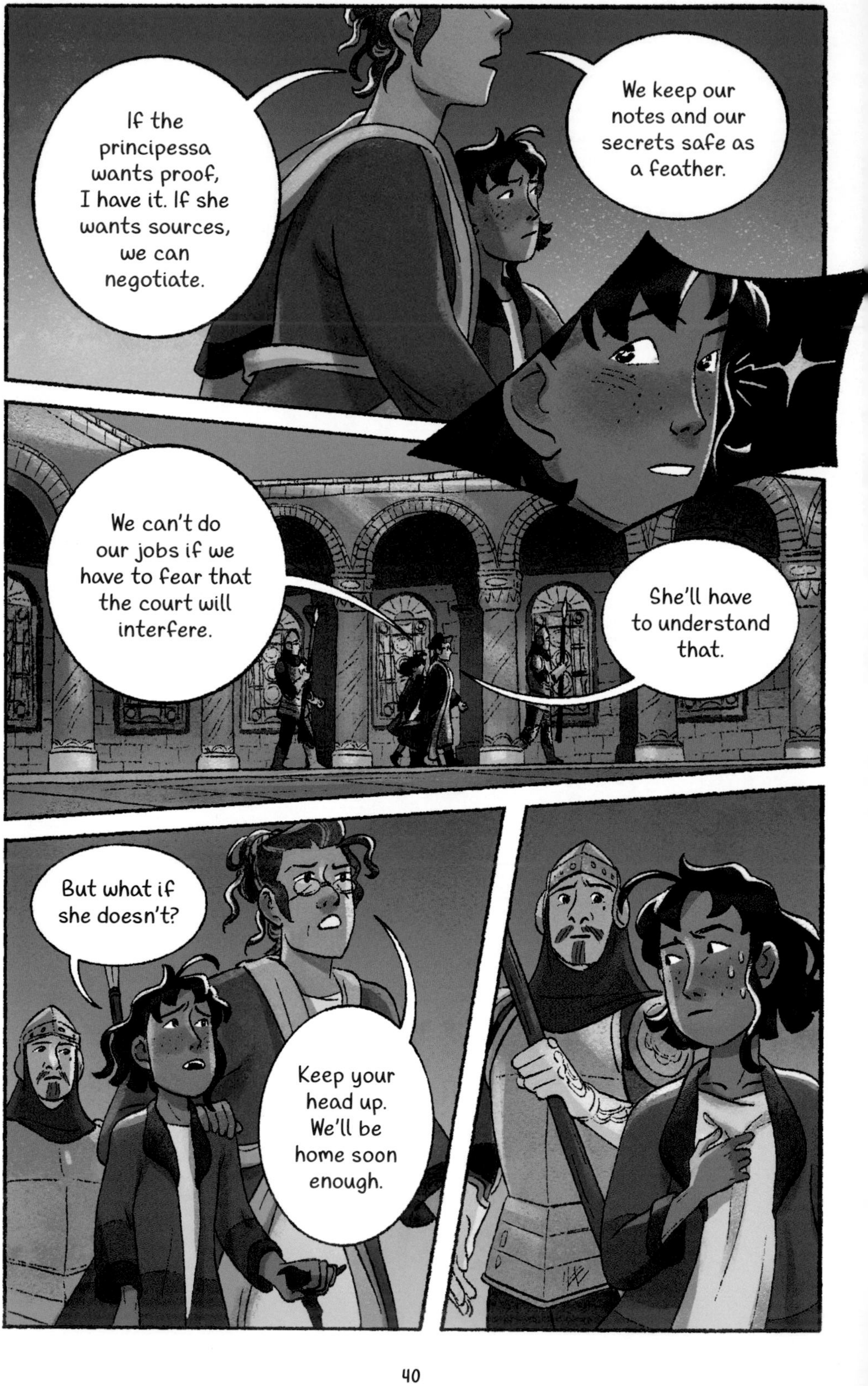
If the principessa wants proof, I have it. If she wants sources, we can negotiate.
We keep our notes and our secrets safe as a feather.
We can't do our jobs if we have to fear that the court will interfere.
She'll have to understand that.
But what if she doesn't?
Keep your head up. We'll be home soon enough.

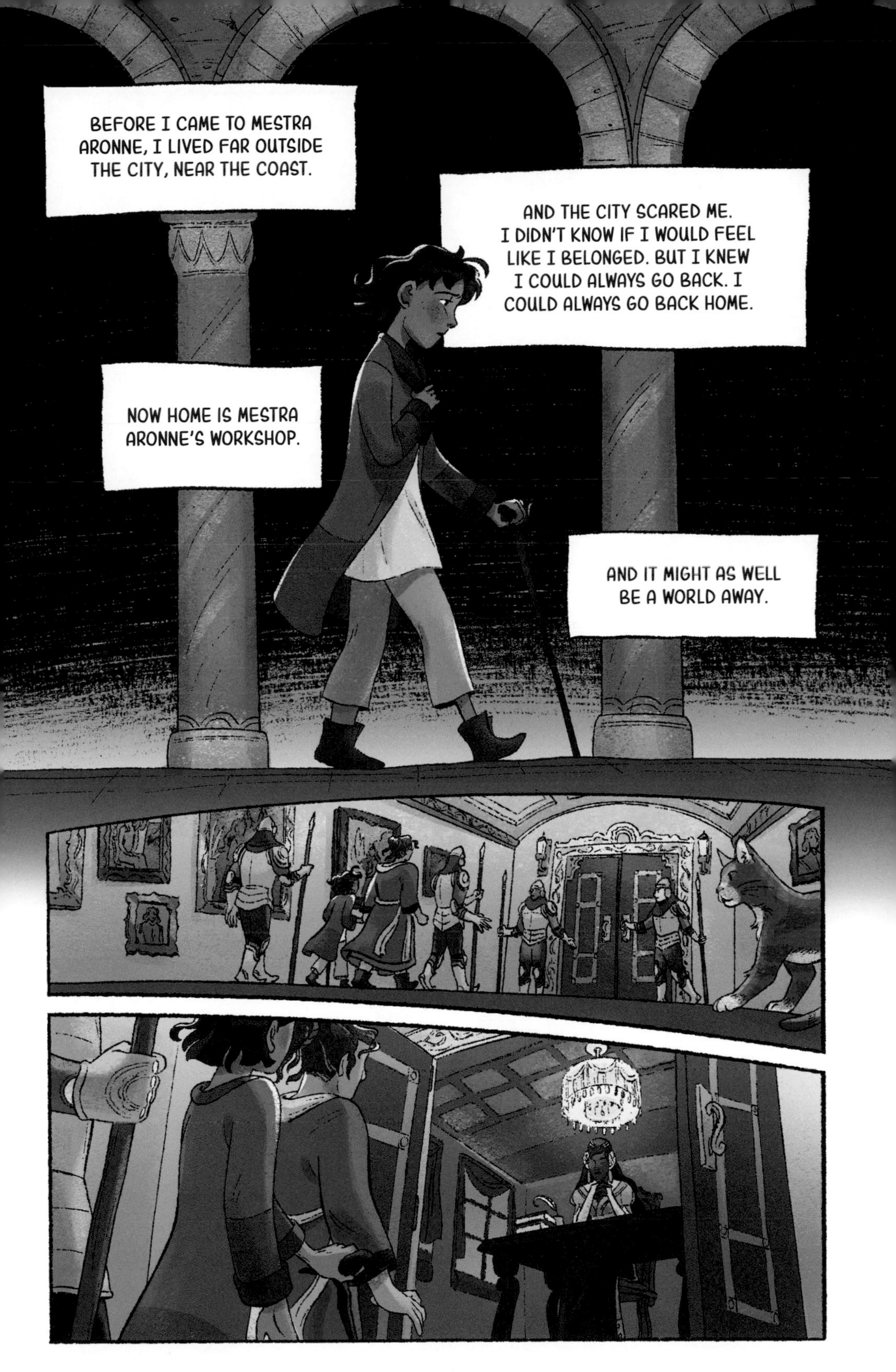
BEFORE I CAME TO MESTRA ARONNE, I LIVED FAR OUTSIDE THE CITY, NEAR THE COAST.
AND THE CITY SCARED ME. I DIDN'T KNOW IF I WOULD FEEL LIKE I BELONGED. BUT I KNEW I COULD ALWAYS GO BACK. I COULD ALWAYS GO BACK HOME.
NOW HOME IS MESTRA ARONNE'S WORKSHOP.
AND IT MIGHT AS WELL BE A WORLD AWAY.

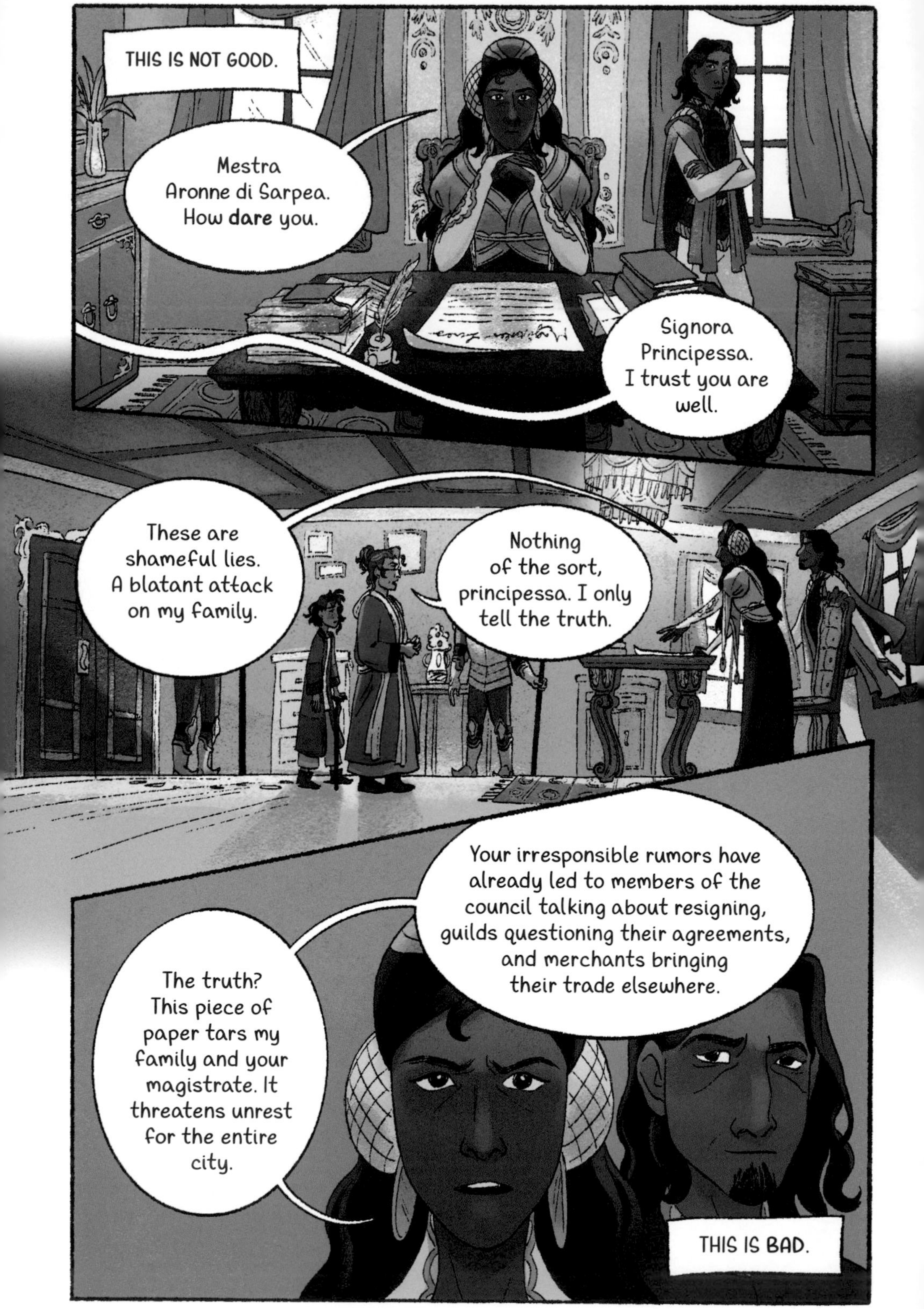
THIS IS NOT GOOD.
Mestra Aronne di Sarpea. How **dare** you.
Signora Principessa. I trust you are well.
These are shameful lies. A blatant attack on my family.
Nothing of the sort, principessa. I only tell the truth.
The truth? This piece of paper tars my family and your magistrate. It threatens unrest for the entire city.
Your irresponsible rumors have already led to members of the council talking about resigning, guilds questioning their agreements, and merchants bringing their trade elsewhere.
THIS IS BAD.

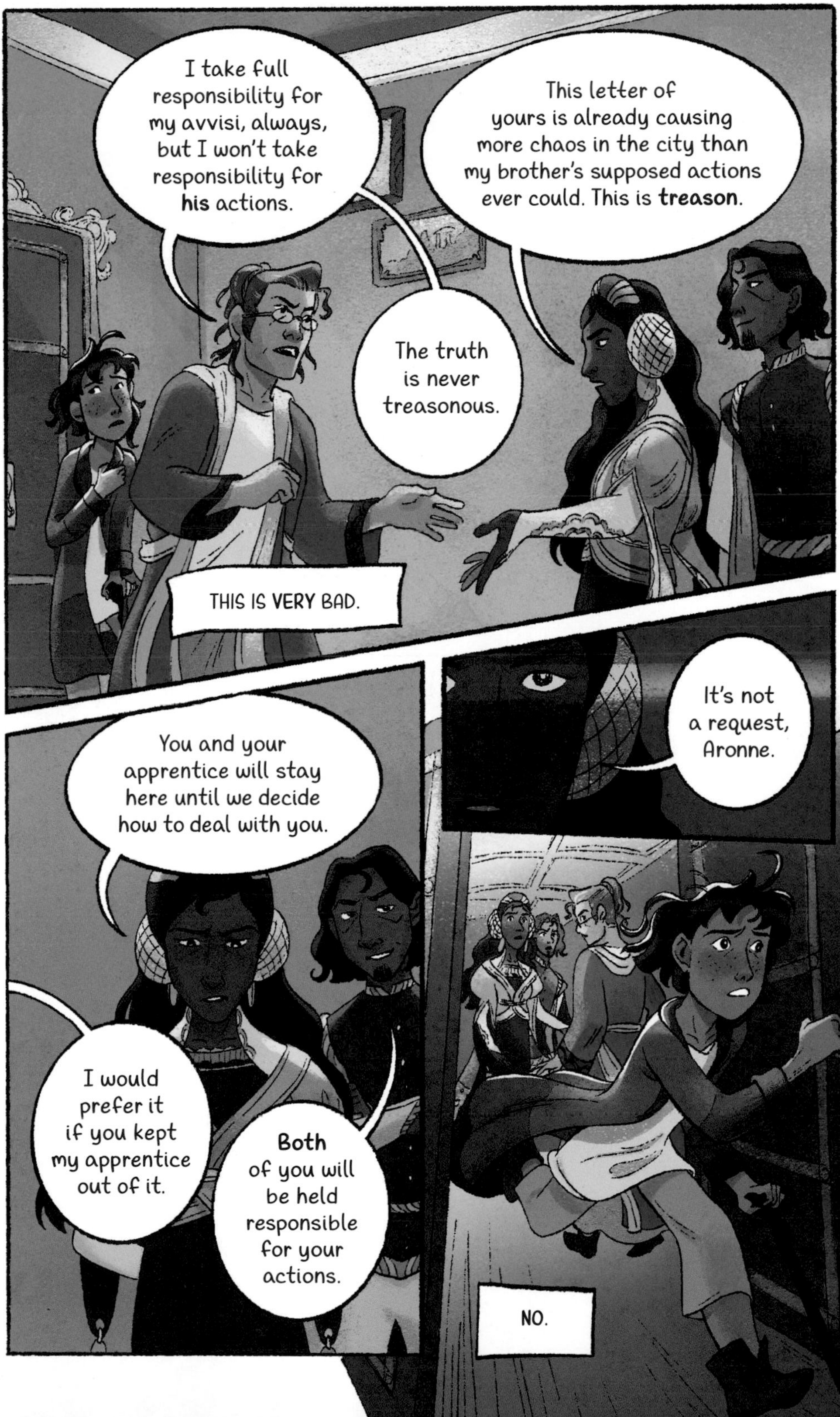
I take full responsibility for my avvisi, always, but I won't take responsibility for **his** actions.
This letter of yours is already causing more chaos in the city than my brother's supposed actions ever could. This is **treason**.
The truth is never treasonous.
THIS IS **VERY** BAD.
It's not a request, Aronne.
You and your apprentice will stay here until we decide how to deal with you.
I would prefer it if you kept my apprentice out of it.
Both of you will be held responsible for your actions.
NO.

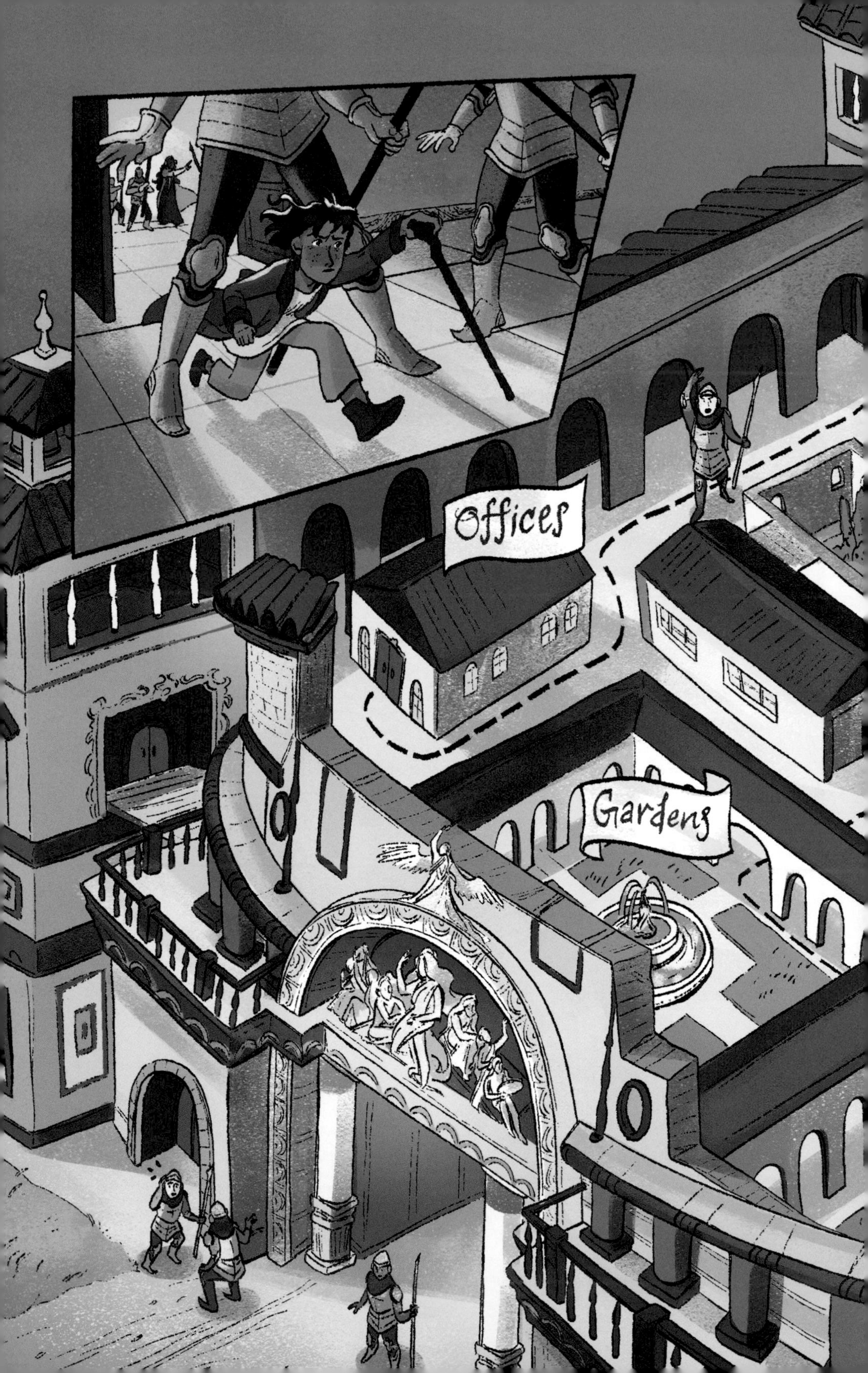
Offices
Gardens

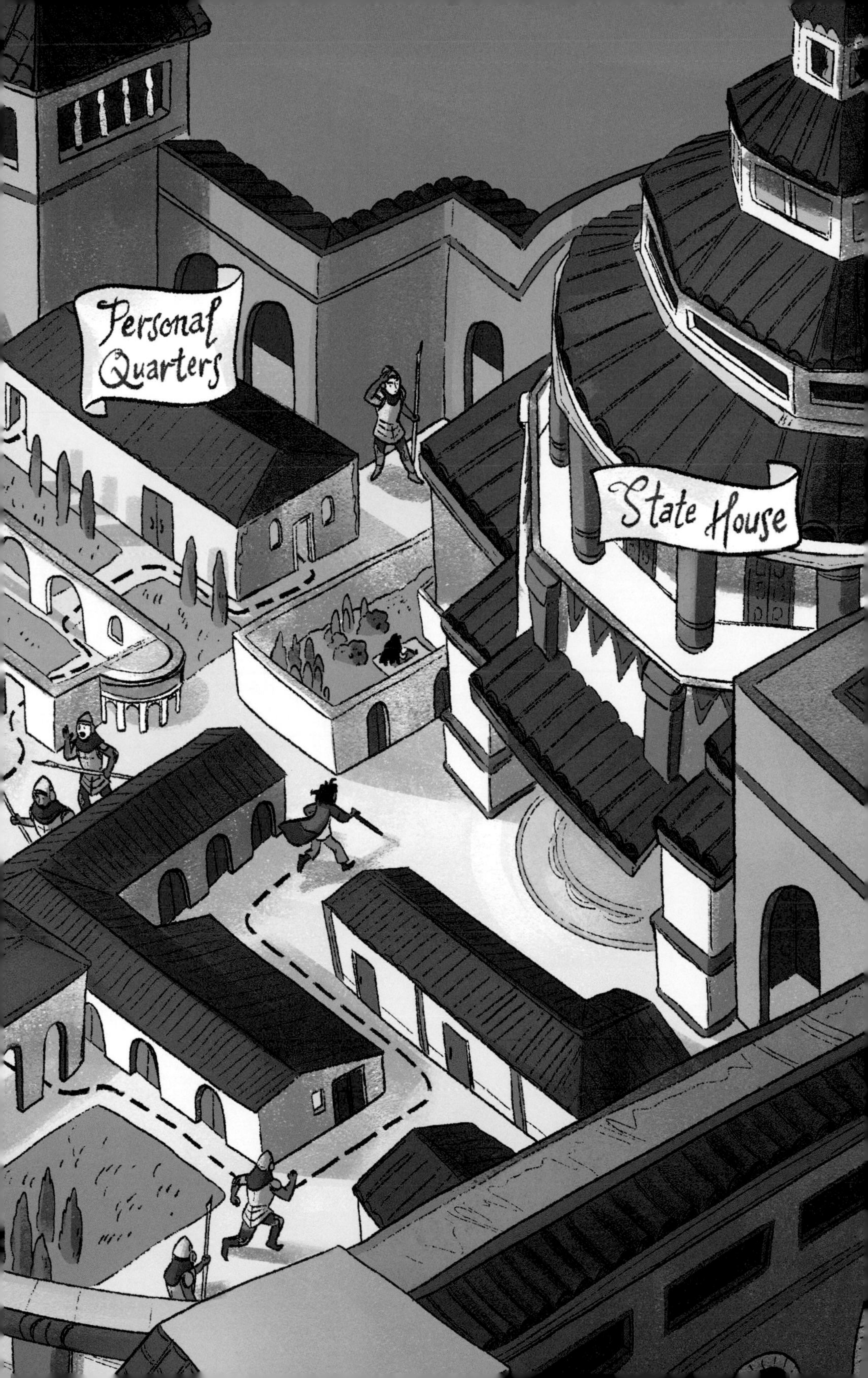
Personal Quarters
State House

"You will stay here until we decide how to deal with you."

"It's not a request."

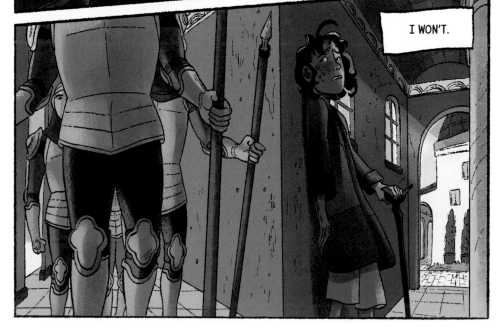

I WON'T.

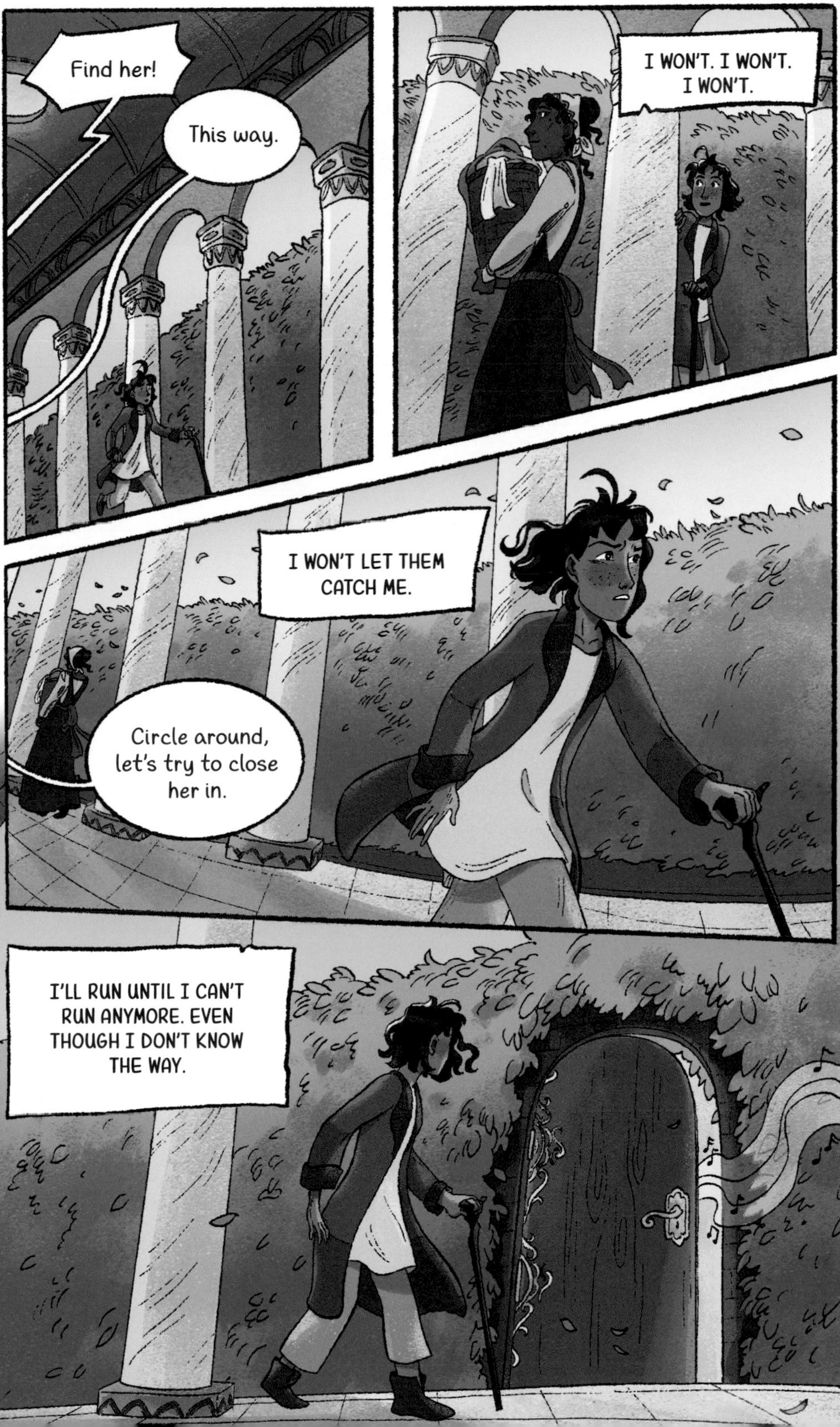
Find her!
This way.
I WON'T. I WON'T. I WON'T.
I WON'T LET THEM CATCH ME.
Circle around, let's try to close her in.
I'LL RUN UNTIL I CAN'T RUN ANYMORE. EVEN THOUGH I DON'T KNOW THE WAY.

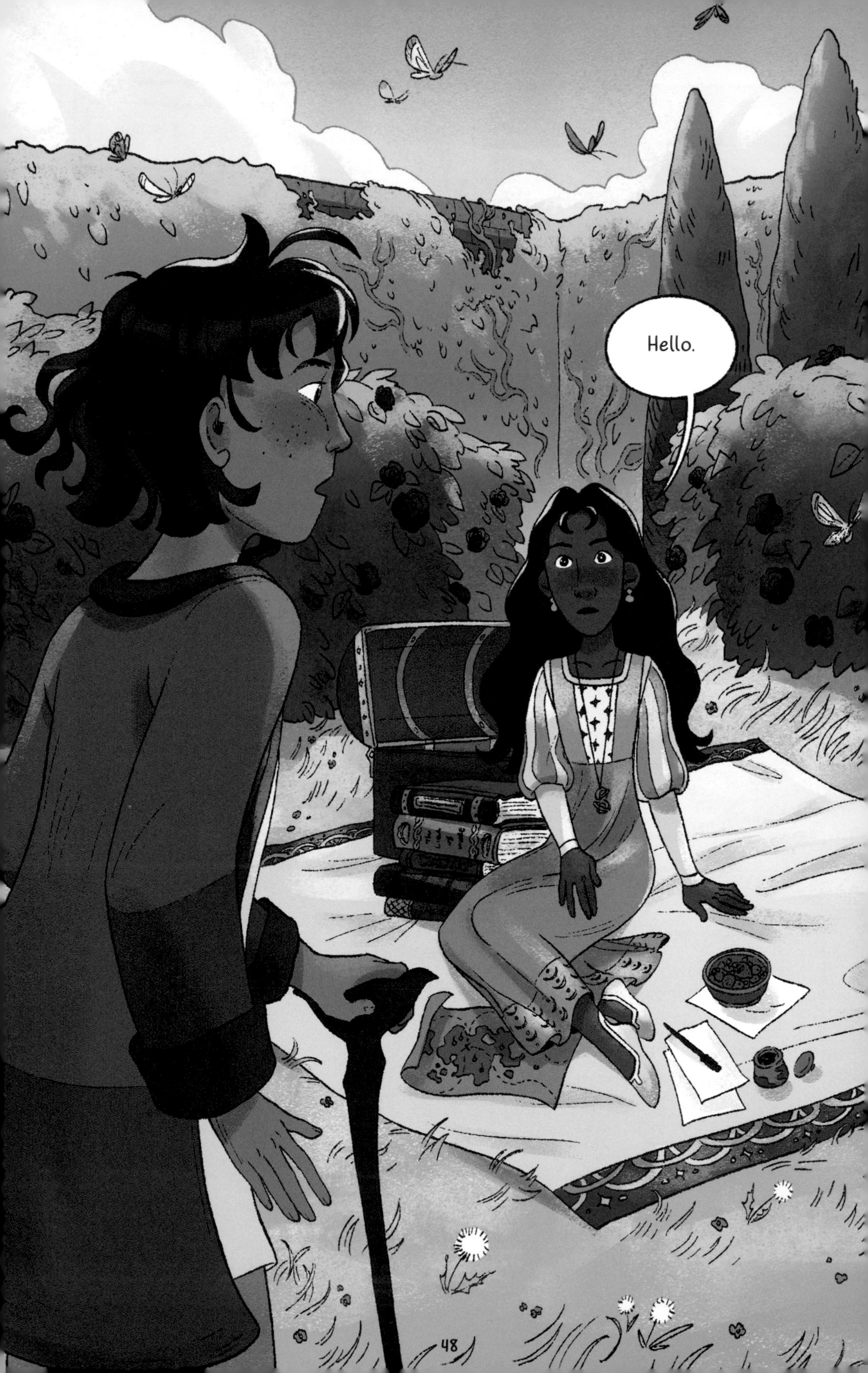
Hello.

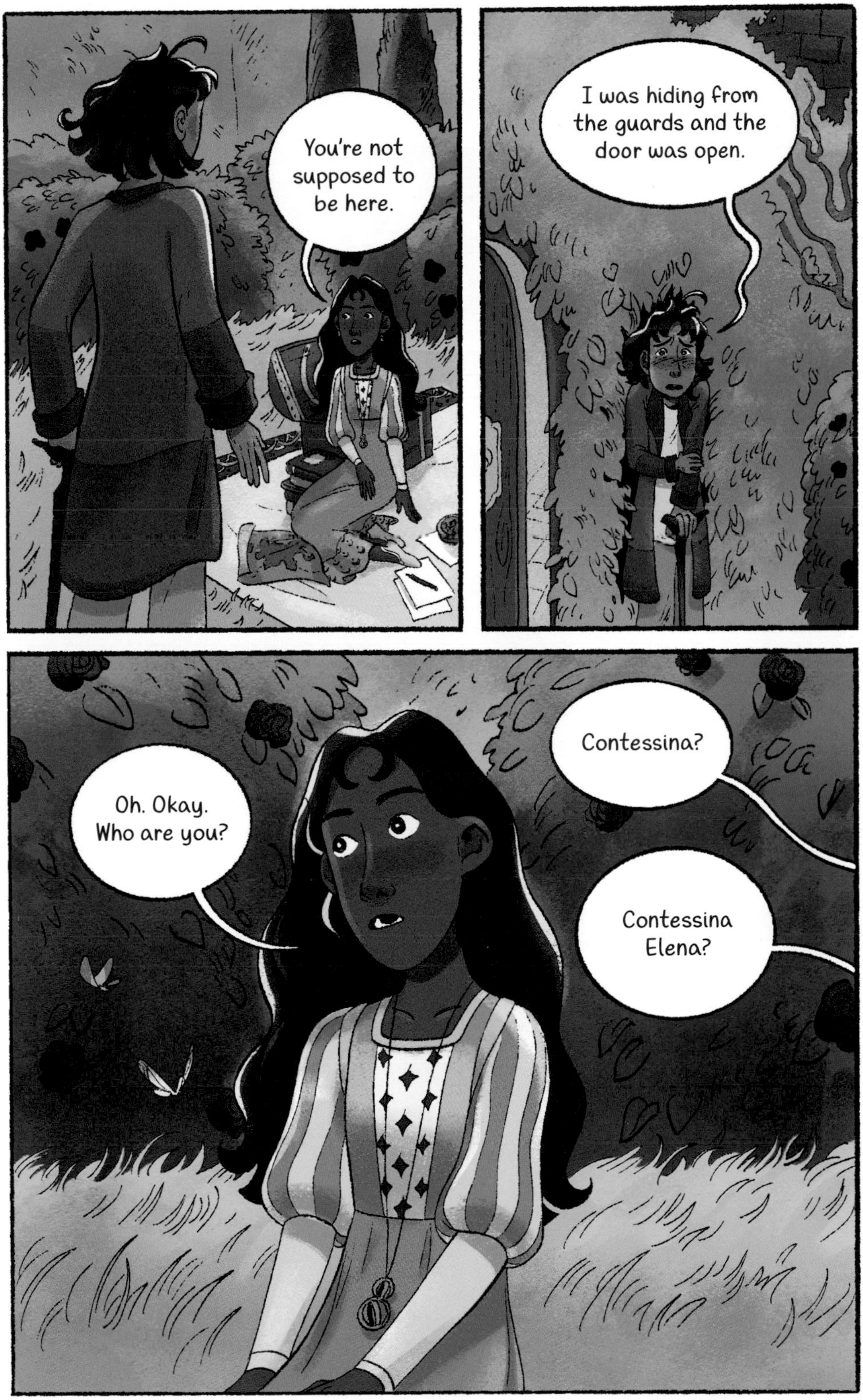
You're not supposed to be here.
I was hiding from the guards and the door was open.
Oh. Okay. Who are you?
Contessina?
Contessina Elena?

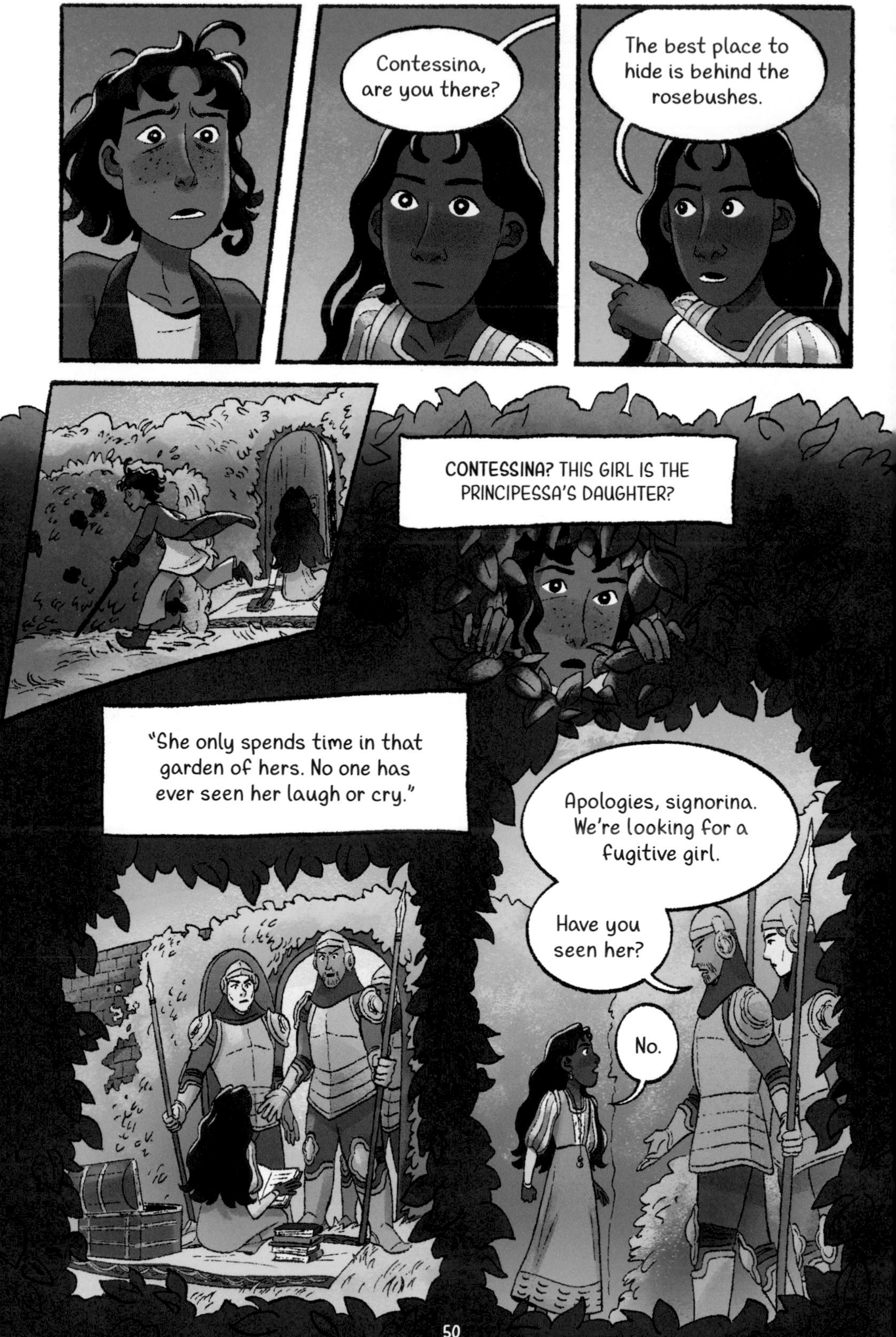
Contessina, are you there?
The best place to hide is behind the rosebushes.
CONTESSINA? THIS GIRL IS THE PRINCIPESSA'S DAUGHTER?
"She only spends time in that garden of hers. No one has ever seen her laugh or cry."
Apologies, signorina. We're looking for a fugitive girl.
Have you seen her?
No.

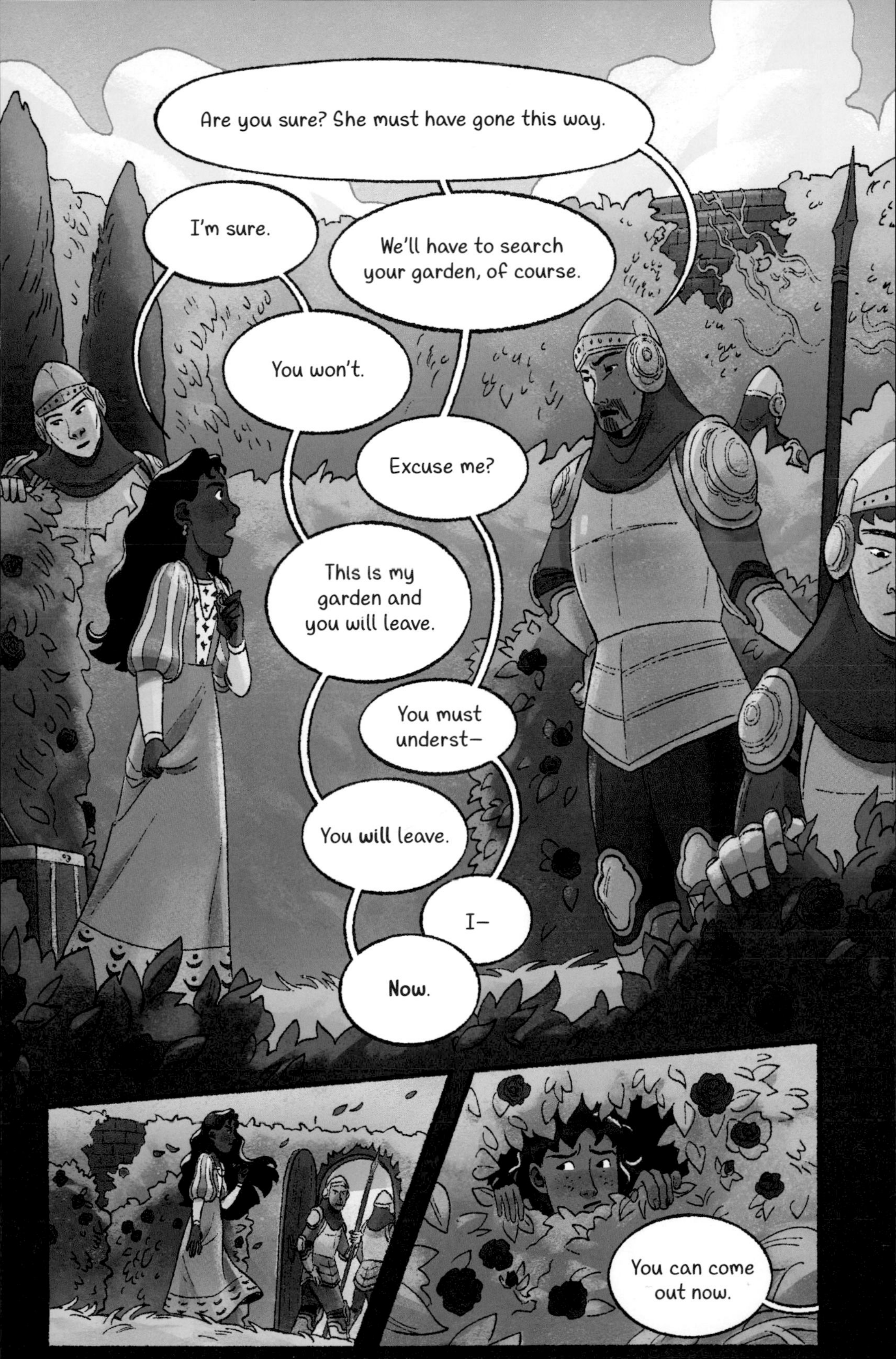
Are you sure? She must have gone this way.
I'm sure.
We'll have to search your garden, of course.
You won't.
Excuse me?
This is my garden and you will leave.
You must underst–
You will leave.
I–
Now.
You can come out now.

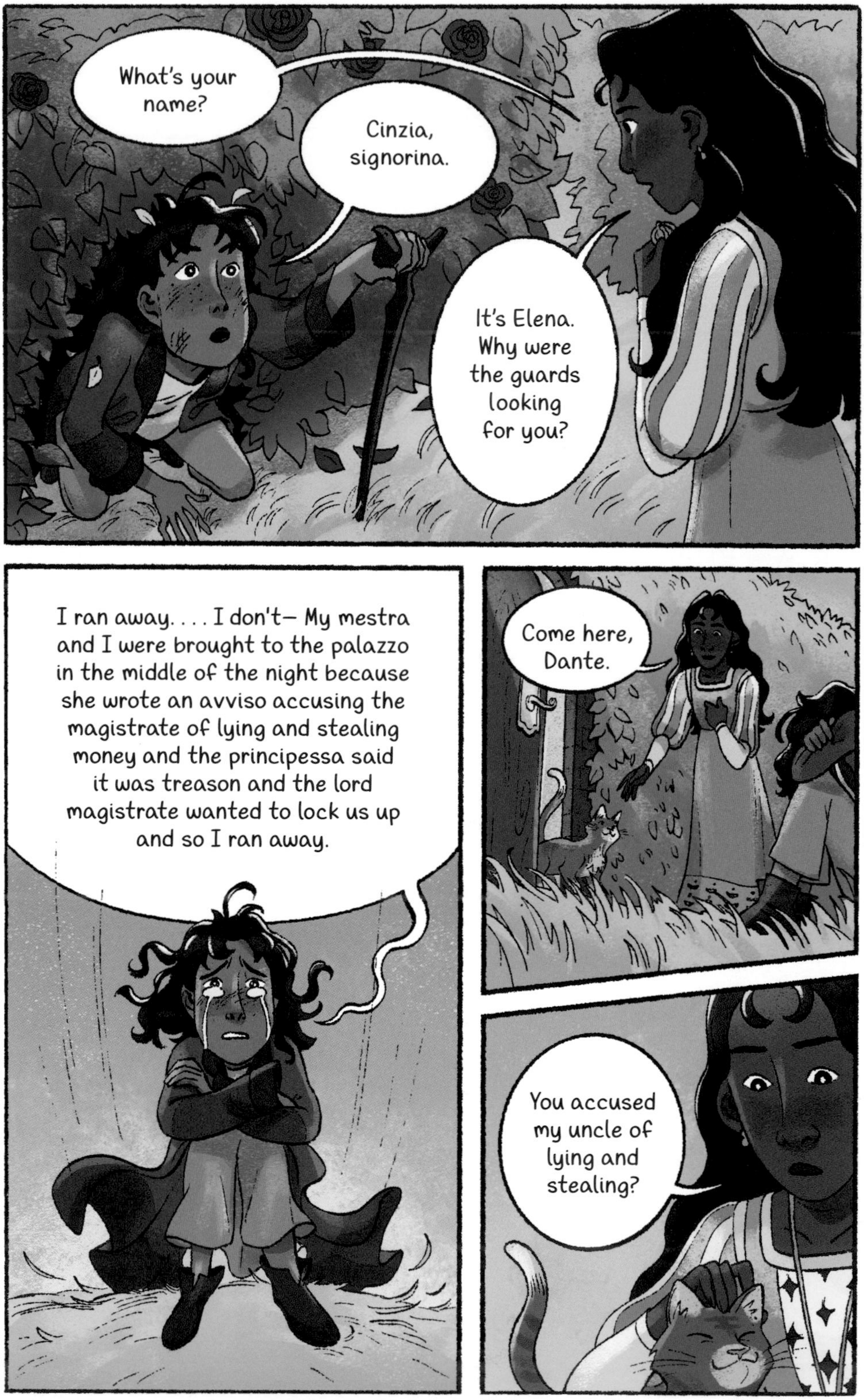
What's your name?
Cinzia, signorina.
It's Elena. Why were the guards looking for you?
I ran away. . . . I don't— My mestra and I were brought to the palazzo in the middle of the night because she wrote an avviso accusing the magistrate of lying and stealing money and the principessa said it was treason and the lord magistrate wanted to lock us up and so I ran away.
Come here, Dante.
You accused my uncle of lying and stealing?

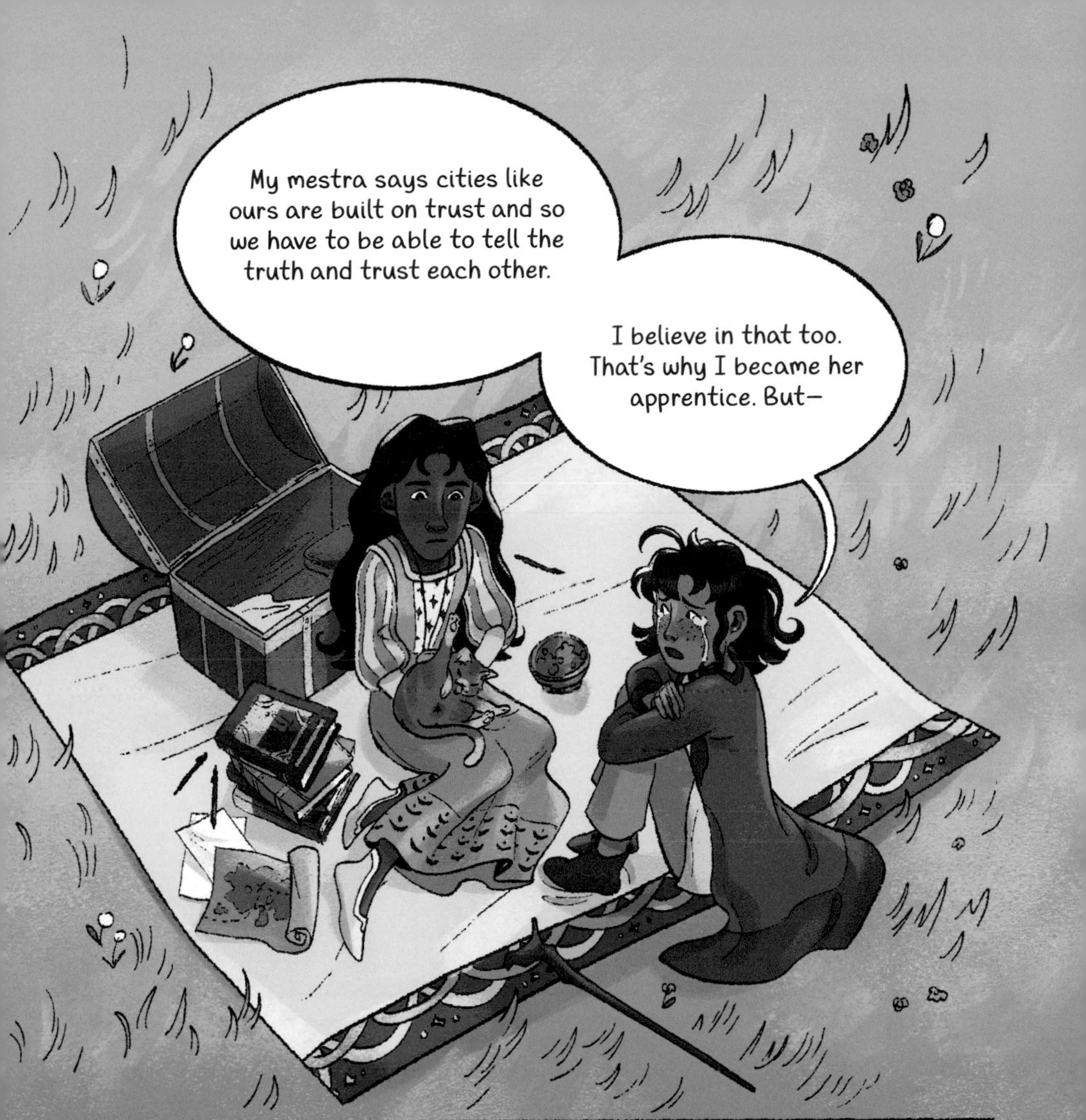
My mestra says cities like ours are built on trust and so we have to be able to tell the truth and trust each other.
I believe in that too. That's why I became her apprentice. But—

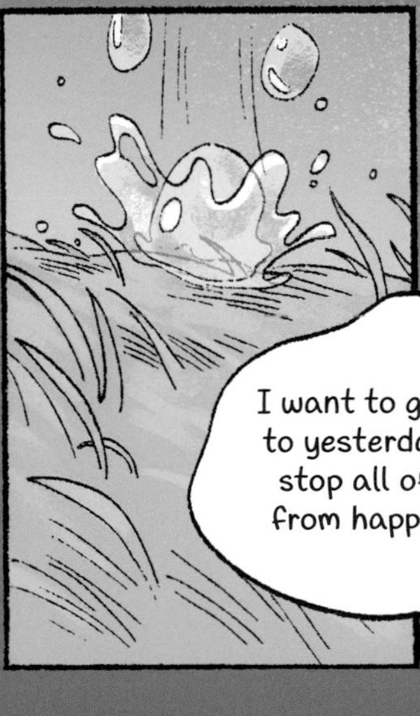

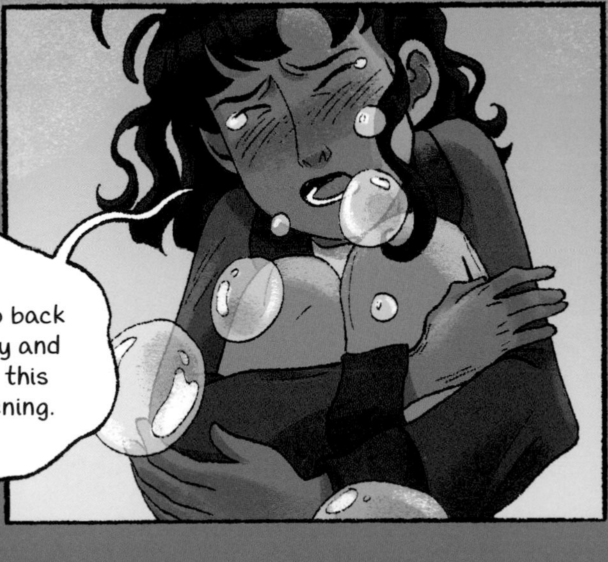
I want to go back to yesterday and stop all of this from happening.

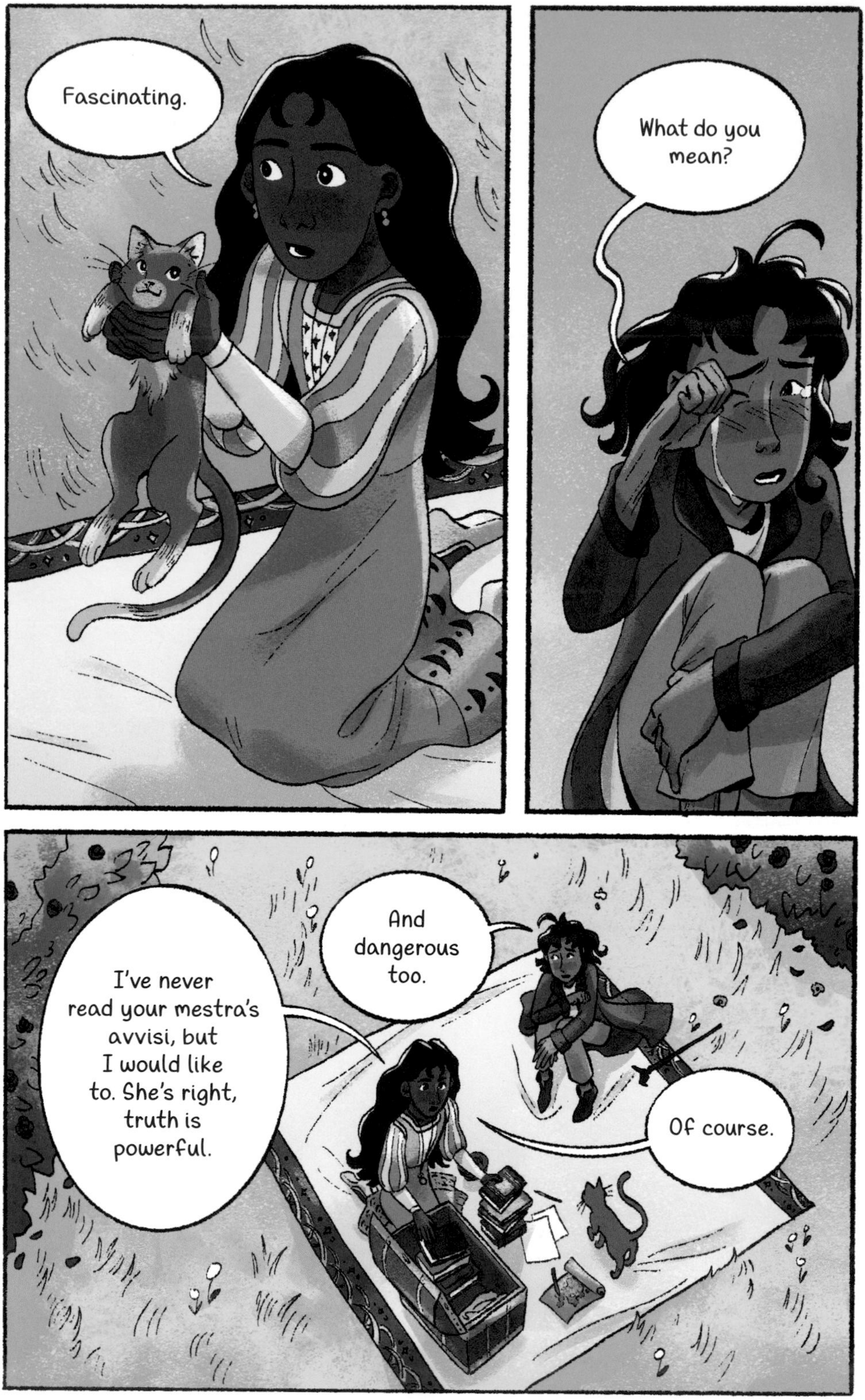
Fascinating.
What do you mean?
I've never read your mestra's avvisi, but I would like to. She's right, truth is powerful.
And dangerous too.
Of course.

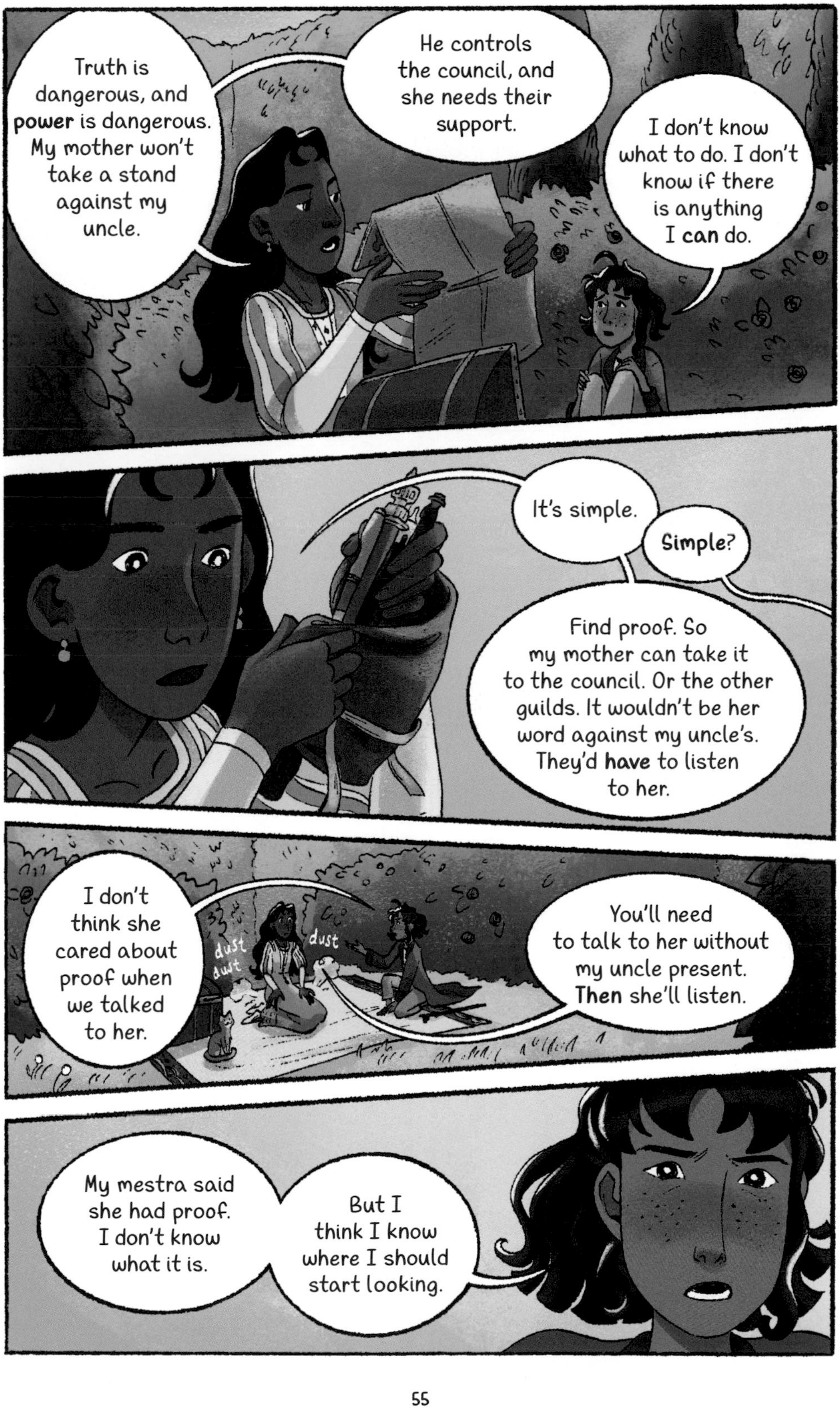
Truth is dangerous, and **power** is dangerous. My mother won't take a stand against my uncle.
He controls the council, and she needs their support.
I don't know what to do. I don't know if there is anything I **can** do.
It's simple.
Simple?
Find proof. So my mother can take it to the council. Or the other guilds. It wouldn't be her word against my uncle's. They'd **have** to listen to her.
I don't think she cared about proof when we talked to her.
dust
dust
dust
You'll need to talk to her without my uncle present. **Then** she'll listen.
My mestra said she had proof. I don't know what it is.
But I think I know where I should start looking.

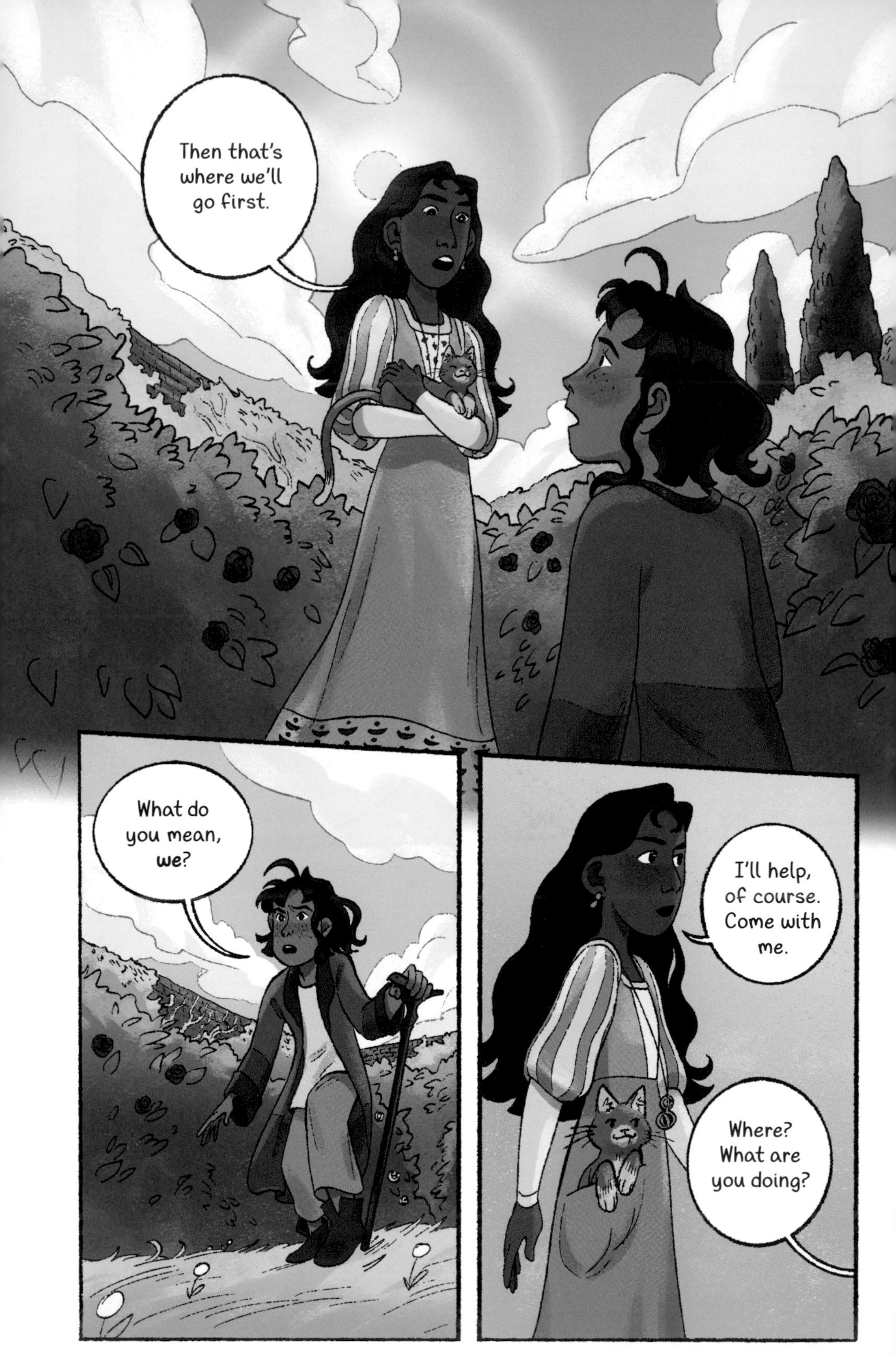
Then that's where we'll go first.
What do you mean, **we**?
I'll help, of course. Come with me.
Where? What are you doing?

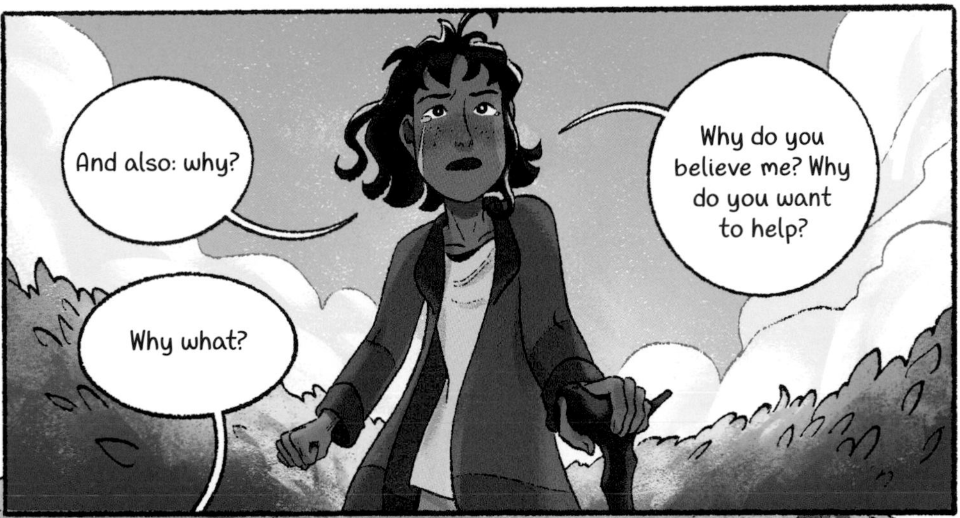
Why do you believe me? Why do you want to help?
And also: why?
Why what?

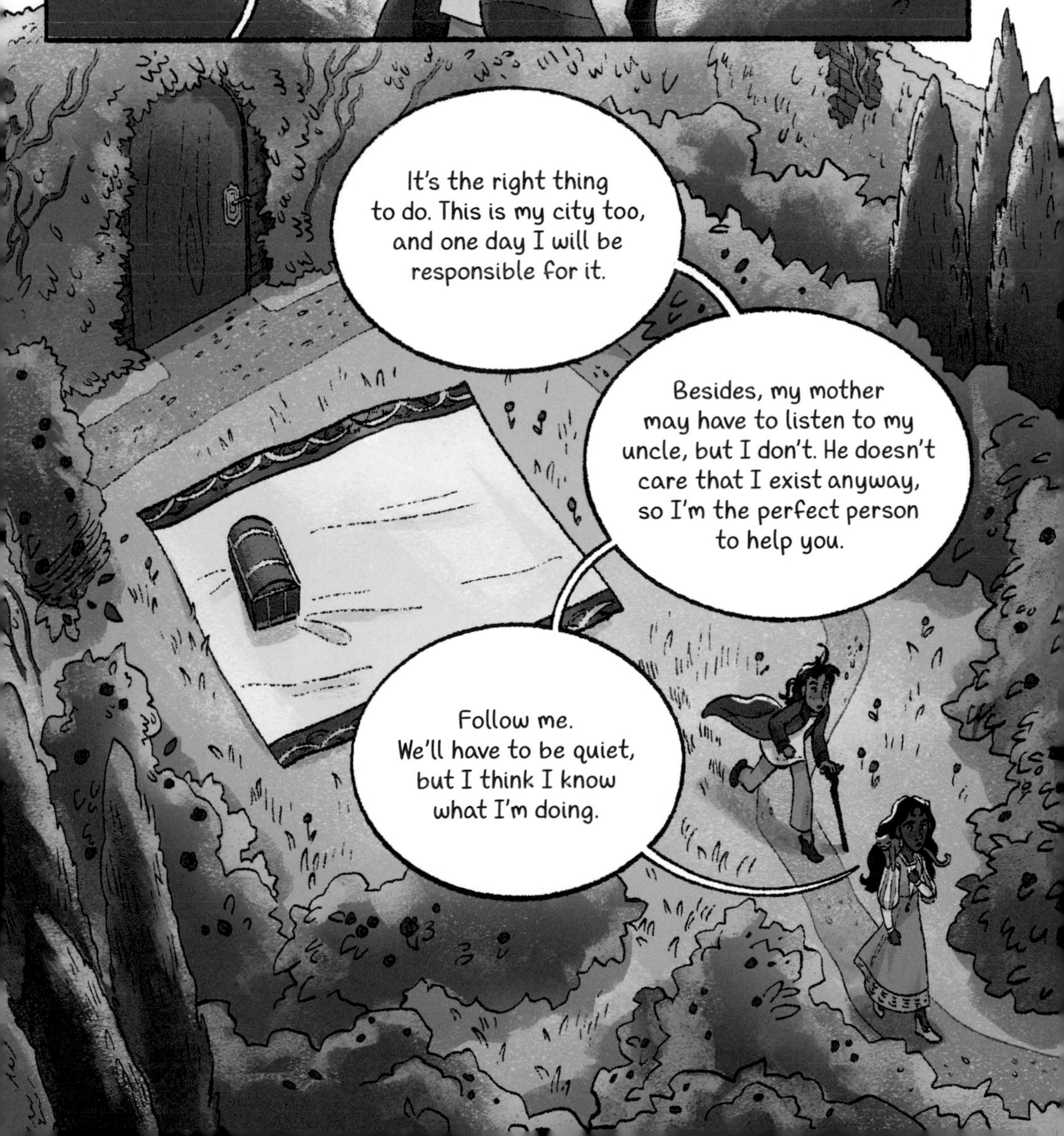
It's the right thing to do. This is my city too, and one day I will be responsible for it.
Besides, my mother may have to listen to my uncle, but I don't. He doesn't care that I exist anyway, so I'm the perfect person to help you.
Follow me. We'll have to be quiet, but I think I know what I'm doing.

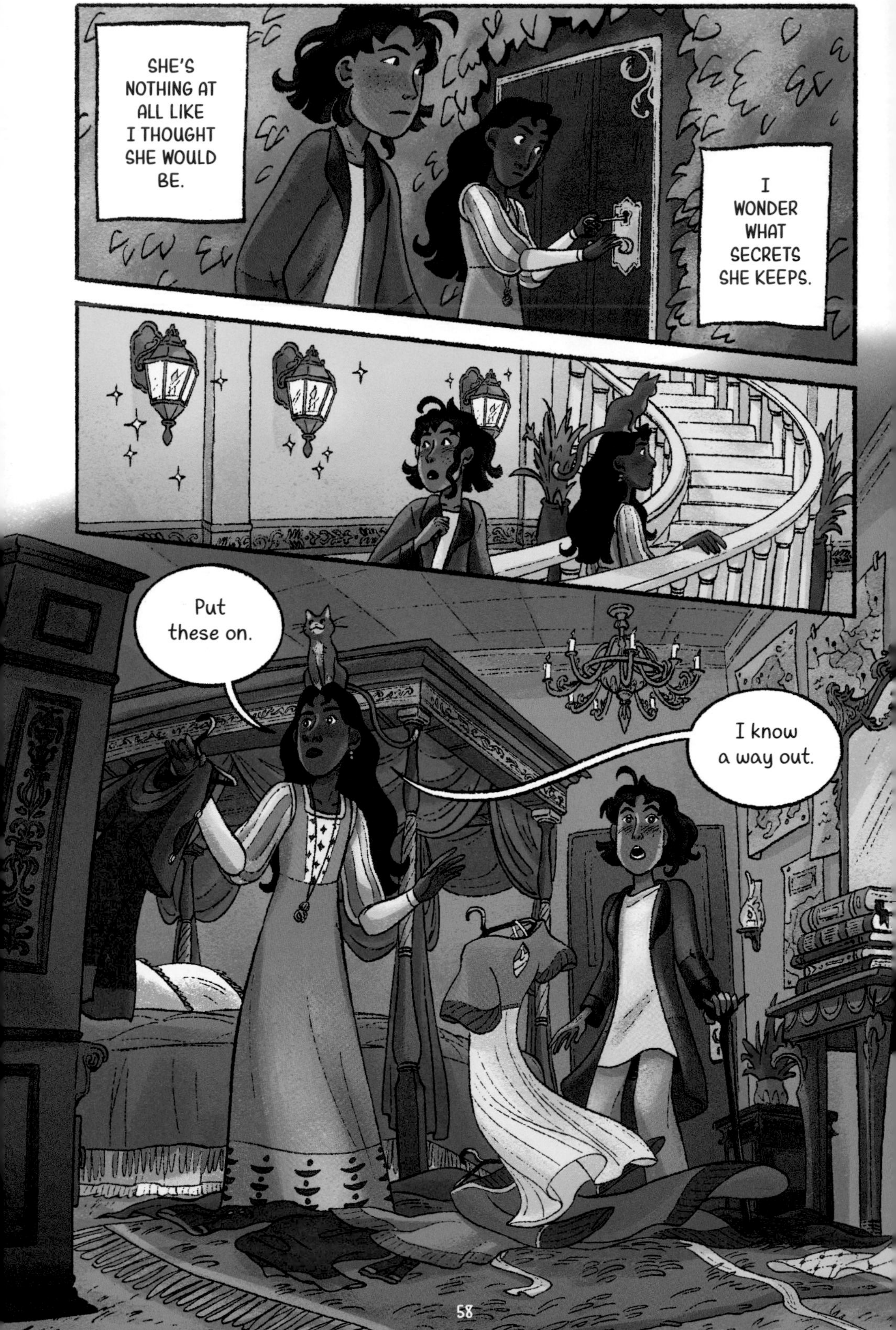
SHE'S NOTHING AT ALL LIKE I THOUGHT SHE WOULD BE.
I WONDER WHAT SECRETS SHE KEEPS.
Put these on.
I know a way out.

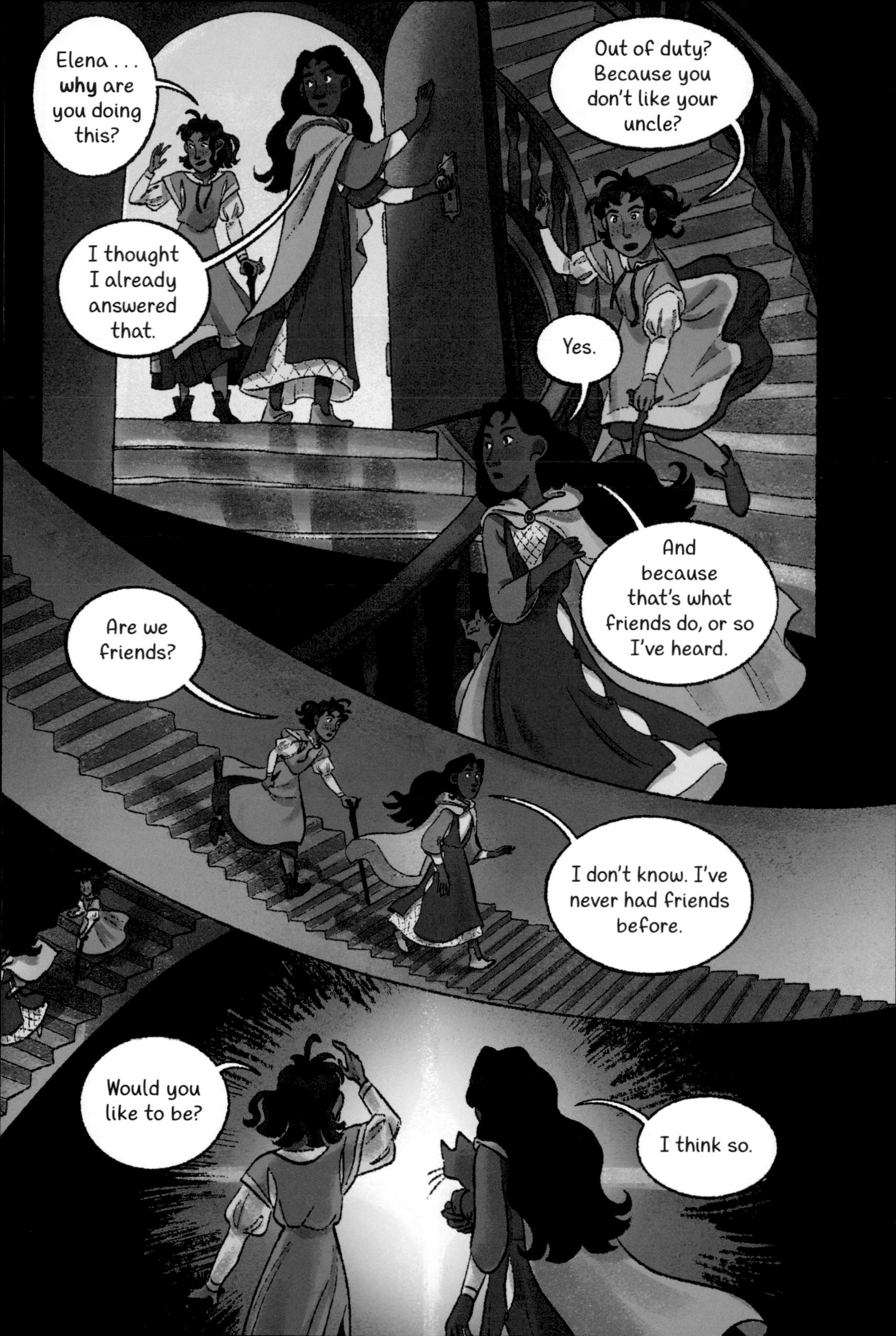
Elena . . . **why** are you doing this?
I thought I already answered that.
Out of duty? Because you don't like your uncle?
Yes.
And because that's what friends do, or so I've heard.
Are we friends?
I don't know. I've never had friends before.
Would you like to be?
I think so.

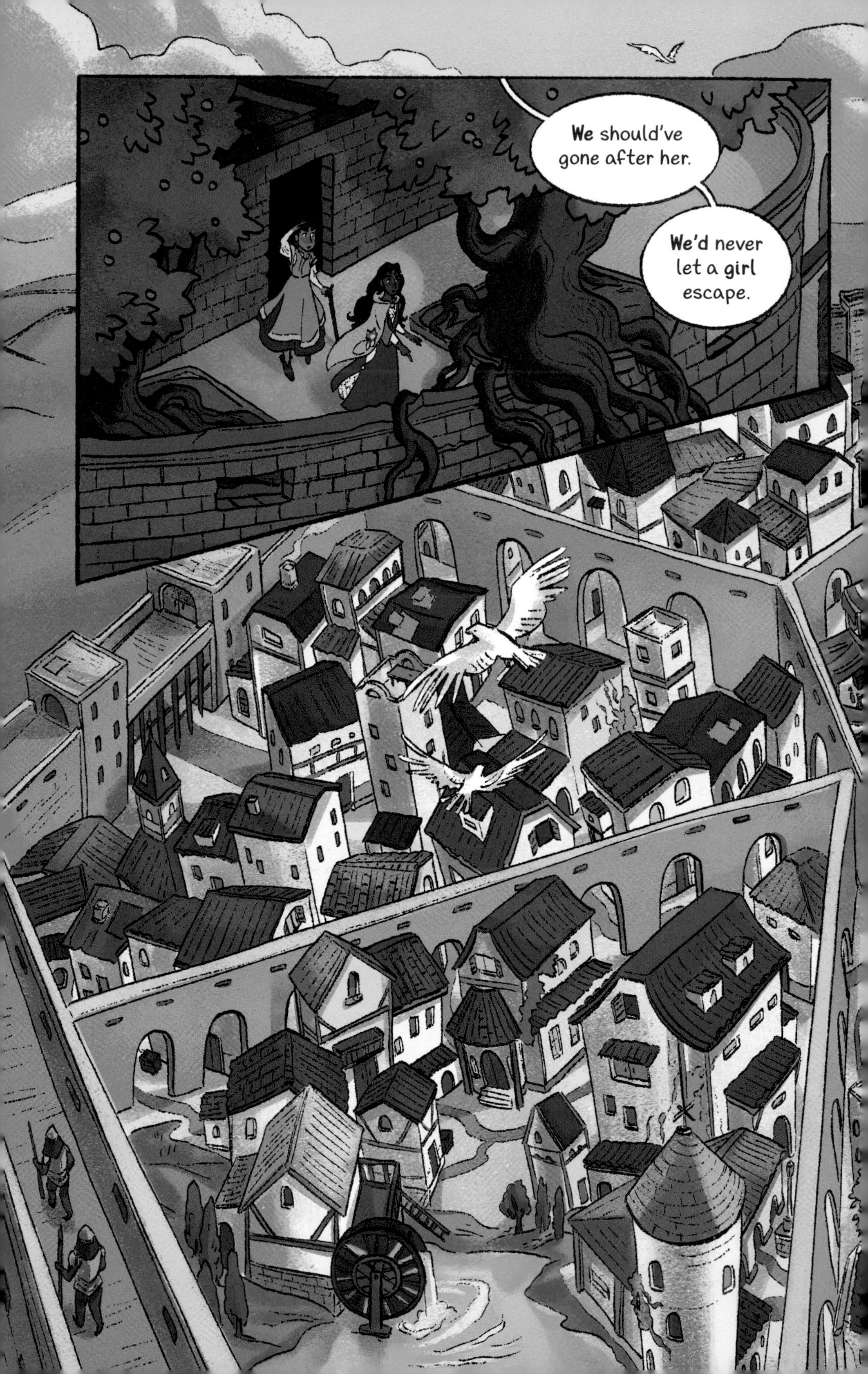
We should've gone after her.
We'd never let a **girl** escape.

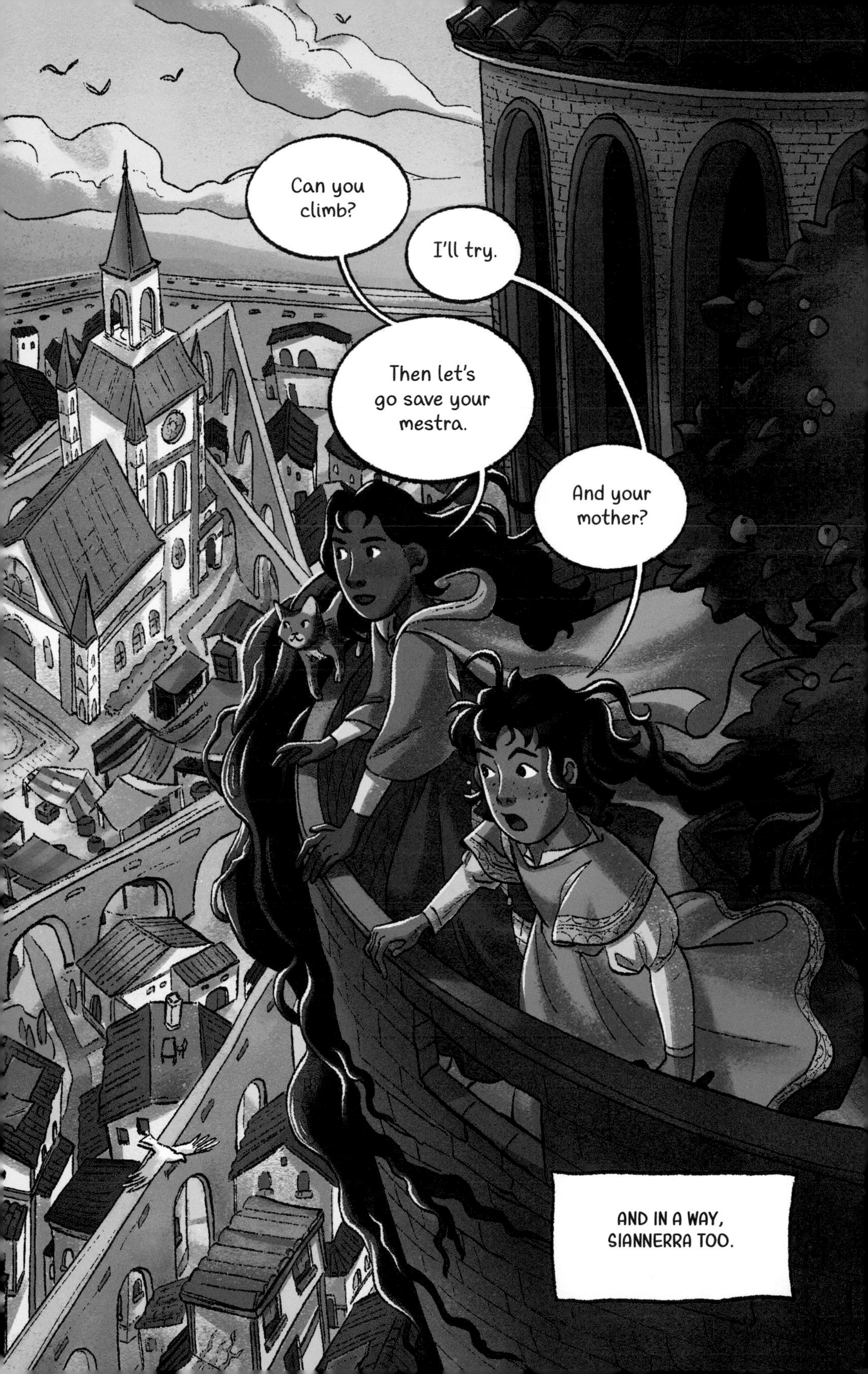
Can you climb?
I'll try.
Then let's go save your mestra.
And your mother?
AND IN A WAY, SIANNERRA TOO.

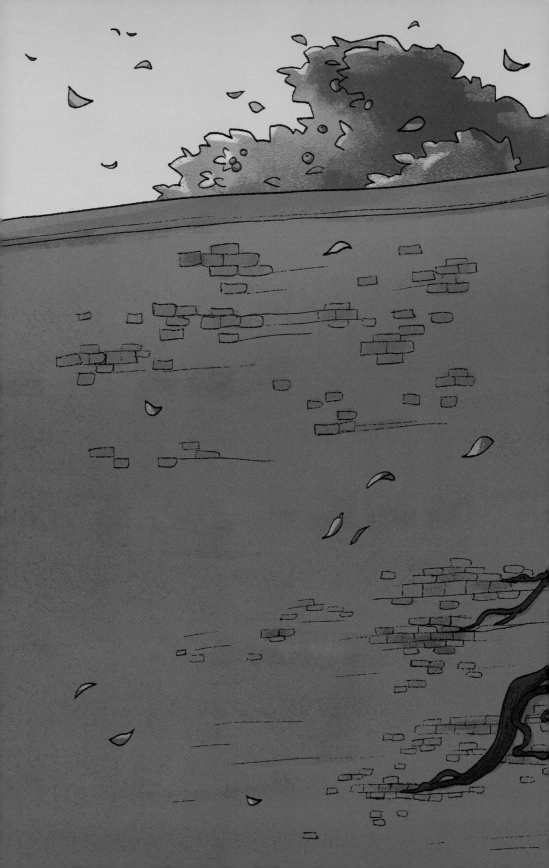

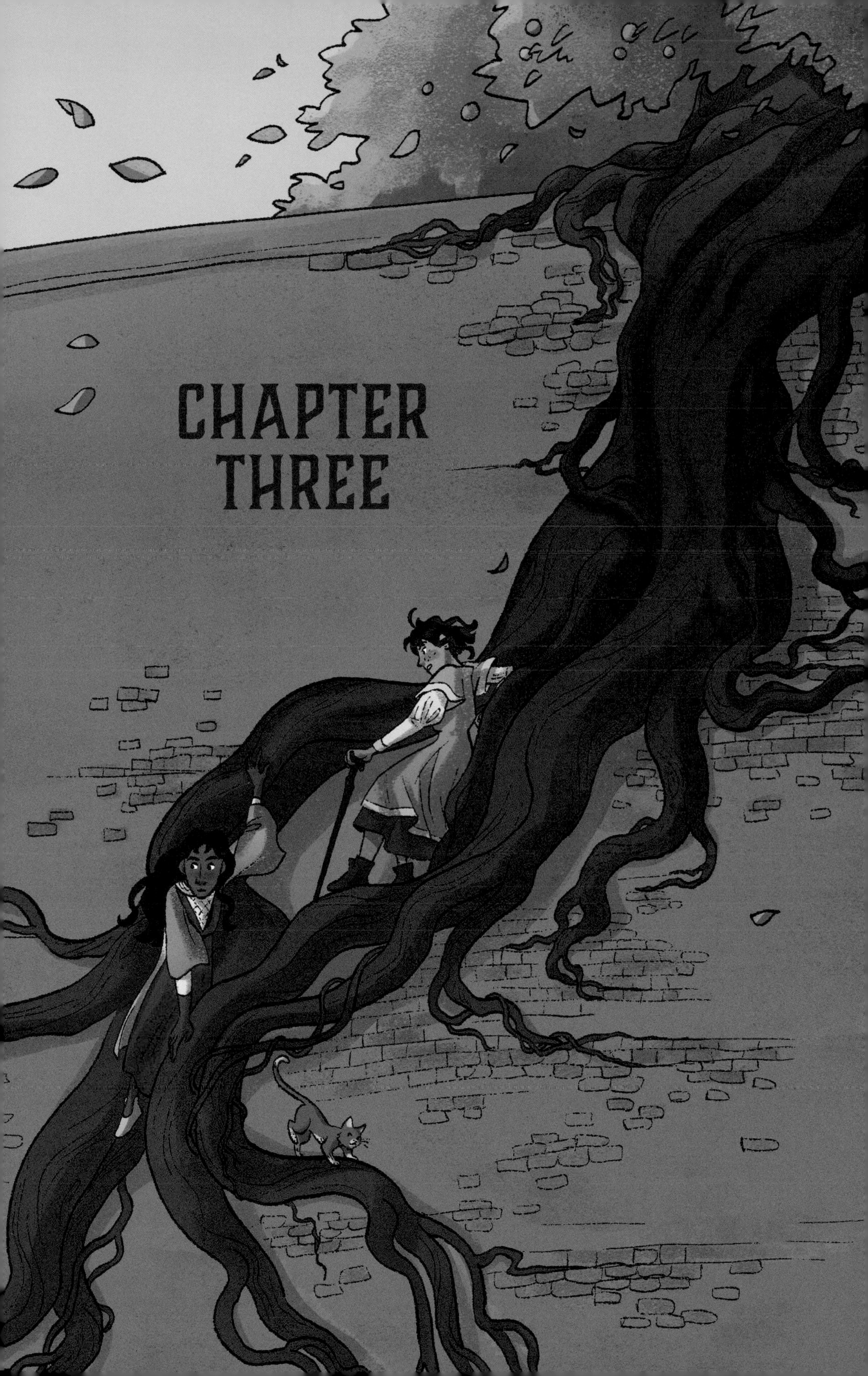
CHAPTER
THREE

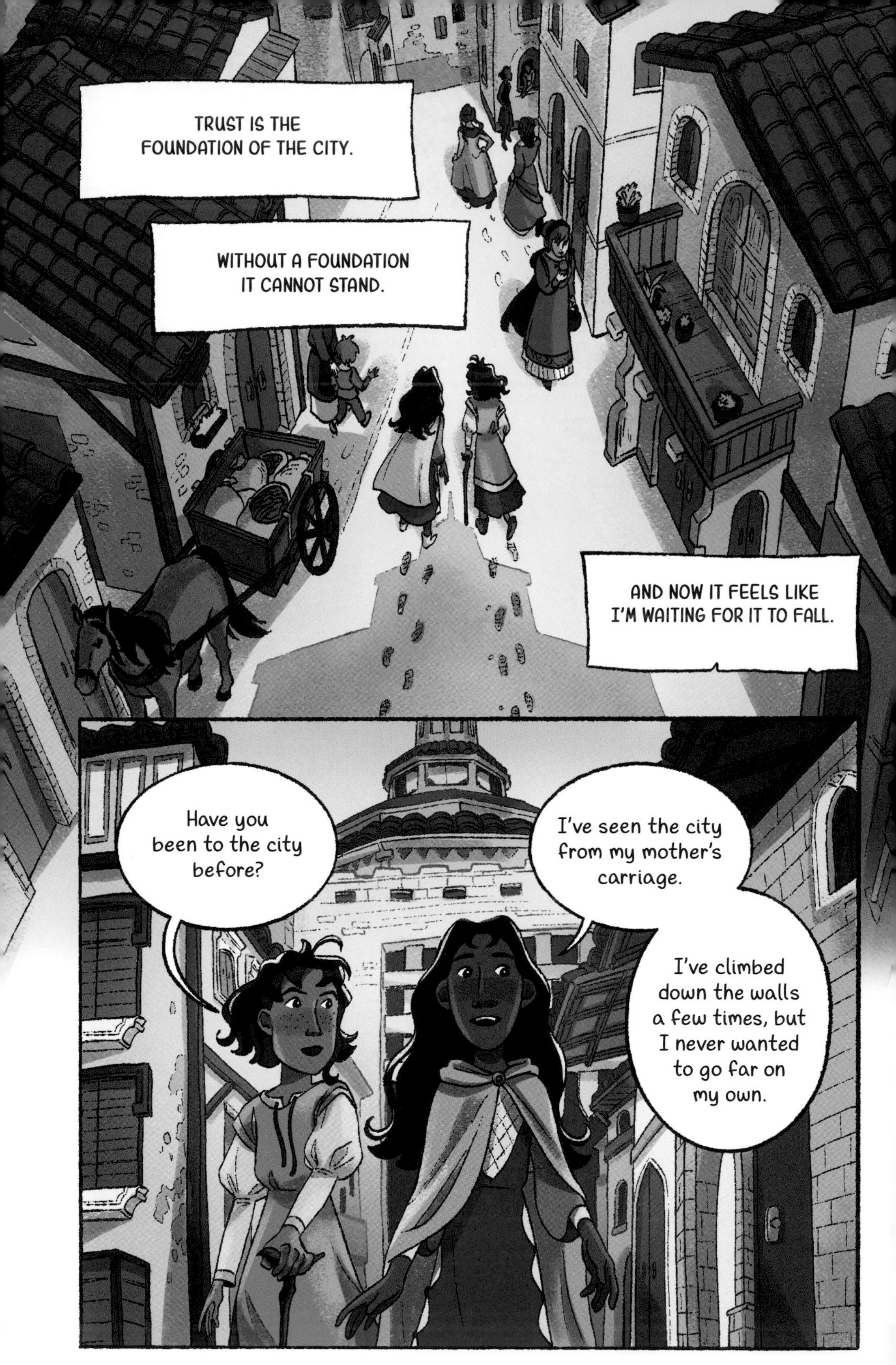
TRUST IS THE FOUNDATION OF THE CITY.
WITHOUT A FOUNDATION IT CANNOT STAND.
AND NOW IT FEELS LIKE I'M WAITING FOR IT TO FALL.
Have you been to the city before?
I've seen the city from my mother's carriage.
I've climbed down the walls a few times, but I never wanted to go far on my own.

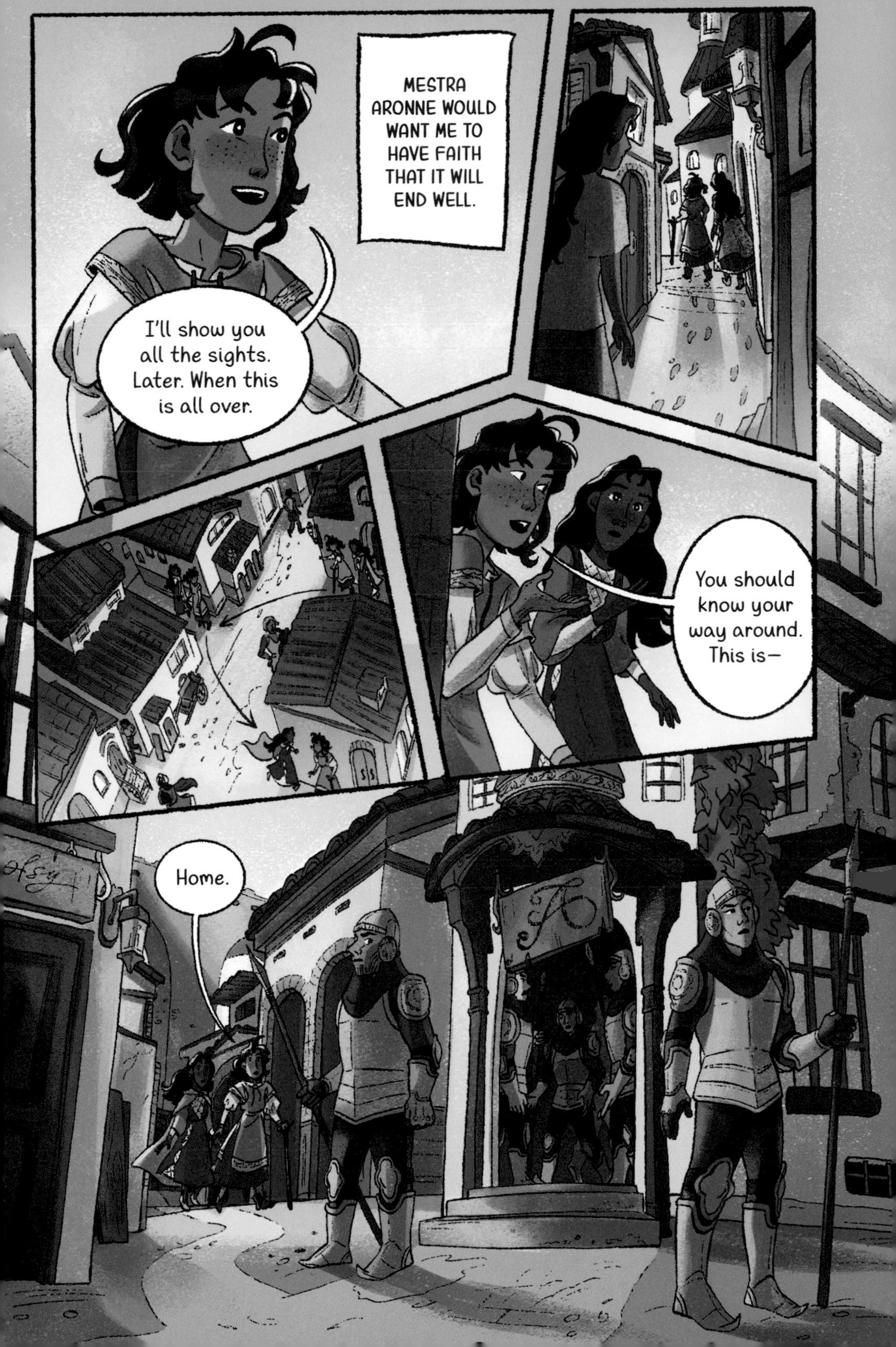
MESTRA ARONNE WOULD WANT ME TO HAVE FAITH THAT IT WILL END WELL.
I'll show you all the sights. Later. When this is all over.
You should know your way around. This is—
Home.

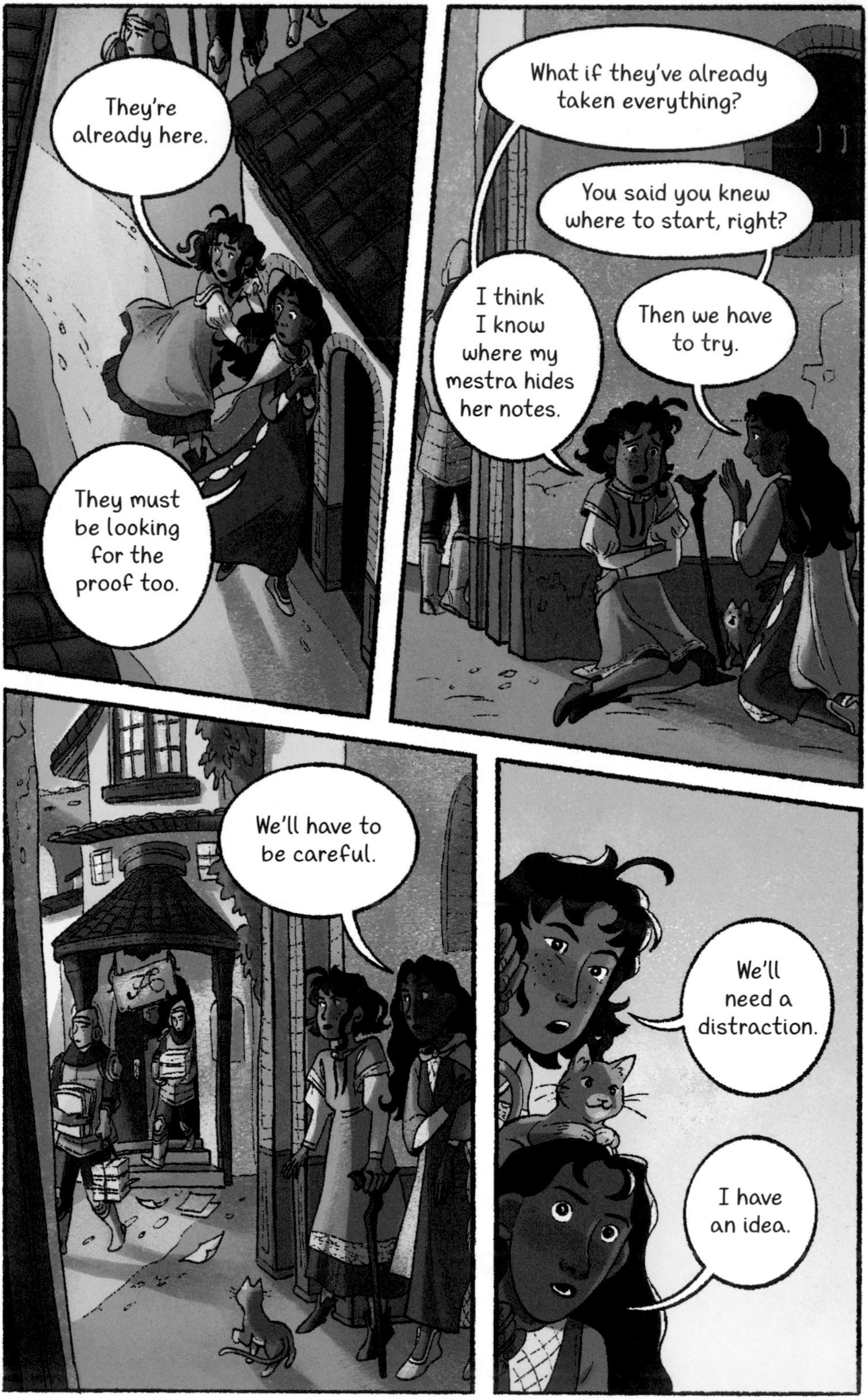
They're already here.
They must be looking for the proof too.
What if they've already taken everything?
You said you knew where to start, right?
I think I know where my mestra hides her notes.
Then we have to try.
We'll have to be careful.
We'll need a distraction.
I have an idea.

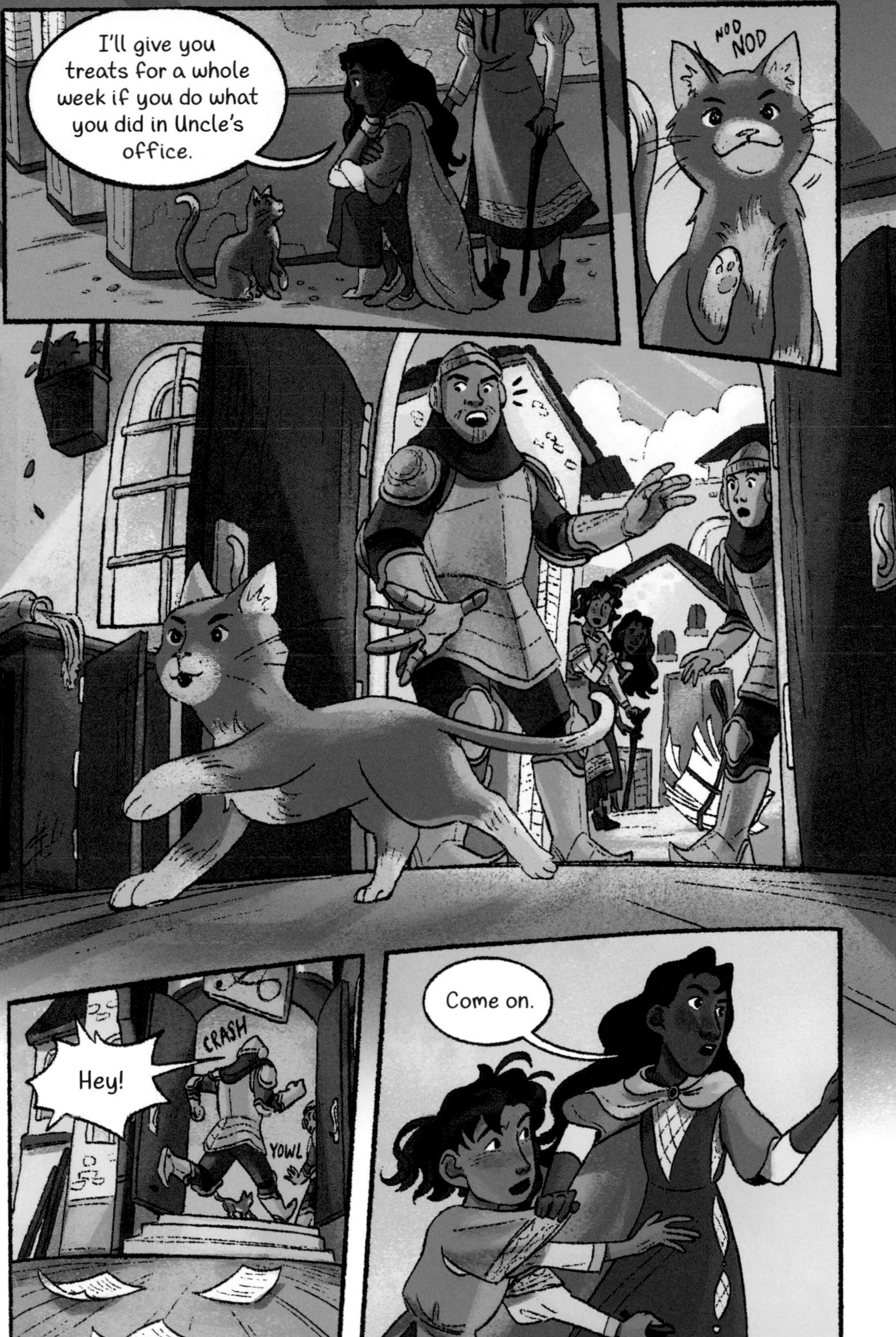
I'll give you treats for a whole week if you do what you did in Uncle's office.
NOD NOD
Hey!
CRASH
YOWL
Come on.

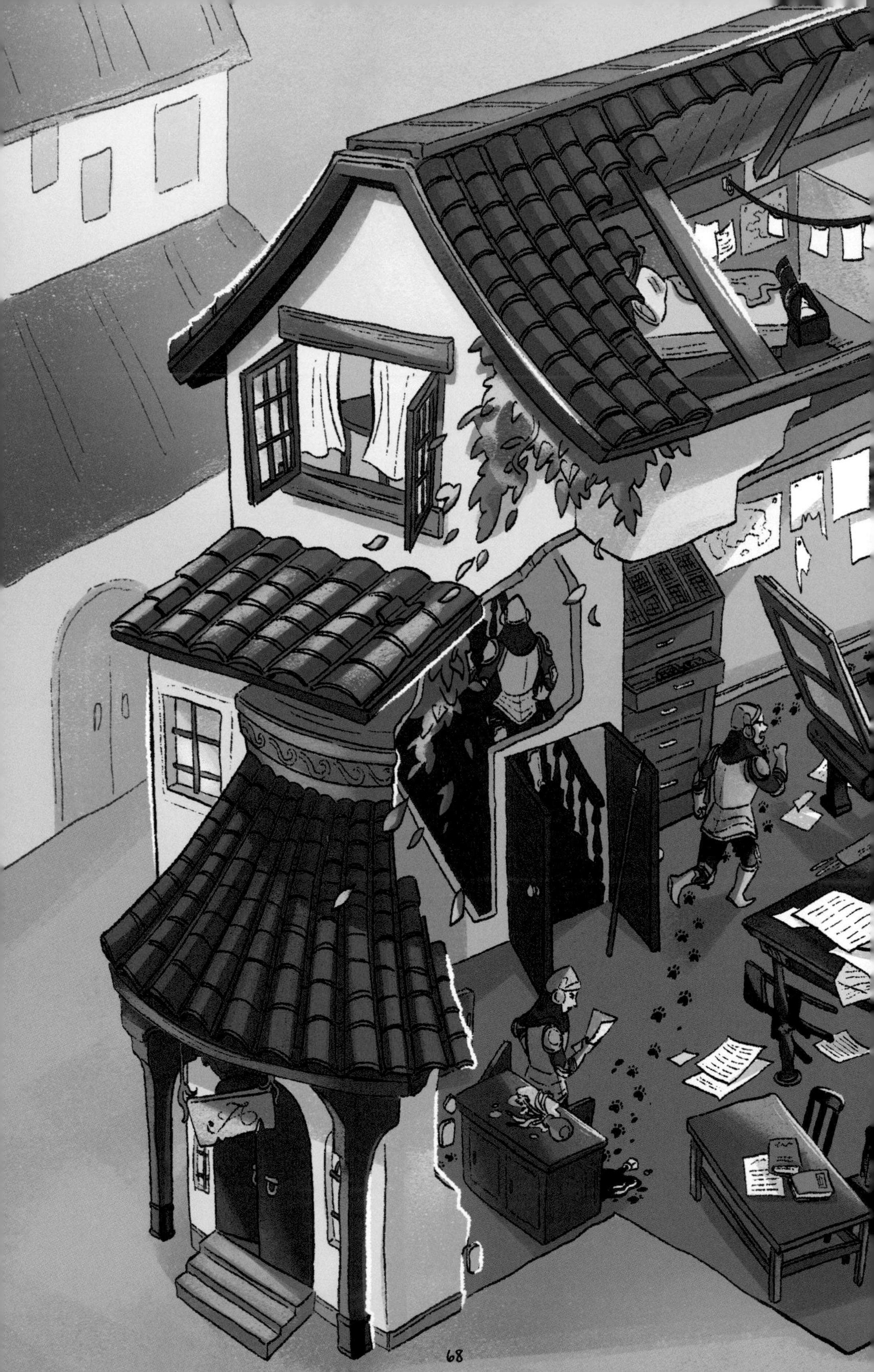

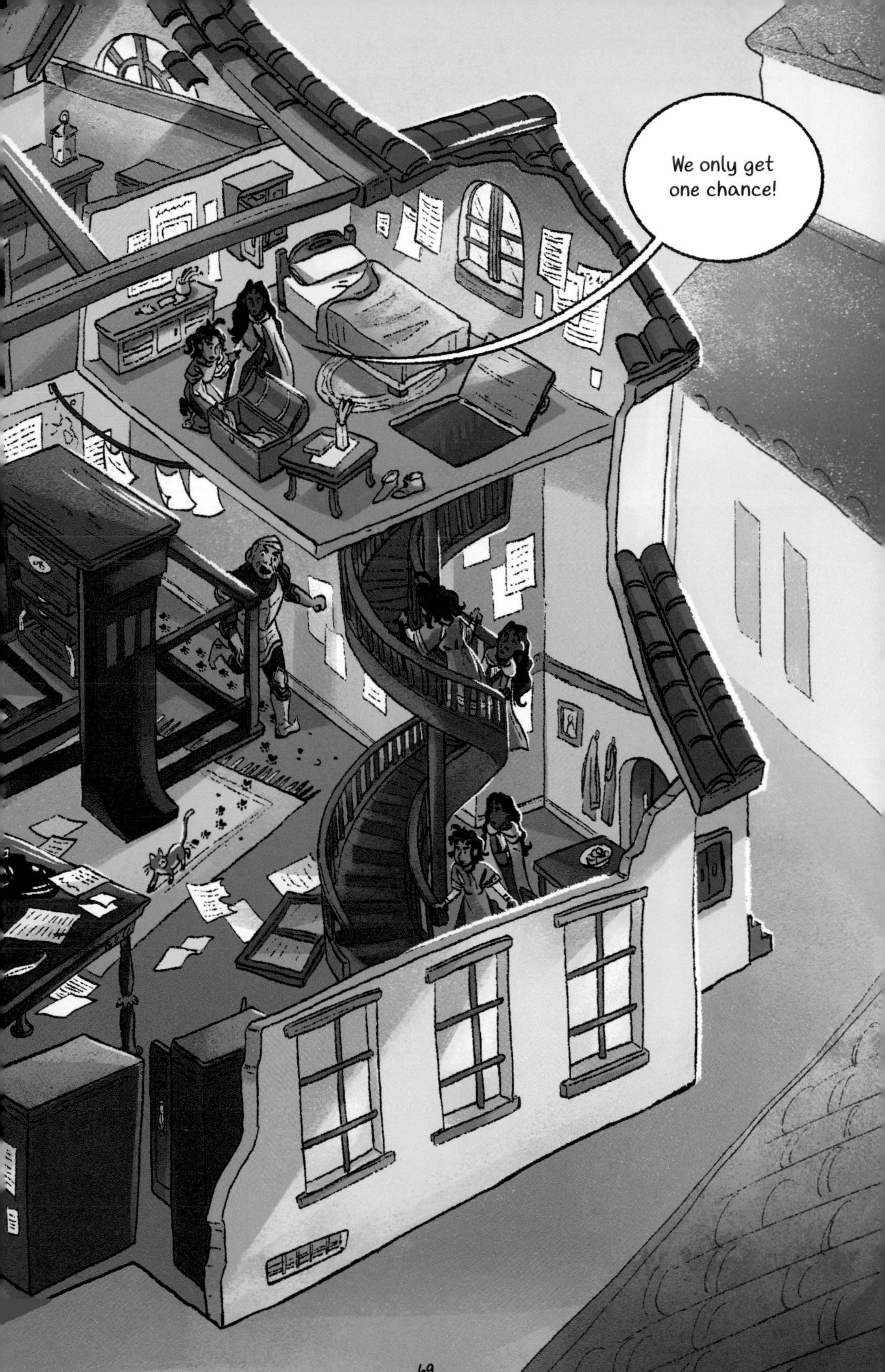
We only get one chance!

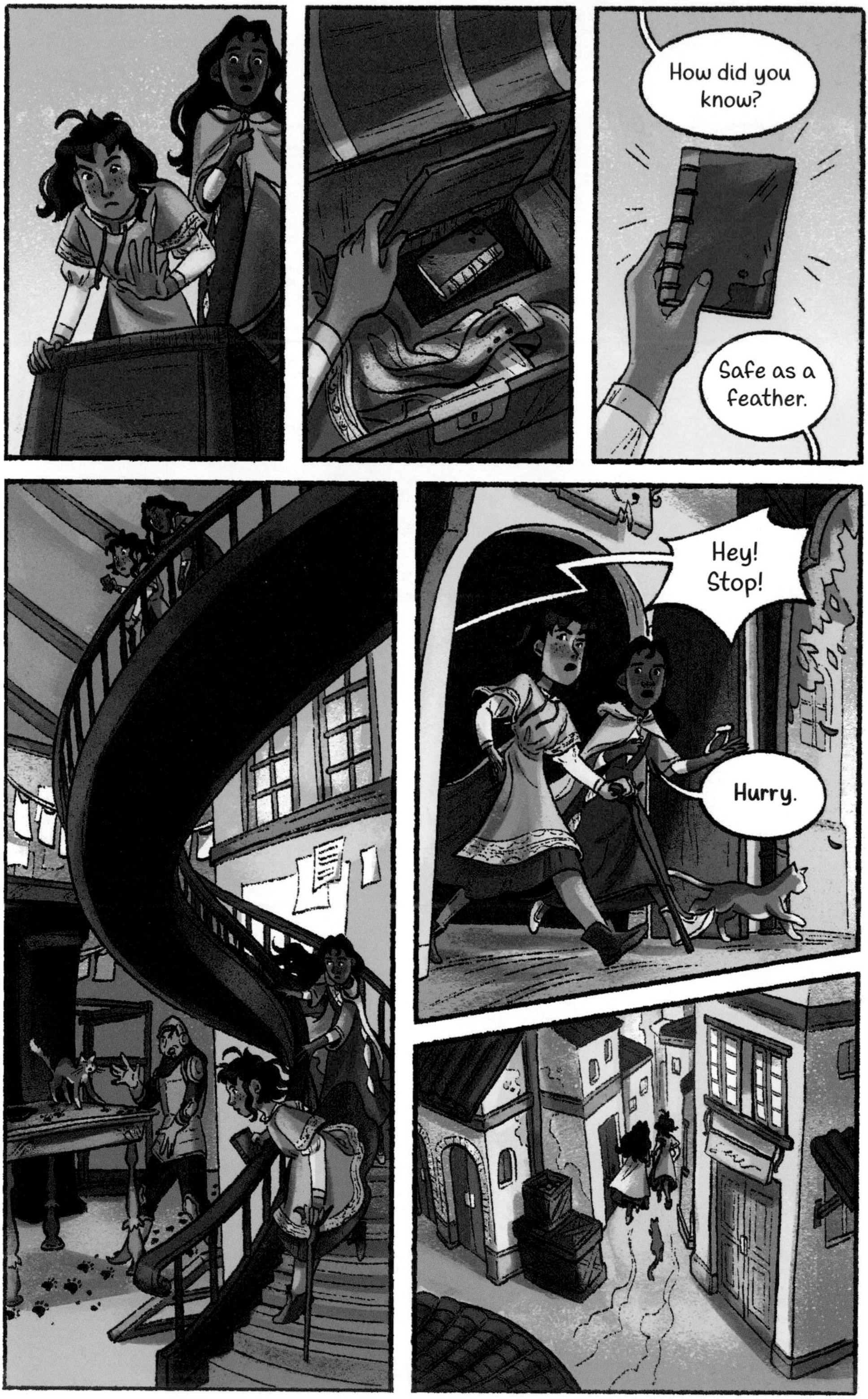
How did you know?
Safe as a feather.
Hey! Stop!
Hurry.

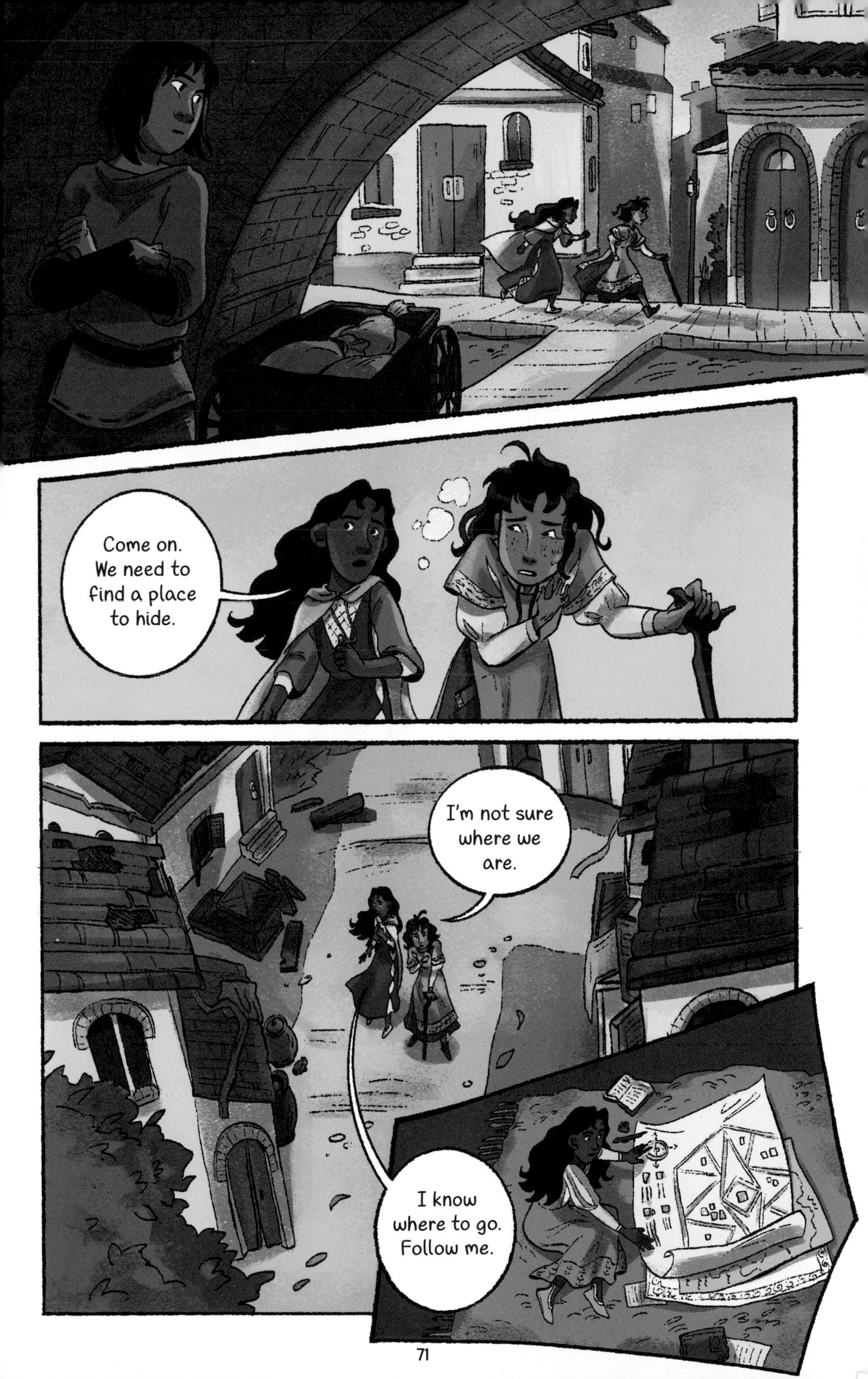
Come on. We need to find a place to hide.
I'm not sure where we are.
I know where to go. Follow me.

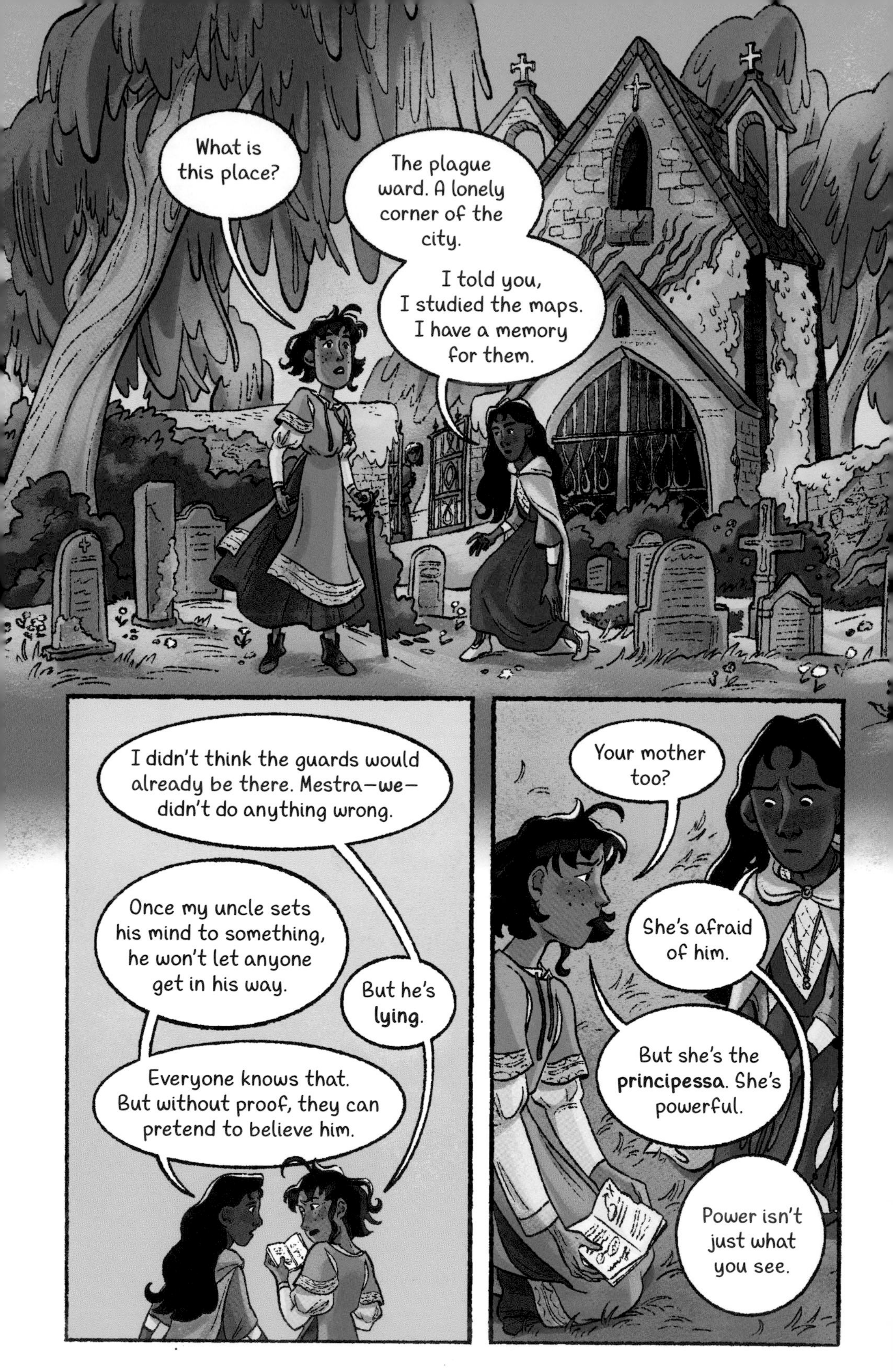
What is this place?
The plague ward. A lonely corner of the city.
I told you, I studied the maps. I have a memory for them.
I didn't think the guards would already be there. Mestra—we—didn't do anything wrong.
Once my uncle sets his mind to something, he won't let anyone get in his way.
But he's **lying**.
Everyone knows that. But without proof, they can pretend to believe him.
Your mother too?
She's afraid of him.
But she's the **principessa**. She's powerful.
Power isn't just what you see.

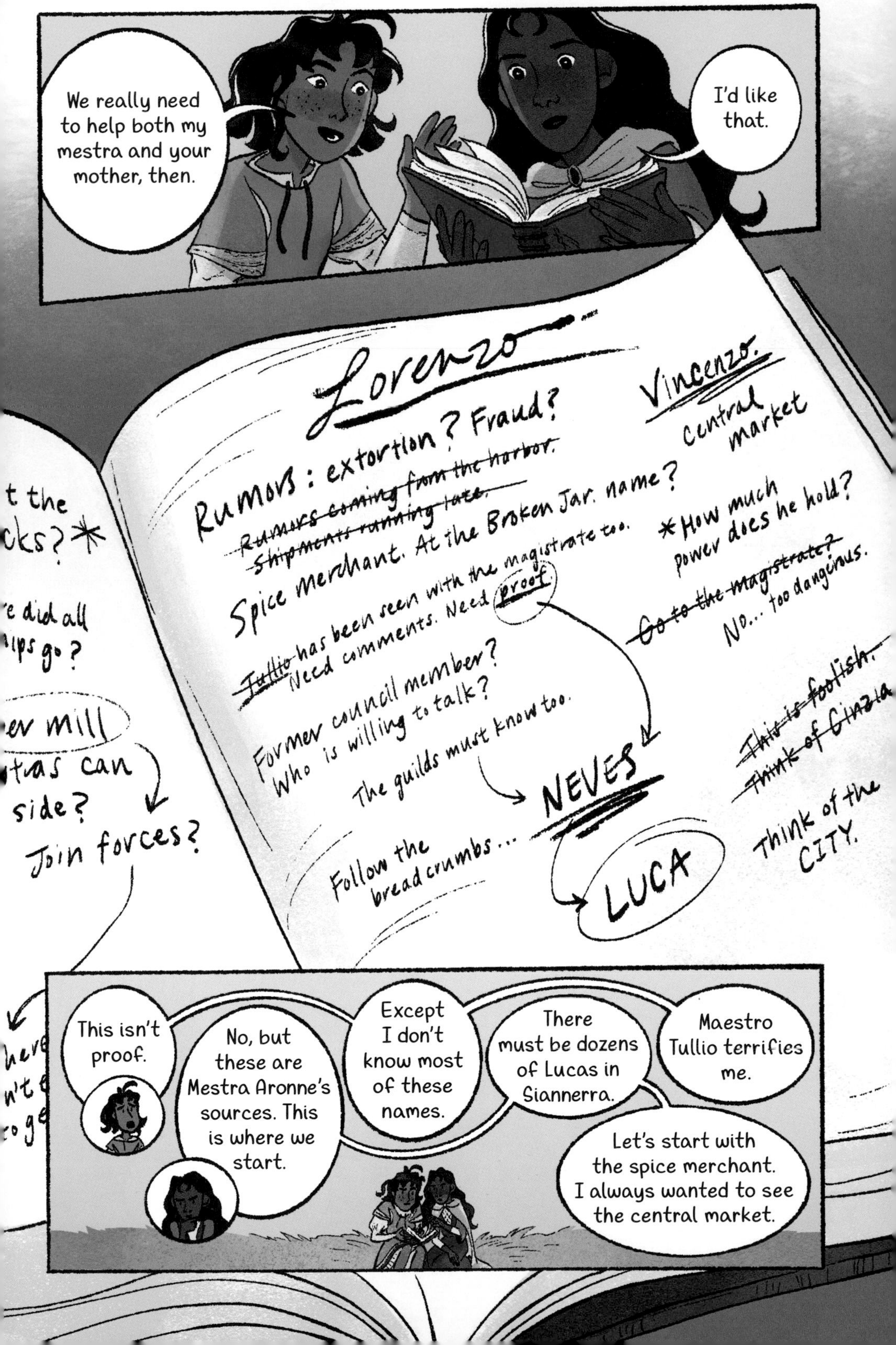
We really need to help both my mestra and your mother, then.
I'd like that.
Lorenzo
Rumors: extortion? Fraud?
Rumors coming from the harbor.
Shipments running late.
Spice merchant. At the Broken Jar. name?
Tullio has been seen with the magistrate too.
Need comments. Need proof
Former council member?
Who is willing to talk?
The guilds must know too.
NEVES
Follow the breadcrumbs...
LUCA
Vincenzo.
Central market
* How much power does he hold?
Go to the magistrate?
No... too dangerous.
This is foolish.
Think of the CITY.
side?
Join forces?
This isn't proof.
No, but these are Mestra Aronne's sources. This is where we start.
Except I don't know most of these names.
There must be dozens of Lucas in Siannerra.
Maestro Tullio terrifies me.
Let's start with the spice merchant. I always wanted to see the central market.

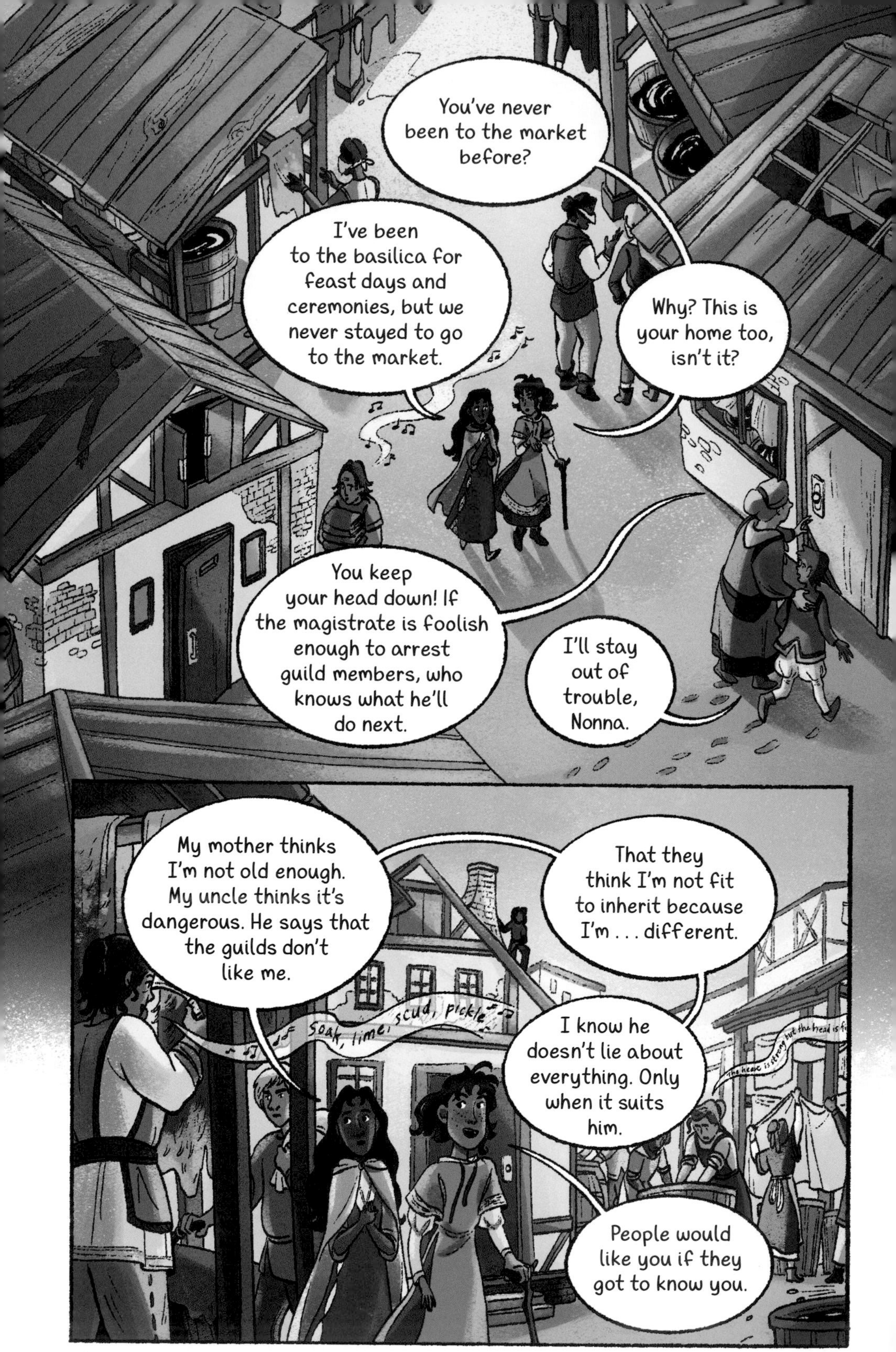
You've never been to the market before?
I've been to the basilica for feast days and ceremonies, but we never stayed to go to the market.
Why? This is your home too, isn't it?
You keep your head down! If the magistrate is foolish enough to arrest guild members, who knows what he'll do next.
I'll stay out of trouble, Nonna.
My mother thinks I'm not old enough. My uncle thinks it's dangerous. He says that the guilds don't like me.
That they think I'm not fit to inherit because I'm . . . different.
Soak, lime, scud, pickle
I know he doesn't lie about everything. Only when it suits him.
People would like you if they got to know you.

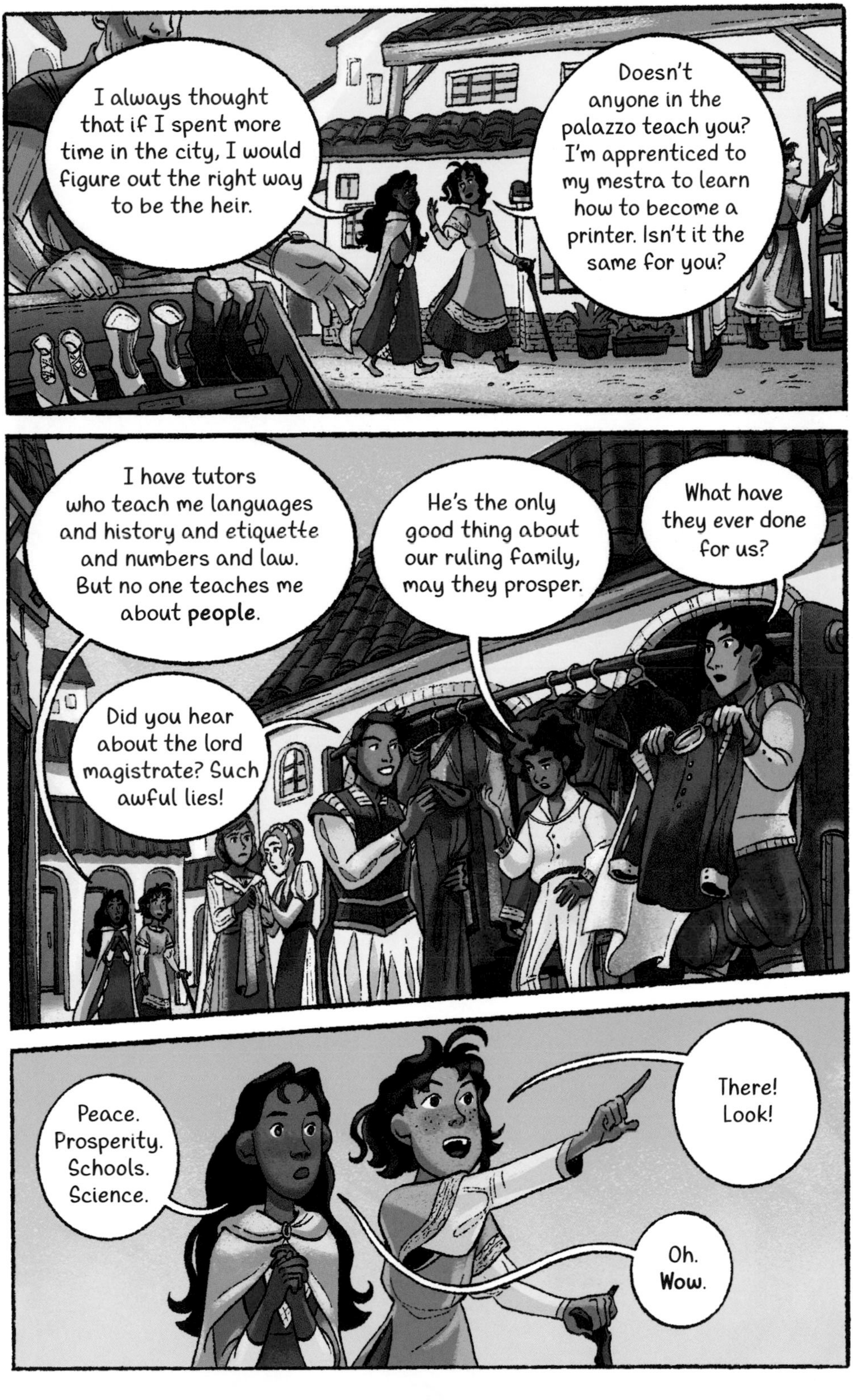
I always thought that if I spent more time in the city, I would figure out the right way to be the heir.
Doesn't anyone in the palazzo teach you? I'm apprenticed to my mestra to learn how to become a printer. Isn't it the same for you?
I have tutors who teach me languages and history and etiquette and numbers and law. But no one teaches me about **people**.
He's the only good thing about our ruling family, may they prosper.
What have they ever done for us?
Did you hear about the lord magistrate? Such awful lies!
Peace. Prosperity. Schools. Science.
There! Look!
Oh. **Wow.**

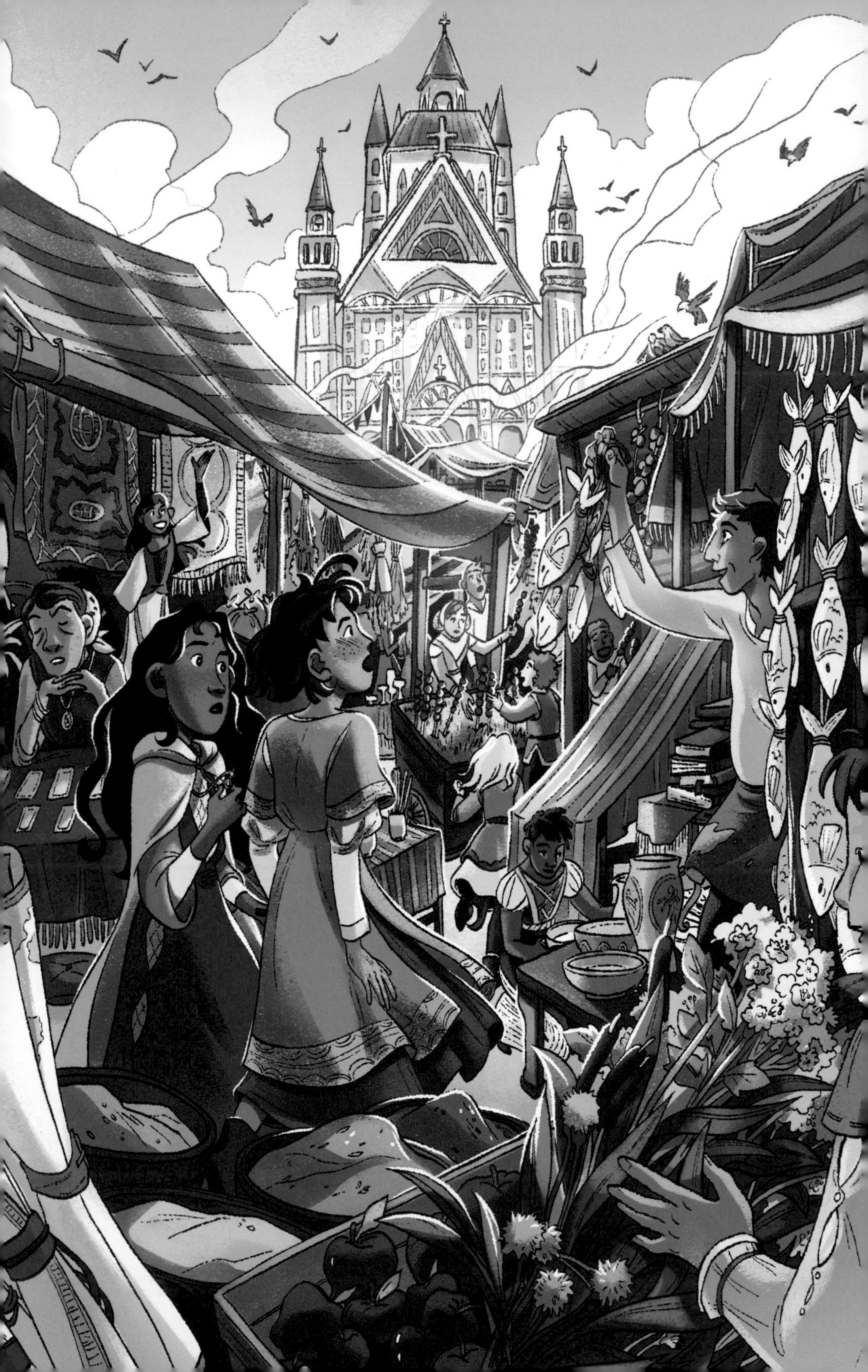

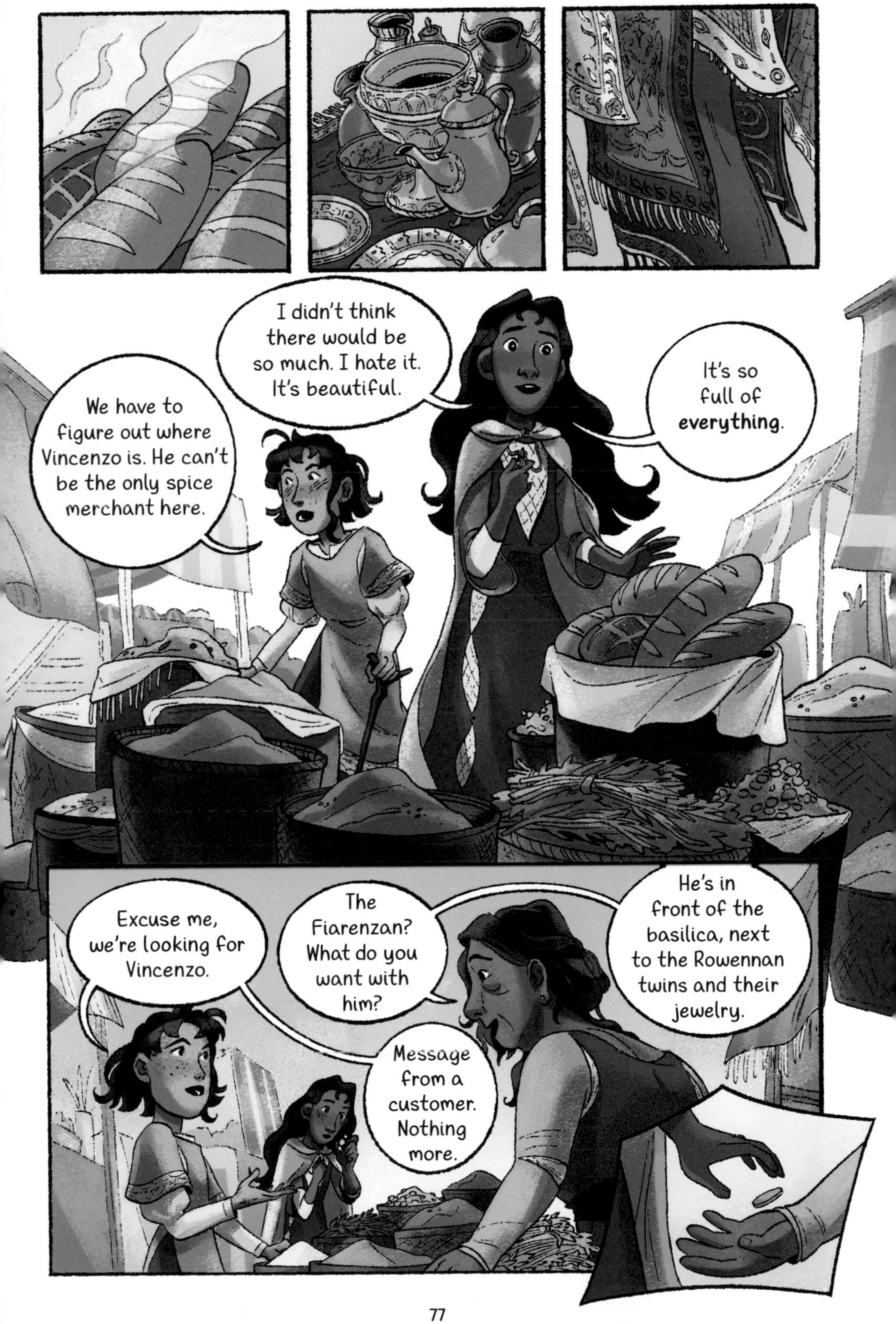
I didn't think there would be so much. I hate it. It's beautiful.
It's so full of **everything**.
We have to figure out where Vincenzo is. He can't be the only spice merchant here.
Excuse me, we're looking for Vincenzo.
The Fiarenzan? What do you want with him?
Message from a customer. Nothing more.
He's in front of the basilica, next to the Rowennan twins and their jewelry.

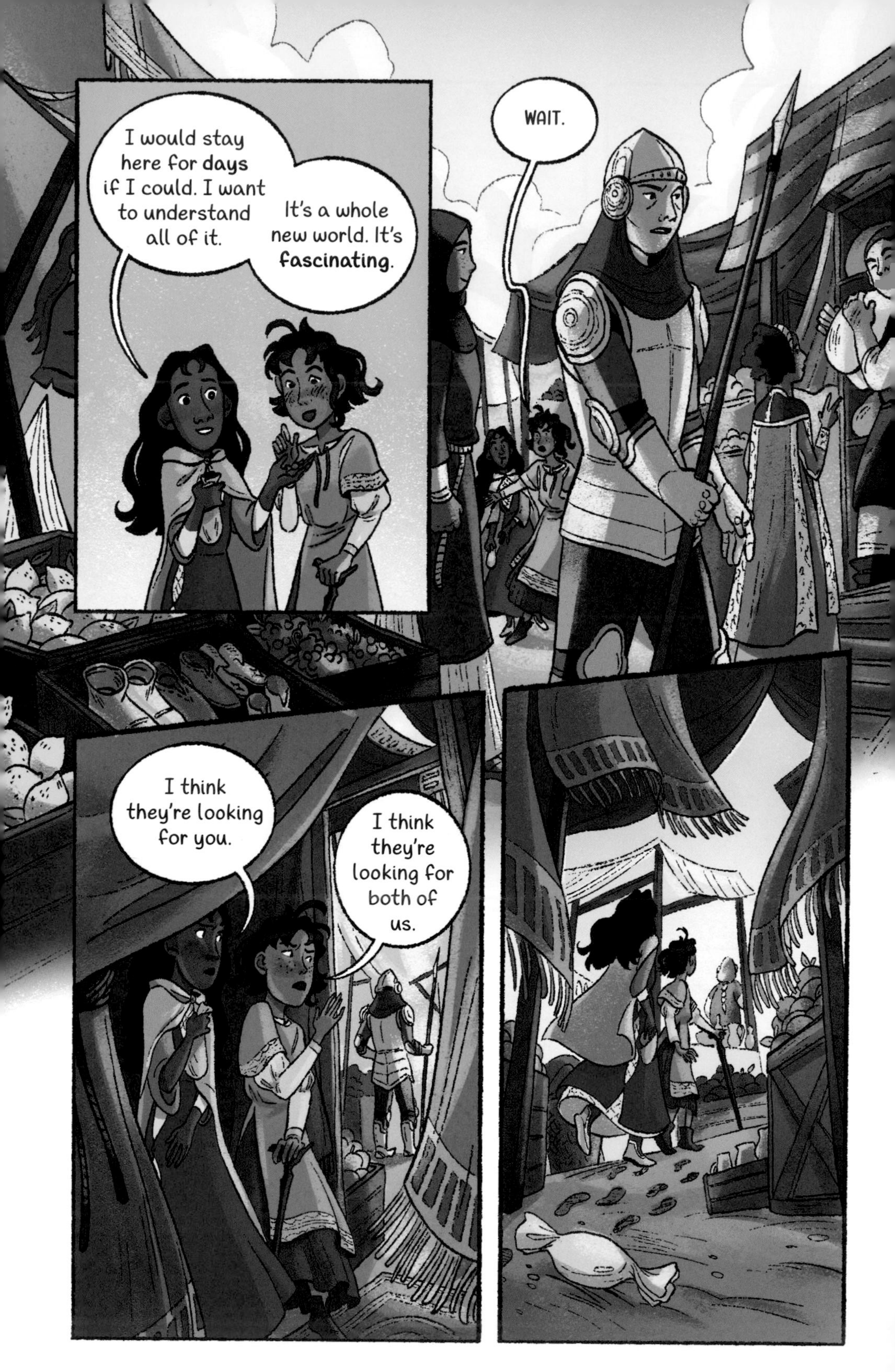
I would stay here for days if I could. I want to understand all of it.
It's a whole new world. It's fascinating.
WAIT.
I think they're looking for you.
I think they're looking for both of us.

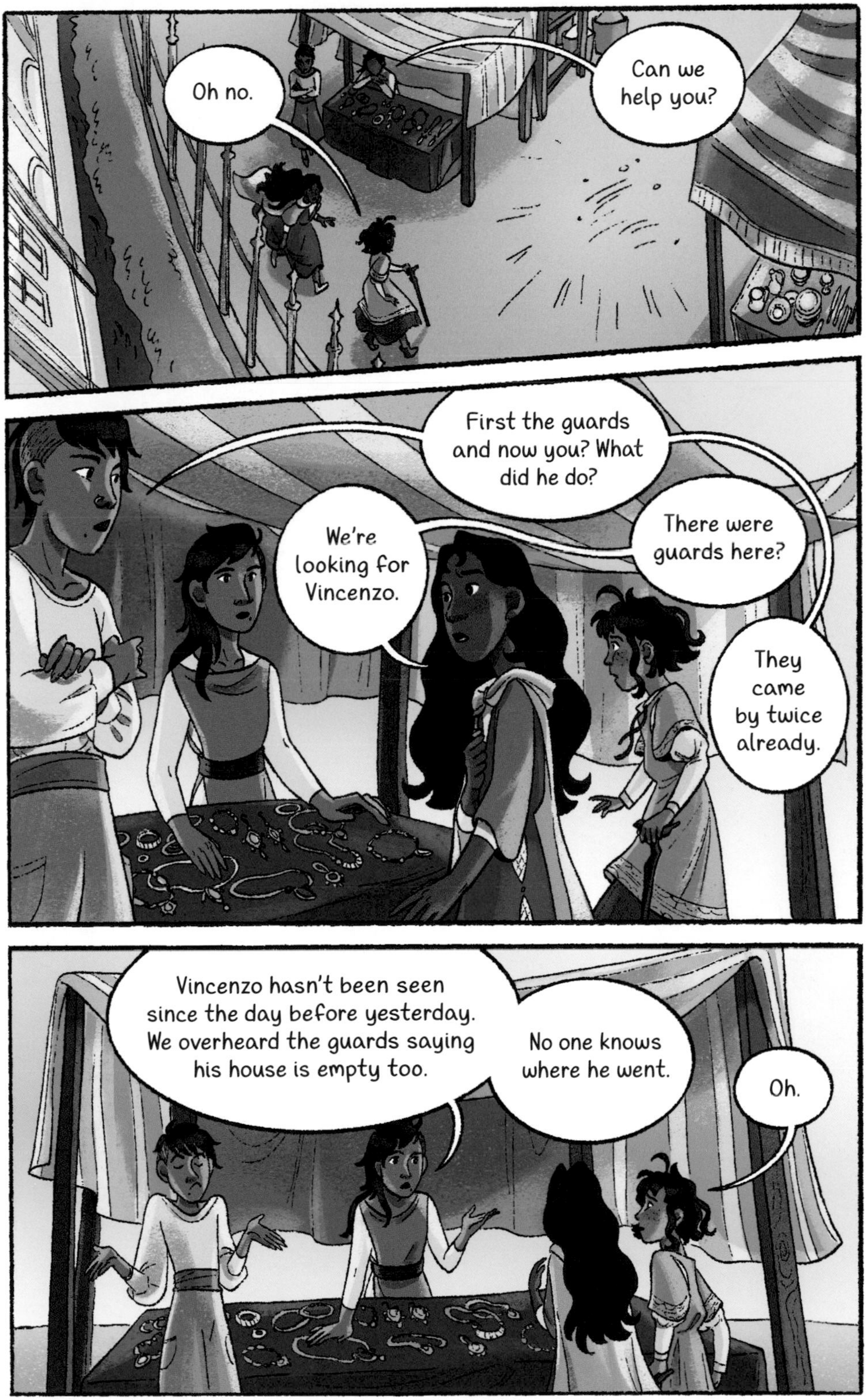
Oh no.
Can we help you?
First the guards and now you? What did he do?
We're looking for Vincenzo.
There were guards here?
They came by twice already.
Vincenzo hasn't been seen since the day before yesterday. We overheard the guards saying his house is empty too.
No one knows where he went.
Oh.

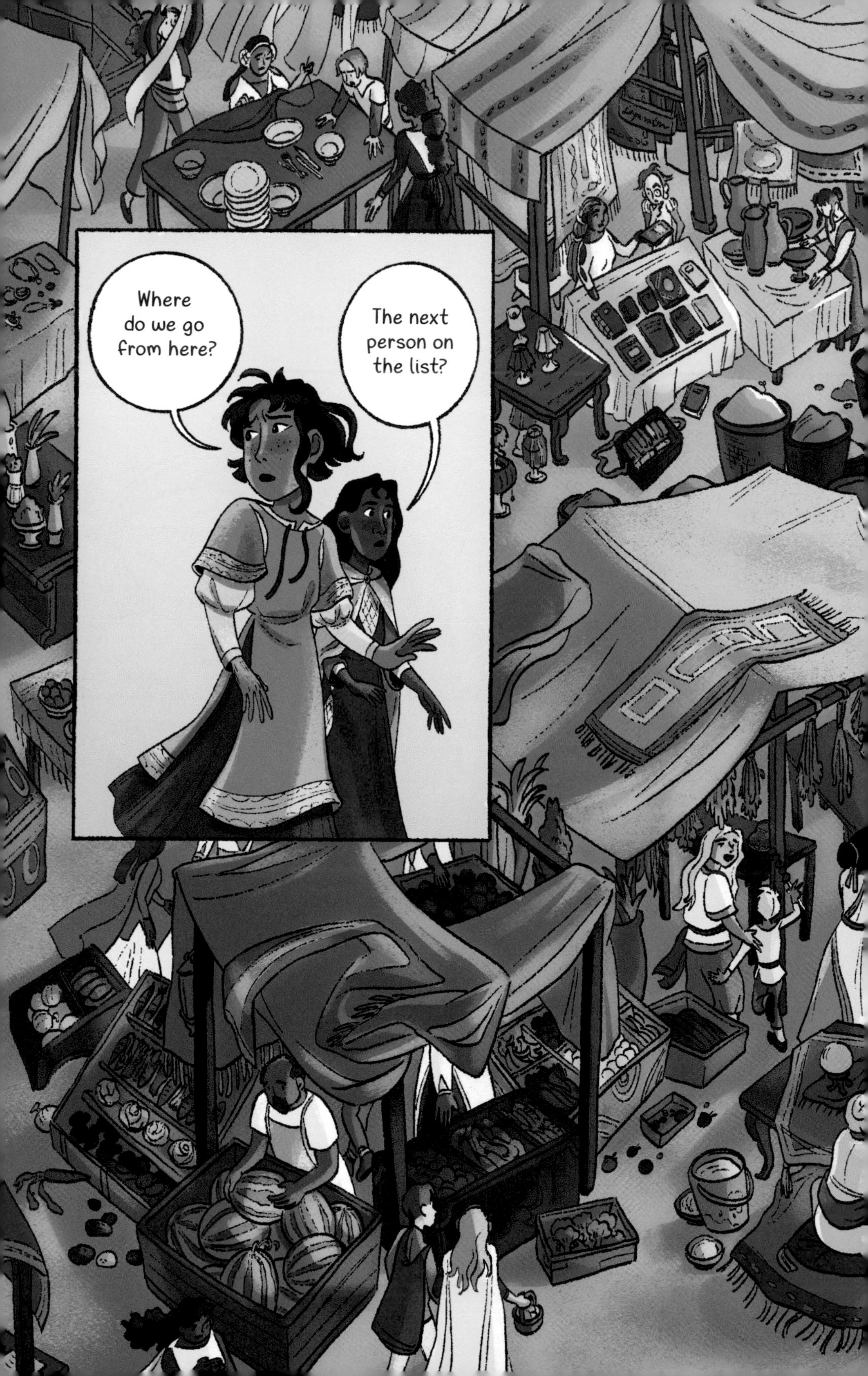
Where do we go from here?
The next person on the list?

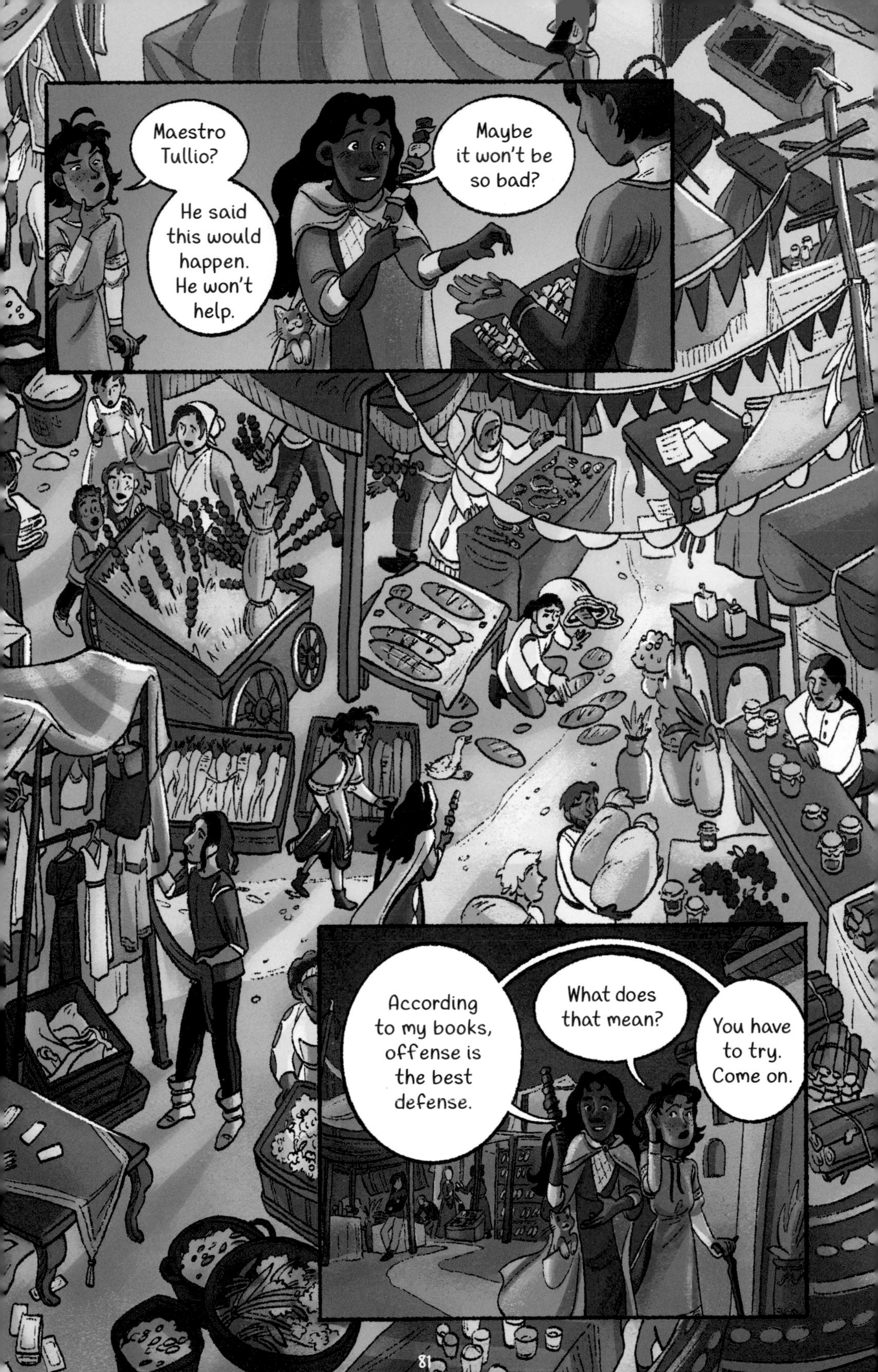
Maestro Tullio?
He said this would happen. He won't help.
Maybe it won't be so bad?
According to my books, offense is the best defense.
What does that mean?
You have to try. Come on.

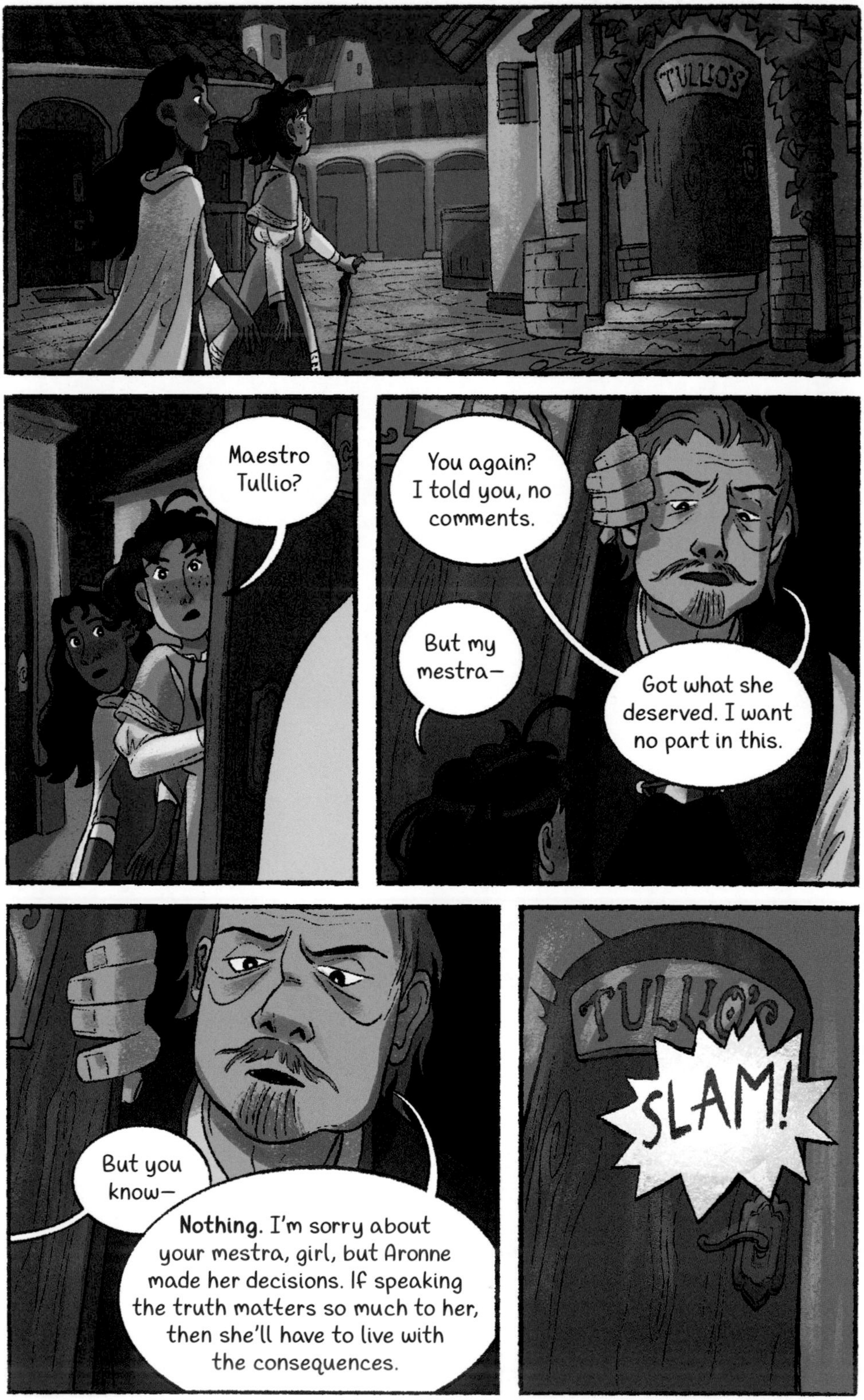
TULLIO'S
Maestro Tullio?
You again? I told you, no comments.
But my mestra—
Got what she deserved. I want no part in this.
But you know—
Nothing. I'm sorry about your mestra, girl, but Aronne made her decisions. If speaking the truth matters so much to her, then she'll have to live with the consequences.
TULLIO'S
SLAM!

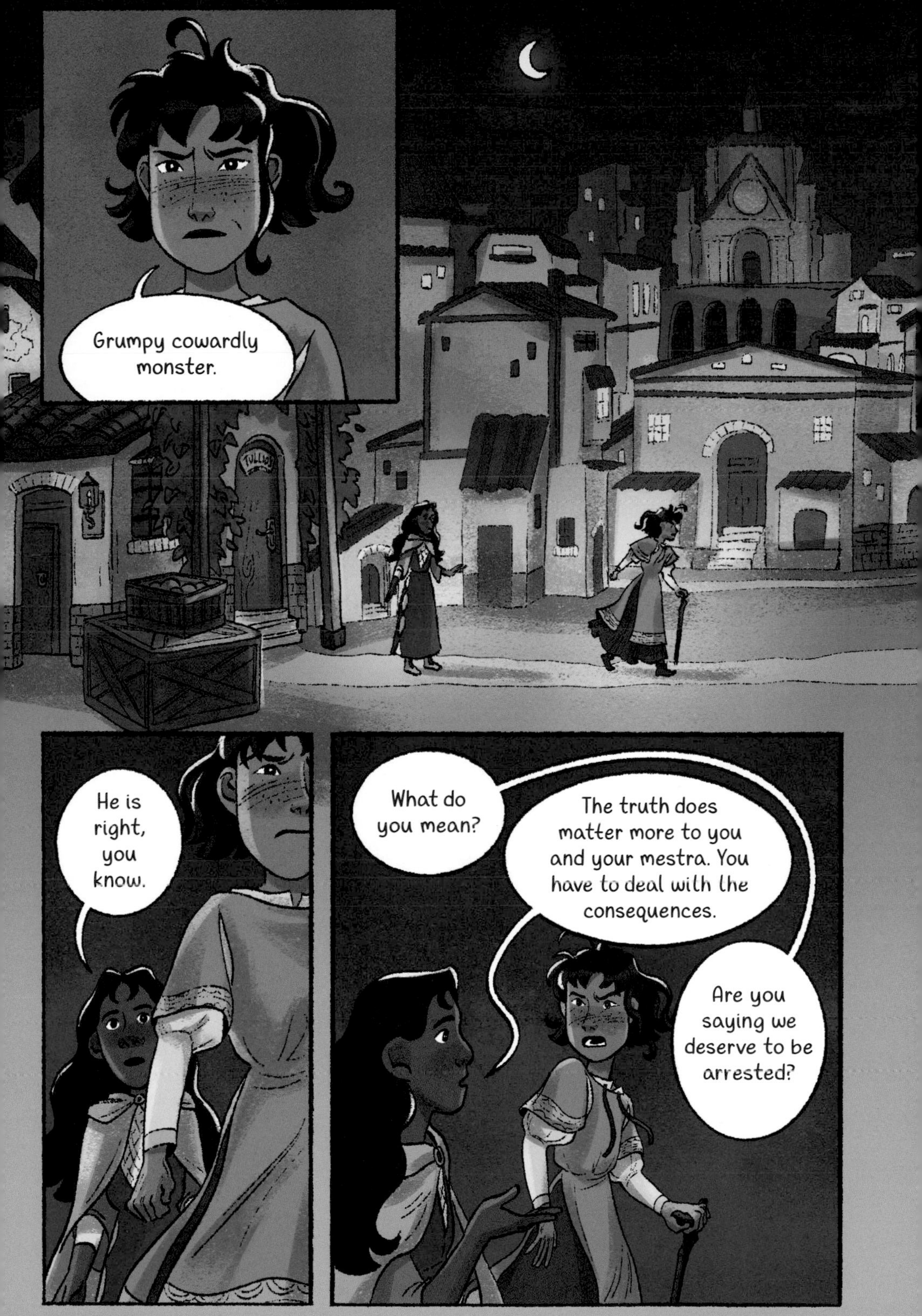
Grumpy cowardly monster.
TULLIO'S
He is right, you know.
What do you mean?
The truth does matter more to you and your mestra. You have to deal with the consequences.
Are you saying we deserve to be arrested?

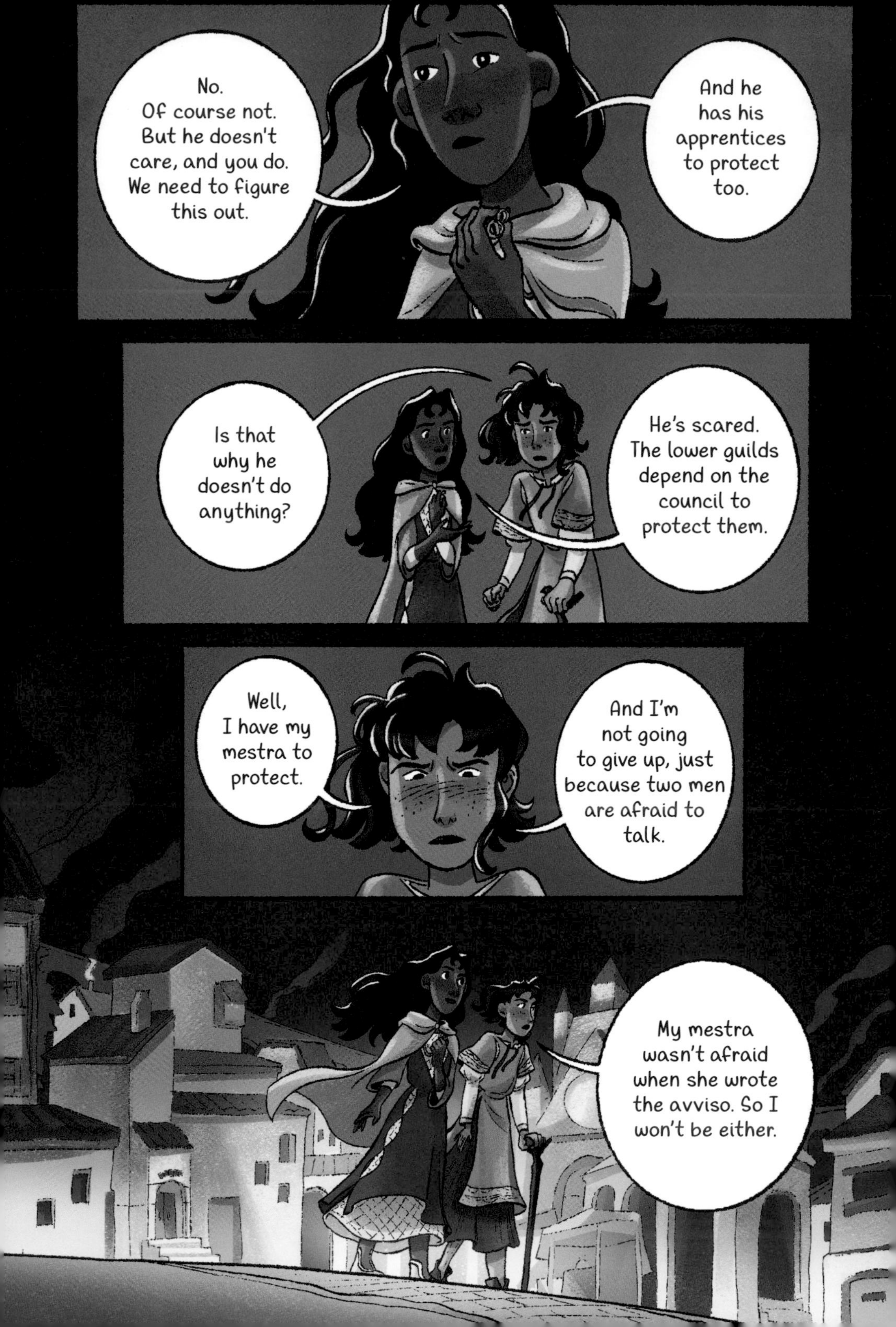
No. Of course not. But he doesn't care, and you do. We need to figure this out.
And he has his apprentices to protect too.
Is that why he doesn't do anything?
He's scared. The lower guilds depend on the council to protect them.
Well, I have my mestra to protect.
And I'm not going to give up, just because two men are afraid to talk.
My mestra wasn't afraid when she wrote the avviso. So I won't be either.

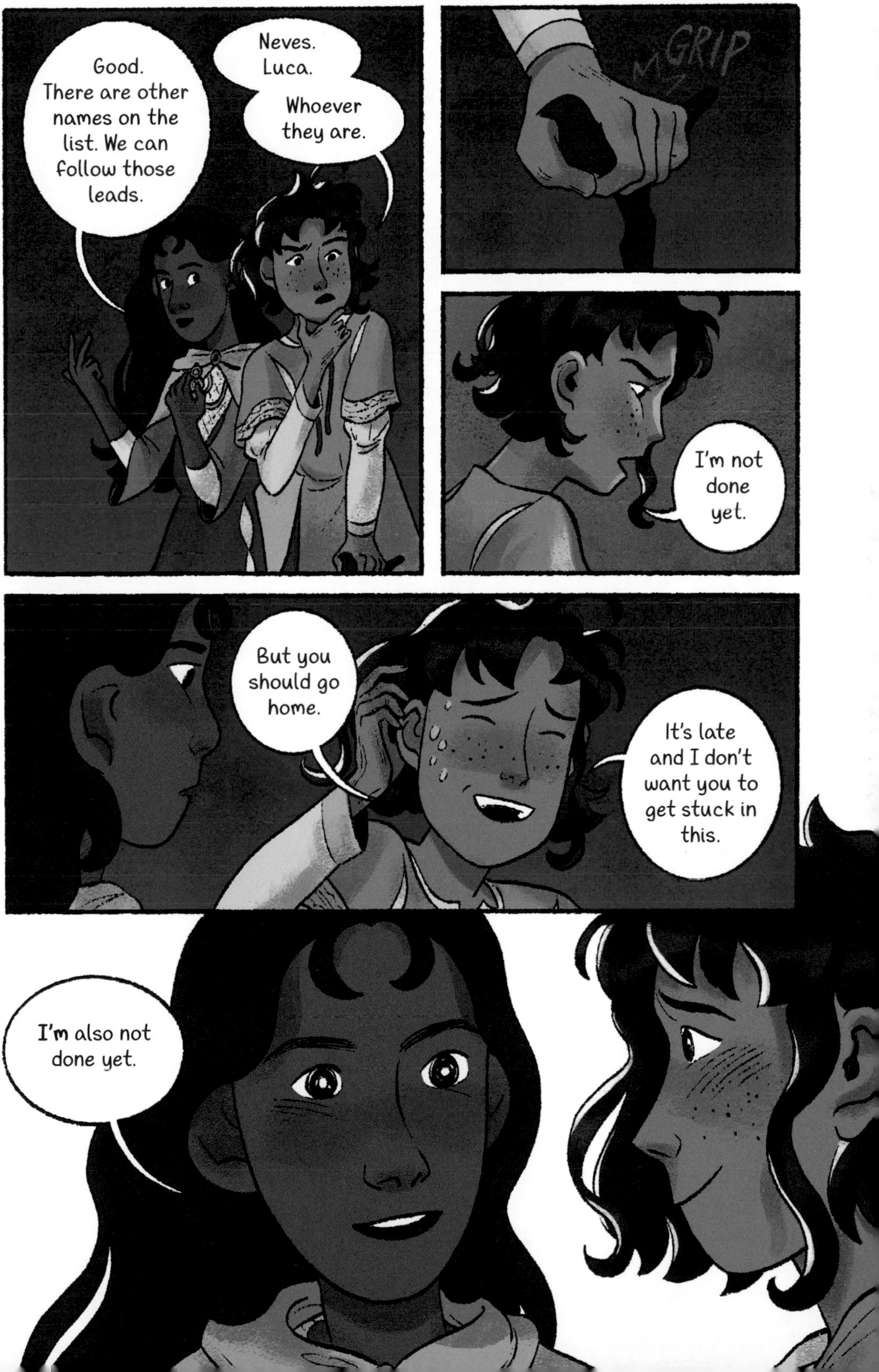
Good. There are other names on the list. We can follow those leads.
Neves. Luca.
Whoever they are.
GRIP
I'm not done yet.
But you should go home.
It's late and I don't want you to get stuck in this.
I'm also not done yet.

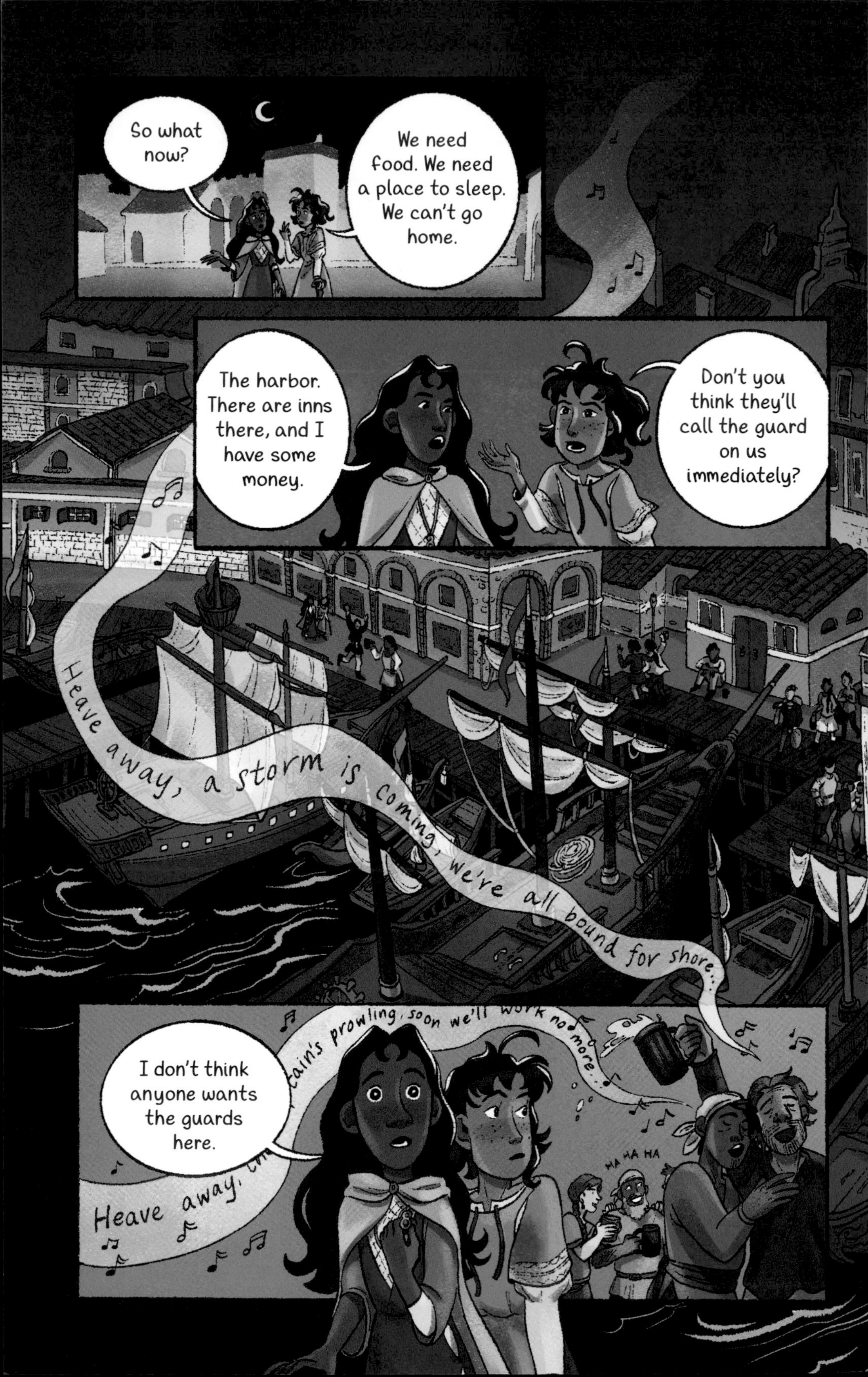

So what now?
We need food. We need a place to sleep. We can't go home.
The harbor. There are inns there, and I have some money.
Don't you think they'll call the guard on us immediately?
Heave away, a storm is coming, we're all bound for shore...
I don't think anyone wants the guards here.
Heave away,
tain's prowling, soon we'll work no more...
HA HA HA

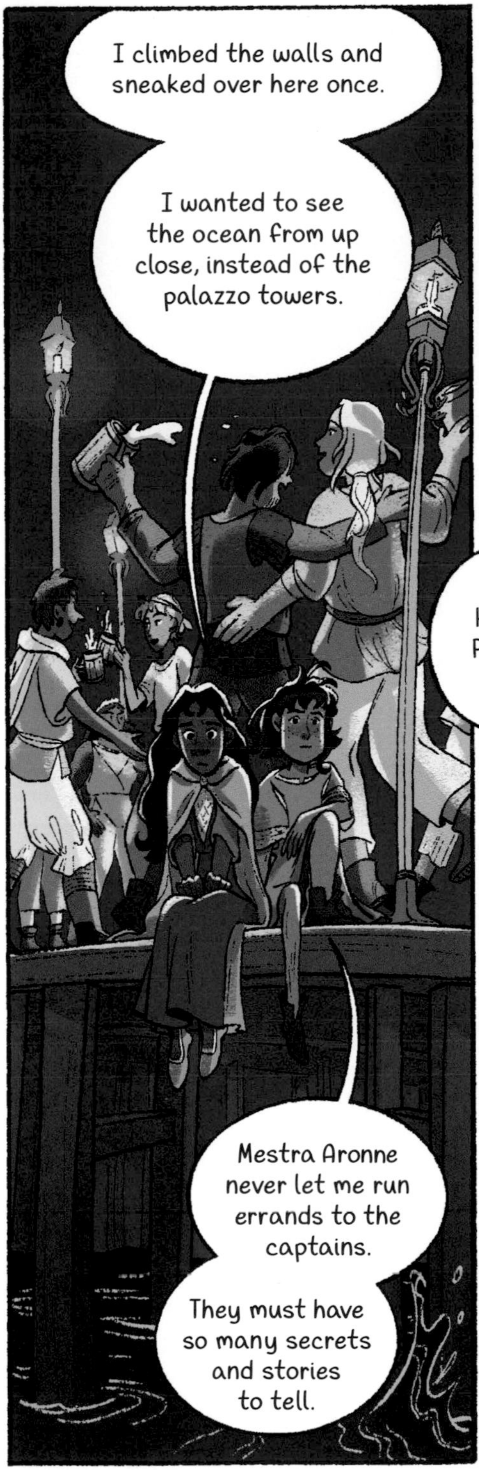
I climbed the walls and sneaked over here once.
I wanted to see the ocean from up close, instead of the palazzo towers.
Mestra Aronne never let me run errands to the captains.
They must have so many secrets and stories to tell.

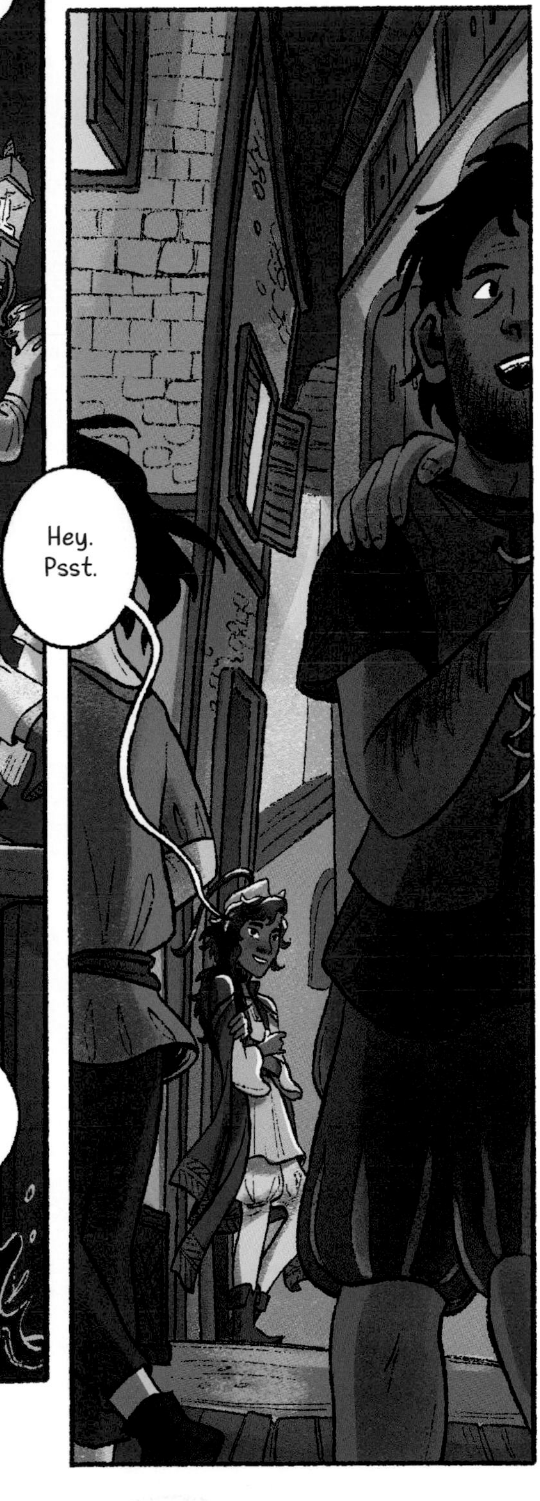
Hey. Psst.

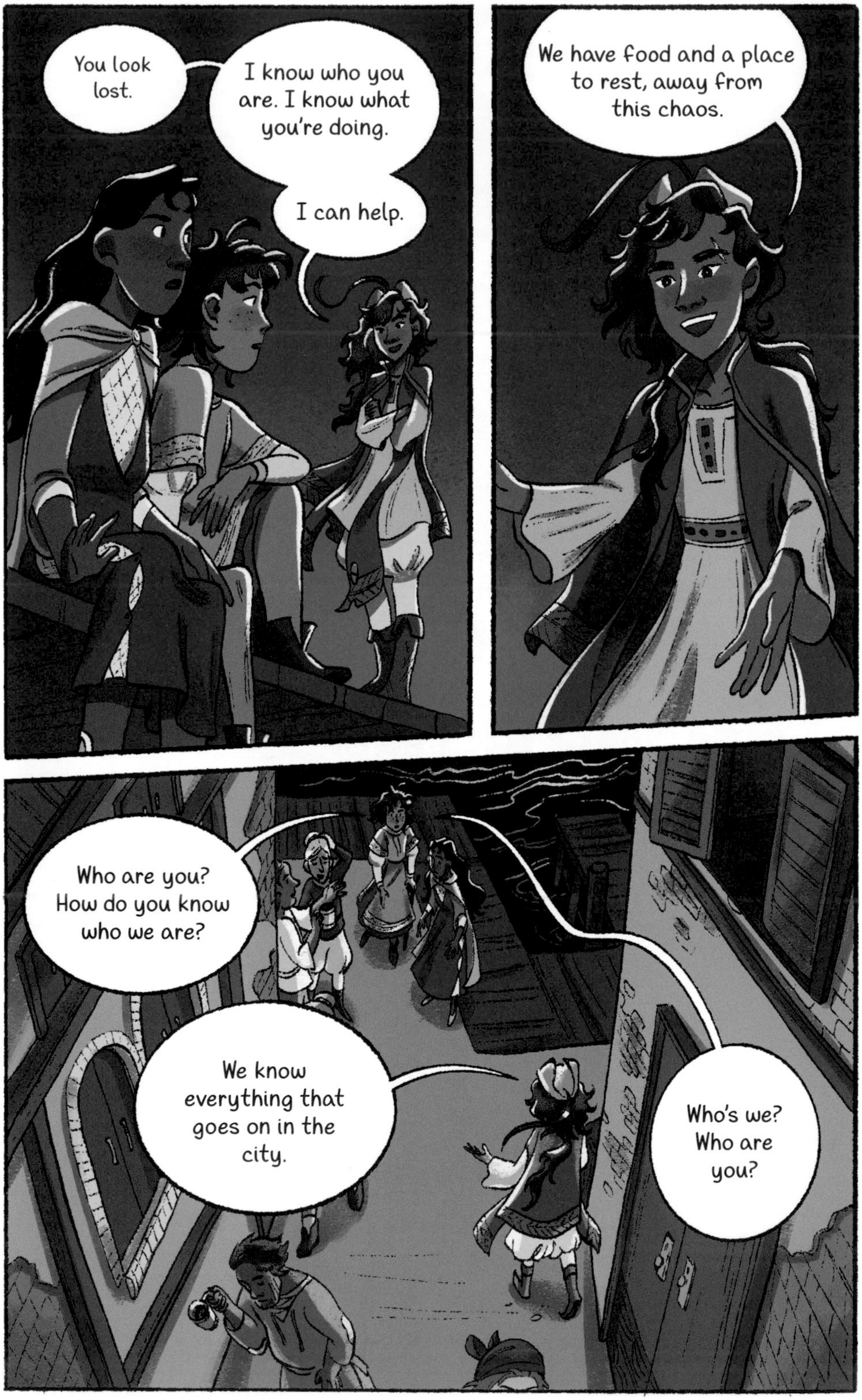
You look lost.
I know who you are. I know what you're doing.
I can help.
We have food and a place to rest, away from this chaos.
Who are you? How do you know who we are?
We know everything that goes on in the city.
Who's we? Who are you?

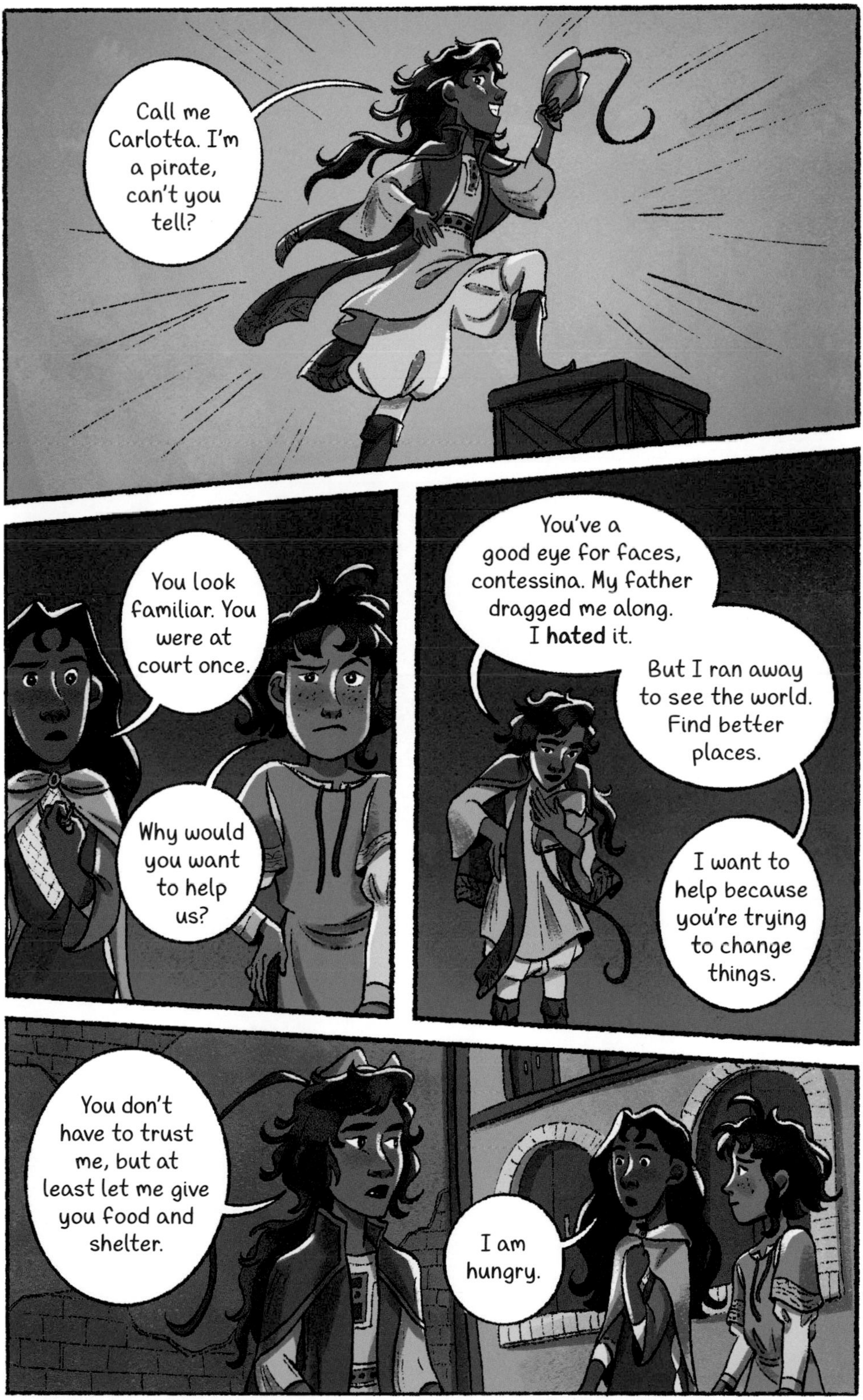
Call me Carlotta. I'm a pirate, can't you tell?
You look familiar. You were at court once.
Why would you want to help us?
You've a good eye for faces, contessina. My father dragged me along. I **hated** it.
But I ran away to see the world. Find better places.
I want to help because you're trying to change things.
You don't have to trust me, but at least let me give you food and shelter.
I am hungry.

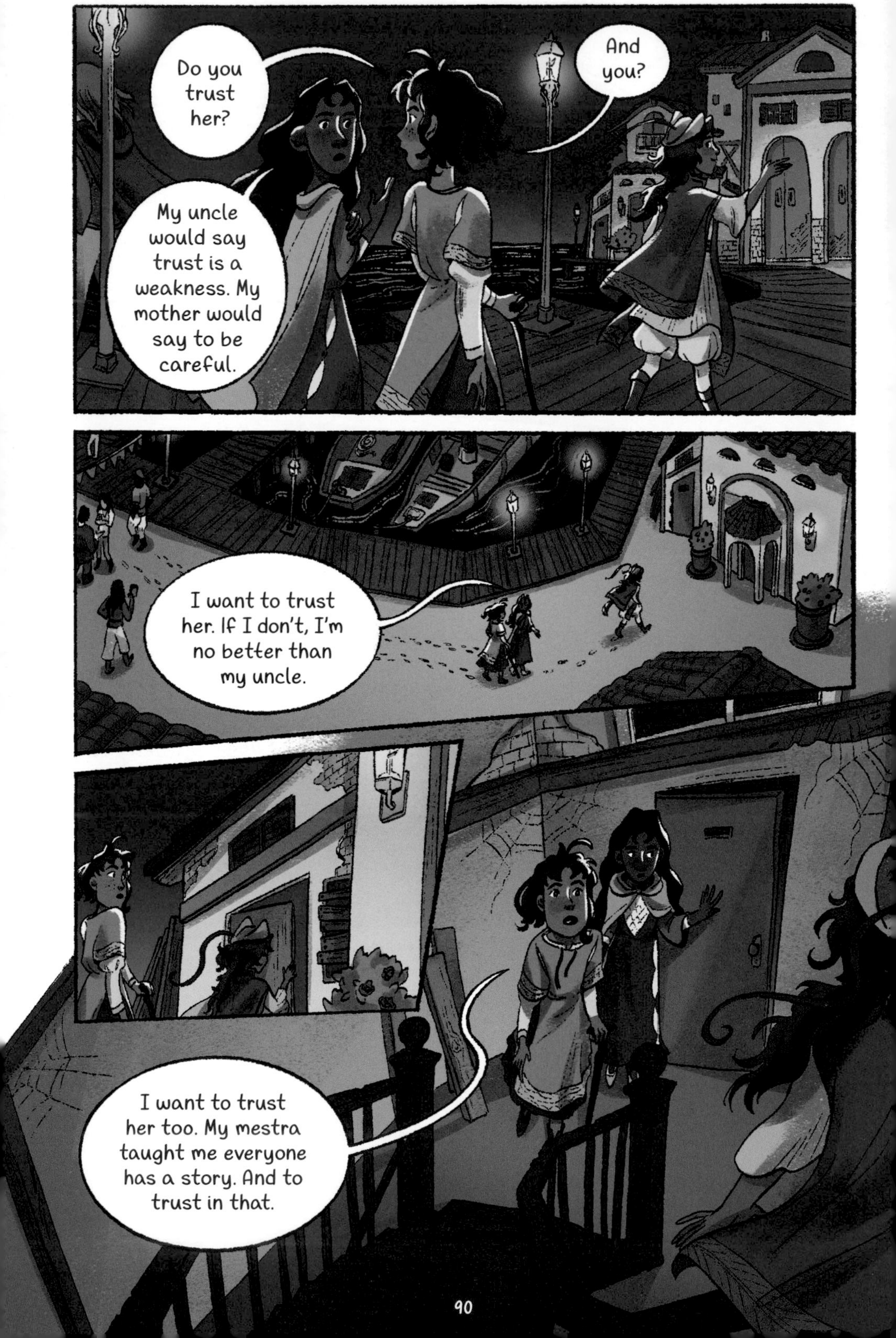
Do you trust her?
And you?
My uncle would say trust is a weakness. My mother would say to be careful.
I want to trust her. If I don't, I'm no better than my uncle.
I want to trust her too. My mestra taught me everyone has a story. And to trust in that.

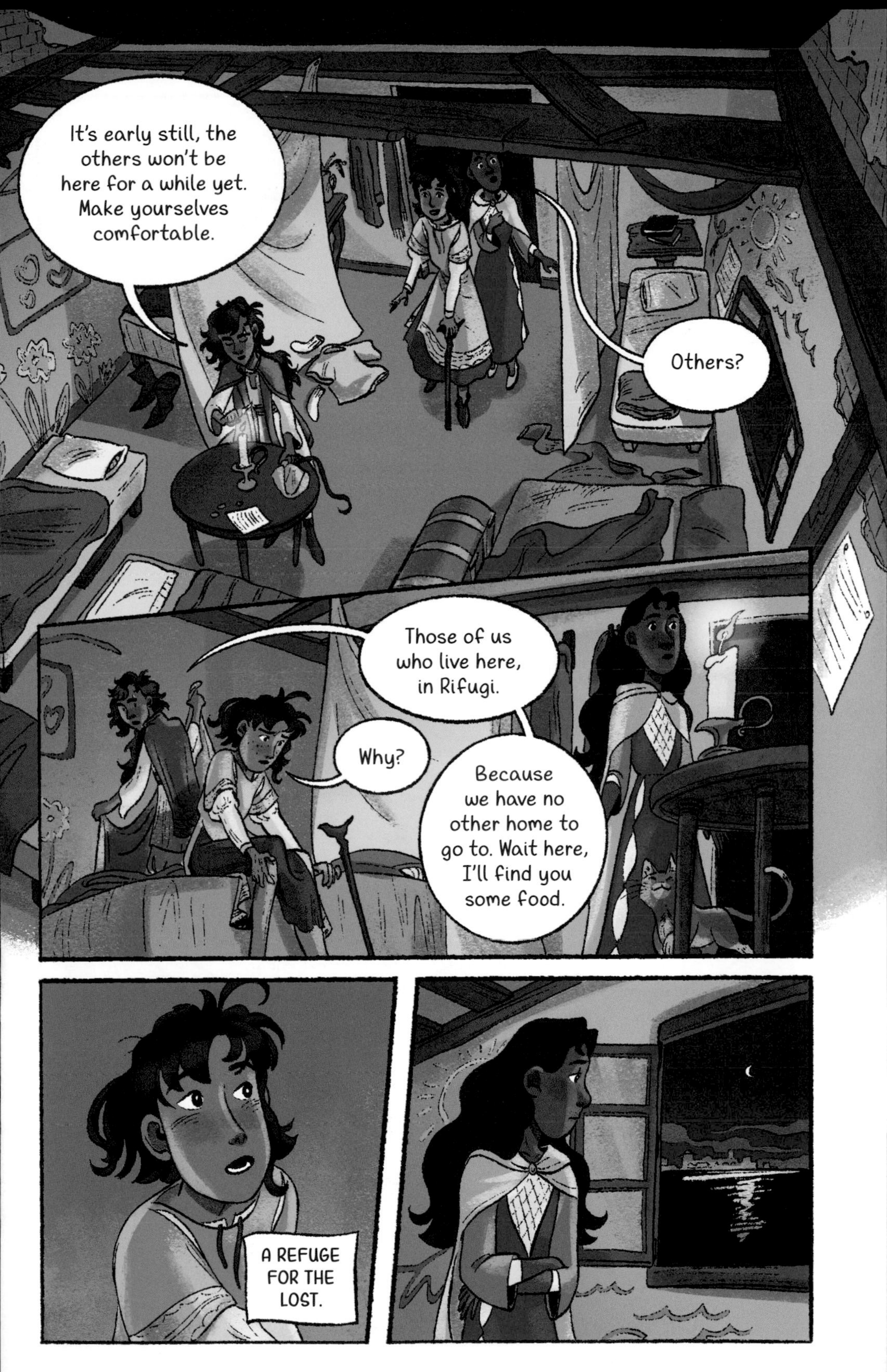

It's early still, the others won't be here for a while yet. Make yourselves comfortable.
Others?
Those of us who live here, in Rifugi.
Why?
Because we have no other home to go to. Wait here, I'll find you some food.
A REFUGE FOR THE LOST.

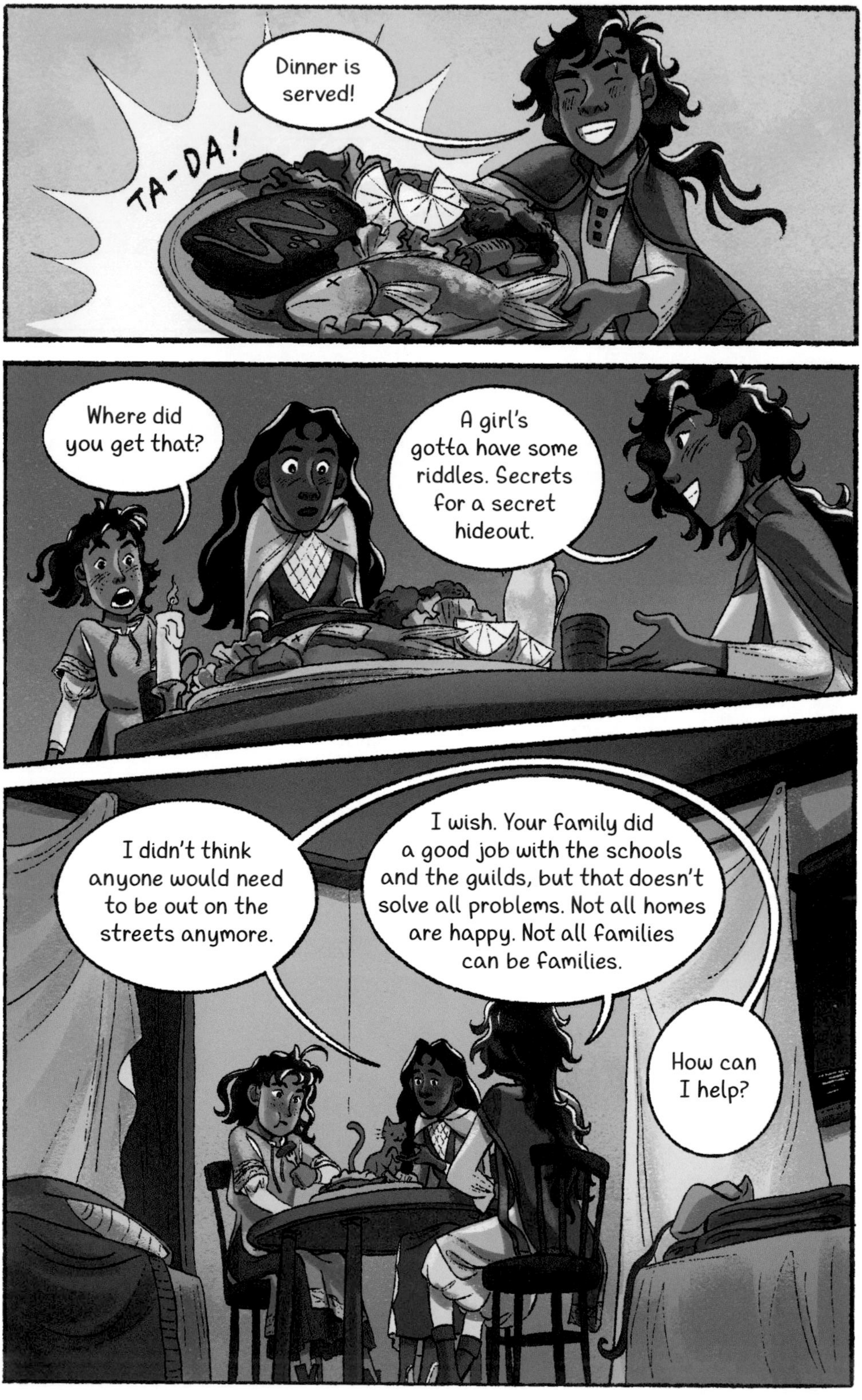
Dinner is served!
TA-DA!
Where did you get that?
A girl's gotta have some riddles. Secrets for a secret hideout.
I didn't think anyone would need to be out on the streets anymore.
I wish. Your family did a good job with the schools and the guilds, but that doesn't solve all problems. Not all homes are happy. Not all families can be families.
How can I help?

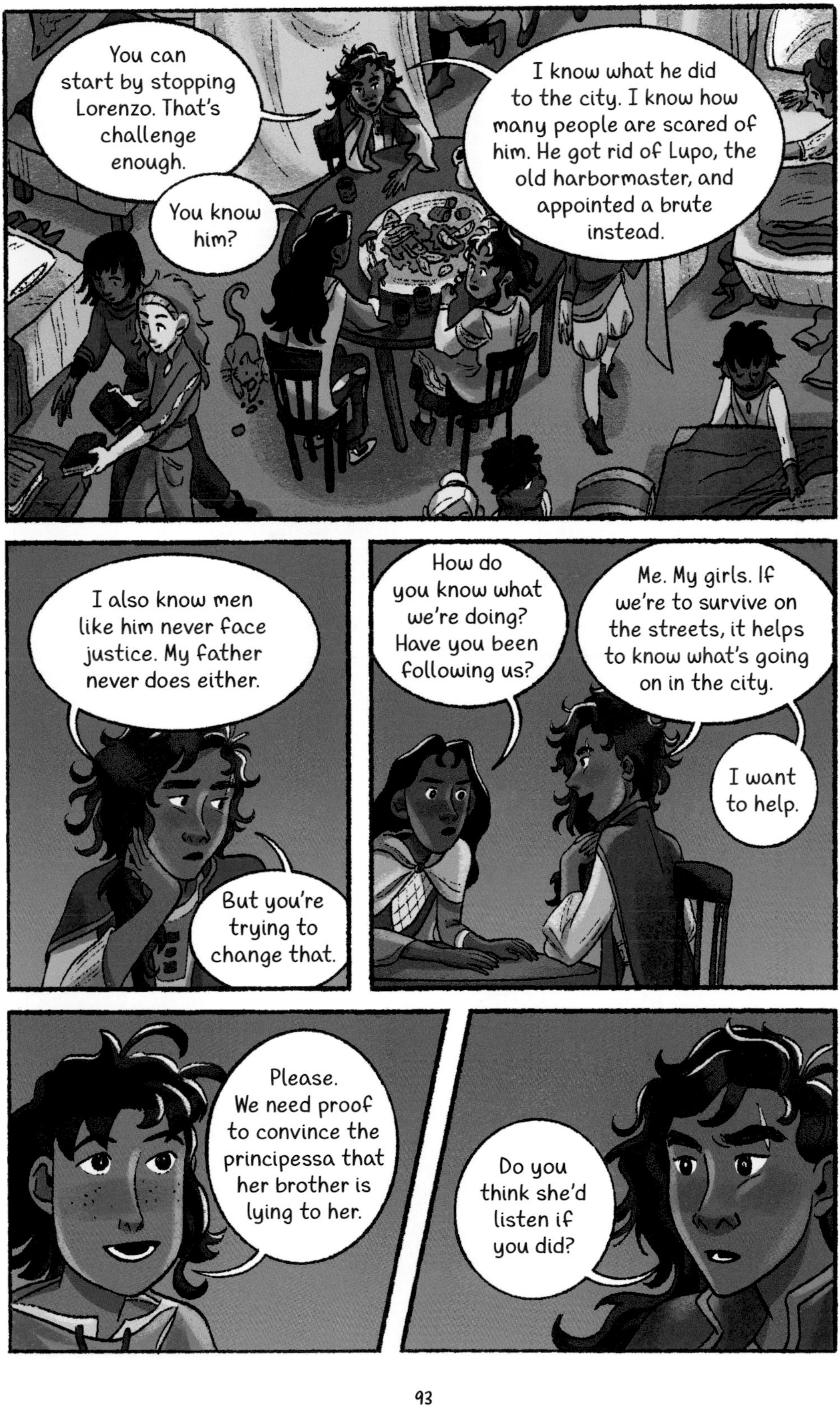
You can start by stopping Lorenzo. That's challenge enough.
You know him?
I know what he did to the city. I know how many people are scared of him. He got rid of Lupo, the old harbormaster, and appointed a brute instead.
I also know men like him never face justice. My father never does either.
But you're trying to change that.
How do you know what we're doing? Have you been following us?
Me. My girls. If we're to survive on the streets, it helps to know what's going on in the city.
I want to help.
Please. We need proof to convince the principessa that her brother is lying to her.
Do you think she'd listen if you did?

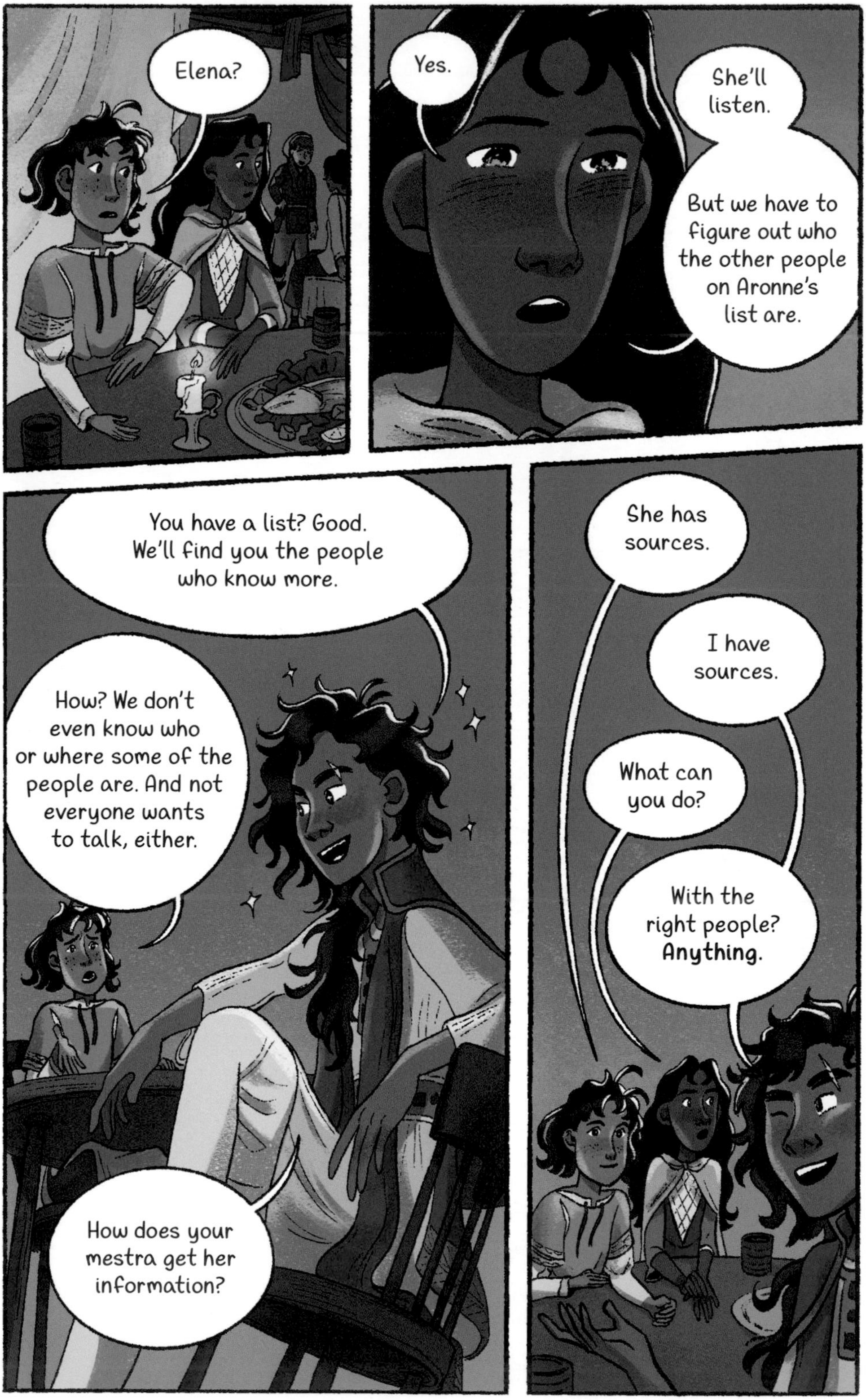
Elena?
Yes.
She'll listen.
But we have to figure out who the other people on Aronne's list are.
You have a list? Good. We'll find you the people who know more.
How? We don't even know who or where some of the people are. And not everyone wants to talk, either.
How does your mestra get her information?
She has sources.
I have sources.
What can you do?
With the right people? **Anything.**

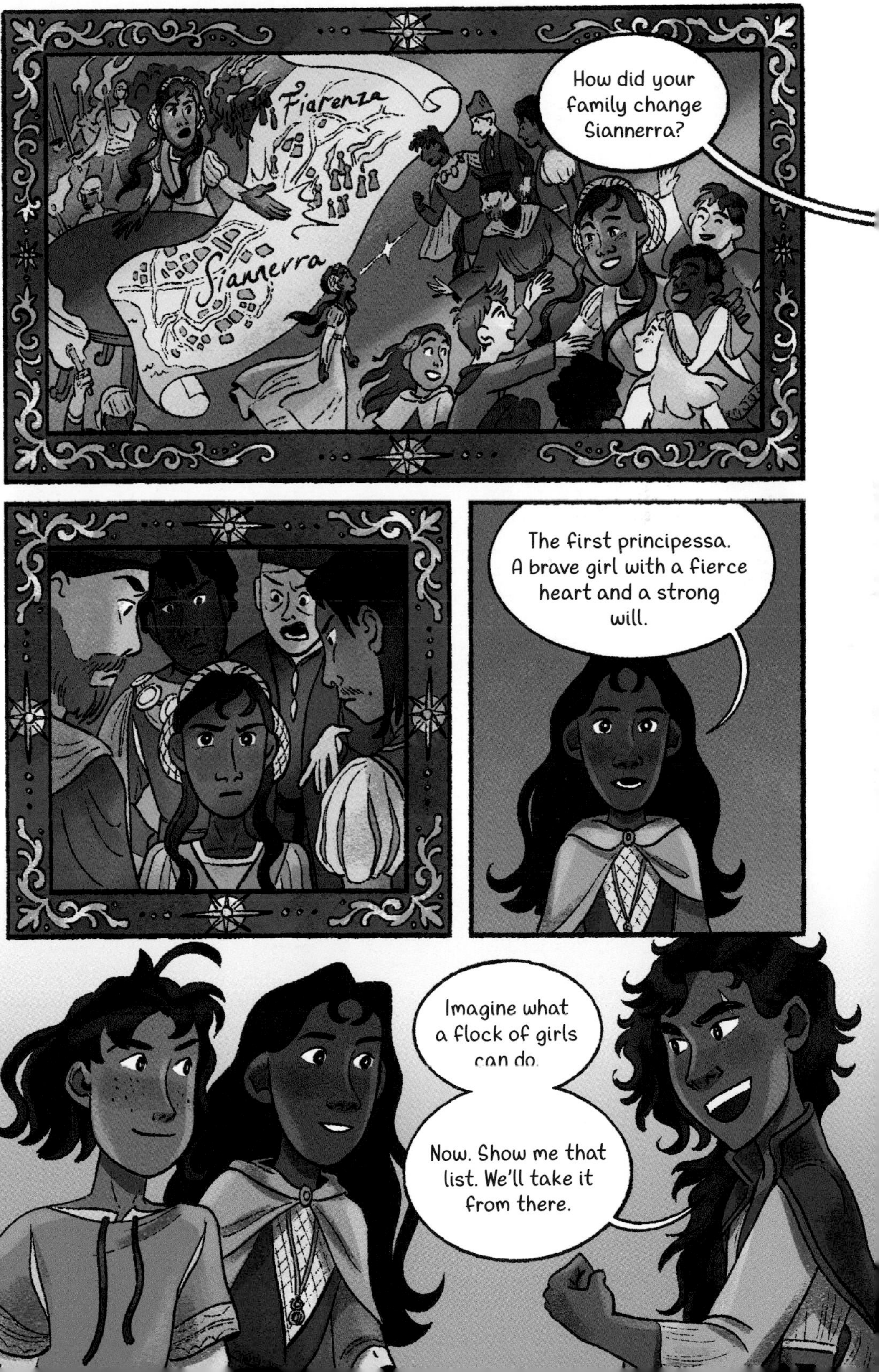

Fiarenza
Siannerra
How did your family change Siannerra?
The first principessa. A brave girl with a fierce heart and a strong will.
Imagine what a flock of girls can do.
Now. Show me that list. We'll take it from there.

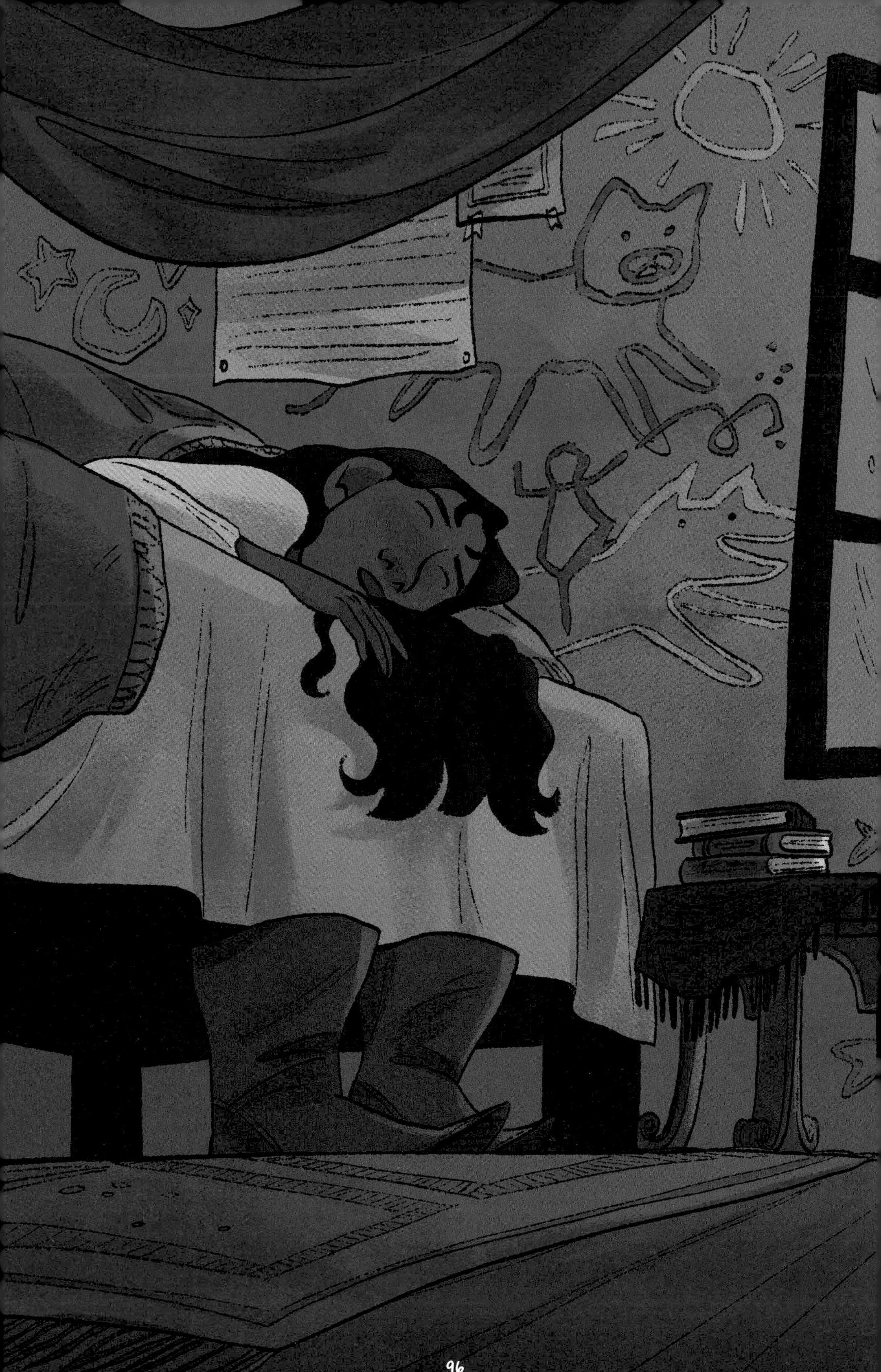

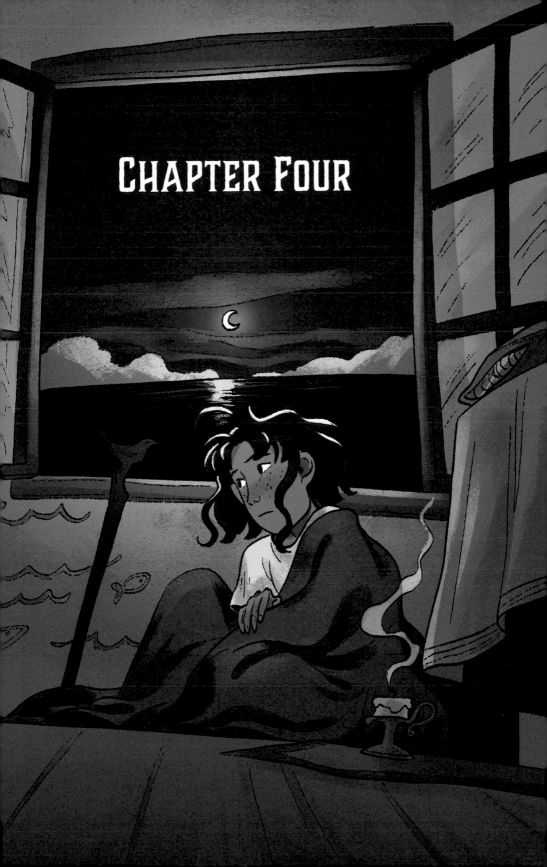

CHAPTER FOUR

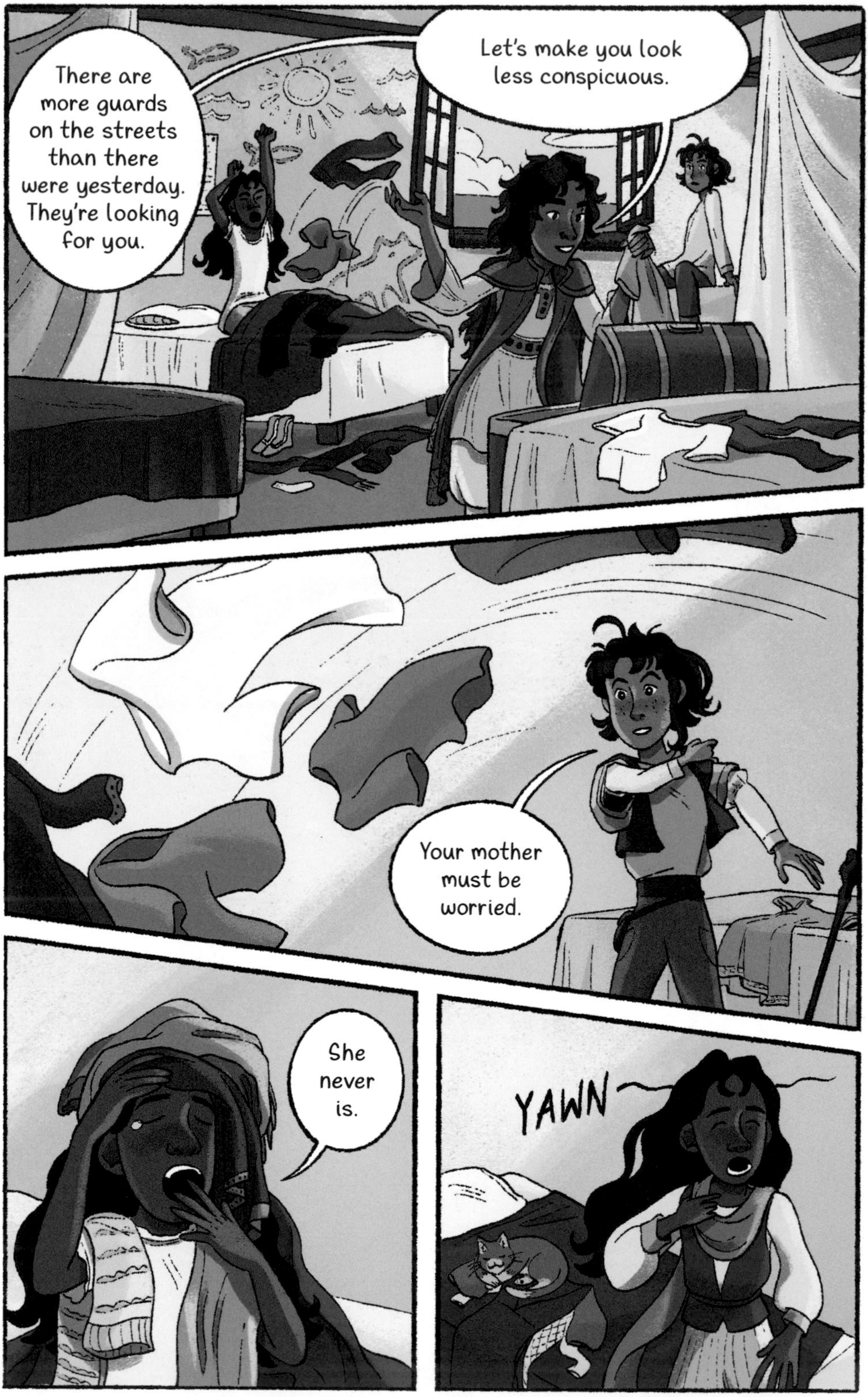
There are more guards on the streets than there were yesterday. They're looking for you.
Let's make you look less conspicuous.
Your mother must be worried.
She never is.
YAWN

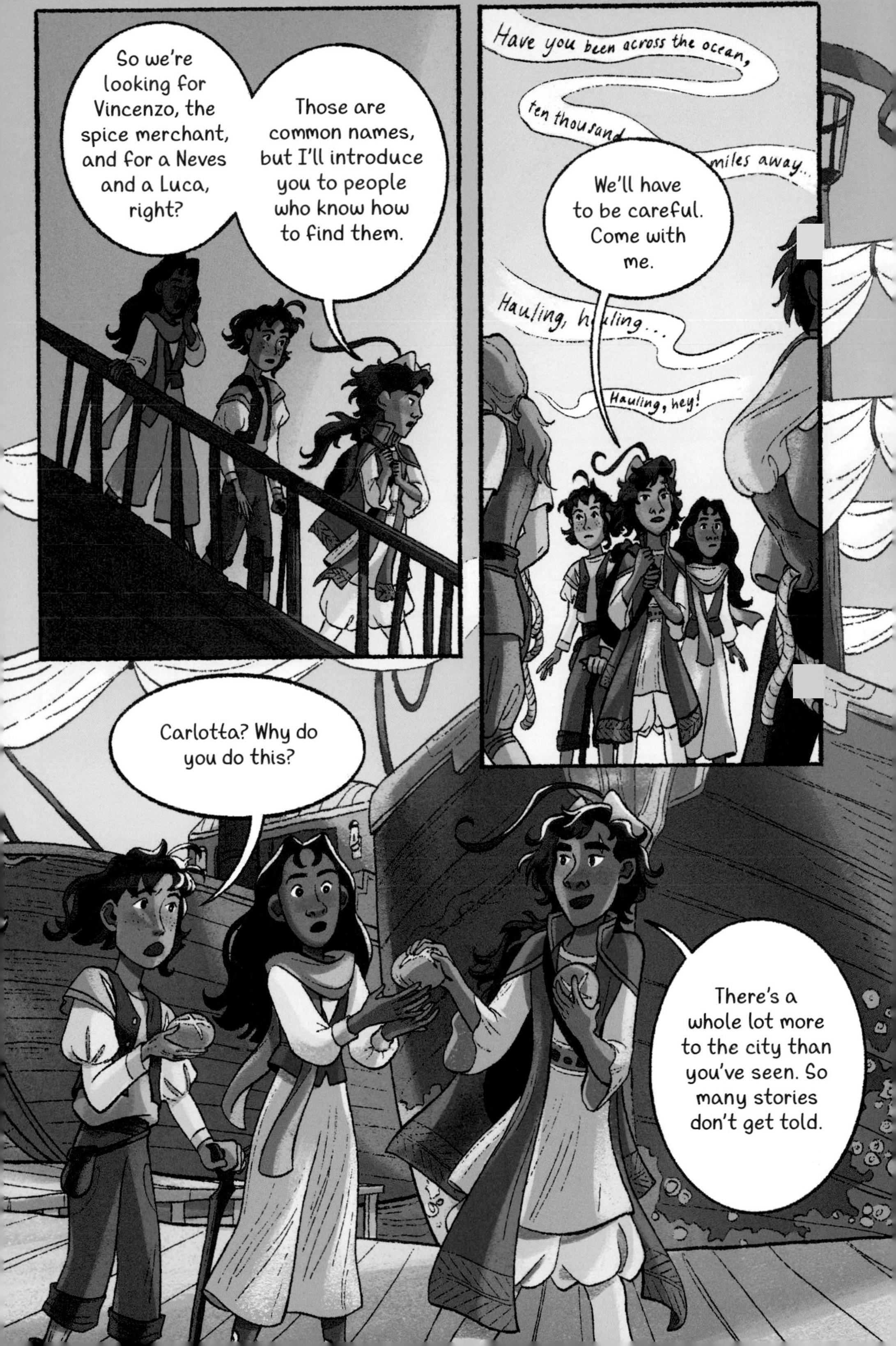
So we're looking for Vincenzo, the spice merchant, and for a Neves and a Luca, right?
Those are common names, but I'll introduce you to people who know how to find them.
Have you been across the ocean,
ten thousand
miles away...
We'll have to be careful. Come with me.
Hauling, hauling...
Hauling, hey!
Carlotta? Why do you do this?
There's a whole lot more to the city than you've seen. So many stories don't get told.

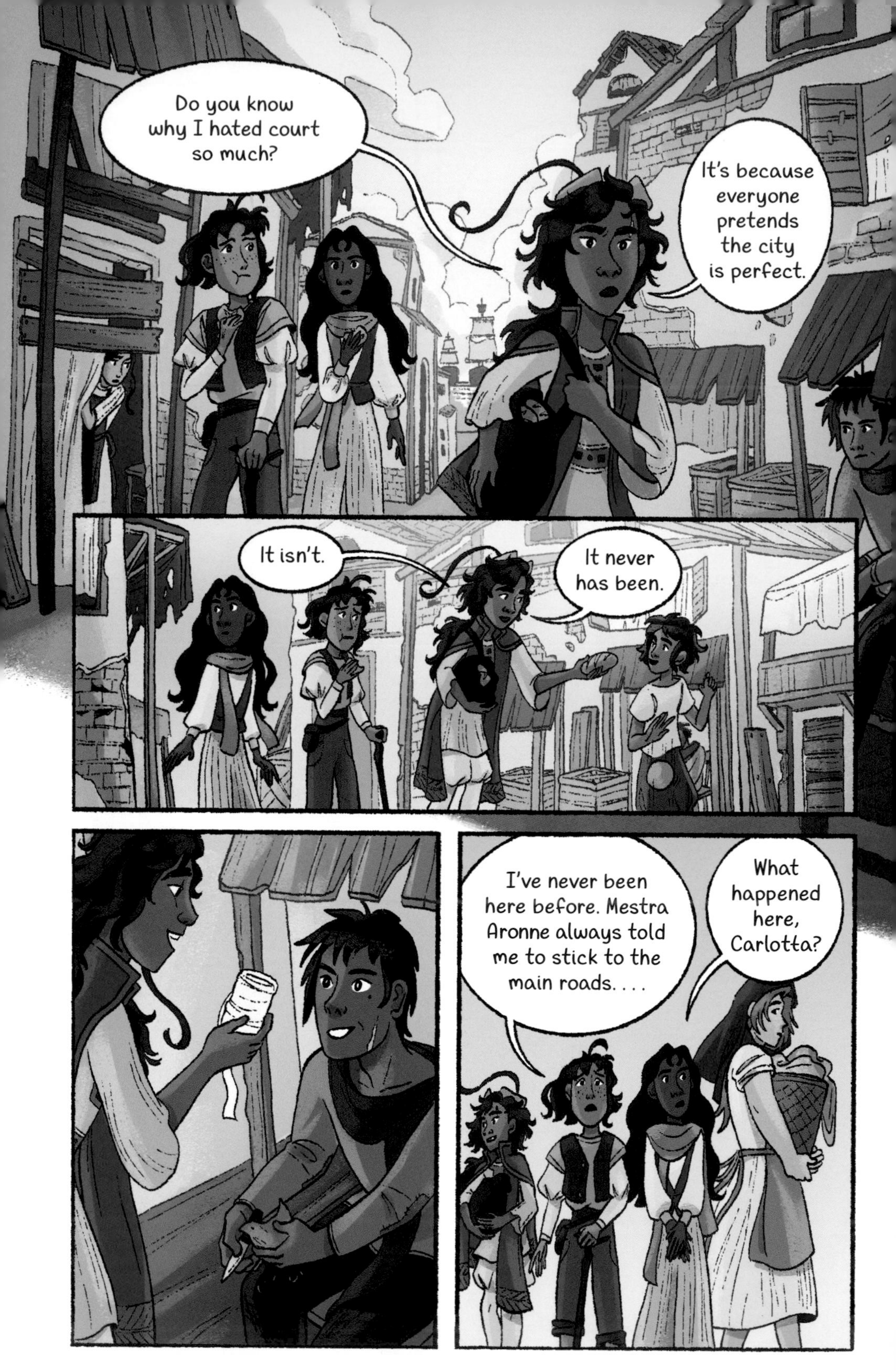

Do you know why I hated court so much?
It's because everyone pretends the city is perfect.
It isn't.
It never has been.
I've never been here before. Mestra Aronne always told me to stick to the main roads. . . .
What happened here, Carlotta?

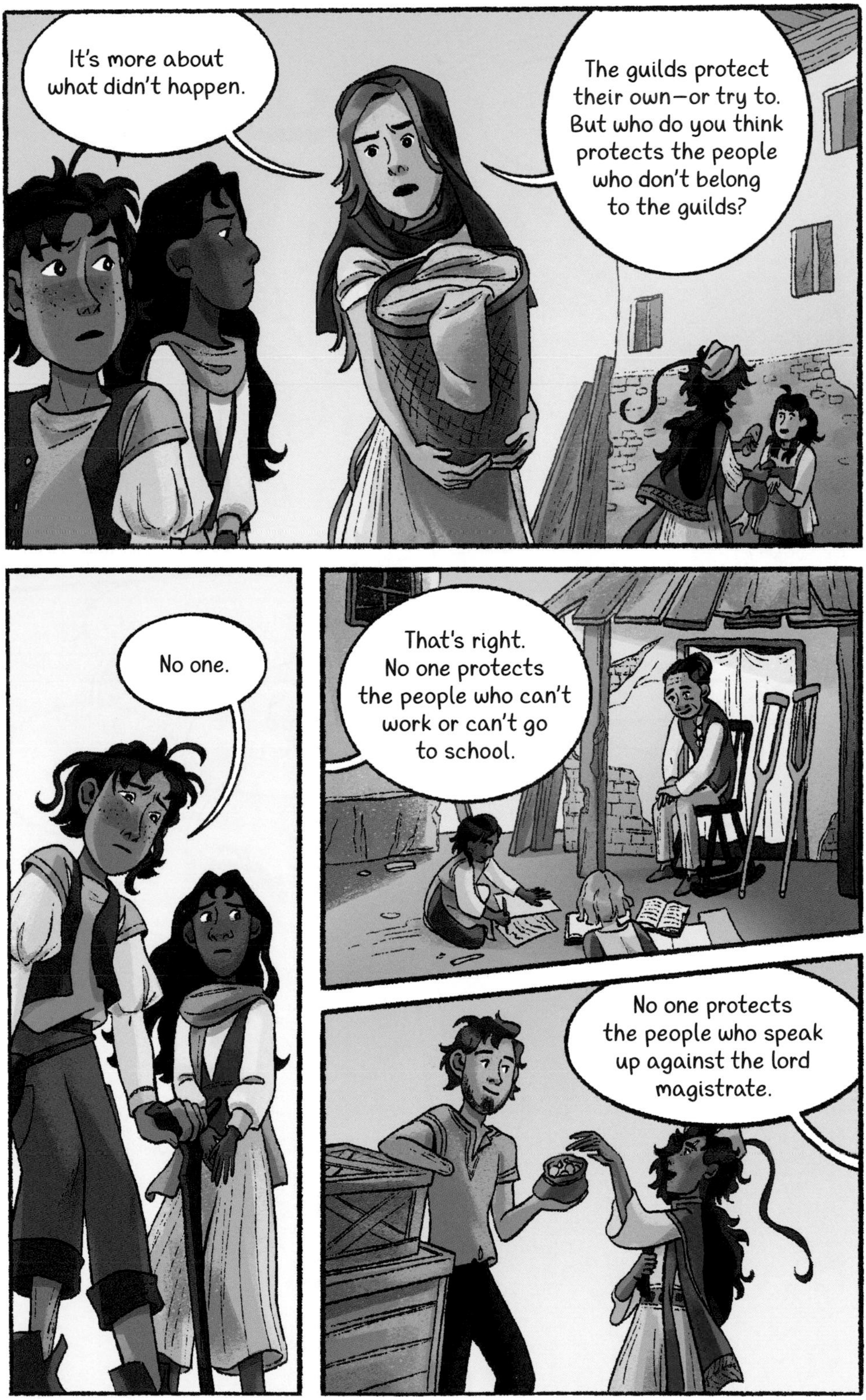
It's more about what didn't happen.
The guilds protect their own—or try to. But who do you think protects the people who don't belong to the guilds?
No one.
That's right. No one protects the people who can't work or can't go to school.
No one protects the people who speak up against the lord magistrate.

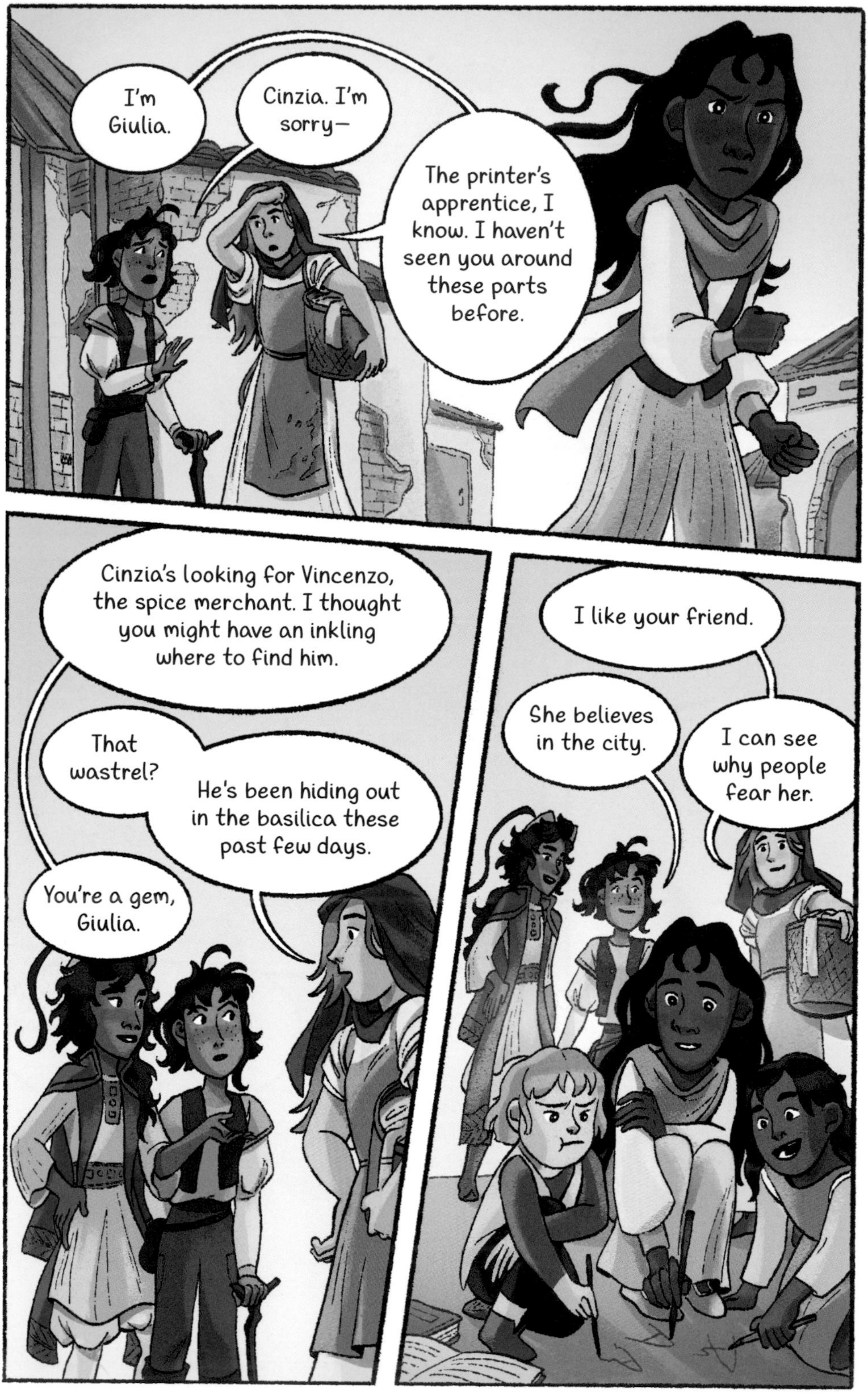
I'm Giulia.
Cinzia. I'm sorry—
The printer's apprentice, I know. I haven't seen you around these parts before.
Cinzia's looking for Vincenzo, the spice merchant. I thought you might have an inkling where to find him.
That wastrel?
He's been hiding out in the basilica these past few days.
You're a gem, Giulia.
I like your friend.
She believes in the city.
I can see why people fear her.

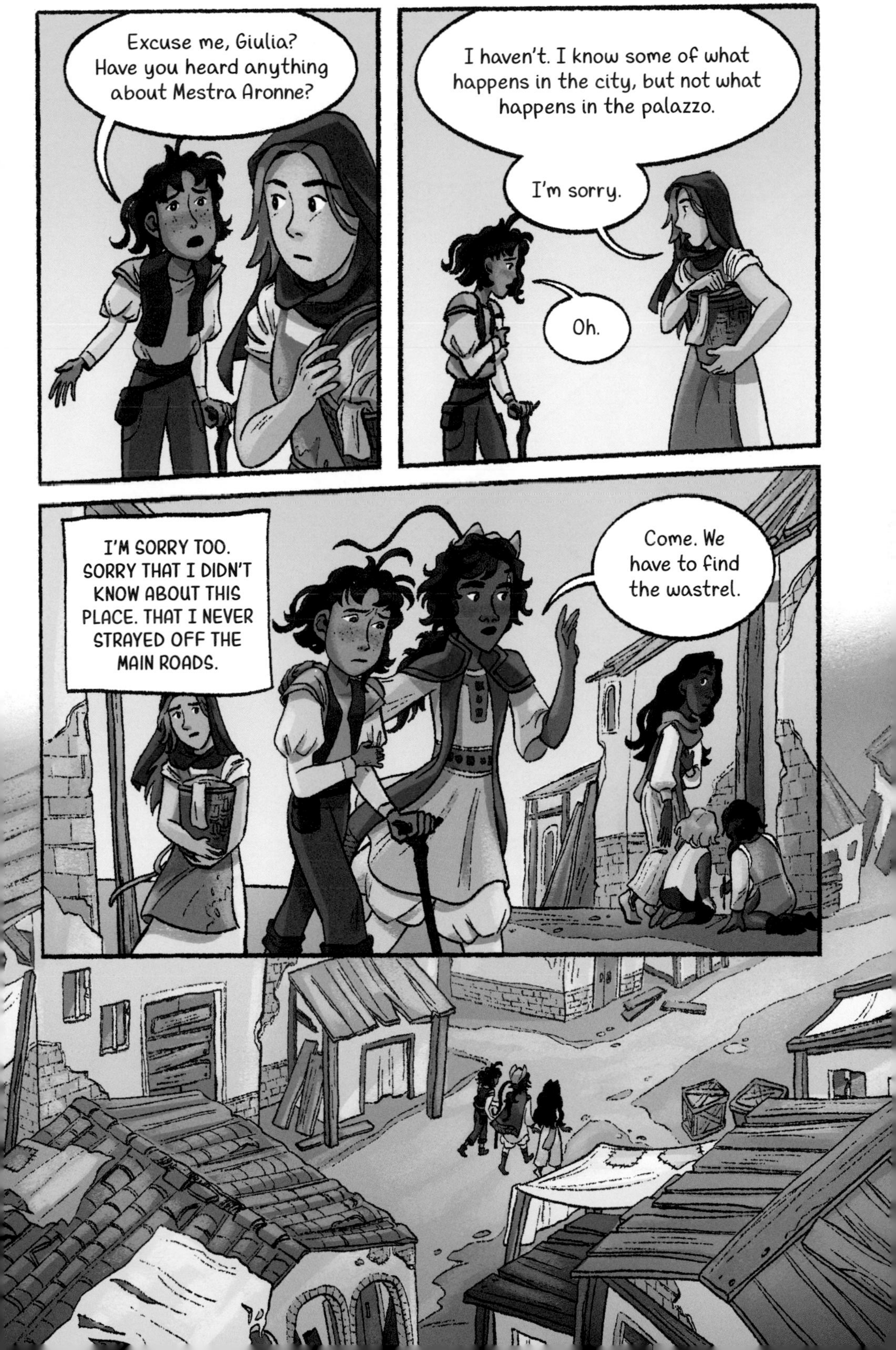
Excuse me, Giulia? Have you heard anything about Mestra Aronne?
I haven't. I know some of what happens in the city, but not what happens in the palazzo.
I'm sorry.
Oh.
I'M SORRY TOO. SORRY THAT I DIDN'T KNOW ABOUT THIS PLACE. THAT I NEVER STRAYED OFF THE MAIN ROADS.
Come. We have to find the wastrel.

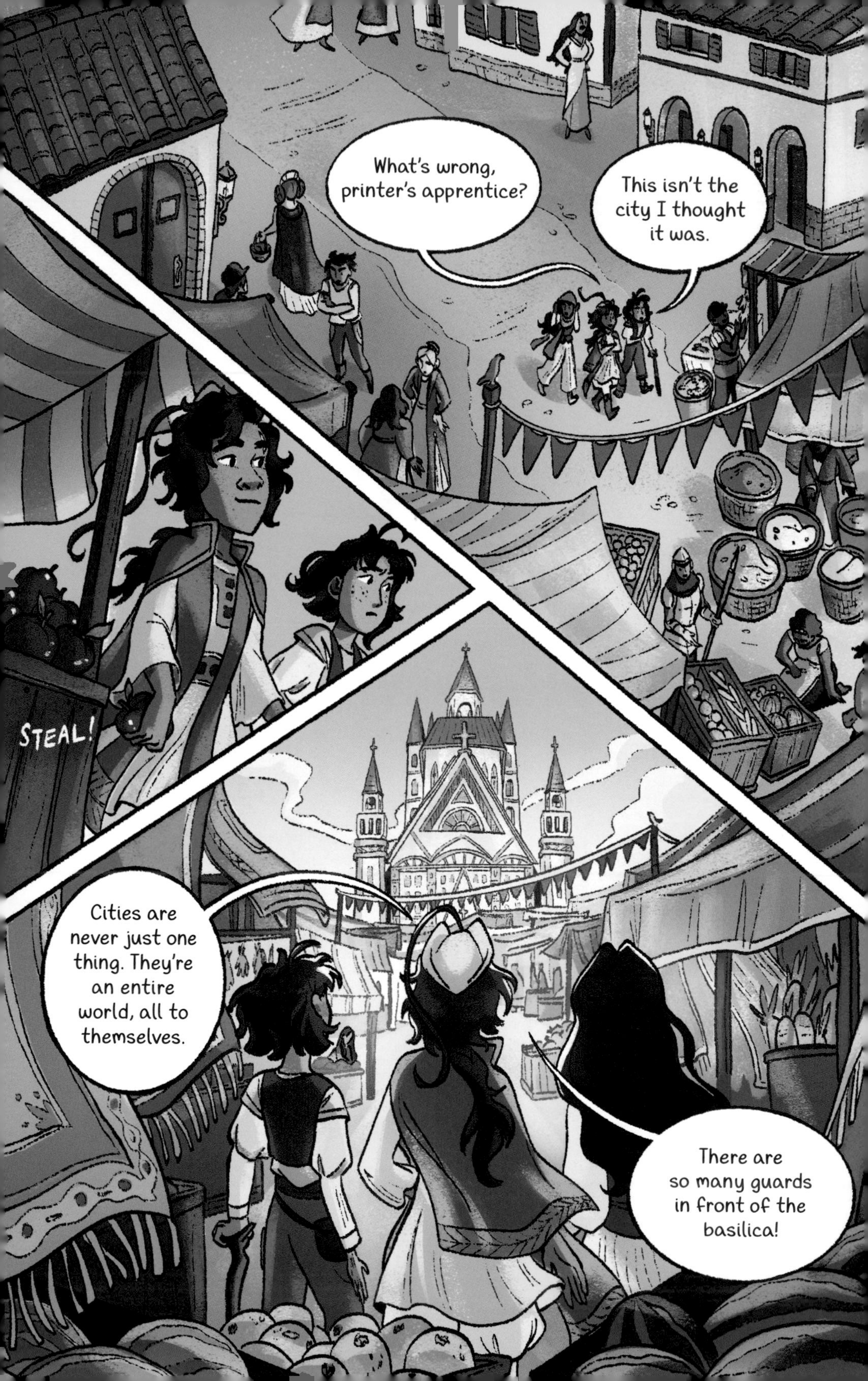
What's wrong, printer's apprentice?
This isn't the city I thought it was.
STEAL!
Cities are never just one thing. They're an entire world, all to themselves.
There are so many guards in front of the basilica!

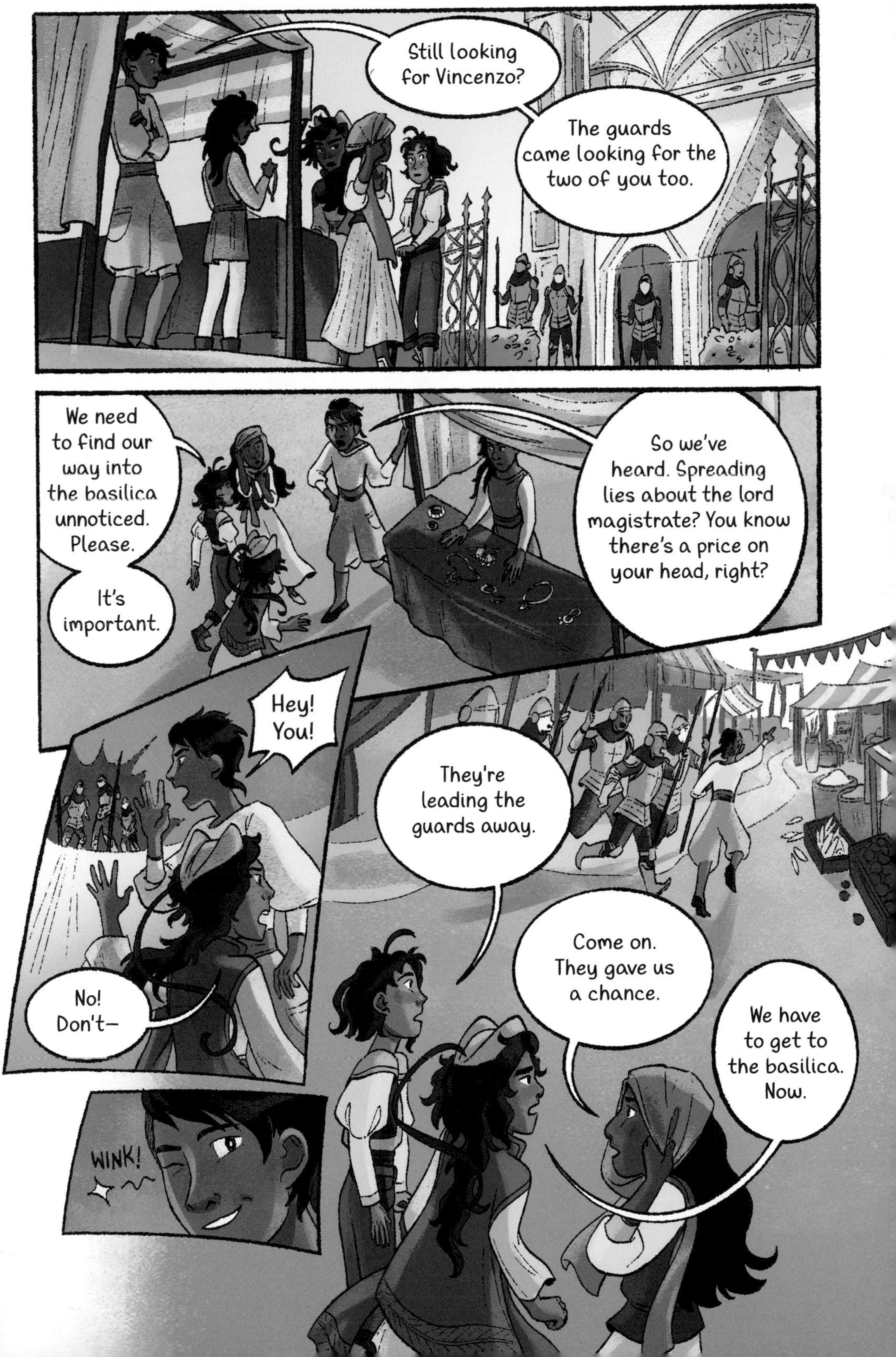
Still looking for Vincenzo?
The guards came looking for the two of you too.
We need to find our way into the basilica unnoticed. Please.
It's important.
So we've heard. Spreading lies about the lord magistrate? You know there's a price on your head, right?
Hey! You!
No! Don't–
They're leading the guards away.
WINK!
Come on. They gave us a chance.
We have to get to the basilica. Now.

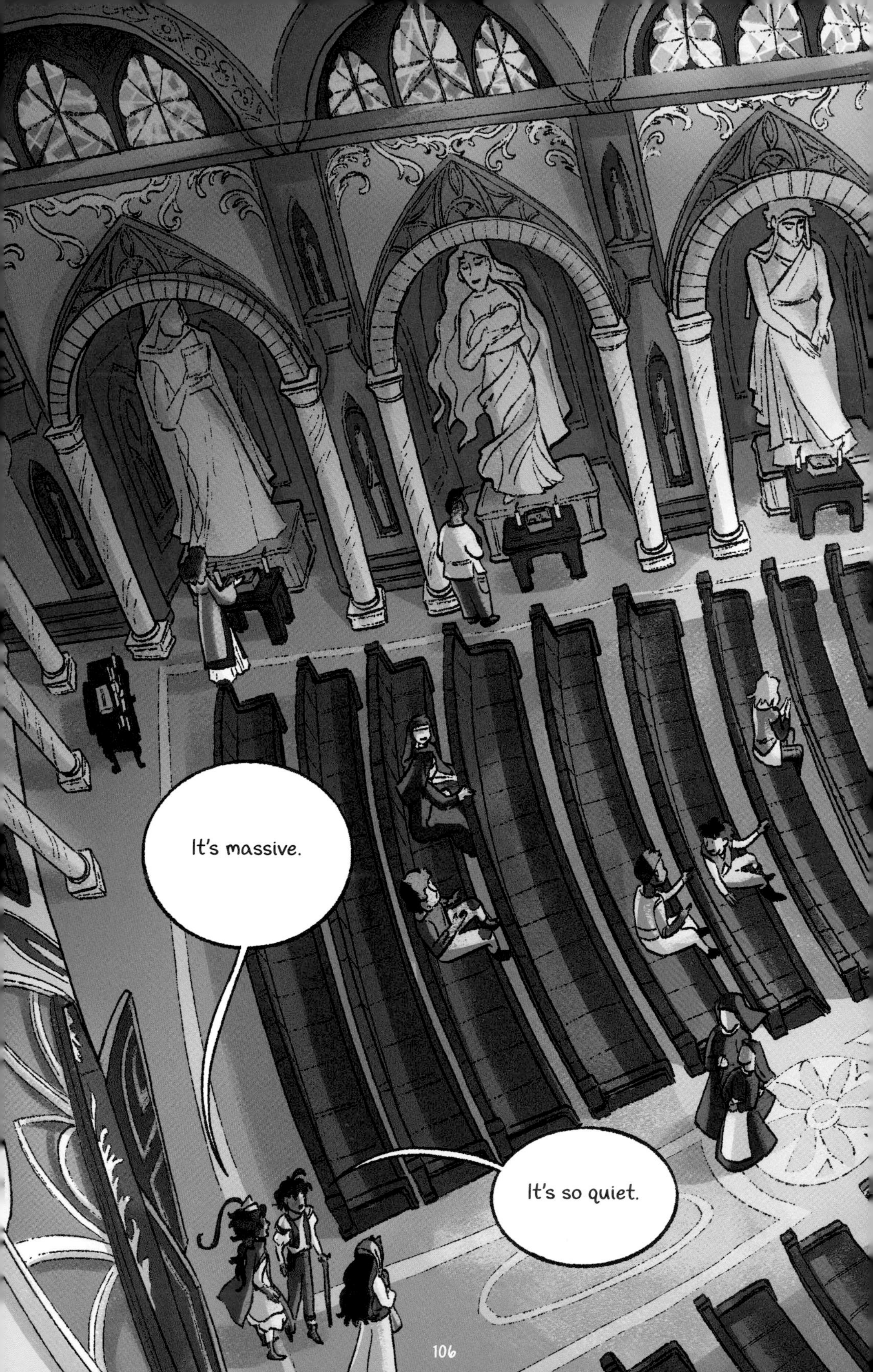
It's massive.
It's so quiet.

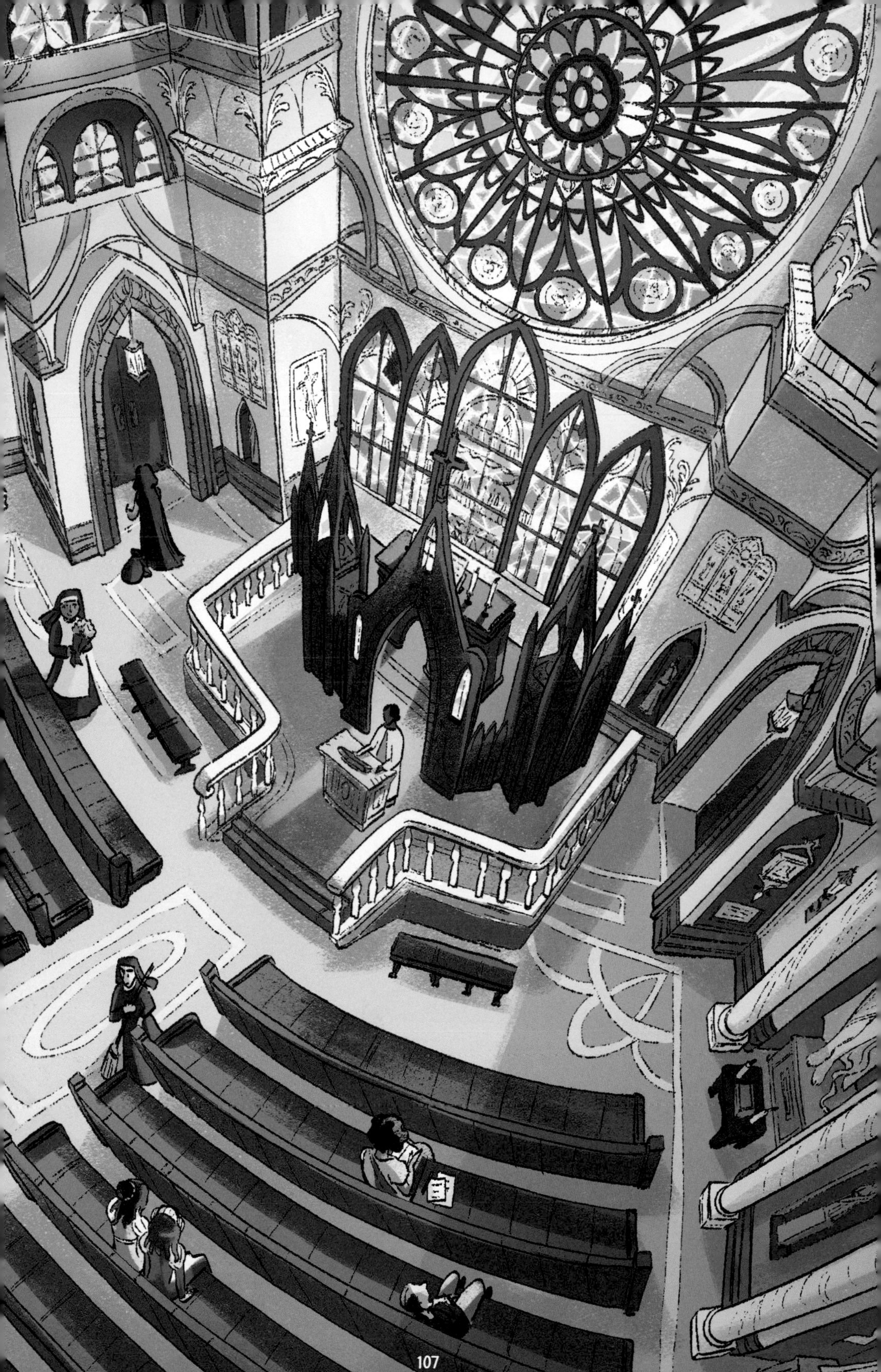

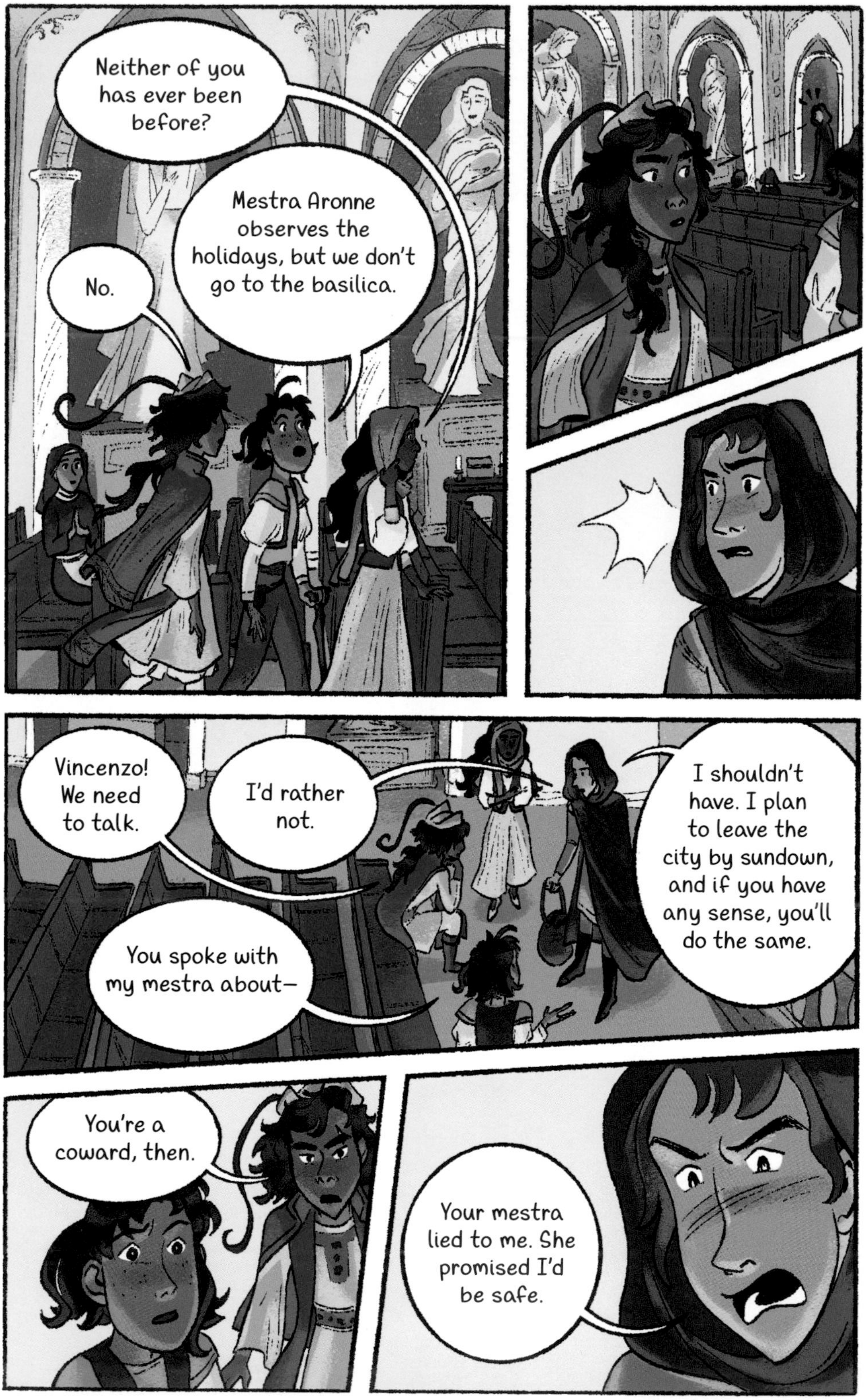
Neither of you has ever been before?
No.
Mestra Aronne observes the holidays, but we don't go to the basilica.
Vincenzo! We need to talk.
I'd rather not.
You spoke with my mestra about—
I shouldn't have. I plan to leave the city by sundown, and if you have any sense, you'll do the same.
You're a coward, then.
Your mestra lied to me. She promised I'd be safe.

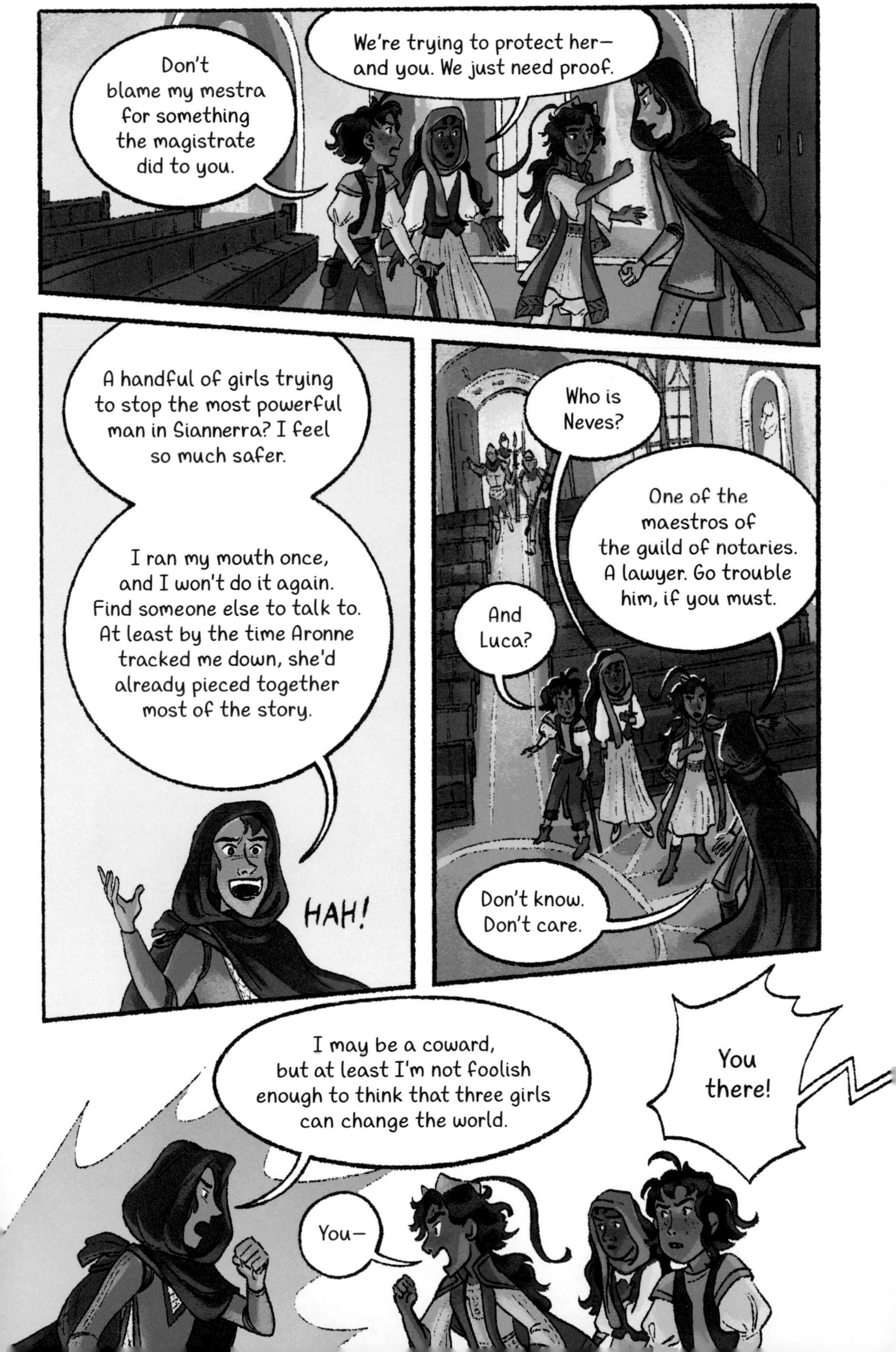

Don't blame my mestra for something the magistrate did to you.
We're trying to protect her— and you. We just need proof.
A handful of girls trying to stop the most powerful man in Siannerra? I feel so much safer.
I ran my mouth once, and I won't do it again. Find someone else to talk to. At least by the time Aronne tracked me down, she'd already pieced together most of the story.
HAH!
Who is Neves?
One of the maestros of the guild of notaries. A lawyer. Go trouble him, if you must.
And Luca?
Don't know. Don't care.
I may be a coward, but at least I'm not foolish enough to think that three girls can change the world.
You there!
You—

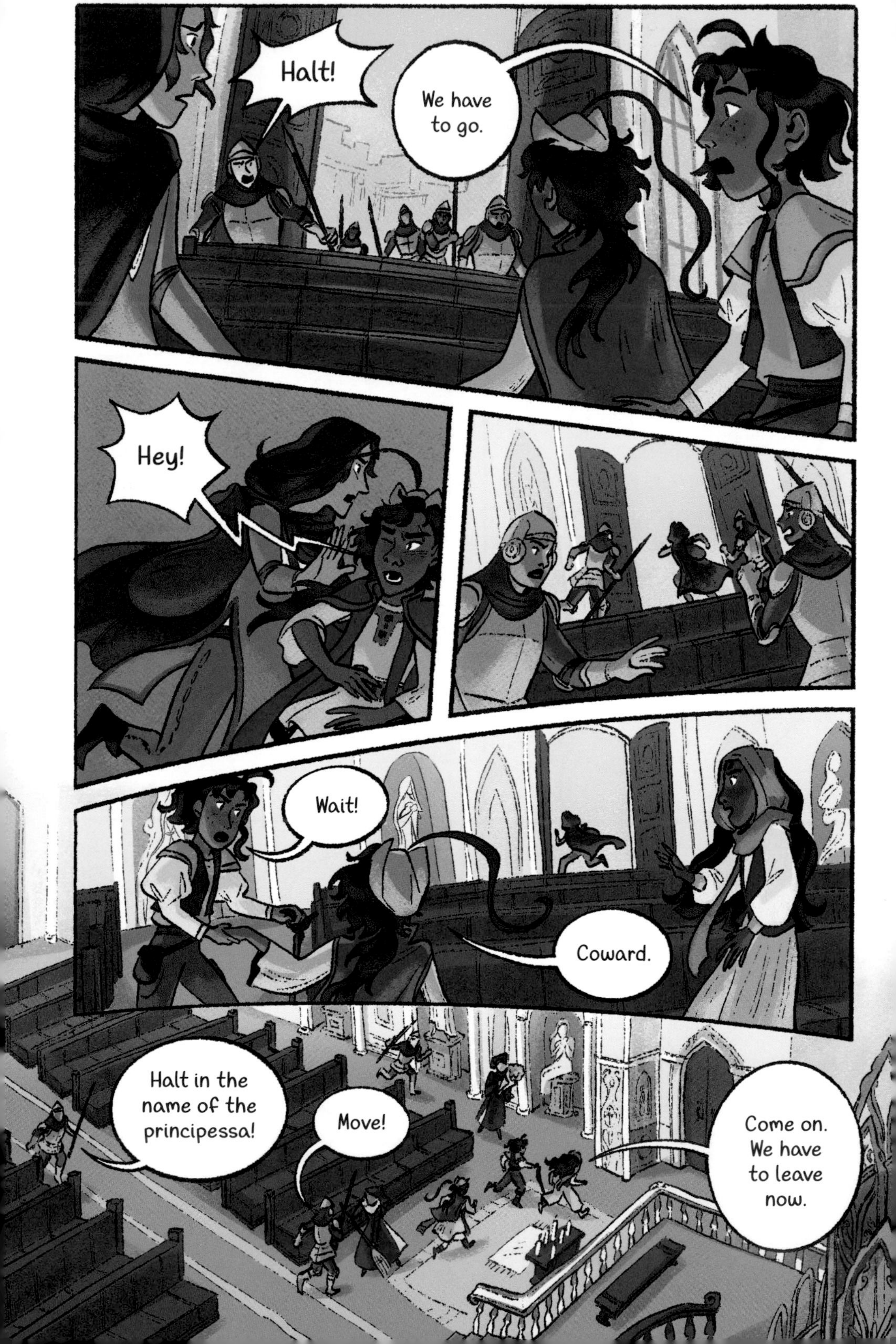
Halt!
We have to go.
Hey!
Wait!
Coward.
Halt in the name of the principessa!
Move!
Come on. We have to leave now.

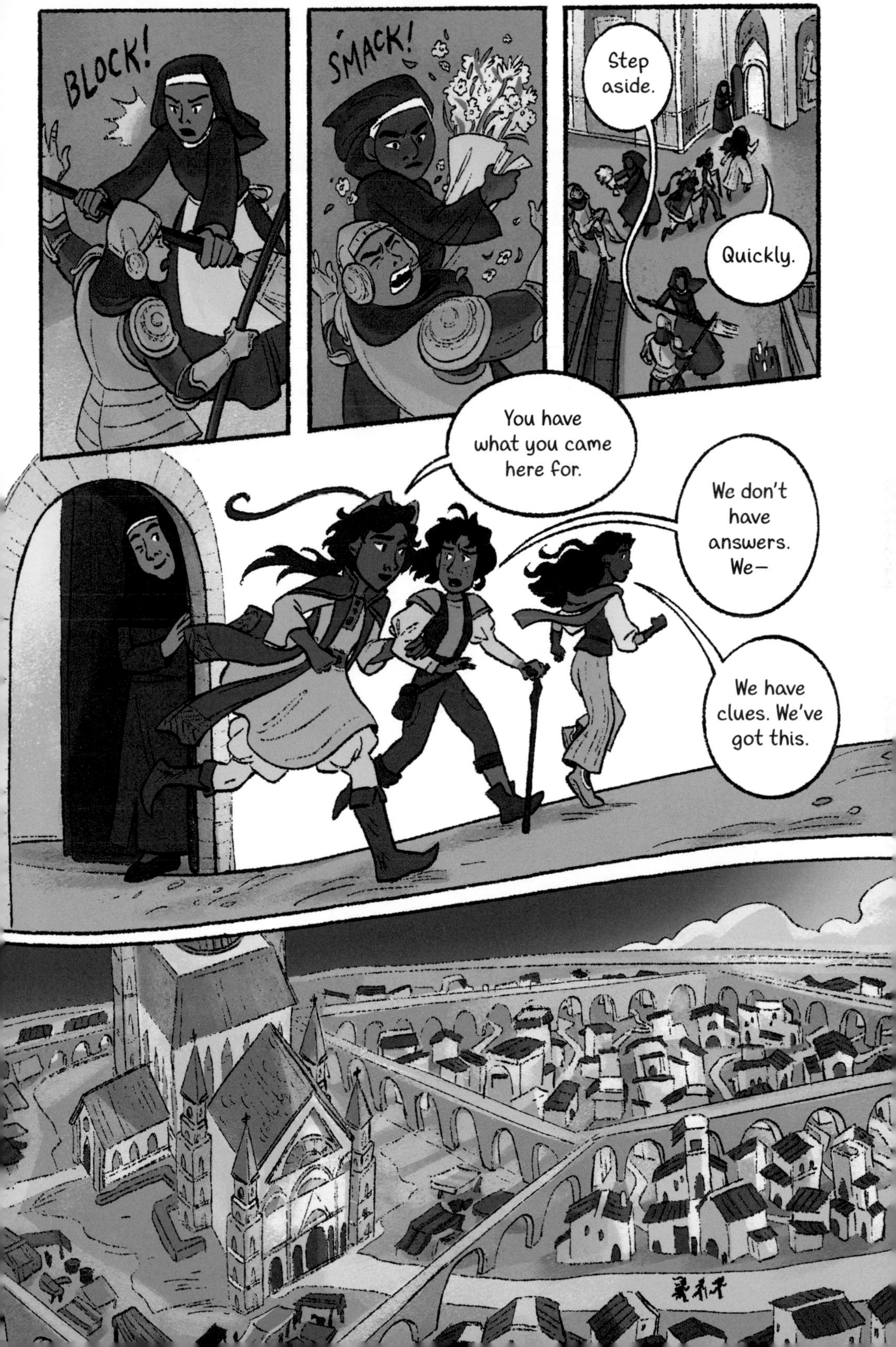
BLOCK!
SMACK!
Step aside.
Quickly.
You have what you came here for.
We don't have answers. We—
We have clues. We've got this.

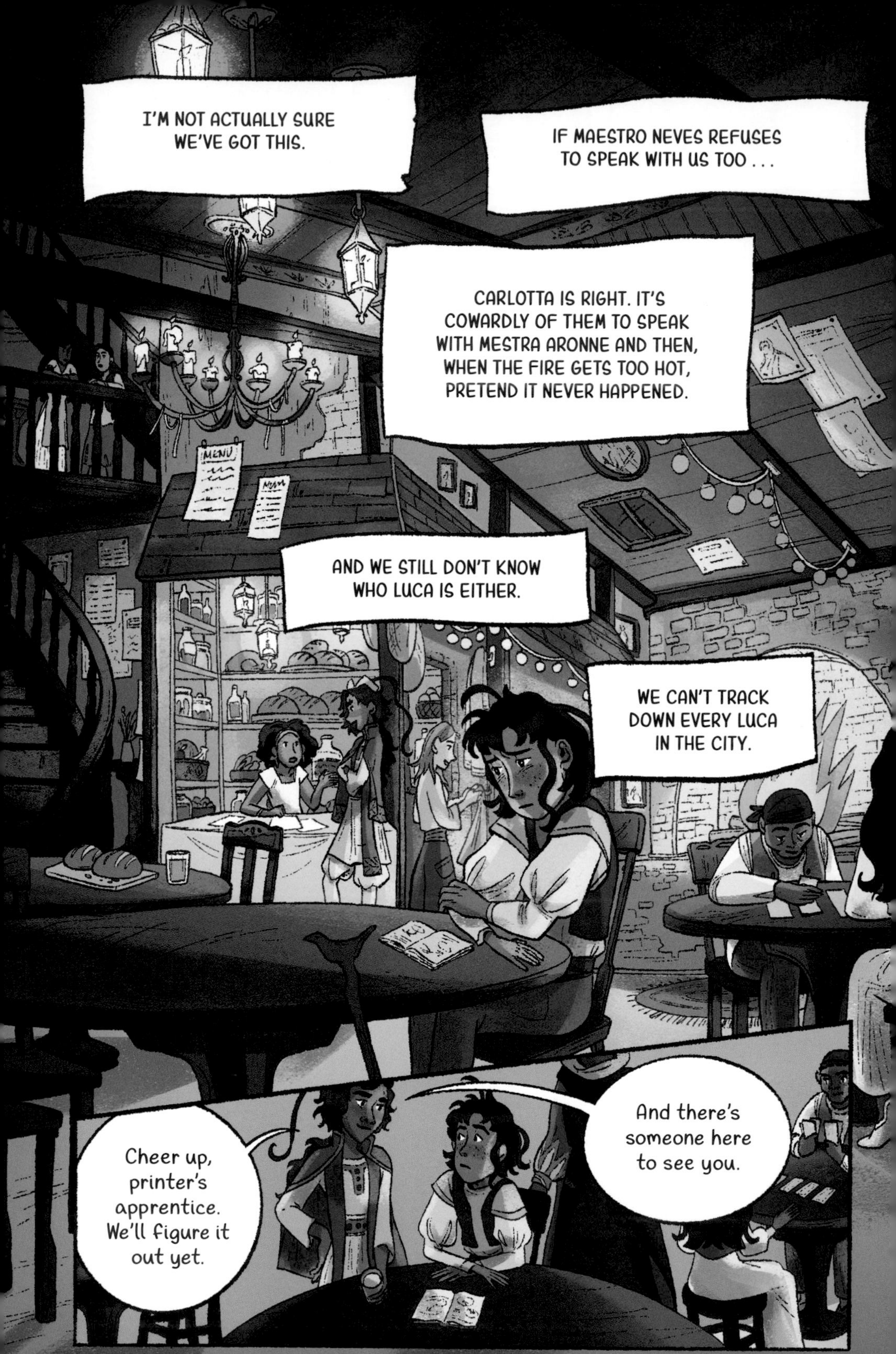
I'M NOT ACTUALLY SURE WE'VE GOT THIS.
IF MAESTRO NEVES REFUSES TO SPEAK WITH US TOO . . .
CARLOTTA IS RIGHT. IT'S COWARDLY OF THEM TO SPEAK WITH MESTRA ARONNE AND THEN, WHEN THE FIRE GETS TOO HOT, PRETEND IT NEVER HAPPENED.
AND WE STILL DON'T KNOW WHO LUCA IS EITHER.
WE CAN'T TRACK DOWN EVERY LUCA IN THE CITY.
Cheer up, printer's apprentice. We'll figure it out yet.
And there's someone here to see you.

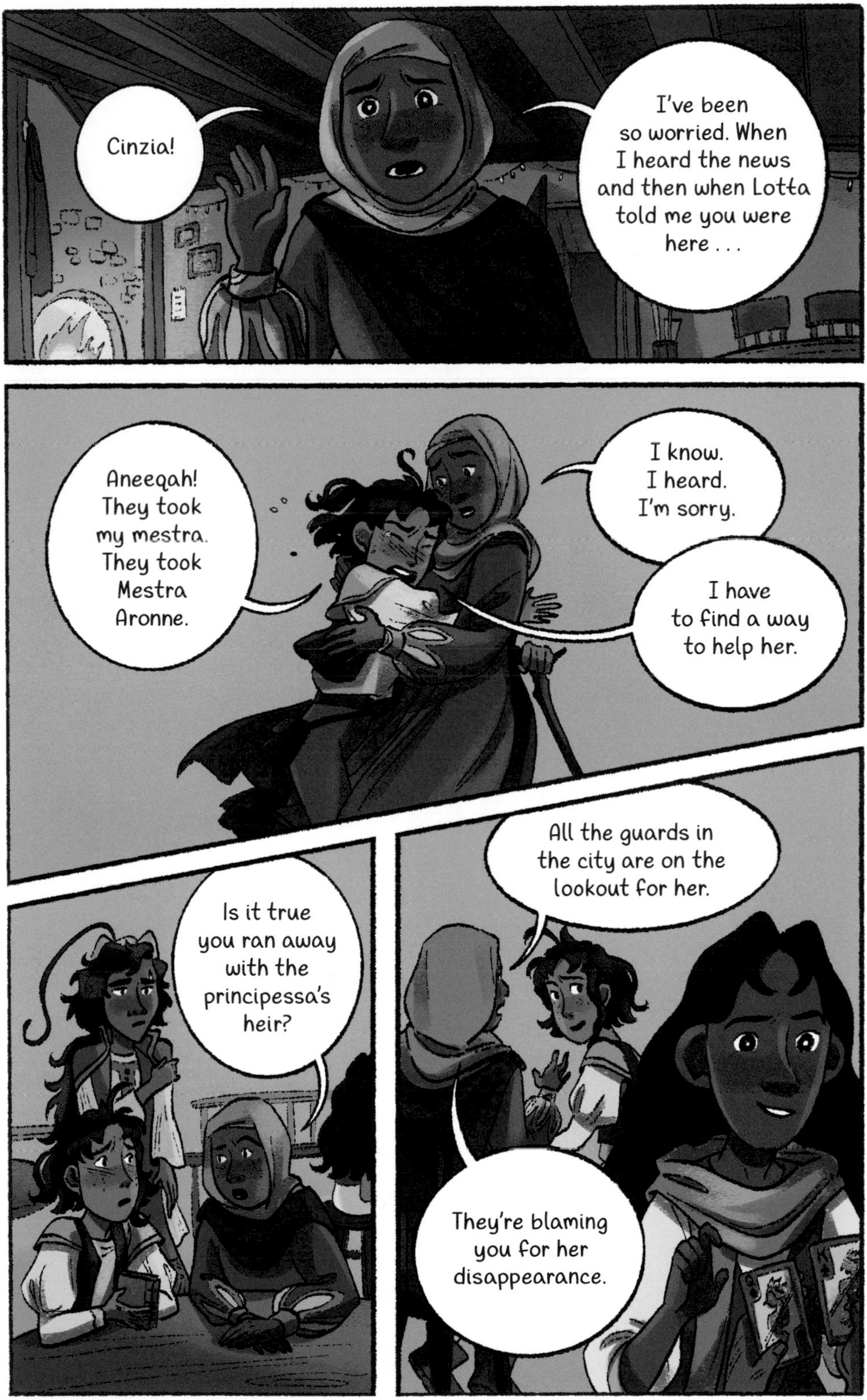
Cinzia!
I've been so worried. When I heard the news and then when Lotta told me you were here . . .
Aneeqah! They took my mestra. They took Mestra Aronne.
I know. I heard. I'm sorry.
I have to find a way to help her.
Is it true you ran away with the principessa's heir?
All the guards in the city are on the lookout for her.
They're blaming you for her disappearance.

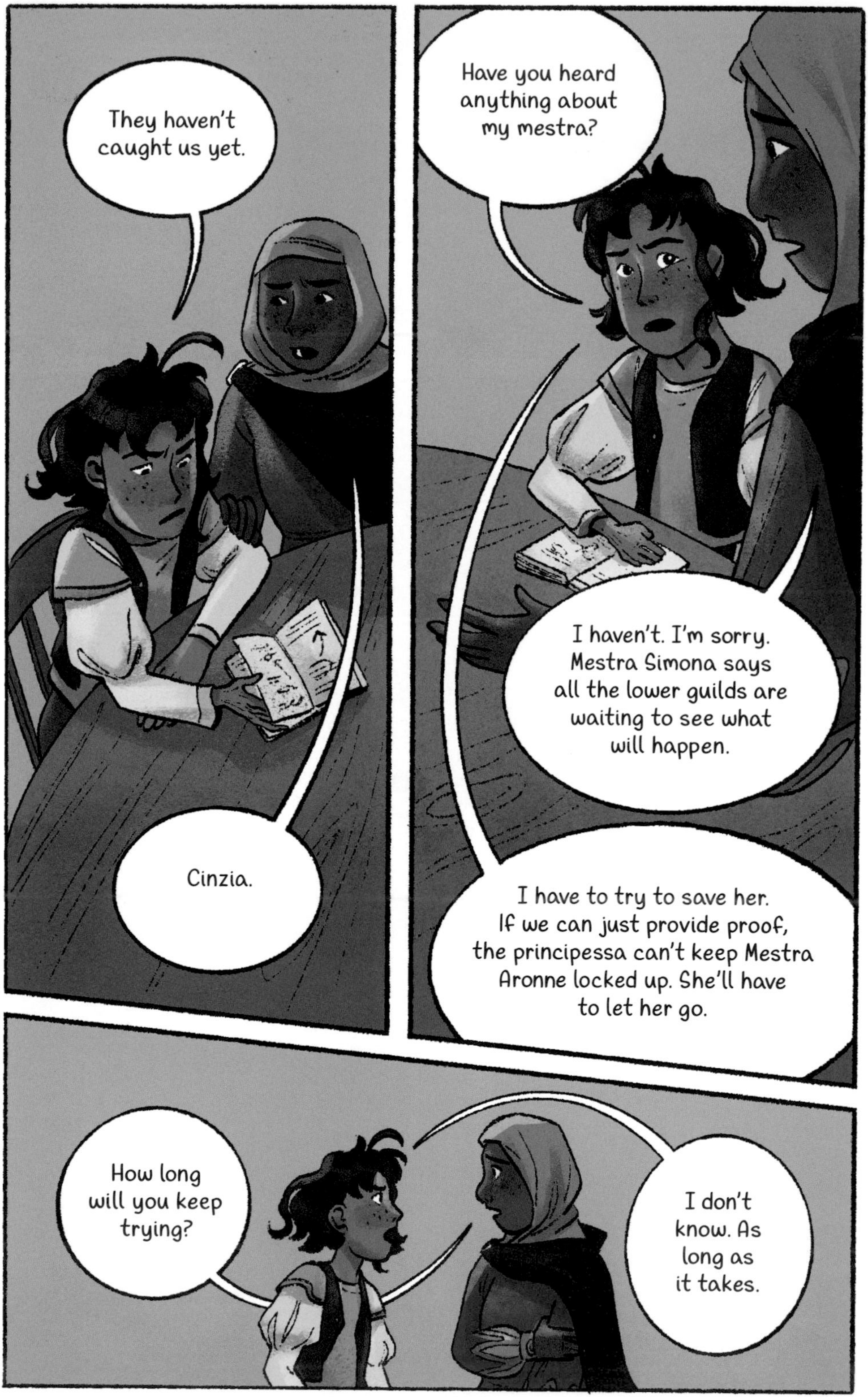
They haven't caught us yet.
Cinzia.
Have you heard anything about my mestra?
I haven't. I'm sorry. Mestra Simona says all the lower guilds are waiting to see what will happen.
I have to try to save her. If we can just provide proof, the principessa can't keep Mestra Aronne locked up. She'll have to let her go.
How long will you keep trying?
I don't know. As long as it takes.

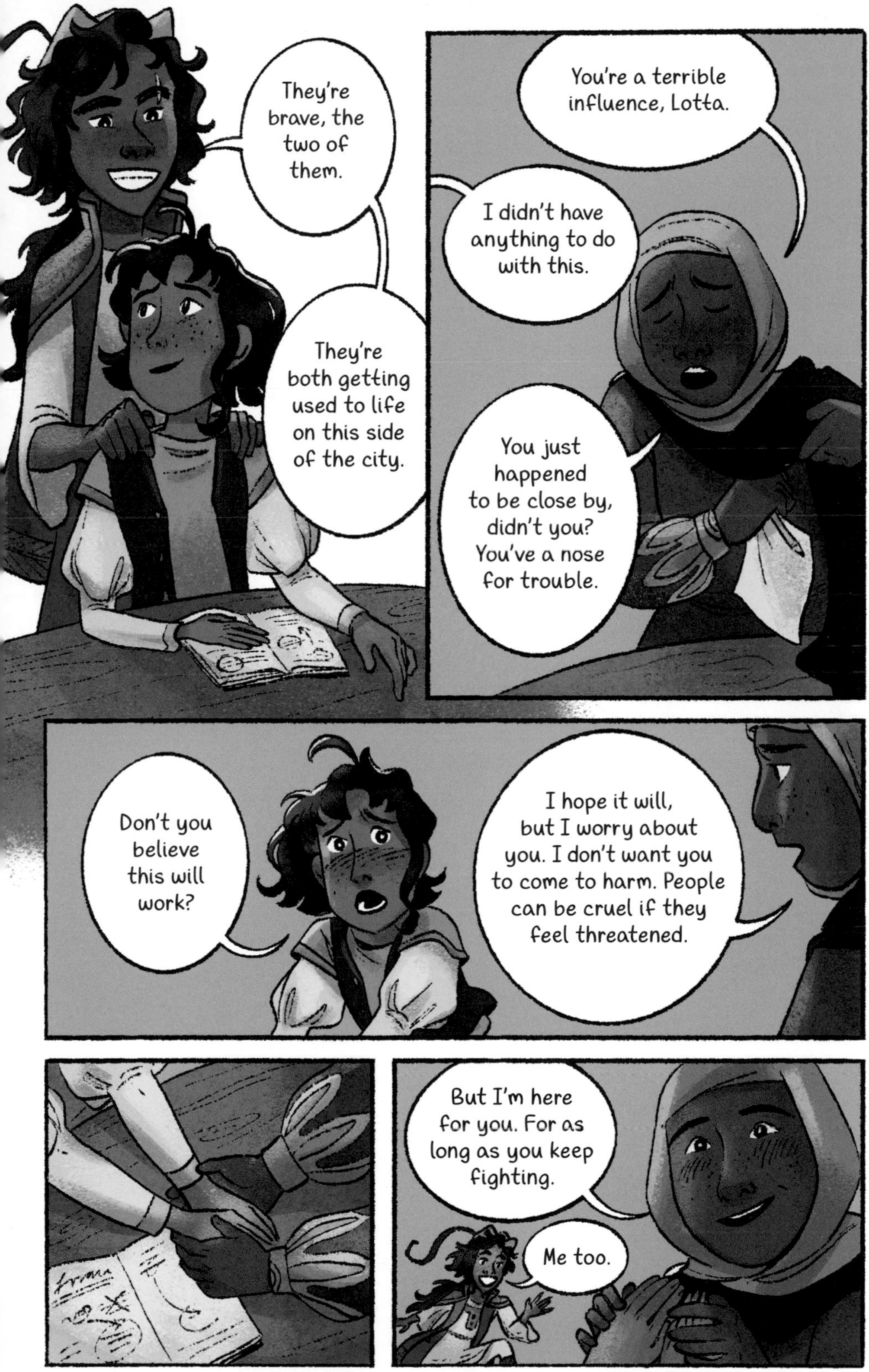
They're brave, the two of them.
They're both getting used to life on this side of the city.
You're a terrible influence, Lotta.
I didn't have anything to do with this.
You just happened to be close by, didn't you? You've a nose for trouble.
Don't you believe this will work?
I hope it will, but I worry about you. I don't want you to come to harm. People can be cruel if they feel threatened.
But I'm here for you. For as long as you keep fighting.
Me too.

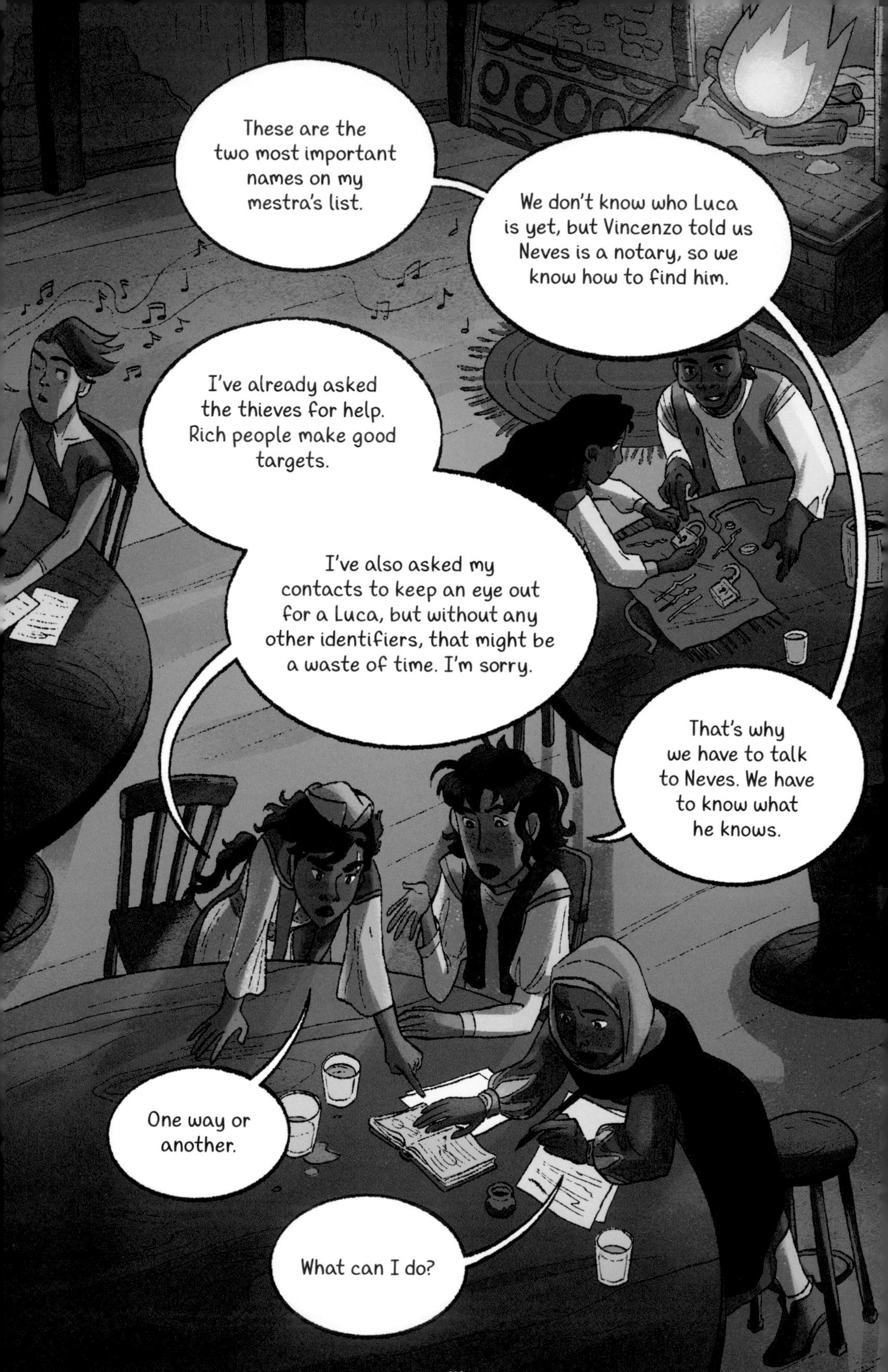
These are the two most important names on my mestra's list.
We don't know who Luca is yet, but Vincenzo told us Neves is a notary, so we know how to find him.
I've already asked the thieves for help. Rich people make good targets.
I've also asked my contacts to keep an eye out for a Luca, but without any other identifiers, that might be a waste of time. I'm sorry.
That's why we have to talk to Neves. We have to know what he knows.
One way or another.
What can I do?

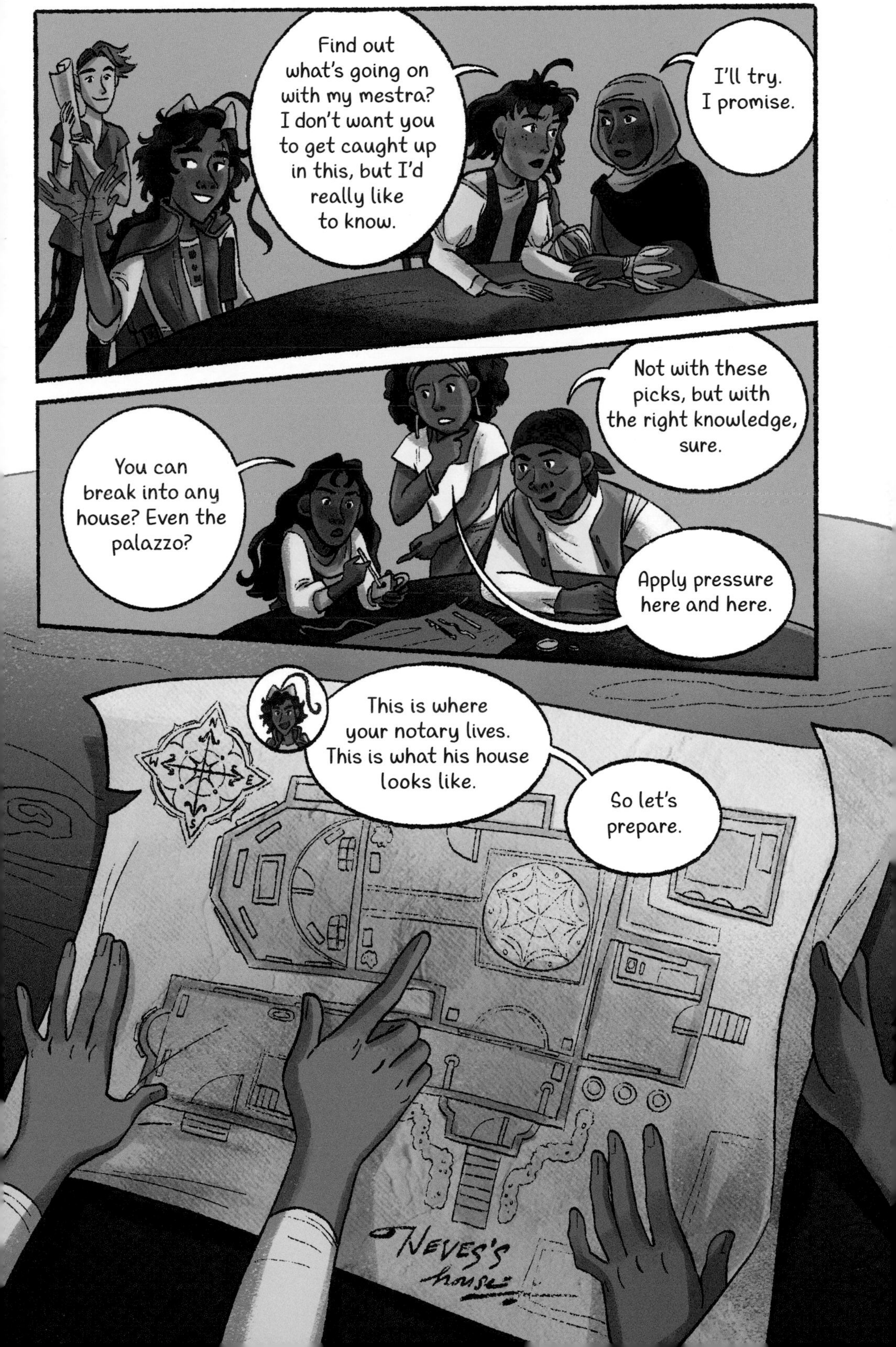
Find out what's going on with my mestra? I don't want you to get caught up in this, but I'd really like to know.
I'll try. I promise.
You can break into any house? Even the palazzo?
Not with these picks, but with the right knowledge, sure.
Apply pressure here and here.
This is where your notary lives. This is what his house looks like.
So let's prepare.
Neves's house

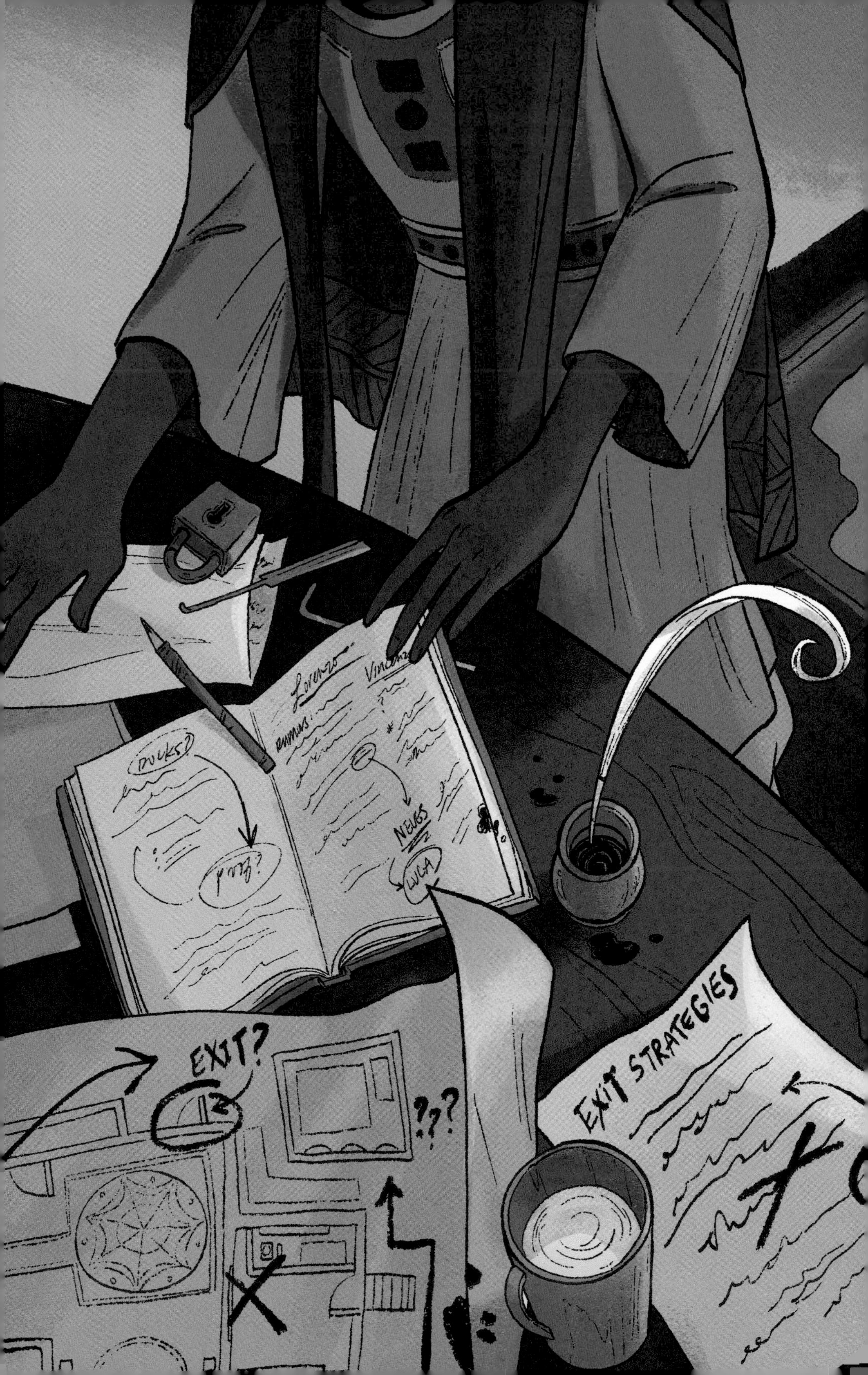

Lorenzo
RUMORS:
NEWS
LUCA
EXIT?
EXIT STRATEGIES

CHAPTER FIVE

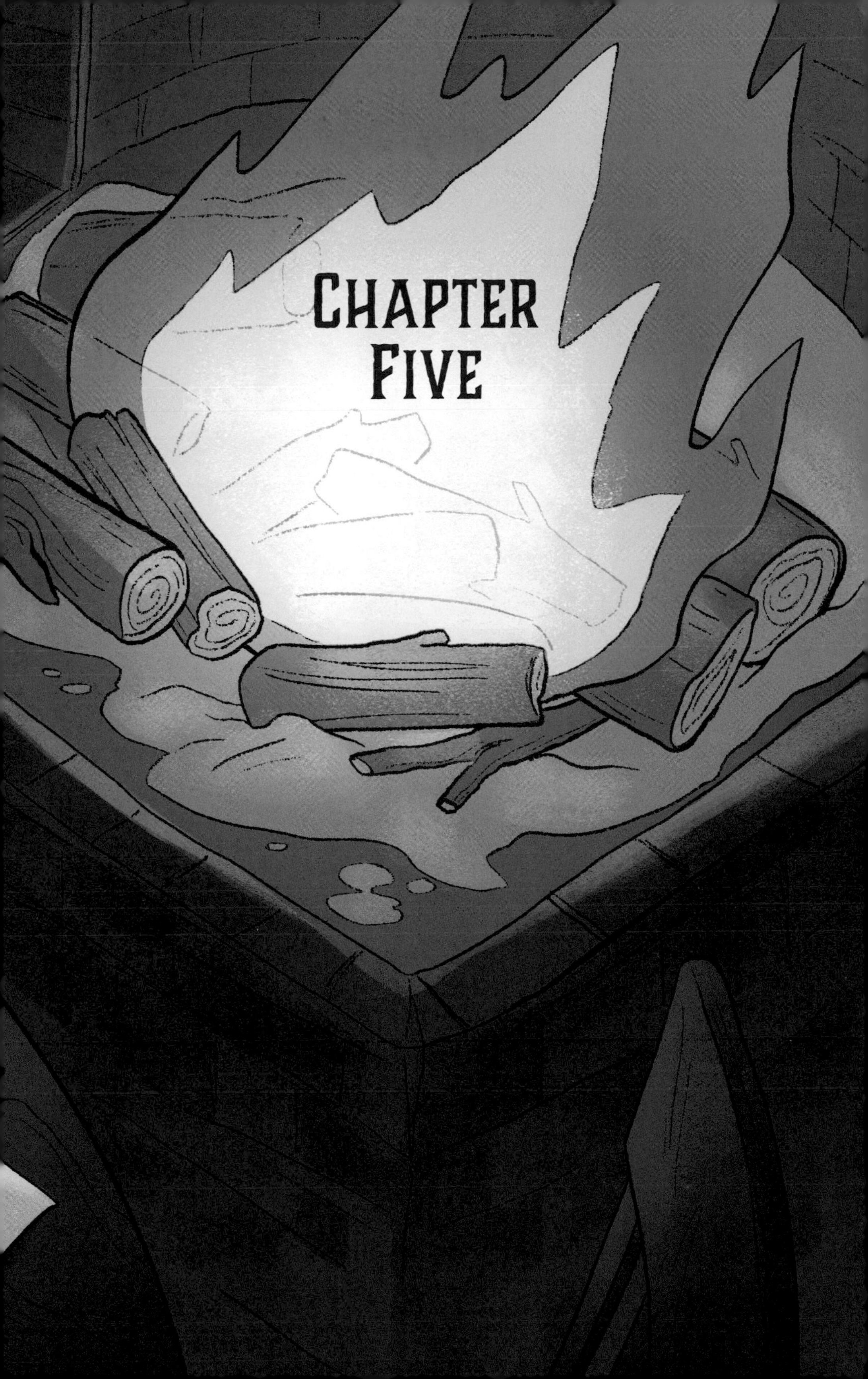

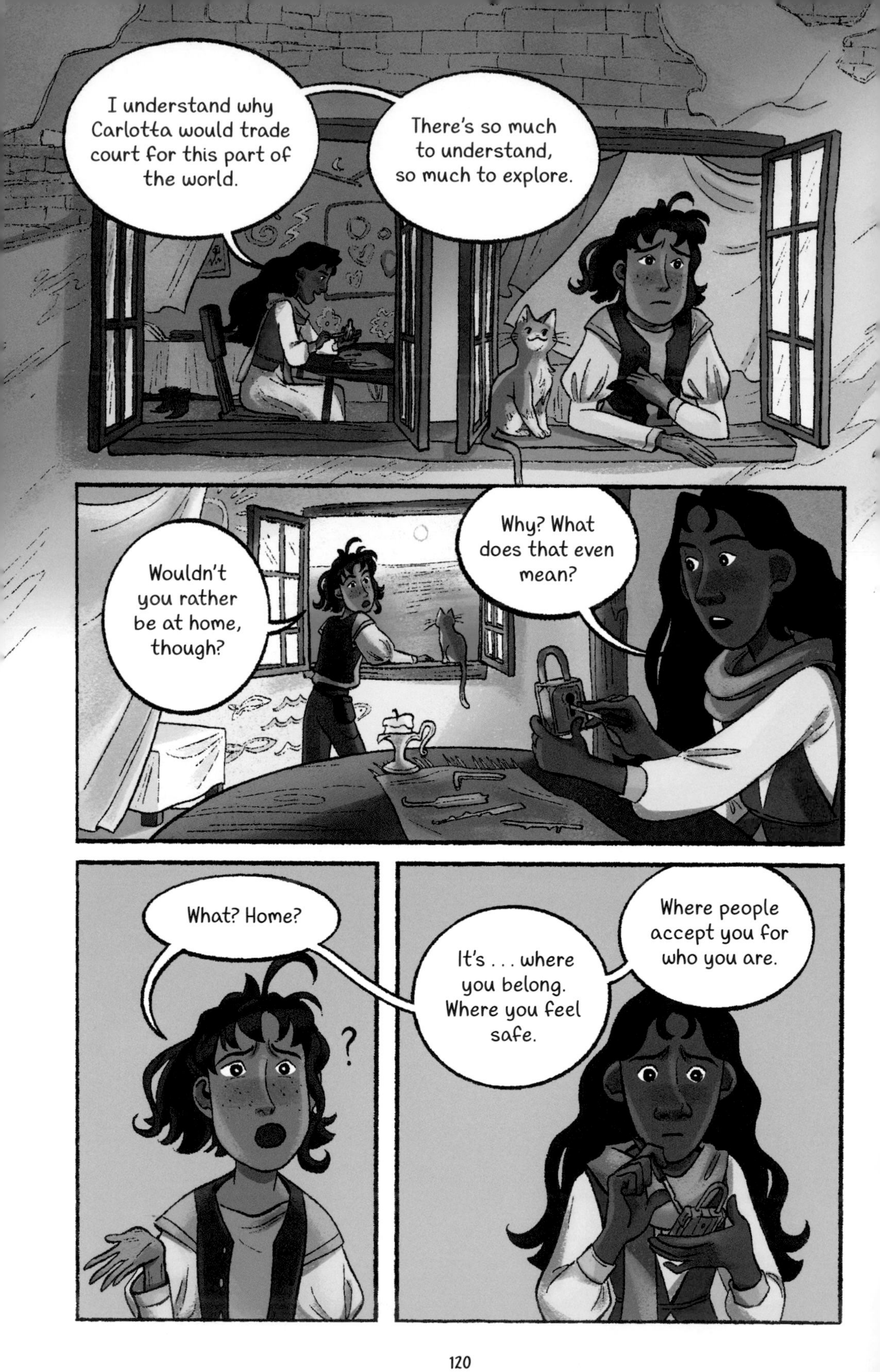
I understand why Carlotta would trade court for this part of the world.
There's so much to understand, so much to explore.
Wouldn't you rather be at home, though?
Why? What does that even mean?
What? Home?
?
It's . . . where you belong. Where you feel safe.
Where people accept you for who you are.

If that's the case, I'm not sure the palazzo counts as home.

Everyone there wants me to be someone I'm not.

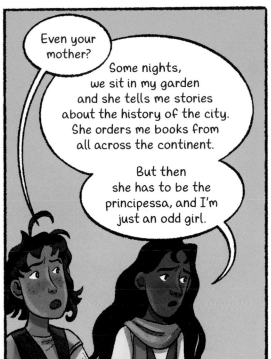

Even your mother?

Some nights, we sit in my garden and she tells me stories about the history of the city. She orders me books from all across the continent.

But then she has to be the principessa, and I'm just an odd girl.

Home is complicated for a lot of us, but you're always welcome here.

I'm sorry.

I'd like to come back here once we prove our case.

I like having friends.

But right now, we have priorities. Let's go talk to Neves and hear what he has to say.

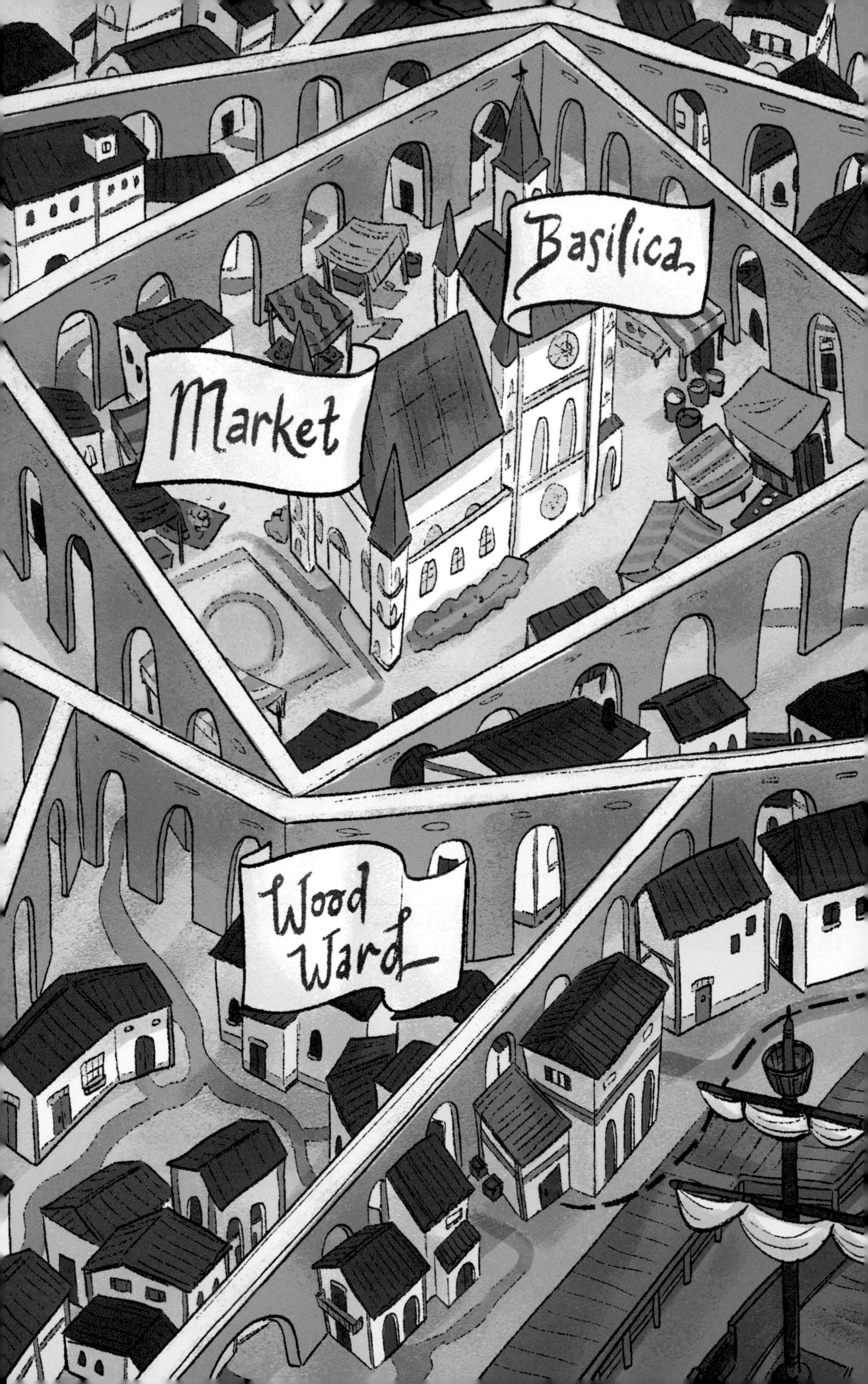
Basilica
Market
Wood
Ward

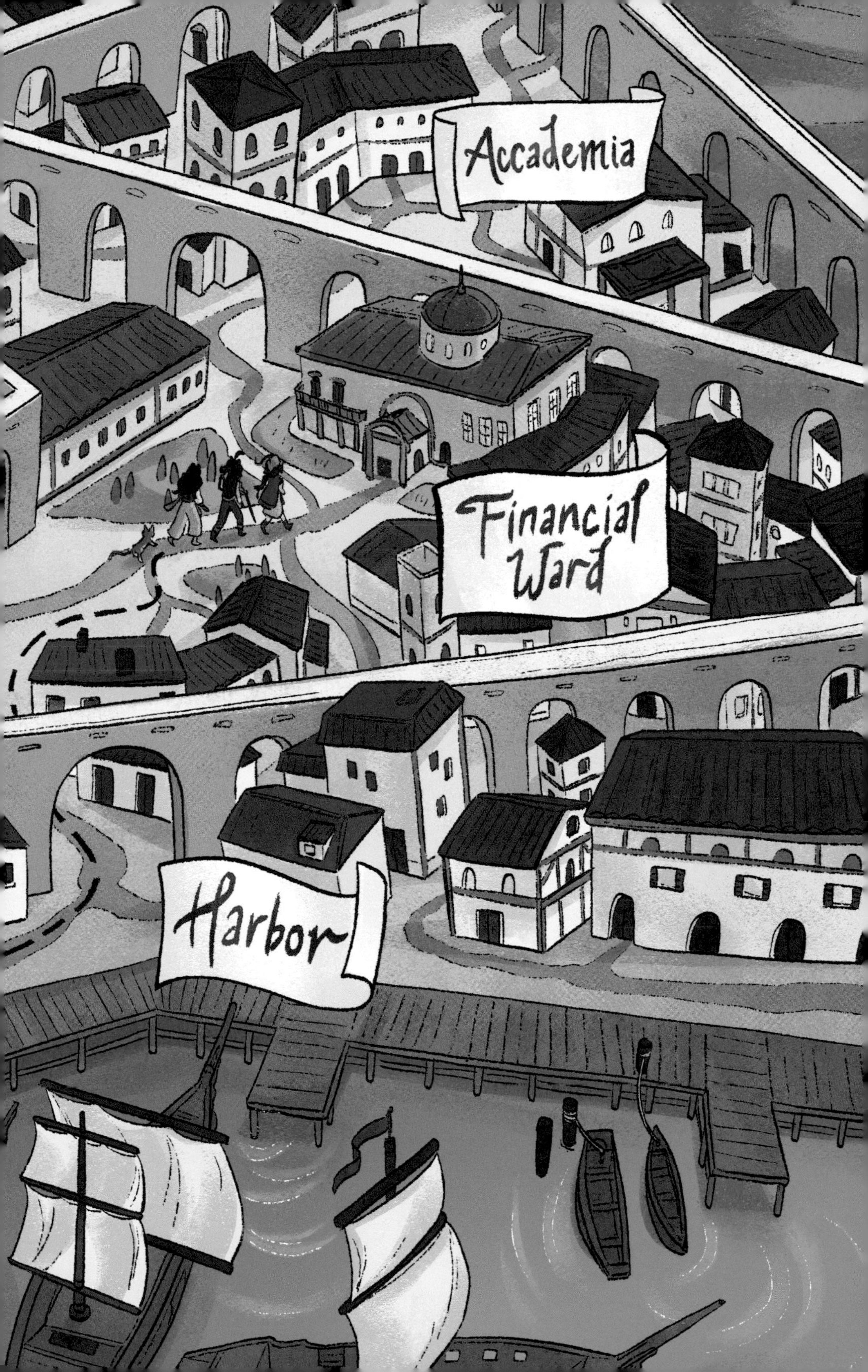
Accademia
Financial Ward
Harbor

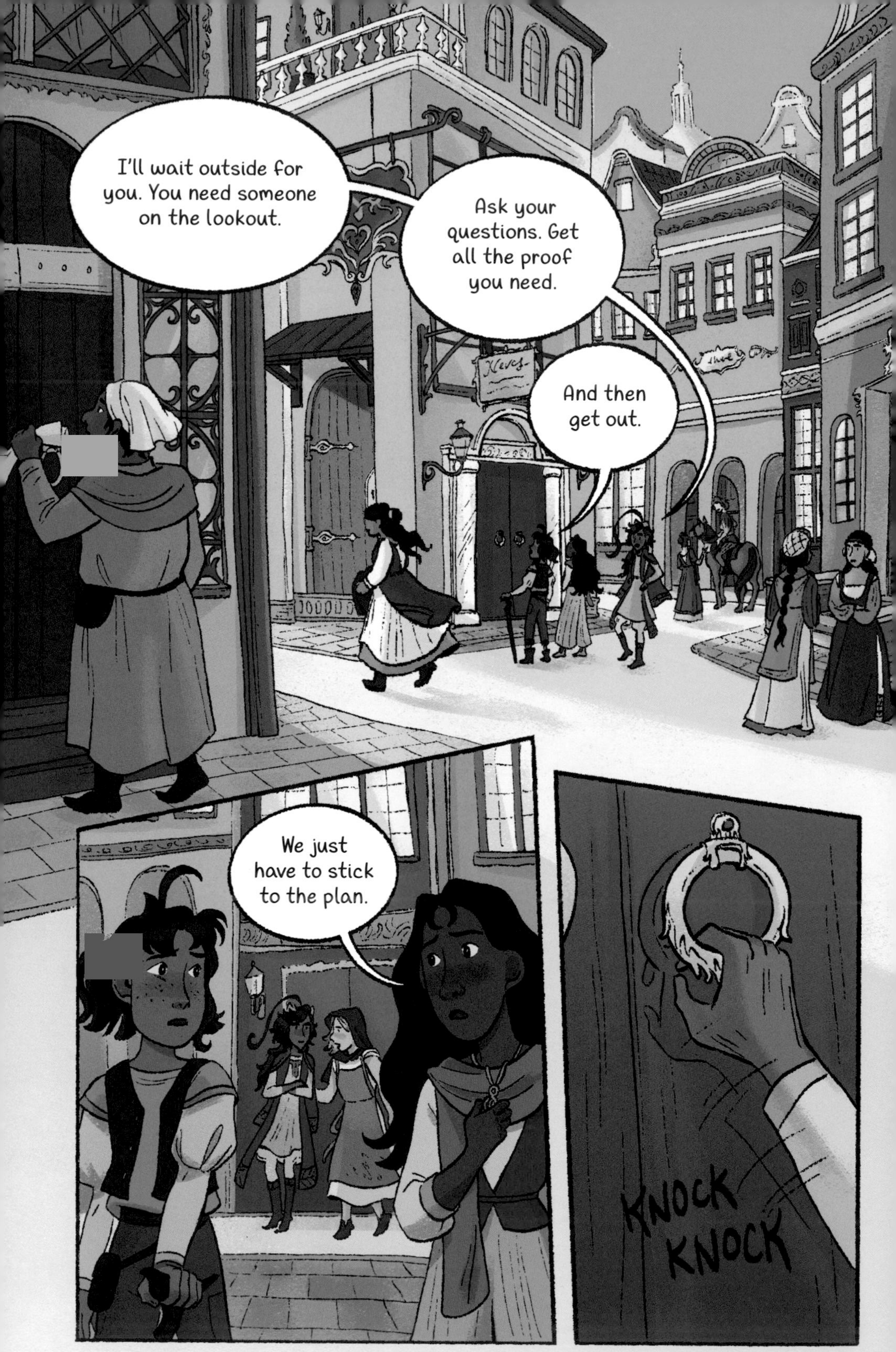
I'll wait outside for you. You need someone on the lookout.
Ask your questions. Get all the proof you need.
And then get out.
We just have to stick to the plan.
KNOCK KNOCK

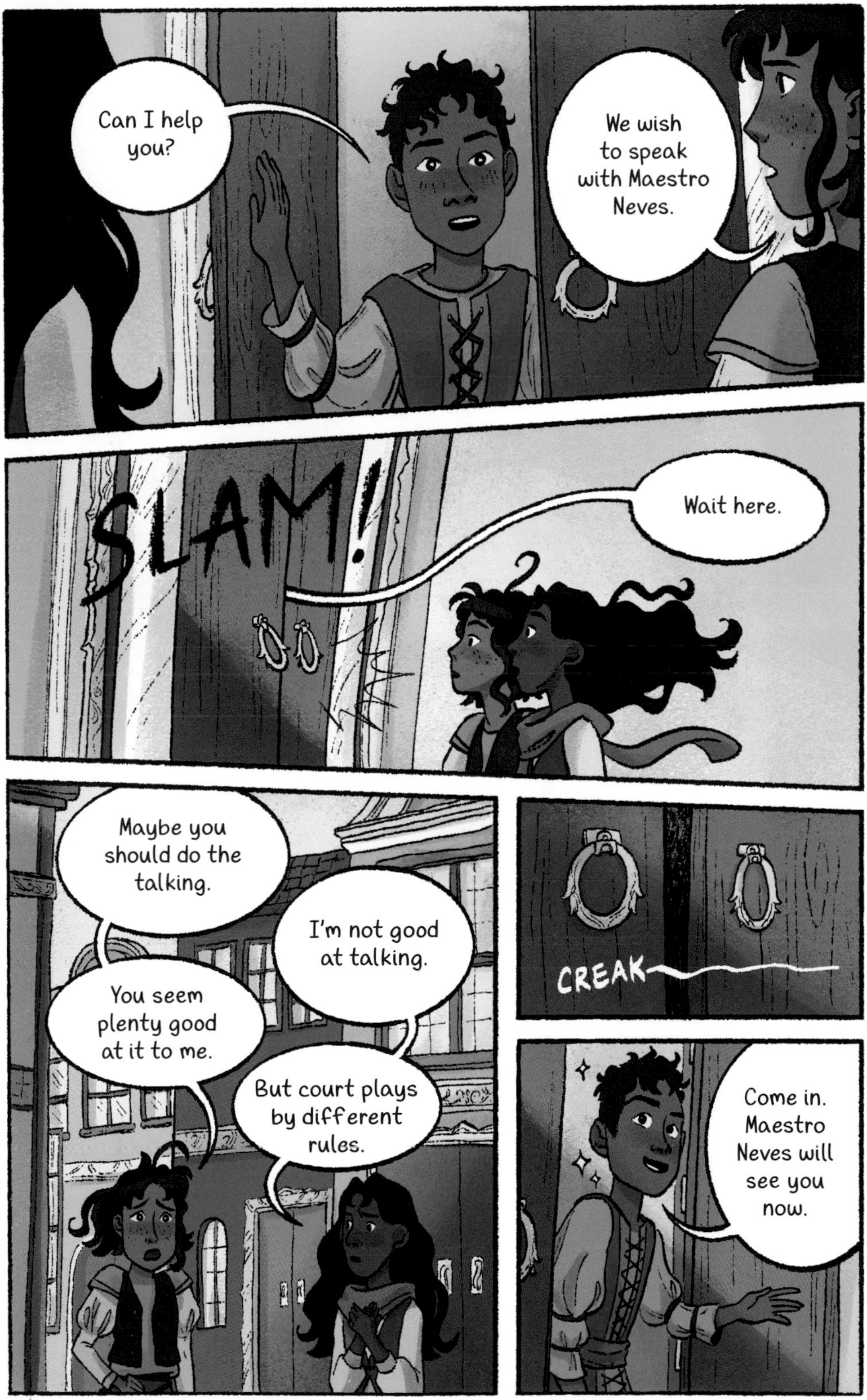
Can I help you?
We wish to speak with Maestro Neves.
SLAM!
Wait here.
Maybe you should do the talking.
I'm not good at talking.
You seem plenty good at it to me.
But court plays by different rules.
CREAK
Come in. Maestro Neves will see you now.

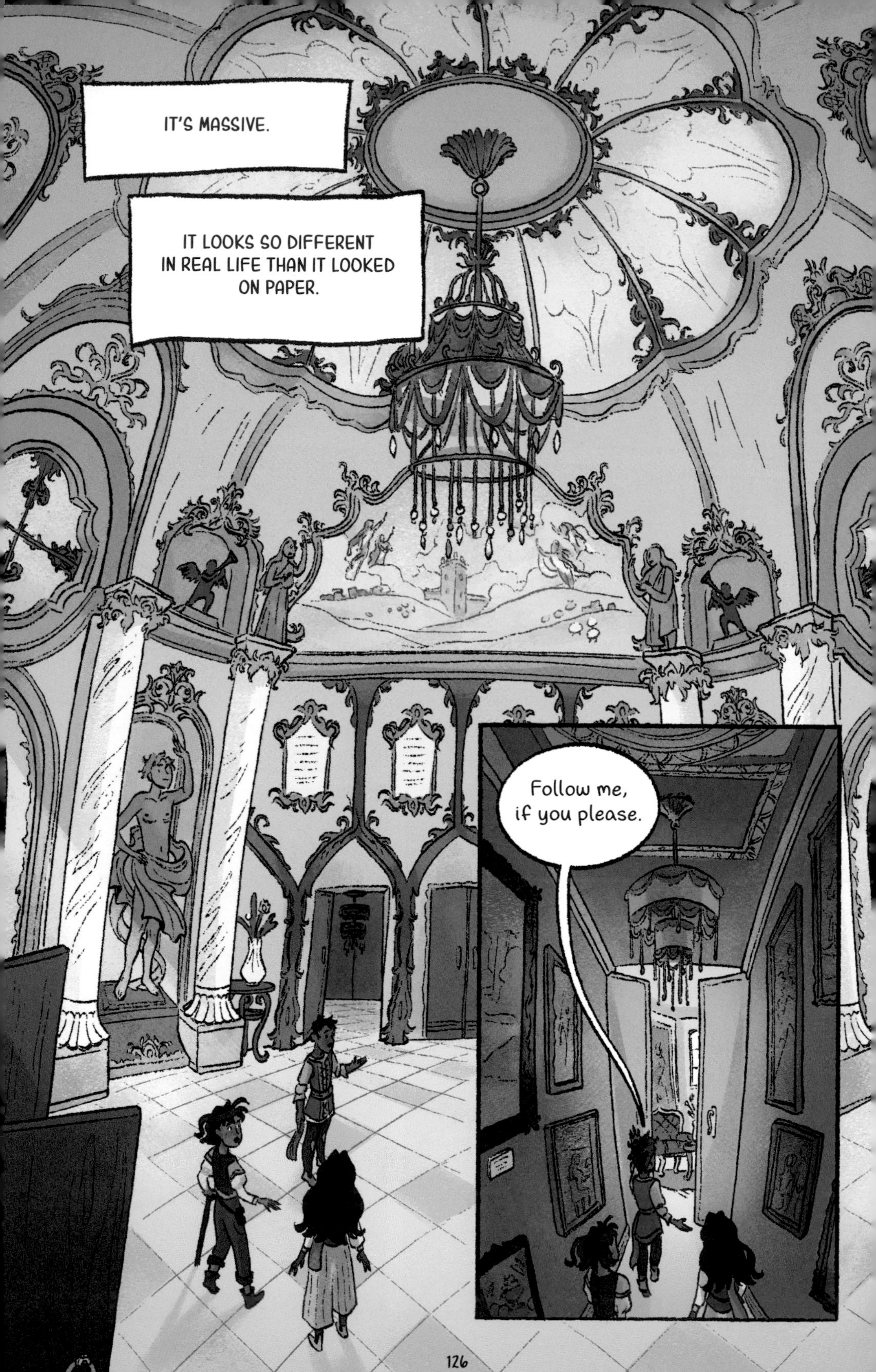
IT'S MASSIVE.
IT LOOKS SO DIFFERENT IN REAL LIFE THAN IT LOOKED ON PAPER.
Follow me, if you please.

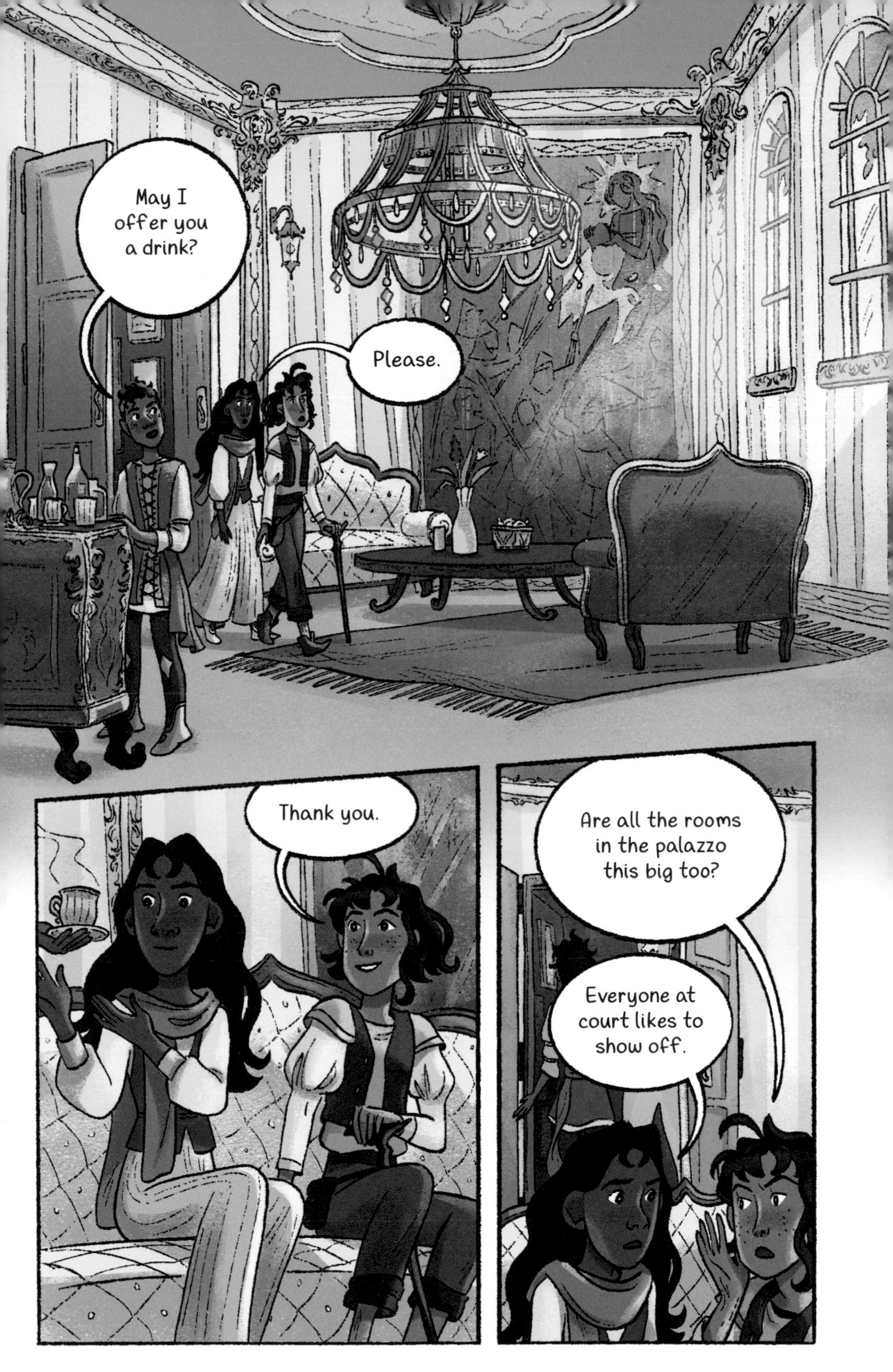
May I offer you a drink?
Please.
Thank you.
Are all the rooms in the palazzo this big too?
Everyone at court likes to show off.

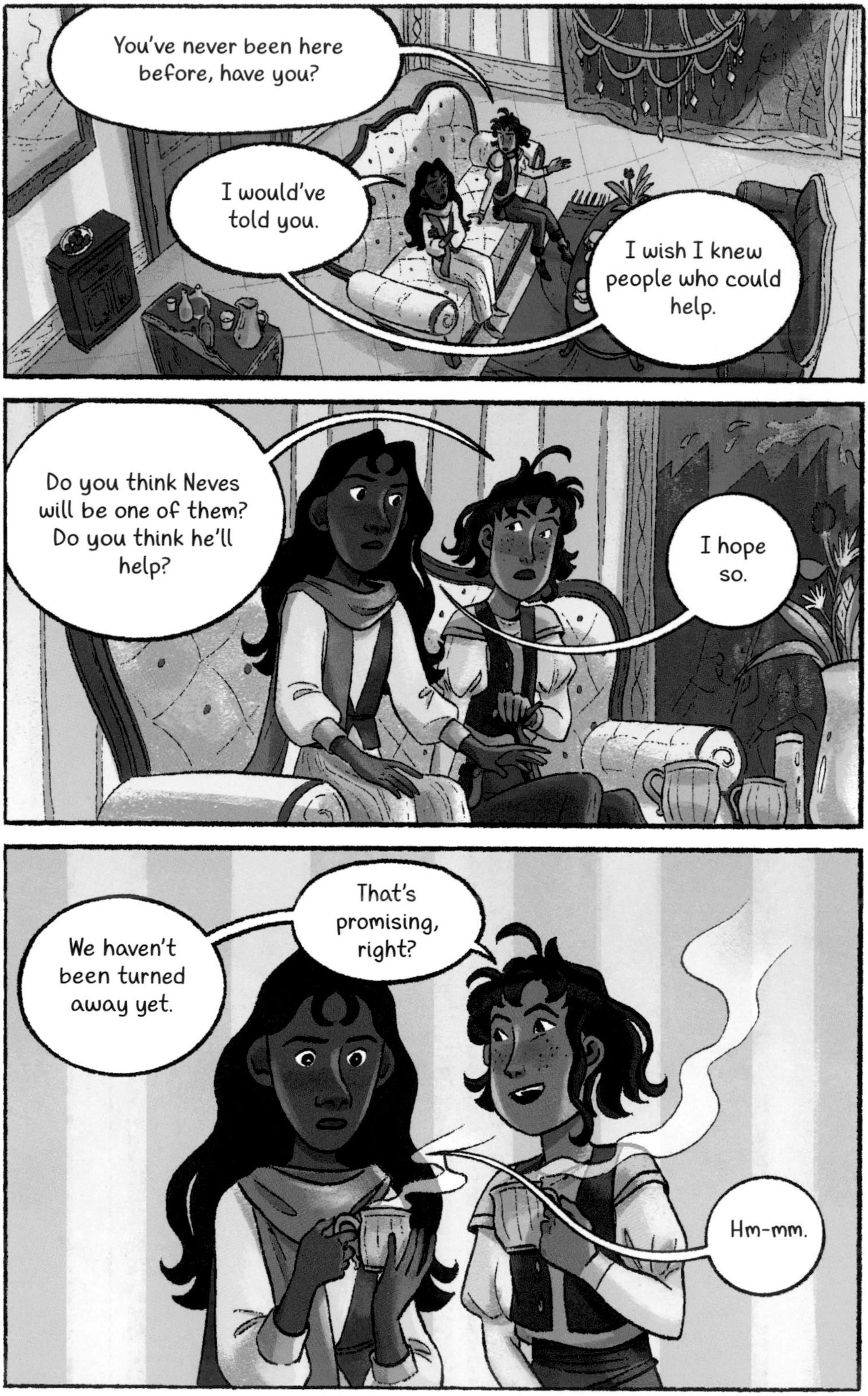
You've never been here before, have you?
I would've told you.
I wish I knew people who could help.
Do you think Neves will be one of them? Do you think he'll help?
I hope so.
We haven't been turned away yet.
That's promising, right?
Hm-mm.

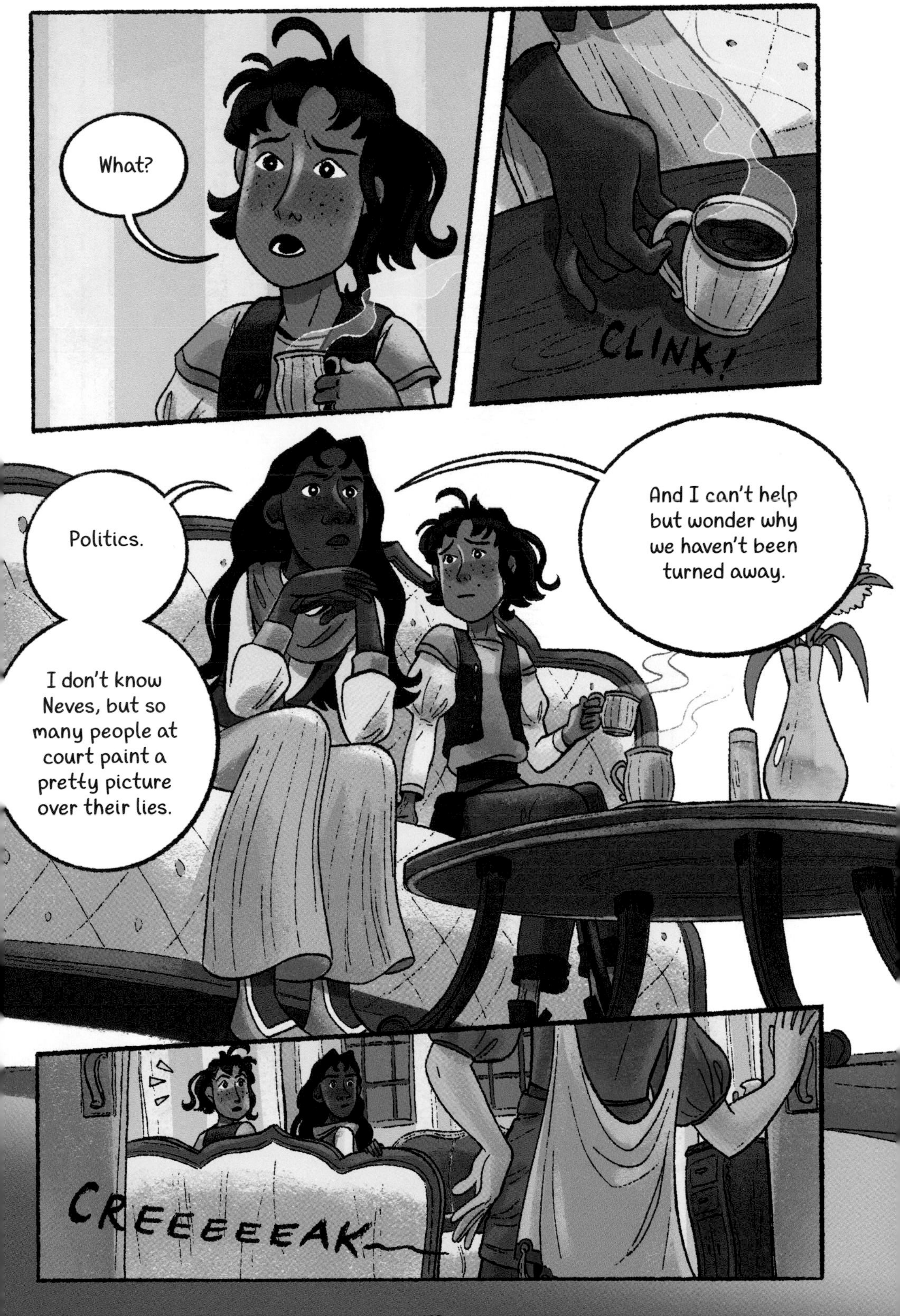

What?
CLINK!
Politics.
I don't know Neves, but so many people at court paint a pretty picture over their lies.
And I can't help but wonder why we haven't been turned away.
CREEEEEEAK

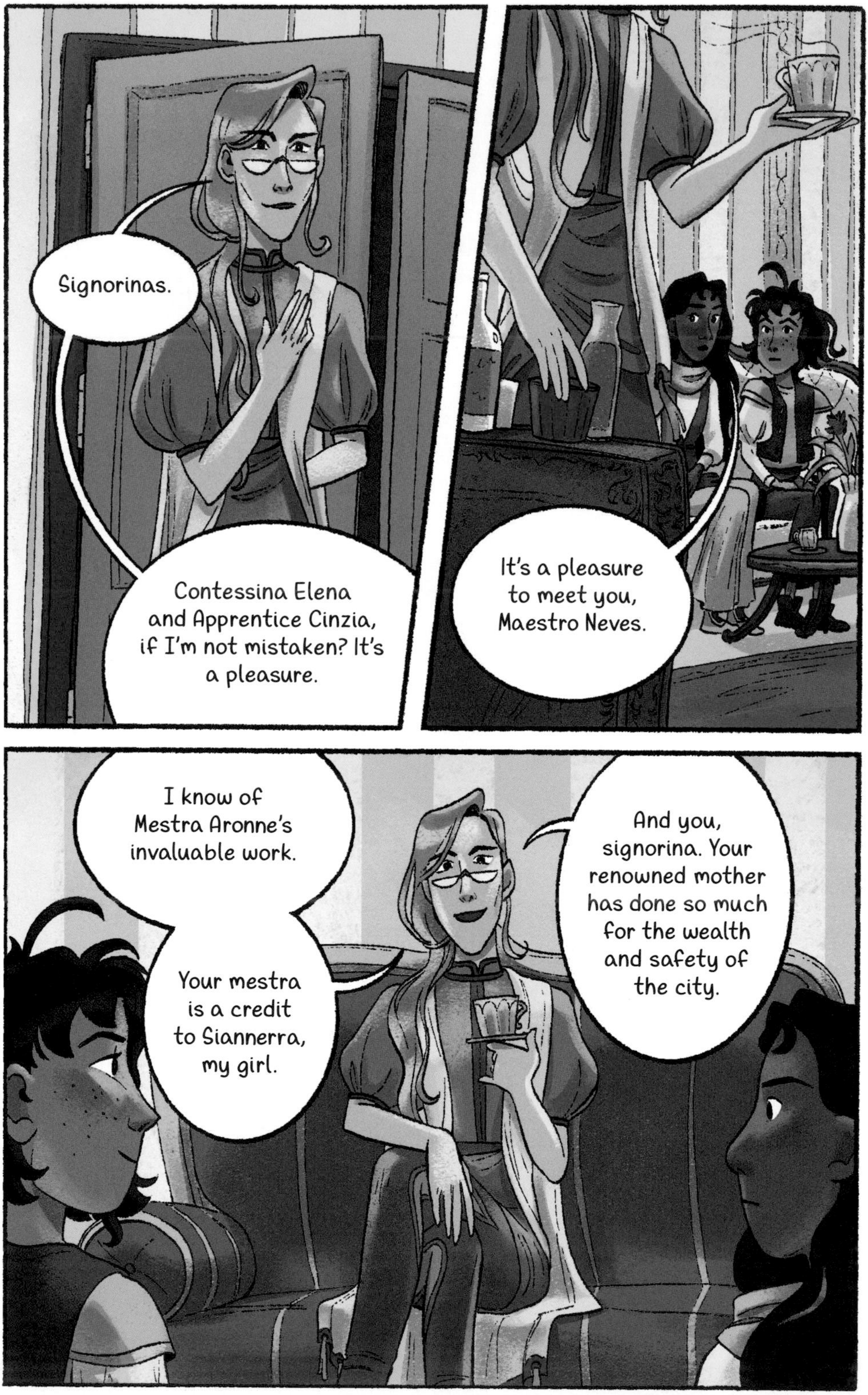
Signorinas.
Contessina Elena and Apprentice Cinzia, if I'm not mistaken? It's a pleasure.
It's a pleasure to meet you, Maestro Neves.
I know of Mestra Aronne's invaluable work.
Your mestra is a credit to Siannerra, my girl.
And you, signorina. Your renowned mother has done so much for the wealth and safety of the city.

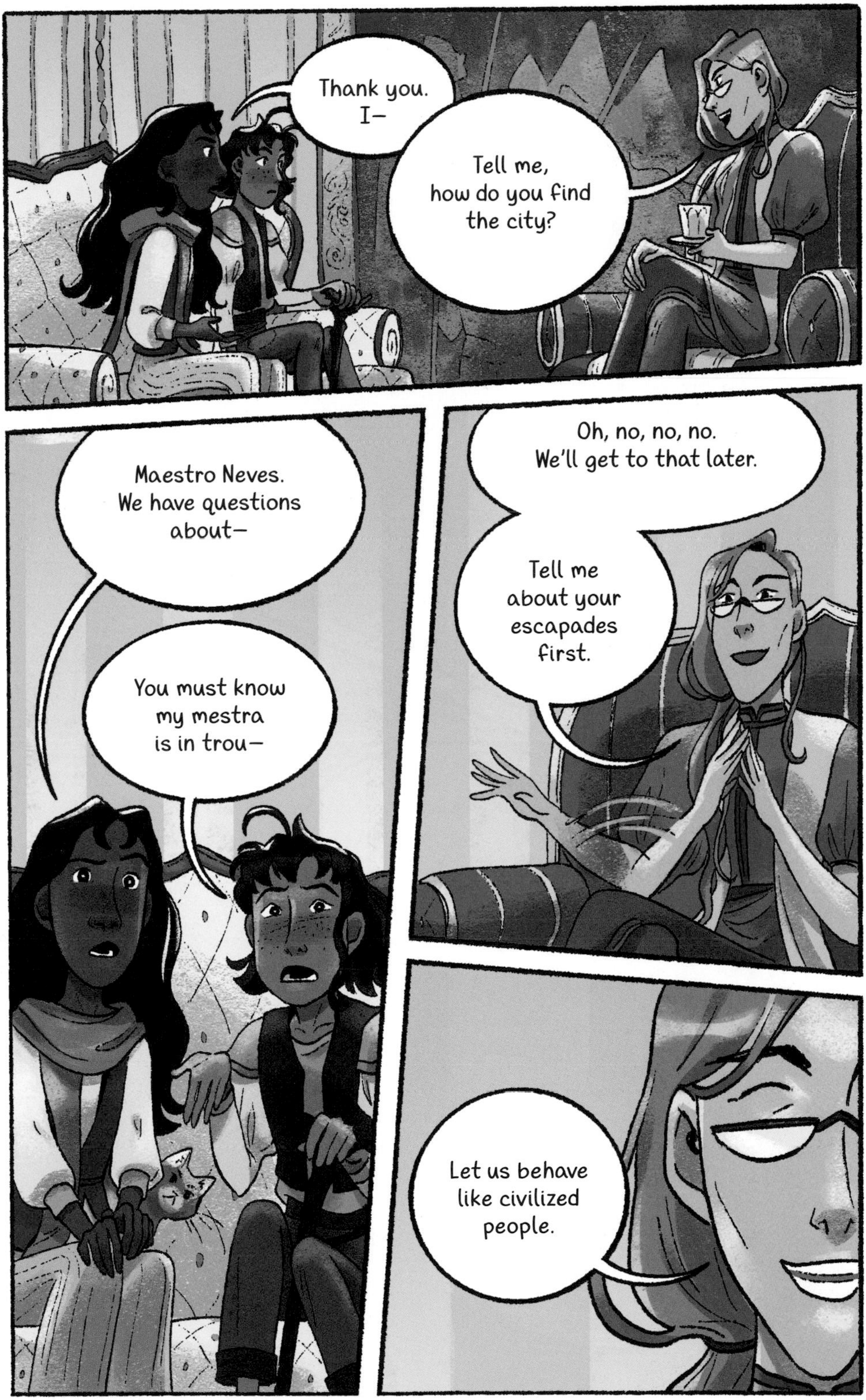
Thank you. I–
Tell me, how do you find the city?
Maestro Neves. We have questions about–
You must know my mestra is in trou–
Oh, no, no, no. We'll get to that later.
Tell me about your escapades first.
Let us behave like civilized people.

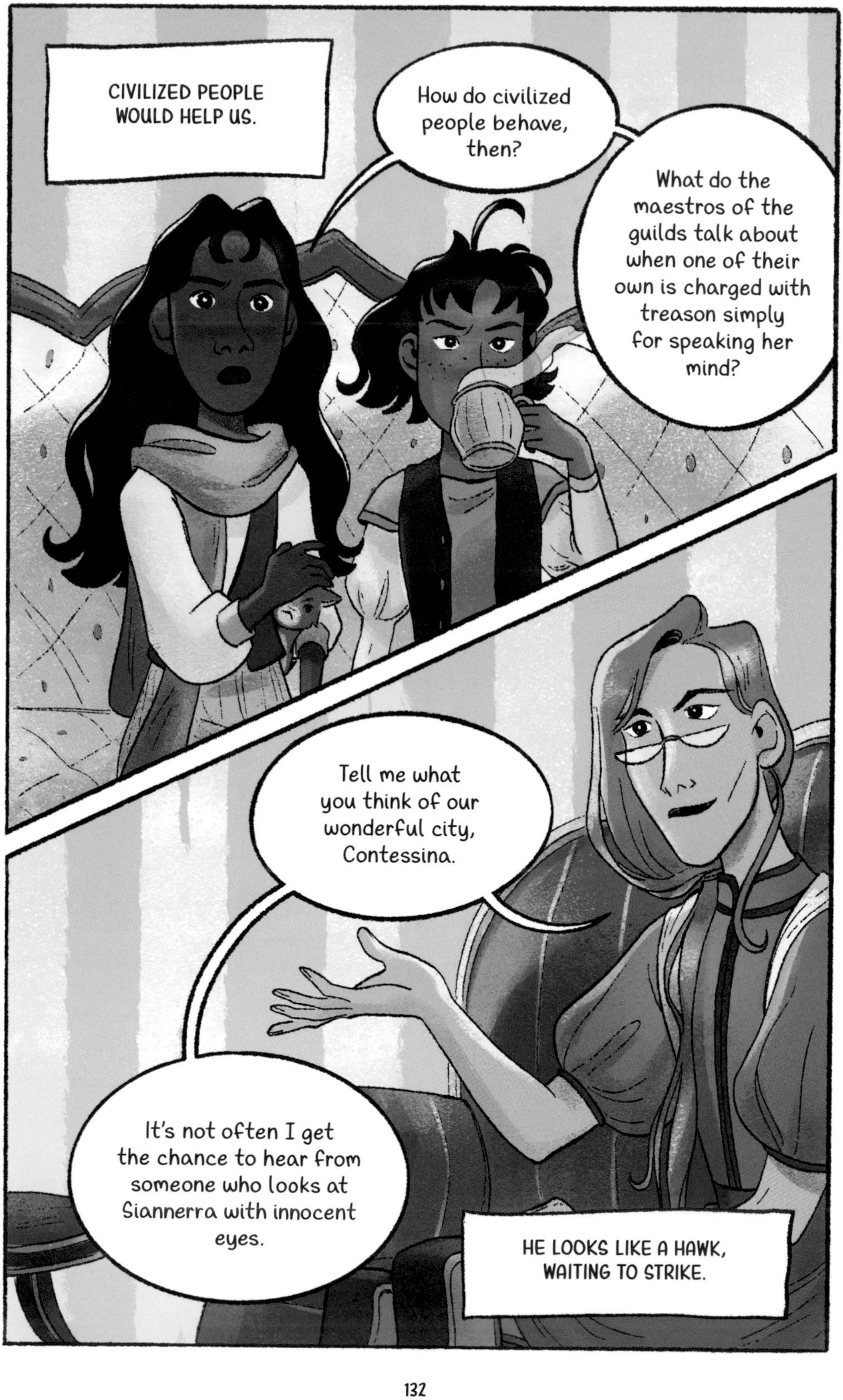
CIVILIZED PEOPLE WOULD HELP US.
How do civilized people behave, then?
What do the maestros of the guilds talk about when one of their own is charged with treason simply for speaking her mind?
Tell me what you think of our wonderful city, Contessina.
It's not often I get the chance to hear from someone who looks at Siannerra with innocent eyes.
HE LOOKS LIKE A HAWK, WAITING TO STRIKE.

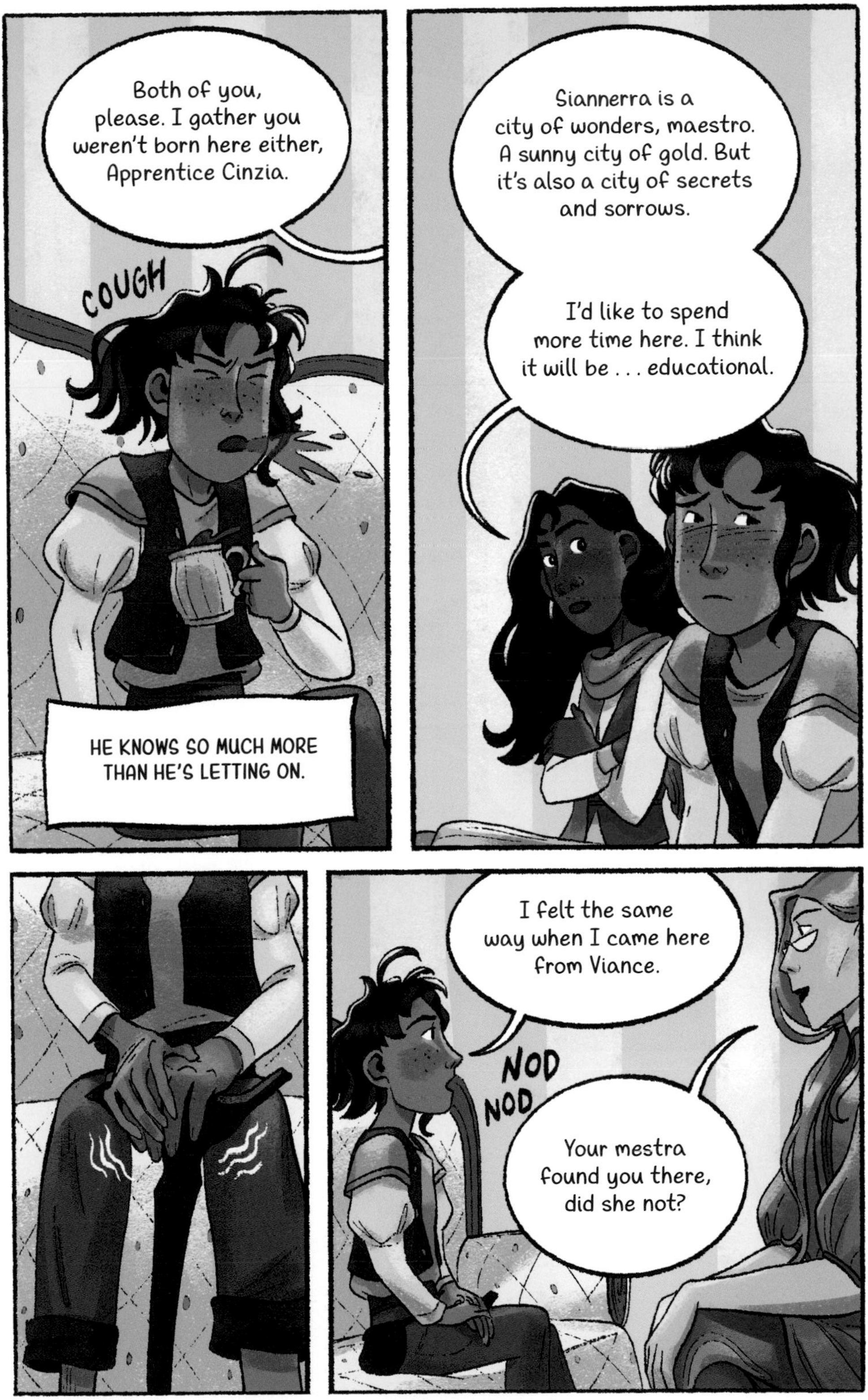
Both of you, please. I gather you weren't born here either, Apprentice Cinzia.
COUGH
HE KNOWS SO MUCH MORE THAN HE'S LETTING ON.
Siannerra is a city of wonders, maestro. A sunny city of gold. But it's also a city of secrets and sorrows.
I'd like to spend more time here. I think it will be . . . educational.
I felt the same way when I came here from Viance.
NOD NOD
Your mestra found you there, did she not?

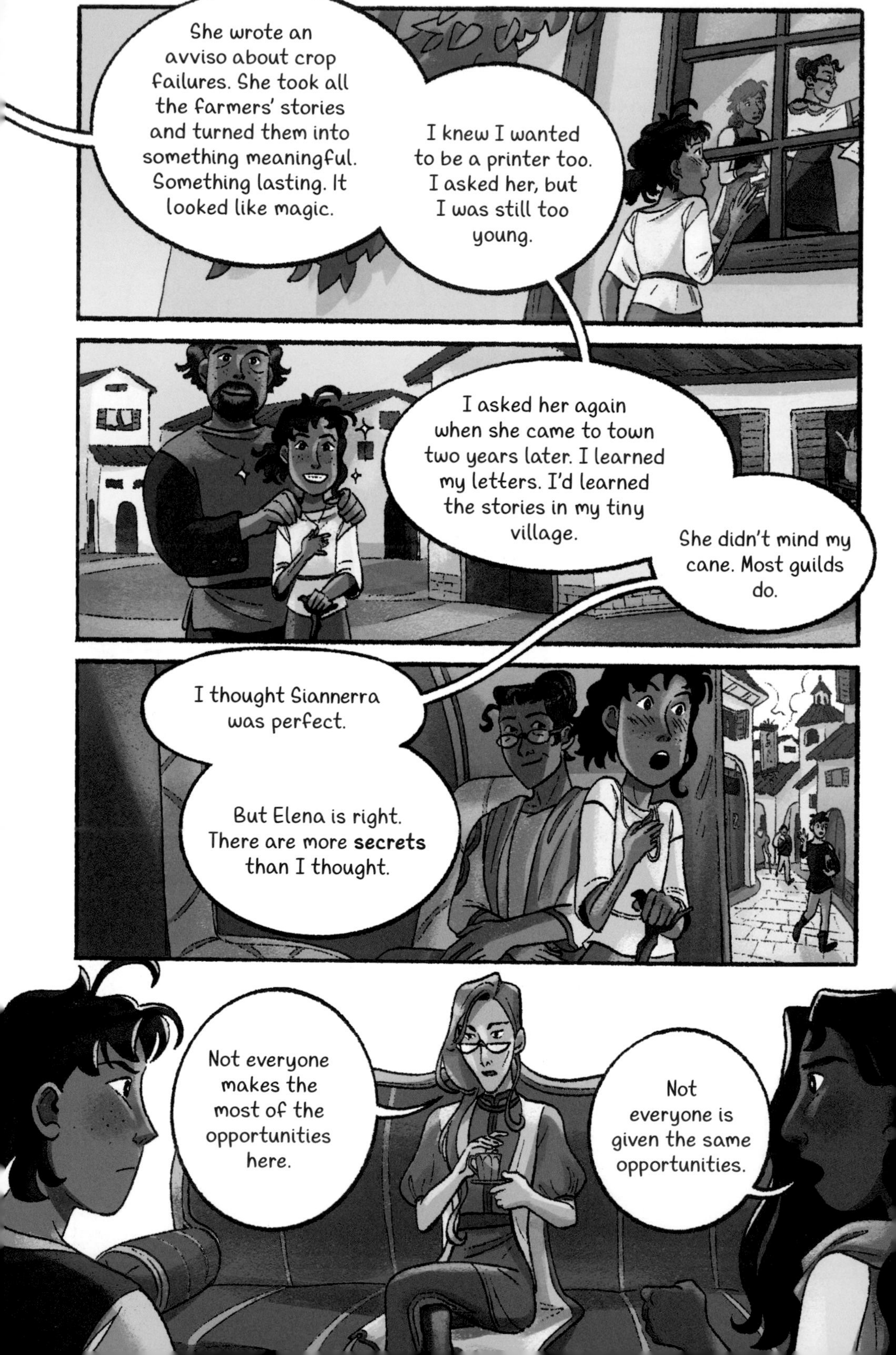
She wrote an avviso about crop failures. She took all the farmers' stories and turned them into something meaningful. Something lasting. It looked like magic.
I knew I wanted to be a printer too. I asked her, but I was still too young.
I asked her again when she came to town two years later. I learned my letters. I'd learned the stories in my tiny village.
She didn't mind my cane. Most guilds do.
I thought Siannerra was perfect.
But Elena is right. There are more **secrets** than I thought.
Not everyone makes the most of the opportunities here.
Not everyone is given the same opportunities.

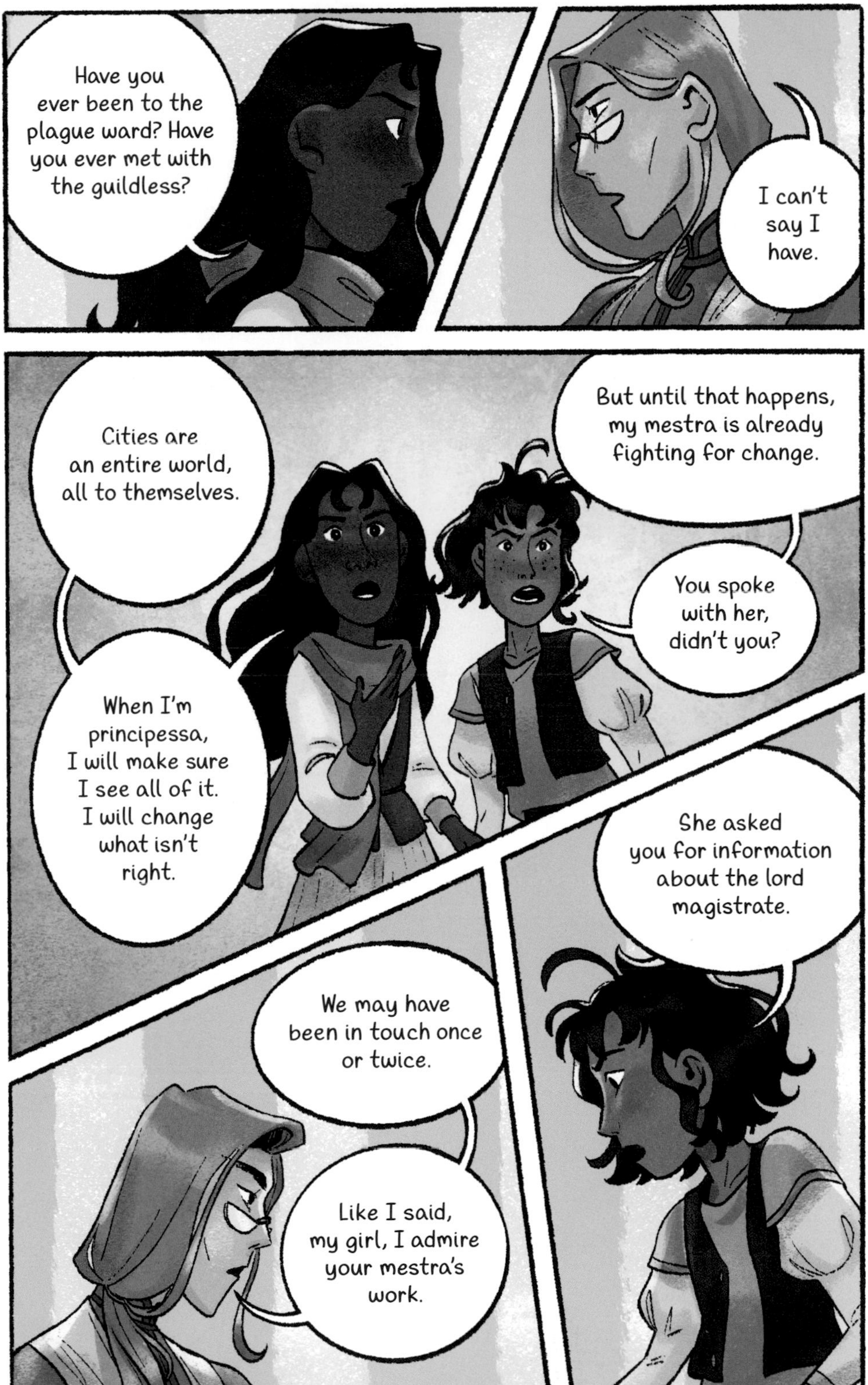
Have you ever been to the plague ward? Have you ever met with the guildless?
I can't say I have.
Cities are an entire world, all to themselves.
When I'm principessa, I will make sure I see all of it. I will change what isn't right.
But until that happens, my mestra is already fighting for change.
You spoke with her, didn't you?
She asked you for information about the lord magistrate.
We may have been in touch once or twice.
Like I said, my girl, I admire your mestra's work.

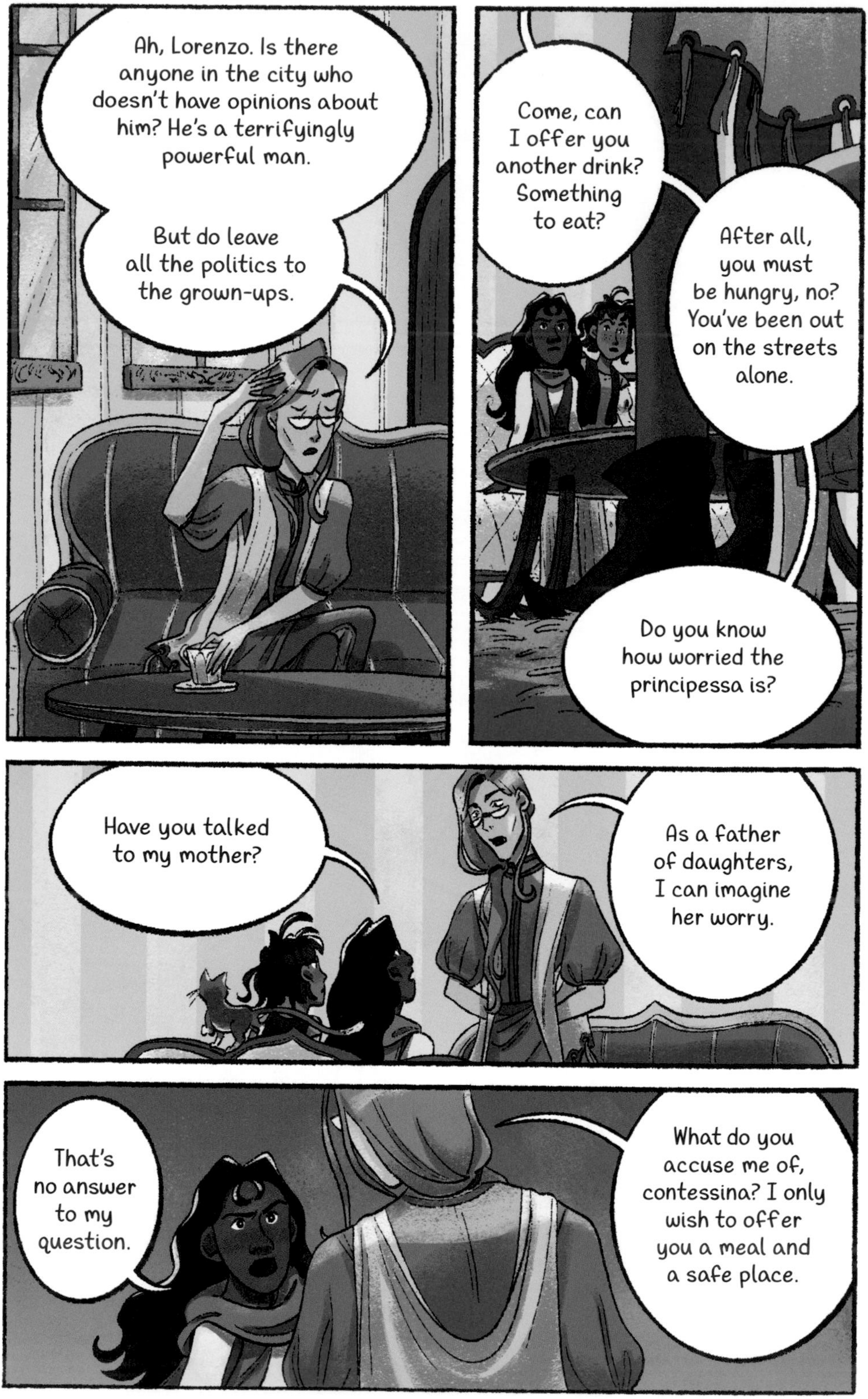
Ah, Lorenzo. Is there anyone in the city who doesn't have opinions about him? He's a terrifyingly powerful man.
But do leave all the politics to the grown-ups.
Come, can I offer you another drink? Something to eat?
After all, you must be hungry, no? You've been out on the streets alone.
Do you know how worried the principessa is?
Have you talked to my mother?
As a father of daughters, I can imagine her worry.
That's no answer to my question.
What do you accuse me of, contessina? I only wish to offer you a meal and a safe place.

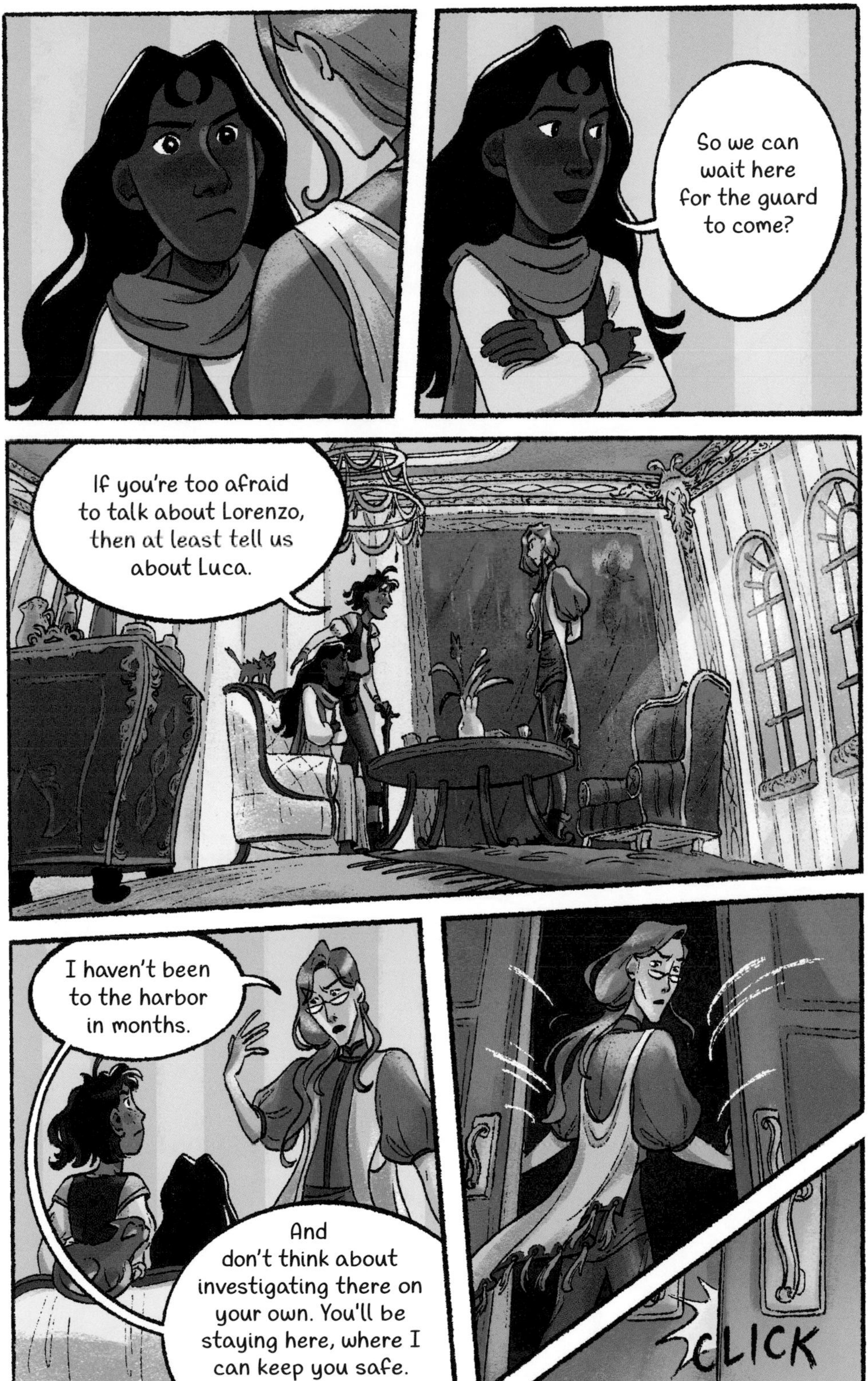

So we can wait here for the guard to come?
If you're too afraid to talk about Lorenzo, then at least tell us about Luca.
I haven't been to the harbor in months.
And don't think about investigating there on your own. You'll be staying here, where I can keep you safe.
CLICK

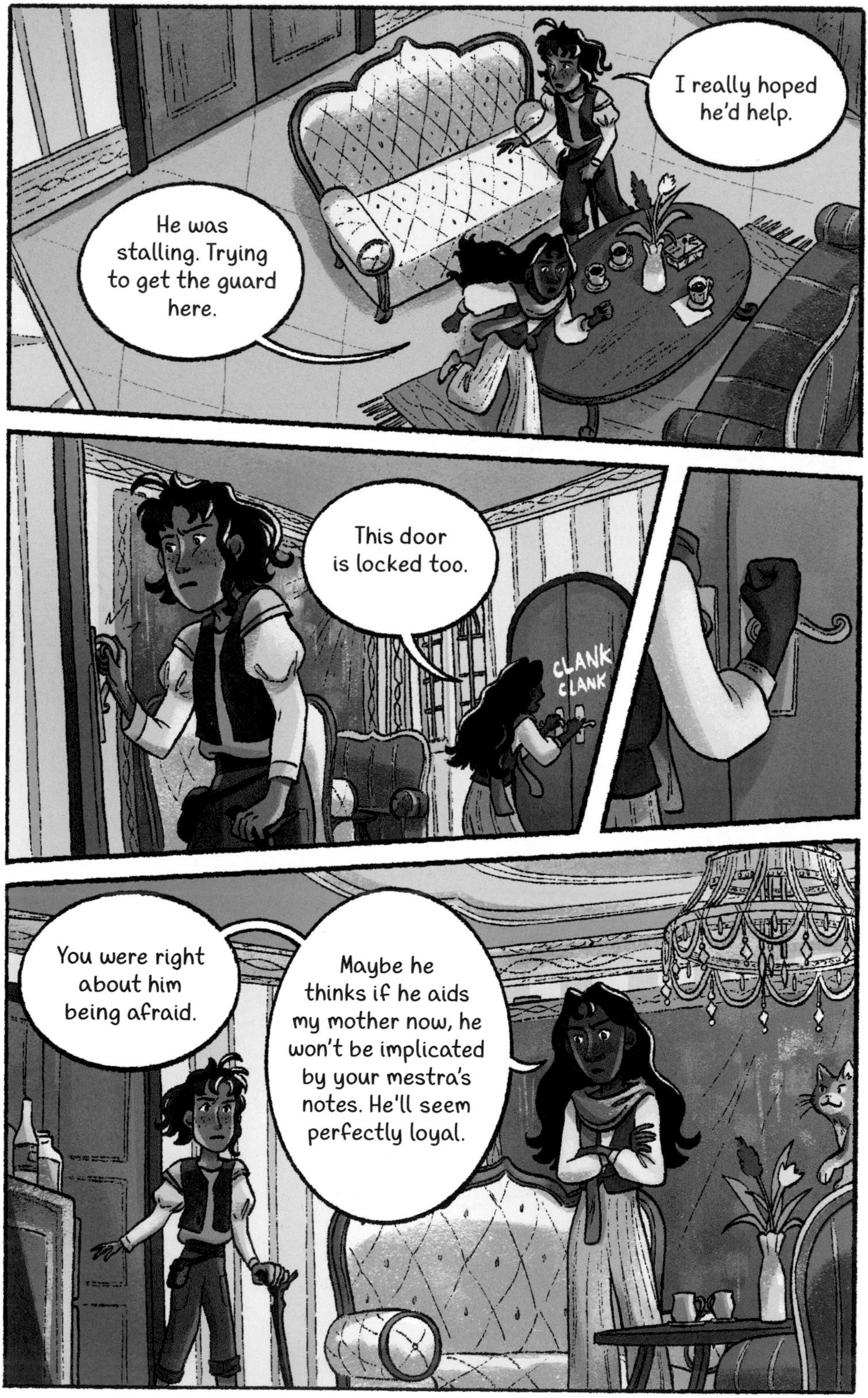
I really hoped he'd help.
He was stalling. Trying to get the guard here.
This door is locked too.
CLANK CLANK
You were right about him being afraid.
Maybe he thinks if he aids my mother now, he won't be implicated by your mestra's notes. He'll seem perfectly loyal.

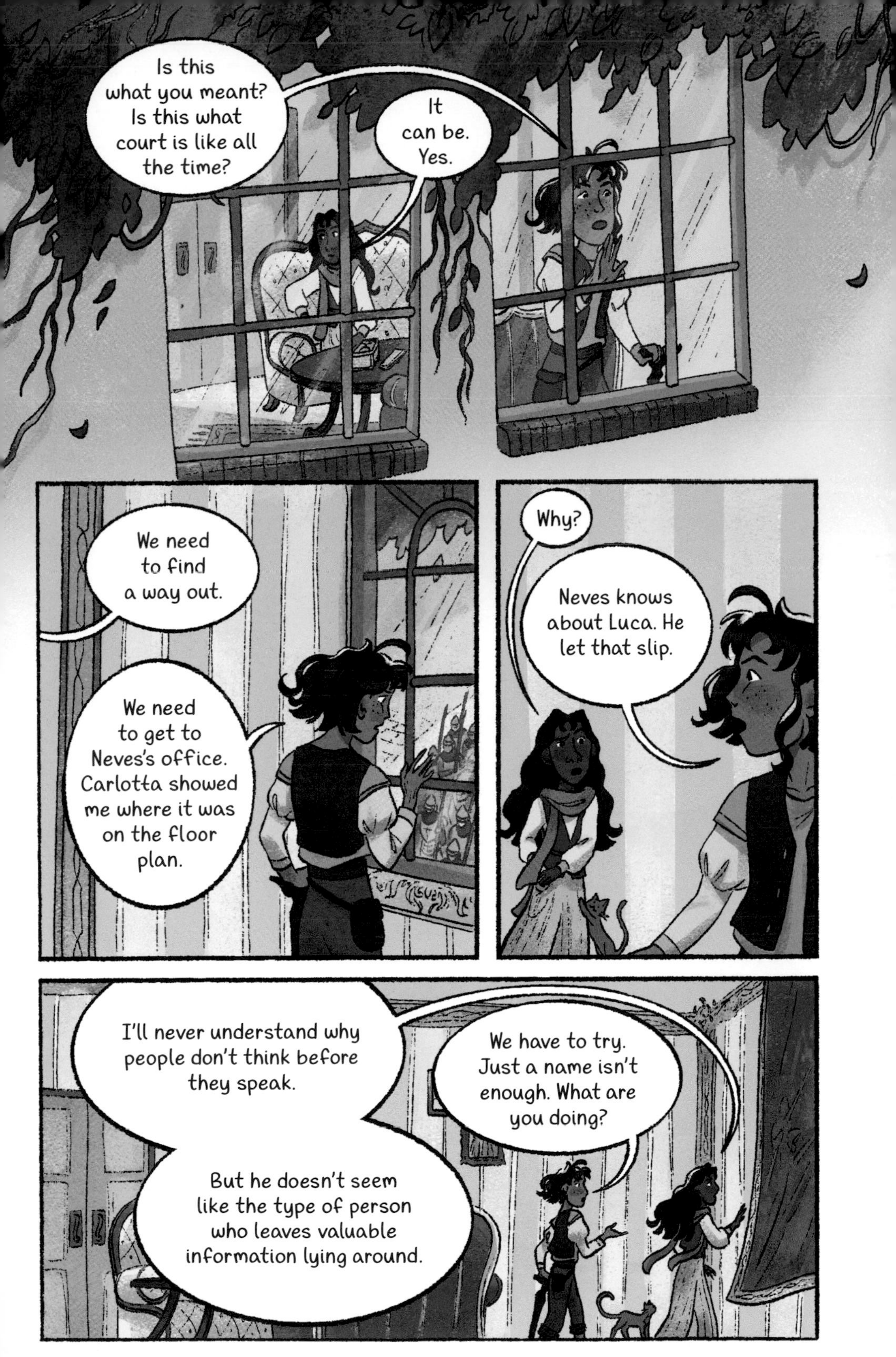

Is this what you meant? Is this what court is like all the time?
It can be. Yes.
We need to find a way out.
We need to get to Neves's office. Carlotta showed me where it was on the floor plan.
Why?
Neves knows about Luca. He let that slip.
I'll never understand why people don't think before they speak.
But he doesn't seem like the type of person who leaves valuable information lying around.
We have to try. Just a name isn't enough. What are you doing?

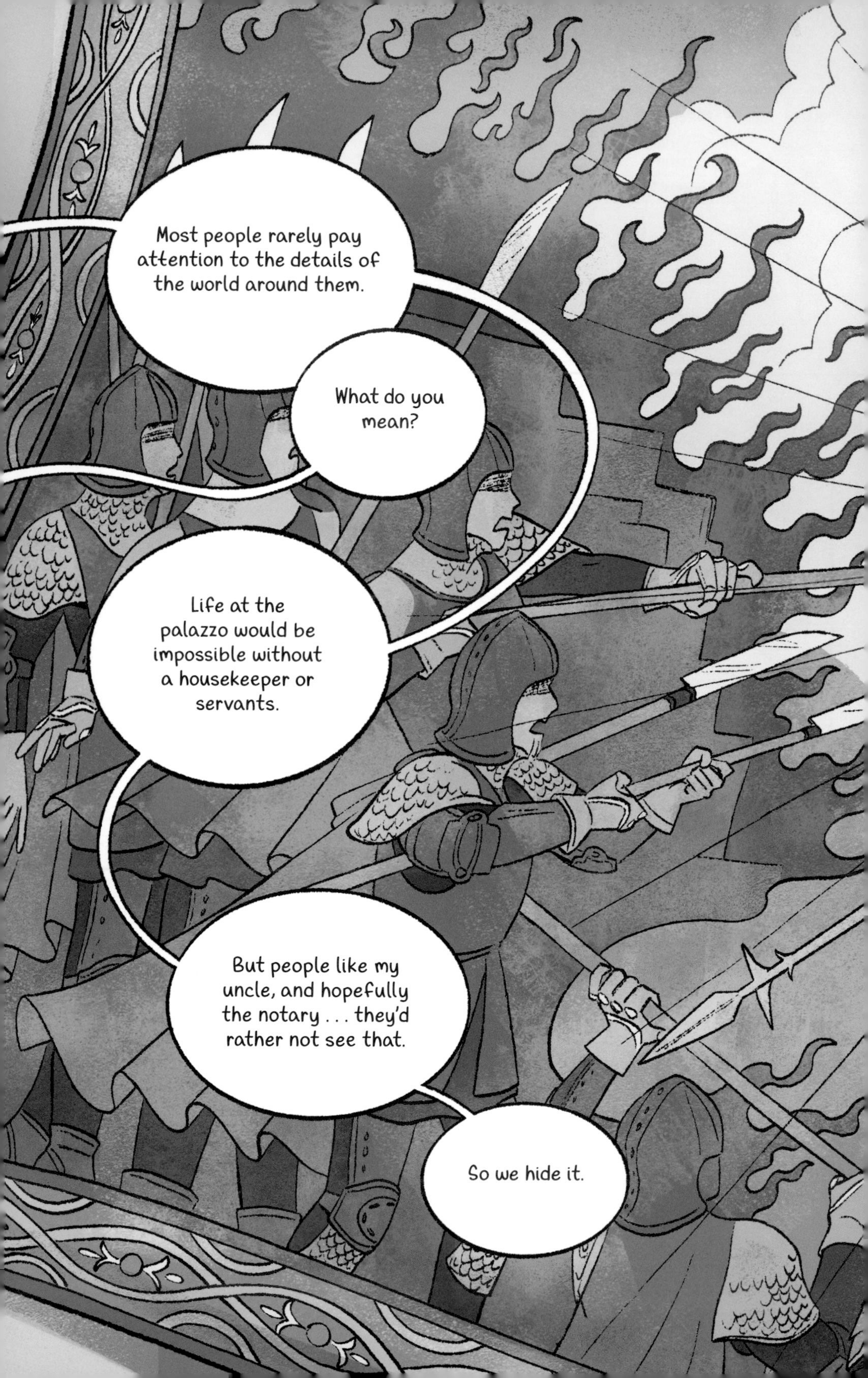
Most people rarely pay attention to the details of the world around them.
What do you mean?
Life at the palazzo would be impossible without a housekeeper or servants.
But people like my uncle, and hopefully the notary . . . they'd rather not see that.
So we hide it.

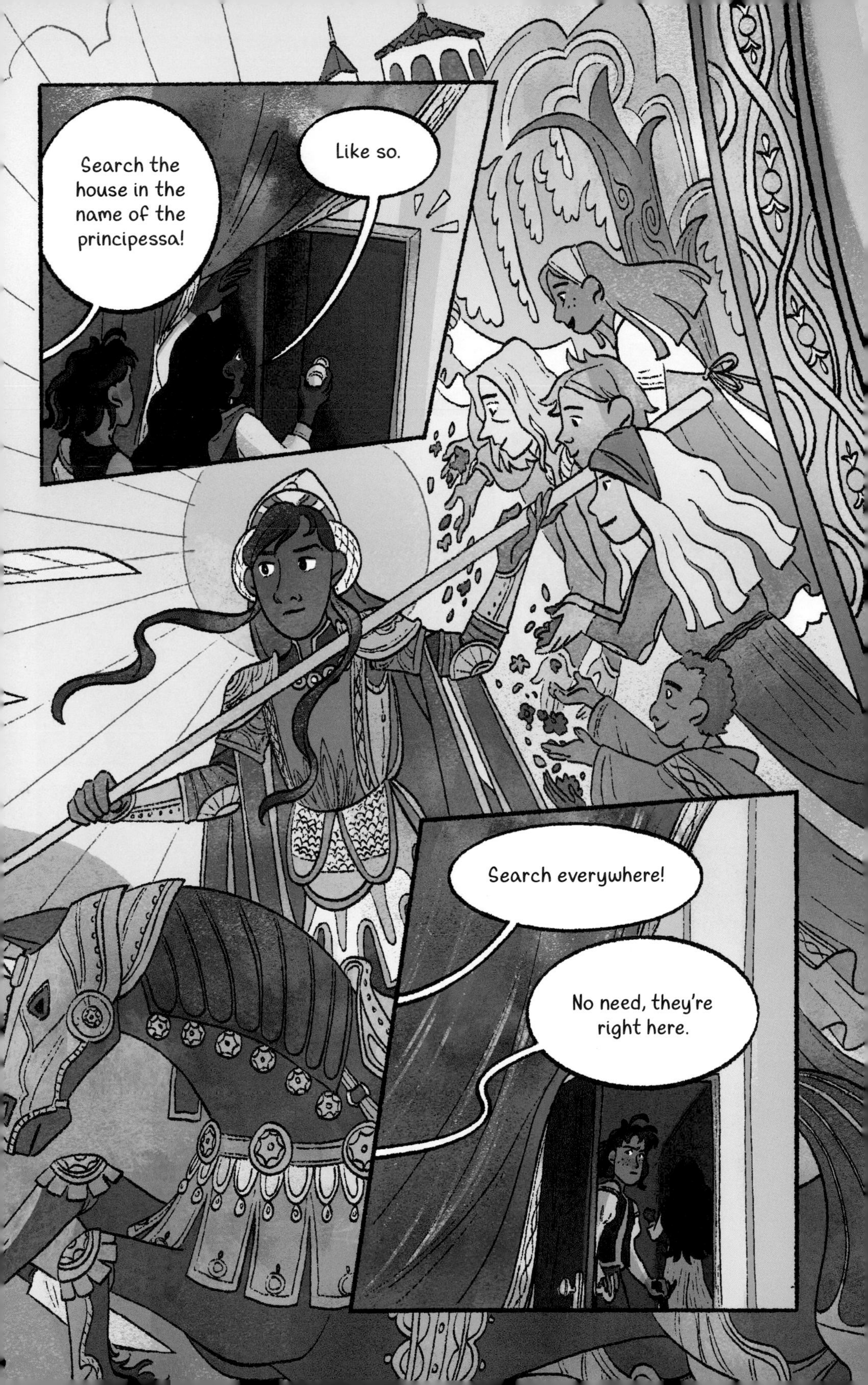
Search the house in the name of the principessa!
Like so.
Search everywhere!
No need, they're right here.

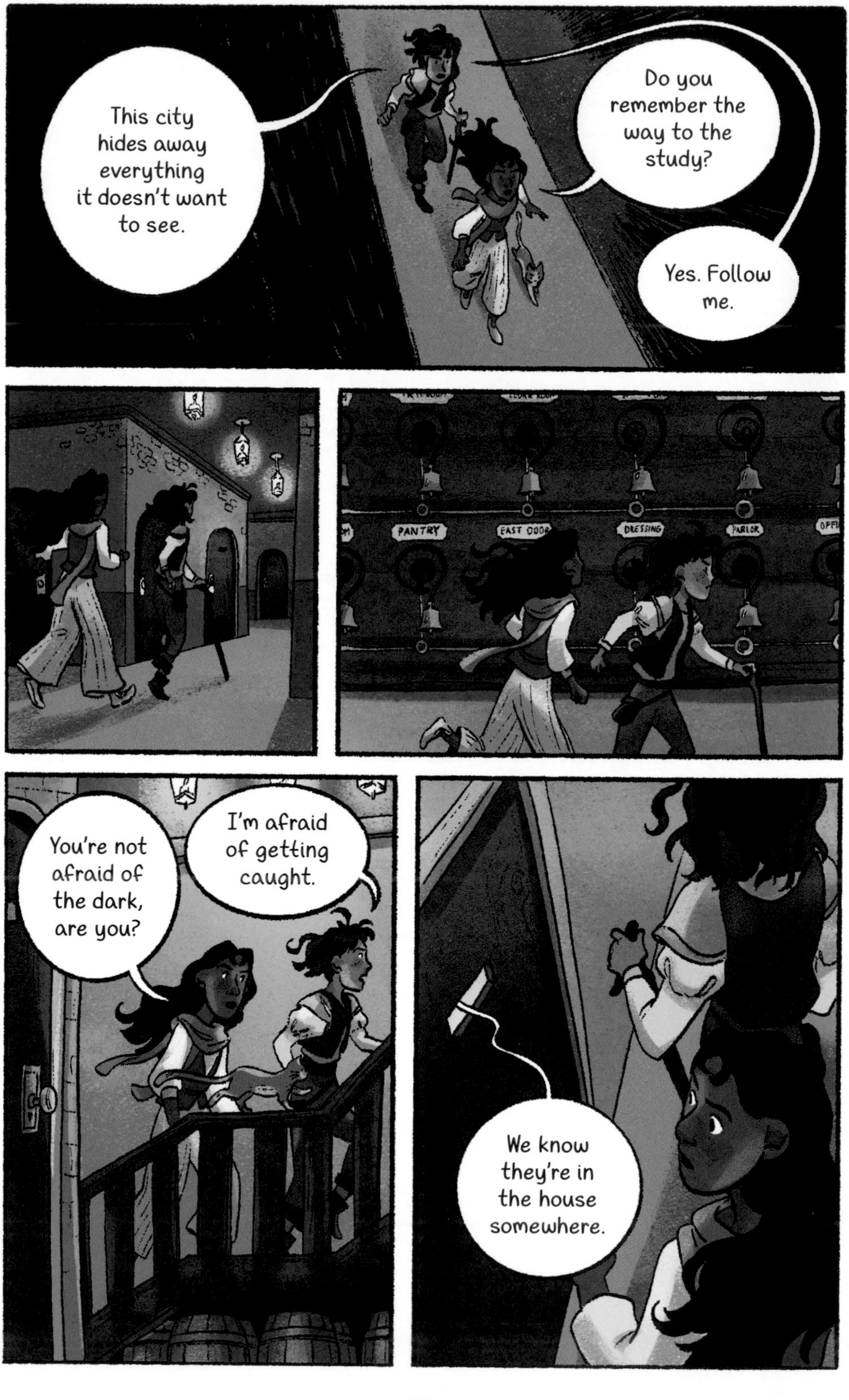
This city hides away everything it doesn't want to see.
Do you remember the way to the study?
Yes. Follow me.
PANTRY
EAST DOOR
DRESSING
PARLOR
You're not afraid of the dark, are you?
I'm afraid of getting caught.
We know they're in the house somewhere.

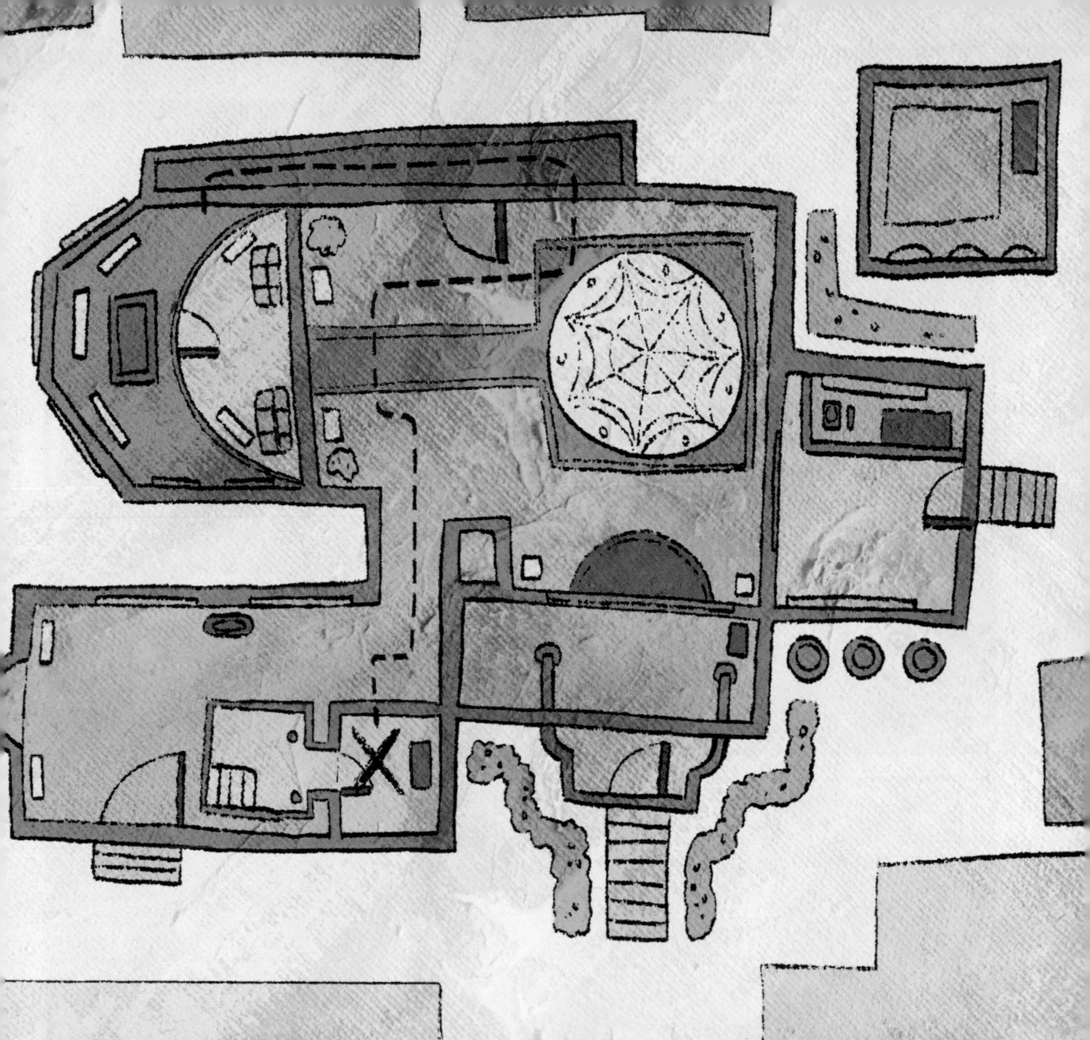

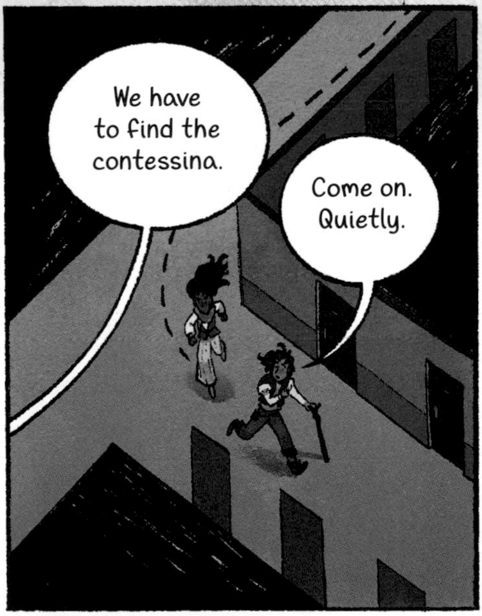

We have to find the contessina.
Come on. Quietly.

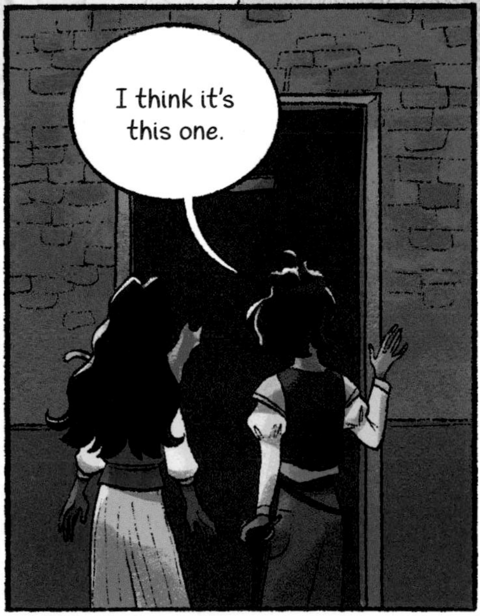

I think it's this one.

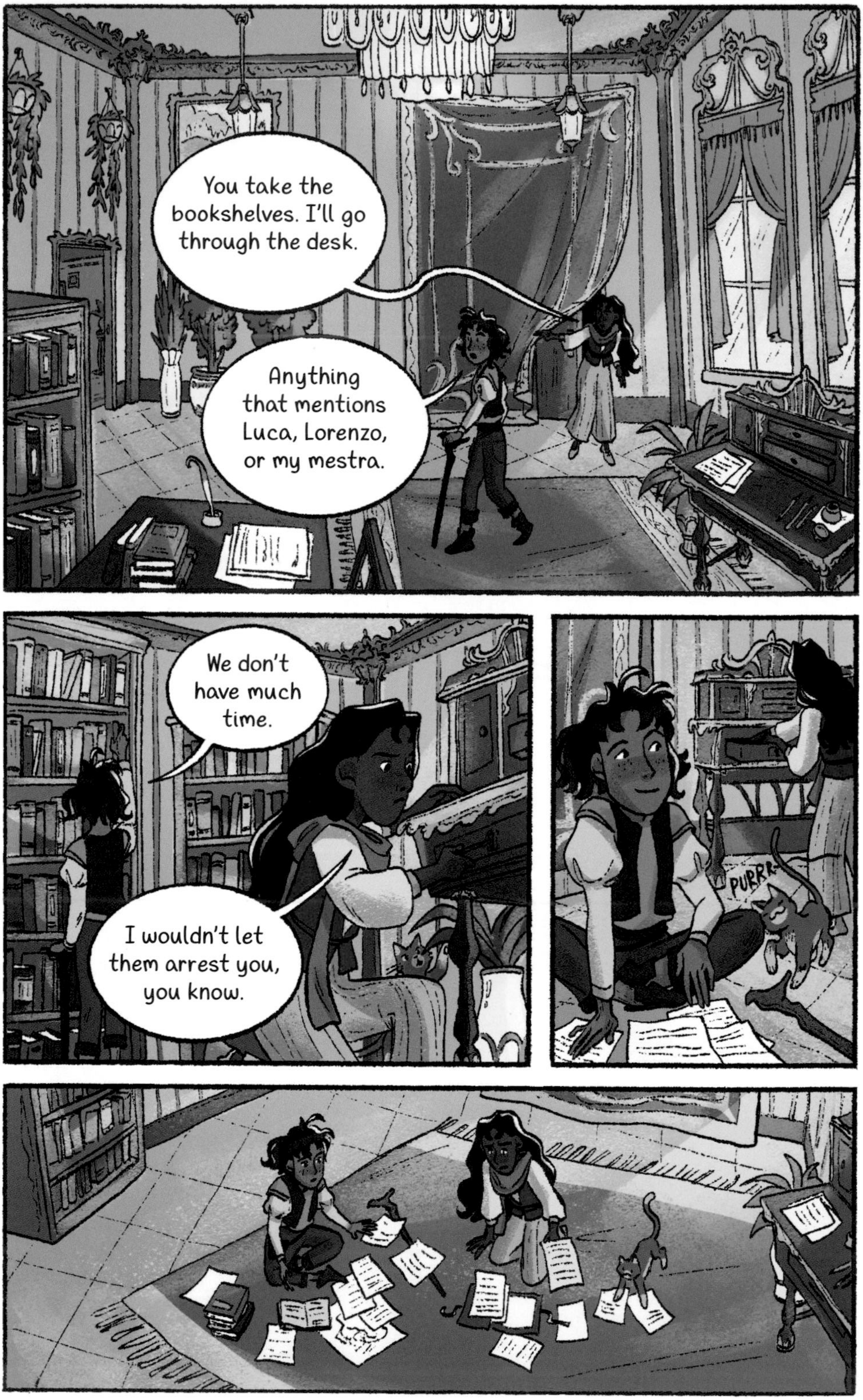
You take the bookshelves. I'll go through the desk.
Anything that mentions Luca, Lorenzo, or my mestra.
We don't have much time.
I wouldn't let them arrest you, you know.
PURRR

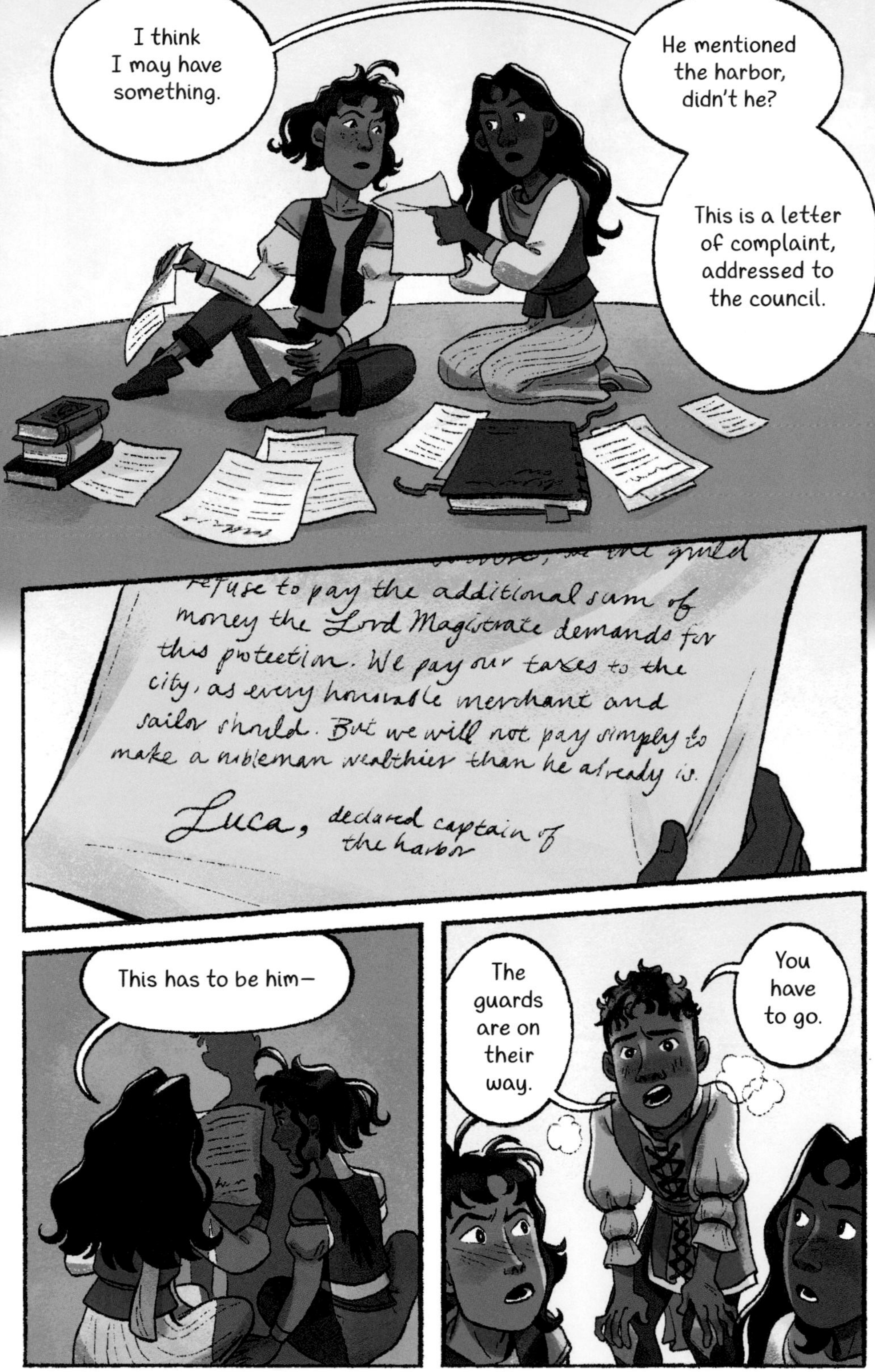
I think I may have something.
He mentioned the harbor, didn't he?
This is a letter of complaint, addressed to the council.
refuse to pay the additional sum of
money the Lord Magistrate demands for
this protection. We pay our taxes to the
city, as every honorable merchant and
sailor should. But we will not pay simply to
make a nobleman wealthier than he already is.
Luca, declared captain of the harbor
This has to be him–
The guards are on their way.
You have to go.

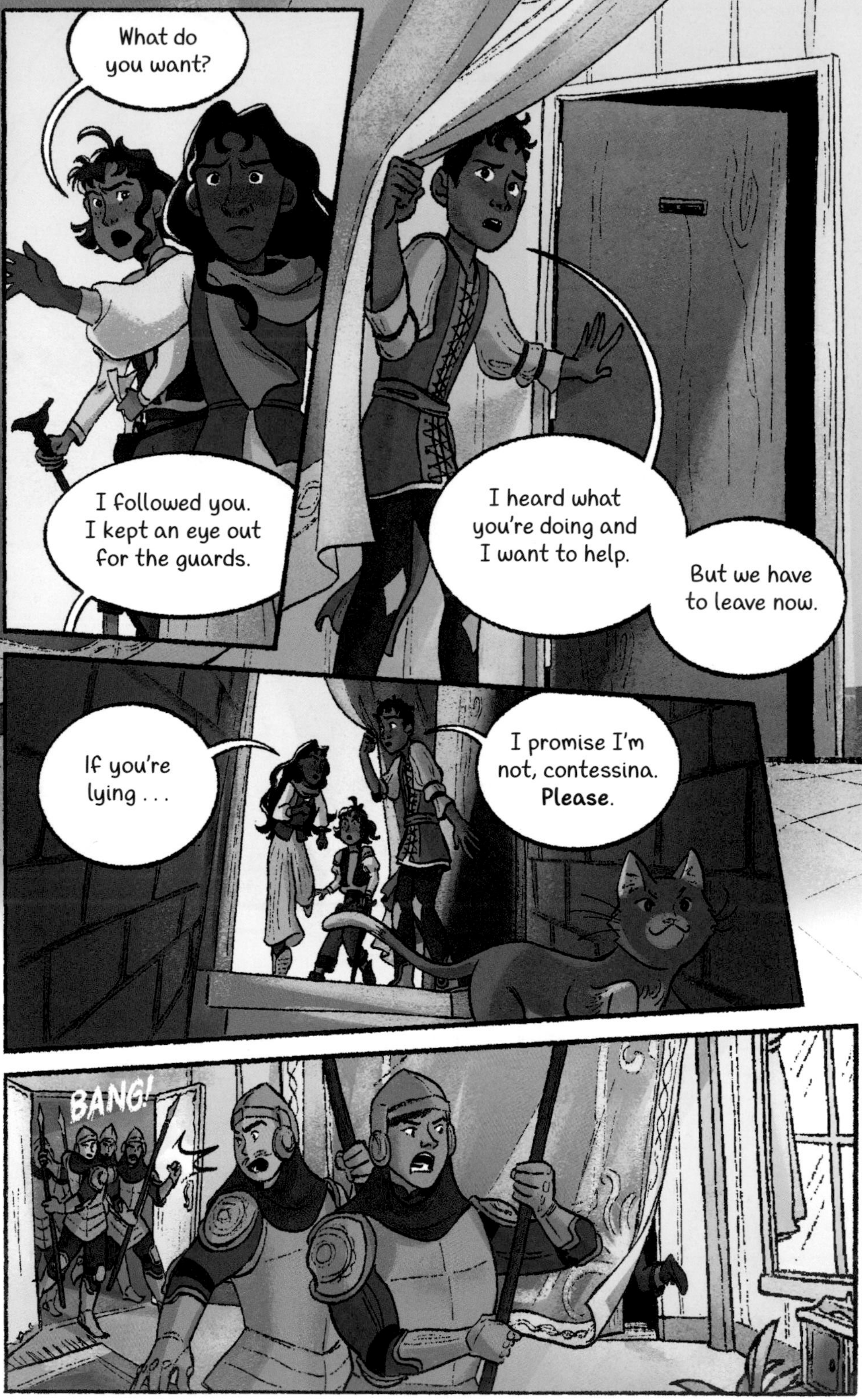

What do you want?
I followed you. I kept an eye out for the guards.
I heard what you're doing and I want to help.
But we have to leave now.
If you're lying . . .
I promise I'm not, contessina. **Please**.
BANG!

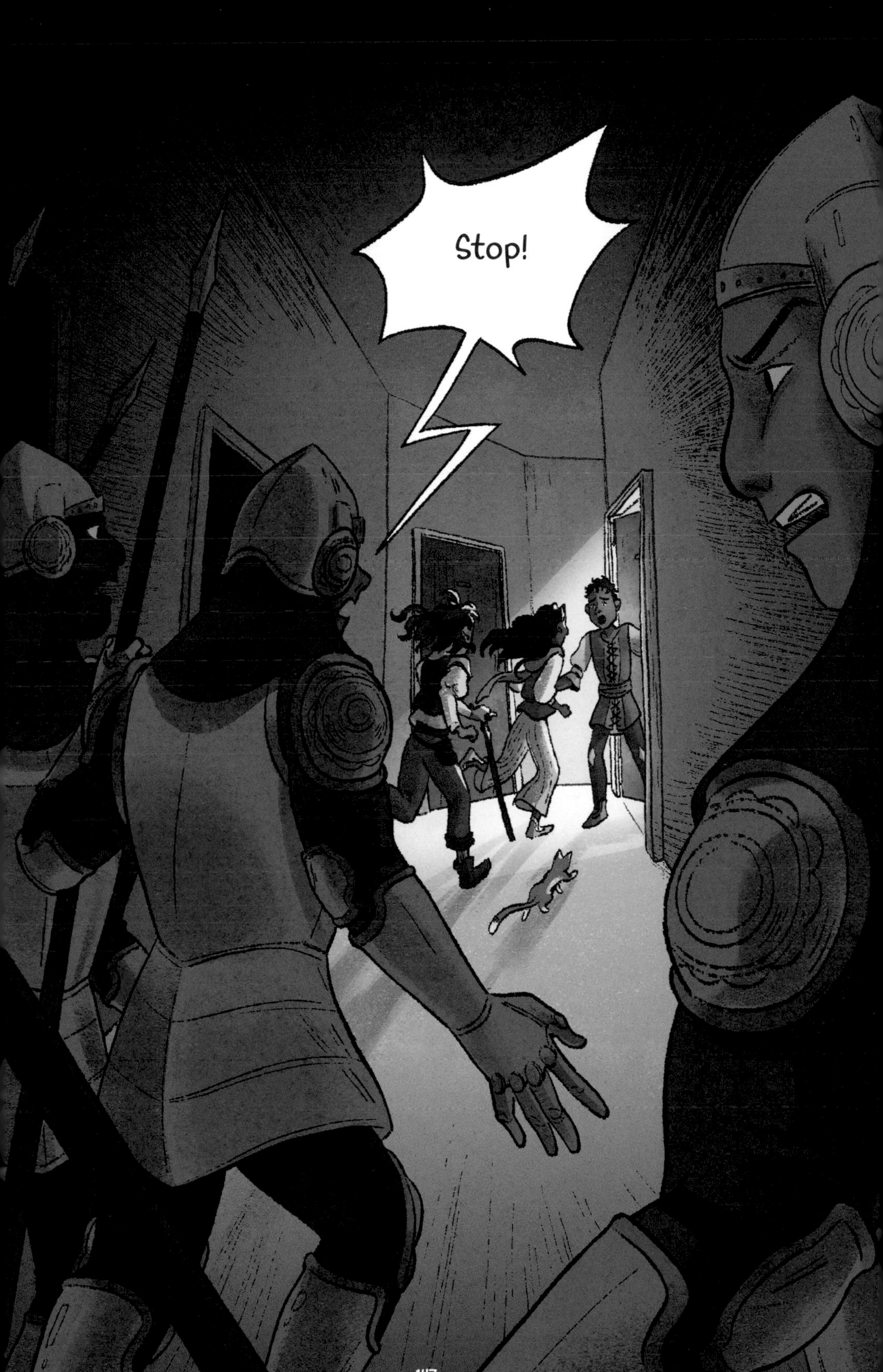
Stop!

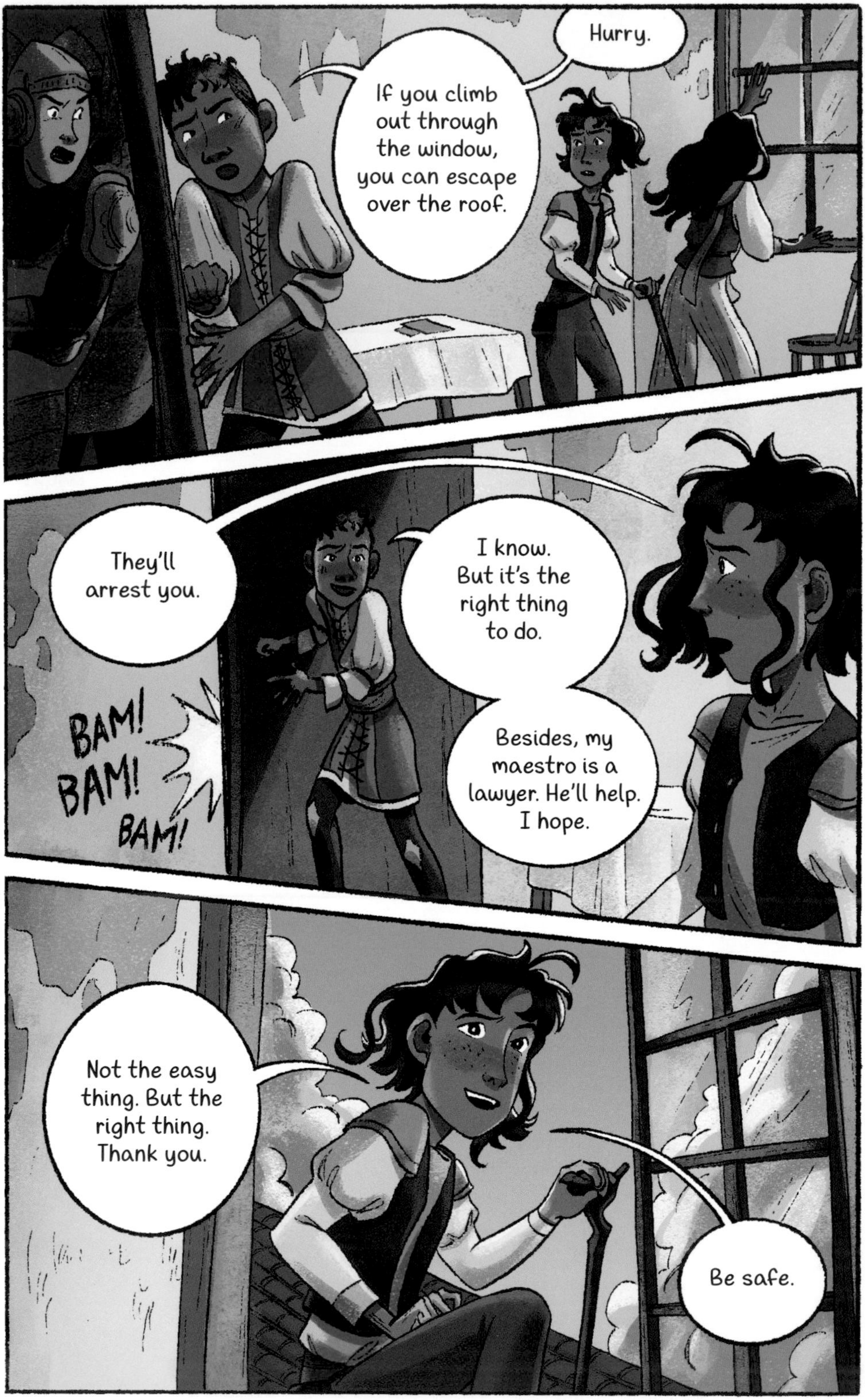
If you climb out through the window, you can escape over the roof.
Hurry.
They'll arrest you.
I know. But it's the right thing to do.
Besides, my maestro is a lawyer. He'll help. I hope.
BAM! BAM! BAM!
Not the easy thing. But the right thing. Thank you.
Be safe.

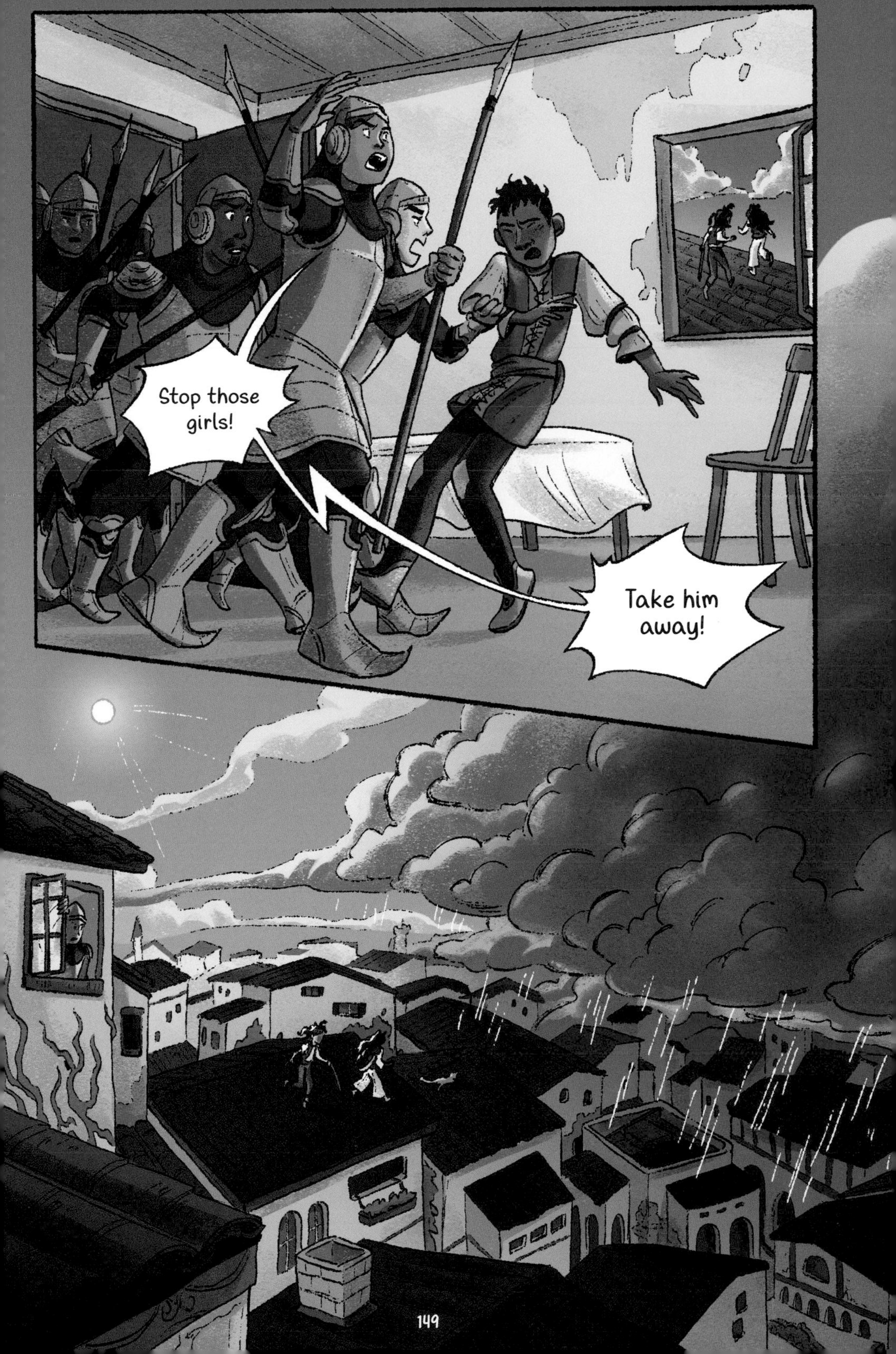
Stop those girls!
Take him away!

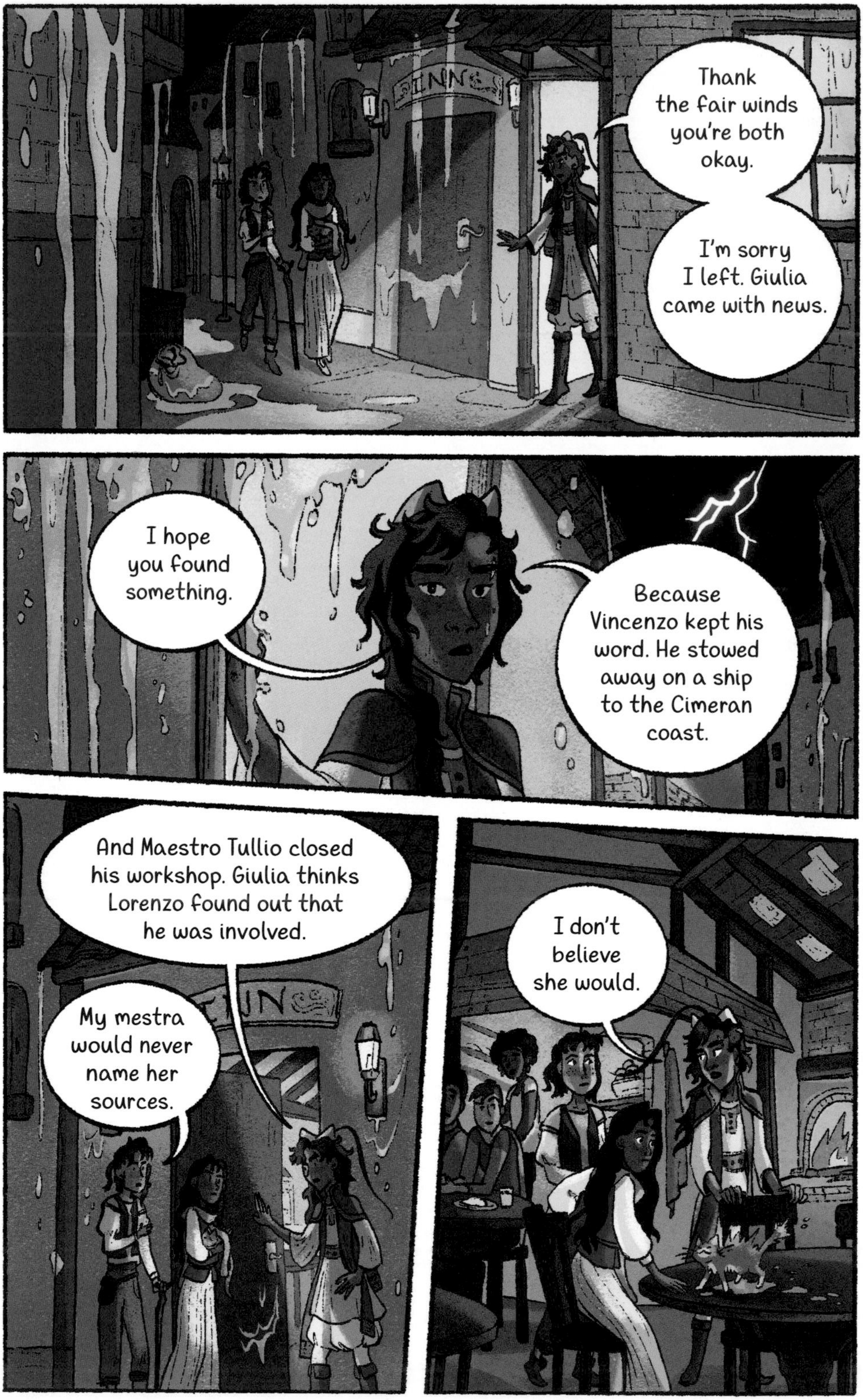
INN
Thank the fair winds you're both okay.
I'm sorry I left. Giulia came with news.
I hope you found something.
Because Vincenzo kept his word. He stowed away on a ship to the Cimeran coast.
And Maestro Tullio closed his workshop. Giulia thinks Lorenzo found out that he was involved.
My mestra would never name her sources.
I don't believe she would.

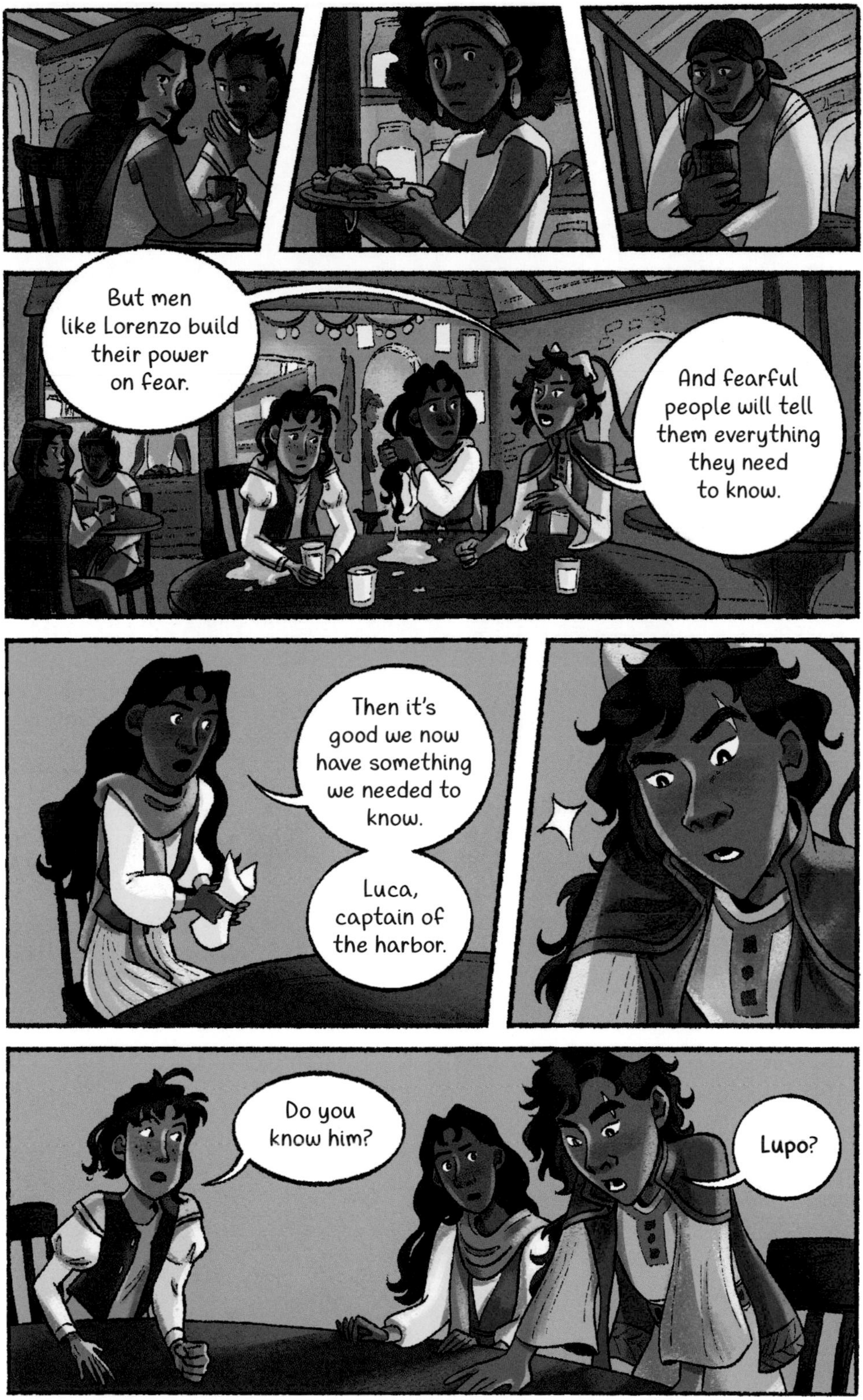
But men like Lorenzo build their power on fear.
And fearful people will tell them everything they need to know.
Then it's good we now have something we needed to know.
Luca, captain of the harbor.
Do you know him?
Lupo?

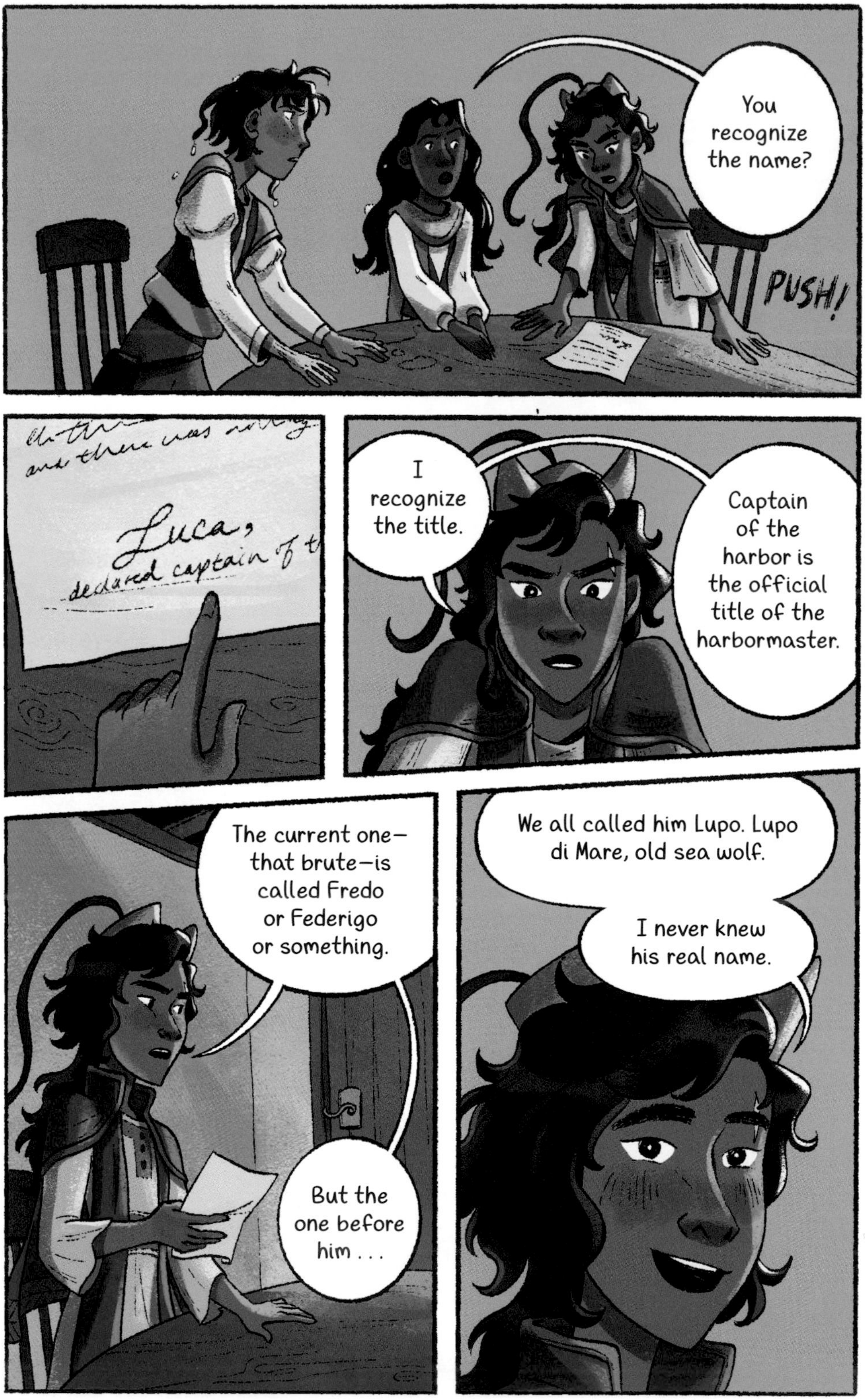
You recognize the name?
PUSH!
Luca,
declared captain of
I recognize the title.
Captain of the harbor is the official title of the harbormaster.
The current one—that brute—is called Fredo or Federigo or something.
But the one before him . . .
We all called him Lupo. Lupo di Mare, old sea wolf.
I never knew his real name.

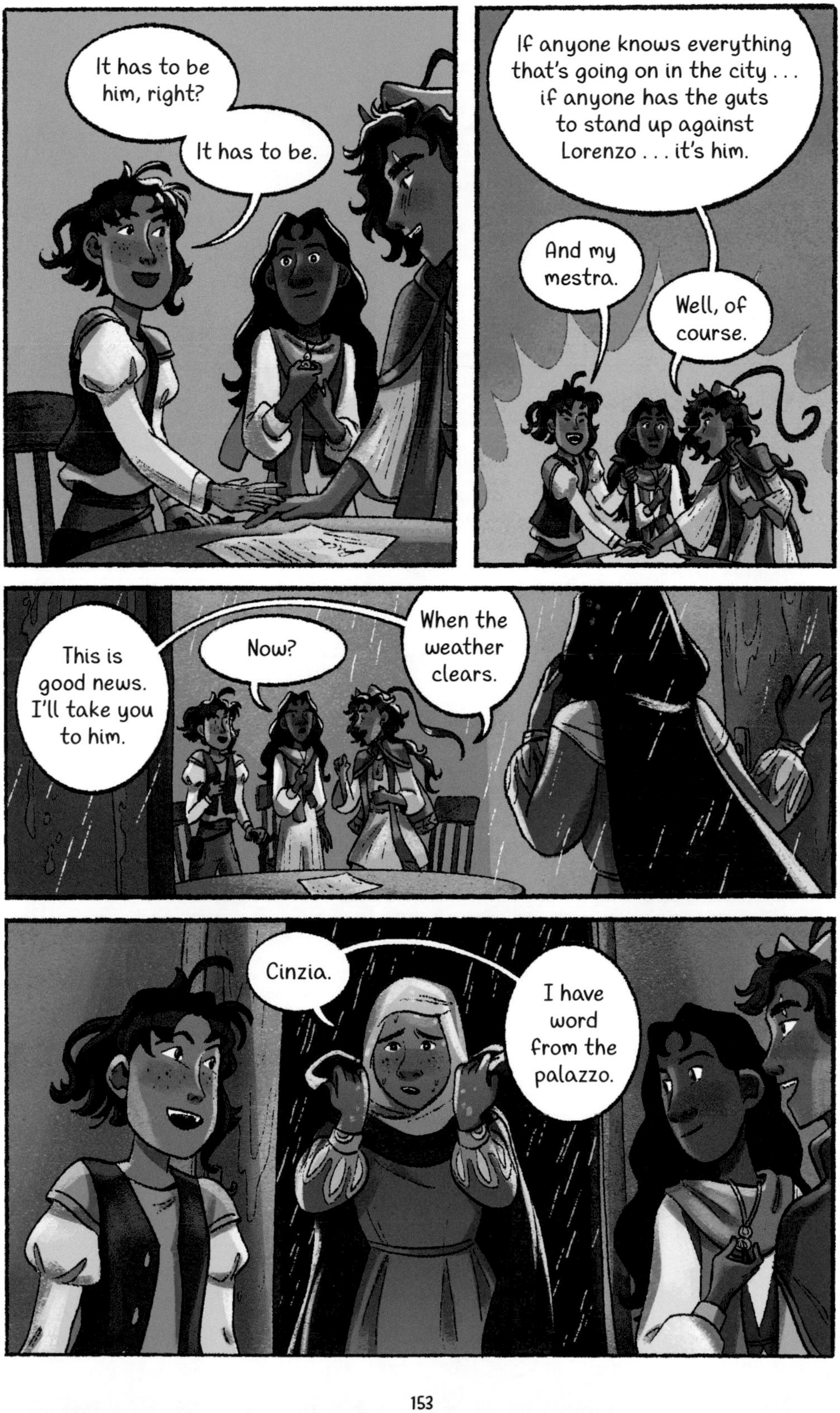
It has to be him, right?
It has to be.
If anyone knows everything that's going on in the city . . . if anyone has the guts to stand up against Lorenzo . . . it's him.
And my mestra.
Well, of course.
This is good news. I'll take you to him.
Now?
When the weather clears.
Cinzia.
I have word from the palazzo.

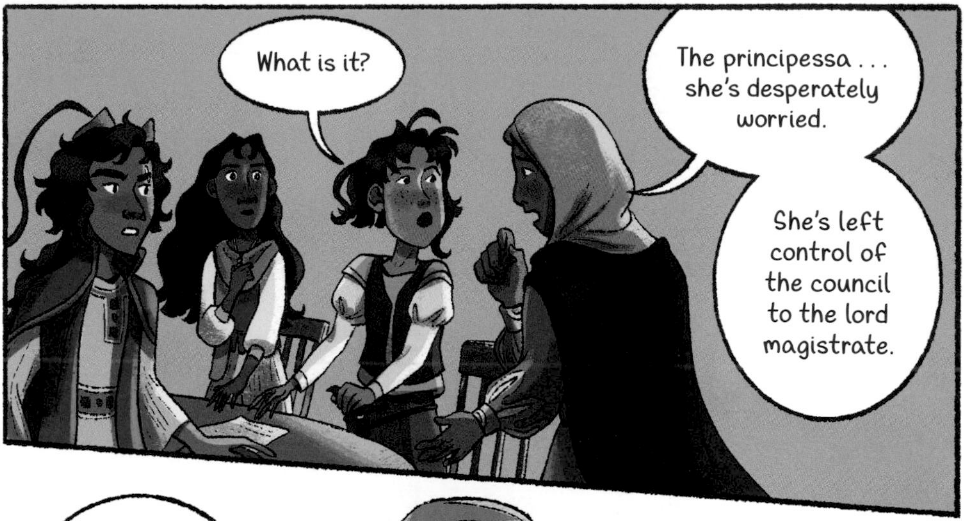
What is it?
The principessa . . . she's desperately worried.
She's left control of the council to the lord magistrate.

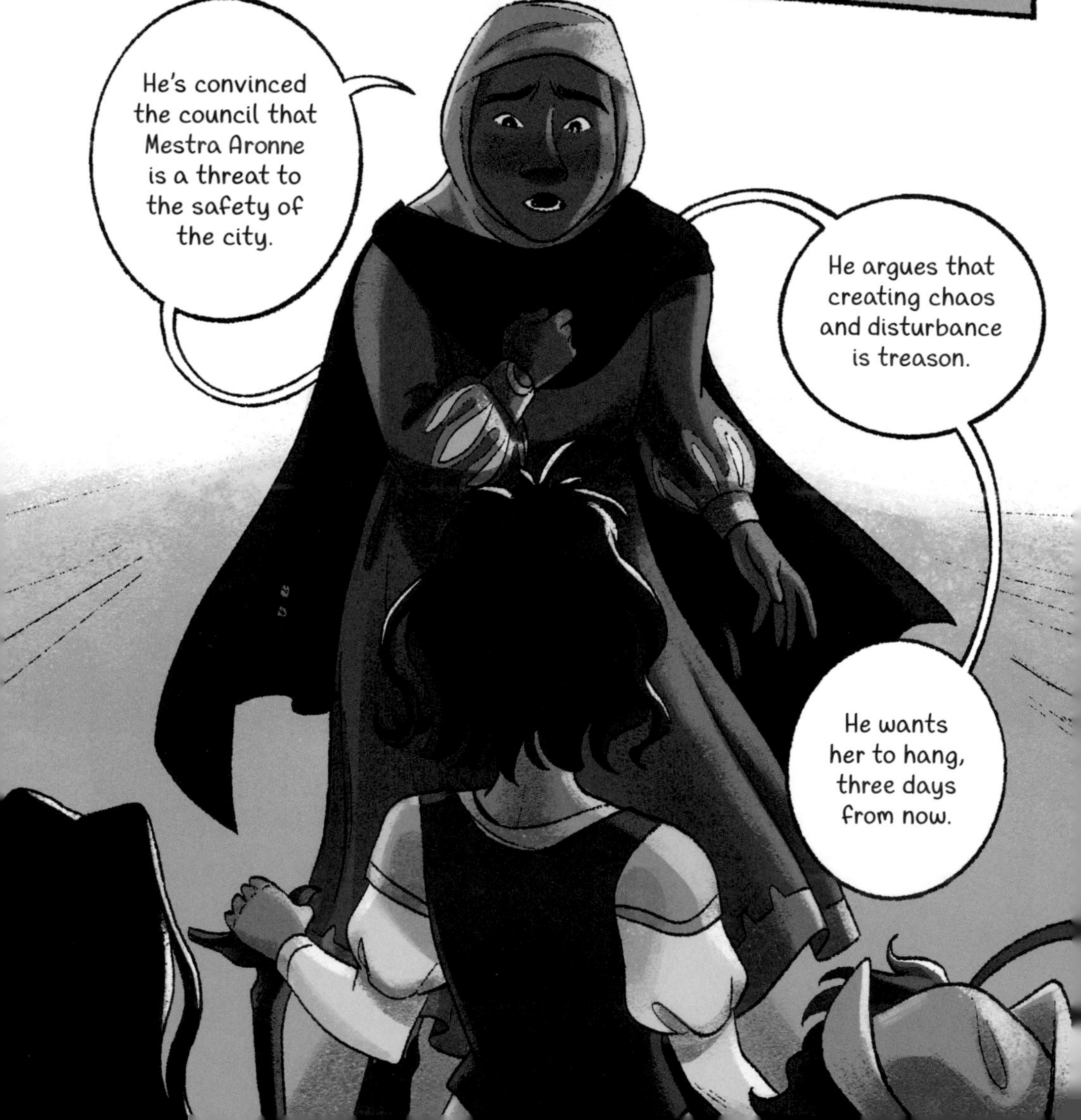
He's convinced the council that Mestra Aronne is a threat to the safety of the city.
He argues that creating chaos and disturbance is treason.
He wants her to hang, three days from now.

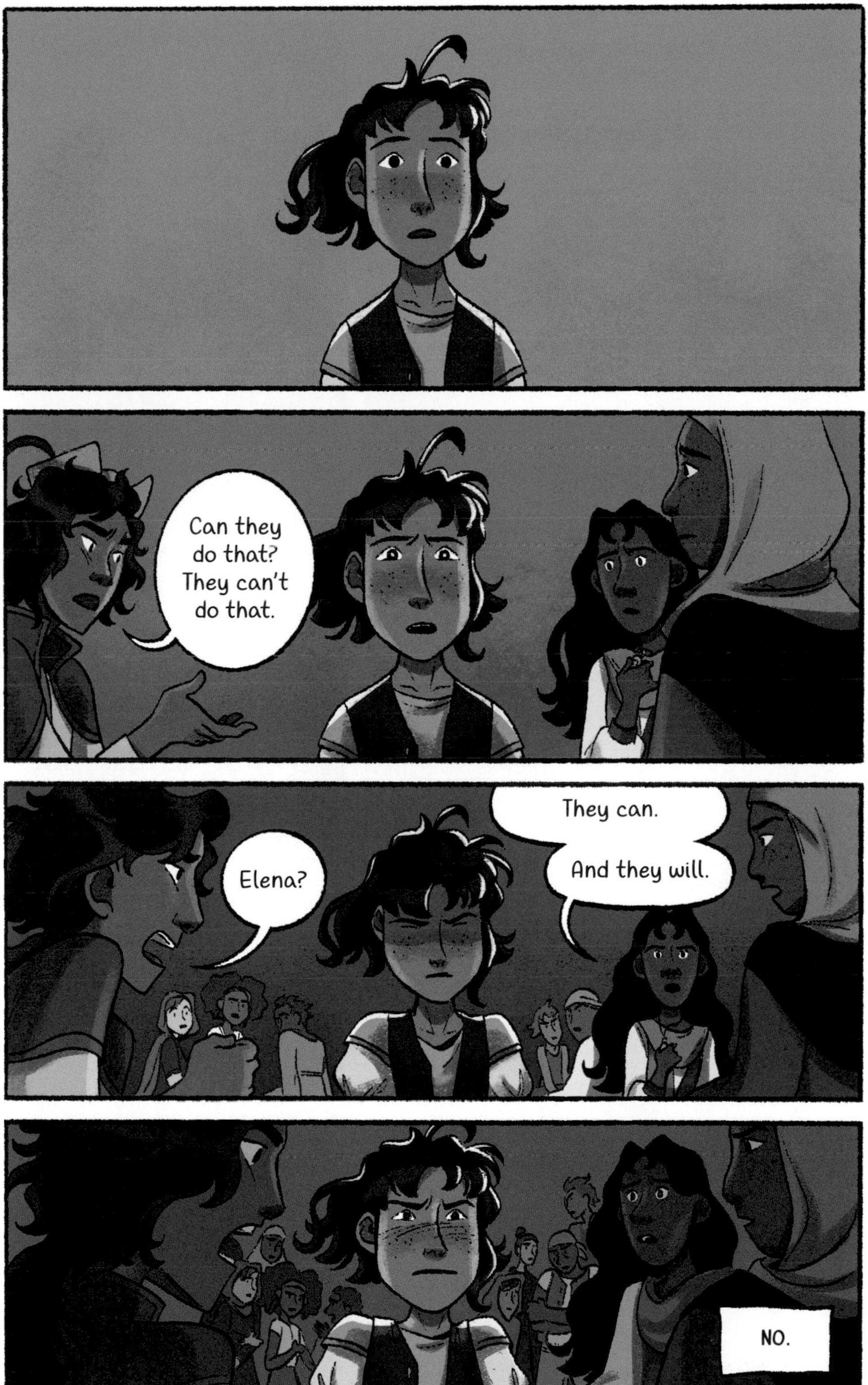
Can they do that? They can't do that.
Elena?
They can.
And they will.
NO.

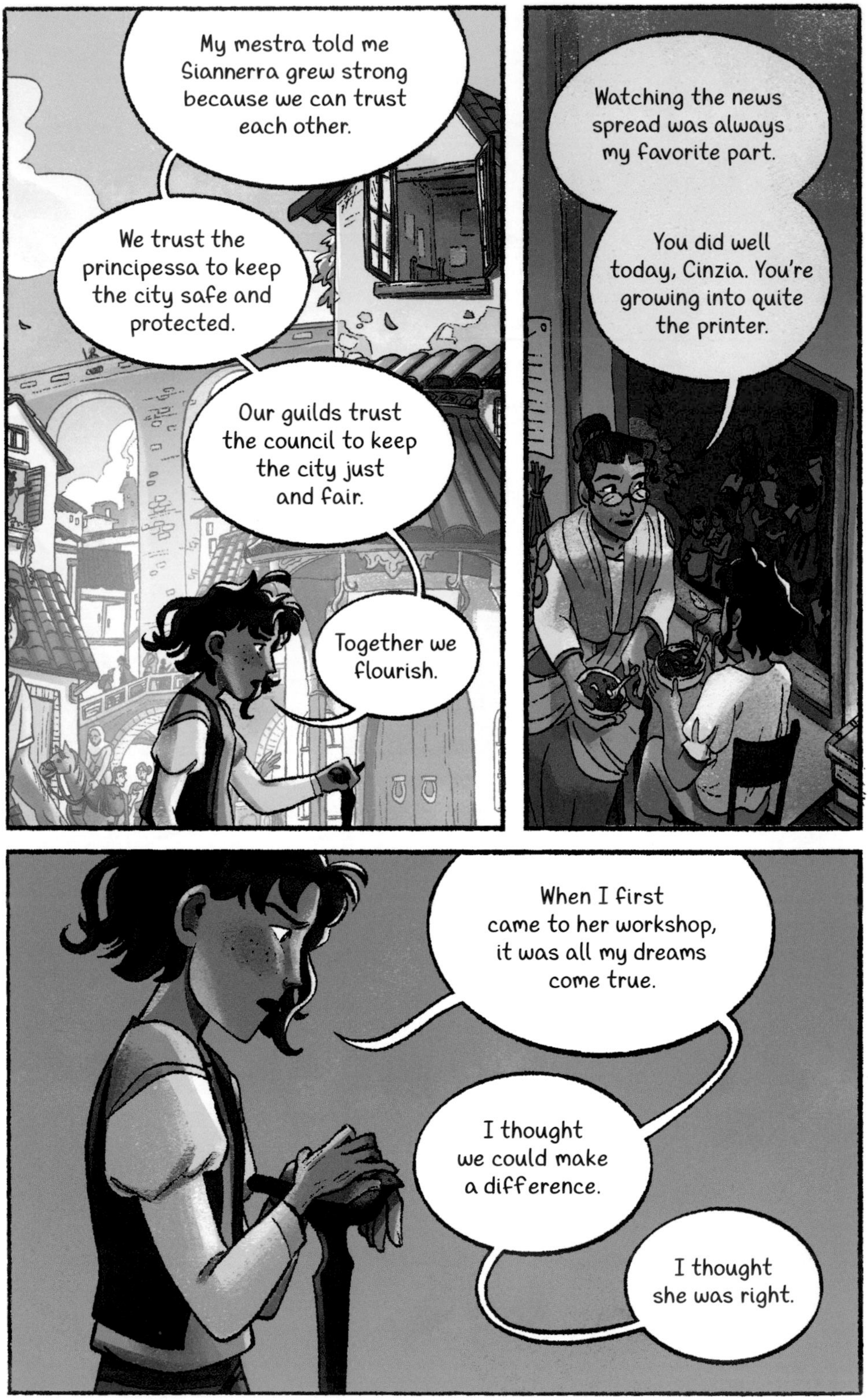

My mestra told me Siannerra grew strong because we can trust each other.
We trust the principessa to keep the city safe and protected.
Our guilds trust the council to keep the city just and fair.
Together we flourish.
Watching the news spread was always my favorite part.
You did well today, Cinzia. You're growing into quite the printer.
When I first came to her workshop, it was all my dreams come true.
I thought we could make a difference.
I thought she was right.

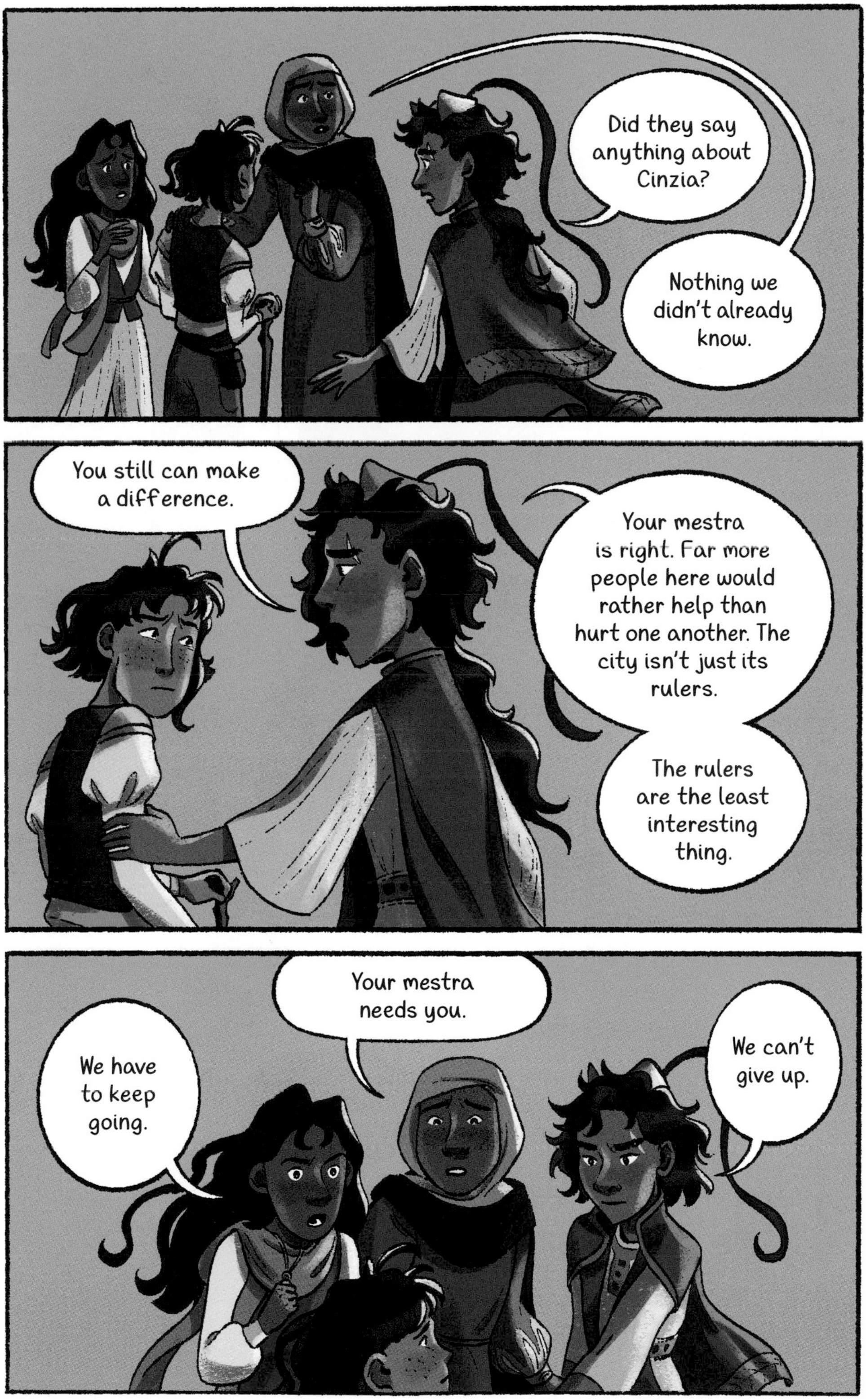
Did they say anything about Cinzia?
Nothing we didn't already know.
You still can make a difference.
Your mestra is right. Far more people here would rather help than hurt one another. The city isn't just its rulers.
The rulers are the least interesting thing.
Your mestra needs you.
We have to keep going.
We can't give up.

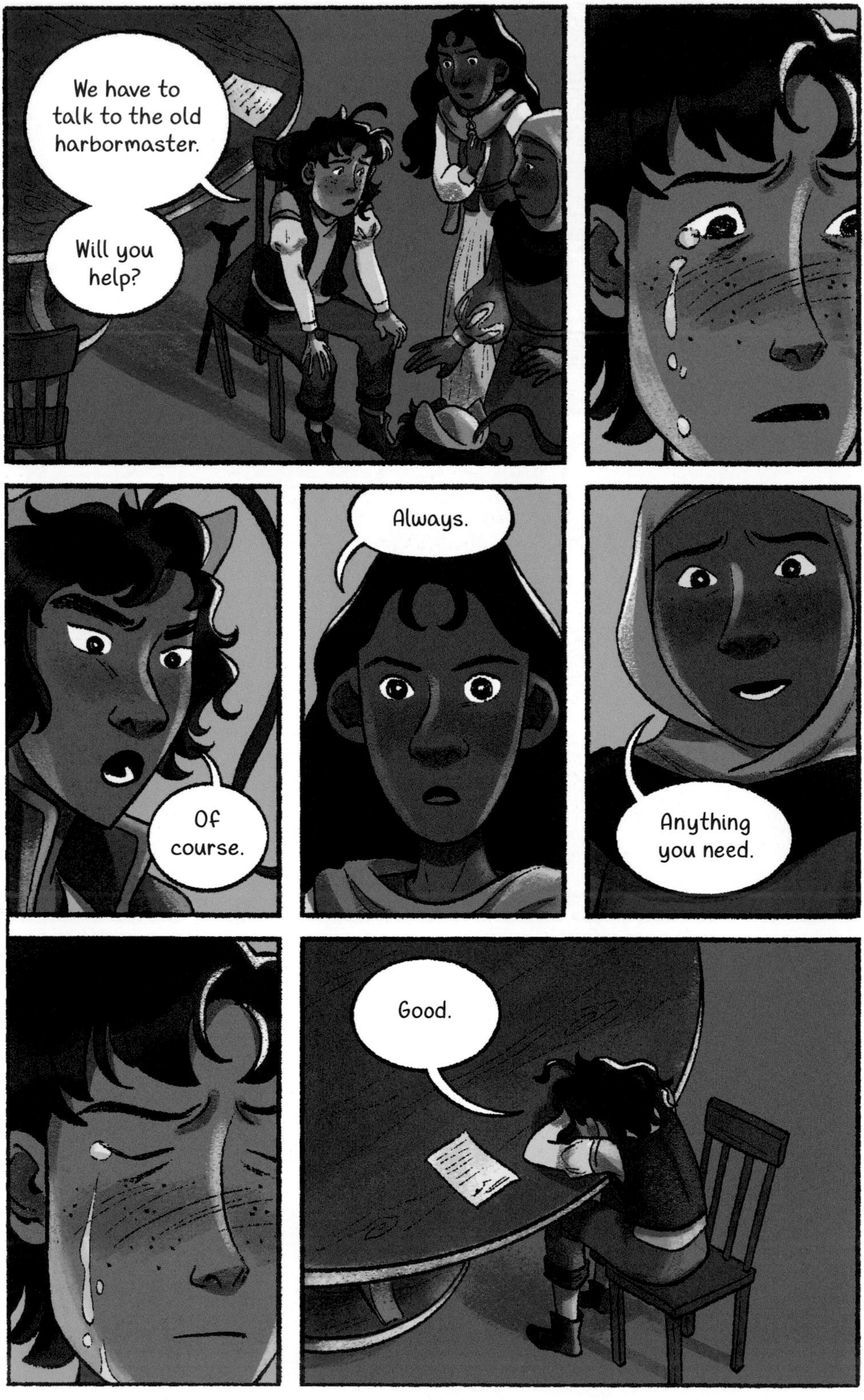
We have to talk to the old harbormaster.
Will you help?
Of course.
Always.
Anything you need.
Good.

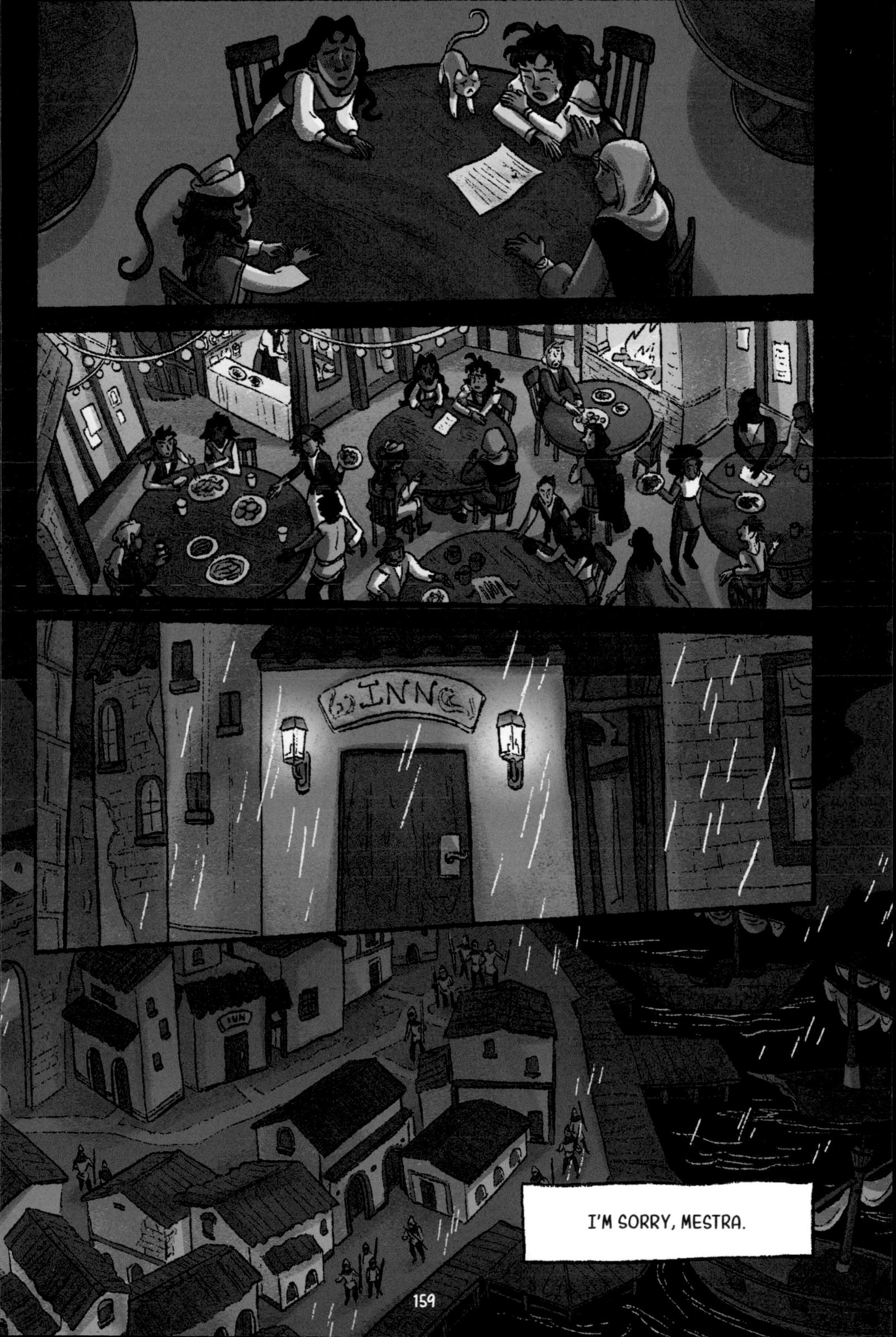
INN
INN
I'M SORRY, MESTRA.

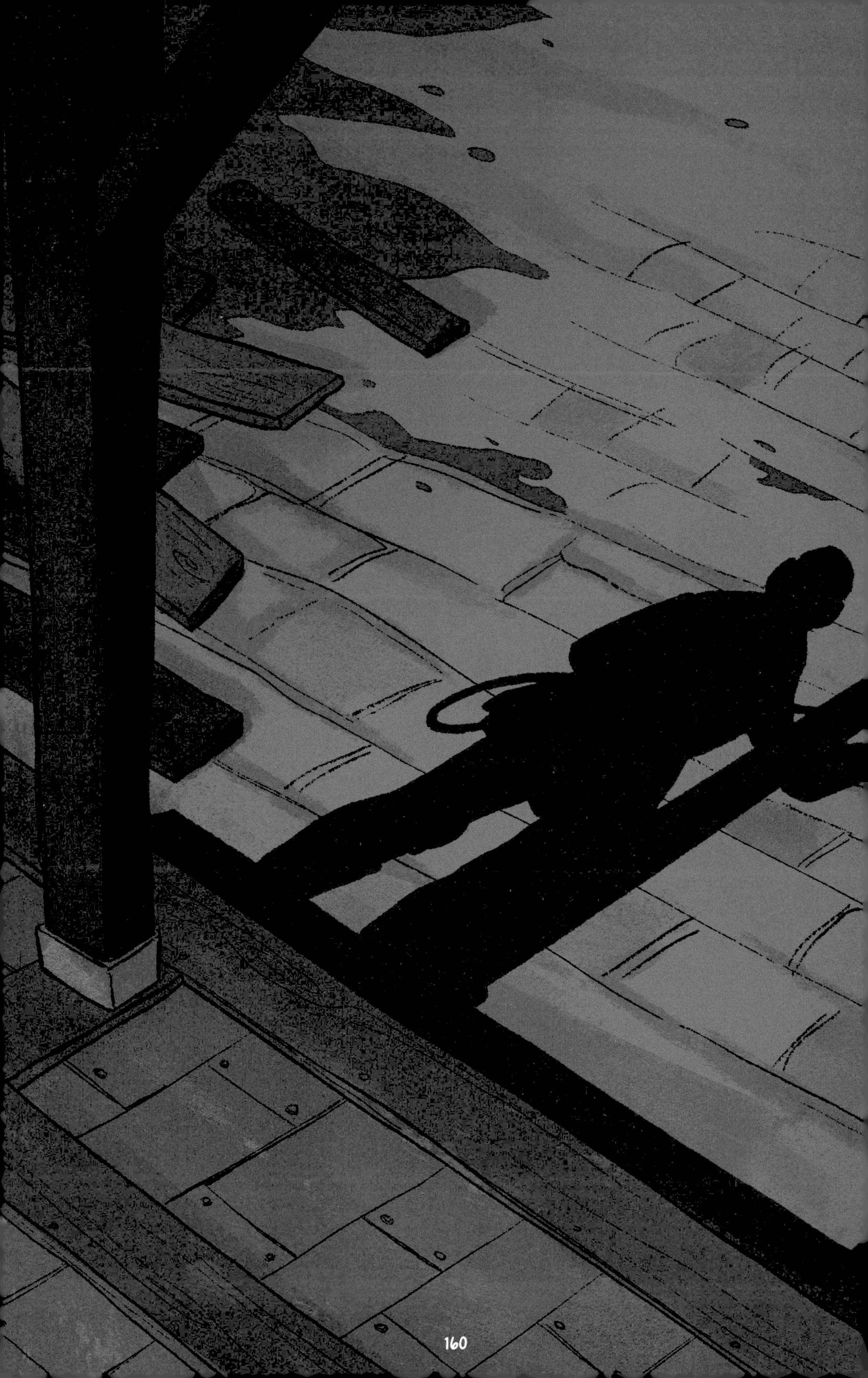

Chapter Six

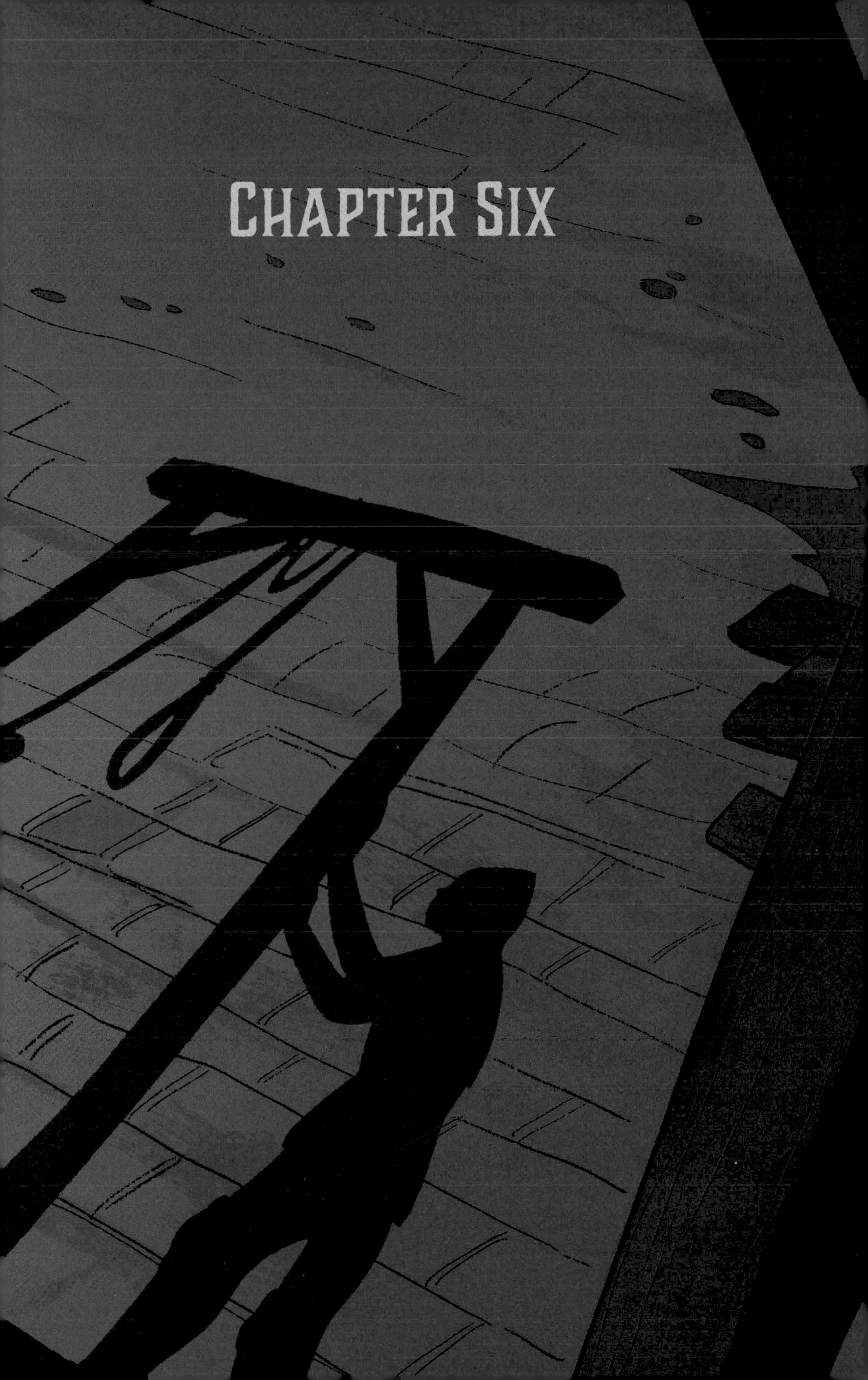

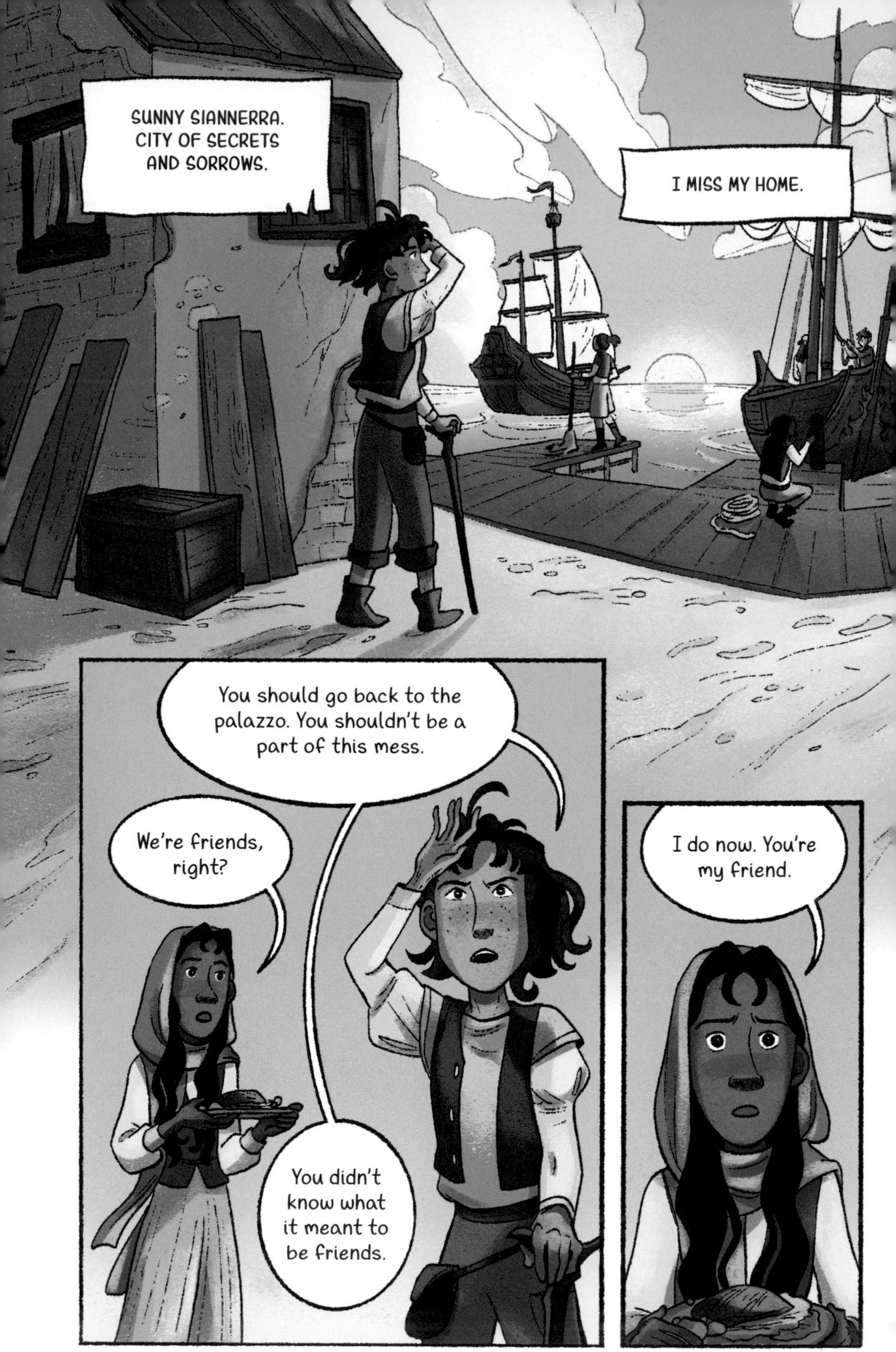
SUNNY SIANNERRA. CITY OF SECRETS AND SORROWS.
I MISS MY HOME.
You should go back to the palazzo. You shouldn't be a part of this mess.
We're friends, right?
You didn't know what it meant to be friends.
I do now. You're my friend.

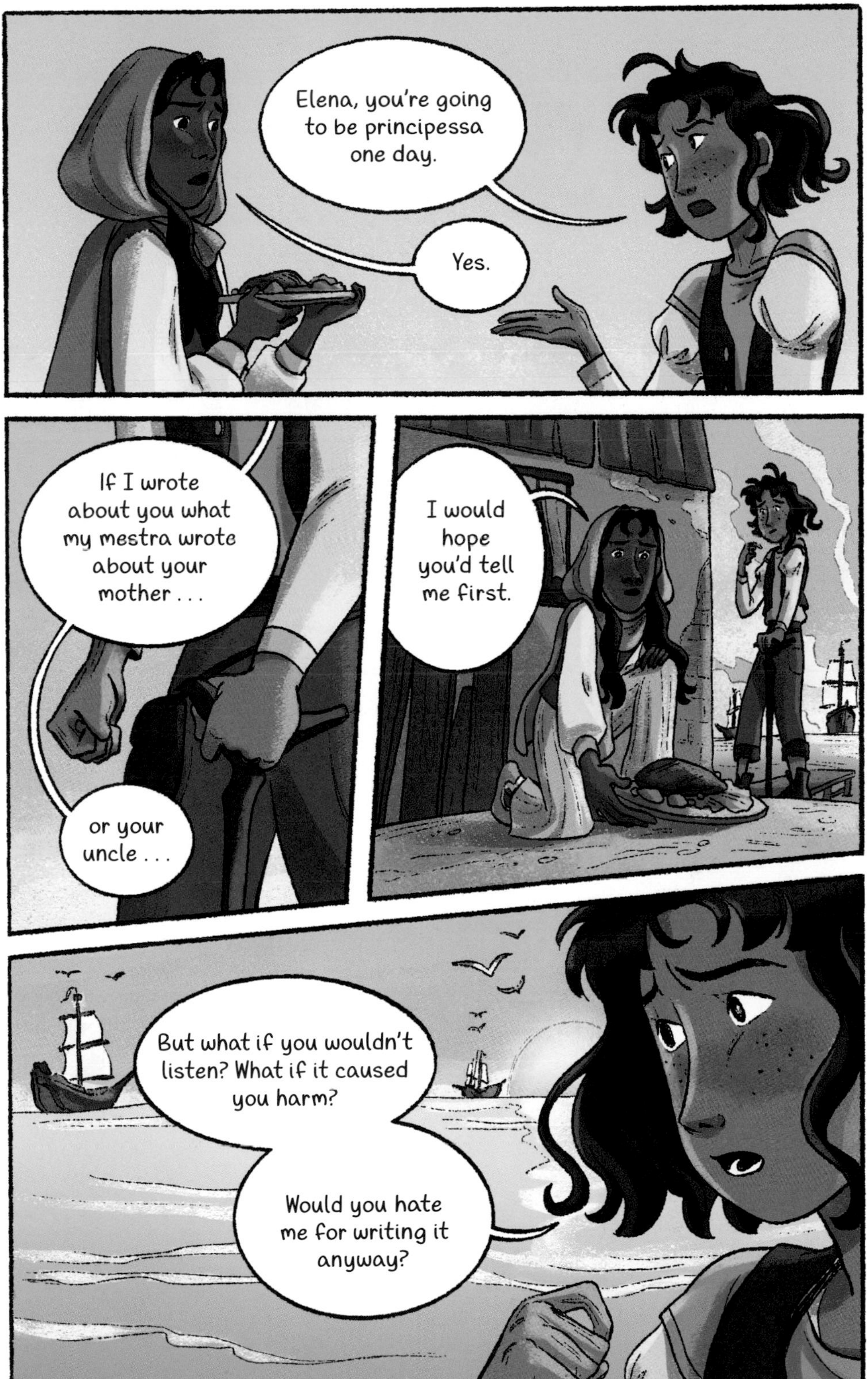
Elena, you're going to be principessa one day.
Yes.
If I wrote about you what my mestra wrote about your mother . . .
or your uncle . . .
I would hope you'd tell me first.
But what if you wouldn't listen? What if it caused you harm?
Would you hate me for writing it anyway?

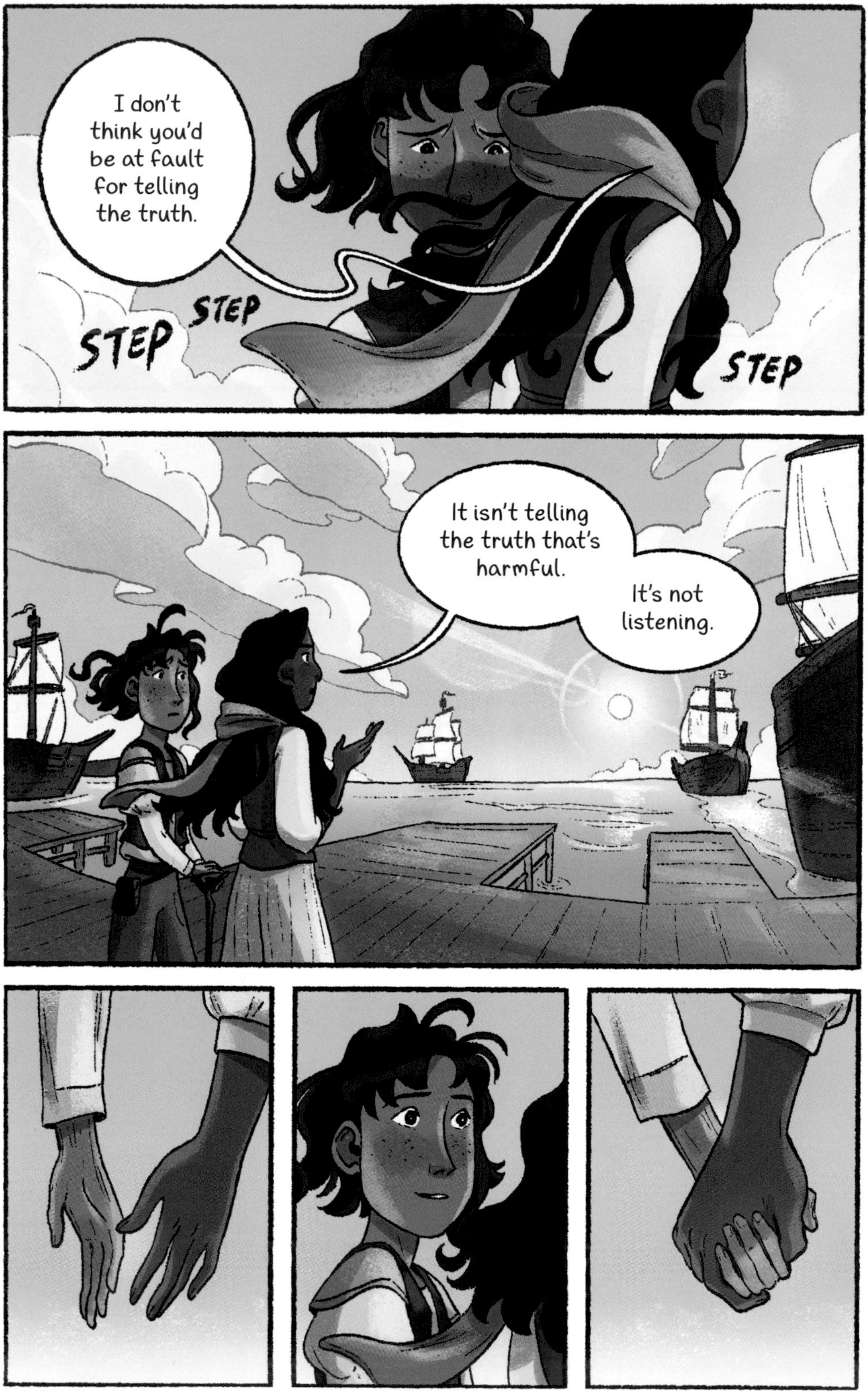
I don't think you'd be at fault for telling the truth.
STEP
STEP
STEP
It isn't telling the truth that's harmful.
It's not listening.

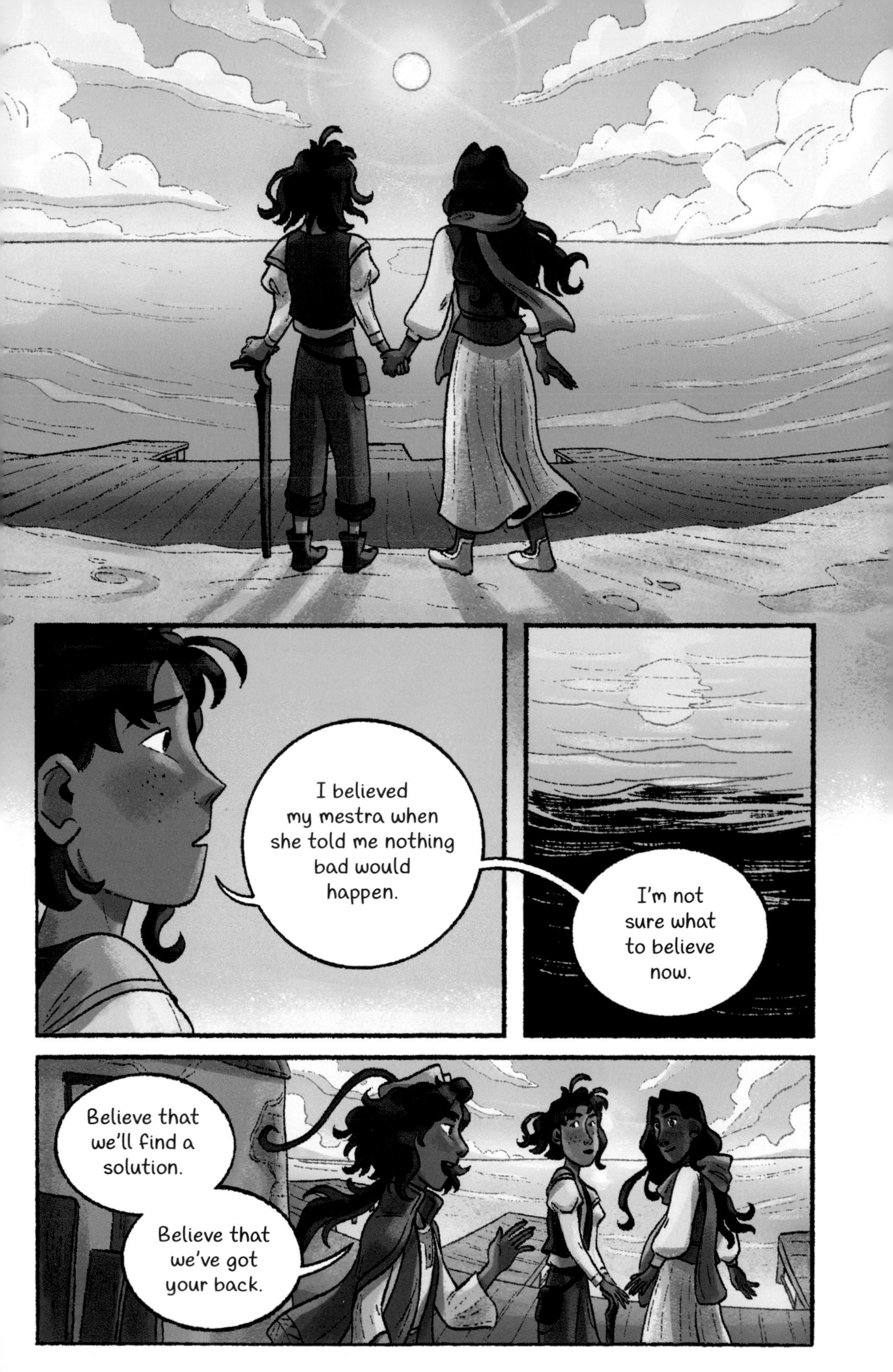
I believed my mestra when she told me nothing bad would happen.
I'm not sure what to believe now.
Believe that we'll find a solution.
Believe that we've got your back.

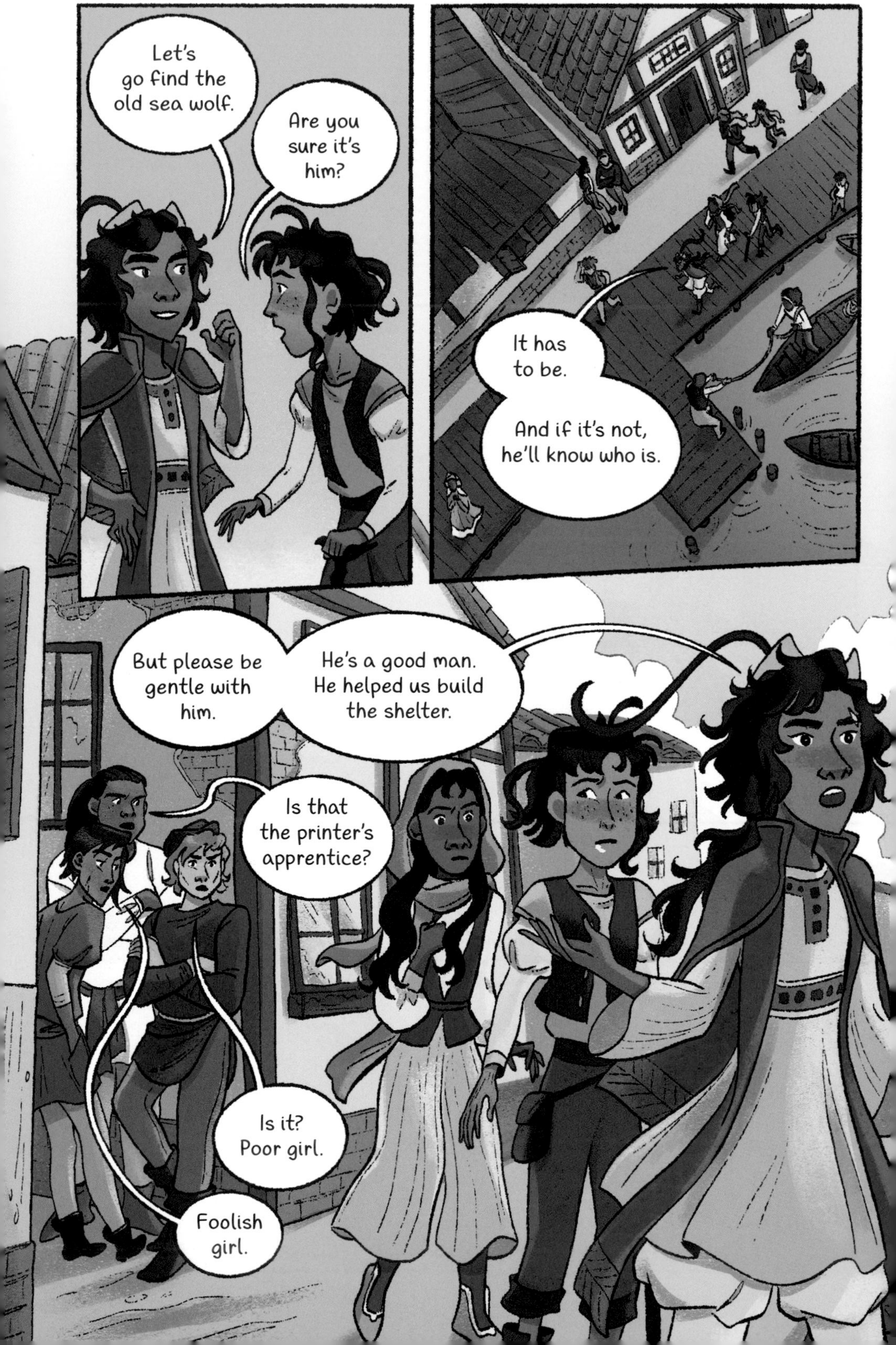
Let's go find the old sea wolf.
Are you sure it's him?
It has to be.
And if it's not, he'll know who is.
But please be gentle with him.
He's a good man. He helped us build the shelter.
Is that the printer's apprentice?
Is it? Poor girl.
Foolish girl.

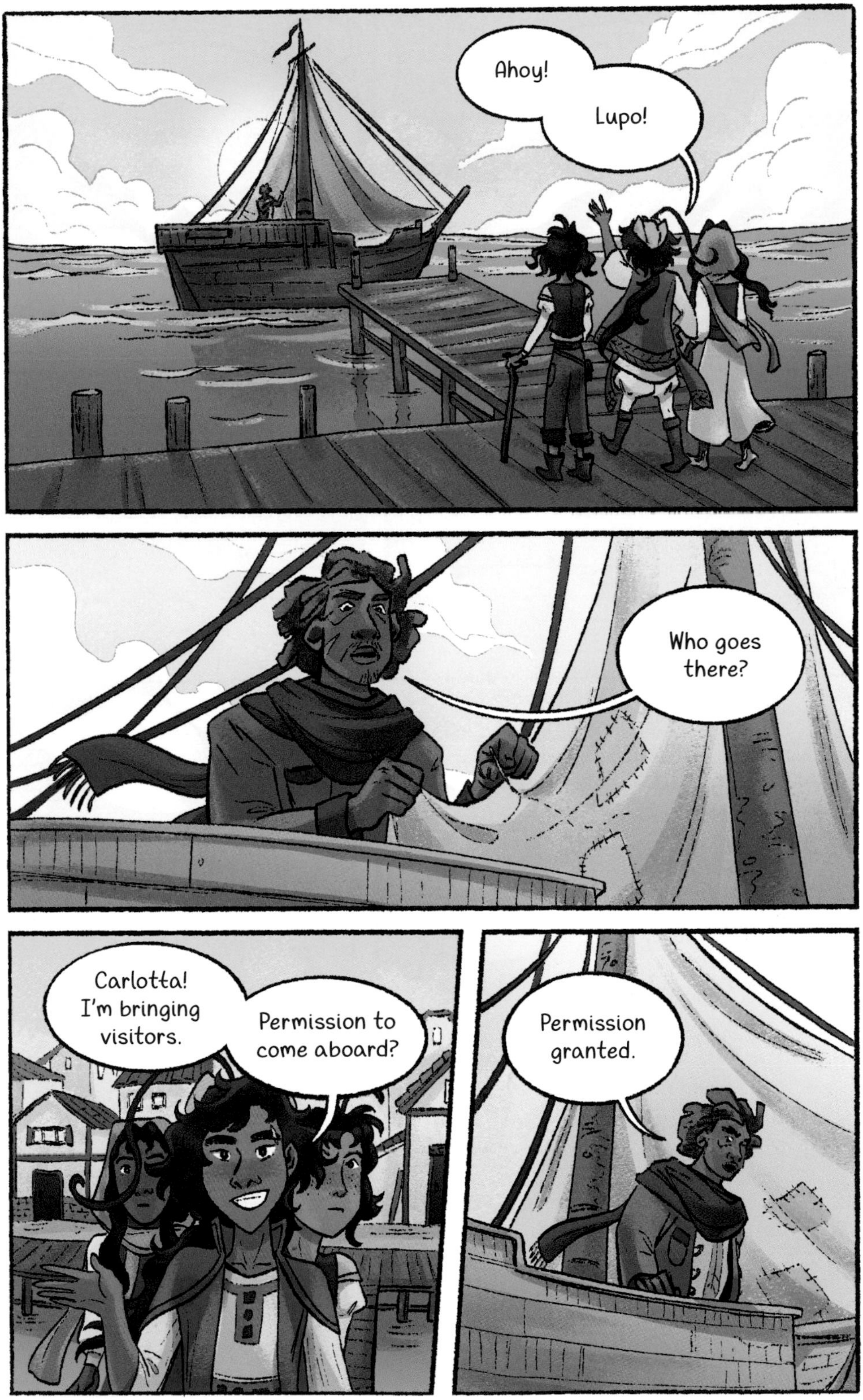
Ahoy!
Lupo!
Who goes there?
Carlotta! I'm bringing visitors.
Permission to come aboard?
Permission granted.

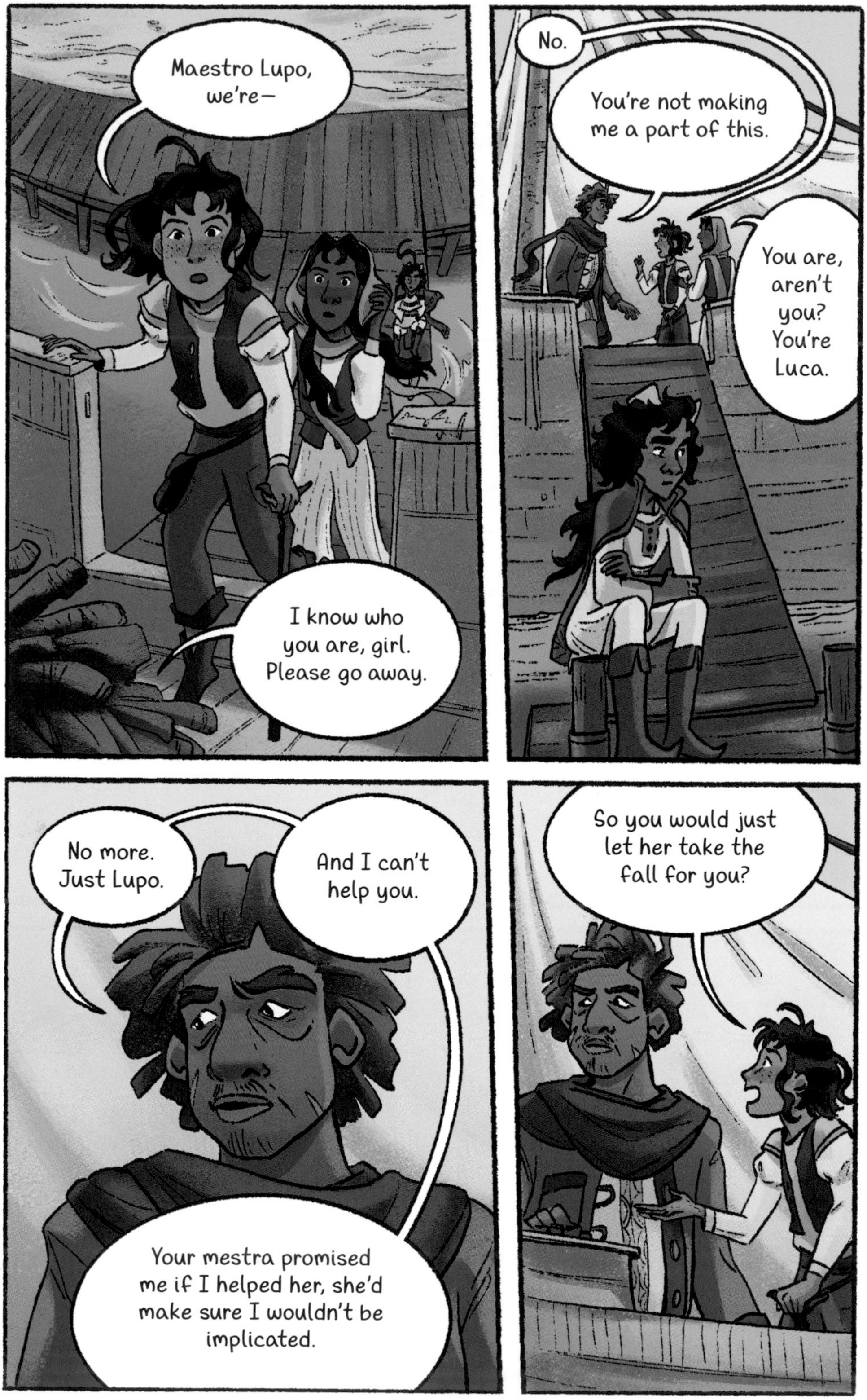
Maestro Lupo, we're—
I know who you are, girl. Please go away.
No.
You're not making me a part of this.
You are, aren't you? You're Luca.
No more. Just Lupo.
And I can't help you.
Your mestra promised me if I helped her, she'd make sure I wouldn't be implicated.
So you would just let her take the fall for you?

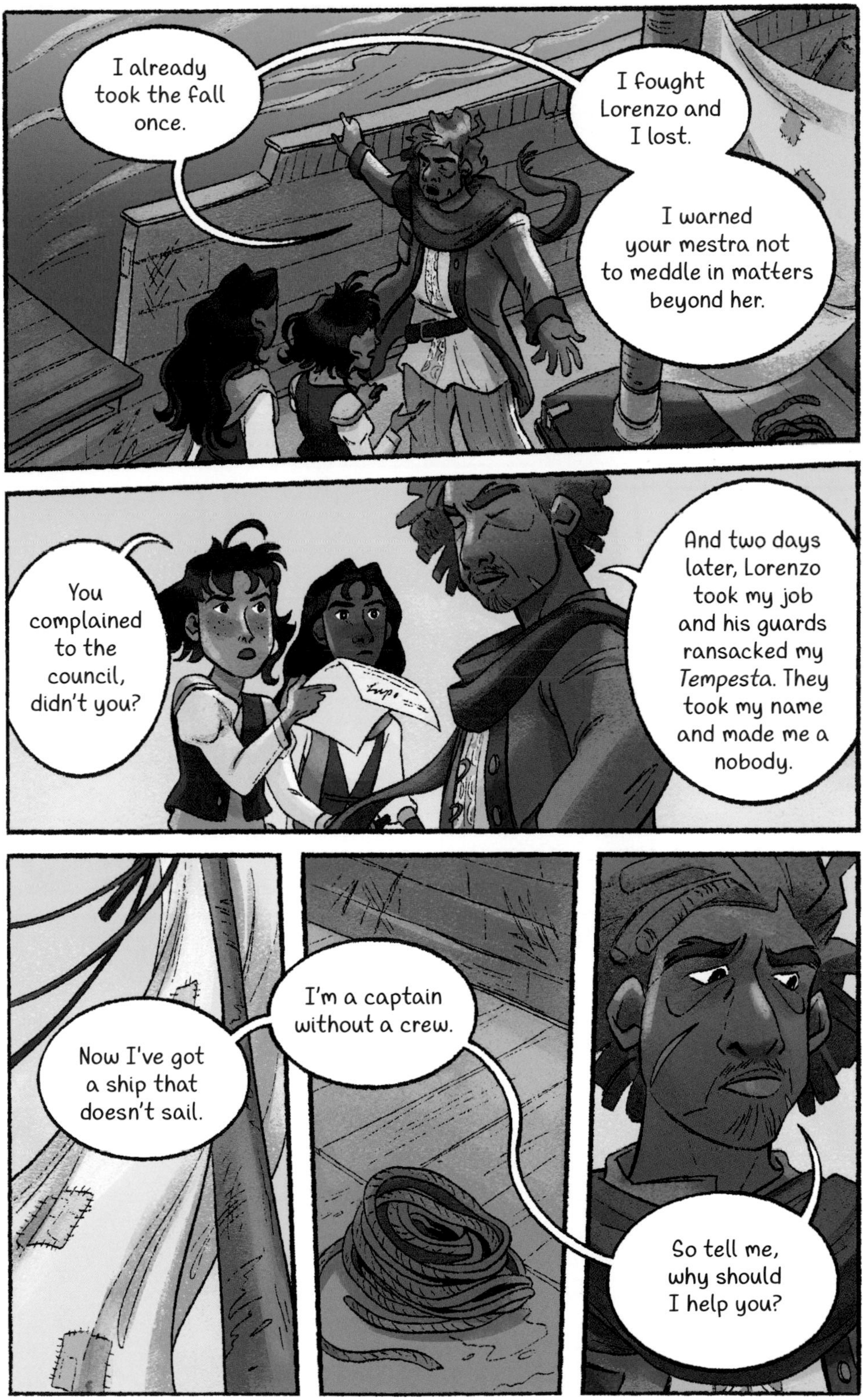

I already took the fall once.
I fought Lorenzo and I lost.
I warned your mestra not to meddle in matters beyond her.
You complained to the council, didn't you?
And two days later, Lorenzo took my job and his guards ransacked my *Tempesta*. They took my name and made me a nobody.
Now I've got a ship that doesn't sail.
I'm a captain without a crew.
So tell me, why should I help you?

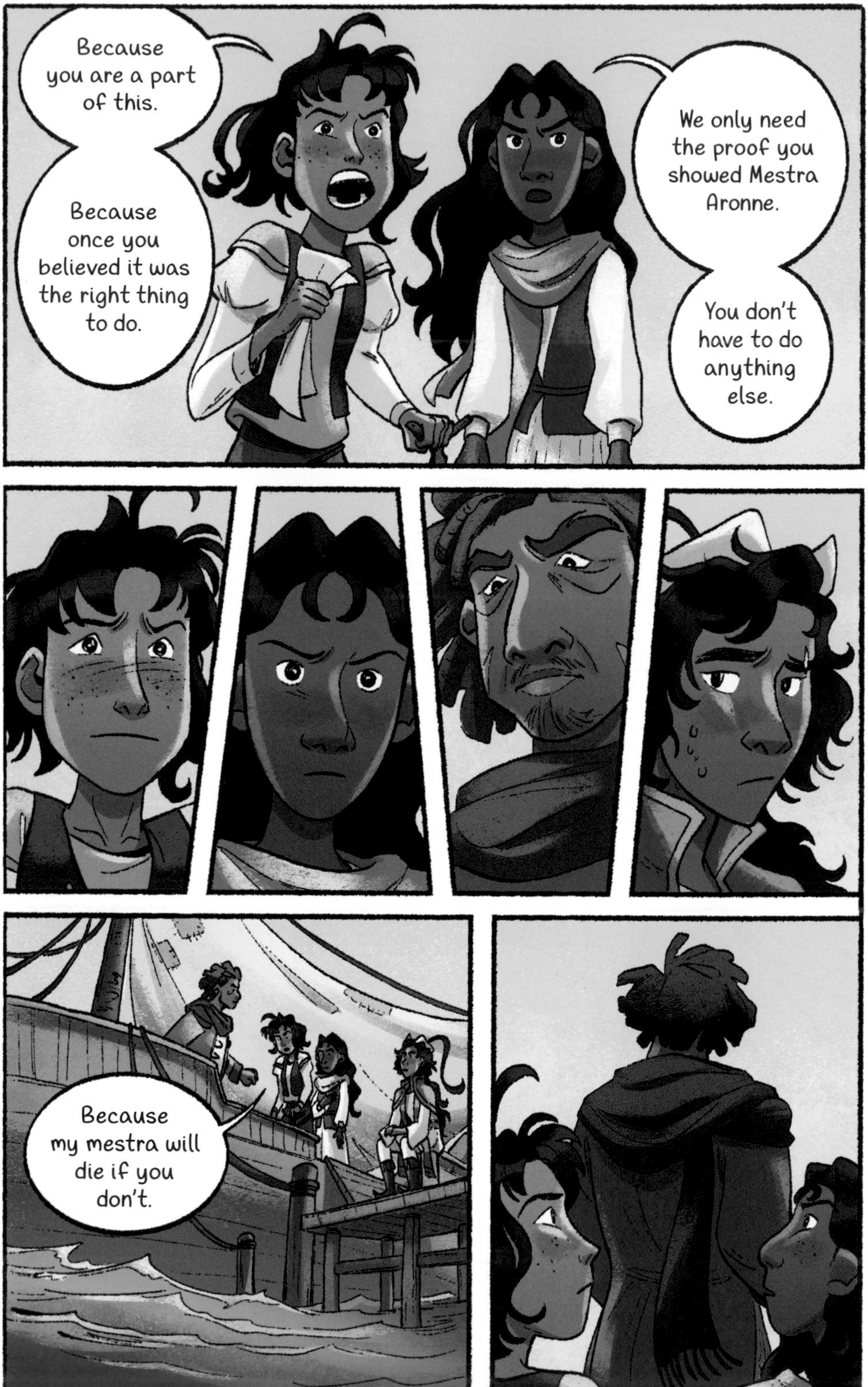
Because you are a part of this.
Because once you believed it was the right thing to do.
We only need the proof you showed Mestra Aronne.
You don't have to do anything else.
Because my mestra will die if you don't.

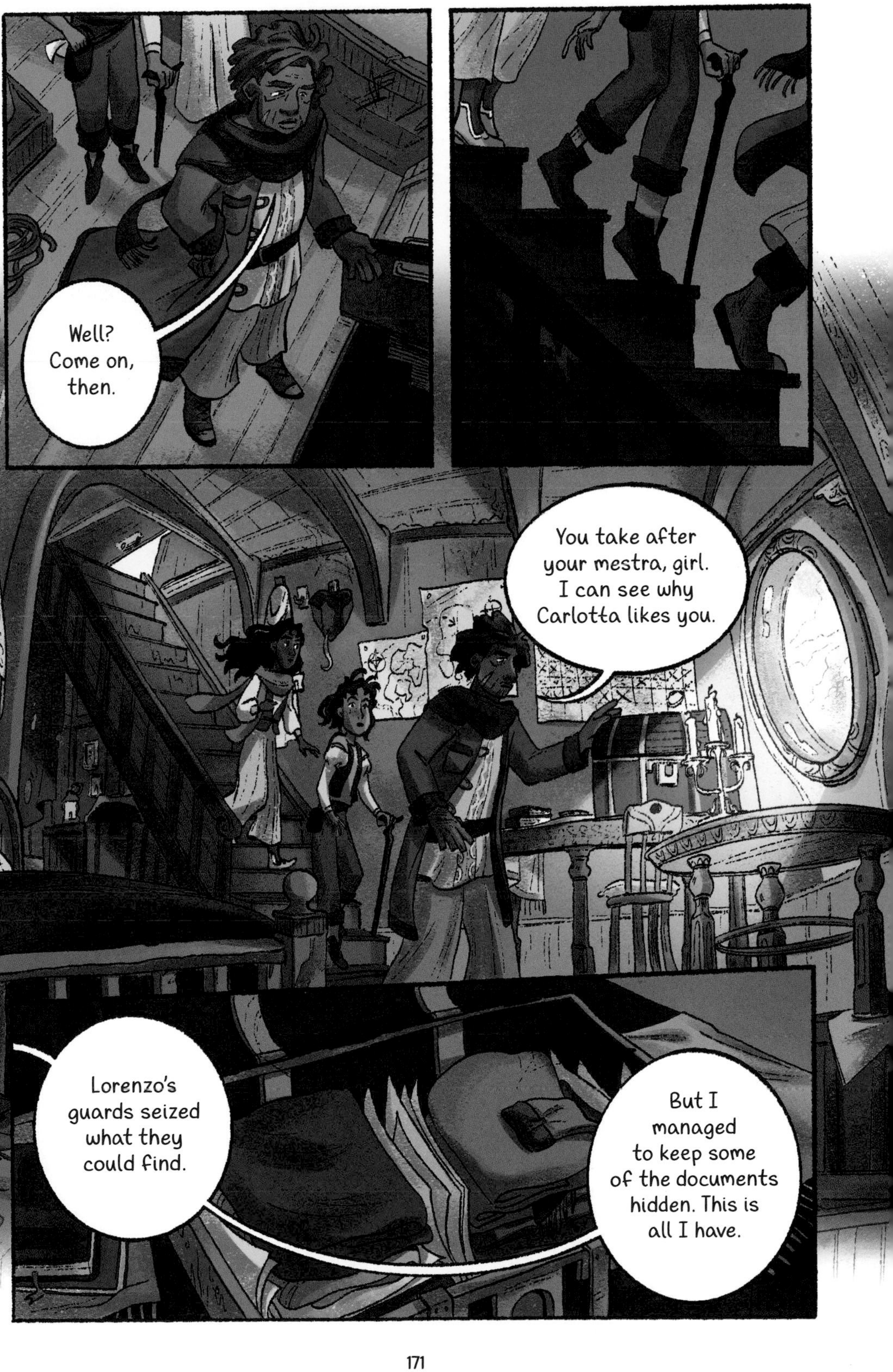
Well? Come on, then.
You take after your mestra, girl. I can see why Carlotta likes you.
Lorenzo's guards seized what they could find.
But I managed to keep some of the documents hidden. This is all I have.

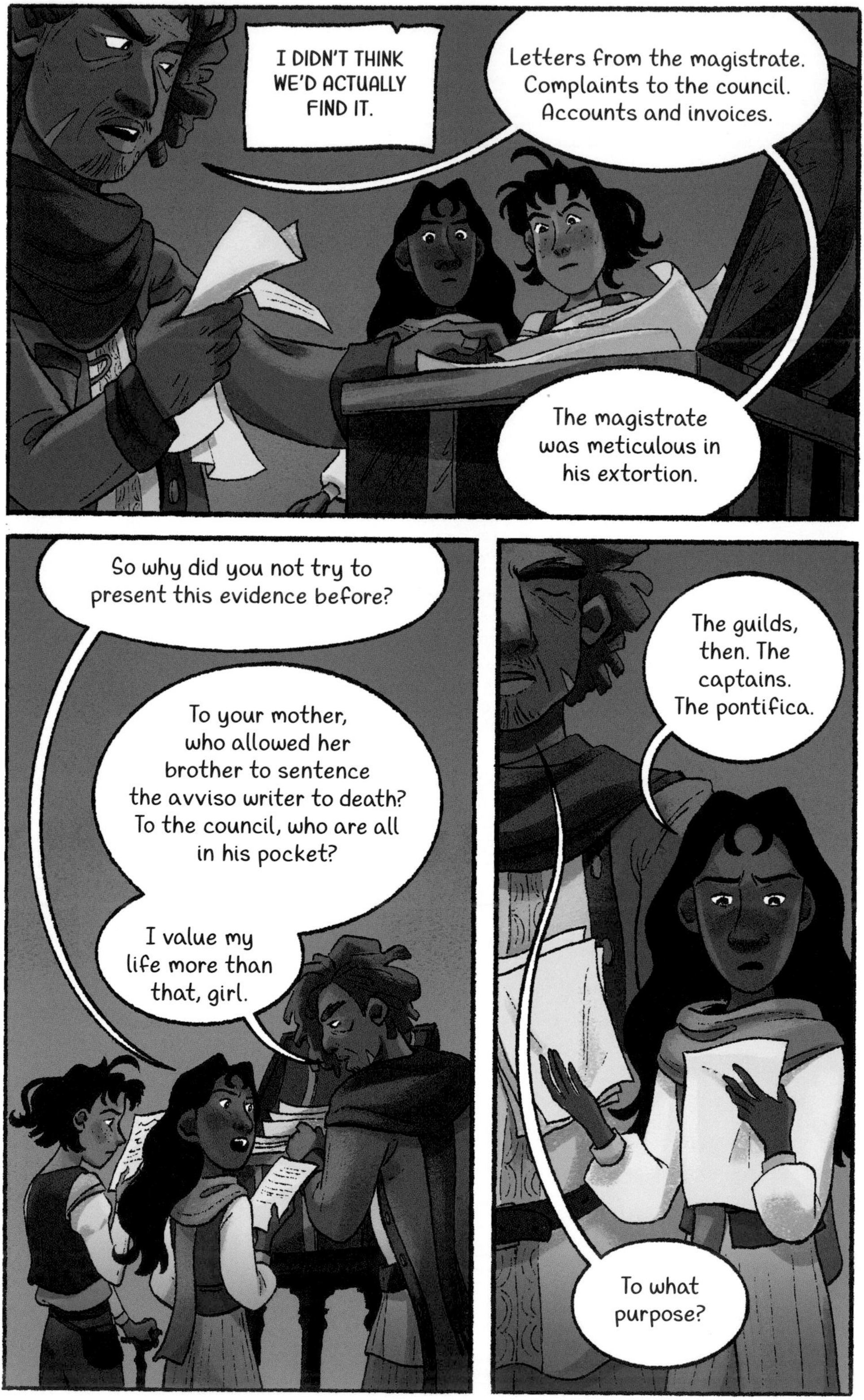
I DIDN'T THINK WE'D ACTUALLY FIND IT.
Letters from the magistrate. Complaints to the council. Accounts and invoices.
The magistrate was meticulous in his extortion.
So why did you not try to present this evidence before?
To your mother, who allowed her brother to sentence the avviso writer to death? To the council, who are all in his pocket?
I value my life more than that, girl.
The guilds, then. The captains. The pontifica.
To what purpose?

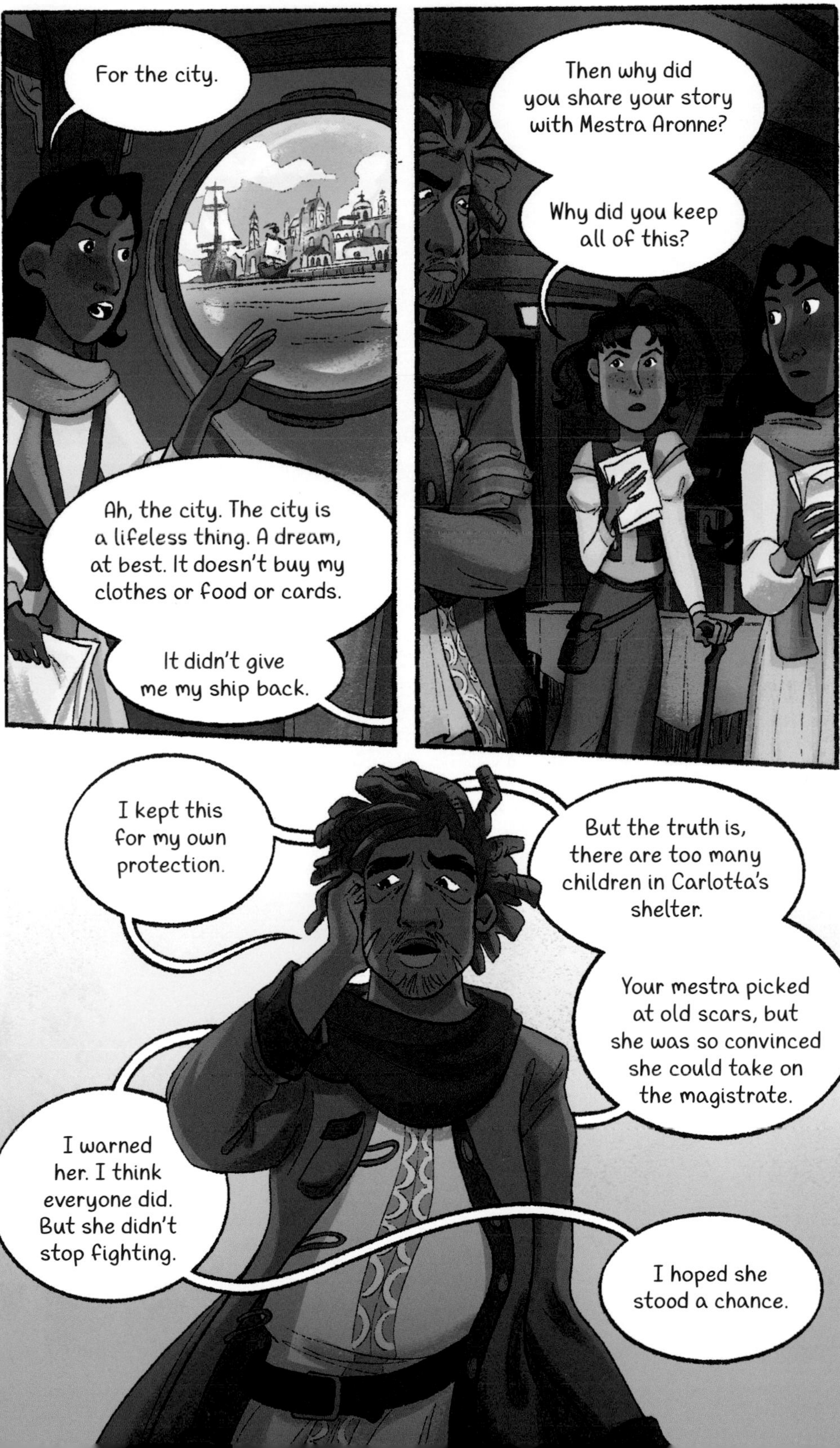
For the city.
Ah, the city. The city is a lifeless thing. A dream, at best. It doesn't buy my clothes or food or cards.
It didn't give me my ship back.
Then why did you share your story with Mestra Aronne?
Why did you keep all of this?
I kept this for my own protection.
But the truth is, there are too many children in Carlotta's shelter.
Your mestra picked at old scars, but she was so convinced she could take on the magistrate.
I warned her. I think everyone did. But she didn't stop fighting.
I hoped she stood a chance.

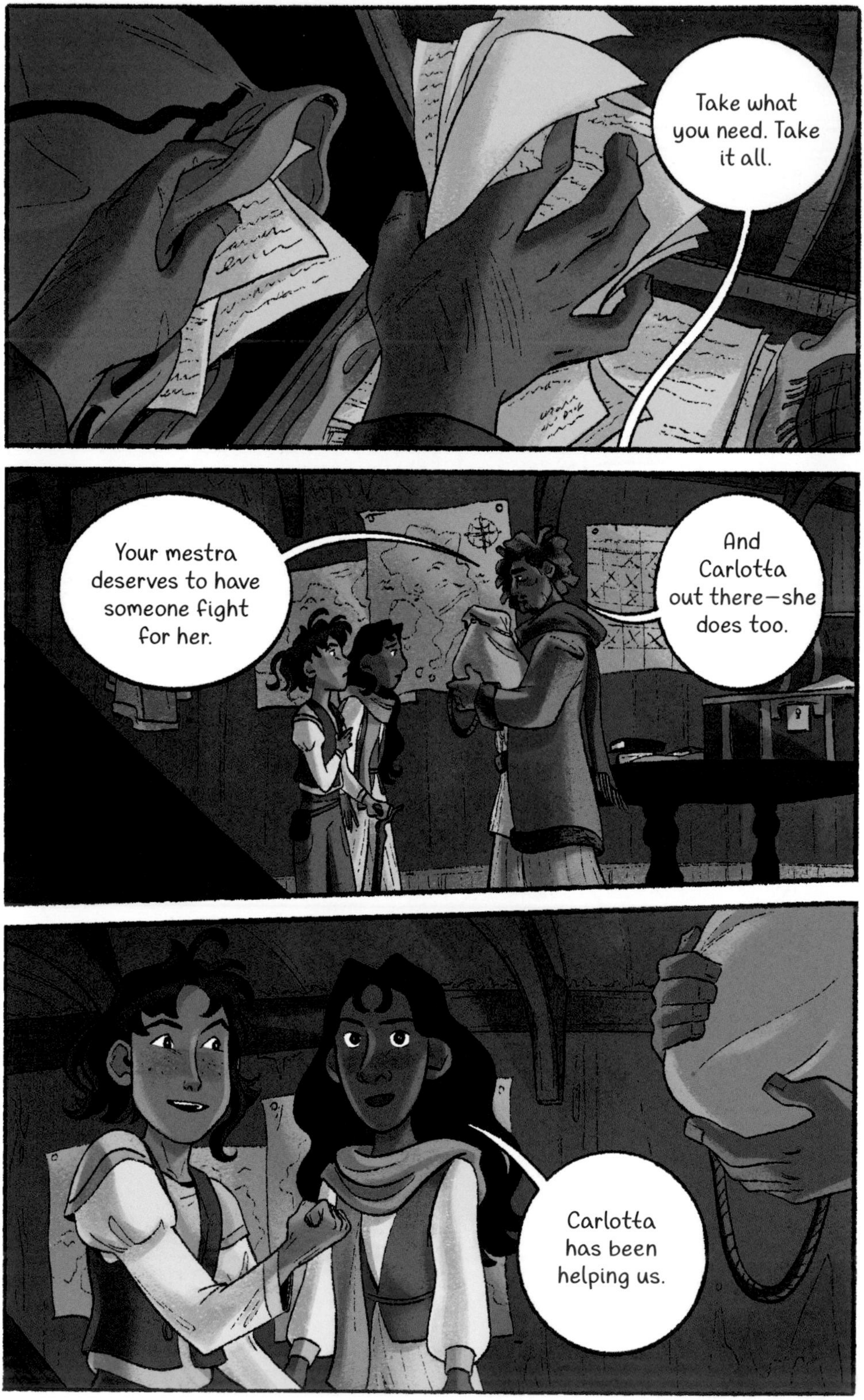
Take what you need. Take it all.
Your mestra deserves to have someone fight for her.
And Carlotta out there—she does too.
Carlotta has been helping us.

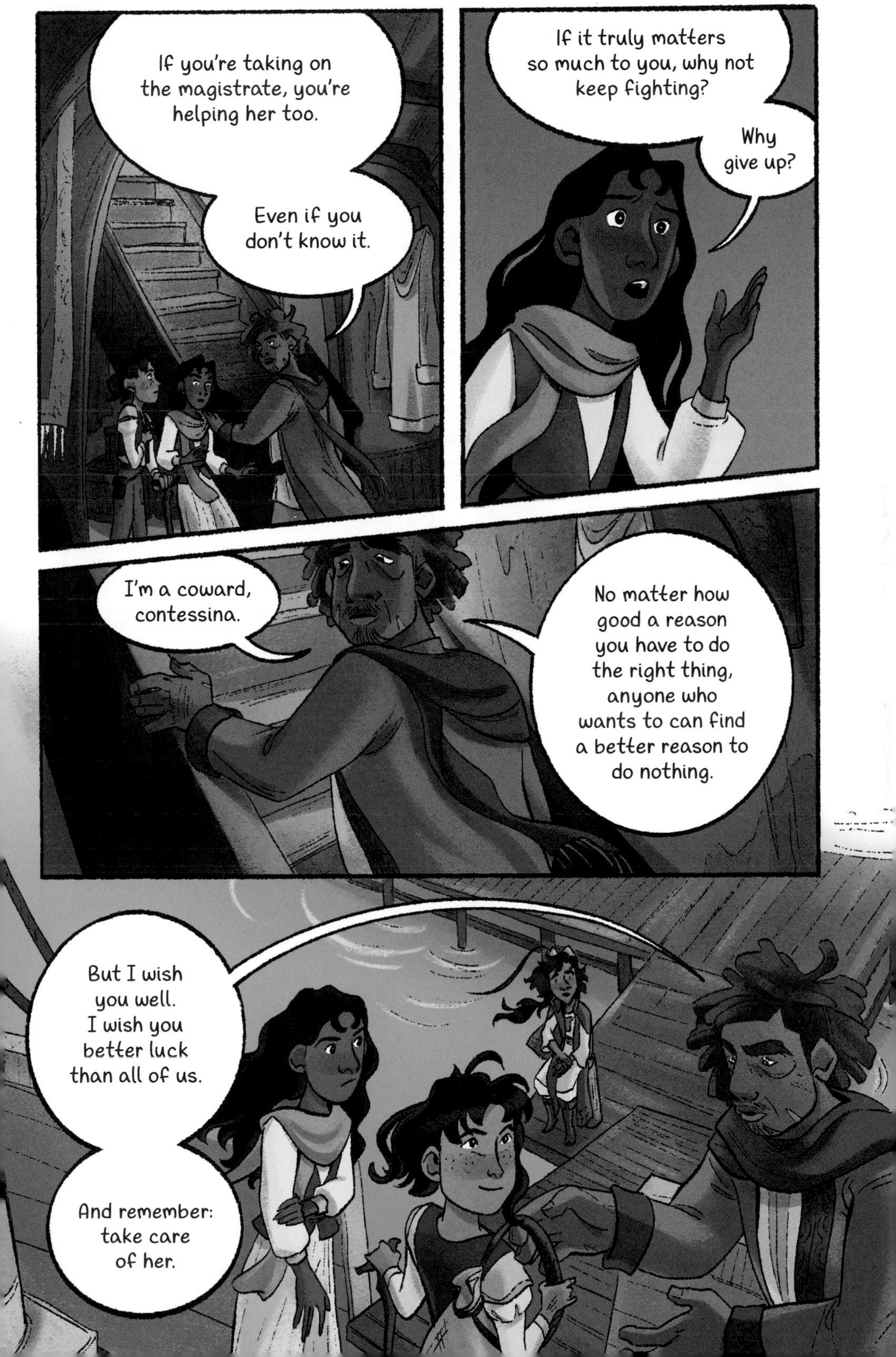
If you're taking on the magistrate, you're helping her too.
Even if you don't know it.
If it truly matters so much to you, why not keep fighting?
Why give up?
I'm a coward, contessina.
No matter how good a reason you have to do the right thing, anyone who wants to can find a better reason to do nothing.
But I wish you well. I wish you better luck than all of us.
And remember: take care of her.

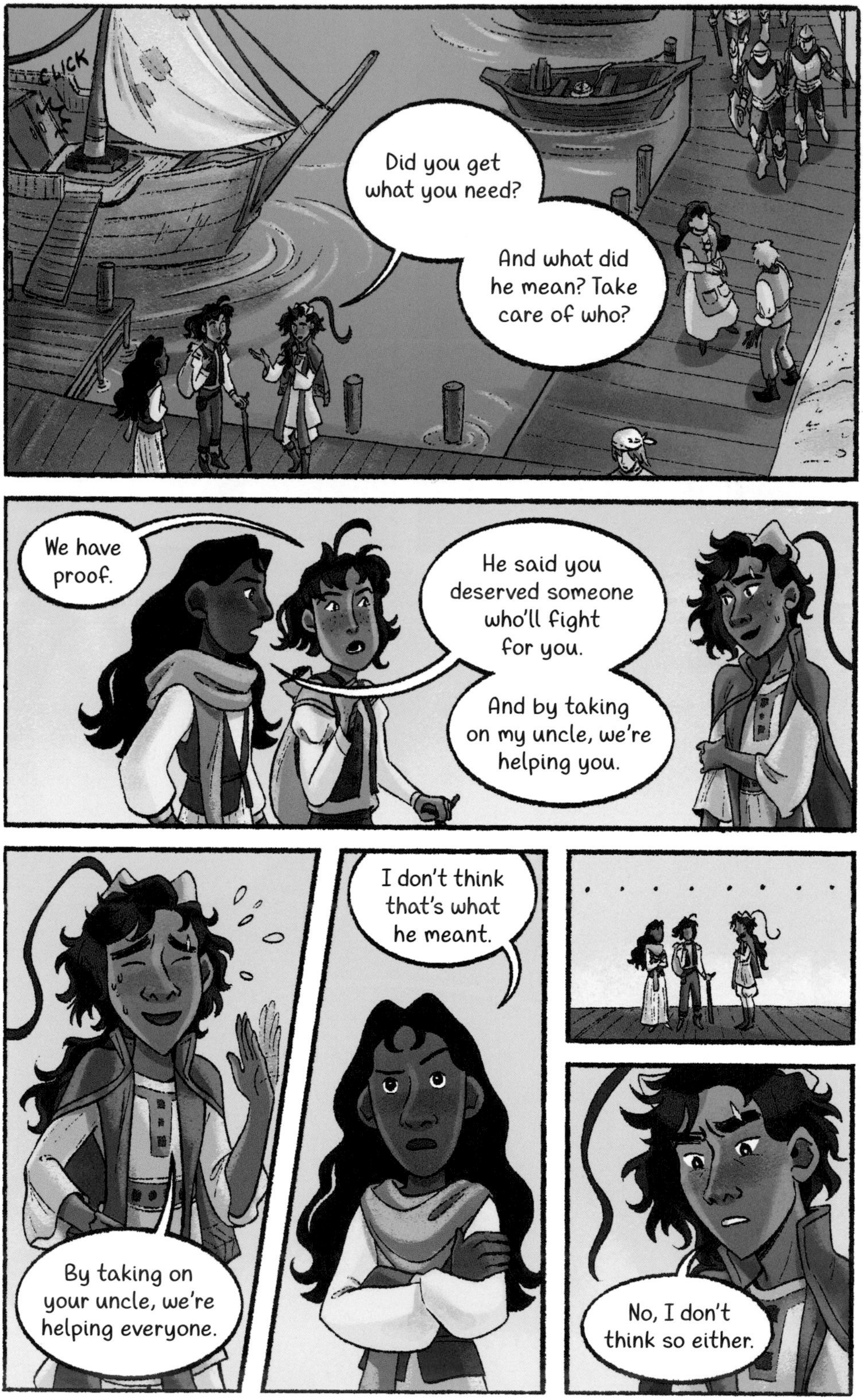
CLICK
Did you get what you need?
And what did he mean? Take care of who?
We have proof.
He said you deserved someone who'll fight for you.
And by taking on my uncle, we're helping you.
By taking on your uncle, we're helping everyone.
I don't think that's what he meant.
. . . .
No, I don't think so either.

People have realized you're here.

You need to get the papers safely to your mother, Elena.

We need to get to the principessa.

No. You need a distraction.

The guard won't harm me. Worst they can do is send me home.

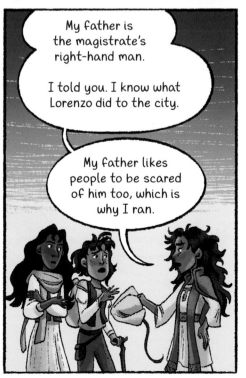

My father is the magistrate's right-hand man.

I told you. I know what Lorenzo did to the city.

My father likes people to be scared of him too, which is why I ran.

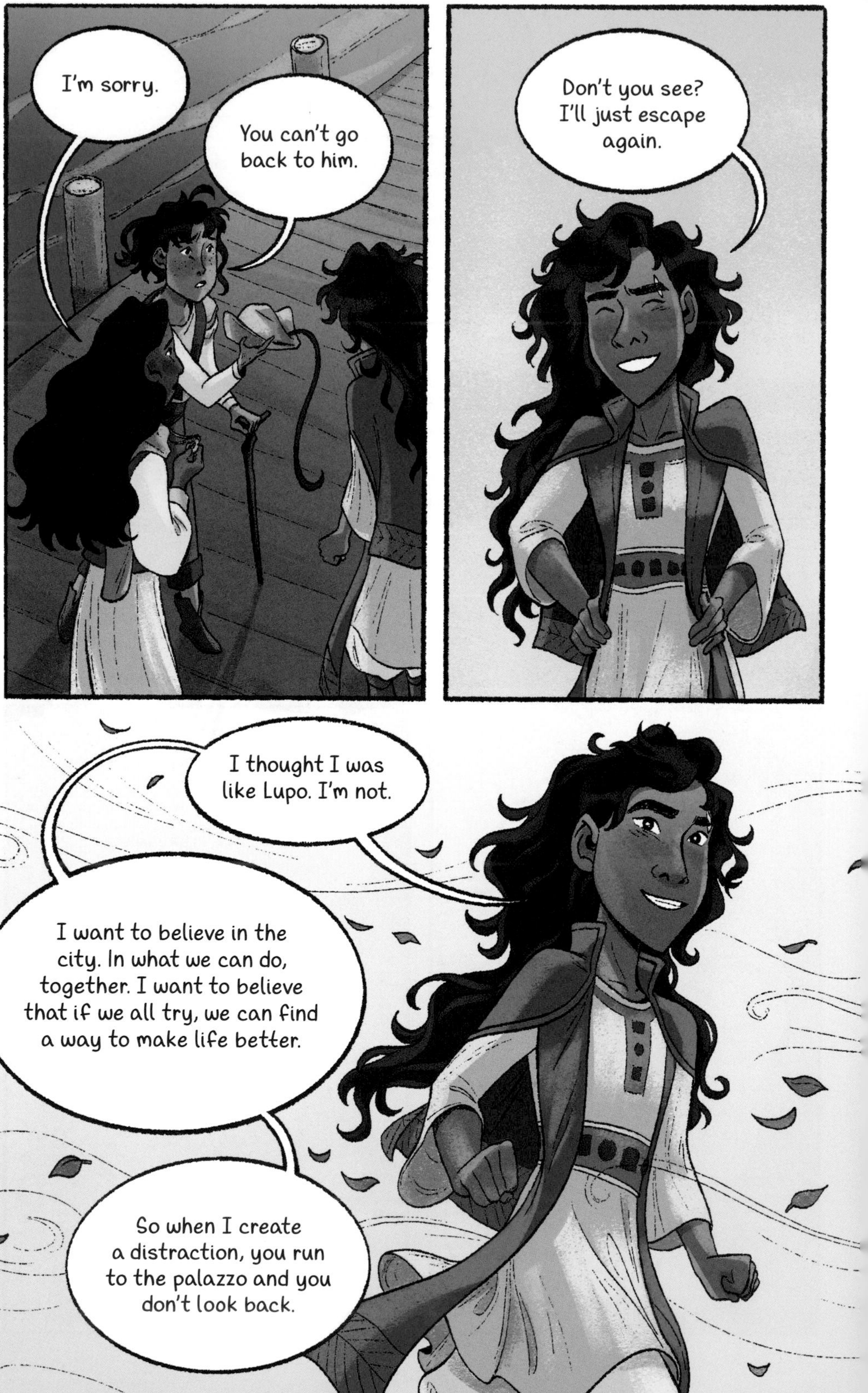
I'm sorry.
You can't go back to him.
Don't you see? I'll just escape again.
I thought I was like Lupo. I'm not.
I want to believe in the city. In what we can do, together. I want to believe that if we all try, we can find a way to make life better.
So when I create a distraction, you run to the palazzo and you don't look back.

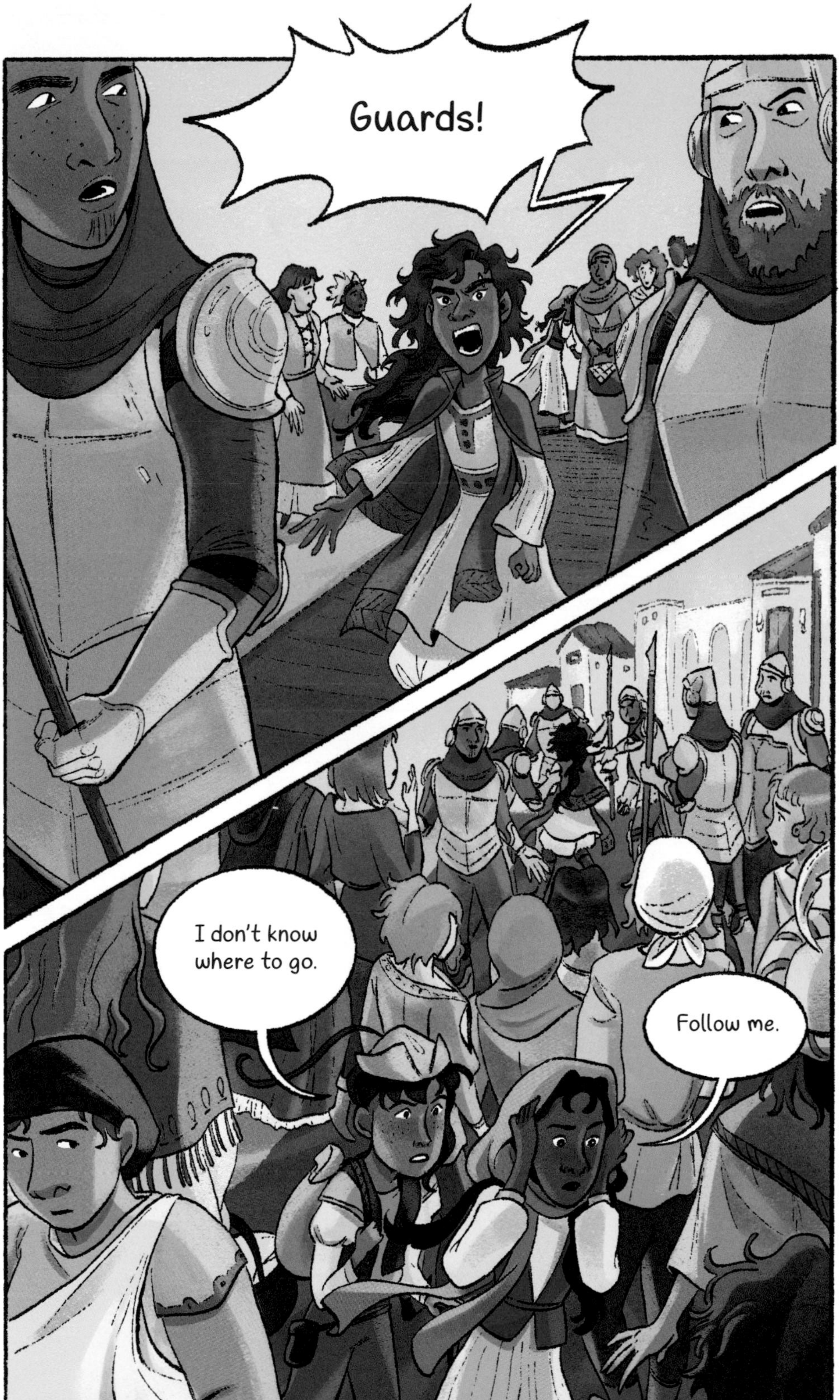
Guards!
I don't know where to go.
Follow me.

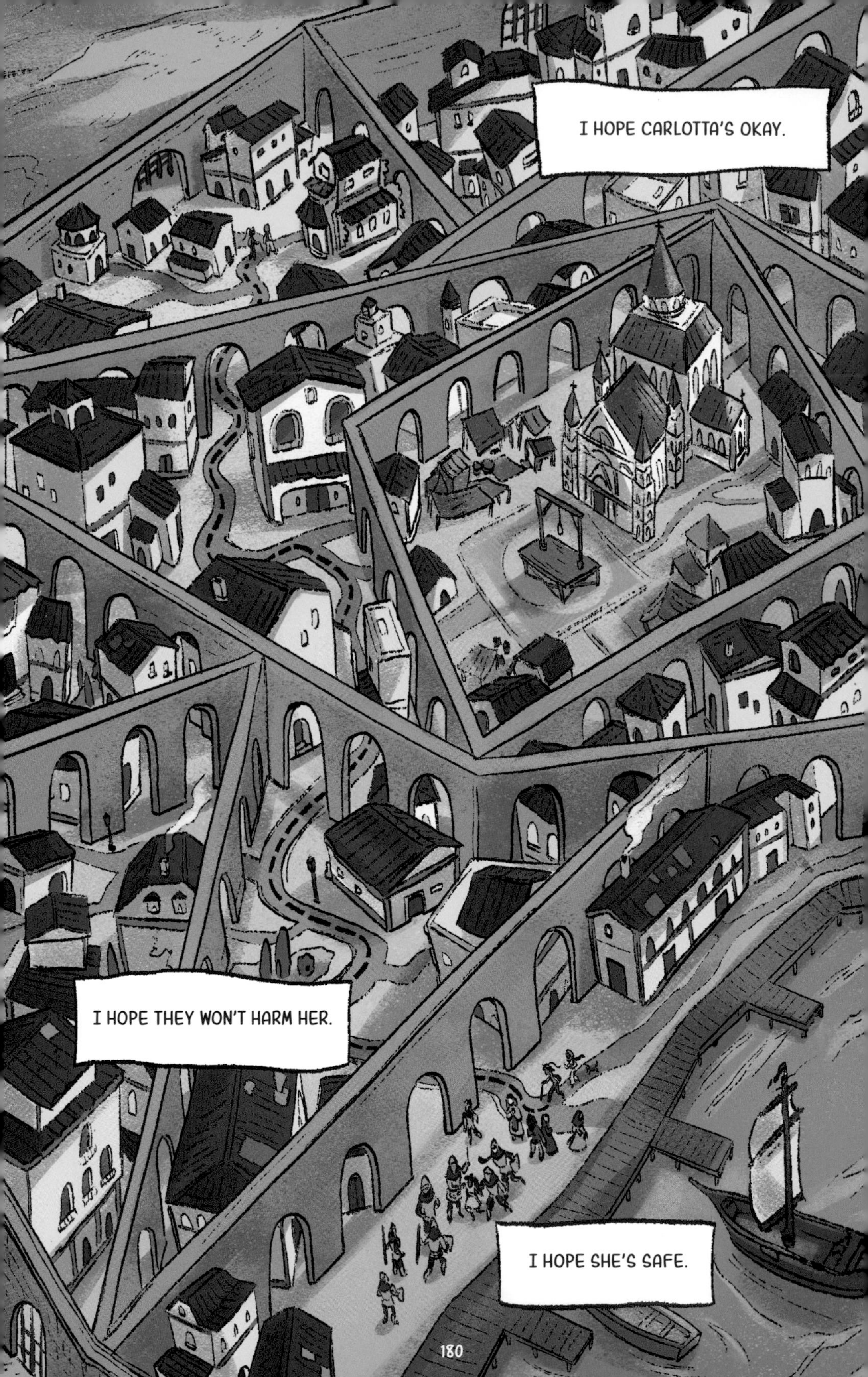
I HOPE CARLOTTA'S OKAY.
I HOPE THEY WON'T HARM HER.
I HOPE SHE'S SAFE.

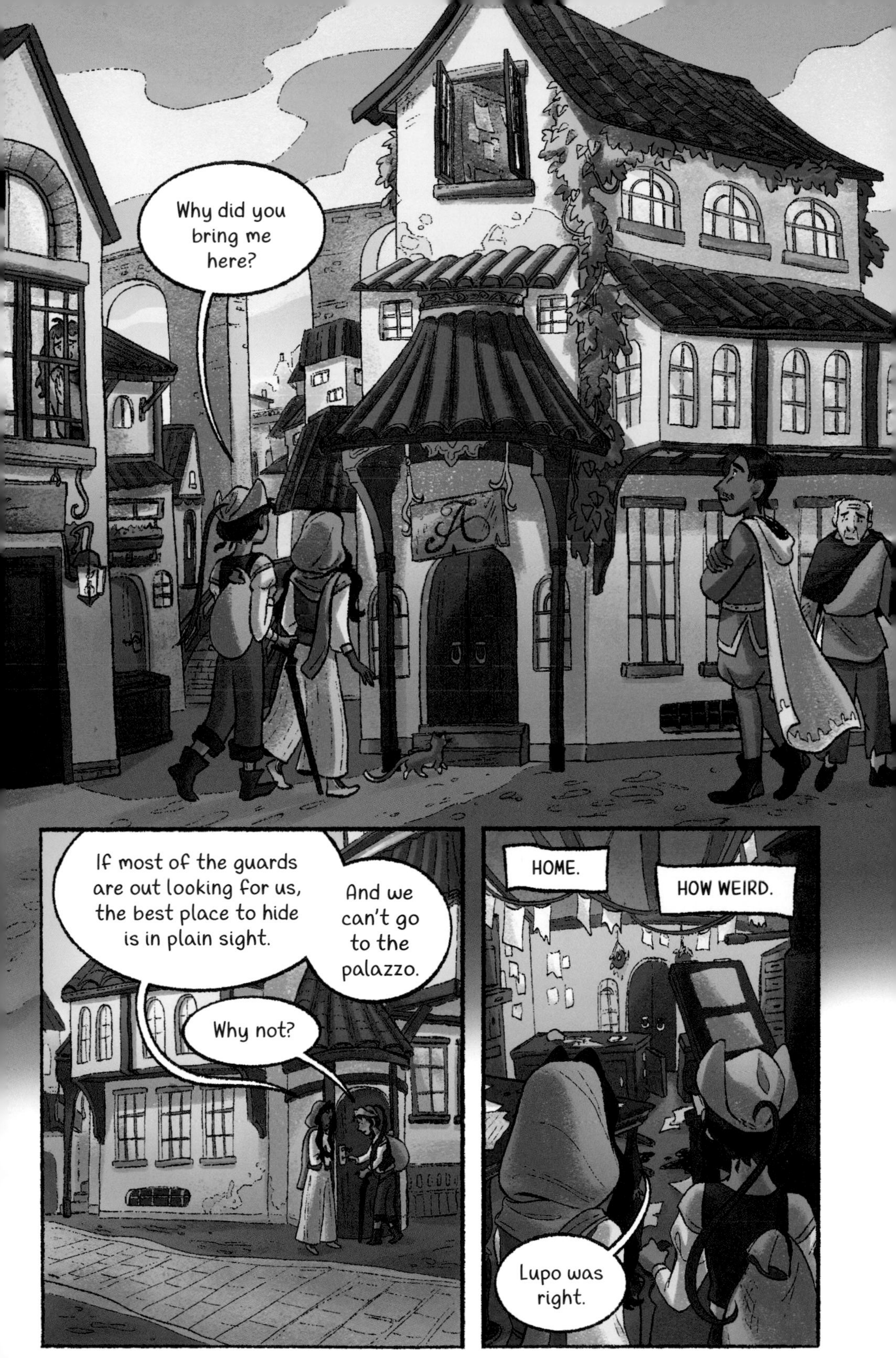
Why did you bring me here?
If most of the guards are out looking for us, the best place to hide is in plain sight.
And we can't go to the palazzo.
Why not?
HOME.
HOW WEIRD.
Lupo was right.

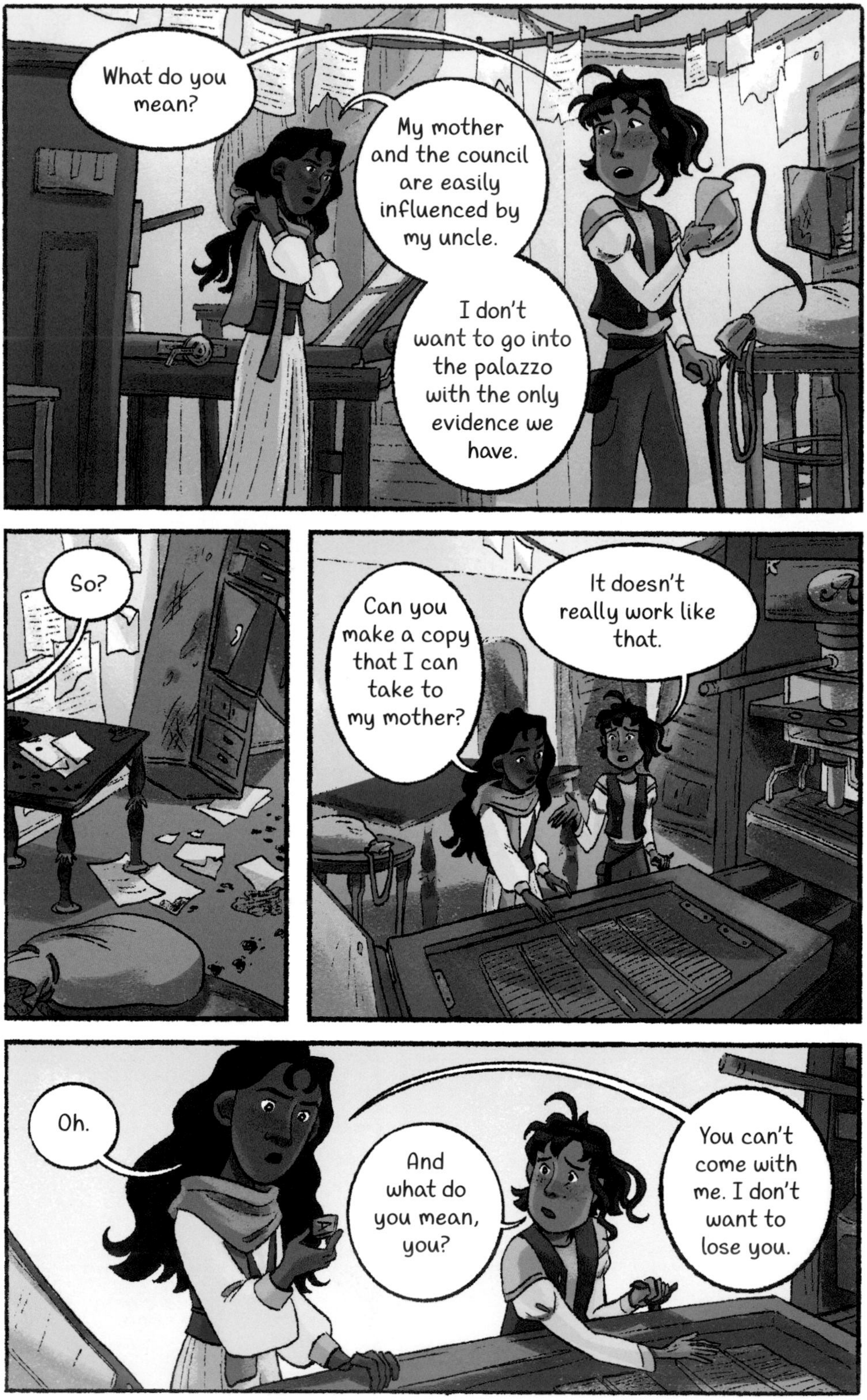
What do you mean?
My mother and the council are easily influenced by my uncle.
I don't want to go into the palazzo with the only evidence we have.
So?
Can you make a copy that I can take to my mother?
It doesn't really work like that.
Oh.
You can't come with me. I don't want to lose you.
And what do you mean, you?

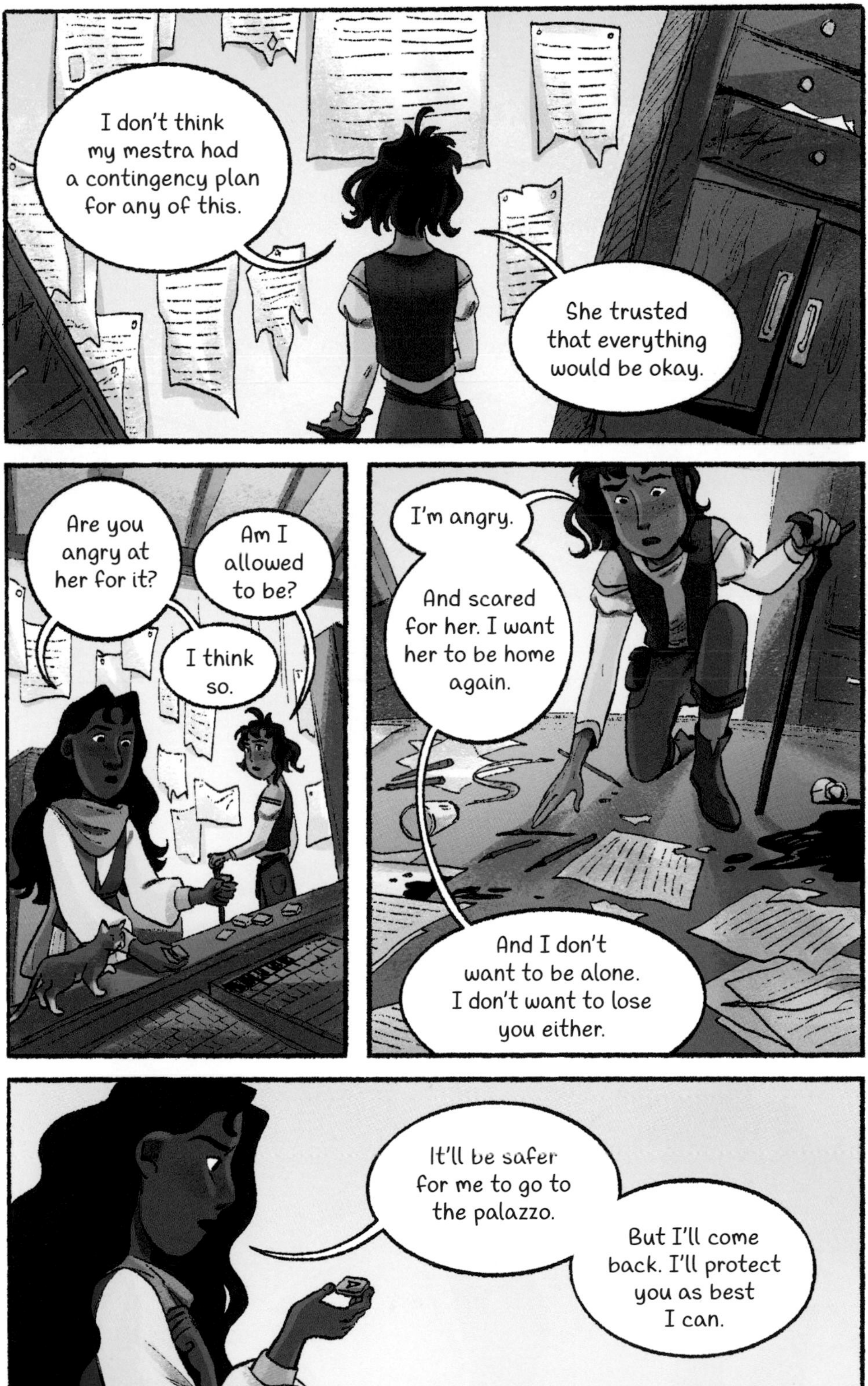
I don't think my mestra had a contingency plan for any of this.
She trusted that everything would be okay.
Are you angry at her for it?
Am I allowed to be?
I think so.
I'm angry.
And scared for her. I want her to be home again.
And I don't want to be alone. I don't want to lose you either.
It'll be safer for me to go to the palazzo.
But I'll come back. I'll protect you as best I can.

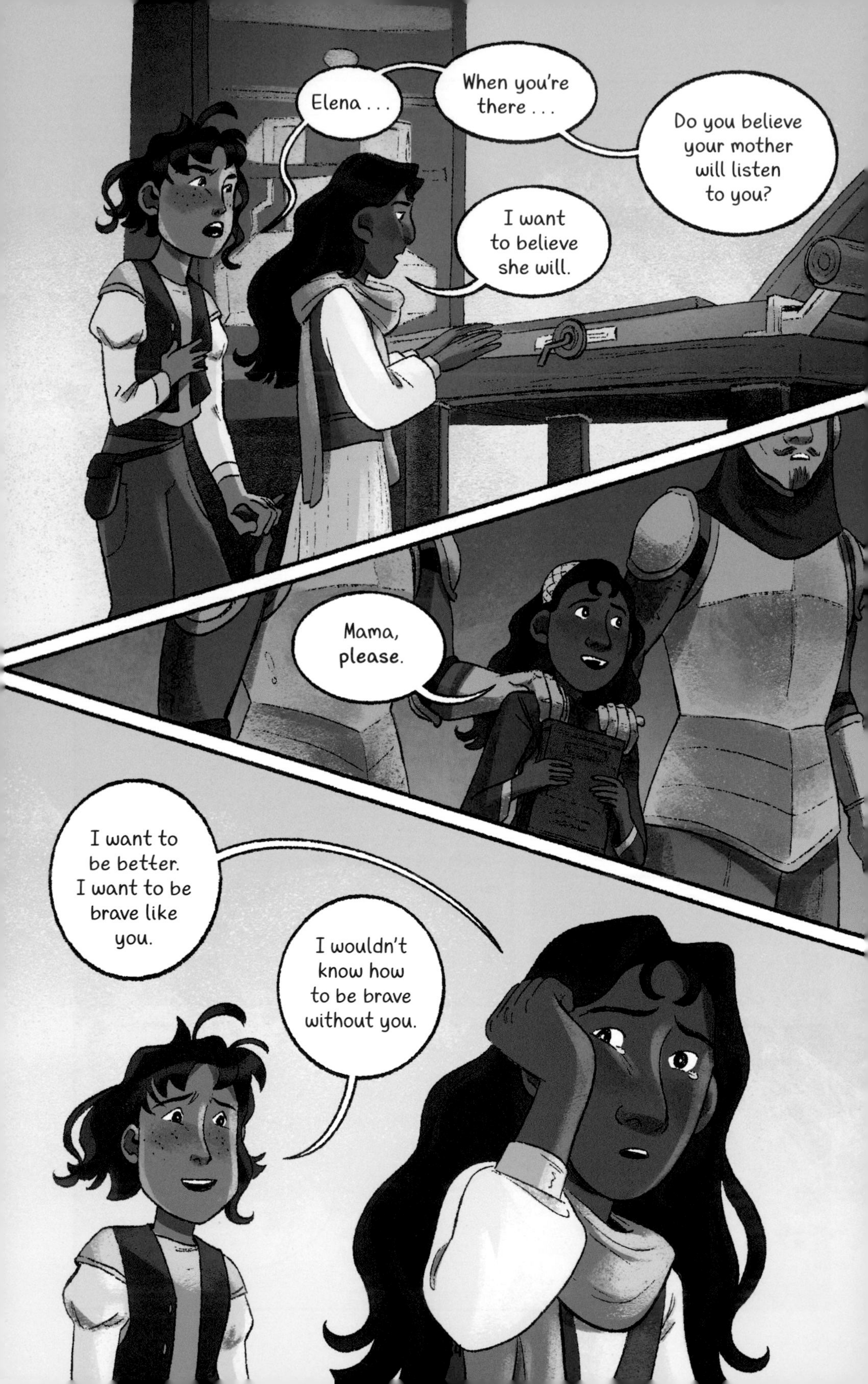
Elena . . .
When you're there . . .
Do you believe your mother will listen to you?
I want to believe she will.
Mama, please.
I want to be better. I want to be brave like you.
I wouldn't know how to be brave without you.

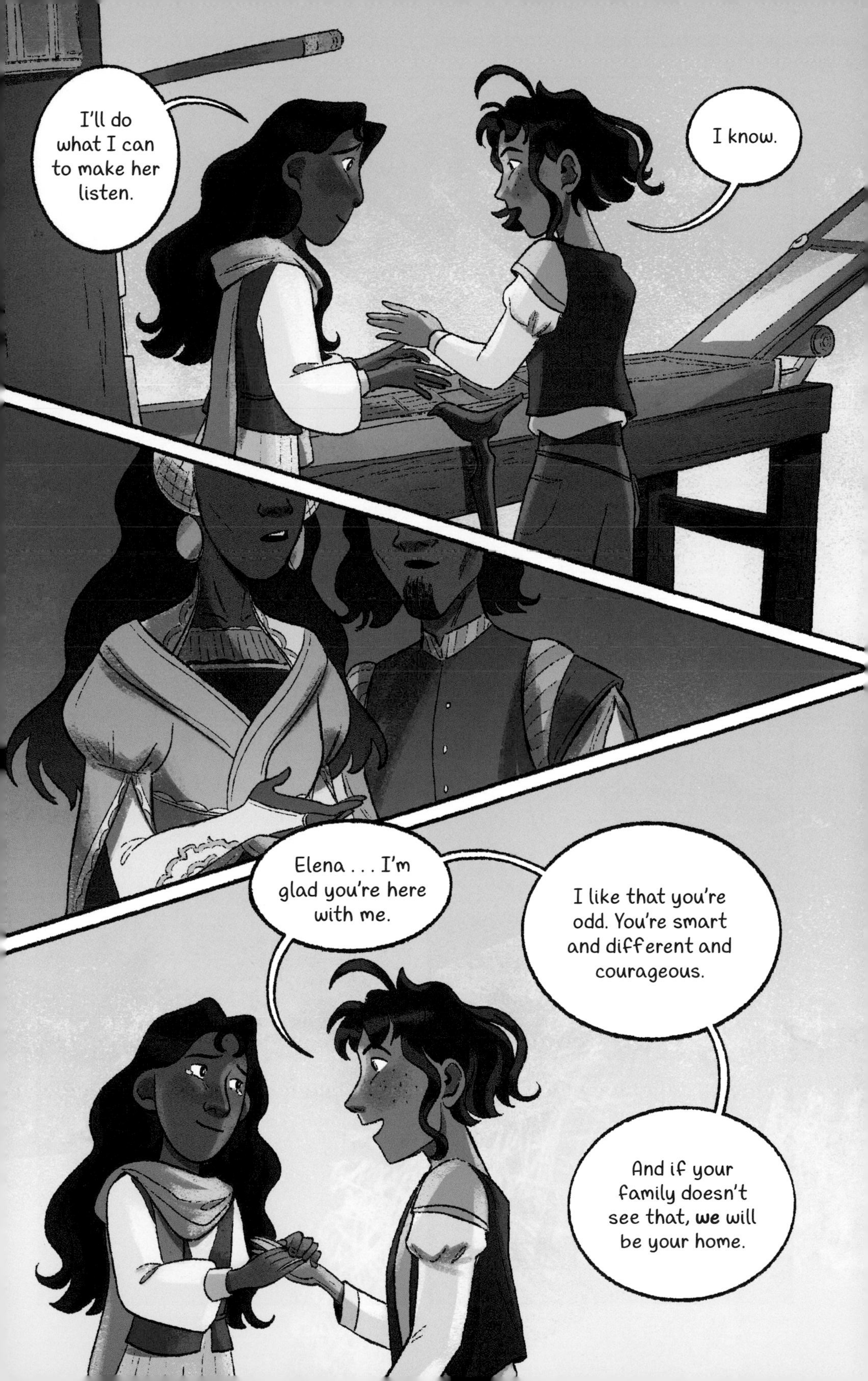
I'll do what I can to make her listen.
I know.
Elena . . . I'm glad you're here with me.
I like that you're odd. You're smart and different and courageous.
And if your family doesn't see that, **we** will be your home.

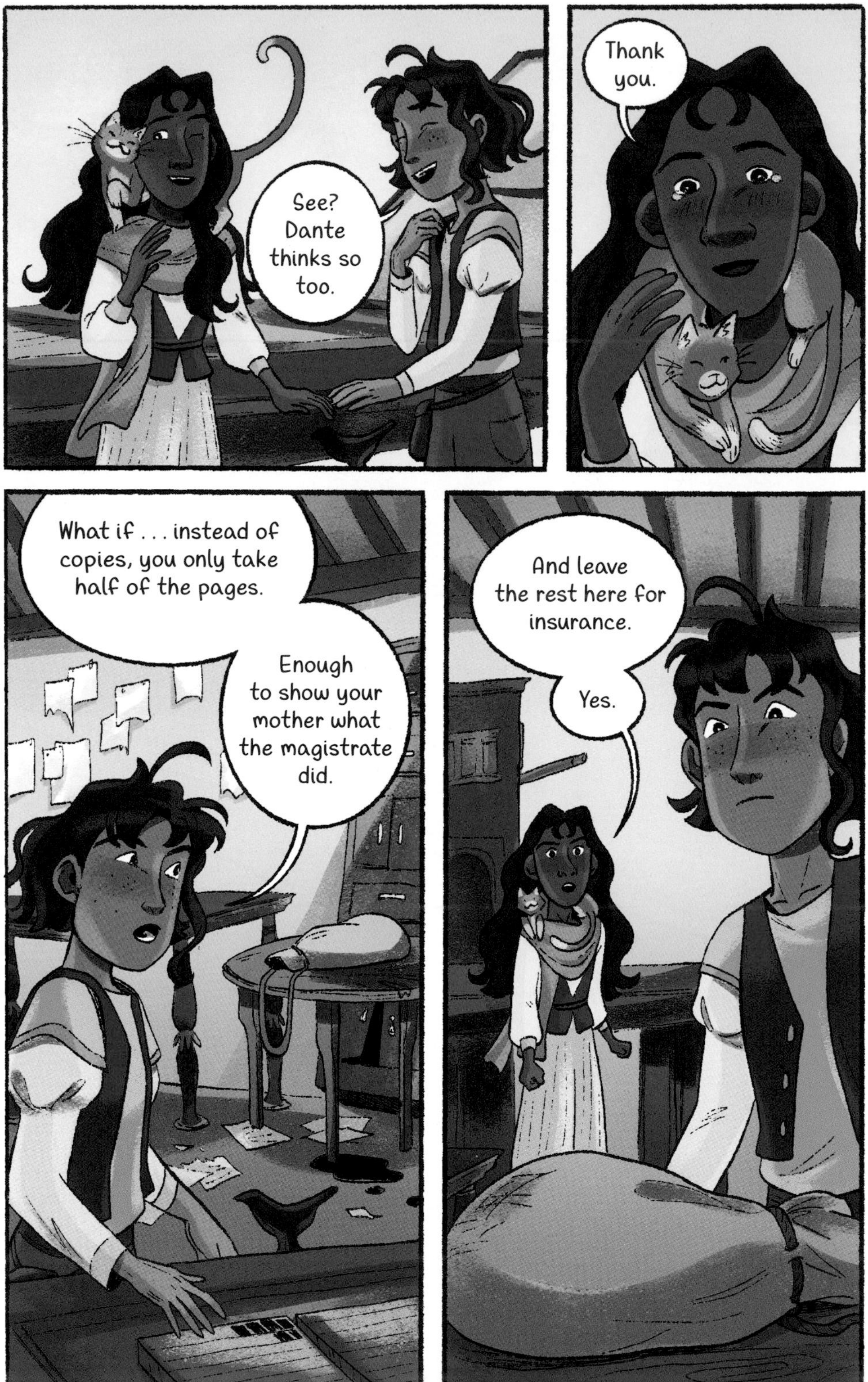
See? Dante thinks so too.
Thank you.
What if . . . instead of copies, you only take half of the pages.
Enough to show your mother what the magistrate did.
And leave the rest here for insurance.
Yes.

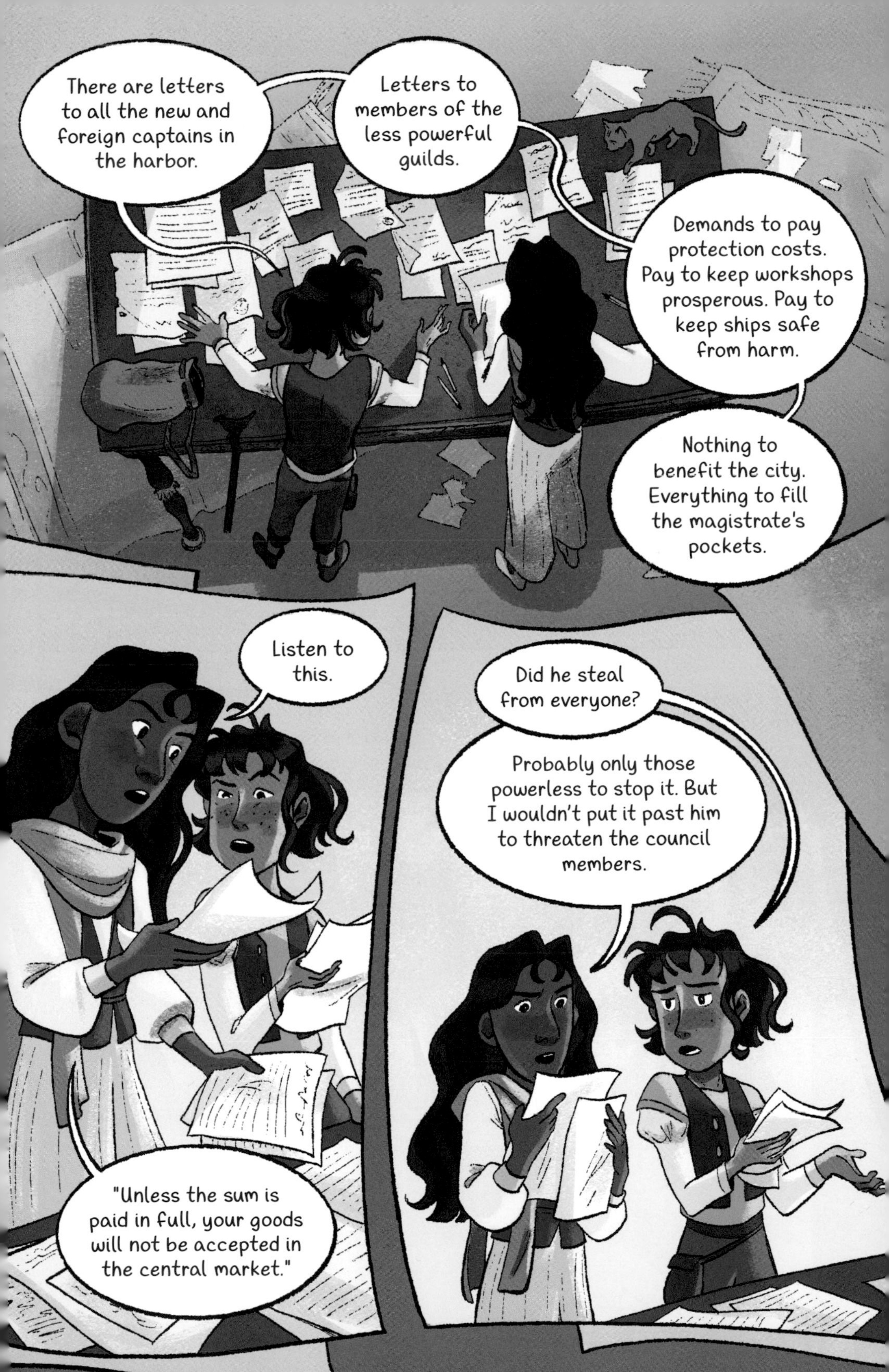
There are letters to all the new and foreign captains in the harbor.
Letters to members of the less powerful guilds.
Demands to pay protection costs. Pay to keep workshops prosperous. Pay to keep ships safe from harm.
Nothing to benefit the city. Everything to fill the magistrate's pockets.
Listen to this.
"Unless the sum is paid in full, your goods will not be accepted in the central market."
Did he steal from everyone?
Probably only those powerless to stop it. But I wouldn't put it past him to threaten the council members.

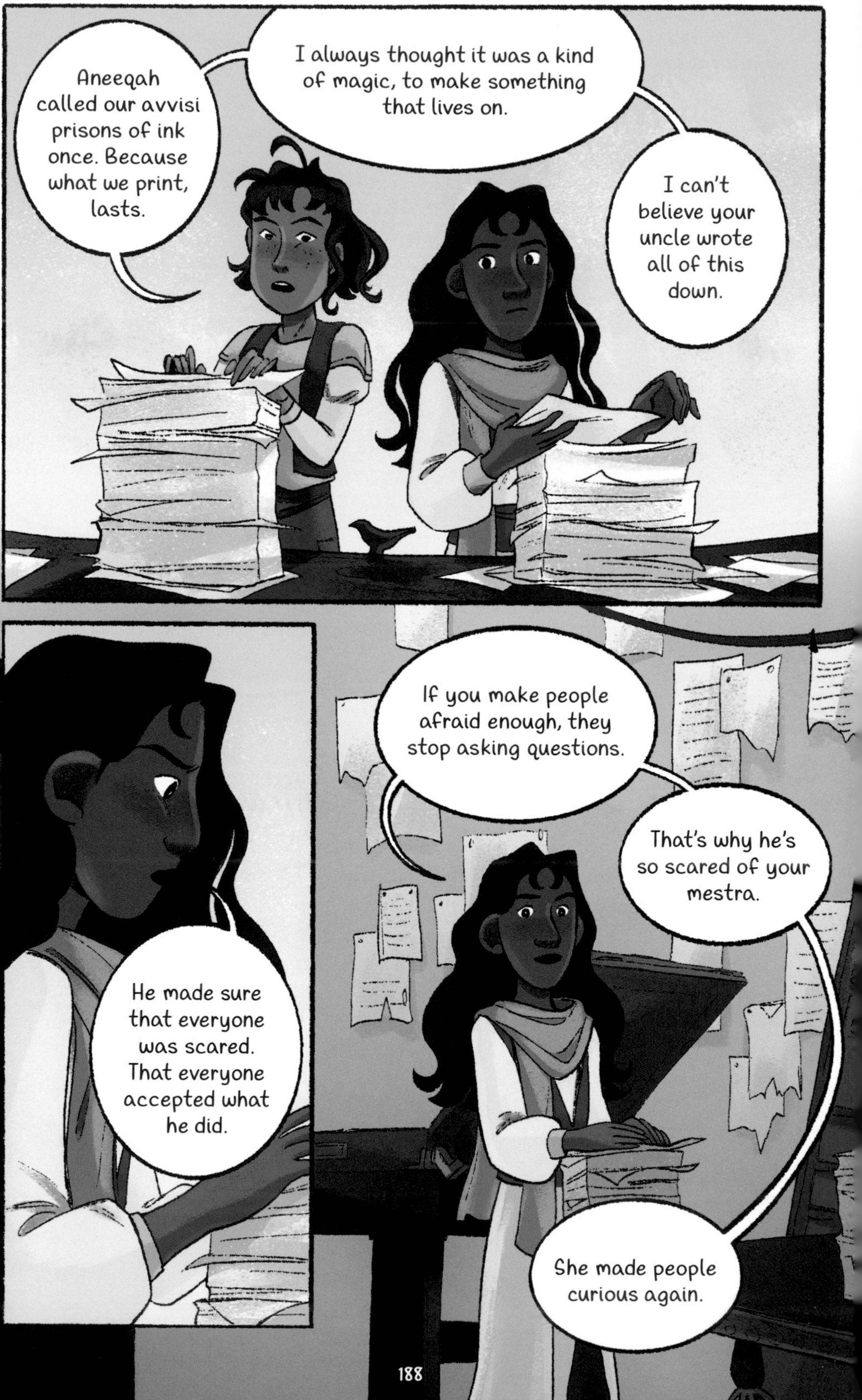
Aneeqah called our avvisi prisons of ink once. Because what we print, lasts.
I always thought it was a kind of magic, to make something that lives on.
I can't believe your uncle wrote all of this down.
He made sure that everyone was scared. That everyone accepted what he did.
If you make people afraid enough, they stop asking questions.
That's why he's so scared of your mestra.
She made people curious again.

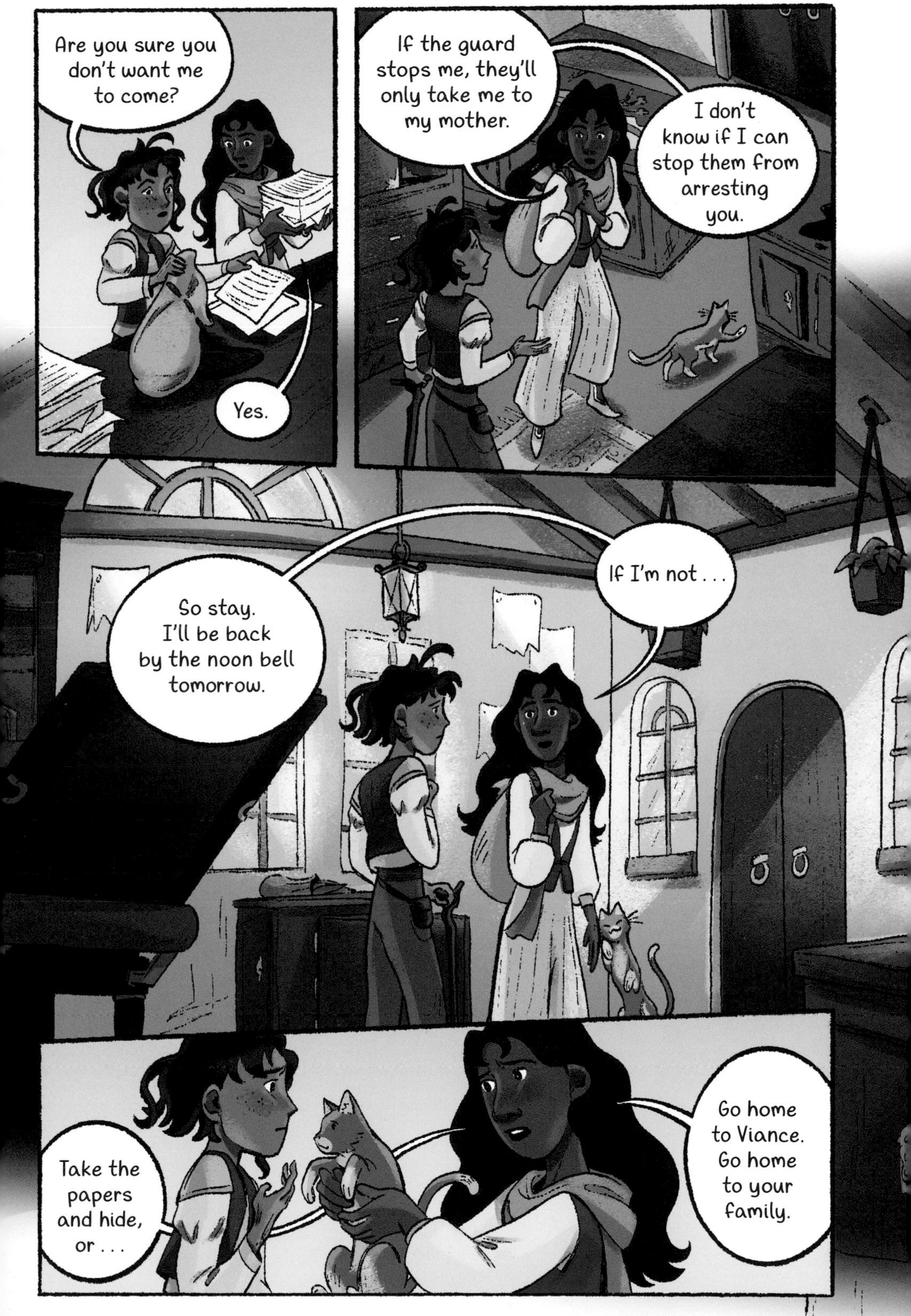

Are you sure you don't want me to come?
Yes.
If the guard stops me, they'll only take me to my mother.
I don't know if I can stop them from arresting you.
So stay. I'll be back by the noon bell tomorrow.
If I'm not . . .
Take the papers and hide, or . . .
Go home to Viance. Go home to your family.

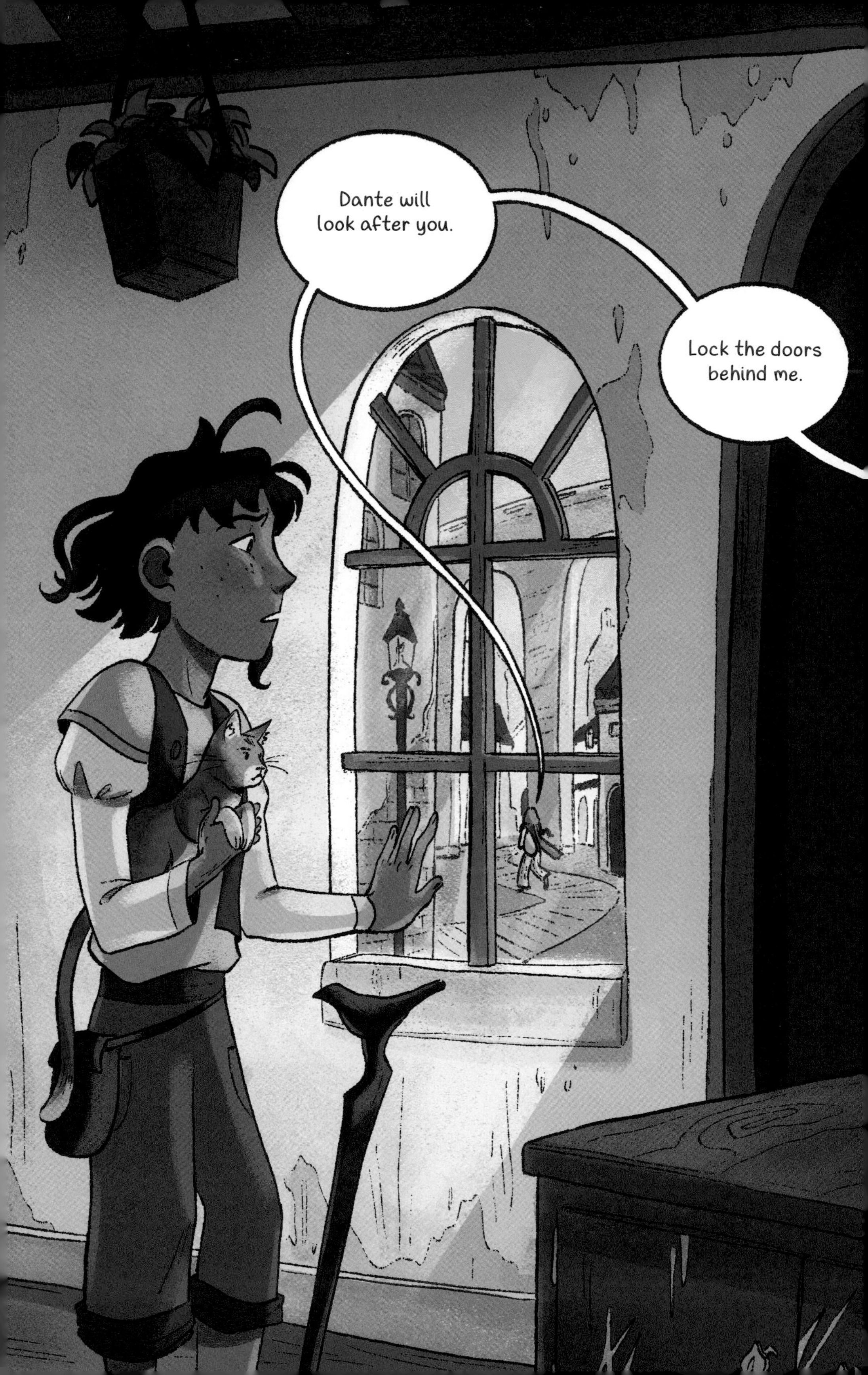
Dante will look after you.
Lock the doors behind me.

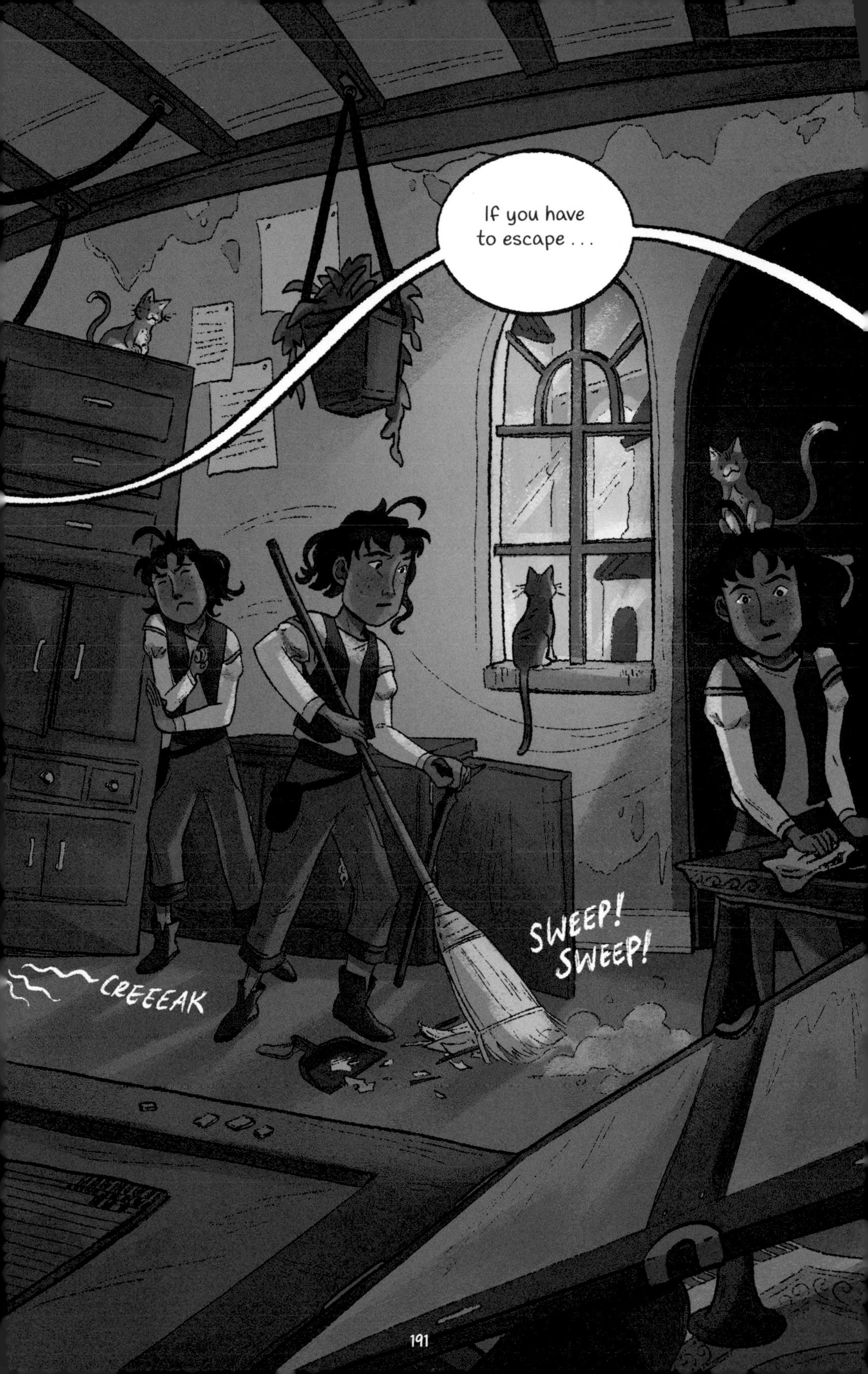
If you have to escape . . .
CREEEAK
SWEEP! SWEEP!

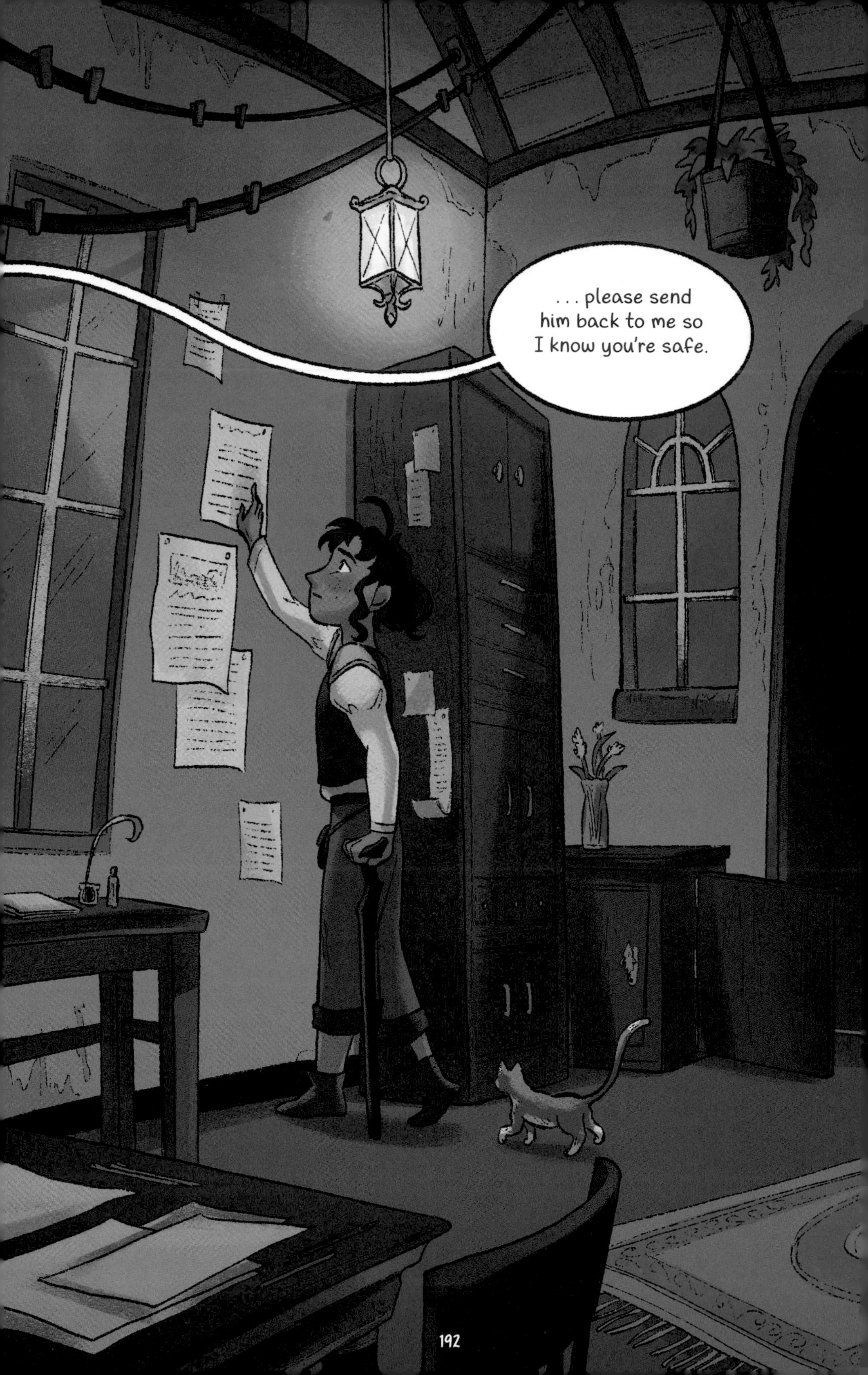
. . . please send him back to me so I know you're safe.

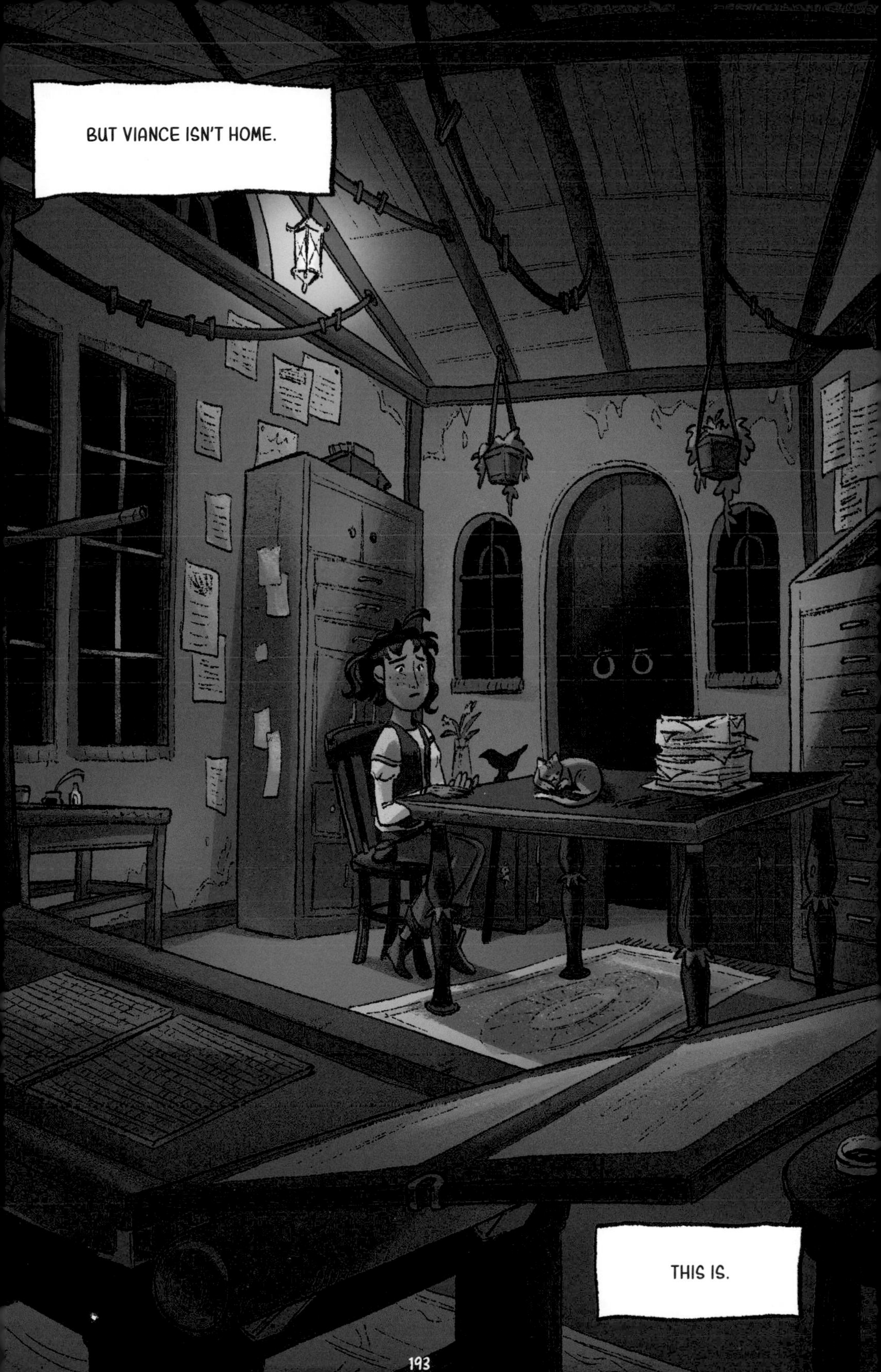
BUT VIANCE ISN'T HOME.
THIS IS.

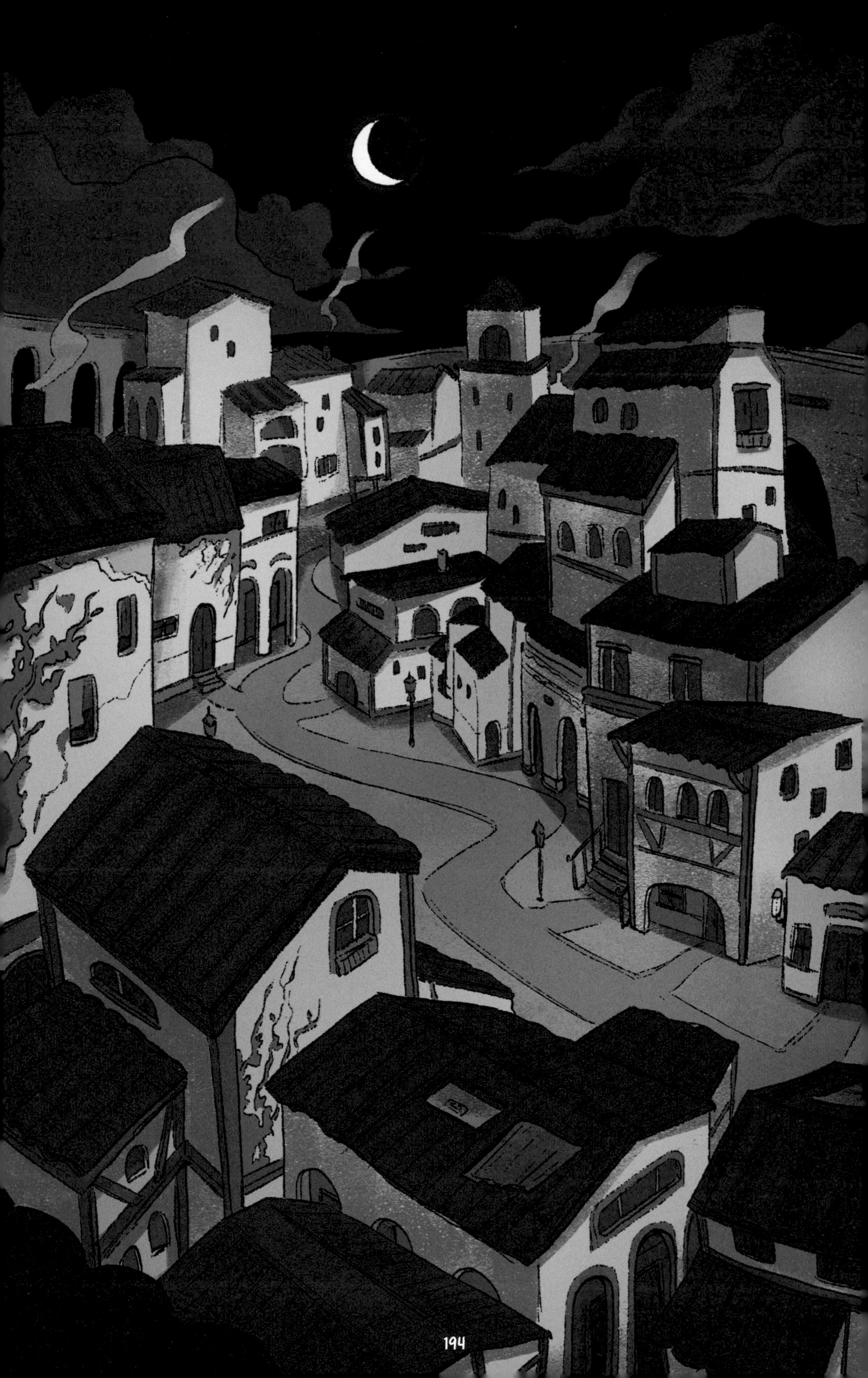

CHAPTER SEVEN

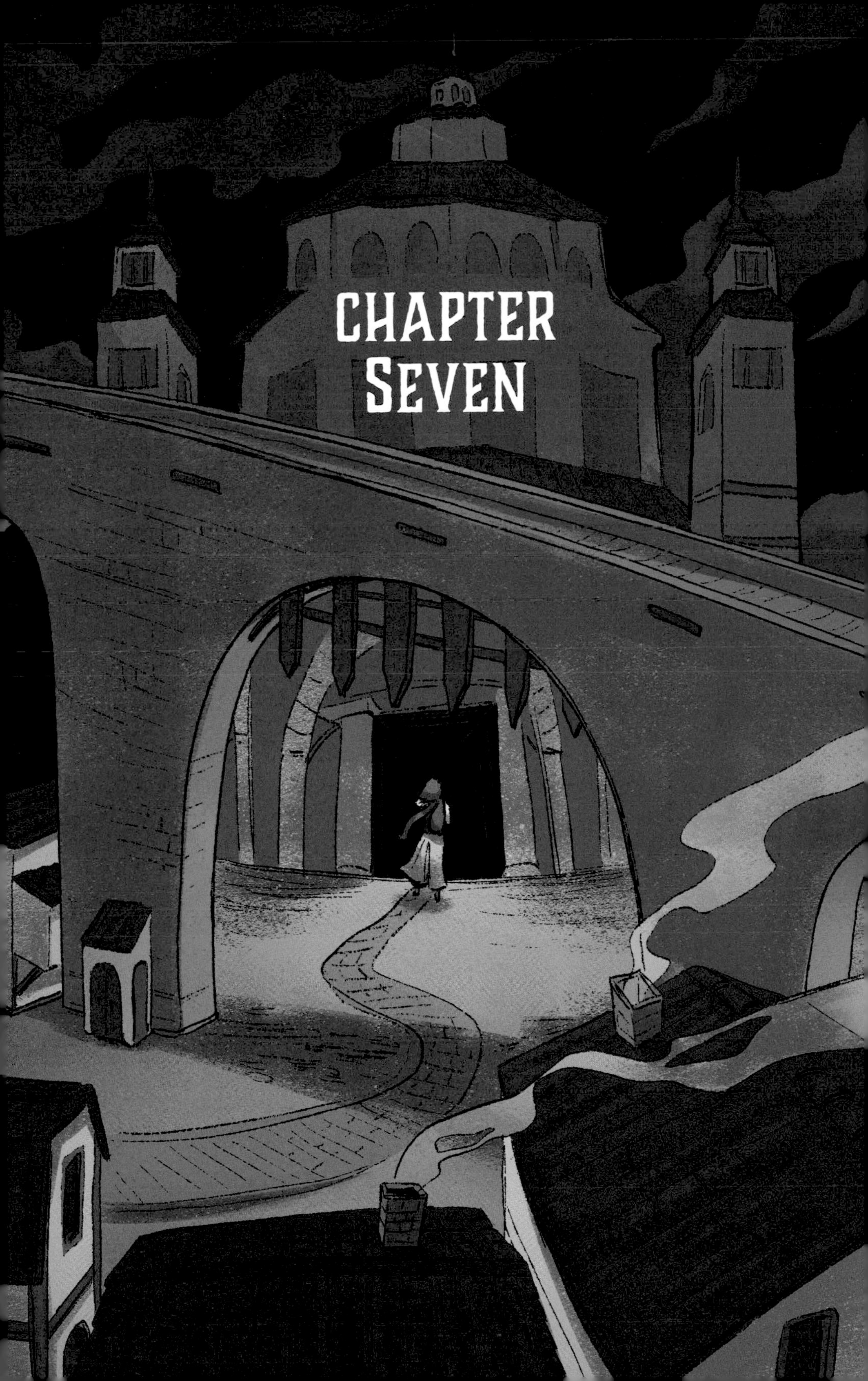

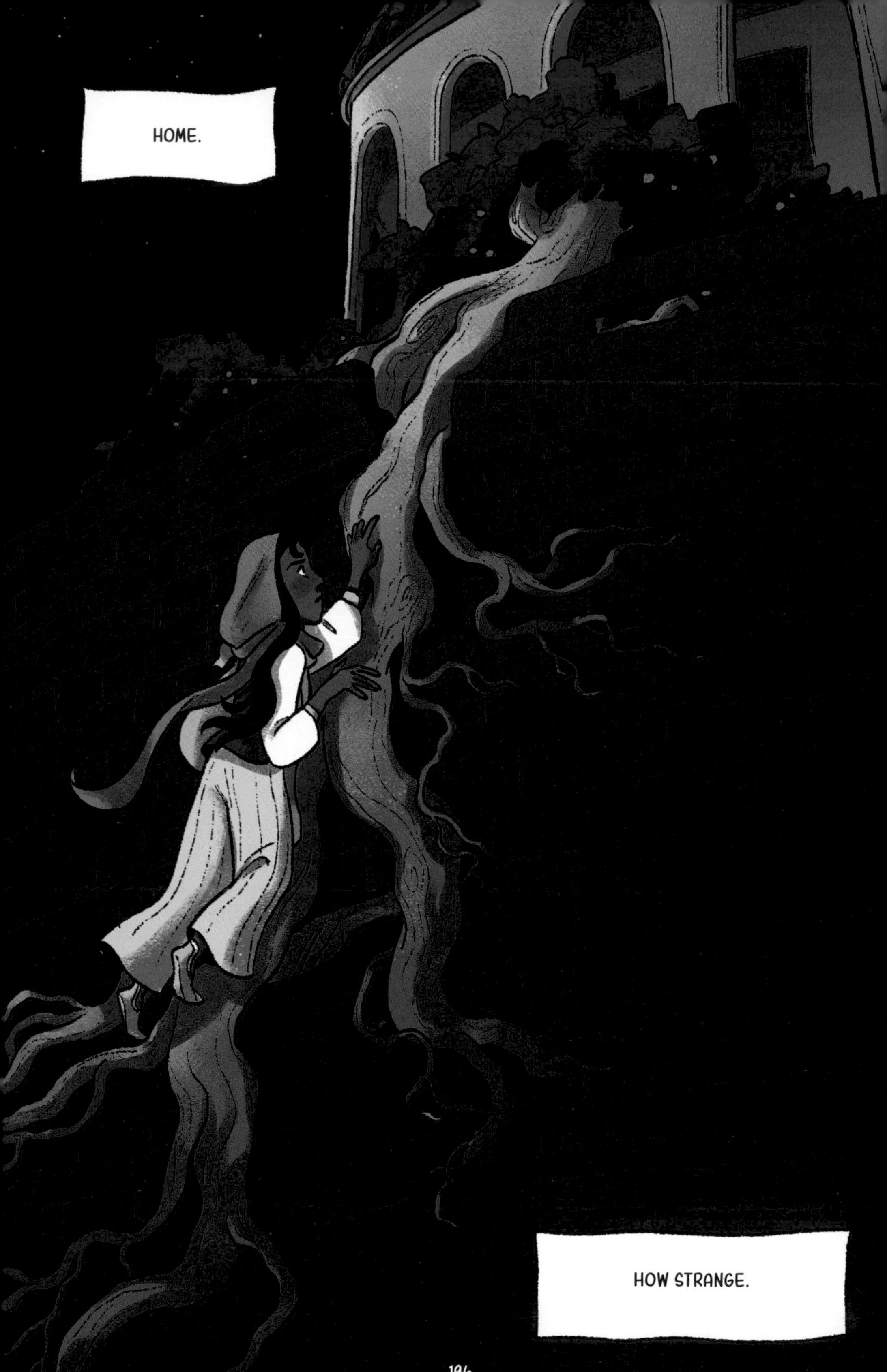
HOME.
HOW STRANGE.

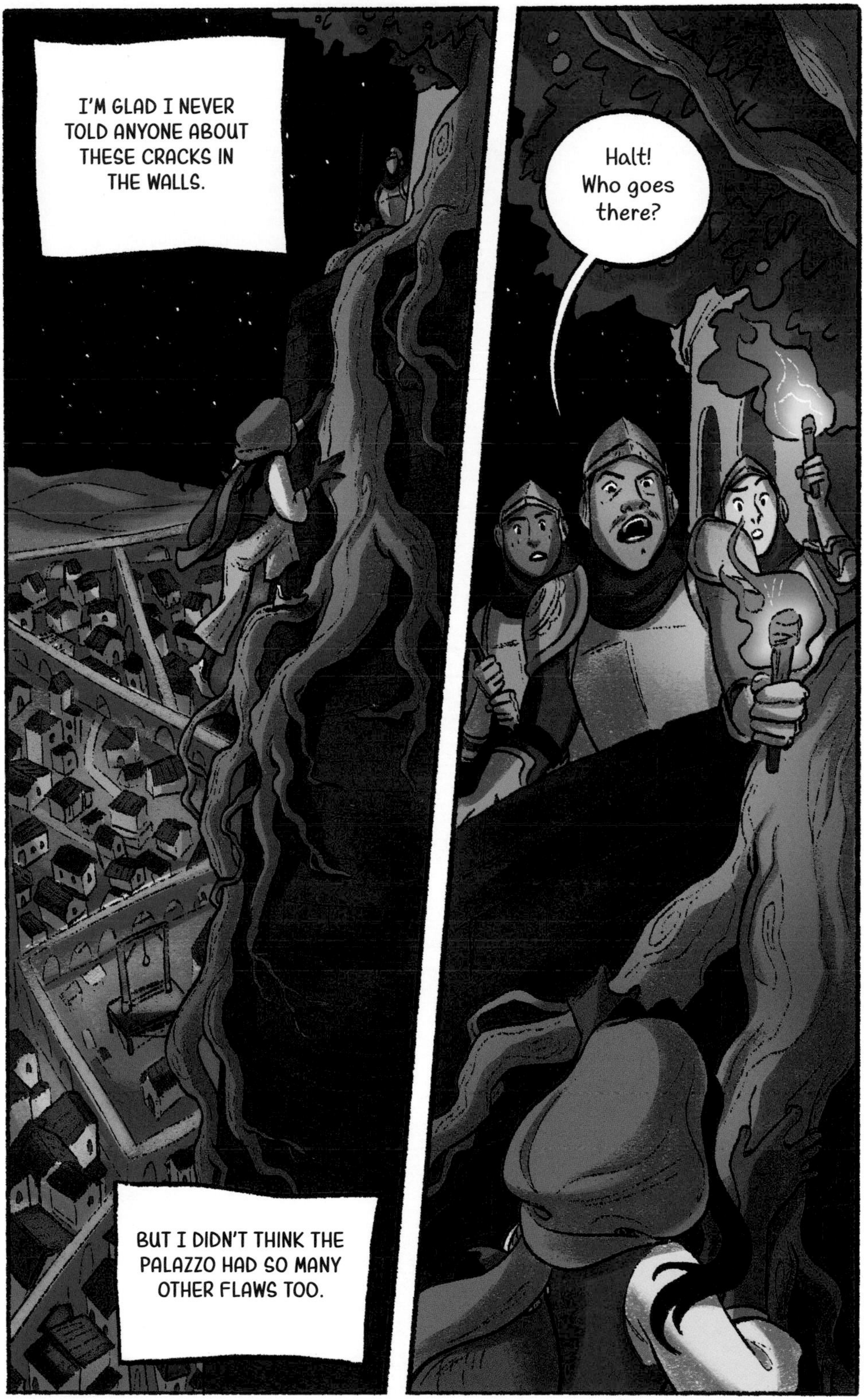
I'M GLAD I NEVER TOLD ANYONE ABOUT THESE CRACKS IN THE WALLS.
BUT I DIDN'T THINK THE PALAZZO HAD SO MANY OTHER FLAWS TOO.
Halt! Who goes there?

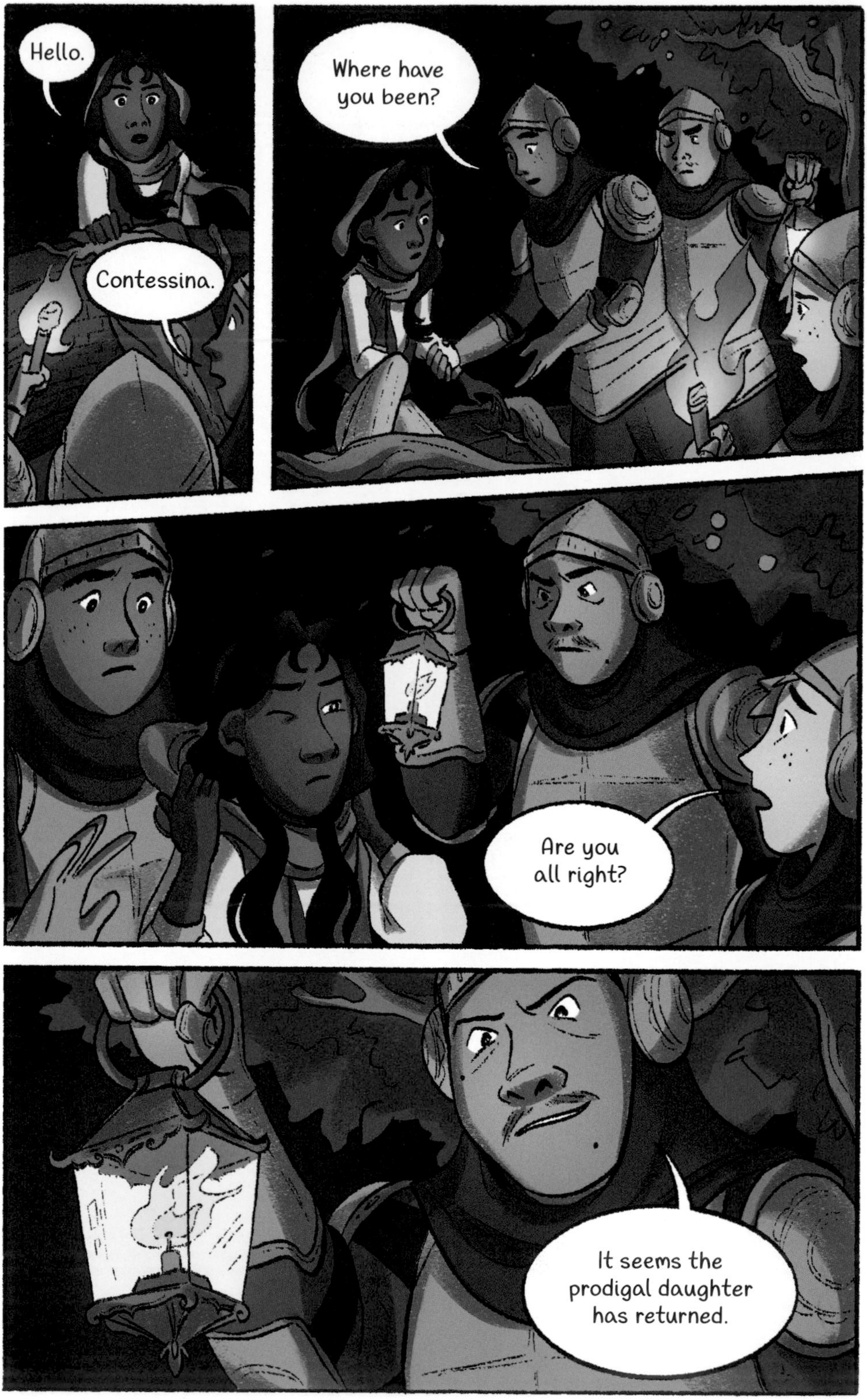
Hello.
Contessina.
Where have you been?
Are you all right?
It seems the prodigal daughter has returned.

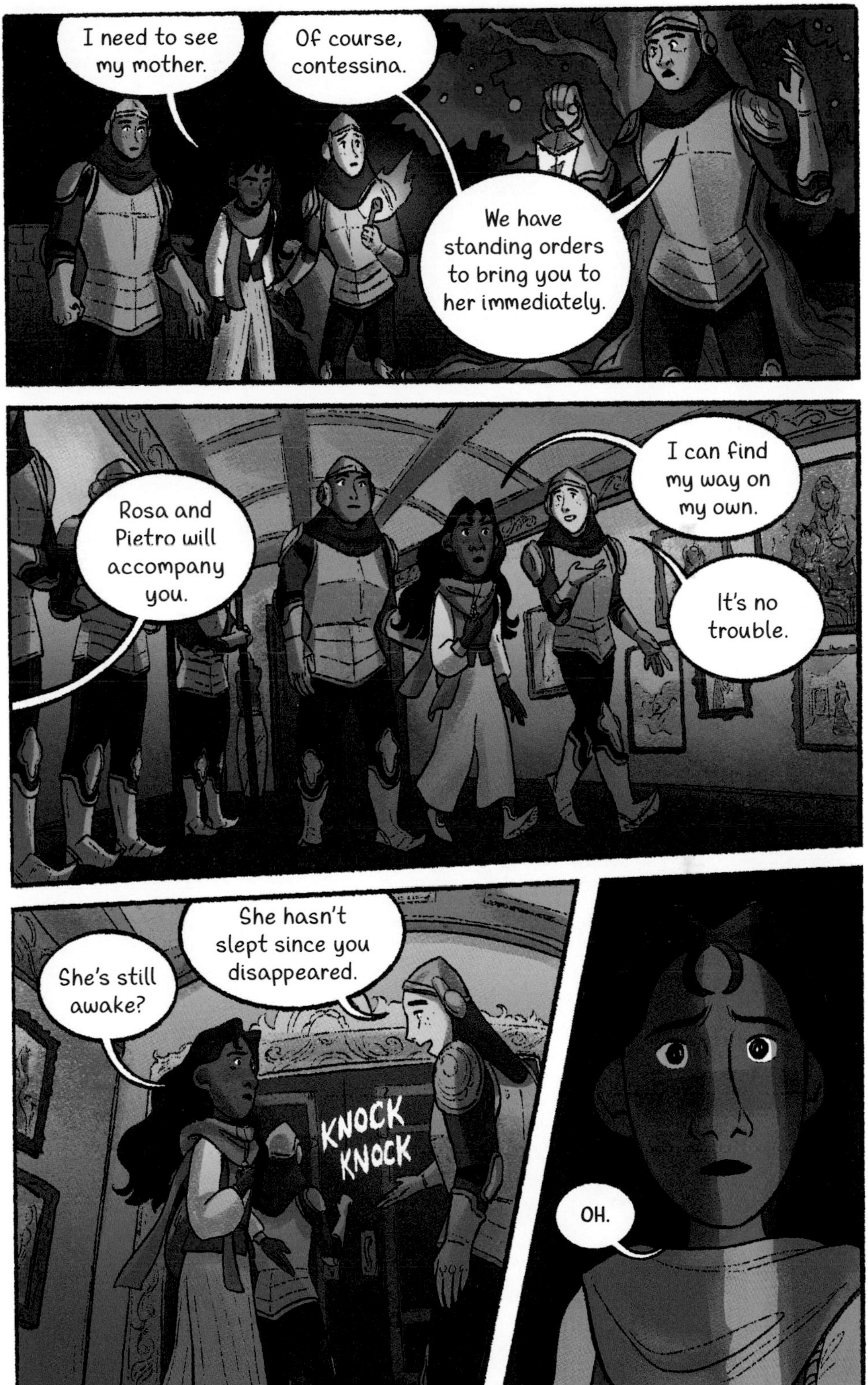

I need to see my mother.
Of course, contessina.
We have standing orders to bring you to her immediately.
Rosa and Pietro will accompany you.
I can find my way on my own.
It's no trouble.
She's still awake?
She hasn't slept since you disappeared.
KNOCK KNOCK
OH.

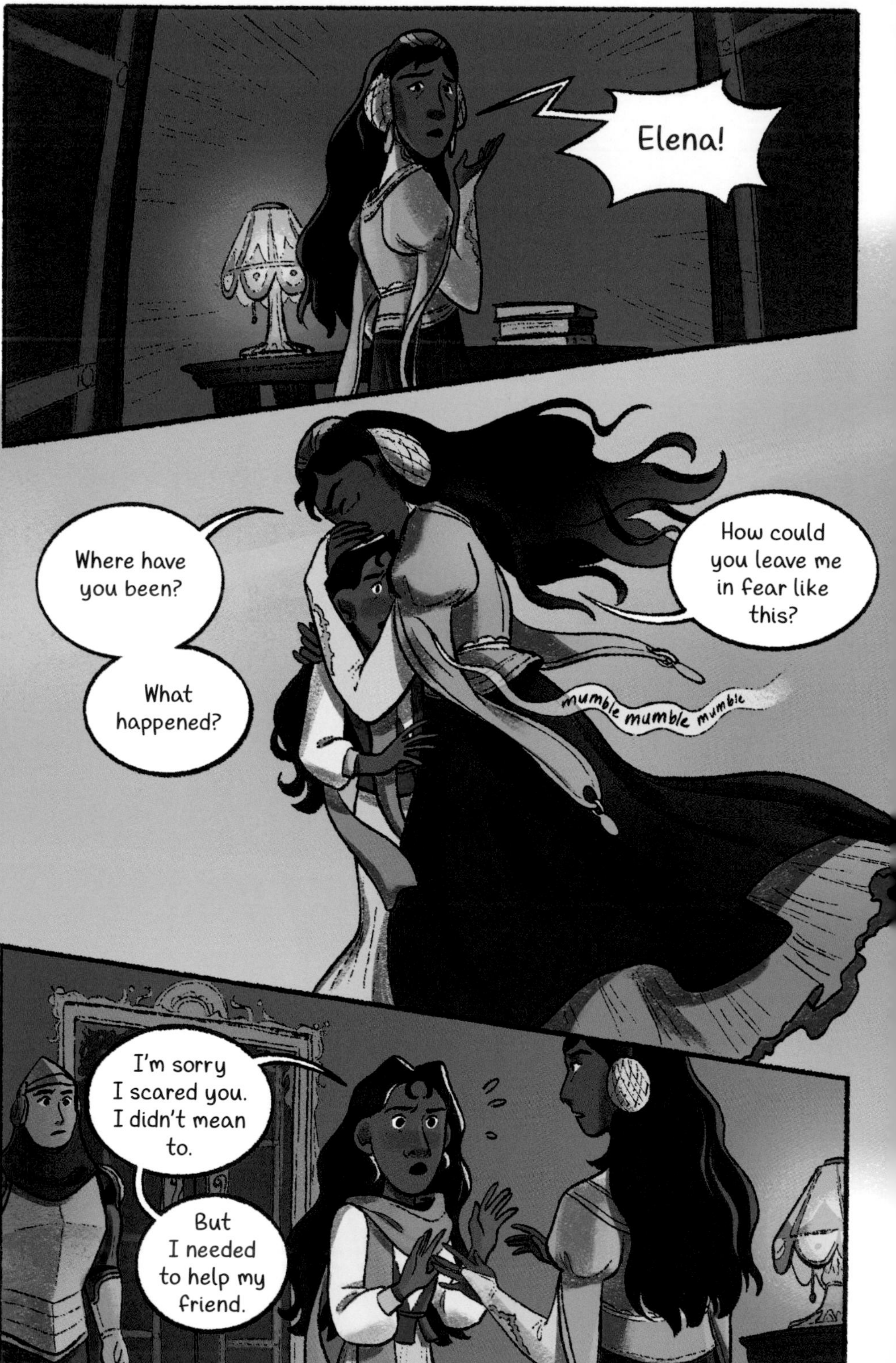
Elena!
Where have you been?
What happened?
How could you leave me in fear like this?
mumble mumble mumble
I'm sorry I scared you. I didn't mean to.
But I needed to help my friend.

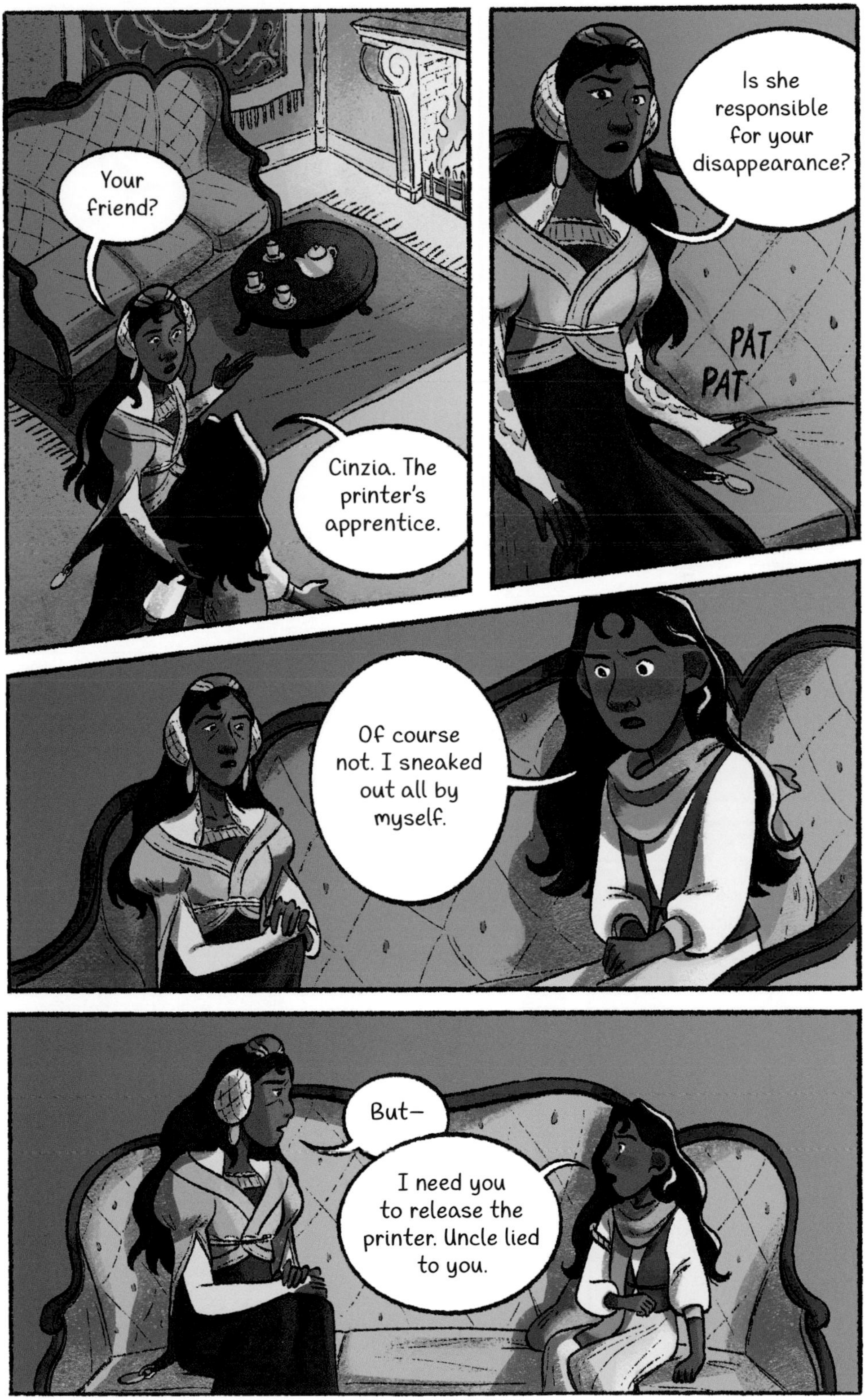
Your friend?
Cinzia. The printer's apprentice.
Is she responsible for your disappearance?
PAT PAT
Of course not. I sneaked out all by myself.
But—
I need you to release the printer. Uncle lied to you.

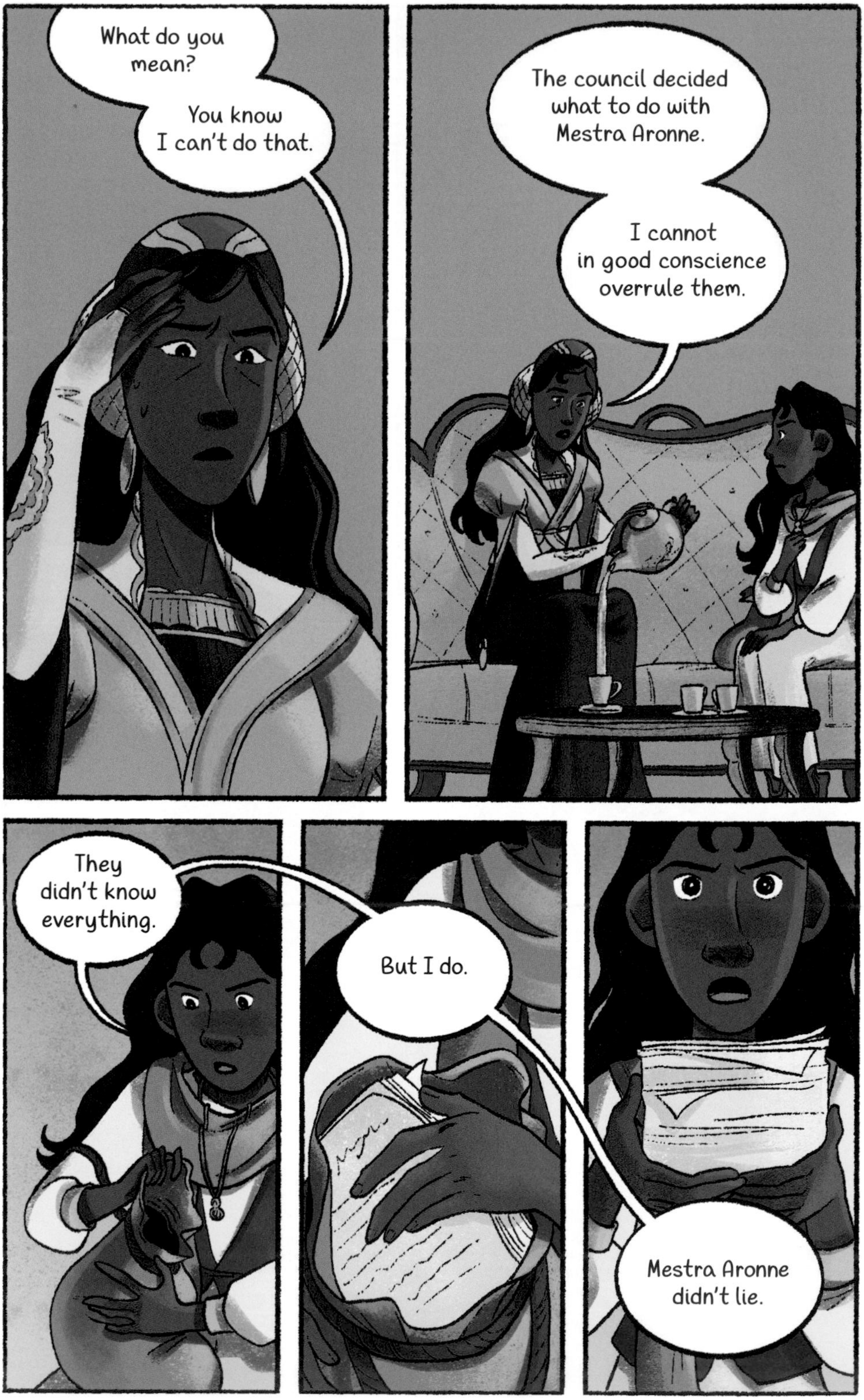
What do you mean?
You know I can't do that.
The council decided what to do with Mestra Aronne.
I cannot in good conscience overrule them.
They didn't know everything.
But I do.
Mestra Aronne didn't lie.

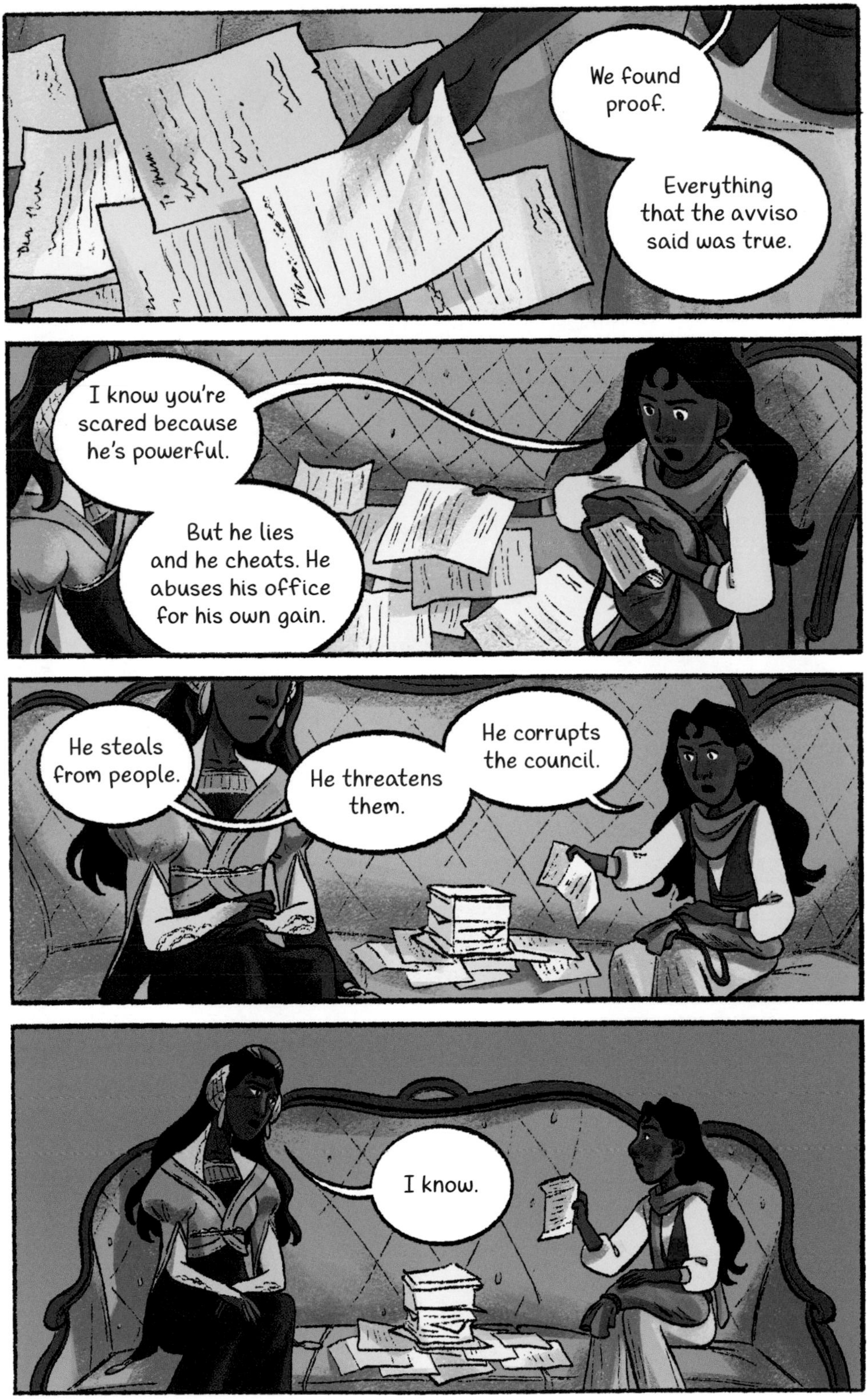
We found proof.
Everything that the avviso said was true.
I know you're scared because he's powerful.
But he lies and he cheats. He abuses his office for his own gain.
He steals from people.
He threatens them.
He corrupts the council.
I know.

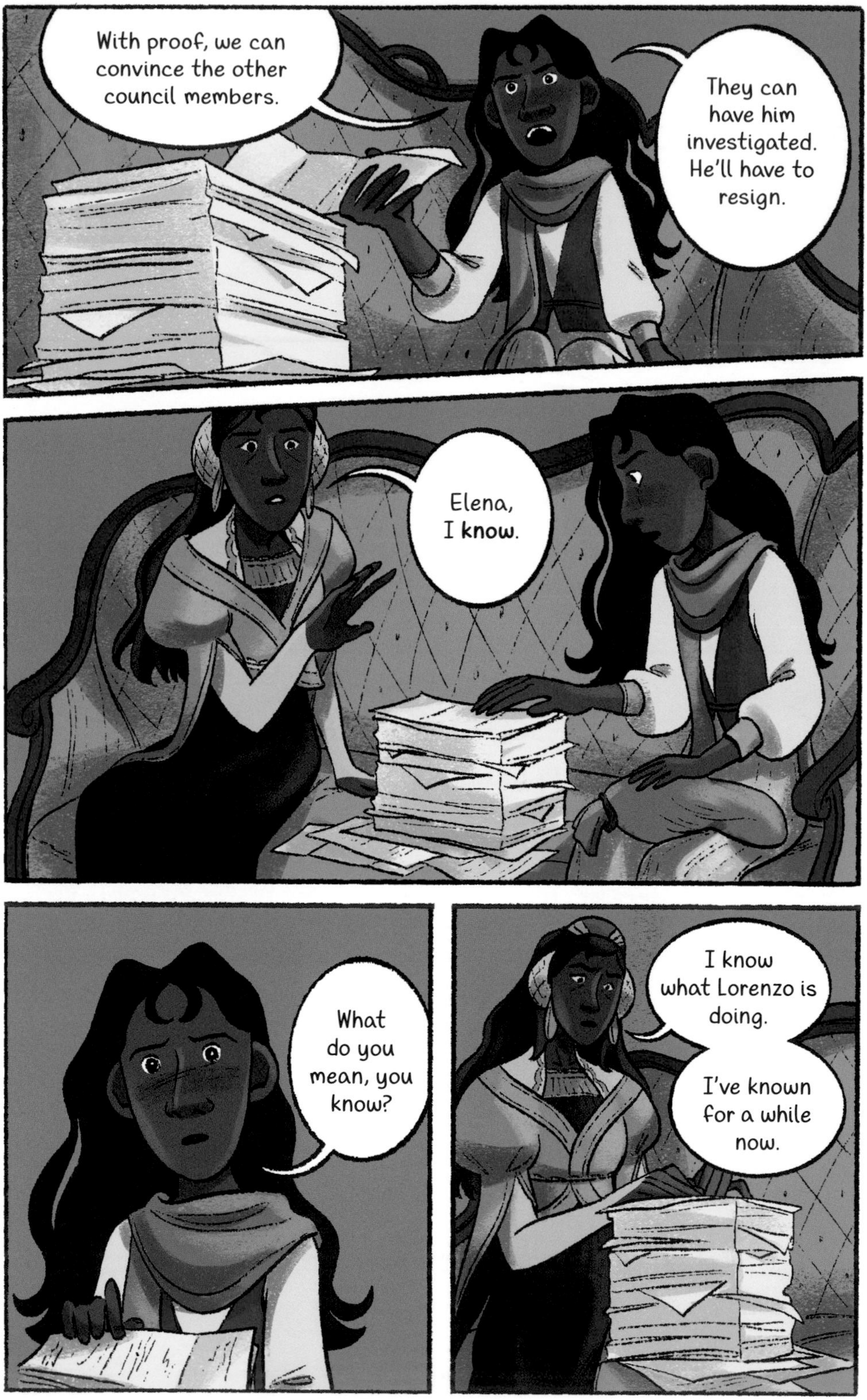

With proof, we can convince the other council members.
They can have him investigated. He'll have to resign.
Elena, I **know**.
What do you mean, you know?
I know what Lorenzo is doing.
I've known for a while now.

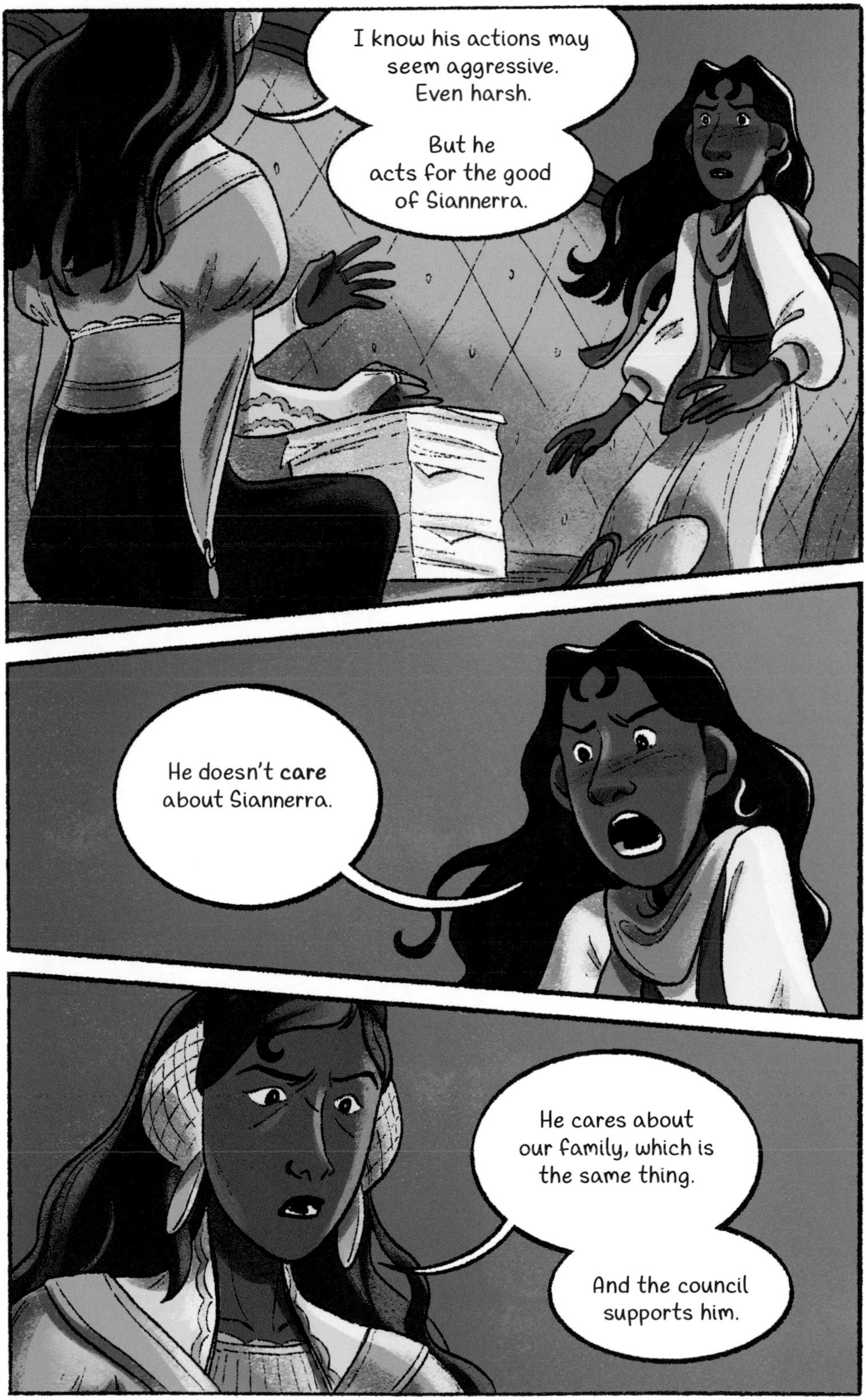
I know his actions may seem aggressive. Even harsh.
But he acts for the good of Siannerra.
He doesn't **care** about Siannerra.
He cares about our family, which is the same thing.
And the council supports him.

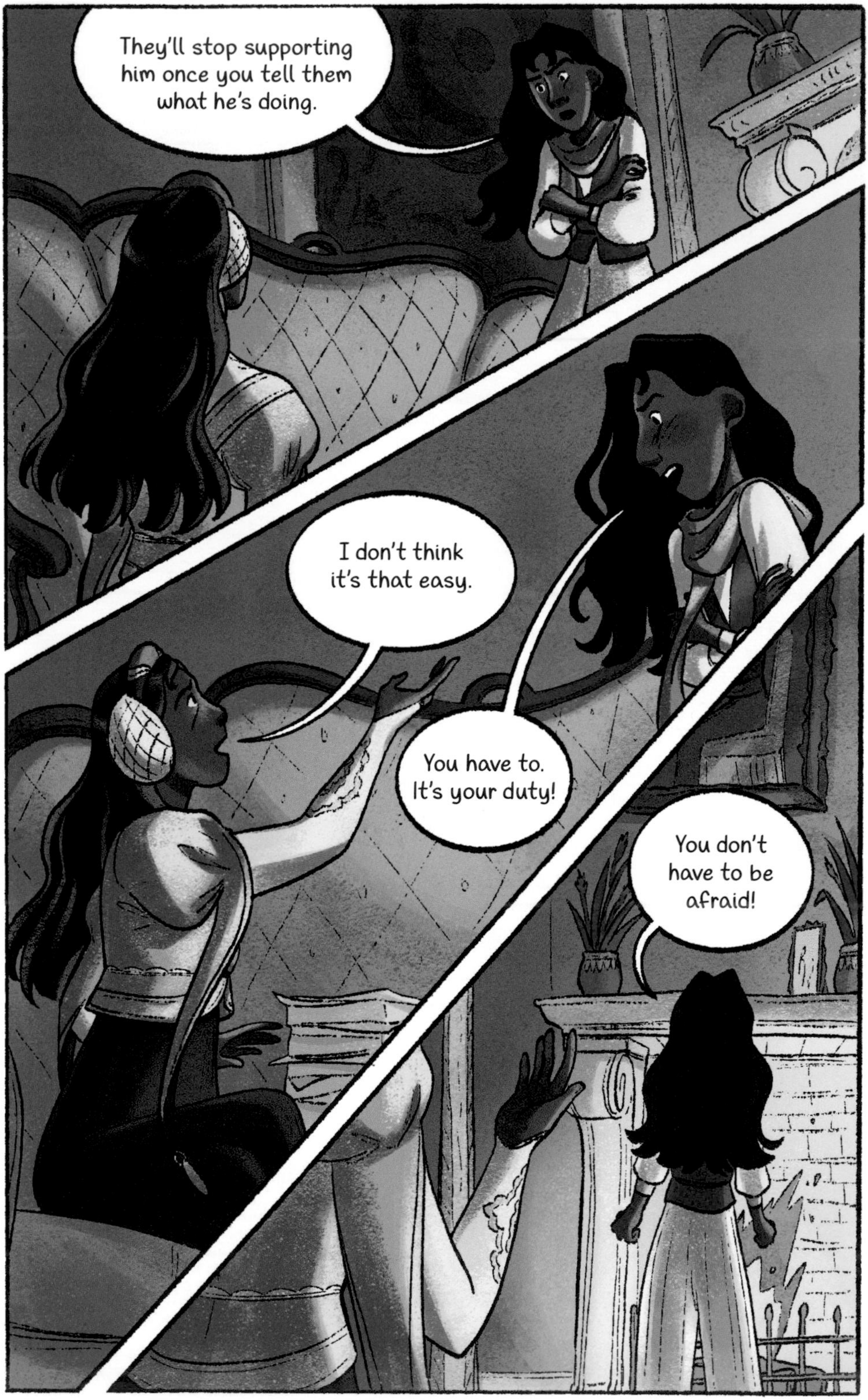
They'll stop supporting him once you tell them what he's doing.
I don't think it's that easy.
You have to. It's your duty!
You don't have to be afraid!

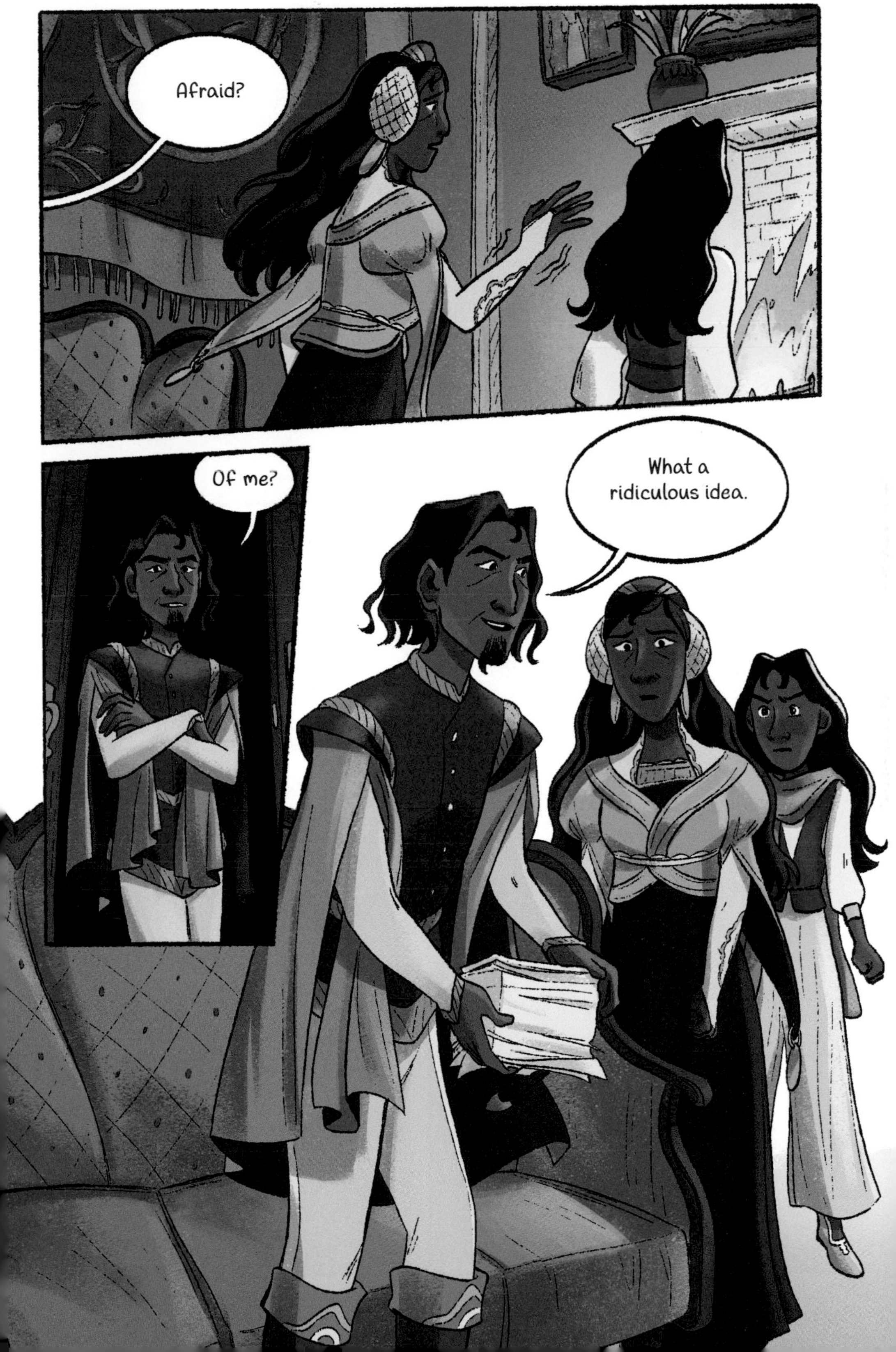
Afraid?
Of me?
What a ridiculous idea.

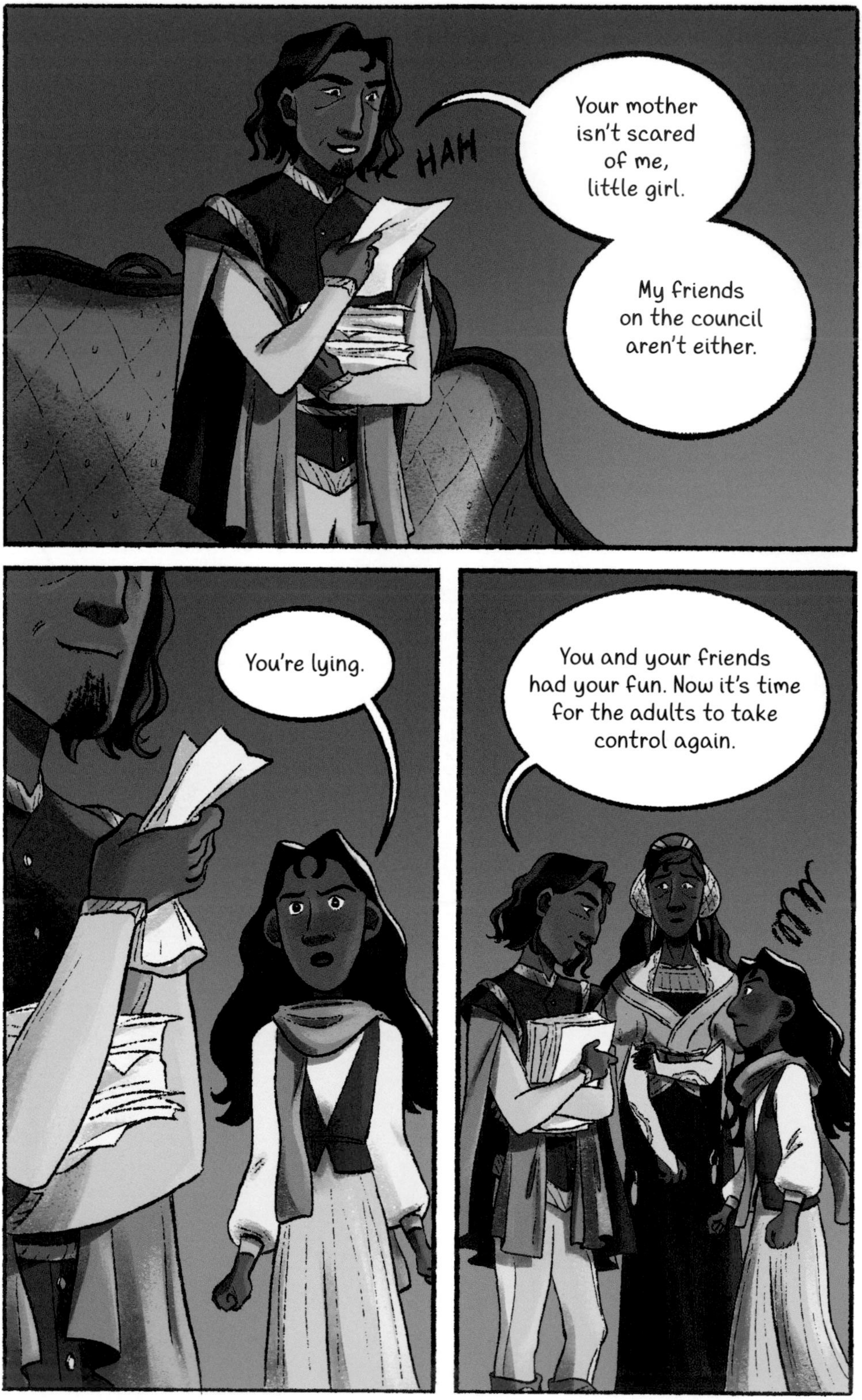
HAH
Your mother isn't scared of me, little girl.
My friends on the council aren't either.
You're lying.
You and your friends had your fun. Now it's time for the adults to take control again.

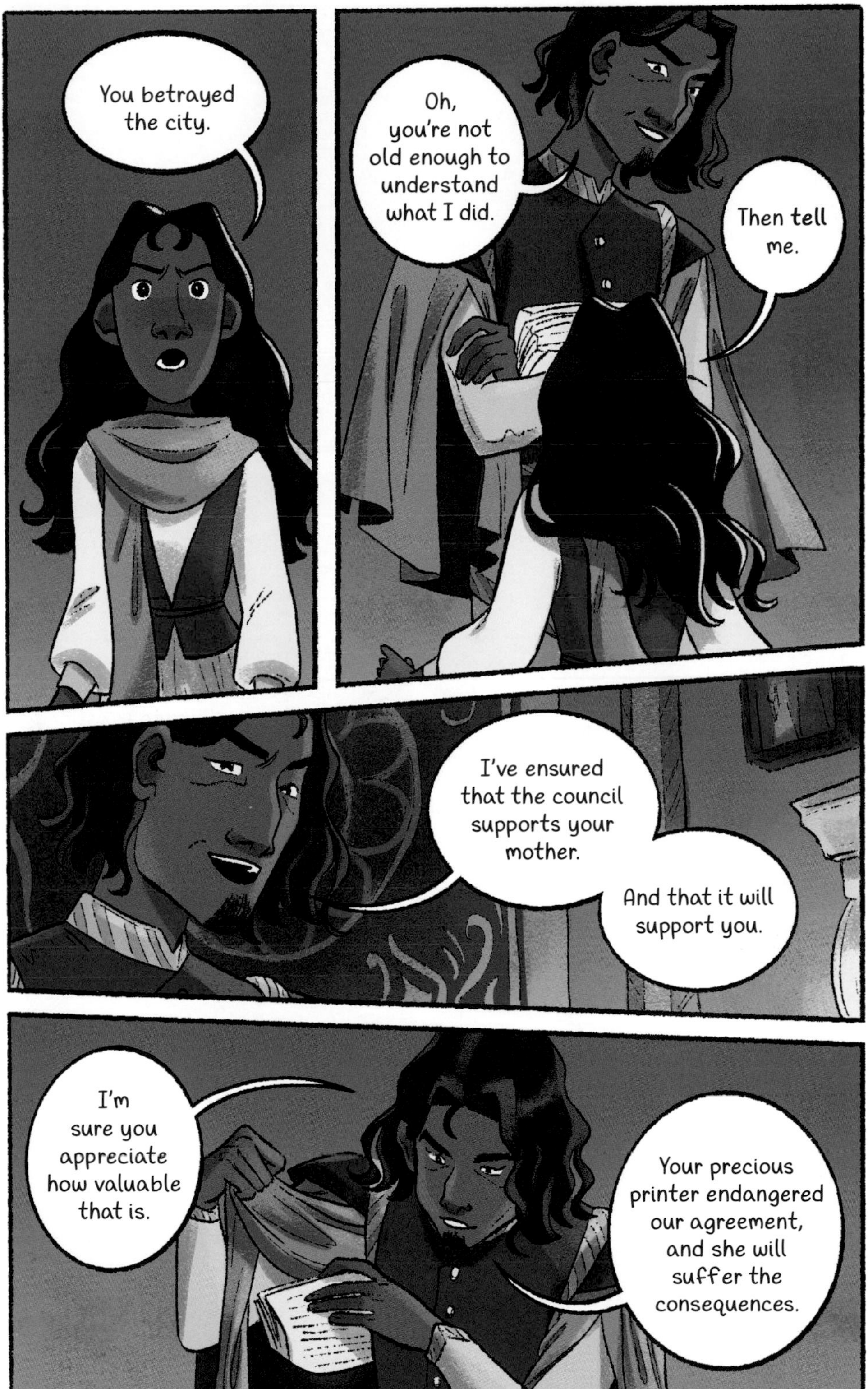
You betrayed the city.
Oh, you're not old enough to understand what I did.
Then **tell** me.
I've ensured that the council supports your mother.
And that it will support you.
I'm sure you appreciate how valuable that is.
Your precious printer endangered our agreement, and she will suffer the consequences.

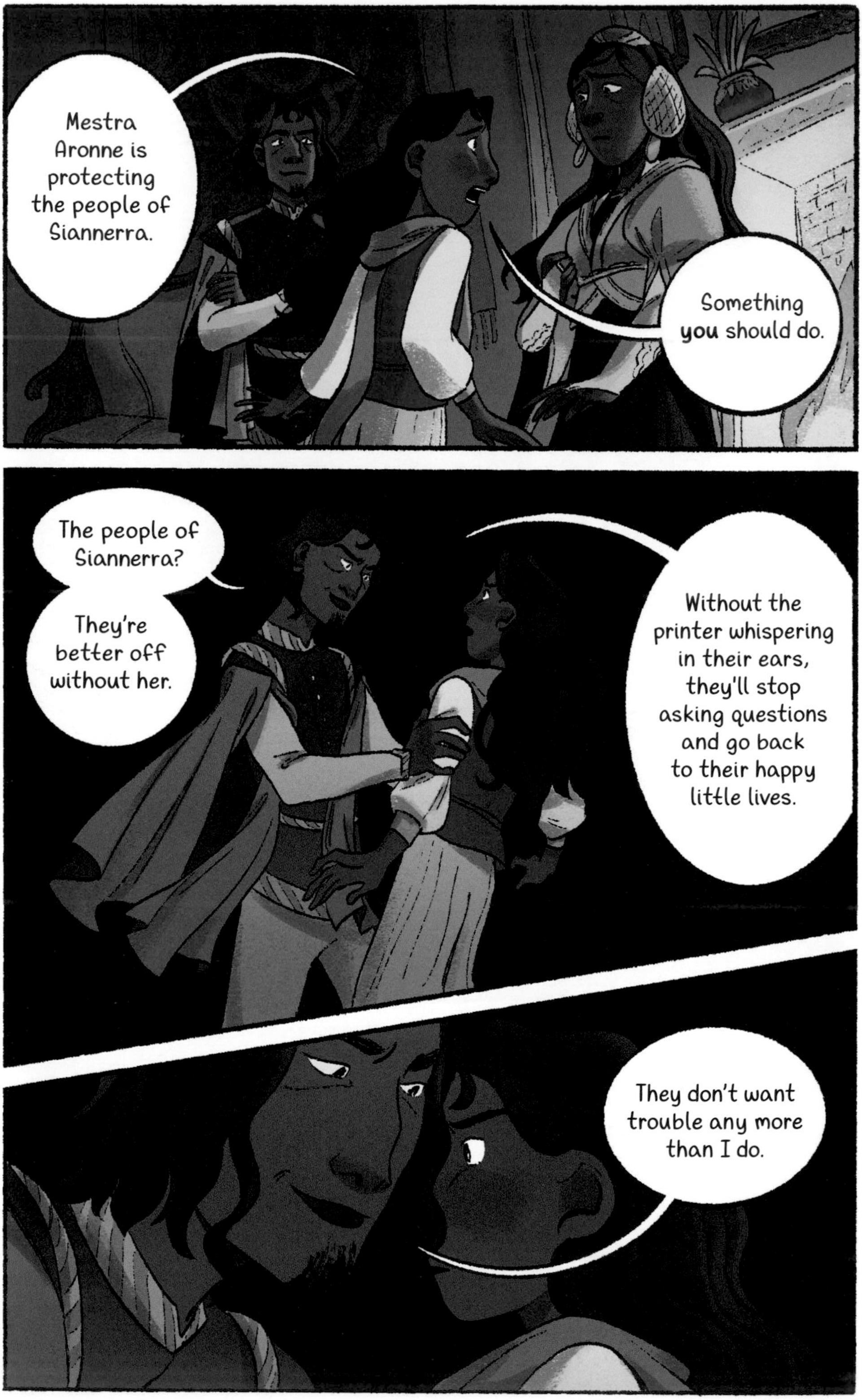

Mestra Aronne is protecting the people of Siannerra.
Something **you** should do.
The people of Siannerra?
They're better off without her.
Without the printer whispering in their ears, they'll stop asking questions and go back to their happy little lives.
They don't want trouble any more than I do.

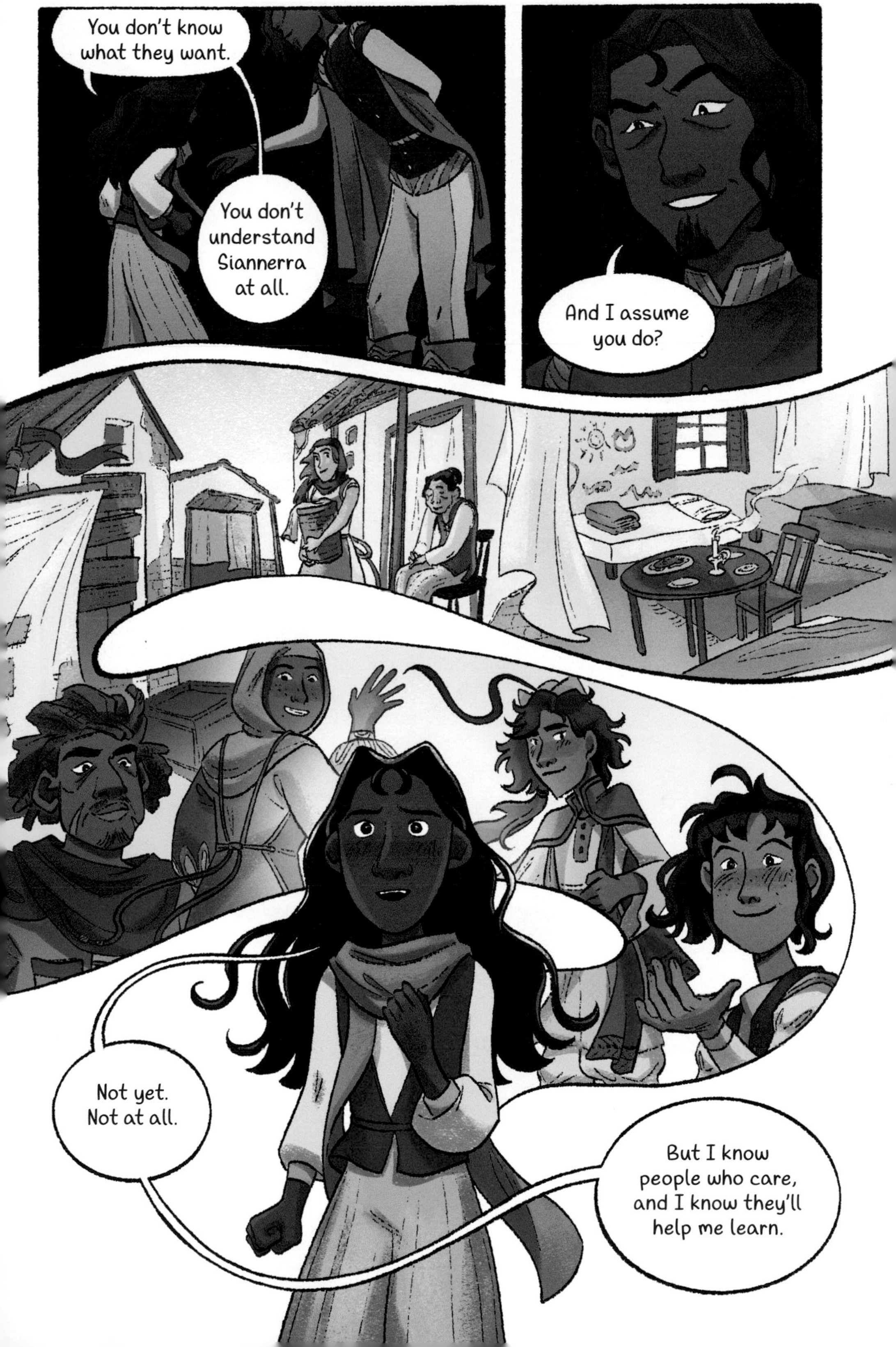
You don't know what they want.
You don't understand Siannerra at all.
And I assume you do?
Not yet. Not at all.
But I know people who care, and I know they'll help me learn.

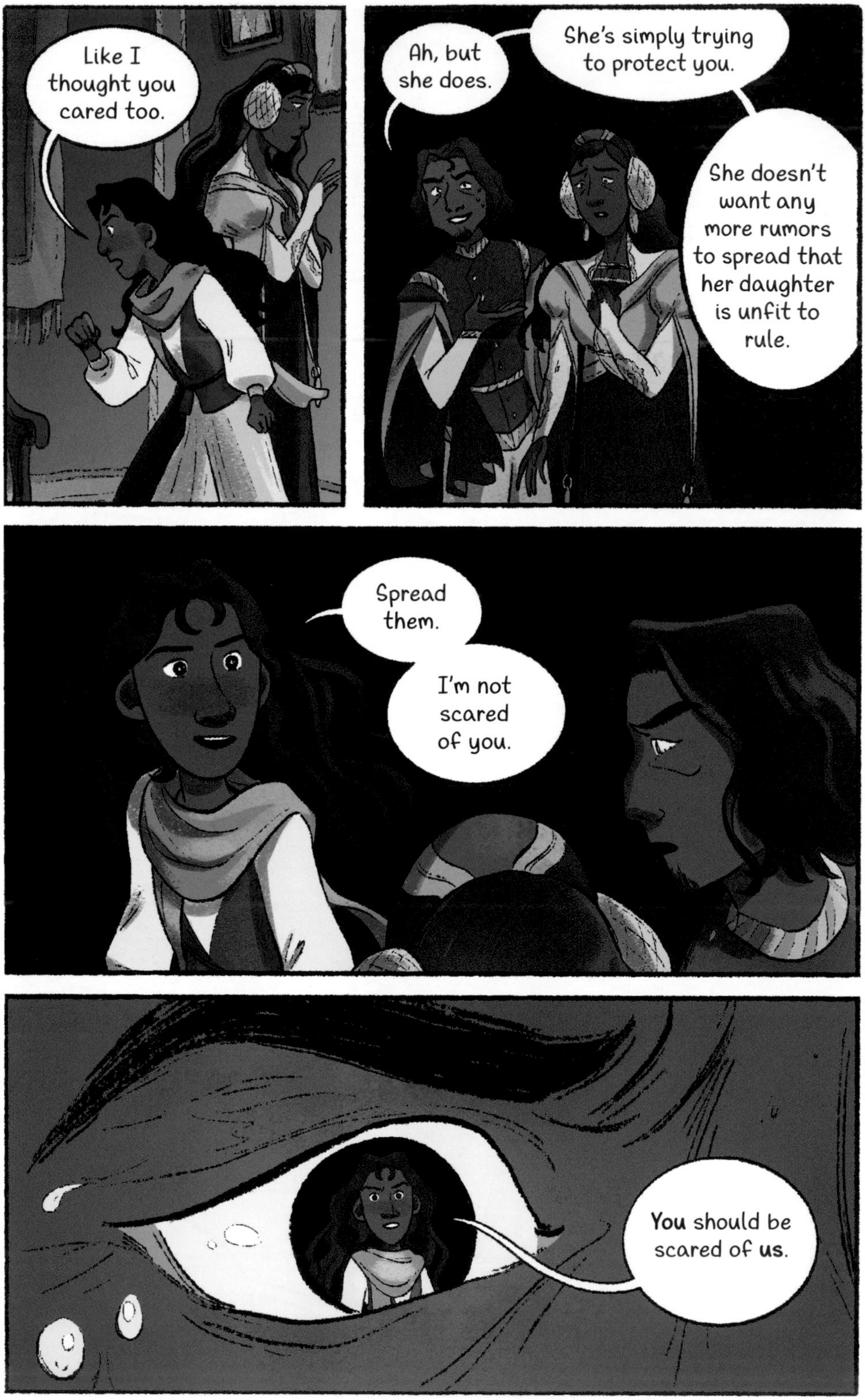
Like I thought you cared too.
Ah, but she does.
She's simply trying to protect you.
She doesn't want any more rumors to spread that her daughter is unfit to rule.
Spread them.
I'm not scared of you.
You should be scared of **us**.

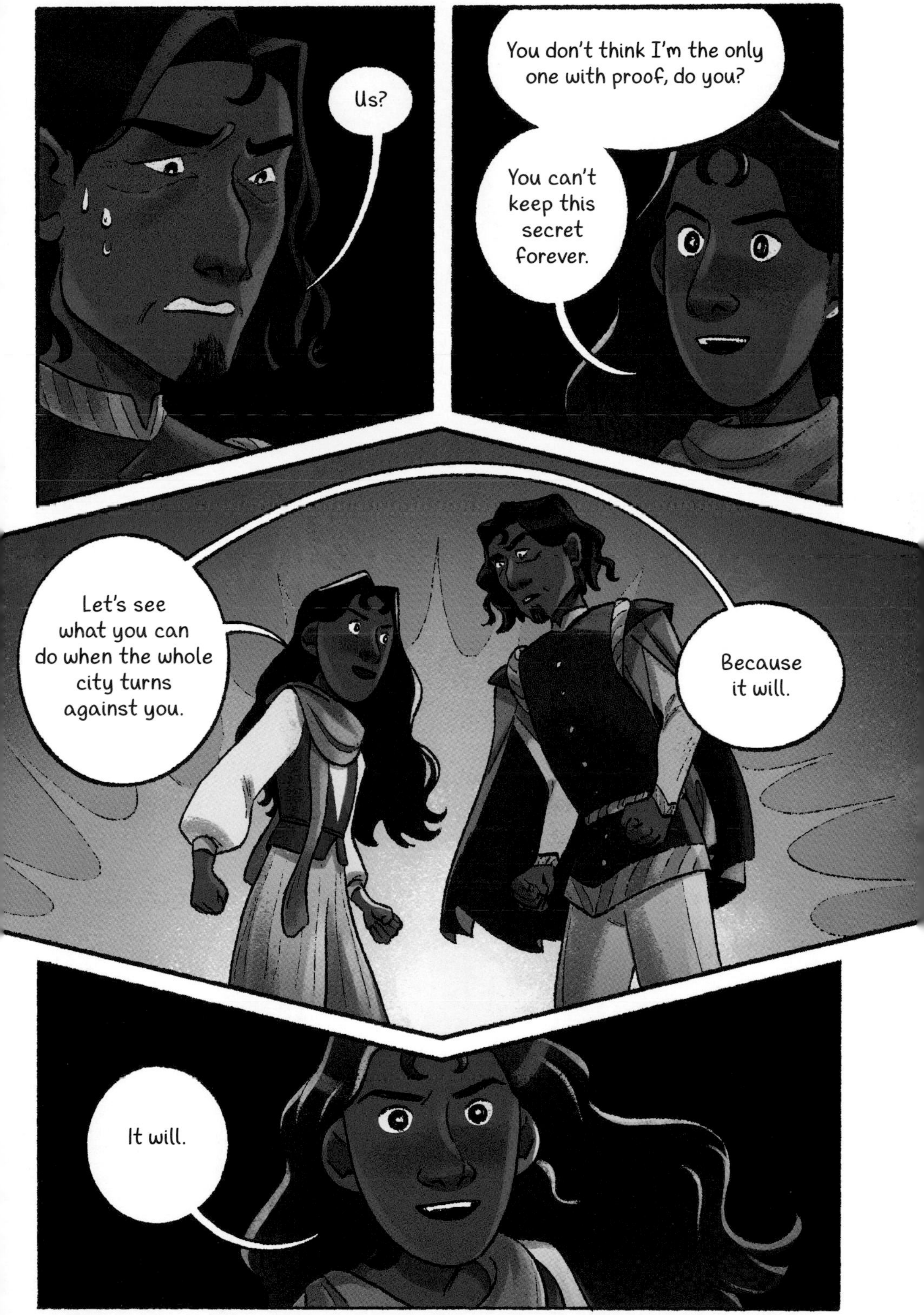
Us?
You don't think I'm the only one with proof, do you?
You can't keep this secret forever.
Let's see what you can do when the whole city turns against you.
Because it will.
It will.

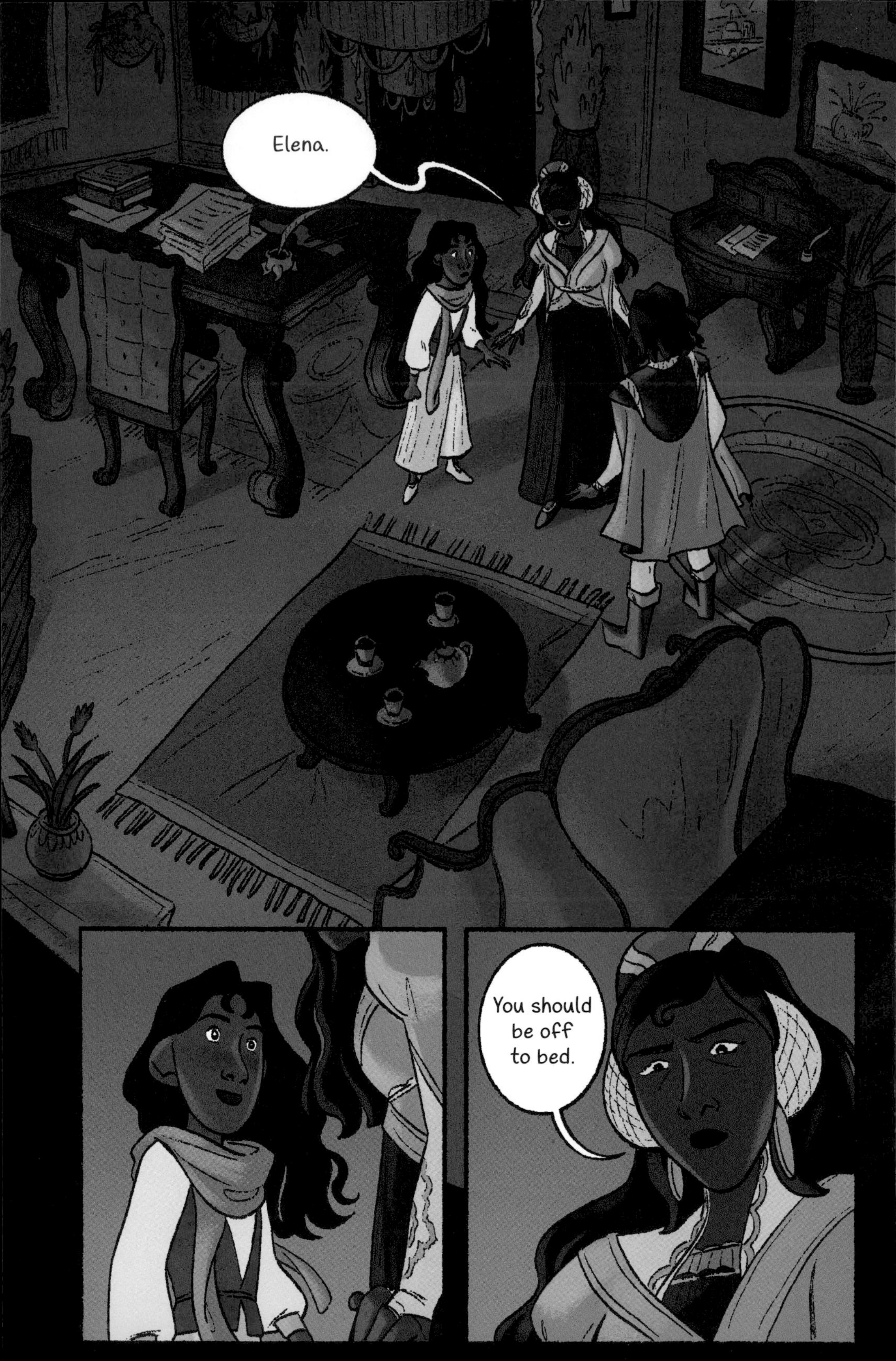
Elena.
You should be off to bed.

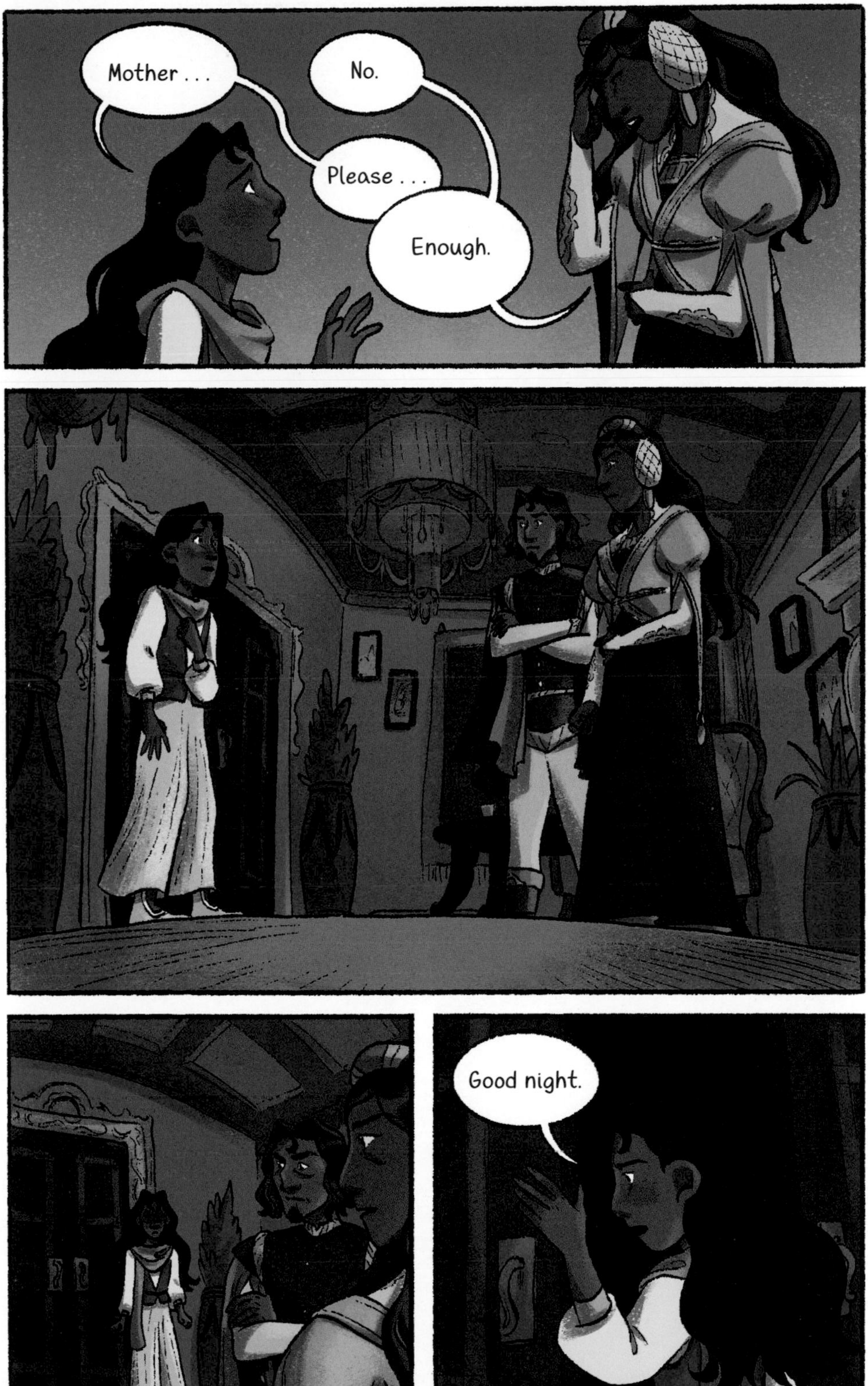
Mother . . .
No.
Please . . .
Enough.
Good night.

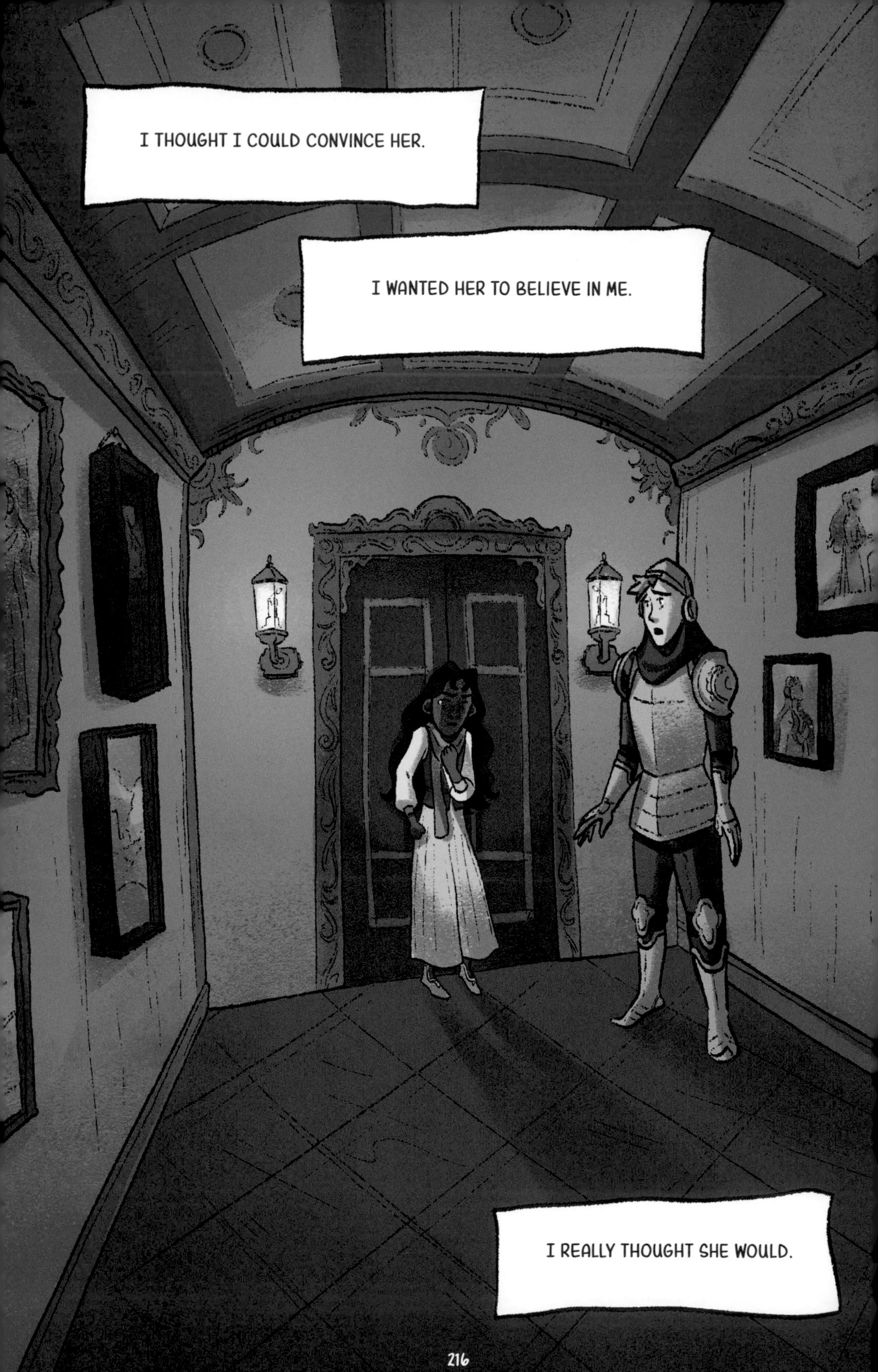
I THOUGHT I COULD CONVINCE HER.
I WANTED HER TO BELIEVE IN ME.
I REALLY THOUGHT SHE WOULD.

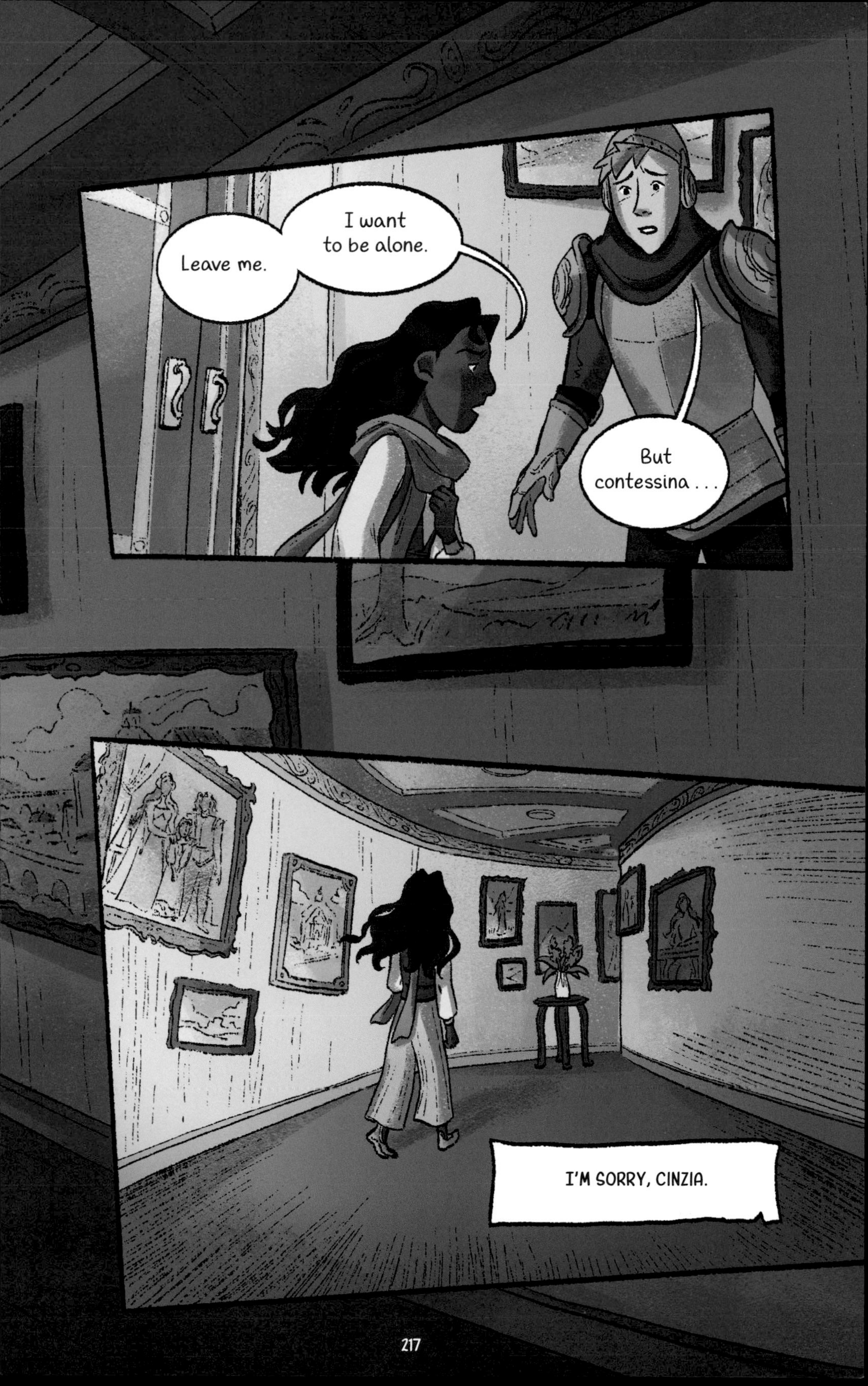
Leave me.
I want to be alone.
But contessina . . .
I'M SORRY, CINZIA.

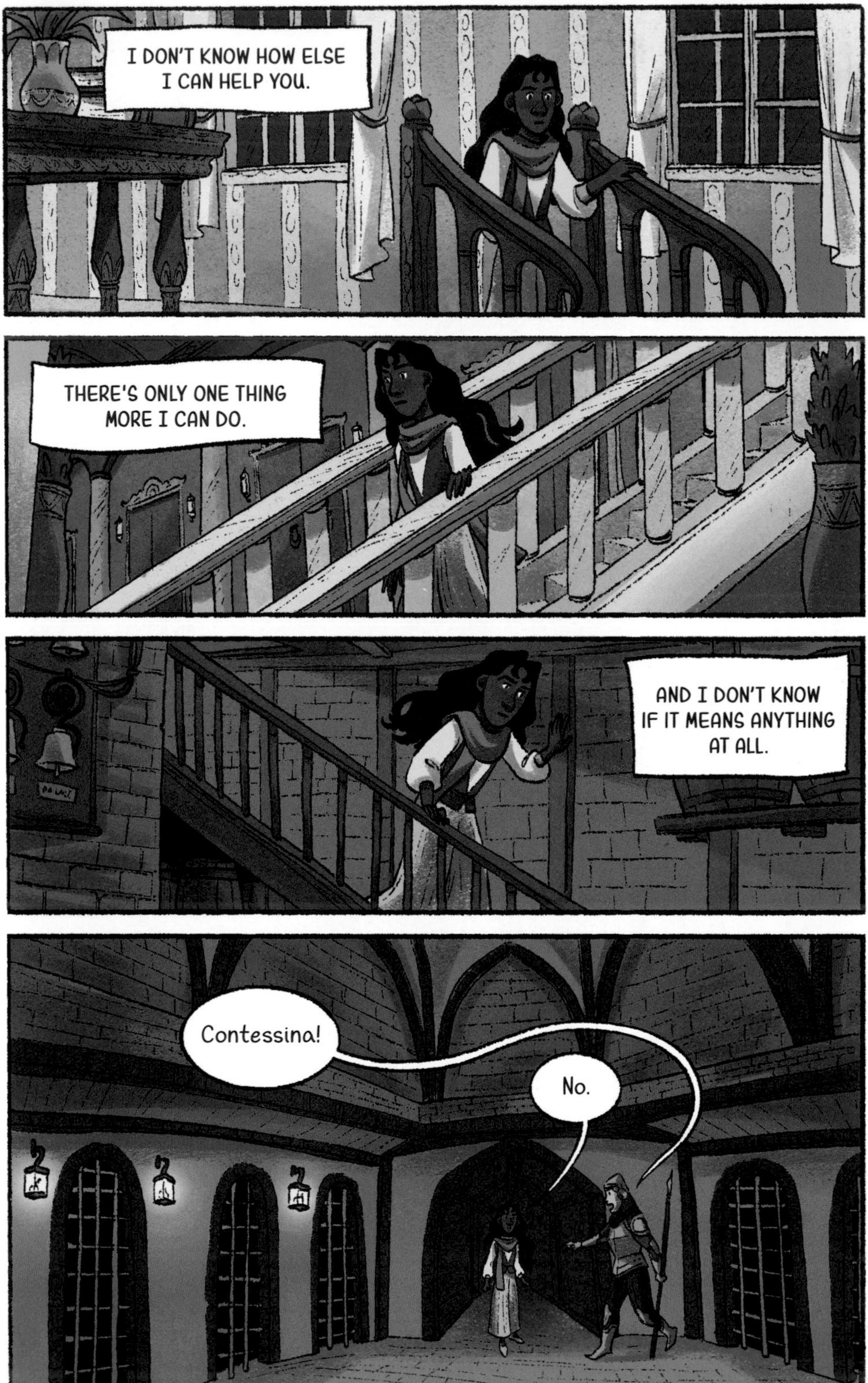
I DON'T KNOW HOW ELSE I CAN HELP YOU.
THERE'S ONLY ONE THING MORE I CAN DO.
AND I DON'T KNOW IF IT MEANS ANYTHING AT ALL.
Contessina!
No.

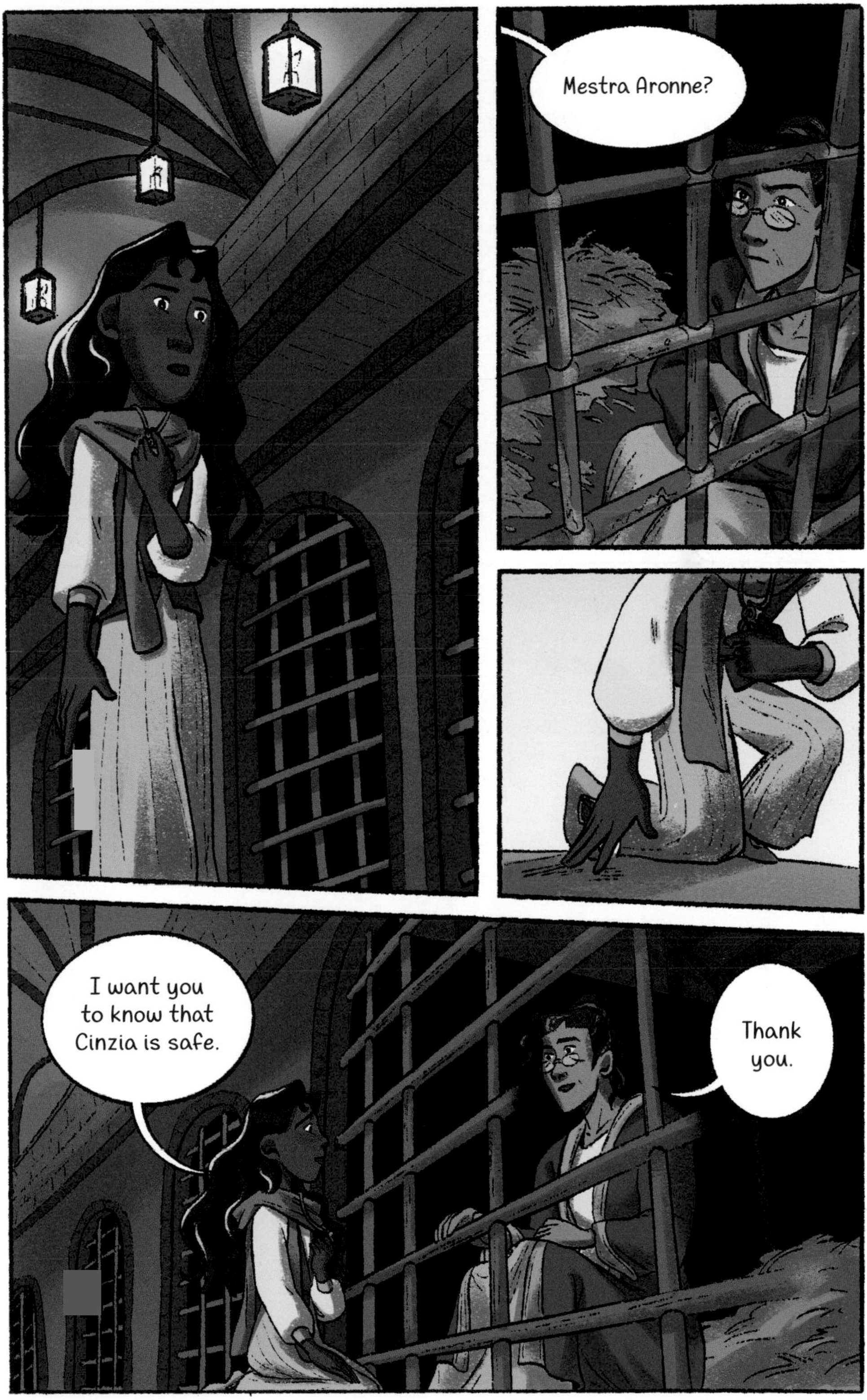
Mestra Aronne?
I want you to know that Cinzia is safe.
Thank you.

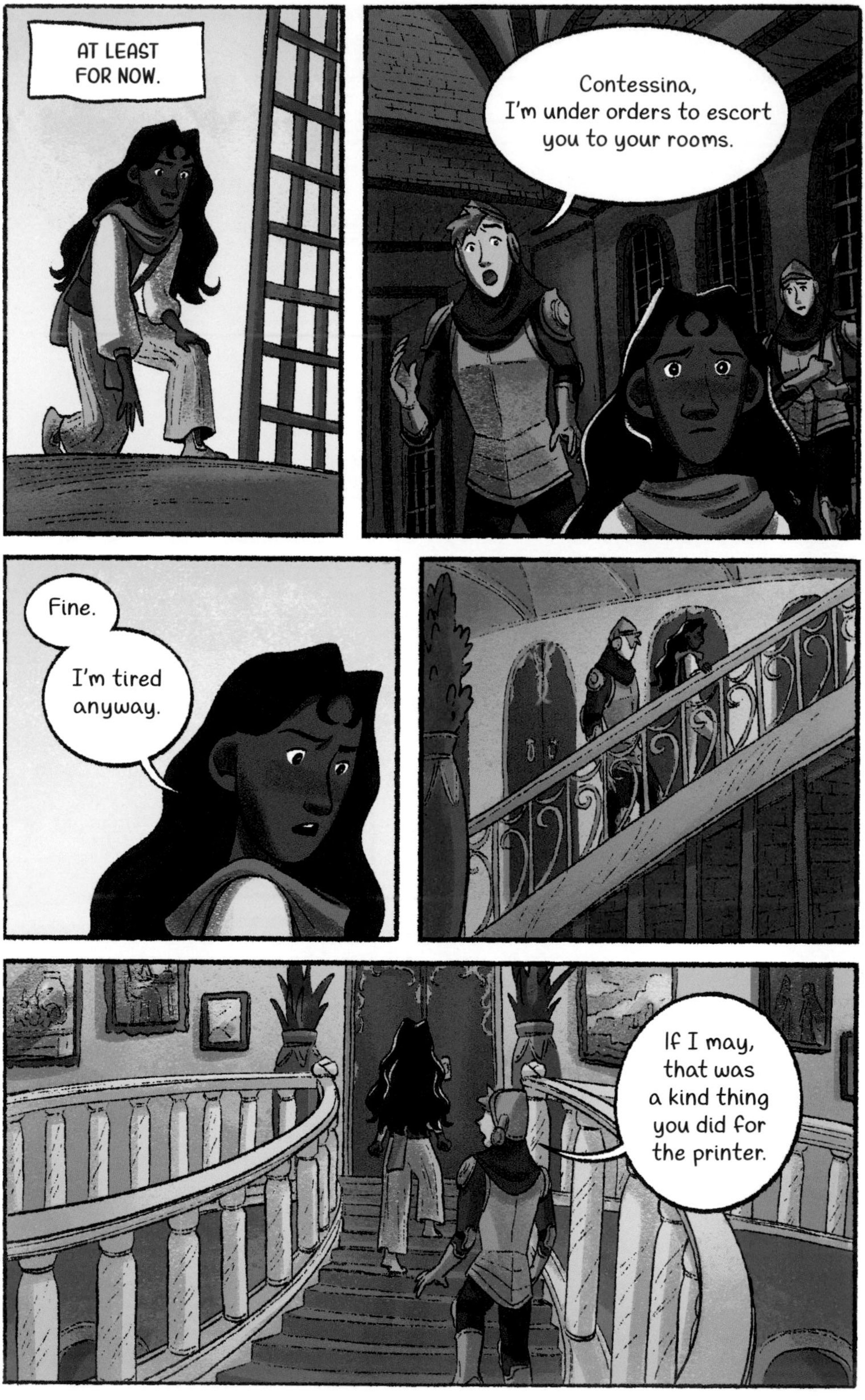
AT LEAST FOR NOW.
Contessina, I'm under orders to escort you to your rooms.
Fine.
I'm tired anyway.
If I may, that was a kind thing you did for the printer.

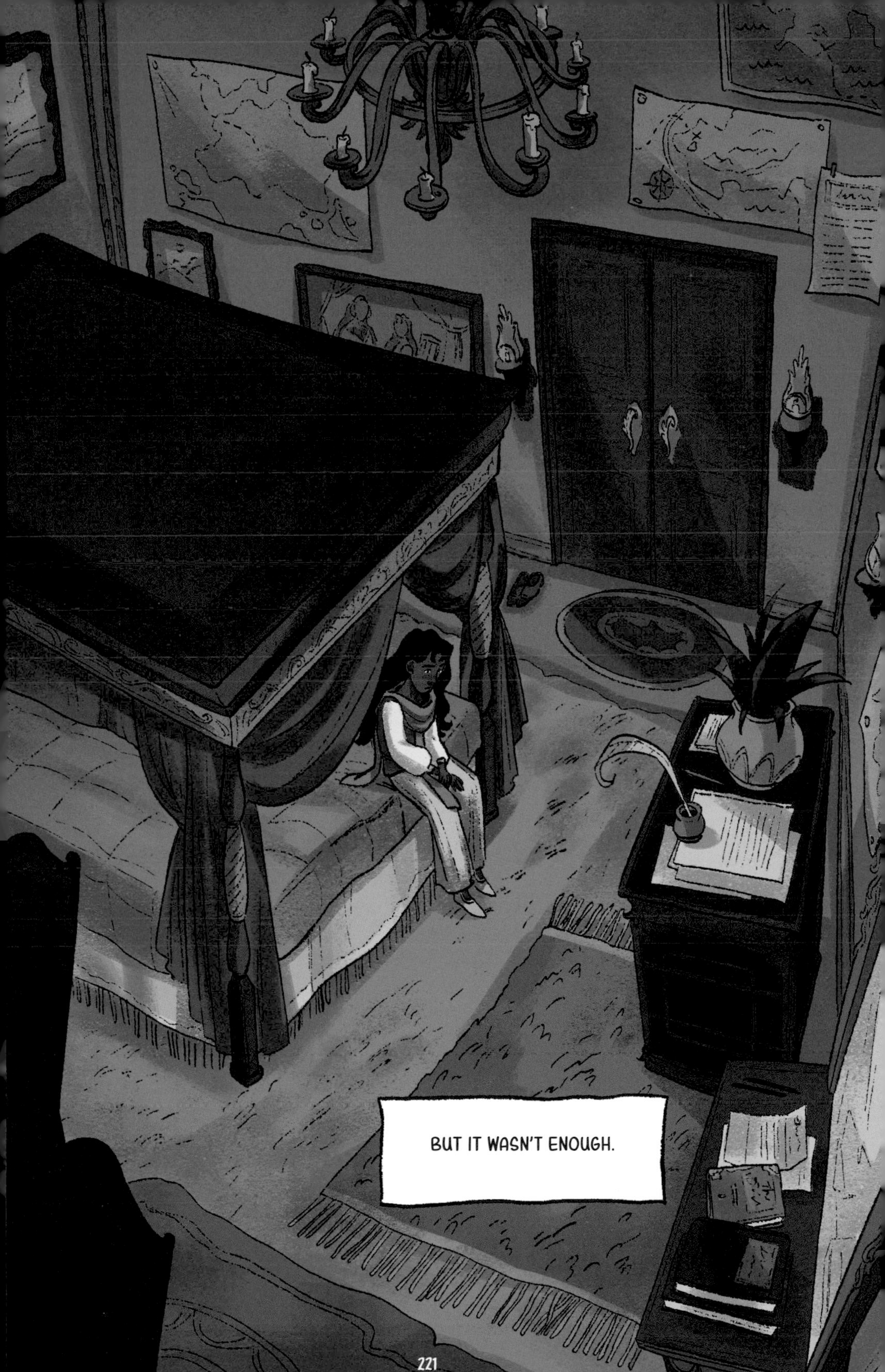
BUT IT WASN'T ENOUGH.

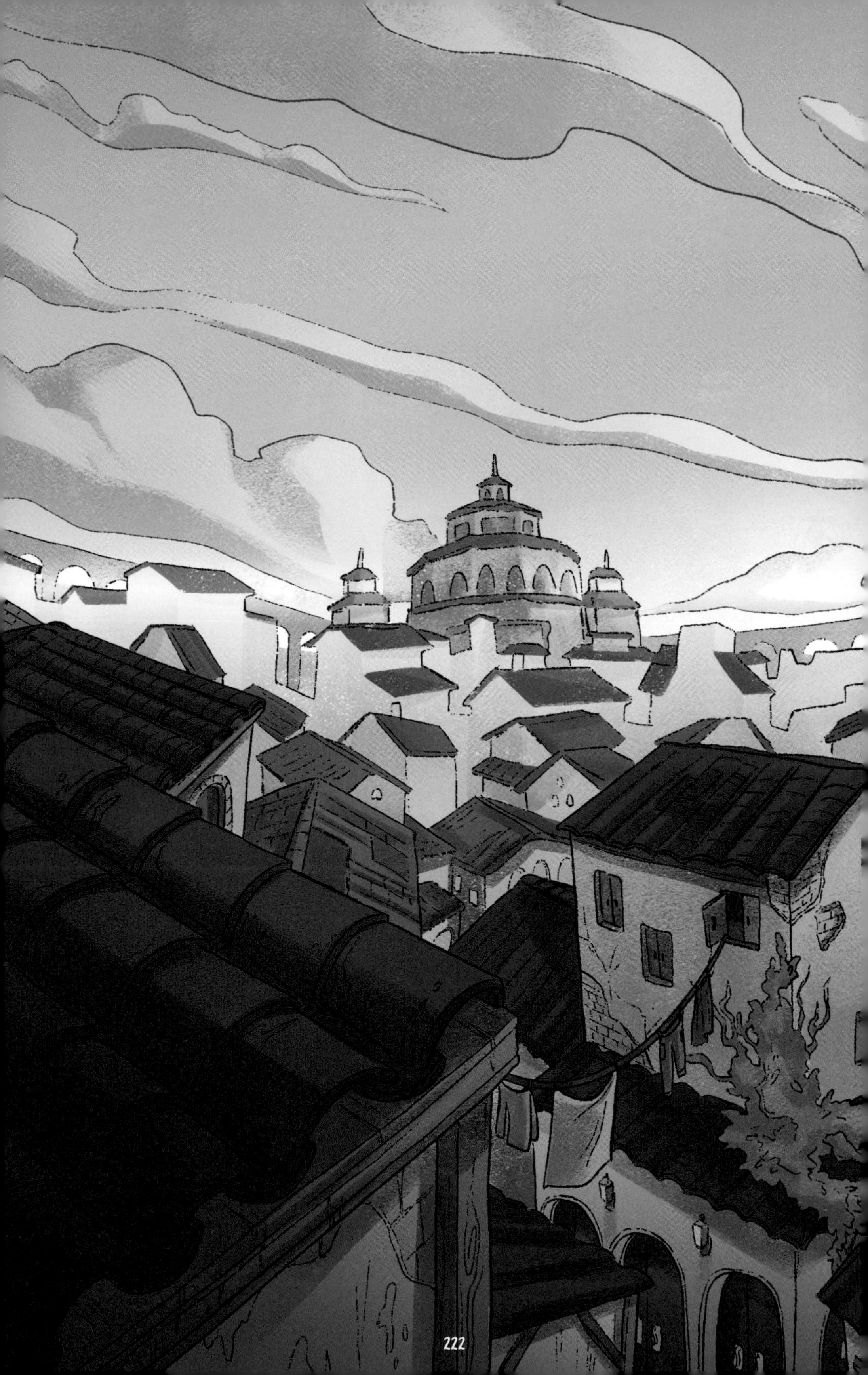

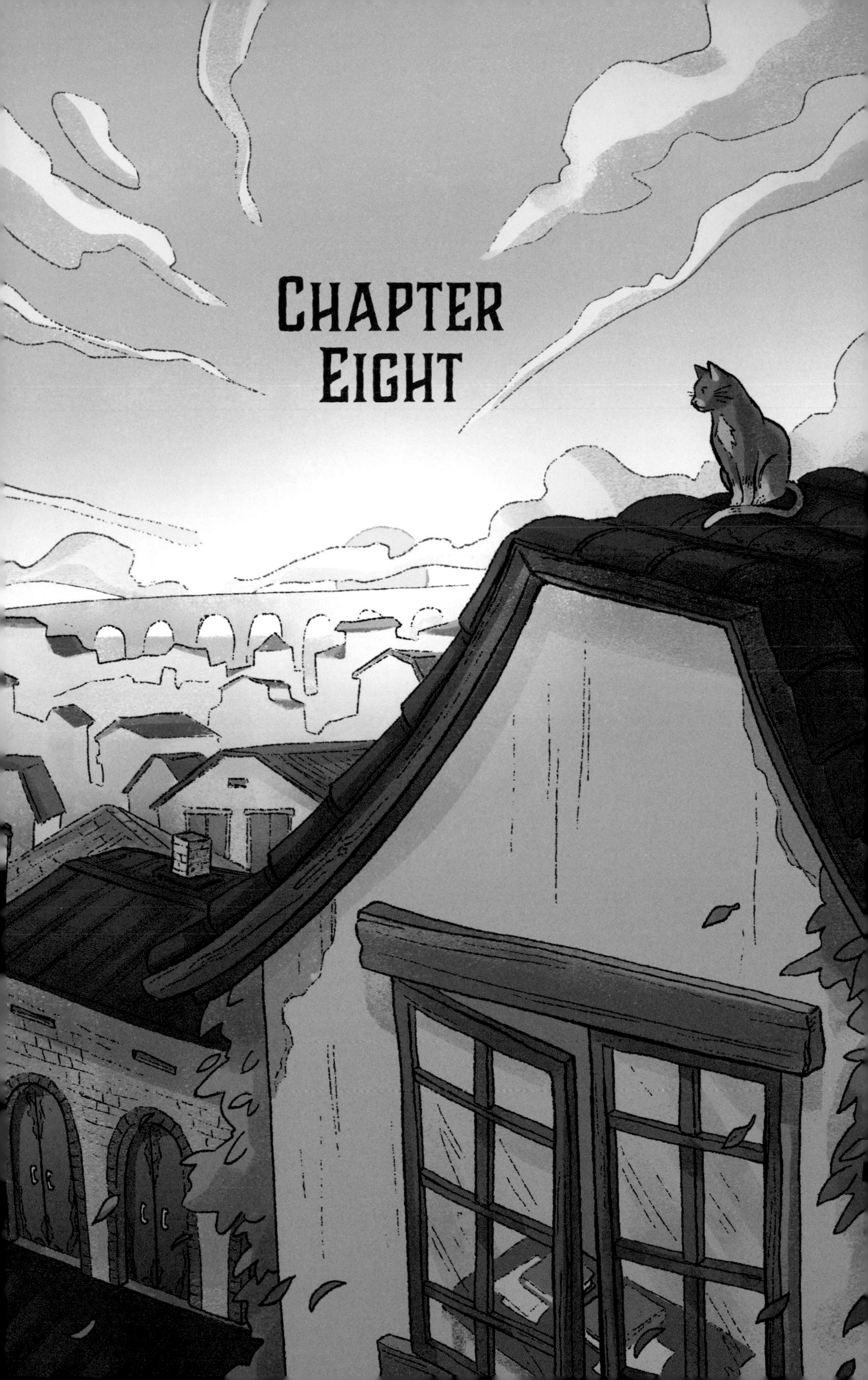
CHAPTER
EIGHT

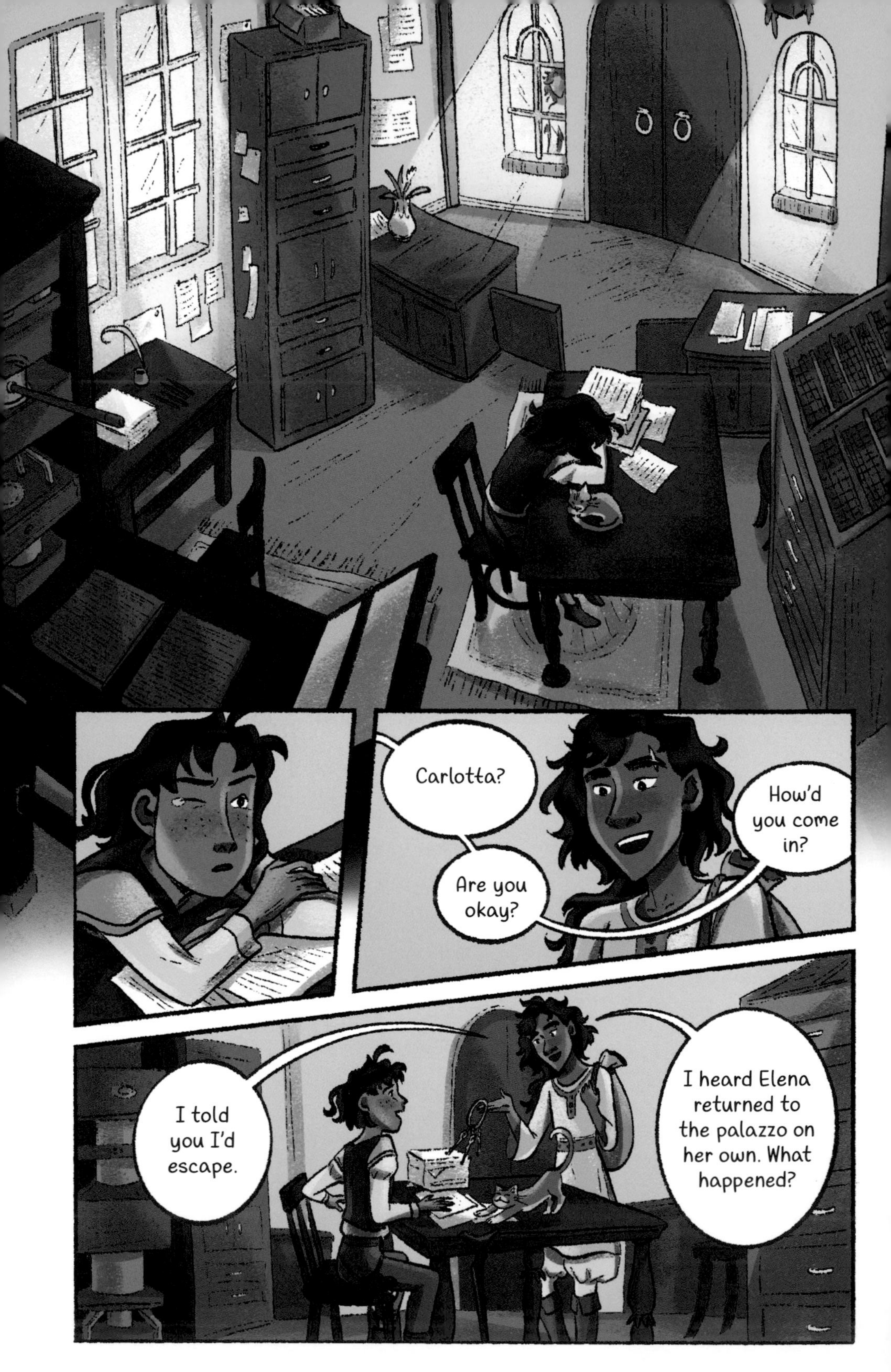
Carlotta?
Are you okay?
How'd you come in?
I told you I'd escape.
I heard Elena returned to the palazzo on her own. What happened?

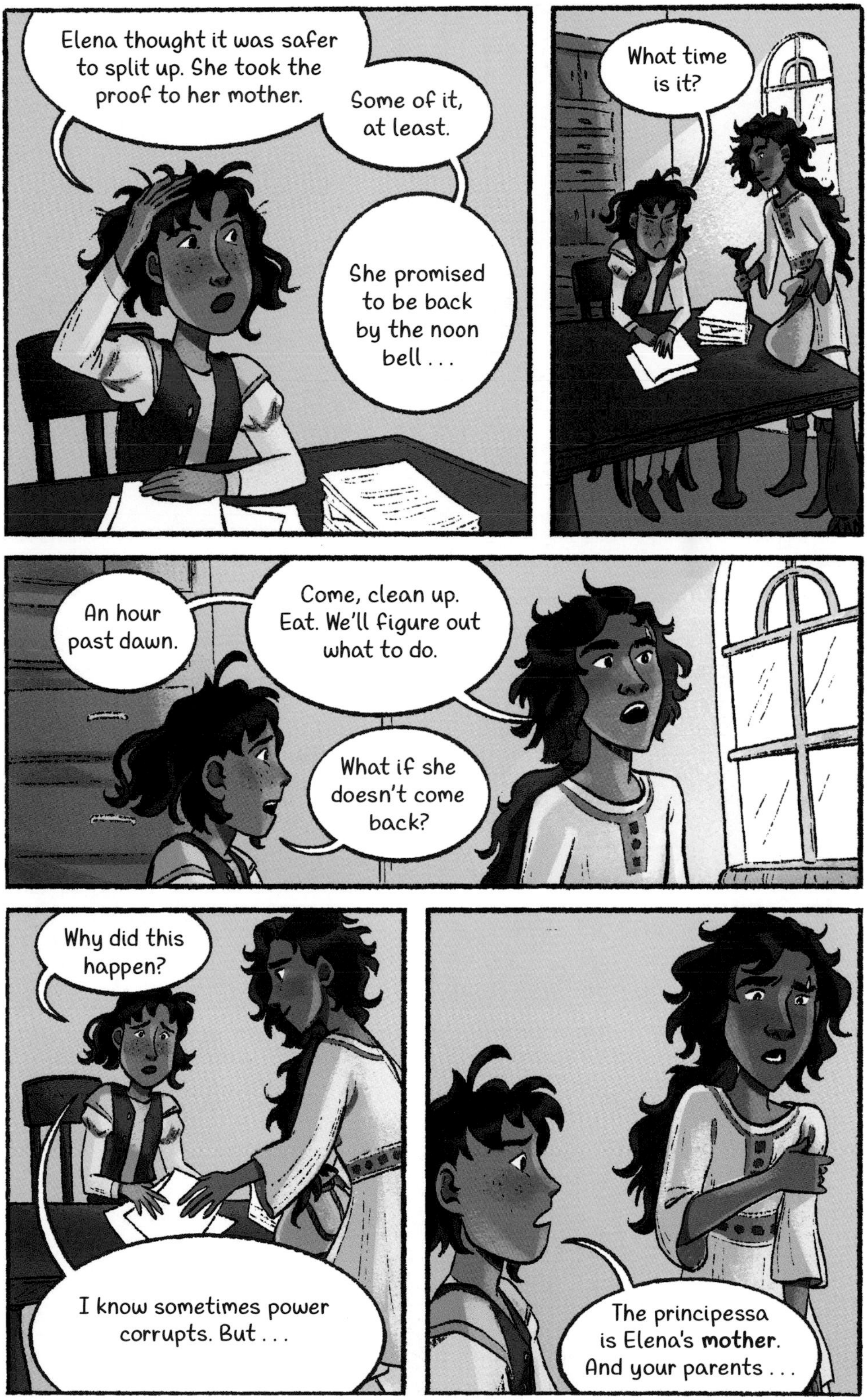
Elena thought it was safer to split up. She took the proof to her mother.
Some of it, at least.
She promised to be back by the noon bell . . .
What time is it?
An hour past dawn.
Come, clean up. Eat. We'll figure out what to do.
What if she doesn't come back?
Why did this happen?
I know sometimes power corrupts. But . . .
The principessa is Elena's **mother**. And your parents . . .

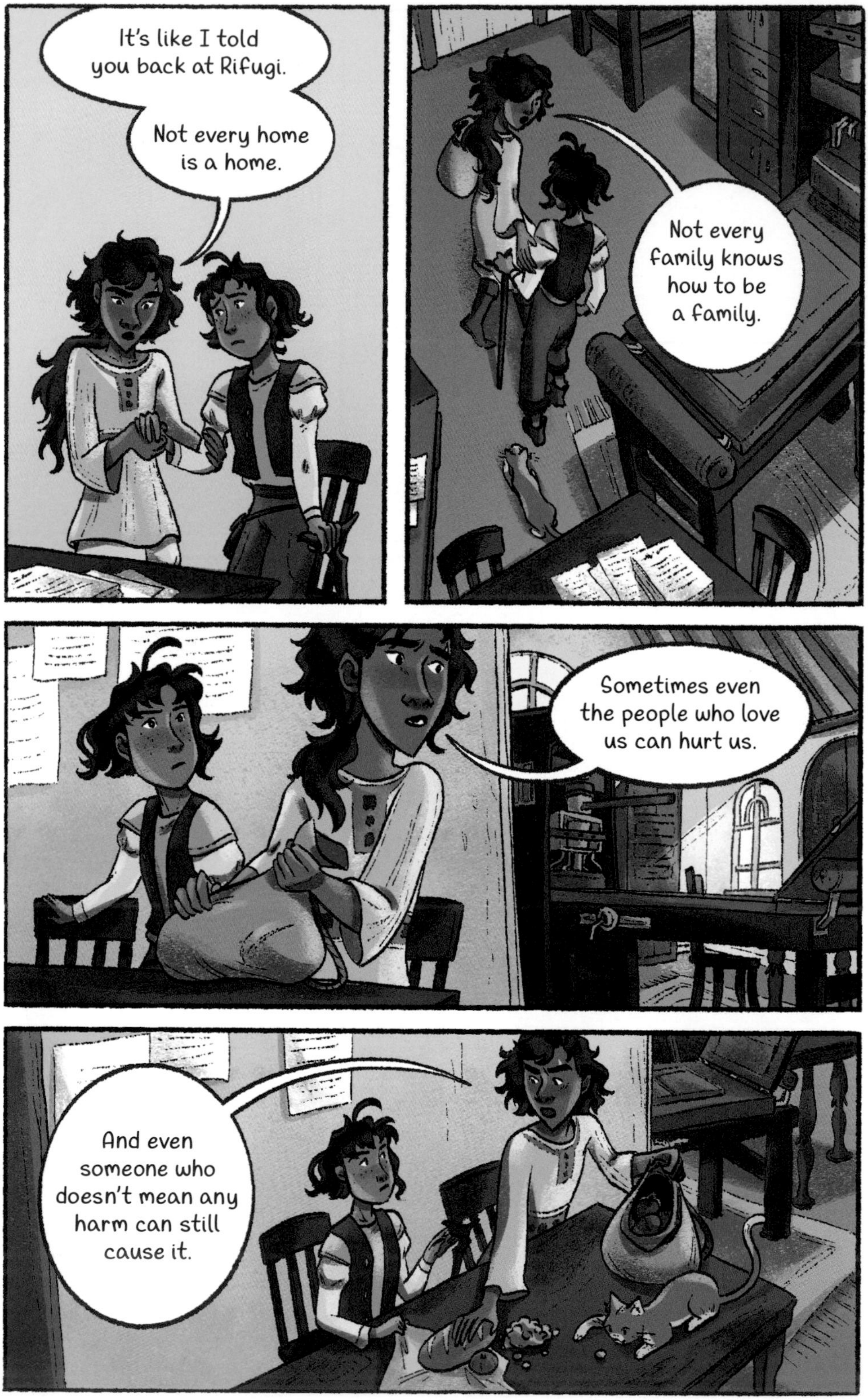
It's like I told you back at Rifugi.
Not every home is a home.
Not every family knows how to be a family.
Sometimes even the people who love us can hurt us.
And even someone who doesn't mean any harm can still cause it.

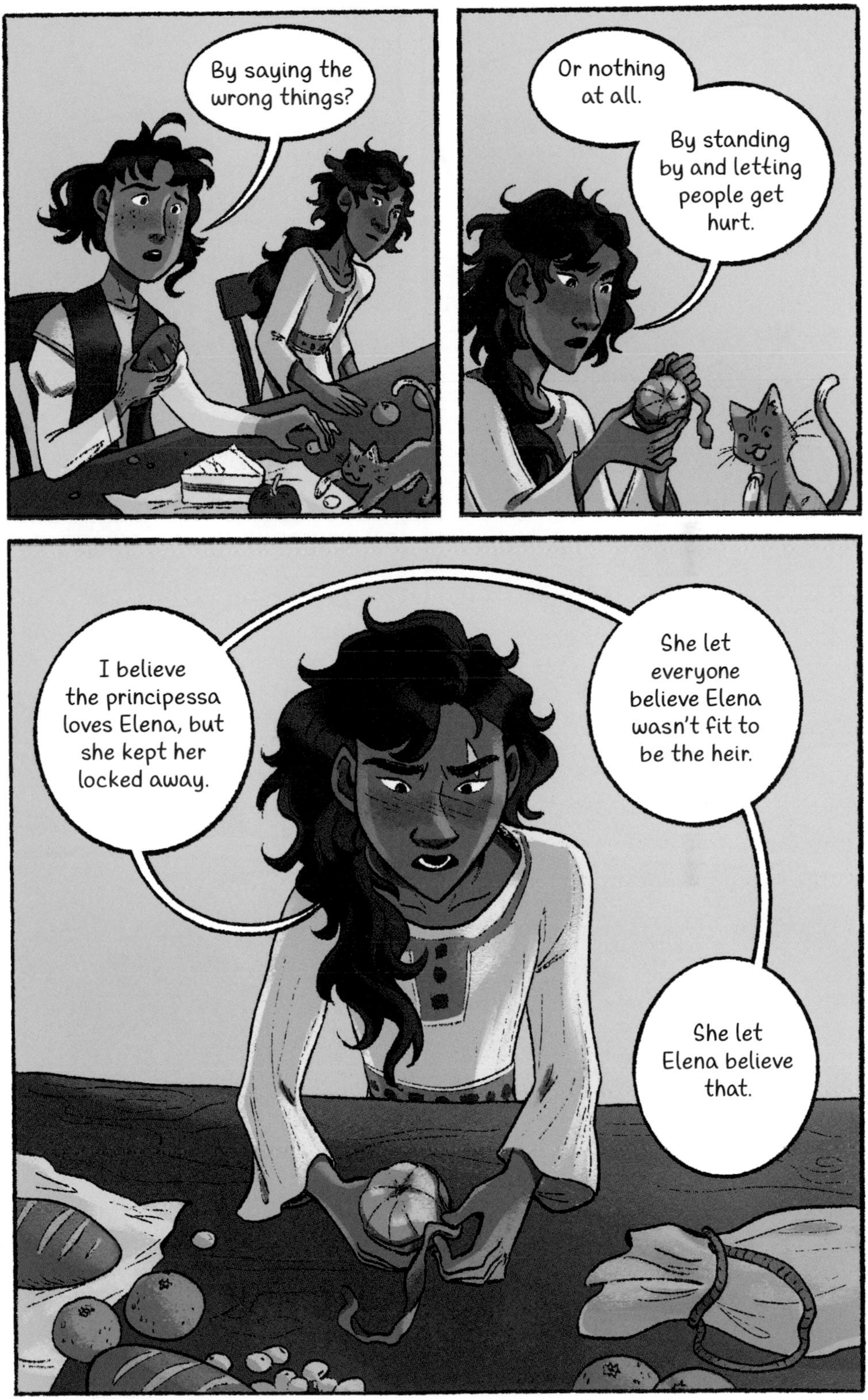
By saying the wrong things?
Or nothing at all.
By standing by and letting people get hurt.
I believe the principessa loves Elena, but she kept her locked away.
She let everyone believe Elena wasn't fit to be the heir.
She let Elena believe that.

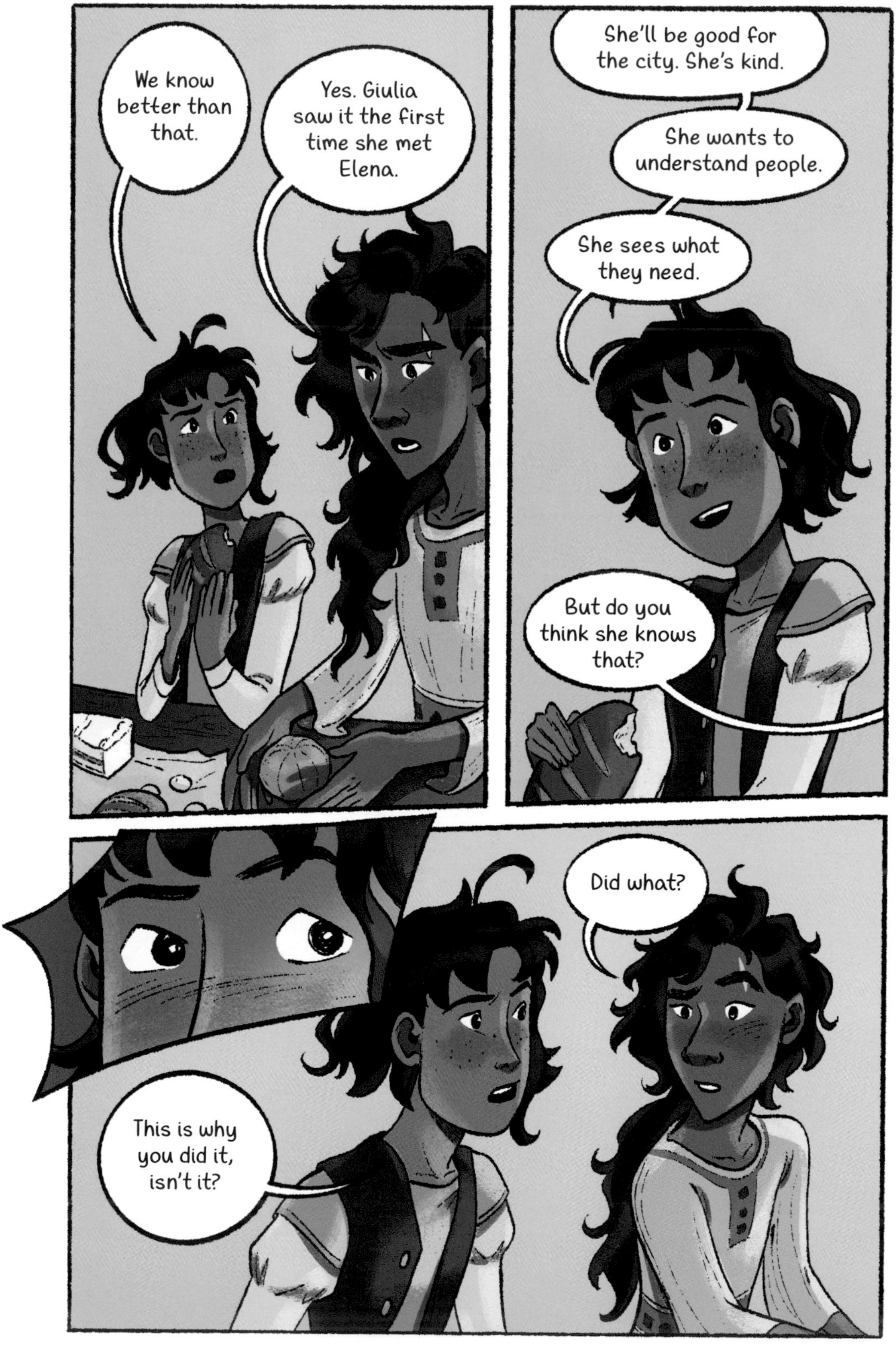
We know better than that.
Yes. Giulia saw it the first time she met Elena.
She'll be good for the city. She's kind.
She wants to understand people.
She sees what they need.
But do you think she knows that?
Did what?
This is why you did it, isn't it?

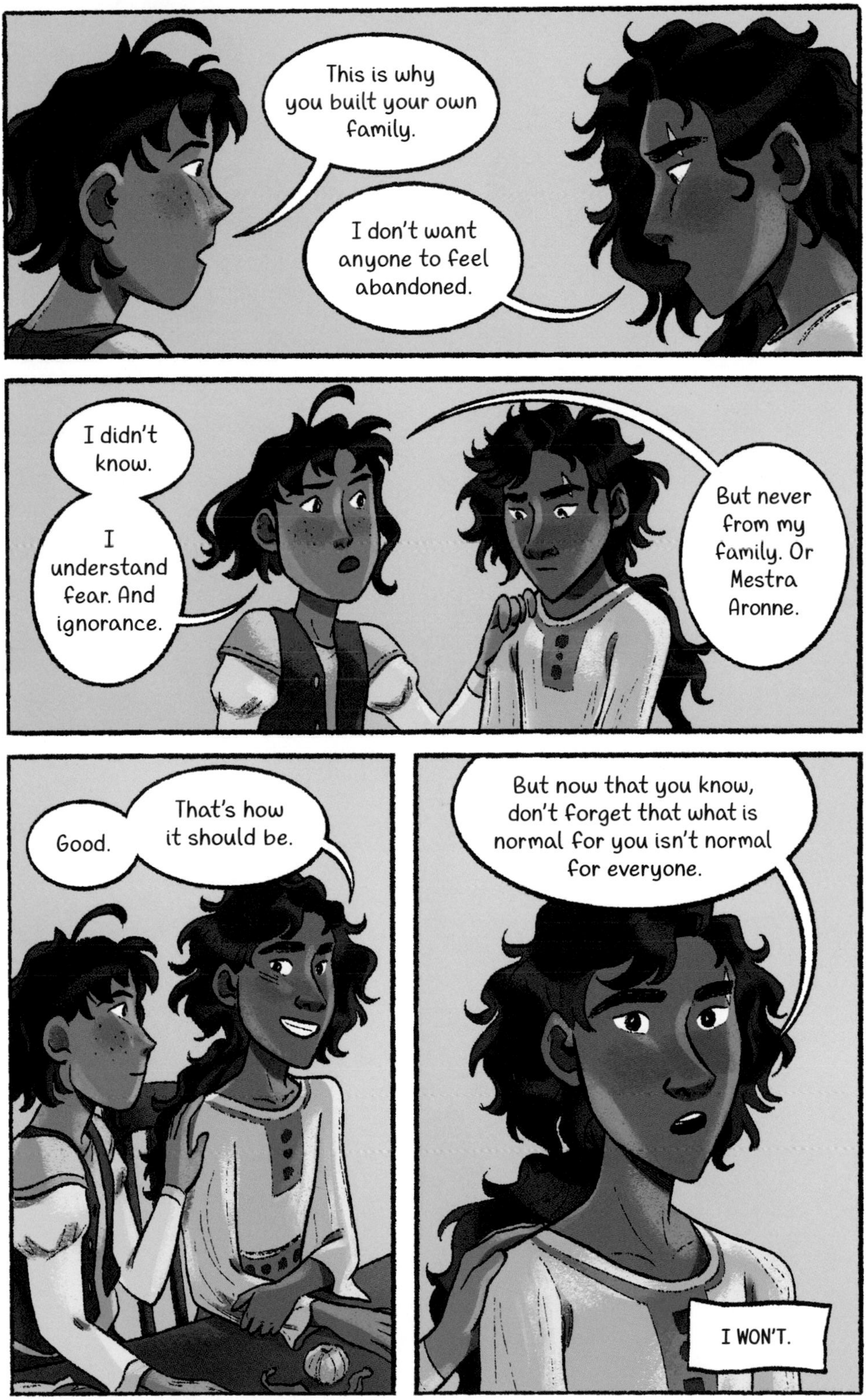
This is why you built your own family.
I don't want anyone to feel abandoned.
I didn't know.
I understand fear. And ignorance.
But never from my family. Or Mestra Aronne.
Good.
That's how it should be.
But now that you know, don't forget that what is normal for you isn't normal for everyone.
I WON'T.

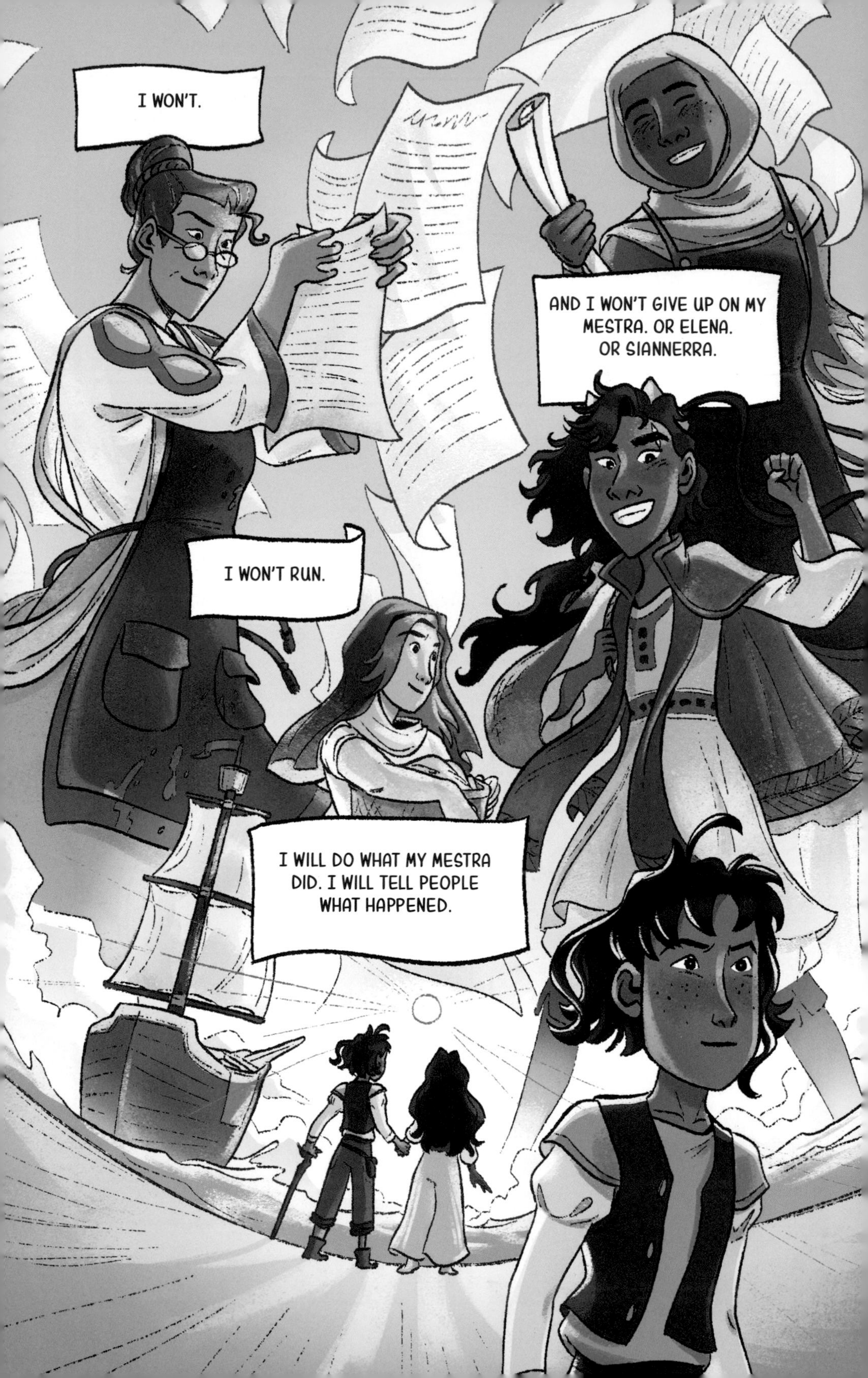
I WON'T.
AND I WON'T GIVE UP ON MY MESTRA. OR ELENA. OR SIANNERRA.
I WON'T RUN.
I WILL DO WHAT MY MESTRA DID. I WILL TELL PEOPLE WHAT HAPPENED.

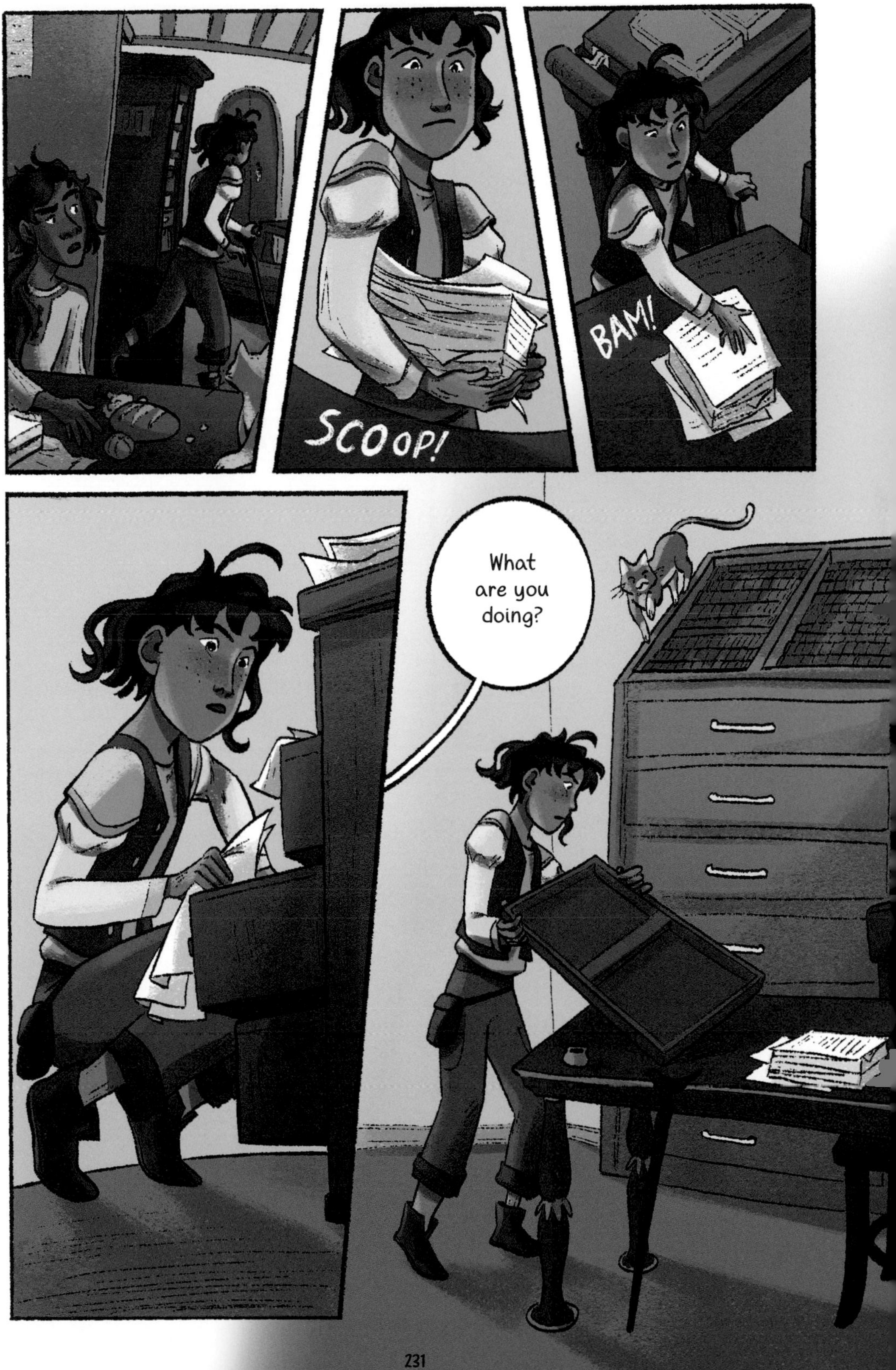
SCOOP!
BAM!
What are you doing?

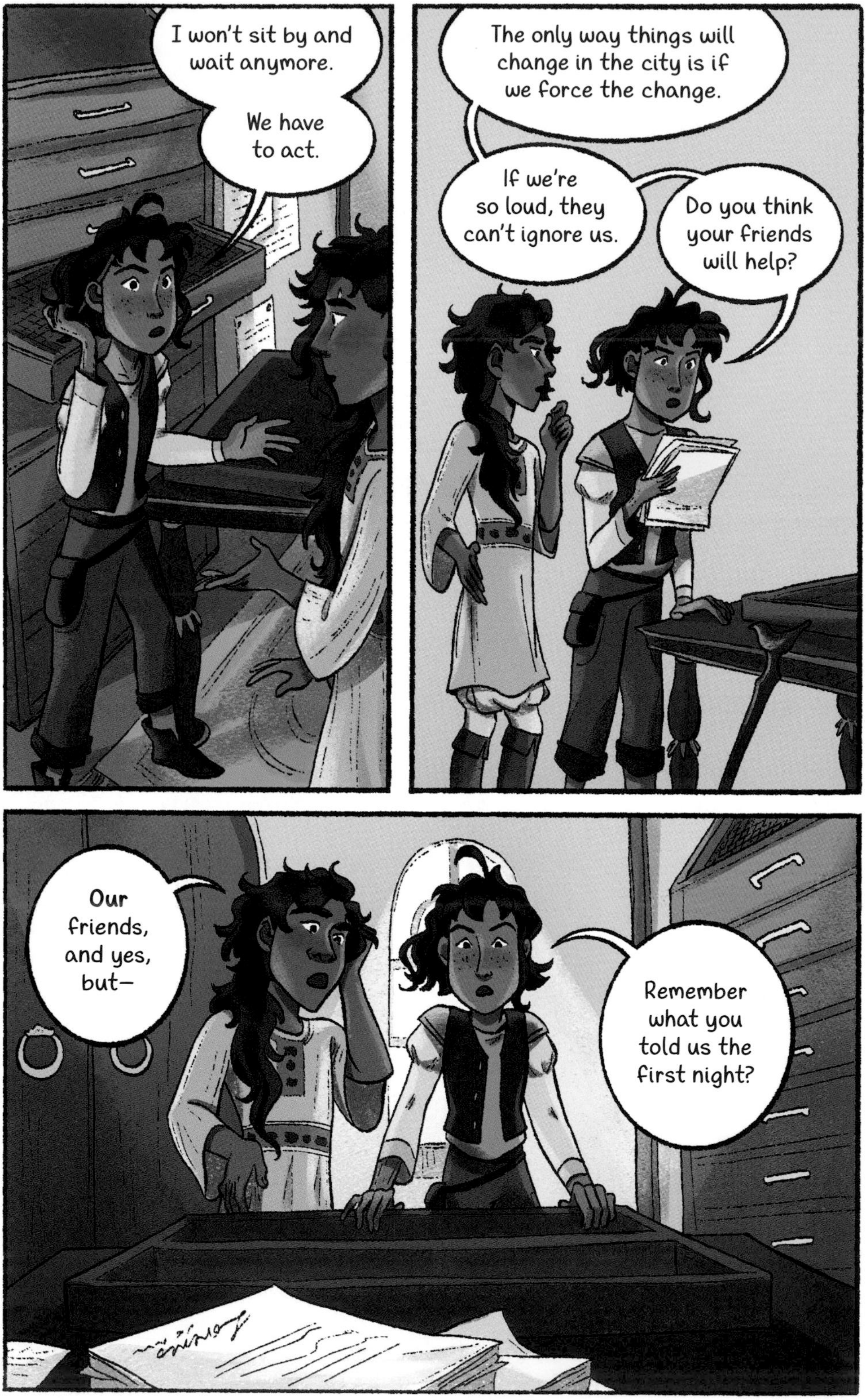

I won't sit by and wait anymore.
We have to act.
The only way things will change in the city is if we force the change.
If we're so loud, they can't ignore us.
Do you think your friends will help?
Our friends, and yes, but—
Remember what you told us the first night?

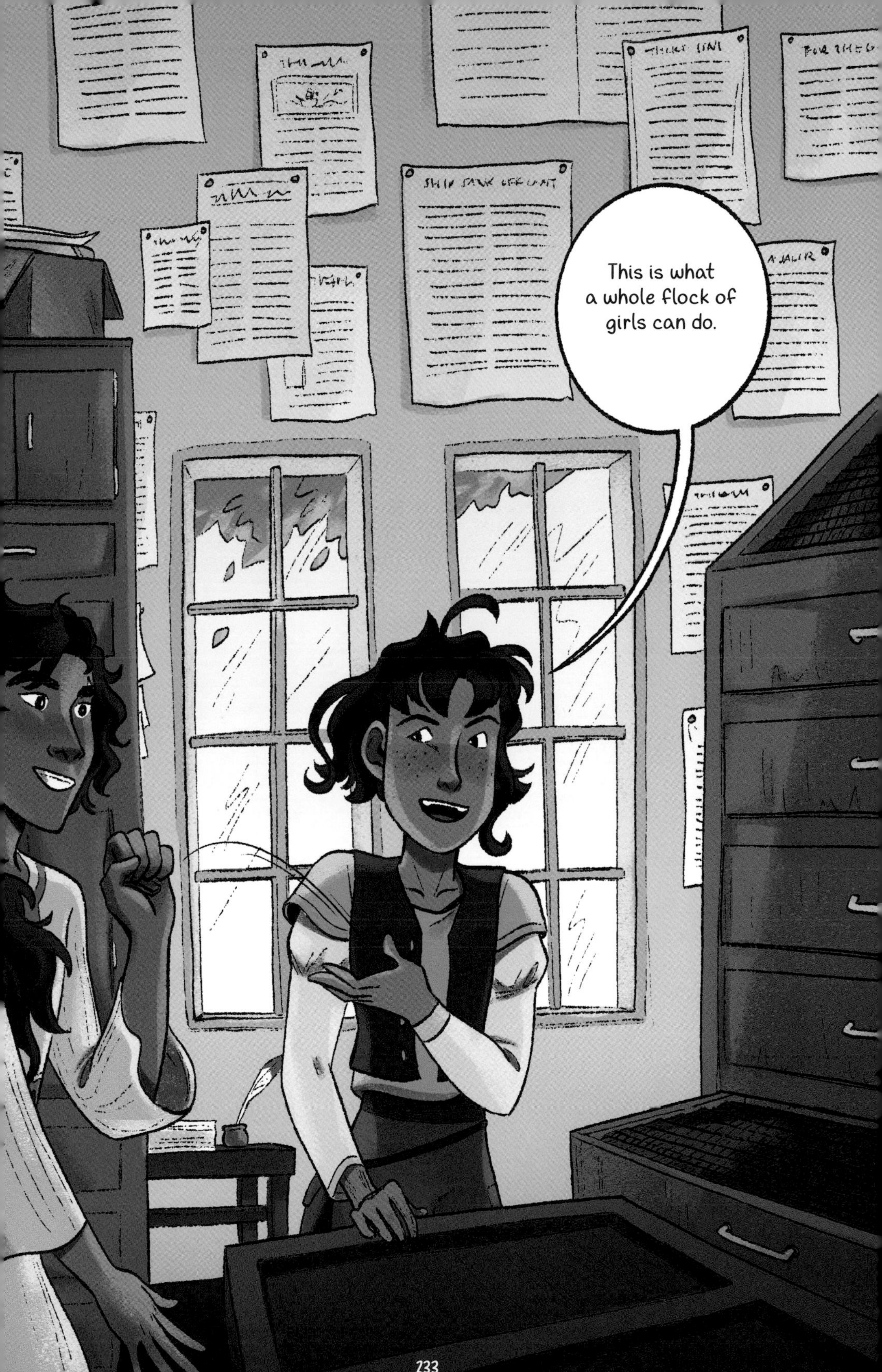
This is what a whole flock of girls can do.

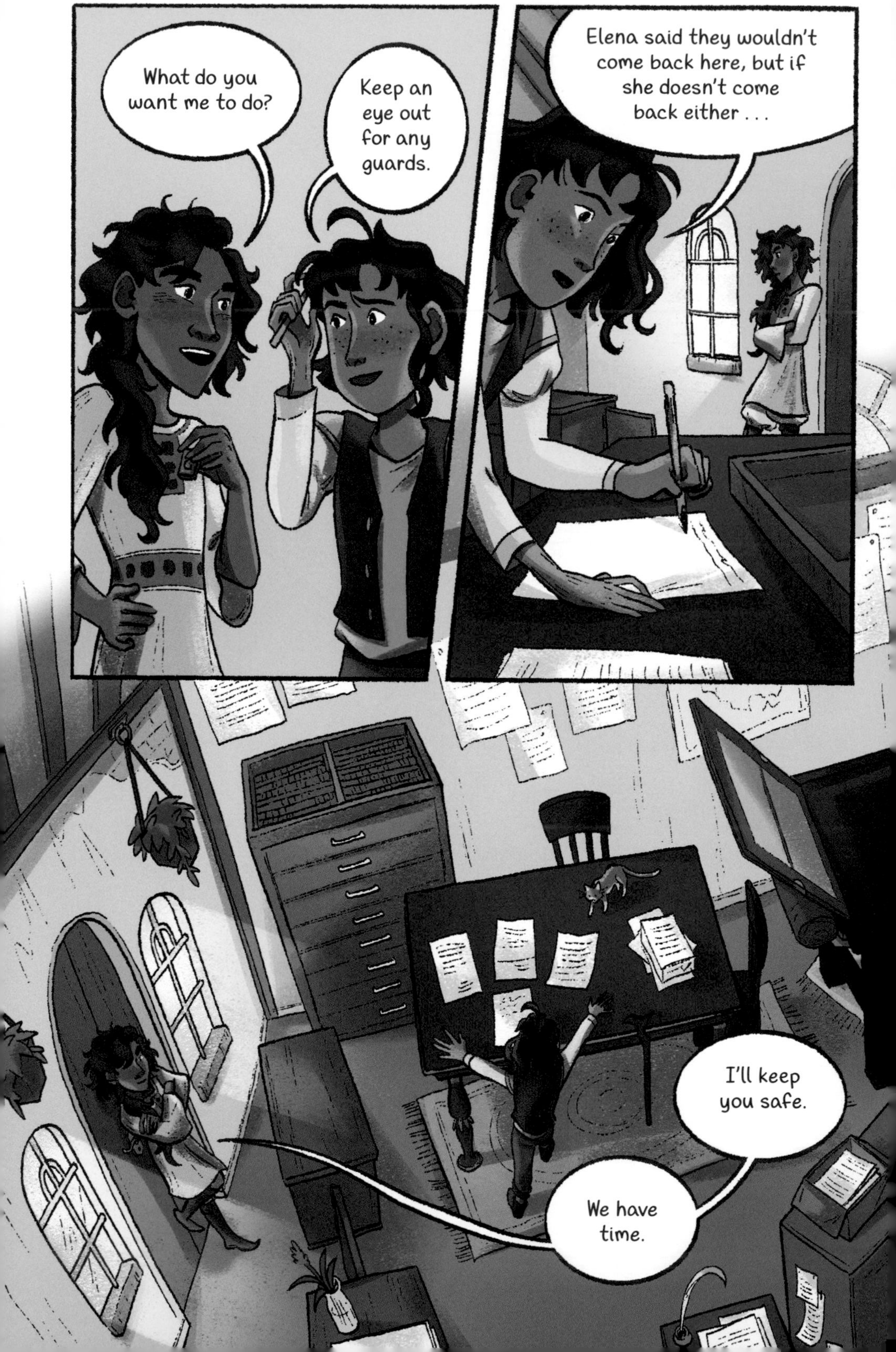
What do you want me to do?
Keep an eye out for any guards.
Elena said they wouldn't come back here, but if she doesn't come back either . . .
I'll keep you safe.
We have time.

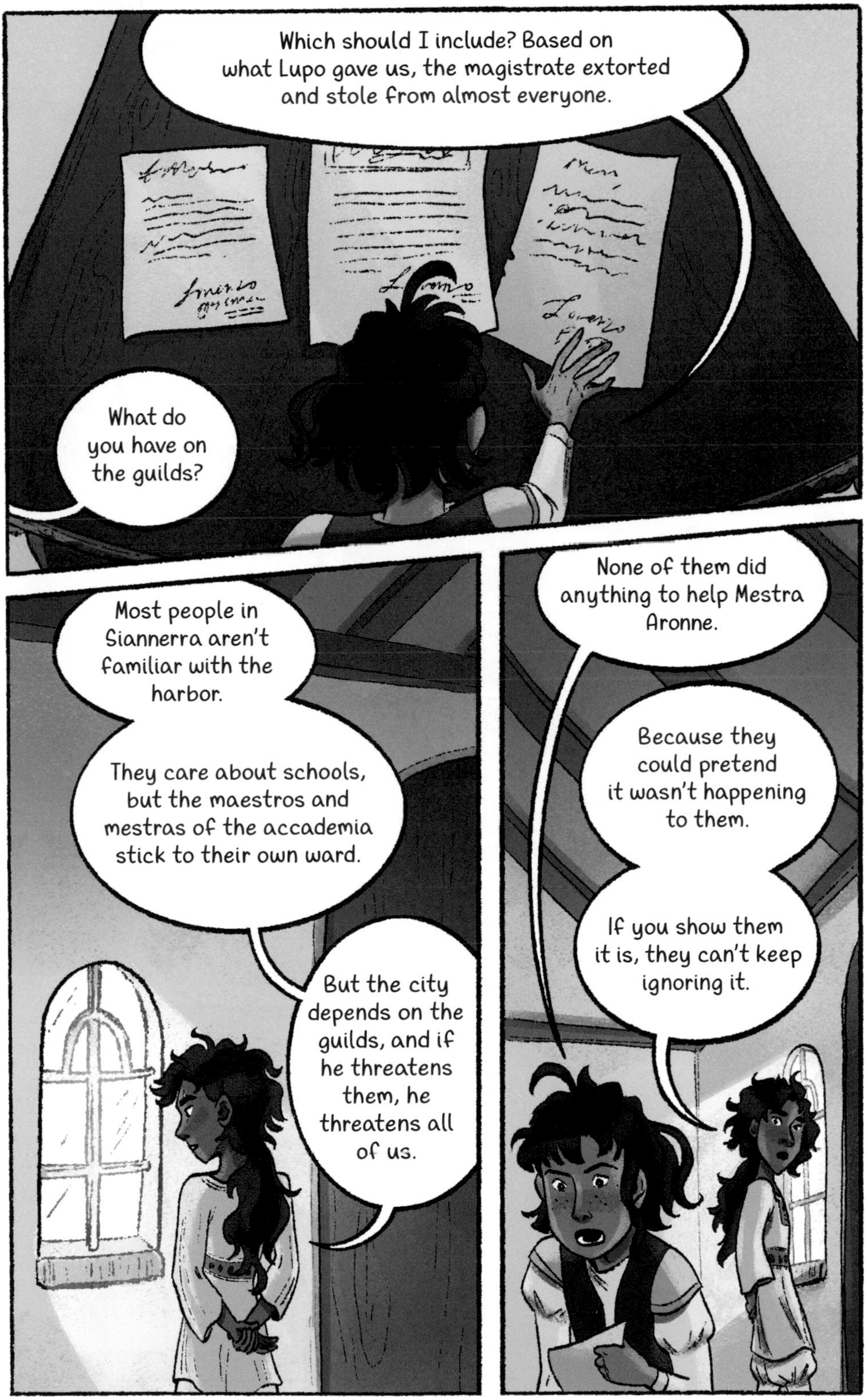
Which should I include? Based on what Lupo gave us, the magistrate extorted and stole from almost everyone.
What do you have on the guilds?
Most people in Siannerra aren't familiar with the harbor.
They care about schools, but the maestros and mestras of the accademia stick to their own ward.
But the city depends on the guilds, and if he threatens them, he threatens all of us.
None of them did anything to help Mestra Aronne.
Because they could pretend it wasn't happening to them.
If you show them it is, they can't keep ignoring it.

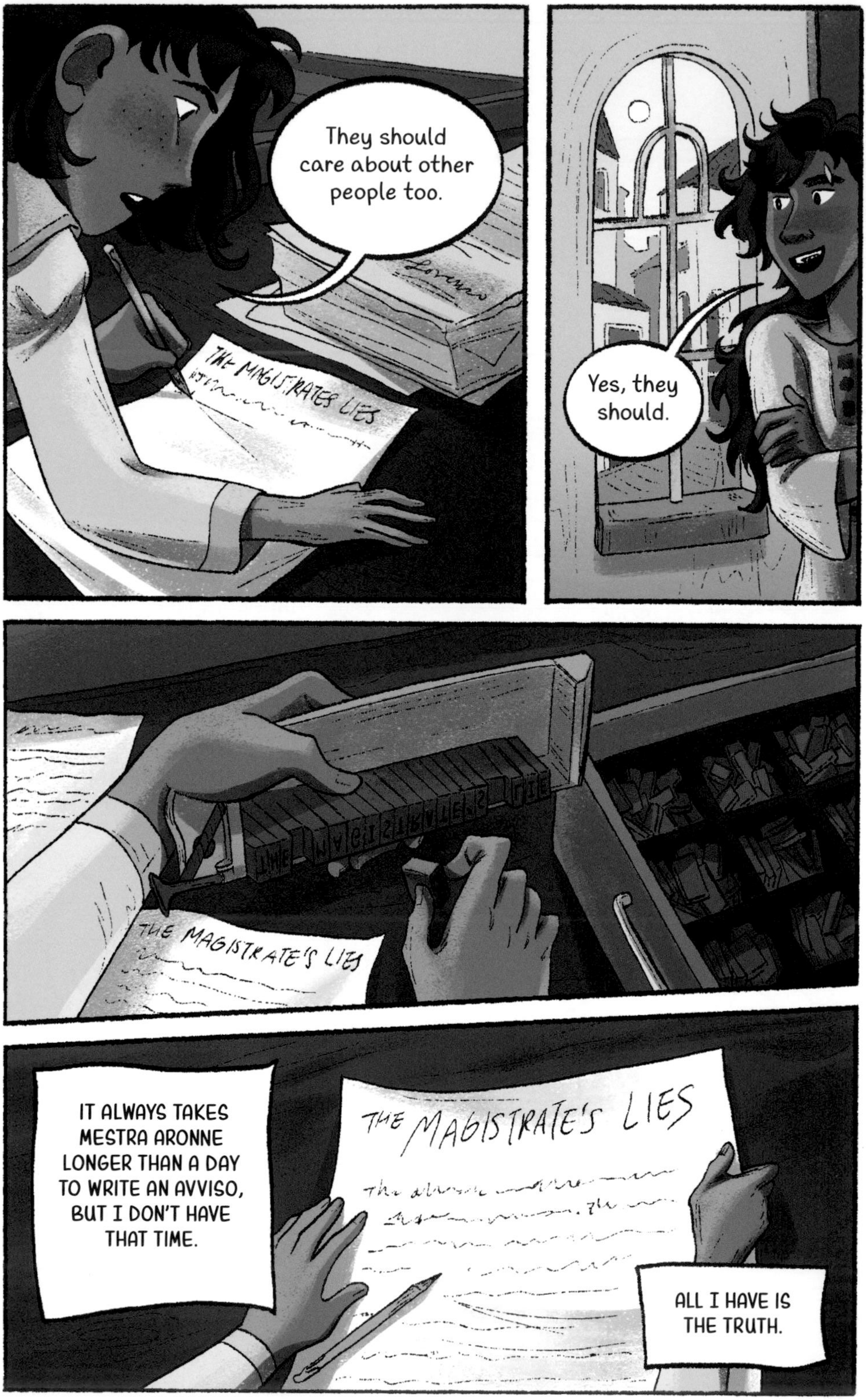
They should care about other people too.
THE MAGISTRATE'S LIES
Yes, they should.
THE MAGISTRATE'S LIES
IT ALWAYS TAKES MESTRA ARONNE LONGER THAN A DAY TO WRITE AN AVVISO, BUT I DON'T HAVE THAT TIME.
THE MAGISTRATE'S LIES
ALL I HAVE IS THE TRUTH.

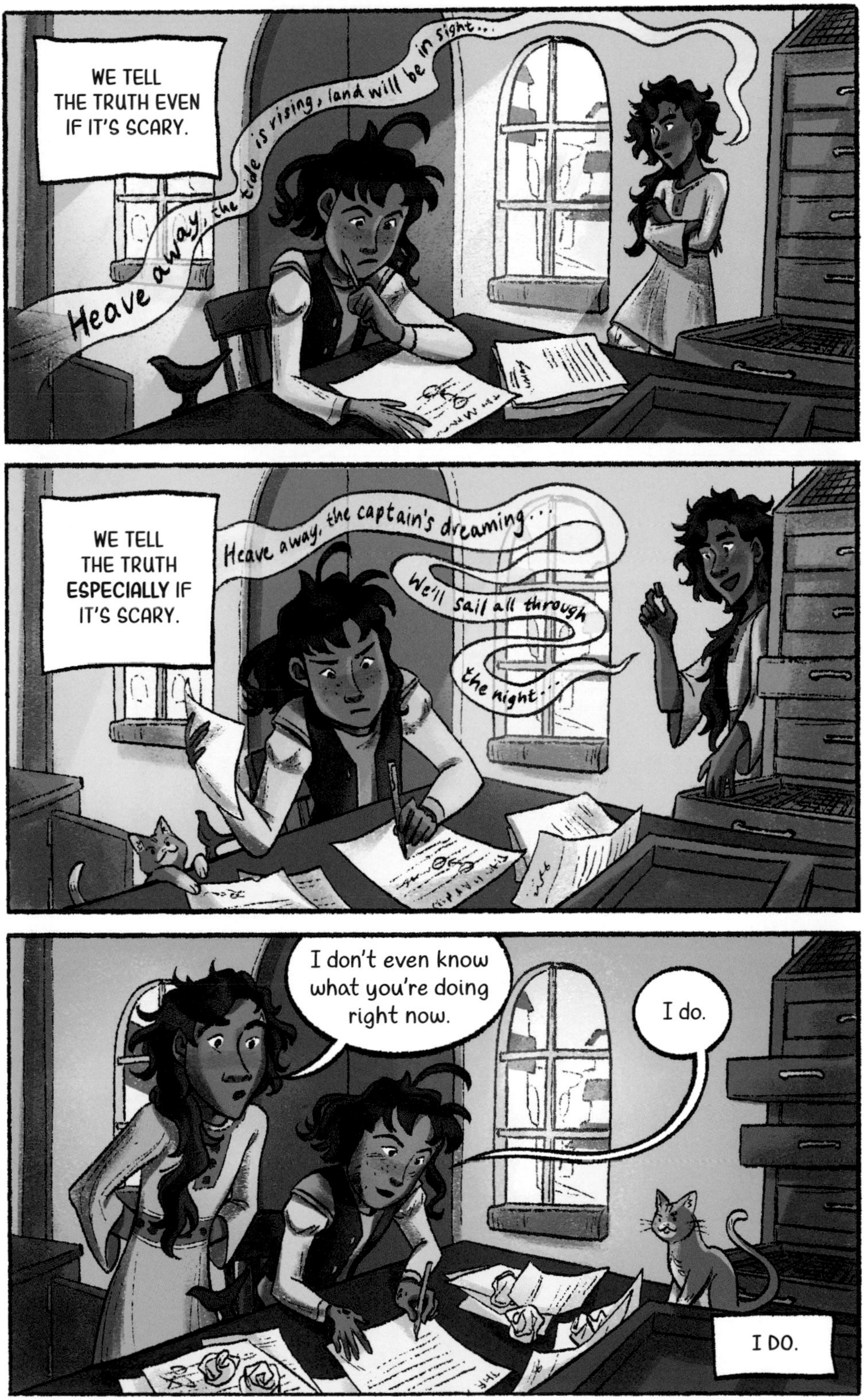
WE TELL THE TRUTH EVEN IF IT'S SCARY.
Heave away, the tide is rising, land will be in sight...
WE TELL THE TRUTH ESPECIALLY IF IT'S SCARY.
Heave away, the captain's dreaming...
We'll sail all through the night...
I don't even know what you're doing right now.
I do.
I DO.

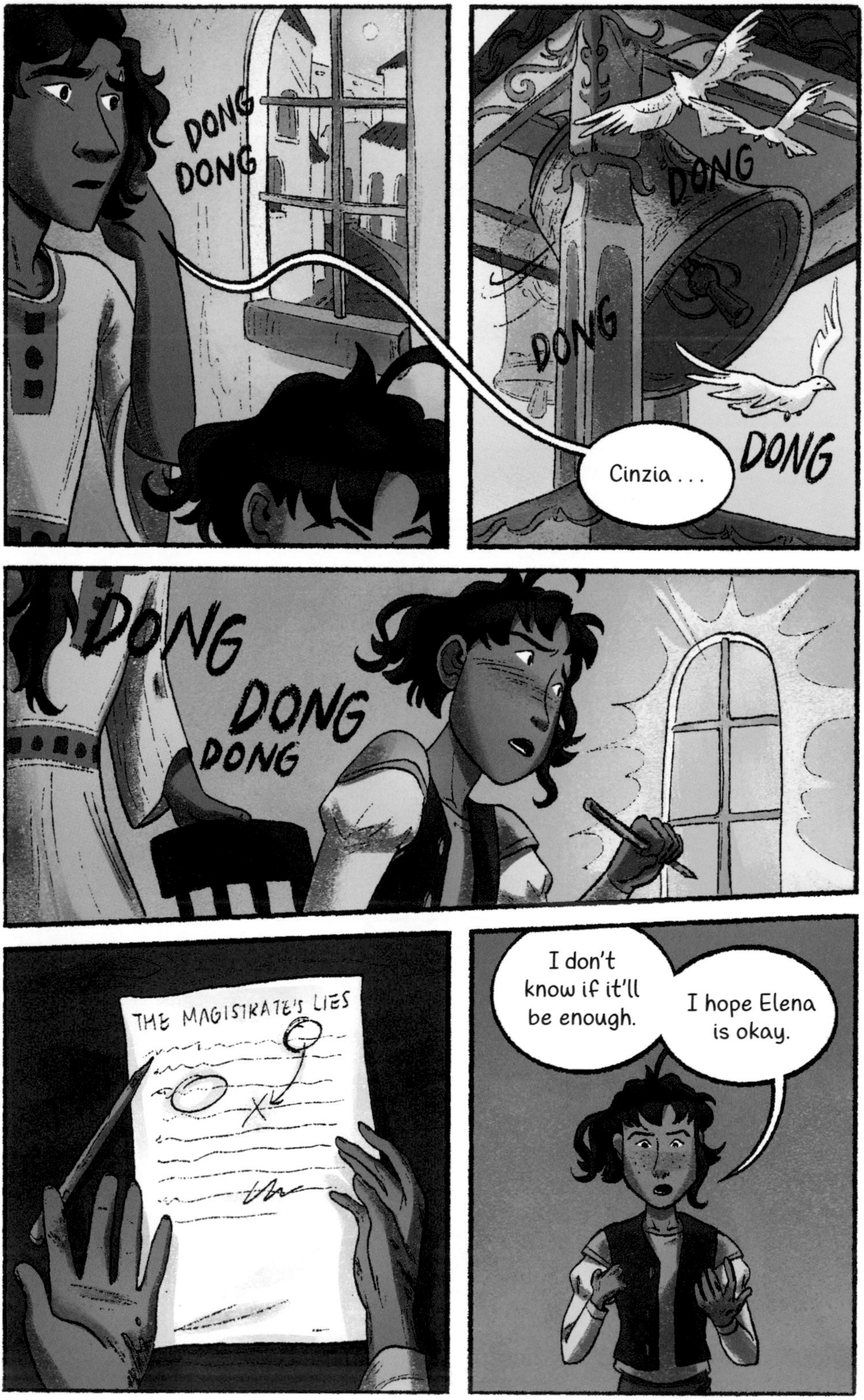
DONG
DONG
DONG
DONG
DONG
Cinzia . . .
DONG
DONG
DONG
THE MAGISTRATE'S LIES
I don't know if it'll be enough.
I hope Elena is okay.

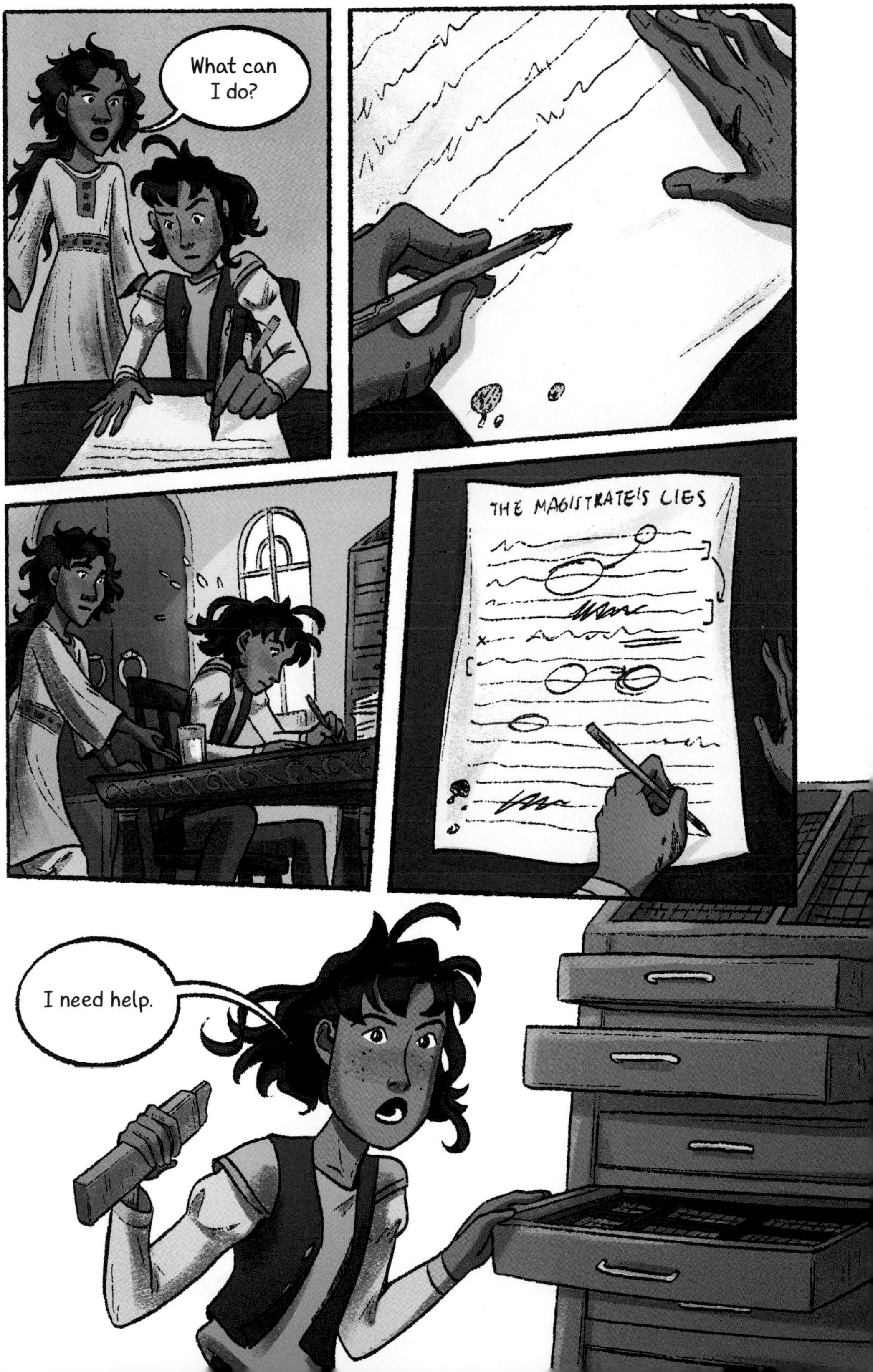
What can I do?
THE MAGISTRATE'S LIES
I need help.

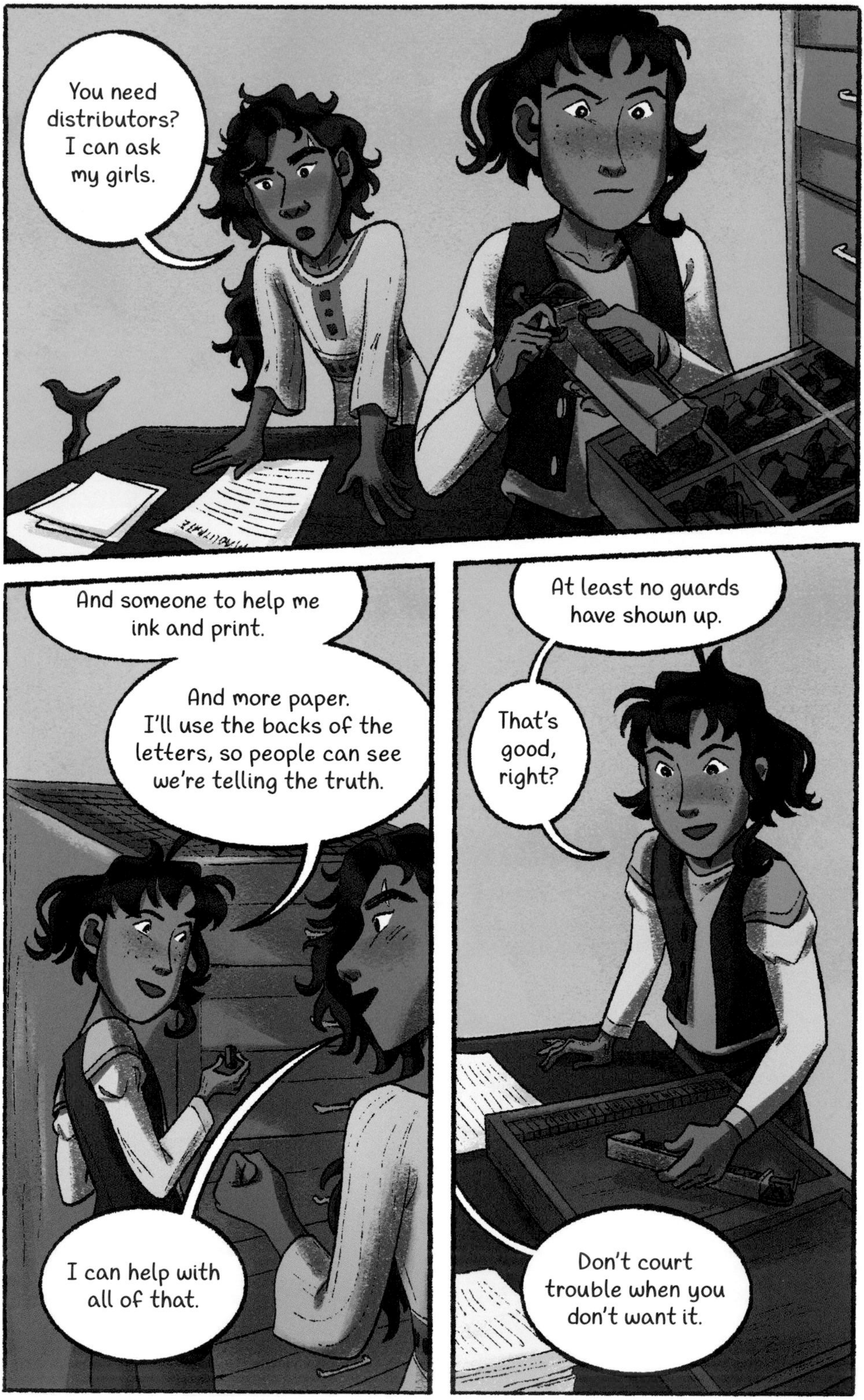
You need distributors? I can ask my girls.
And someone to help me ink and print.
And more paper. I'll use the backs of the letters, so people can see we're telling the truth.
I can help with all of that.
At least no guards have shown up.
That's good, right?
Don't court trouble when you don't want it.

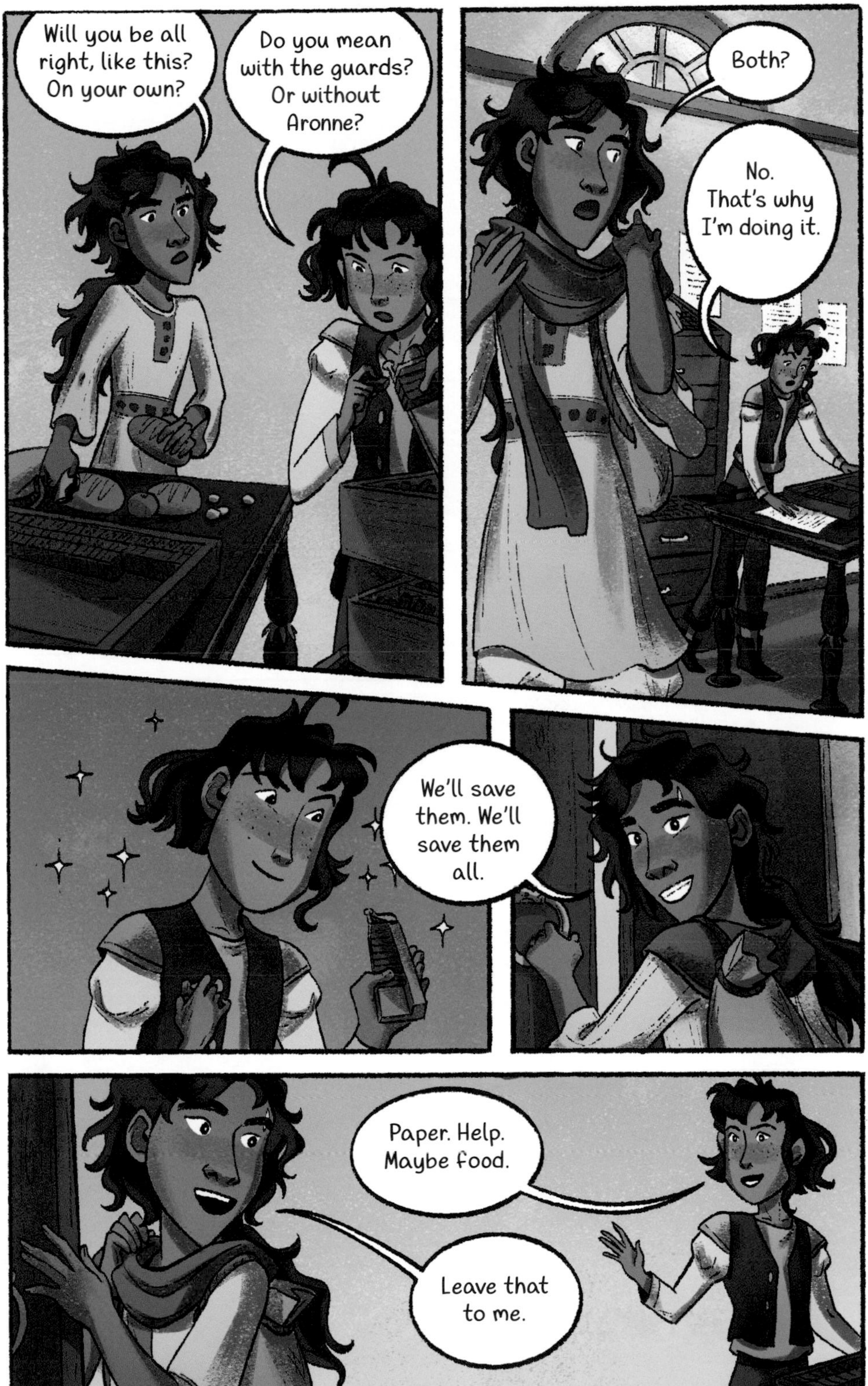
Will you be all right, like this? On your own?
Do you mean with the guards? Or without Aronne?
Both?
No. That's why I'm doing it.
We'll save them. We'll save them all.
Paper. Help. Maybe food.
Leave that to me.

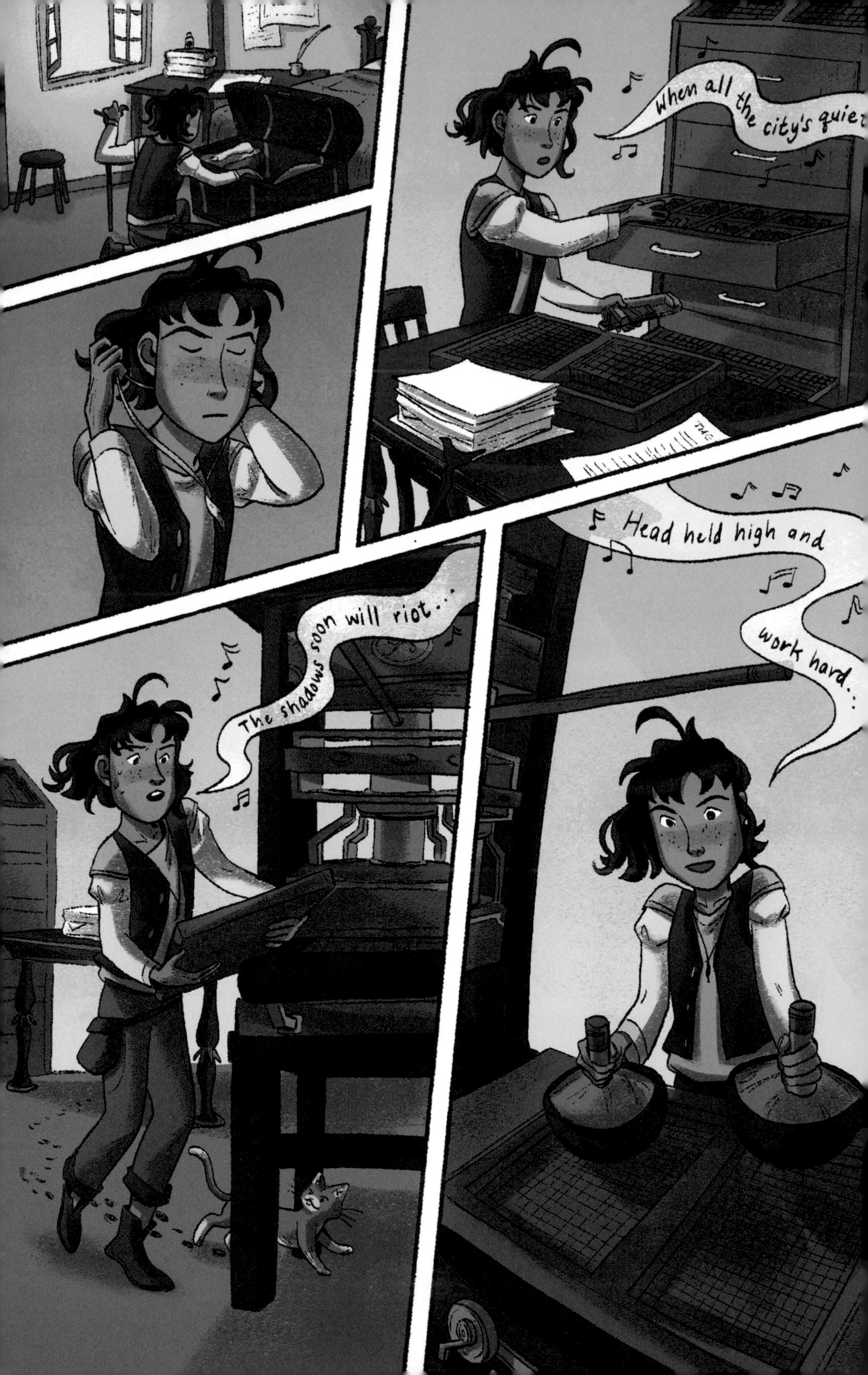
When all the city's quiet
The shadows soon will riot...
Head held high and
work hard...

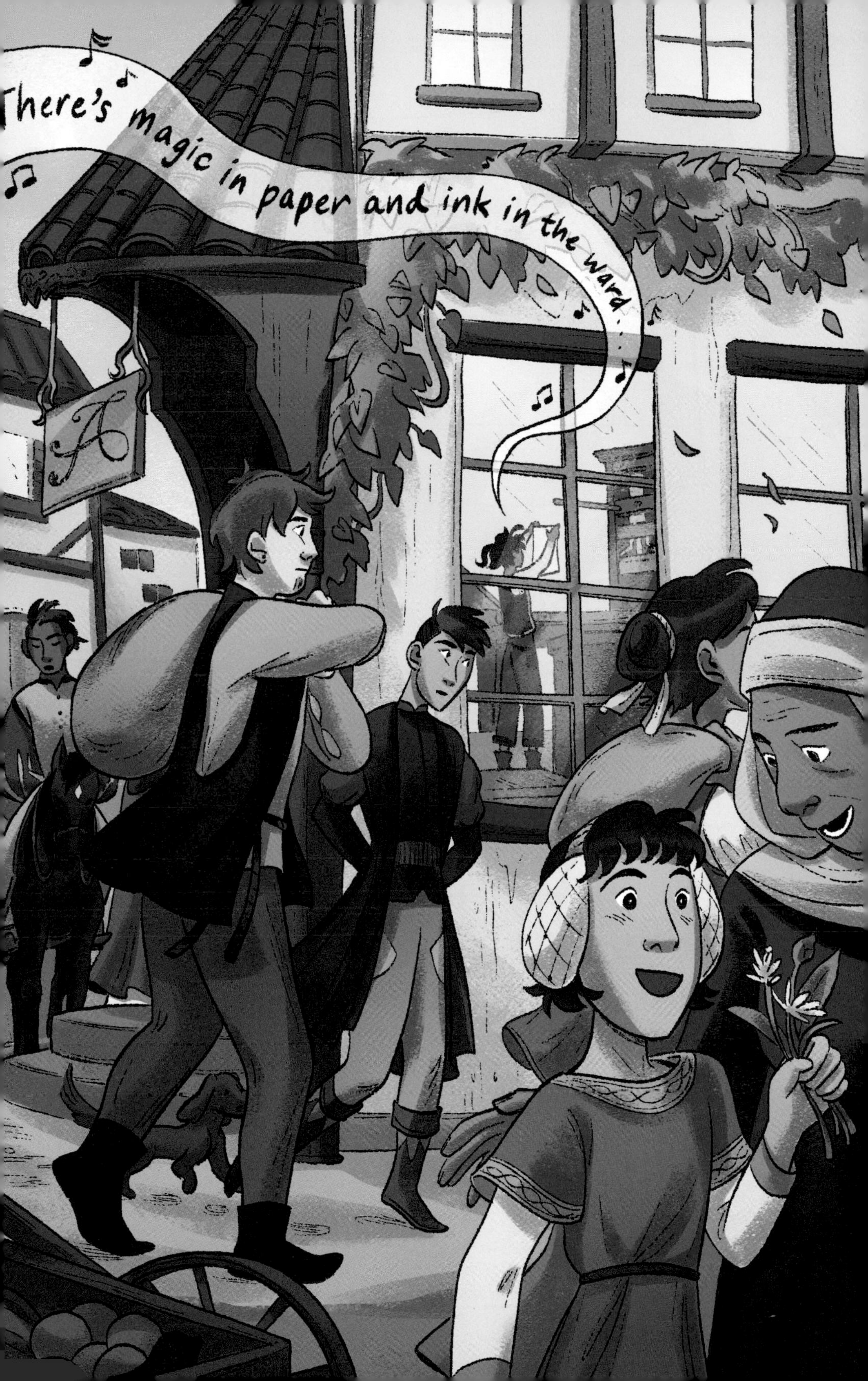
There's magic in paper and ink in the ward. . .

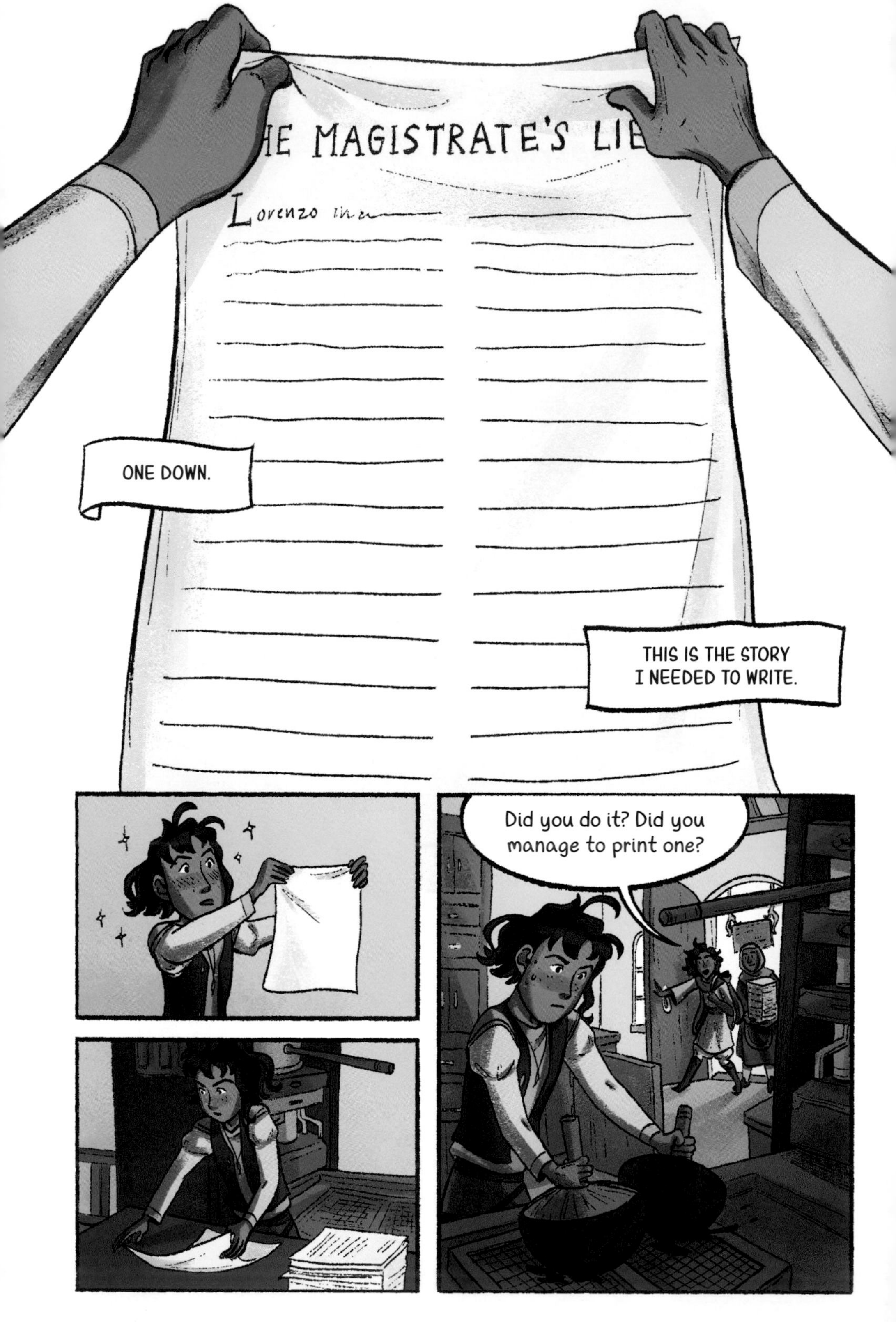
HE MAGISTRATE'S LIE
Lorenzo
ONE DOWN.
THIS IS THE STORY
I NEEDED TO WRITE.
Did you do it? Did you
manage to print one?

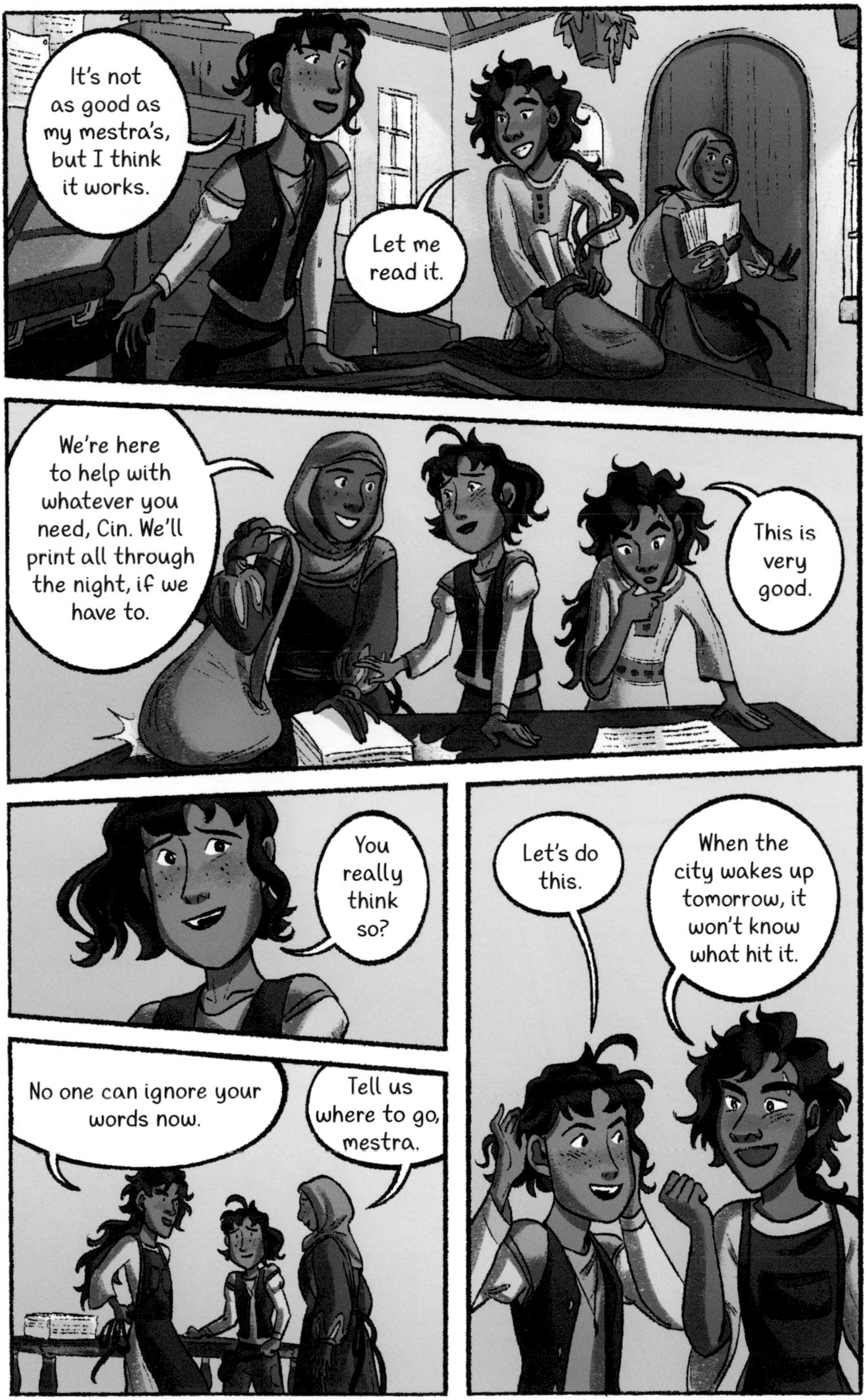
It's not as good as my mestra's, but I think it works.
Let me read it.
We're here to help with whatever you need, Cin. We'll print all through the night, if we have to.
This is very good.
You really think so?
No one can ignore your words now.
Tell us where to go, mestra.
Let's do this.
When the city wakes up tomorrow, it won't know what hit it.

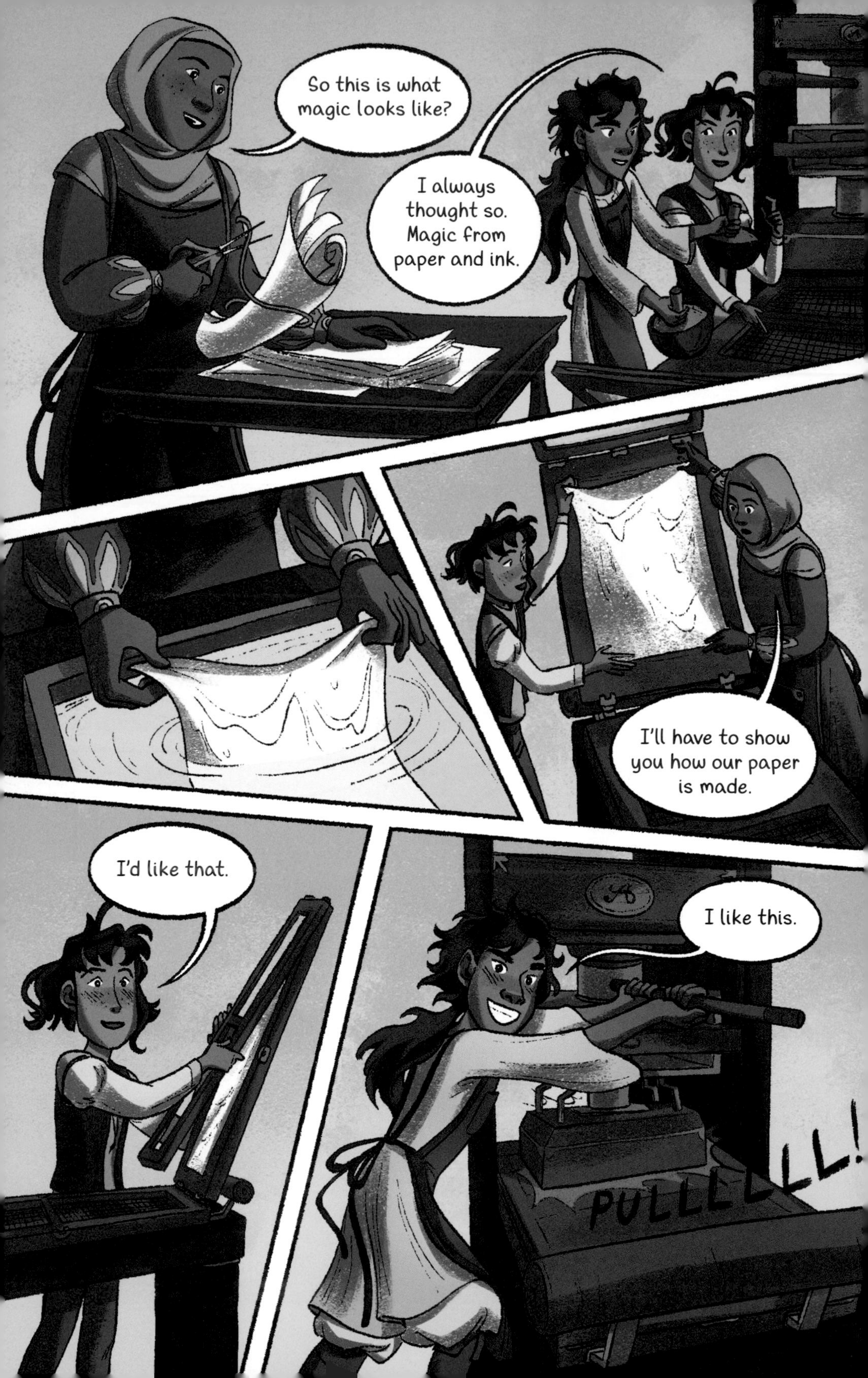

So this is what magic looks like?
I always thought so. Magic from paper and ink.
I'll have to show you how our paper is made.
I'd like that.
I like this.
PULLLLLLL!

WE PRINT OUR LETTERS

AND DEEP IN MY HEART I KNOW

PULL!

THE MAGISTRATE'S LIES

THE M

THE MAGISTRATE'S LIES

THE MAGISTRATE'S LIES

GISTRATE'S LIES

THE MAGISTRATE'S LIES

OUR NEWS WILL SPREAD LIKE A SPLOTCH OF INK TOO.

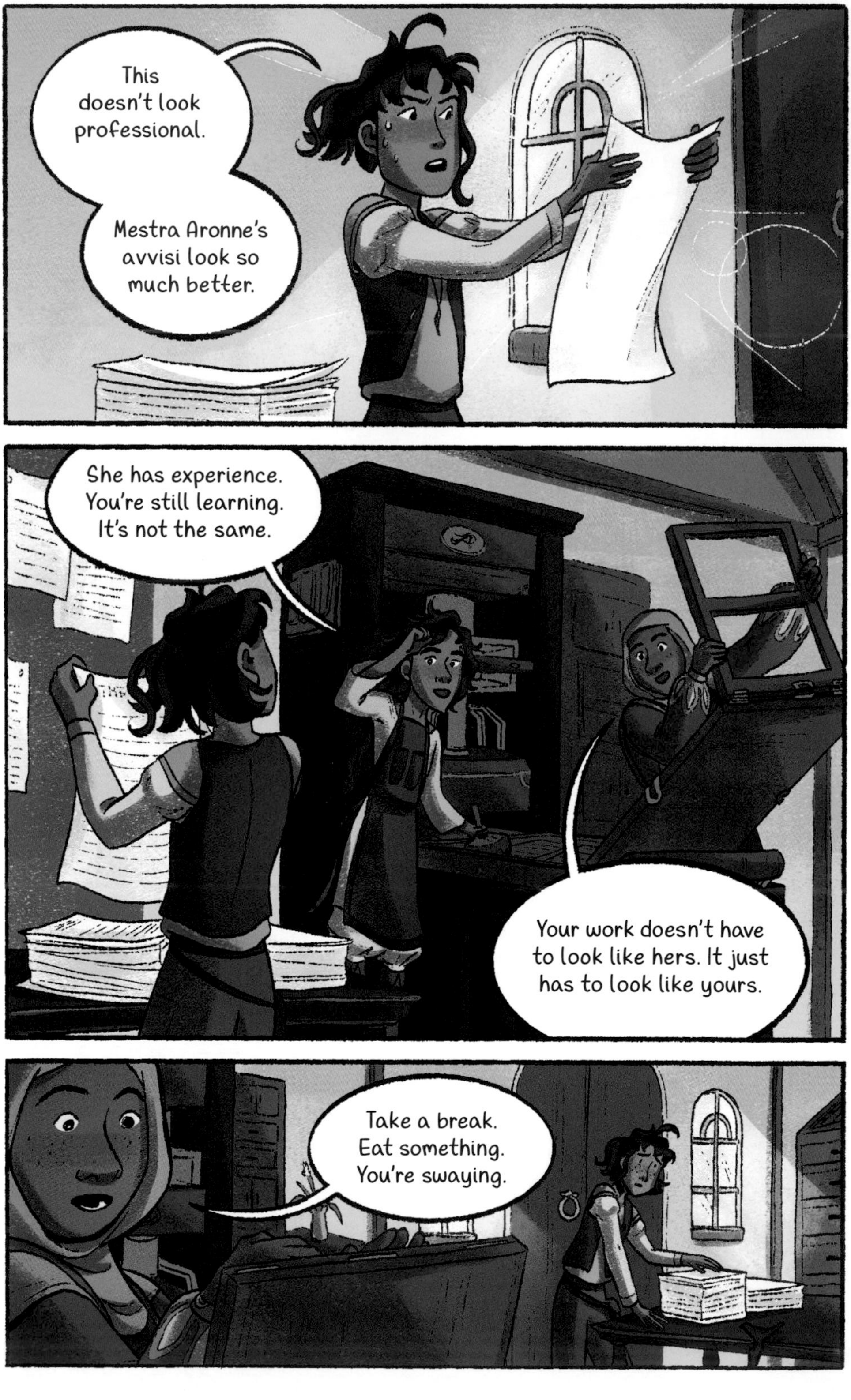
This doesn't look professional.
Mestra Aronne's avvisi look so much better.
She has experience. You're still learning. It's not the same.
Your work doesn't have to look like hers. It just has to look like yours.
Take a break. Eat something. You're swaying.

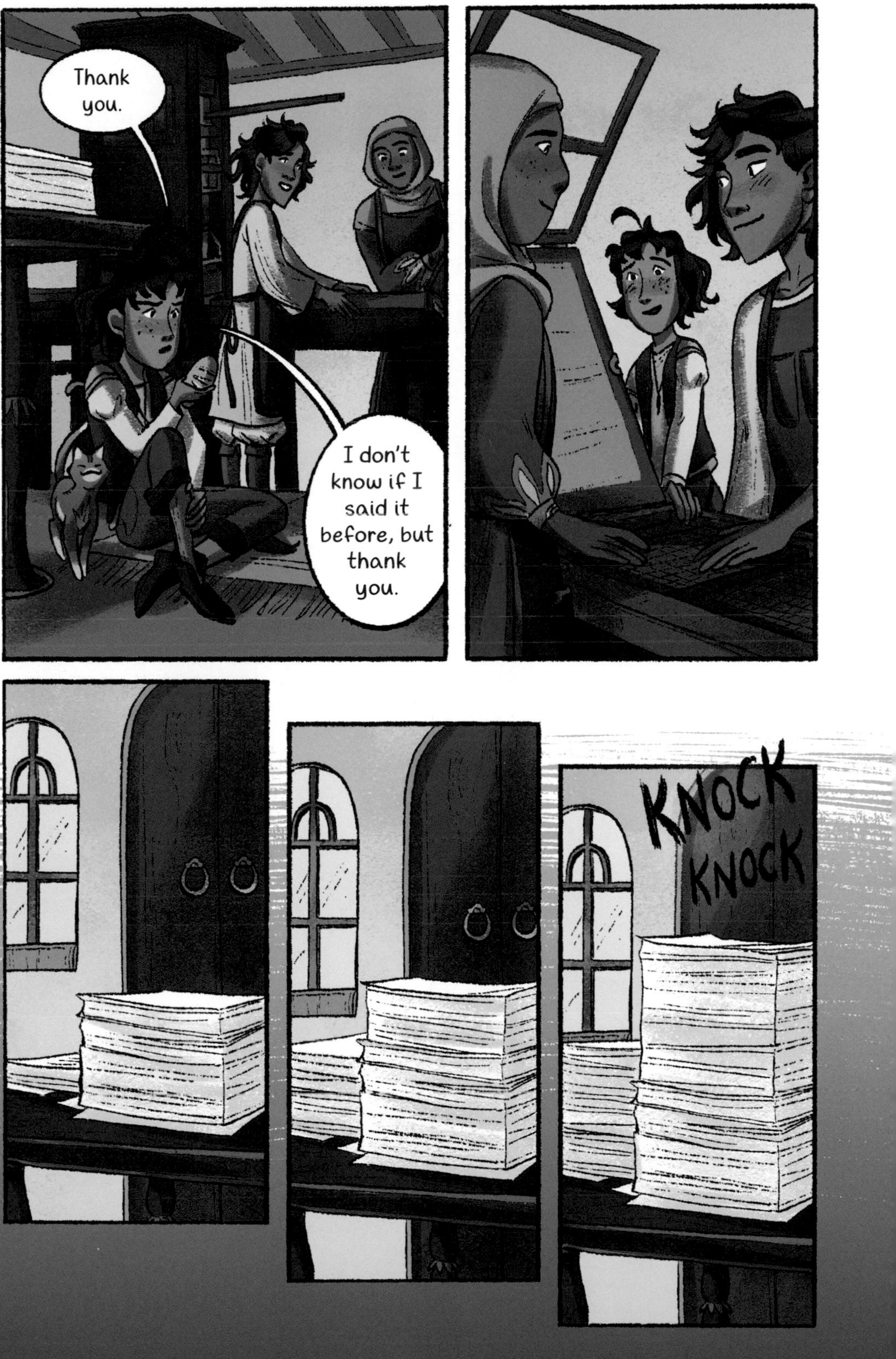
Thank you.
I don't know if I said it before, but thank you.
KNOCK
KNOCK

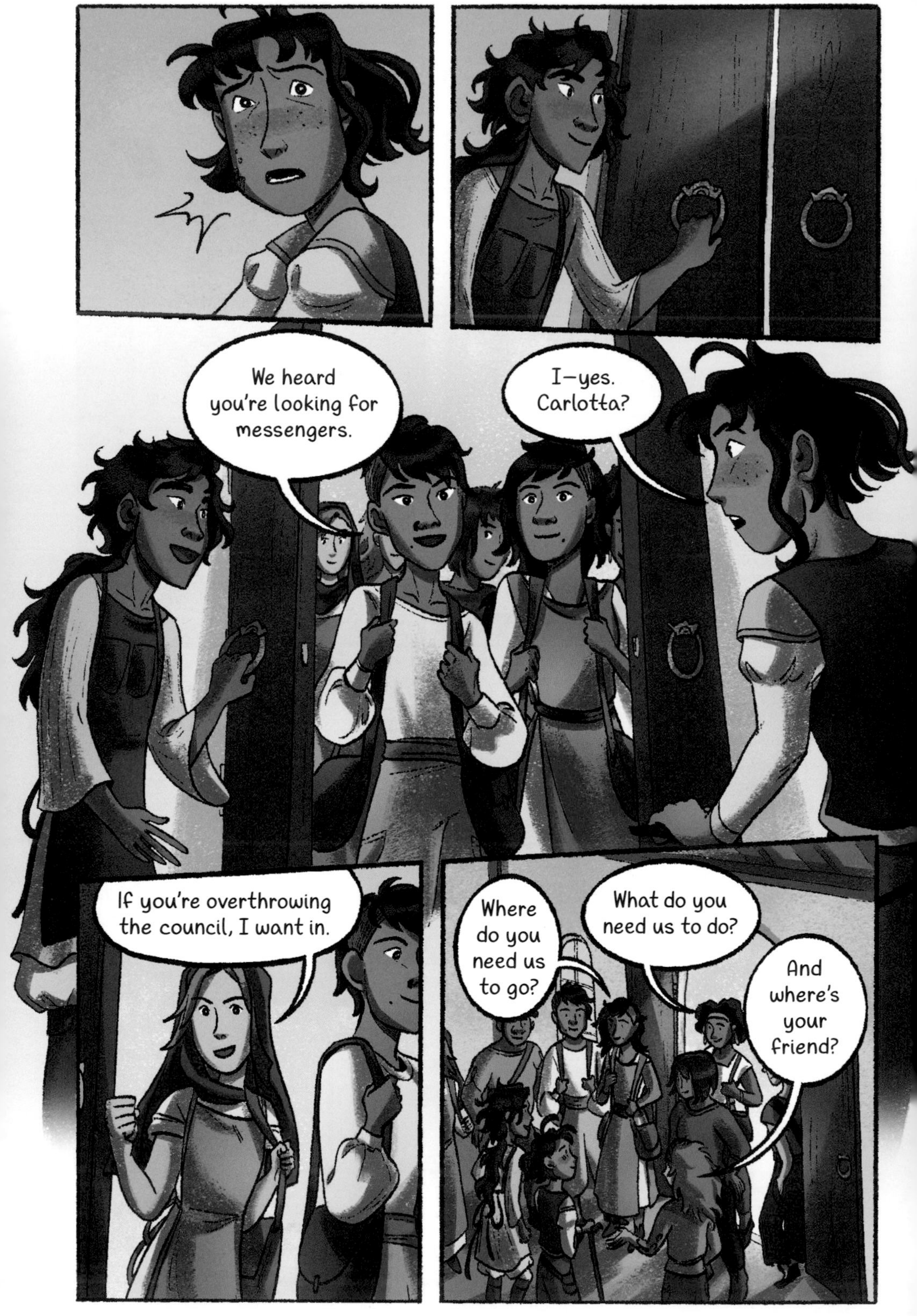
We heard you're looking for messengers.
I—yes. Carlotta?
If you're overthrowing the council, I want in.
Where do you need us to go?
What do you need us to do?
And where's your friend?

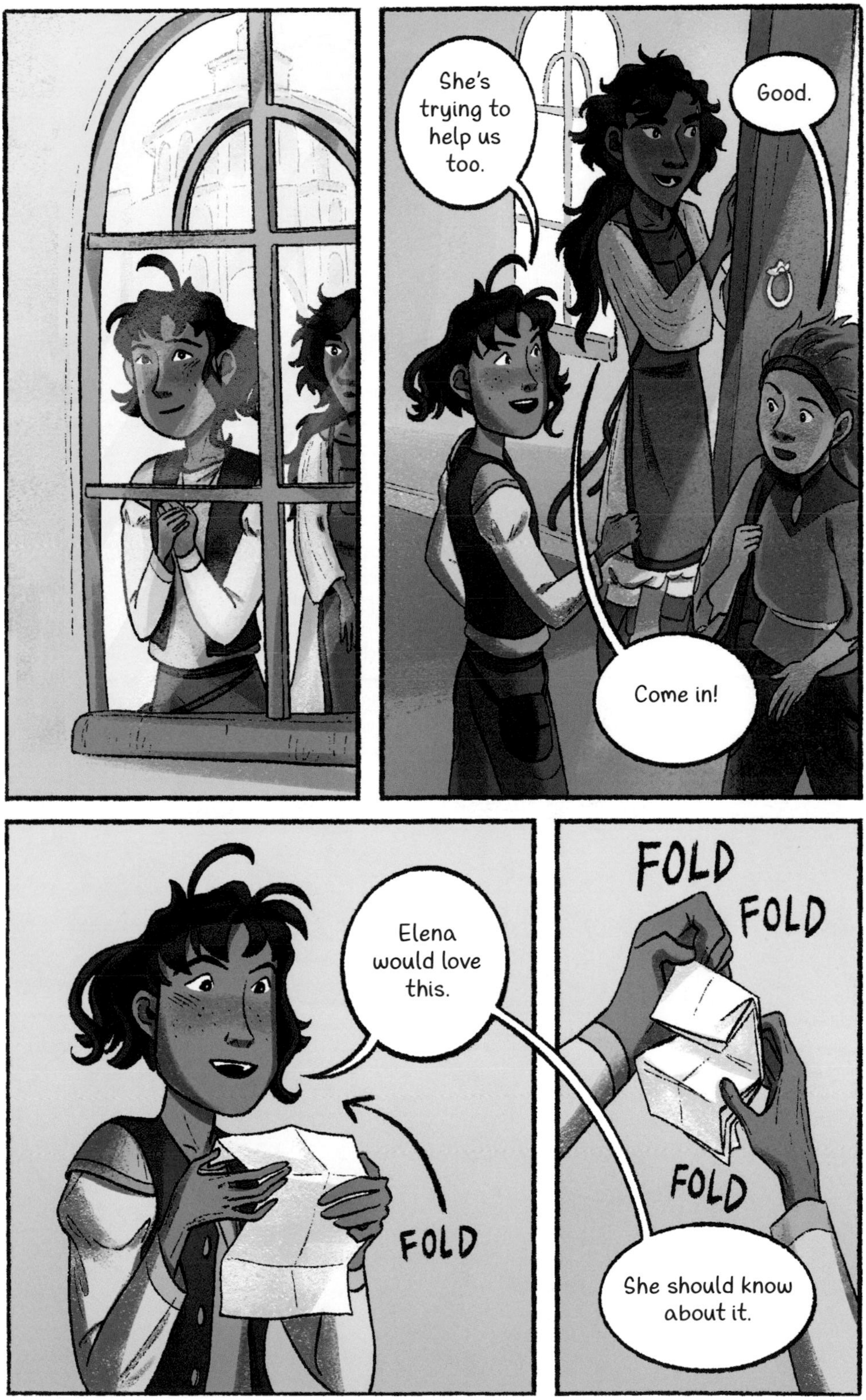

She's trying to help us too.
Good.
Come in!
Elena would love this.
FOLD
FOLD
FOLD
FOLD
She should know about it.

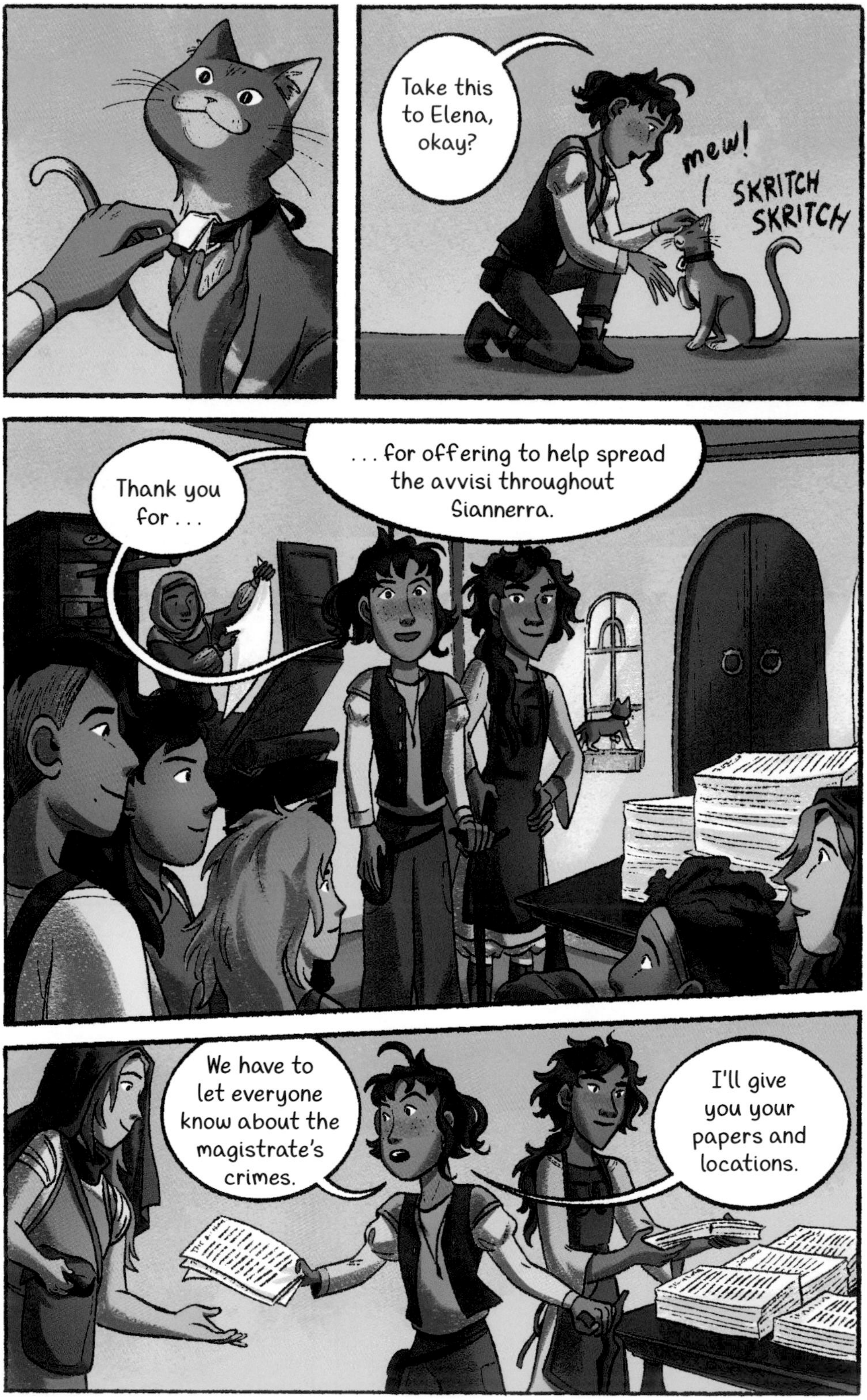
Take this to Elena, okay?
mew!
SKRITCH SKRITCH
Thank you for . . .
. . . for offering to help spread the avvisi throughout Siannerra.
We have to let everyone know about the magistrate's crimes.
I'll give you your papers and locations.

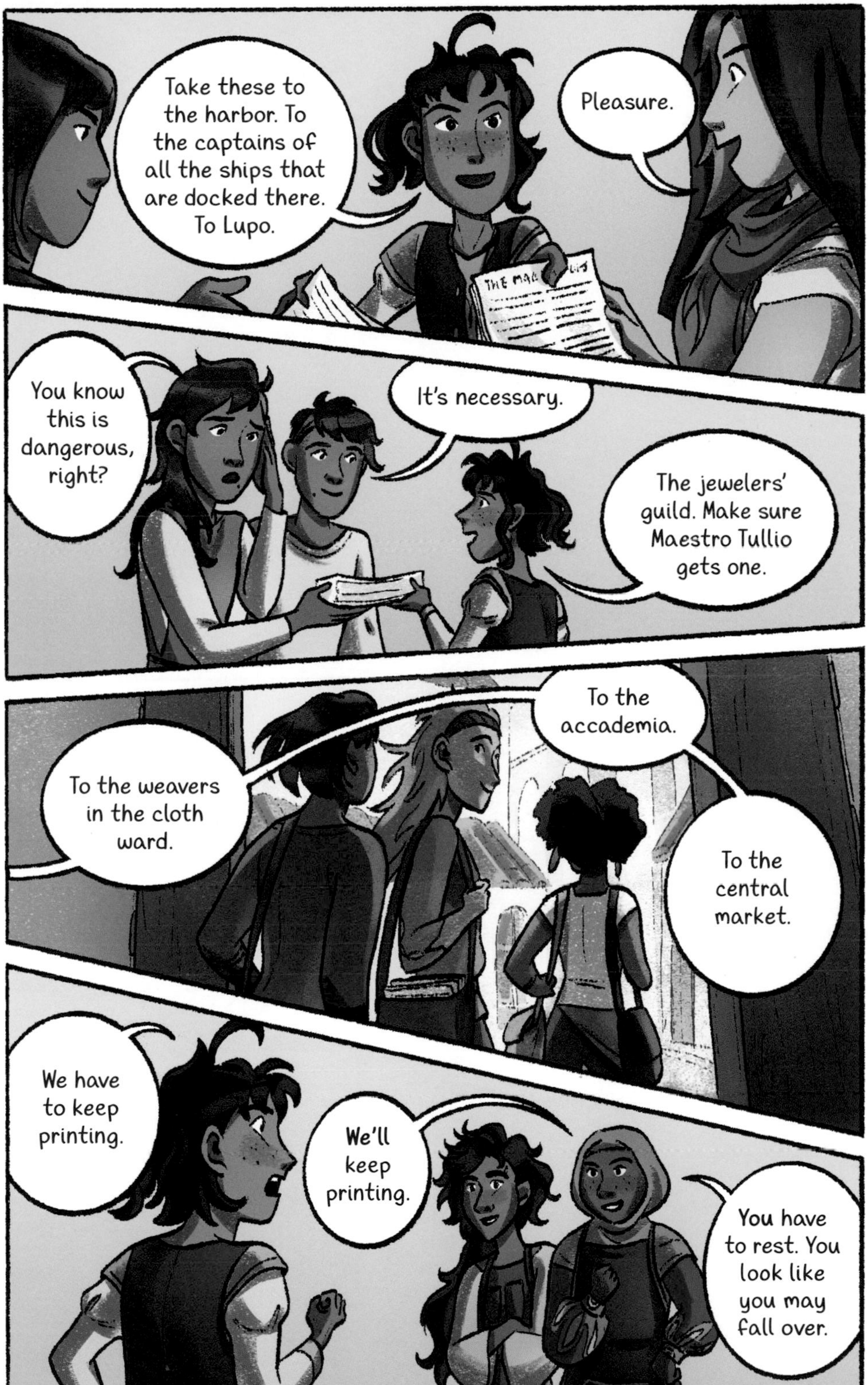
Take these to the harbor. To the captains of all the ships that are docked there. To Lupo.
Pleasure.
THE MA
You know this is dangerous, right?
It's necessary.
The jewelers' guild. Make sure Maestro Tullio gets one.
To the weavers in the cloth ward.
To the accademia.
To the central market.
We have to keep printing.
We'll keep printing.
You have to rest. You look like you may fall over.

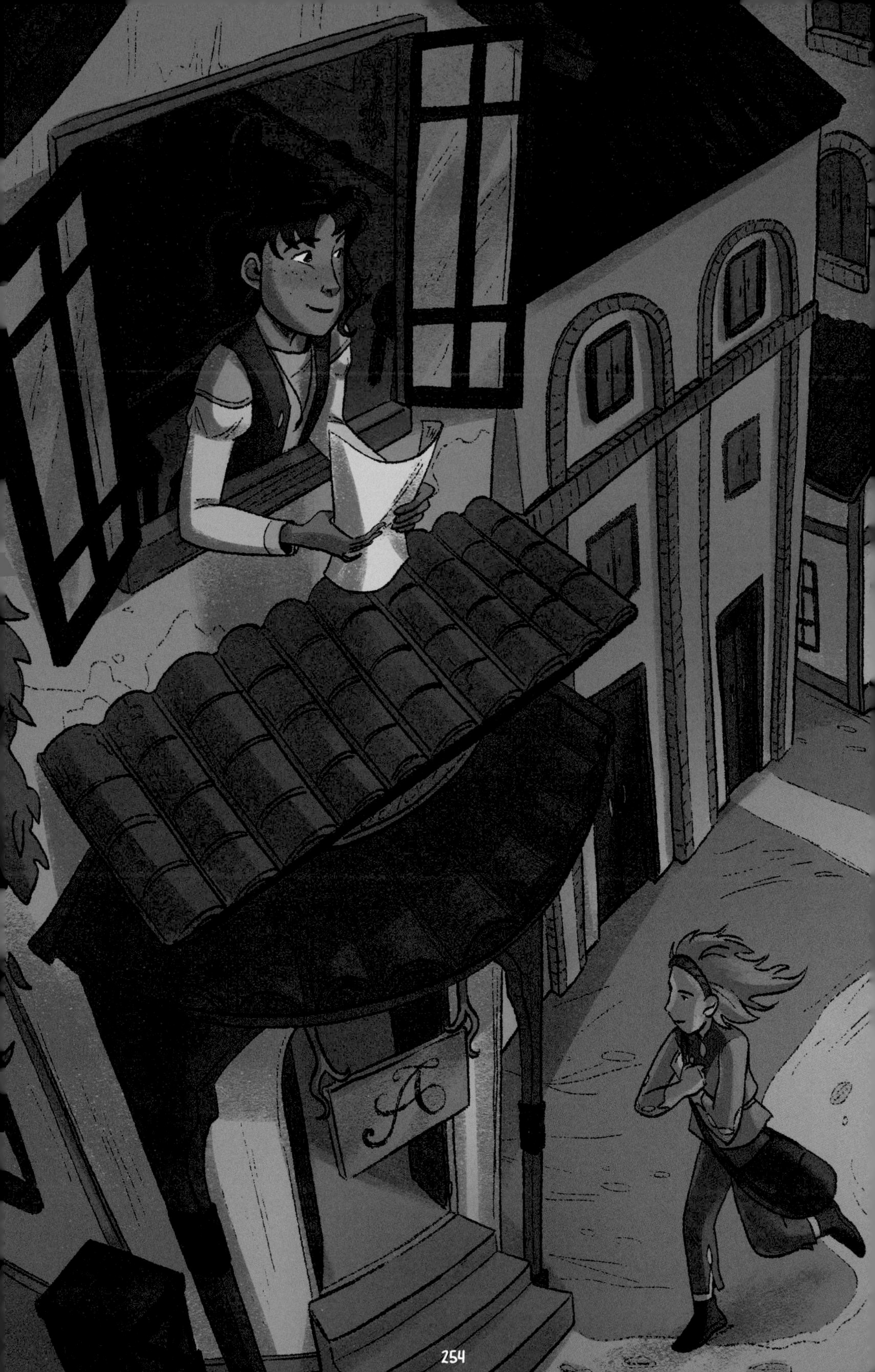

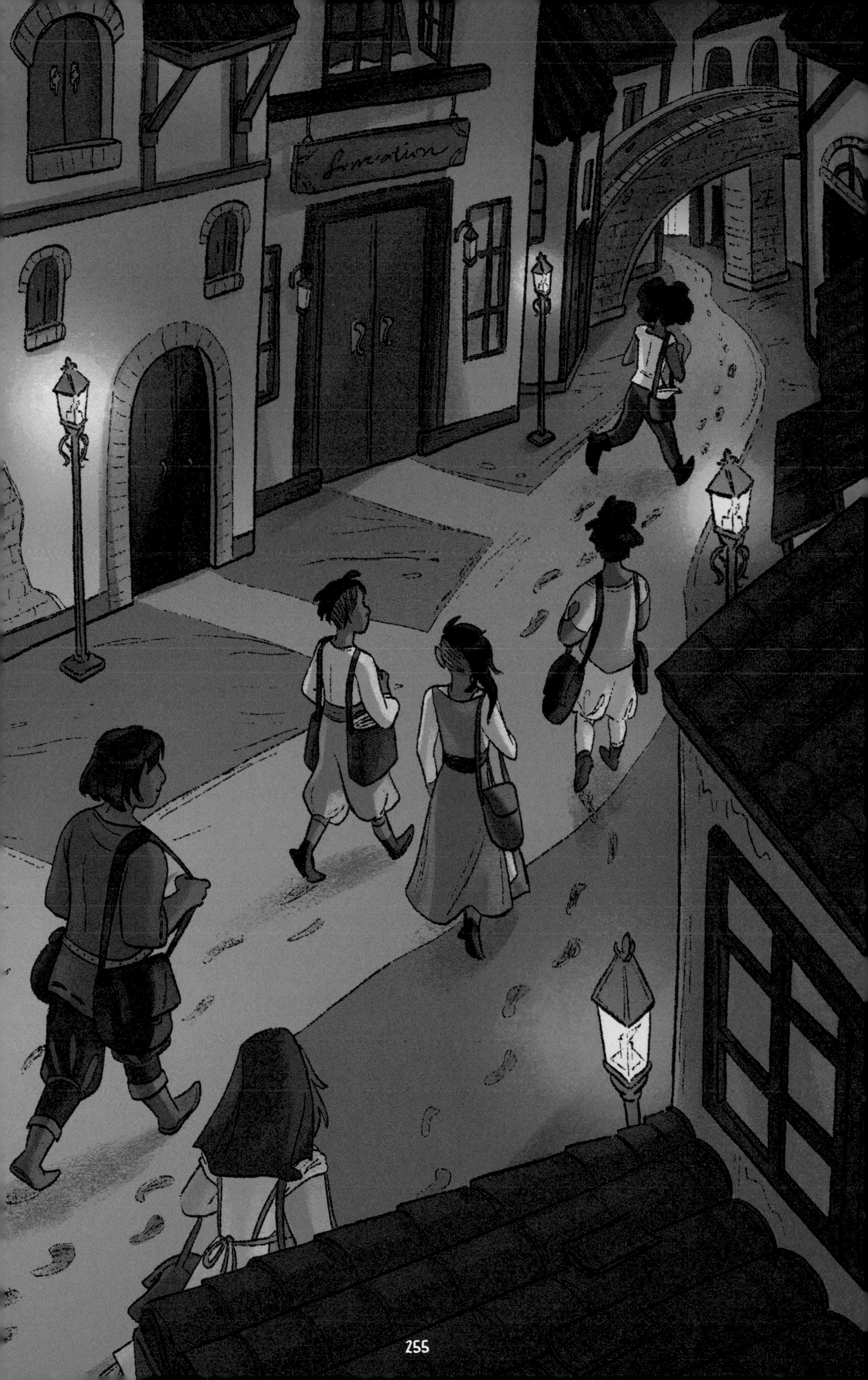

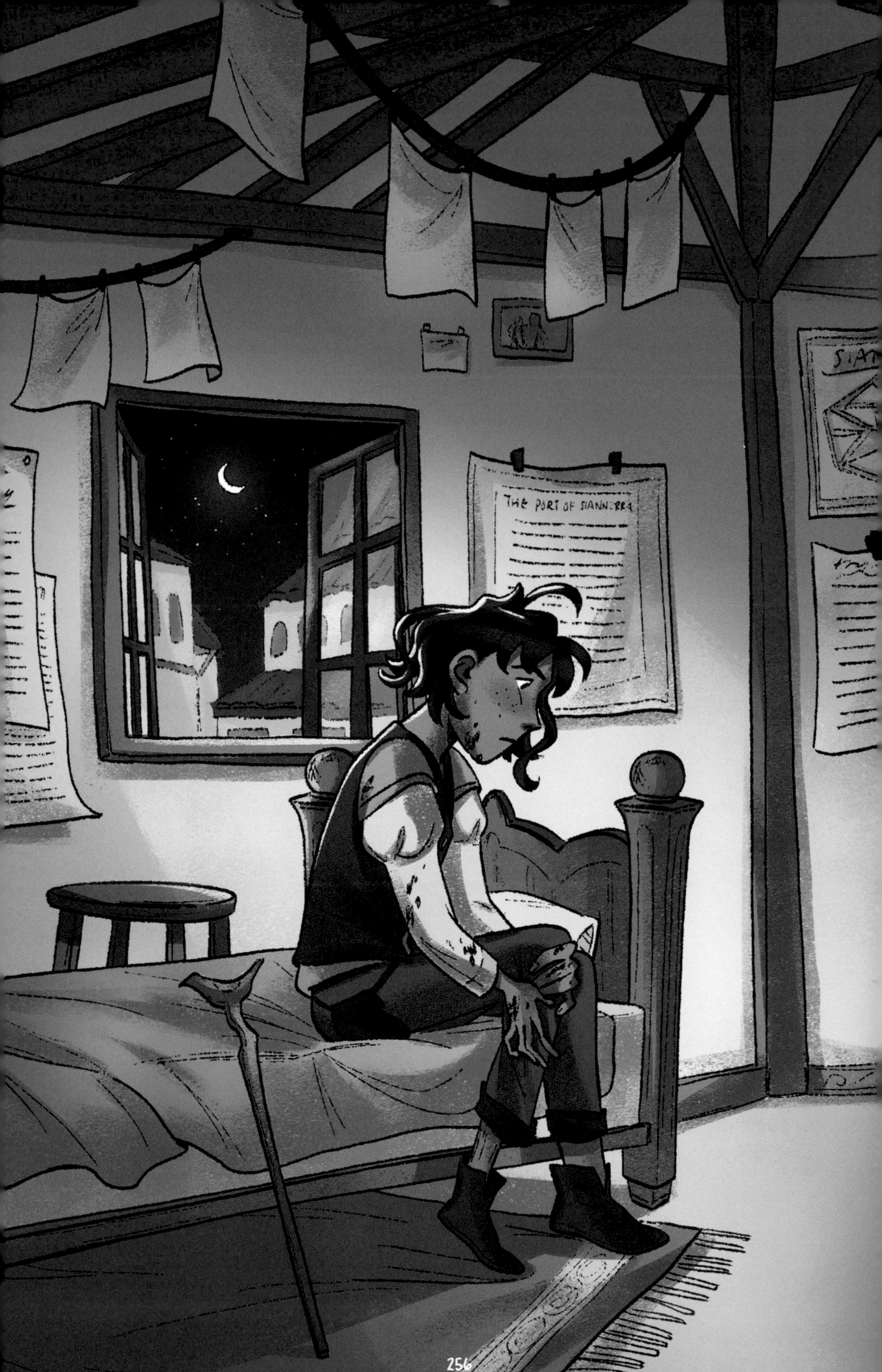

THE PORT OF SIANNORRA

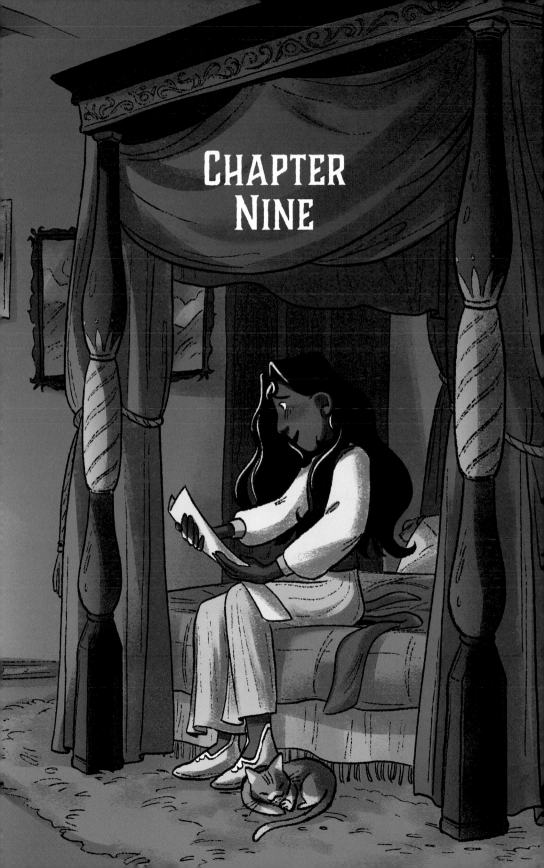

CHAPTER
NINE

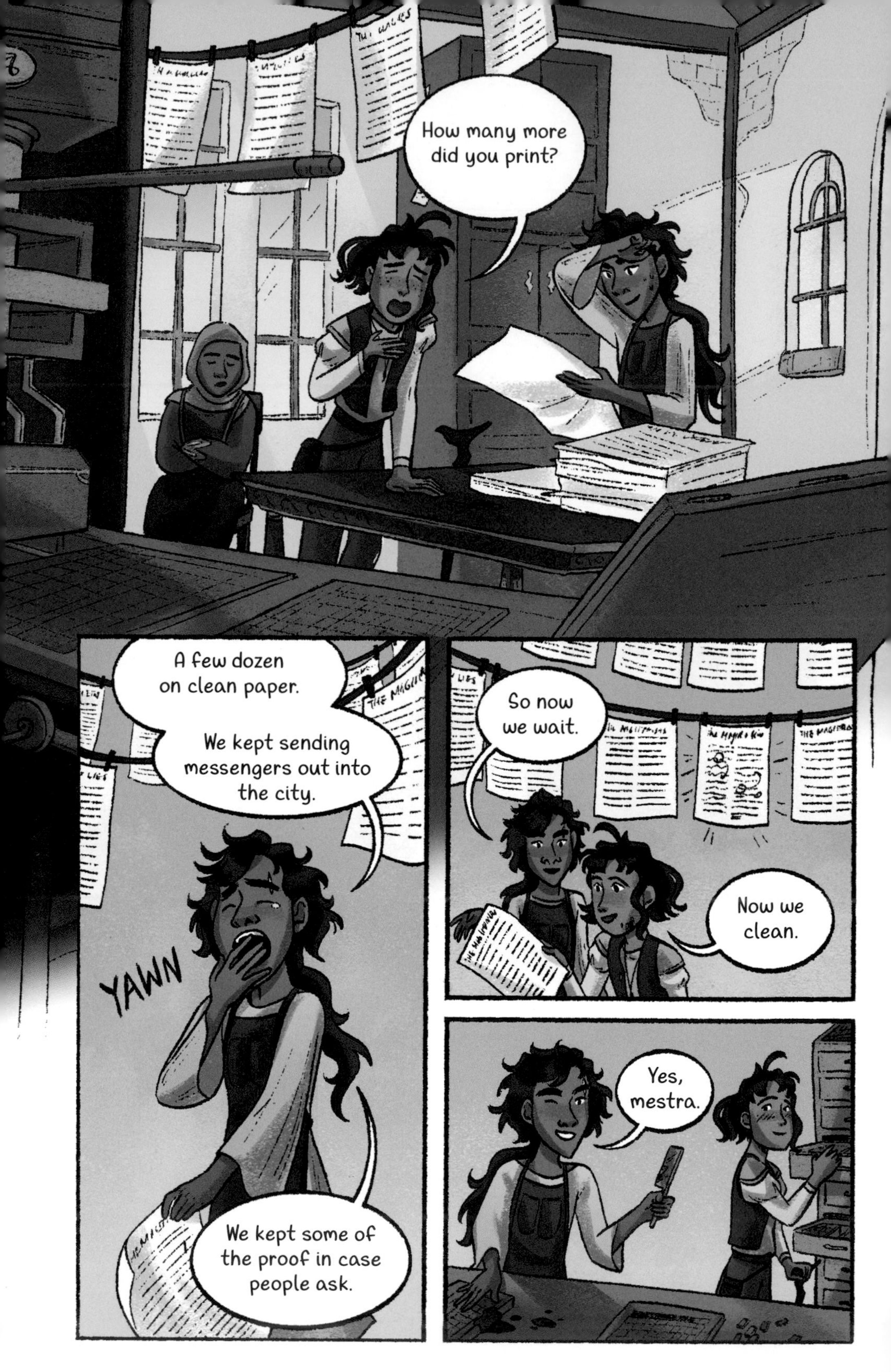
How many more did you print?
A few dozen on clean paper.
We kept sending messengers out into the city.
YAWN
We kept some of the proof in case people ask.
So now we wait.
Now we clean.
Yes, mestra.

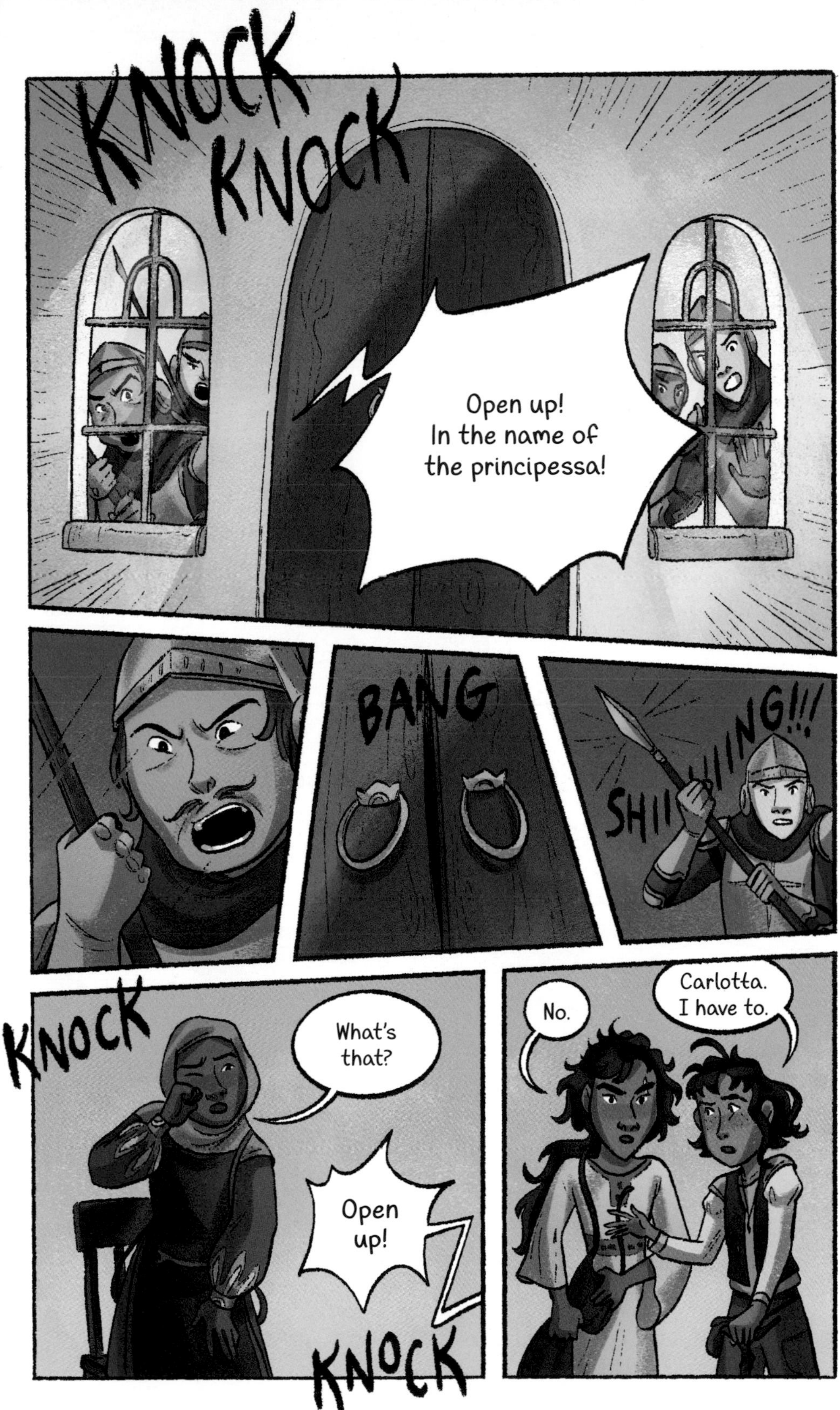
KNOCK
KNOCK
Open up! In the name of the principessa!
BANG
SHIIIIIING!!!
KNOCK
What's that?
Open up!
KNOCK
No.
Carlotta. I have to.

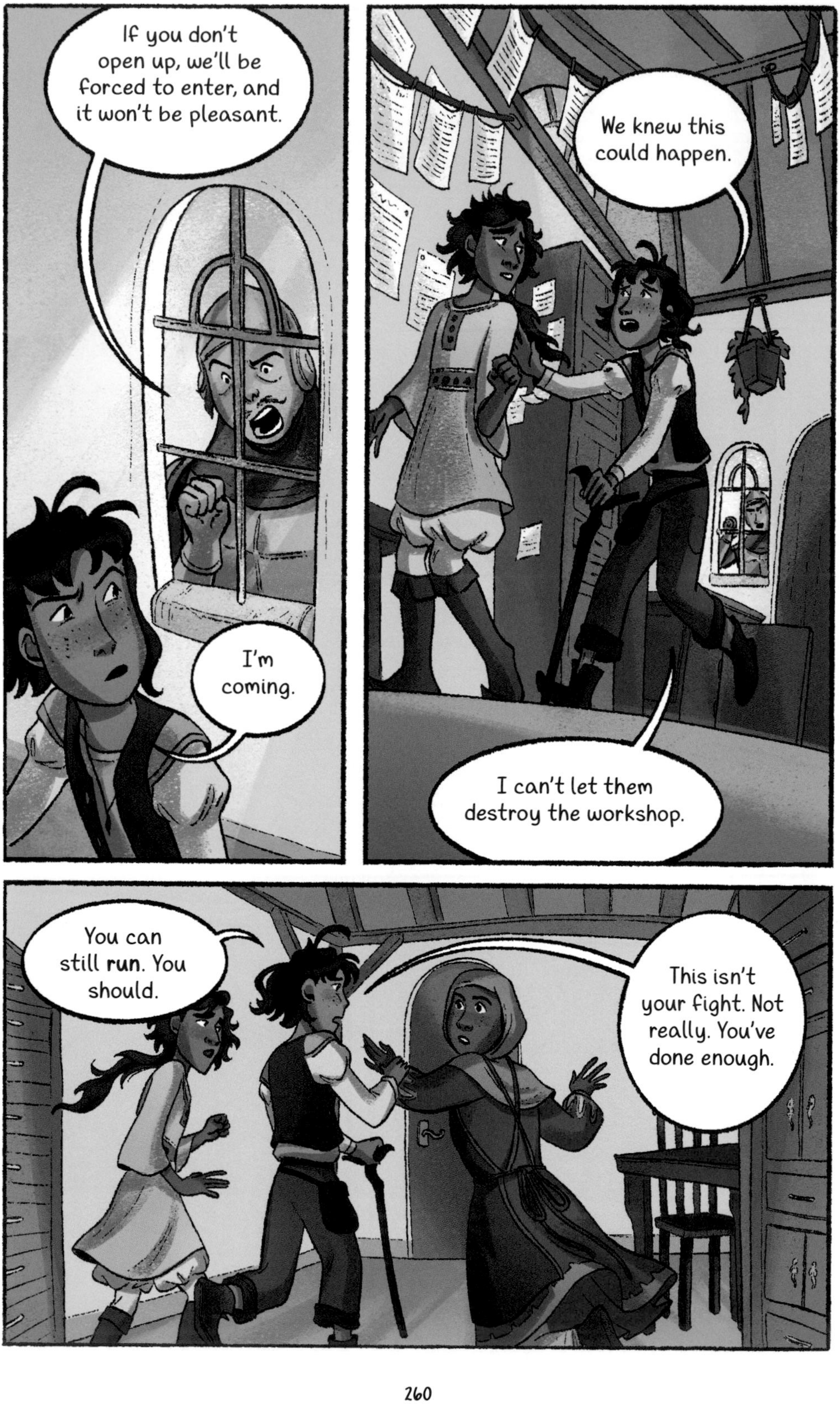
If you don't open up, we'll be forced to enter, and it won't be pleasant.
I'm coming.
We knew this could happen.
I can't let them destroy the workshop.
You can still **run**. You should.
This isn't your fight. Not really. You've done enough.

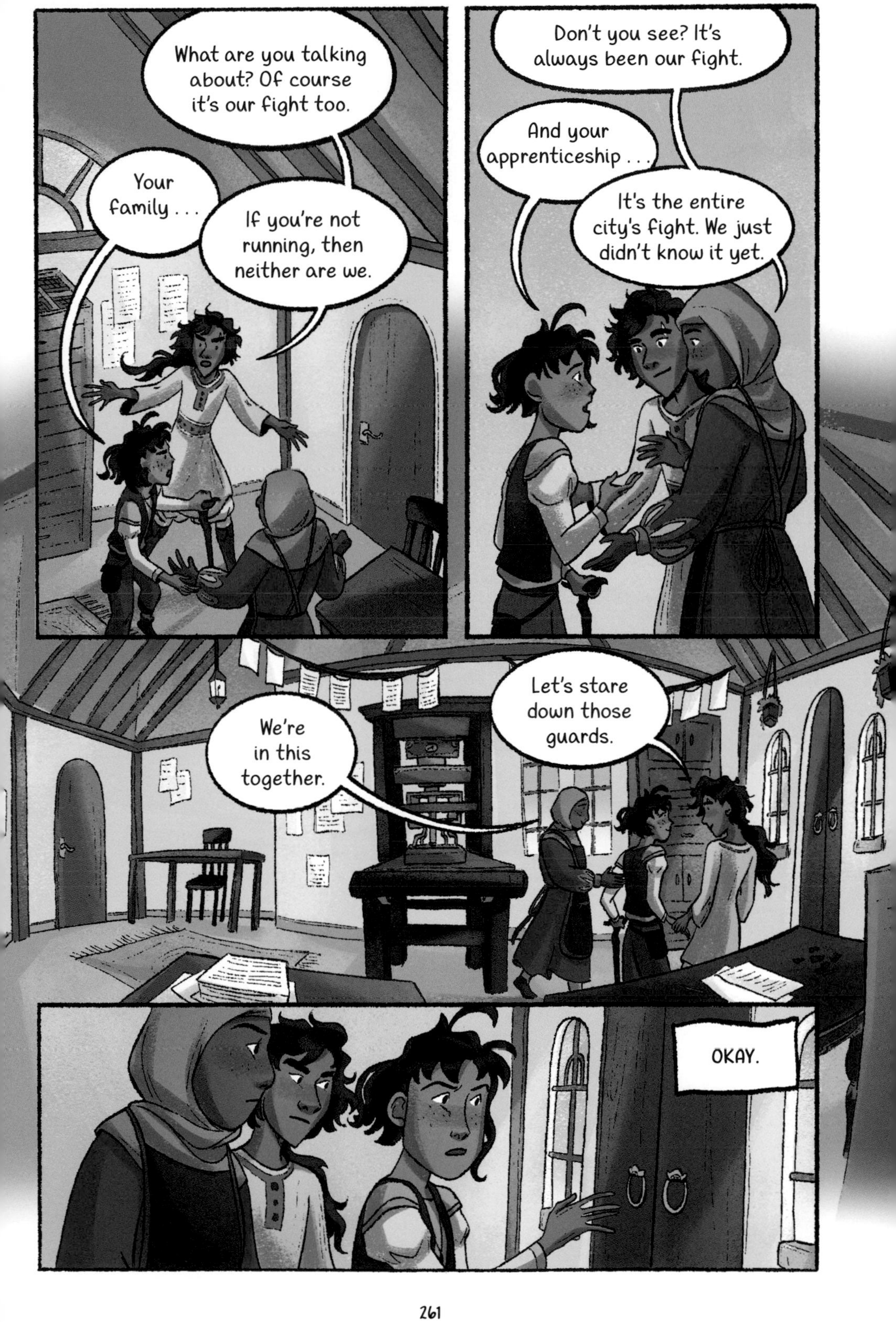

What are you talking about? Of course it's our fight too.
Your family . . .
If you're not running, then neither are we.
Don't you see? It's always been our fight.
And your apprenticeship . . .
It's the entire city's fight. We just didn't know it yet.
We're in this together.
Let's stare down those guards.
OKAY.

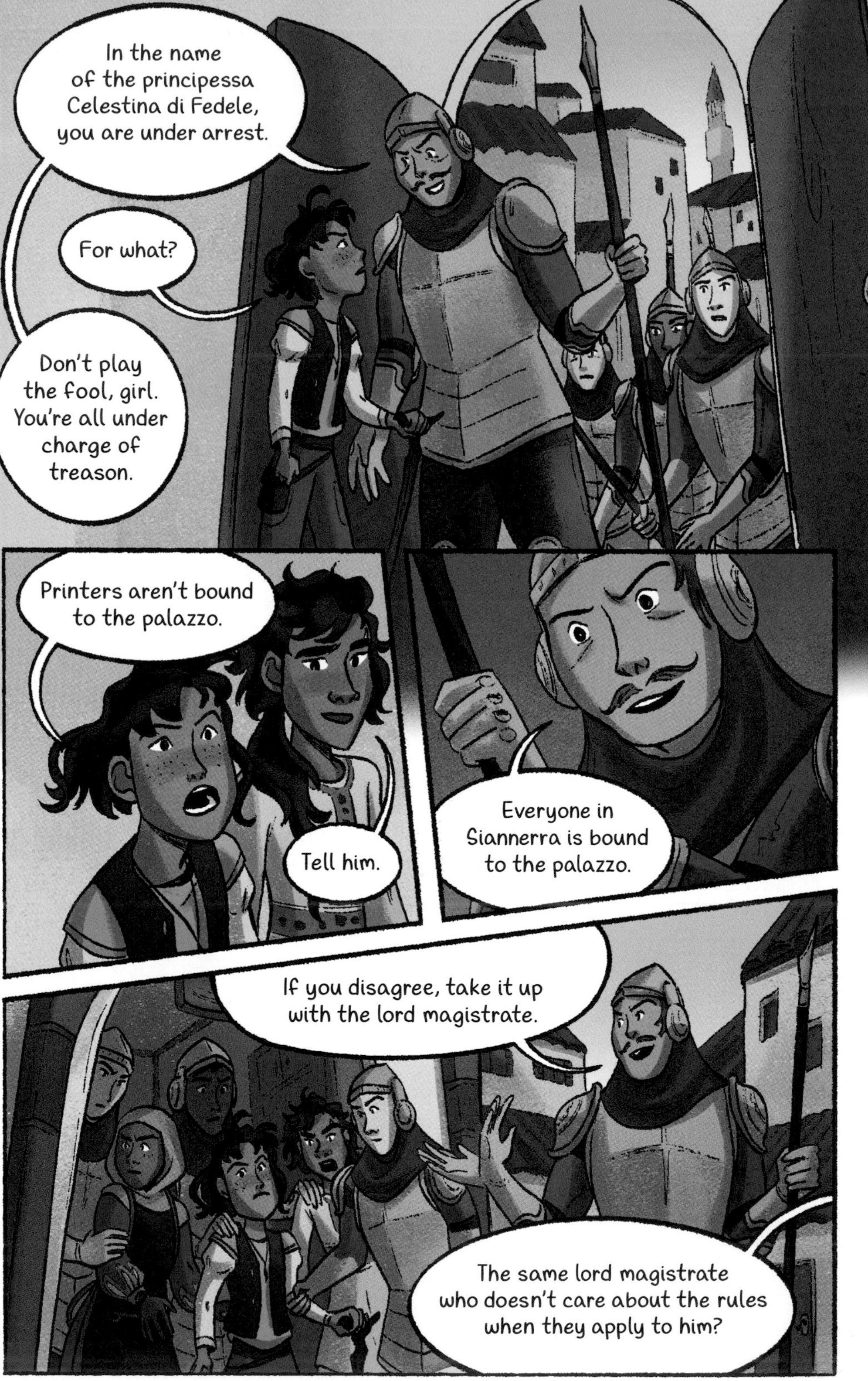
In the name of the principessa Celestina di Fedele, you are under arrest.
For what?
Don't play the fool, girl. You're all under charge of treason.
Printers aren't bound to the palazzo.
Tell him.
Everyone in Siannerra is bound to the palazzo.
If you disagree, take it up with the lord magistrate.
The same lord magistrate who doesn't care about the rules when they apply to him?

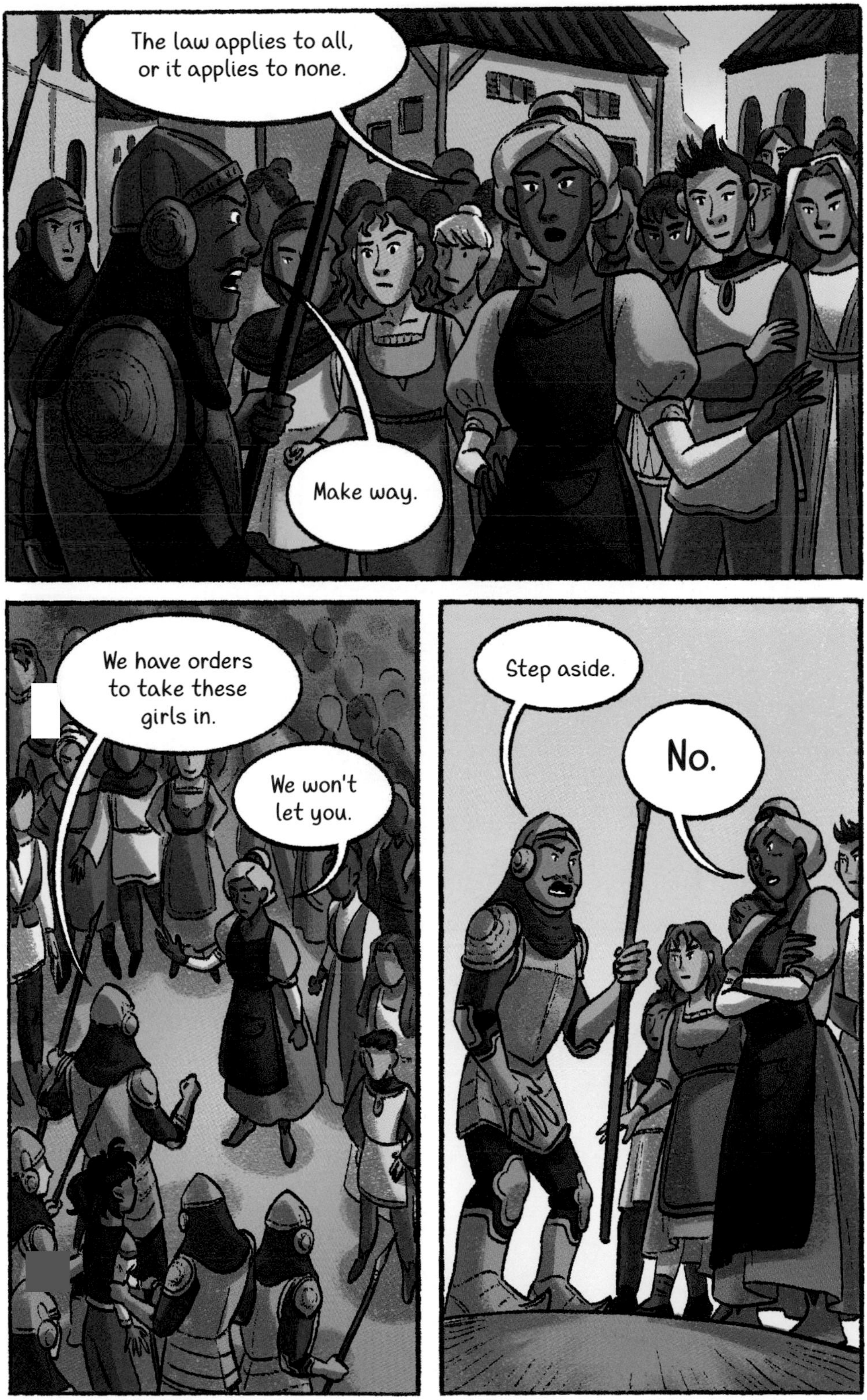
The law applies to all, or it applies to none.
Make way.
We have orders to take these girls in.
We won't let you.
Step aside.
No.

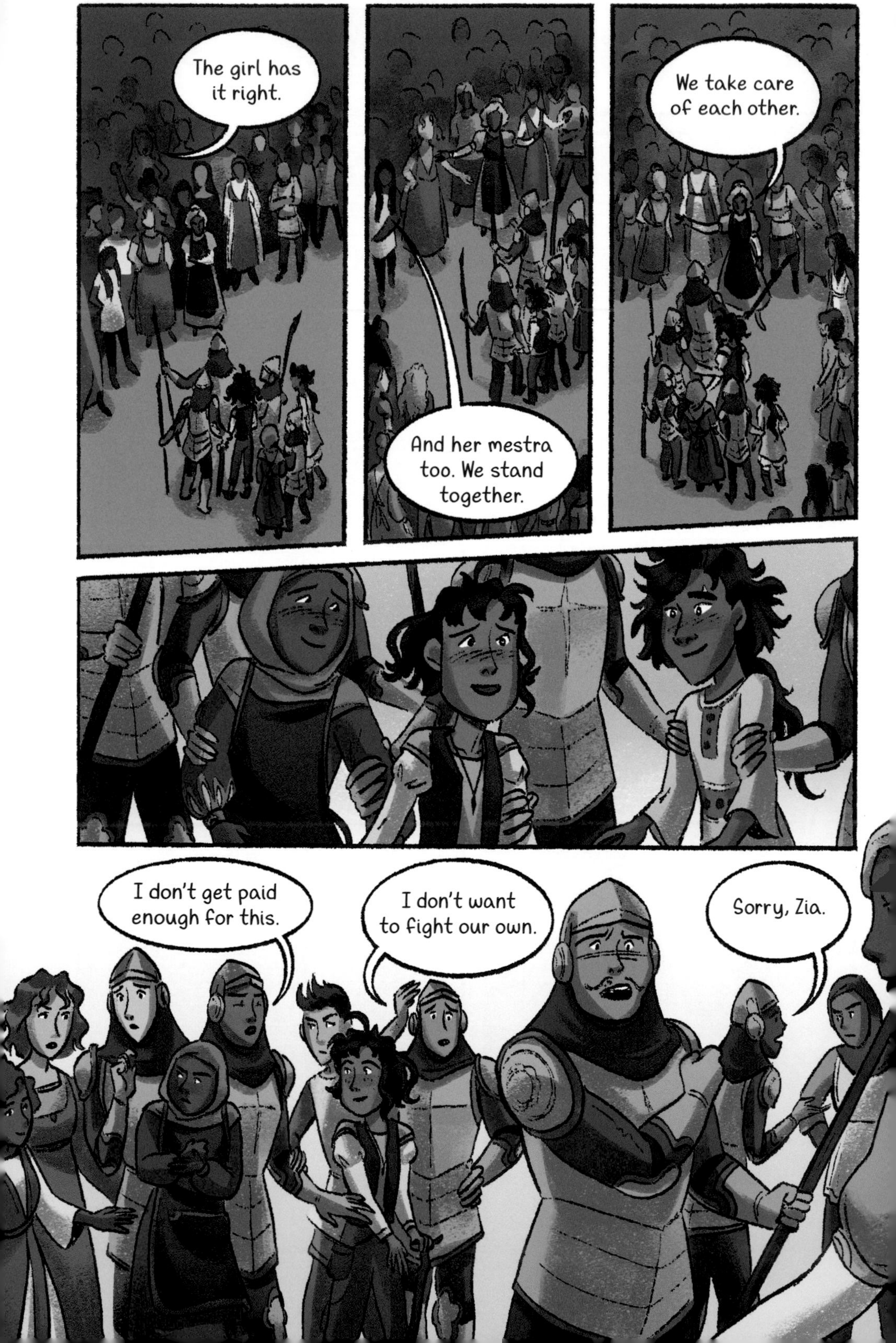
The girl has it right.
And her mestra too. We stand together.
We take care of each other.
I don't get paid enough for this.
I don't want to fight our own.
Sorry, Zia.

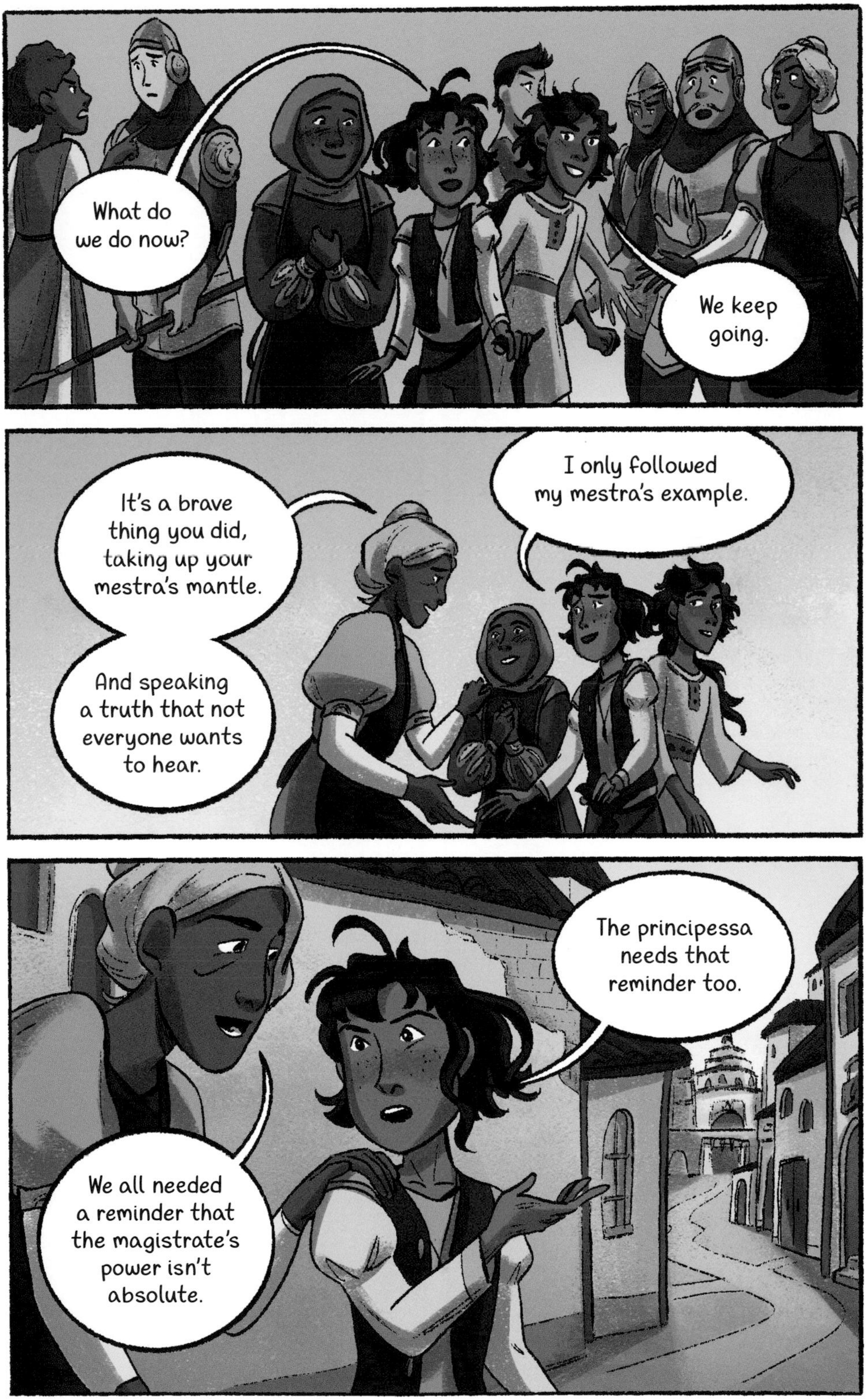
What do we do now?
We keep going.
It's a brave thing you did, taking up your mestra's mantle.
And speaking a truth that not everyone wants to hear.
I only followed my mestra's example.
We all needed a reminder that the magistrate's power isn't absolute.
The principessa needs that reminder too.

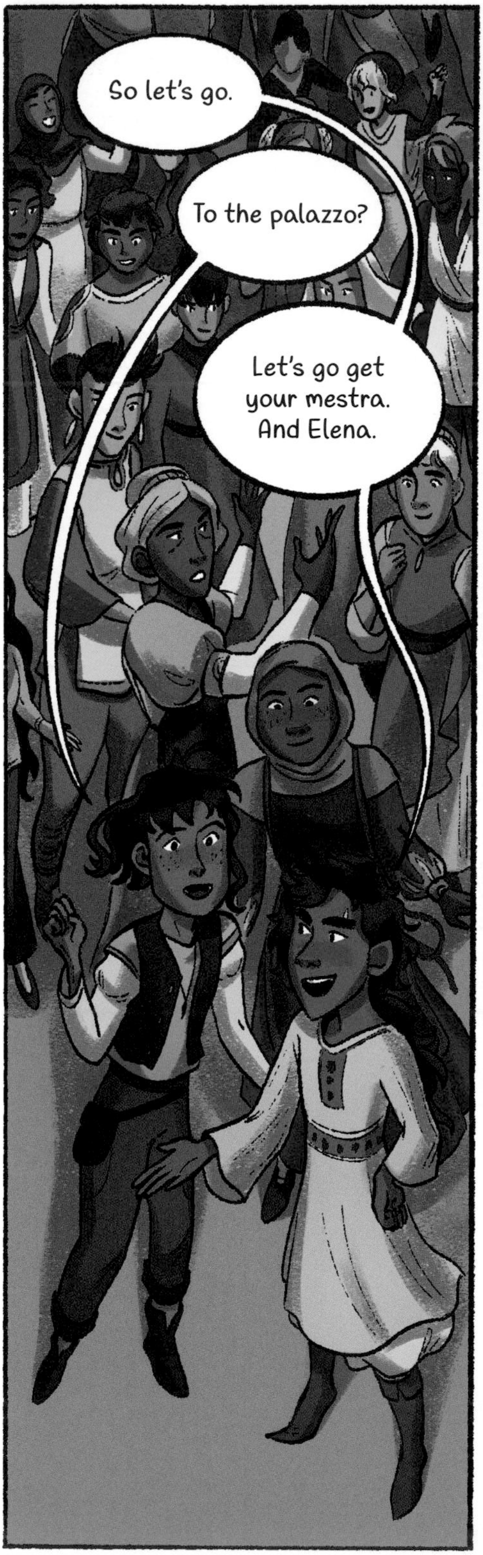
So let's go.
To the palazzo?
Let's go get your mestra. And Elena.

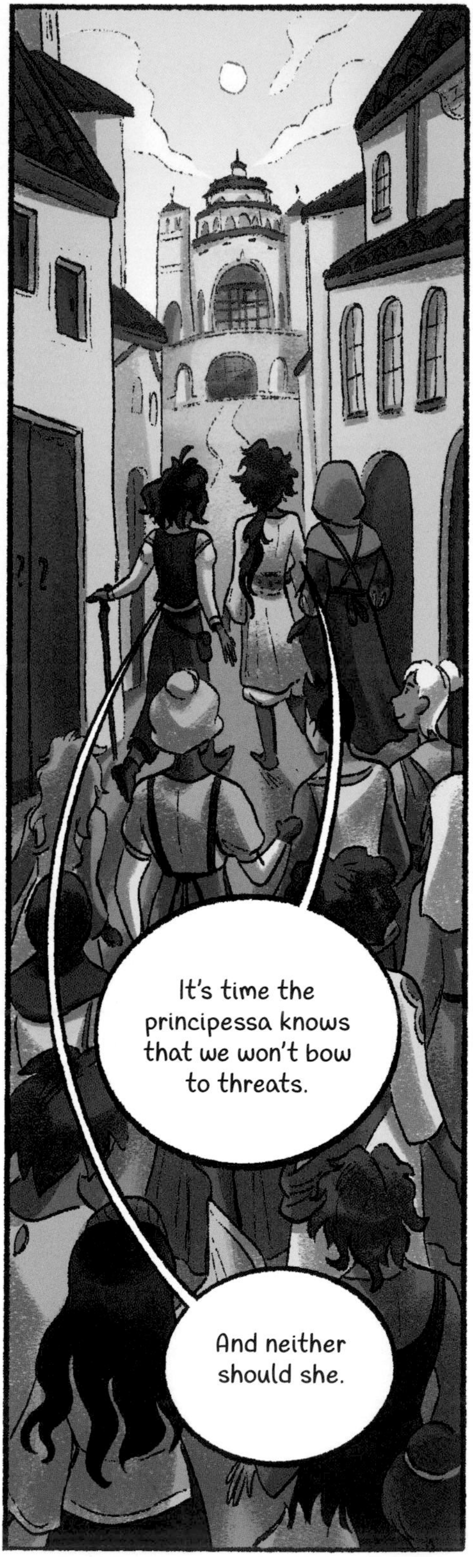
It's time the principessa knows that we won't bow to threats.
And neither should she.

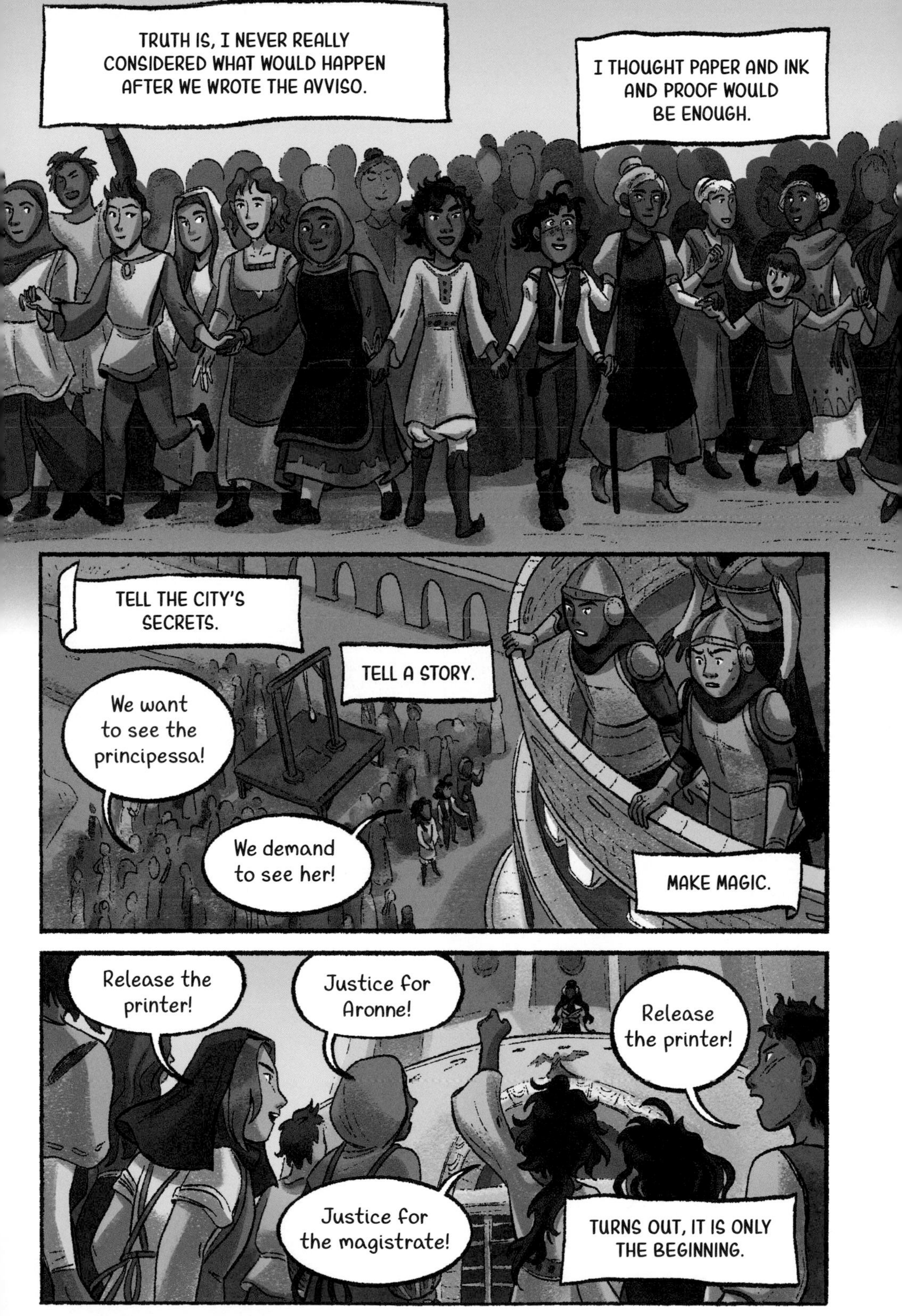
TRUTH IS, I NEVER REALLY CONSIDERED WHAT WOULD HAPPEN AFTER WE WROTE THE AVVISO.
I THOUGHT PAPER AND INK AND PROOF WOULD BE ENOUGH.
TELL THE CITY'S SECRETS.
TELL A STORY.
We want to see the principessa!
We demand to see her!
MAKE MAGIC.
Release the printer!
Justice for Aronne!
Release the printer!
Justice for the magistrate!
TURNS OUT, IT IS ONLY THE BEGINNING.

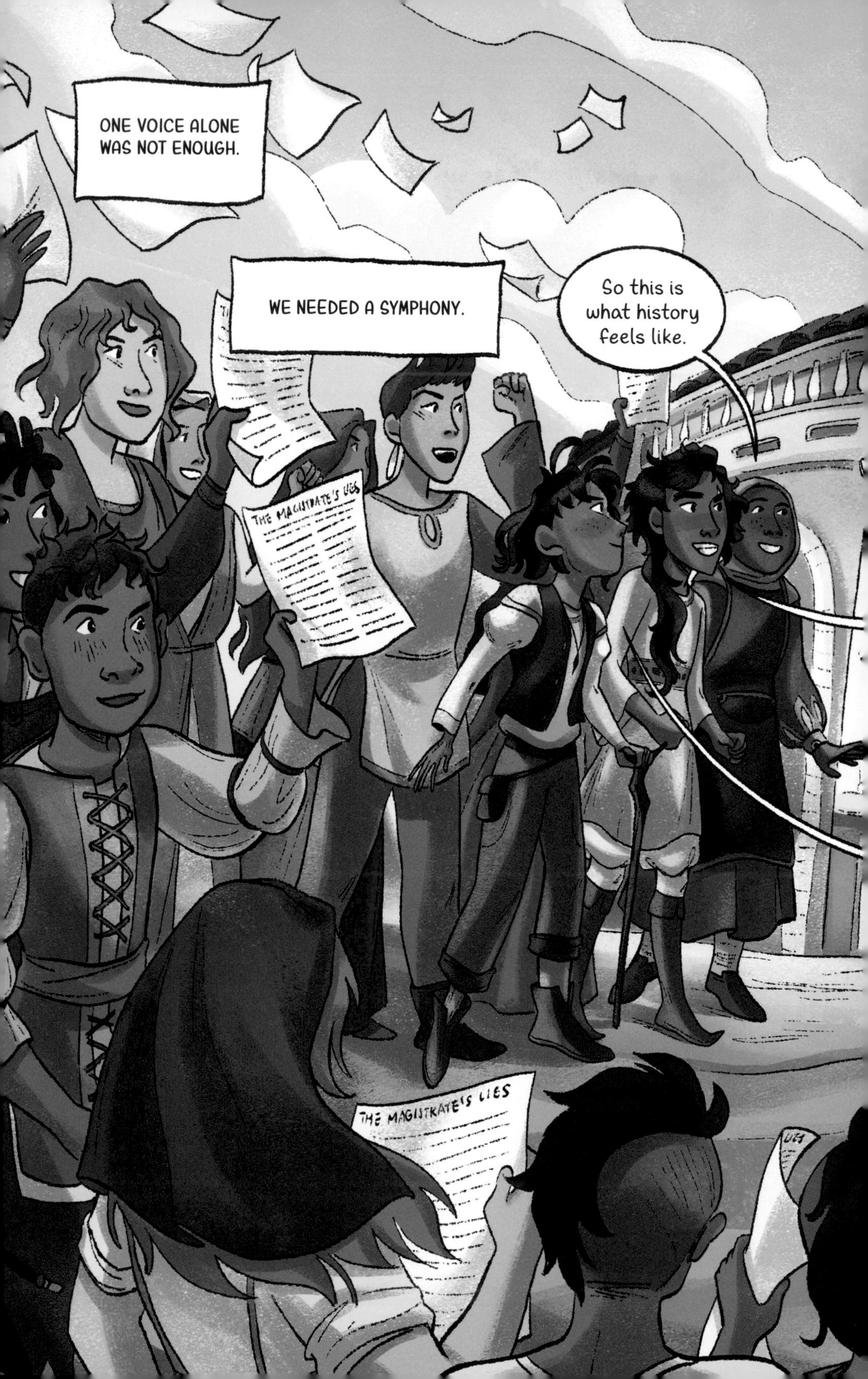
ONE VOICE ALONE WAS NOT ENOUGH.
WE NEEDED A SYMPHONY.
So this is what history feels like.
THE MAGISTRATE'S LIES
THE MAGISTRATE'S LIES

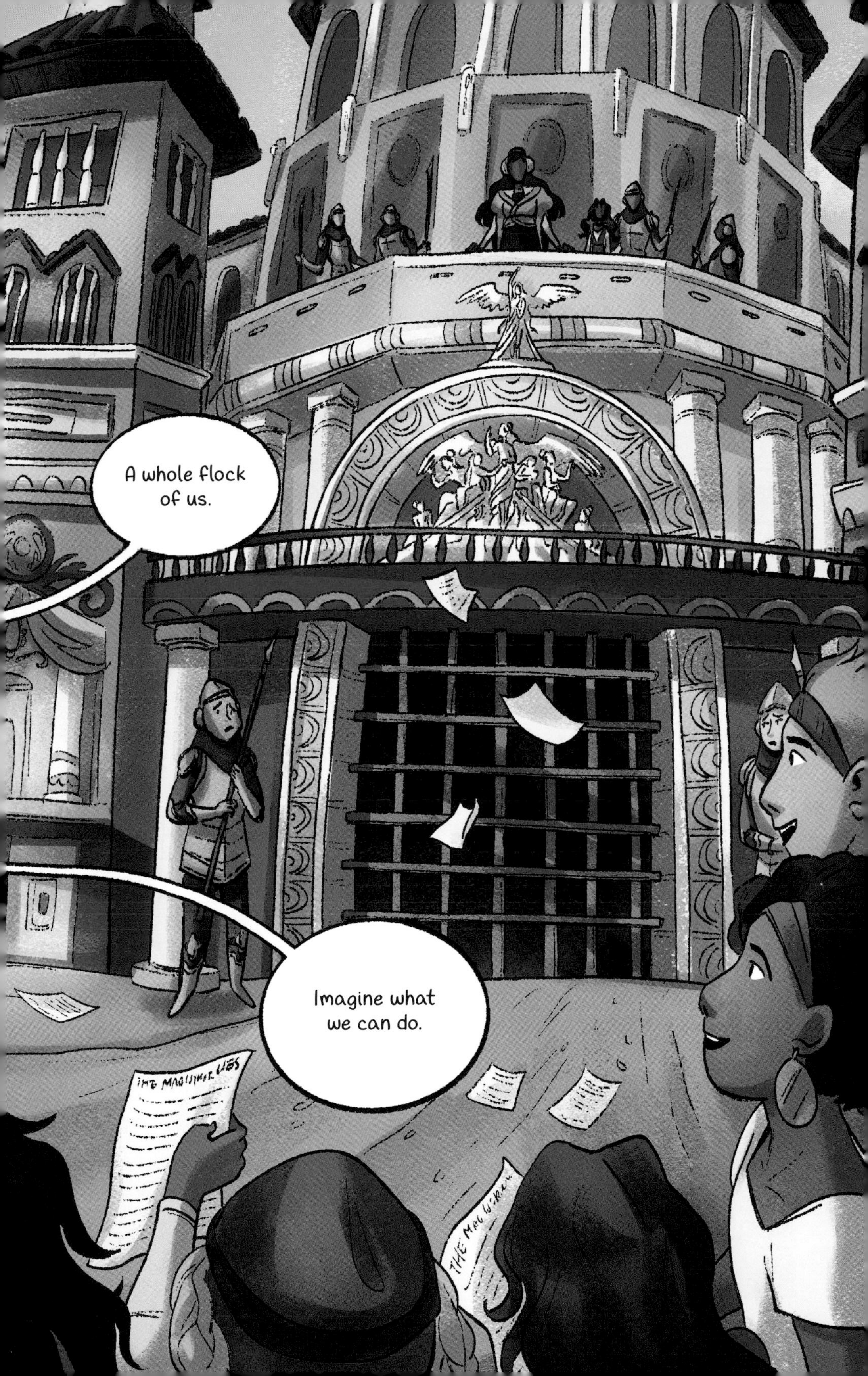
A whole flock of us.
Imagine what we can do.

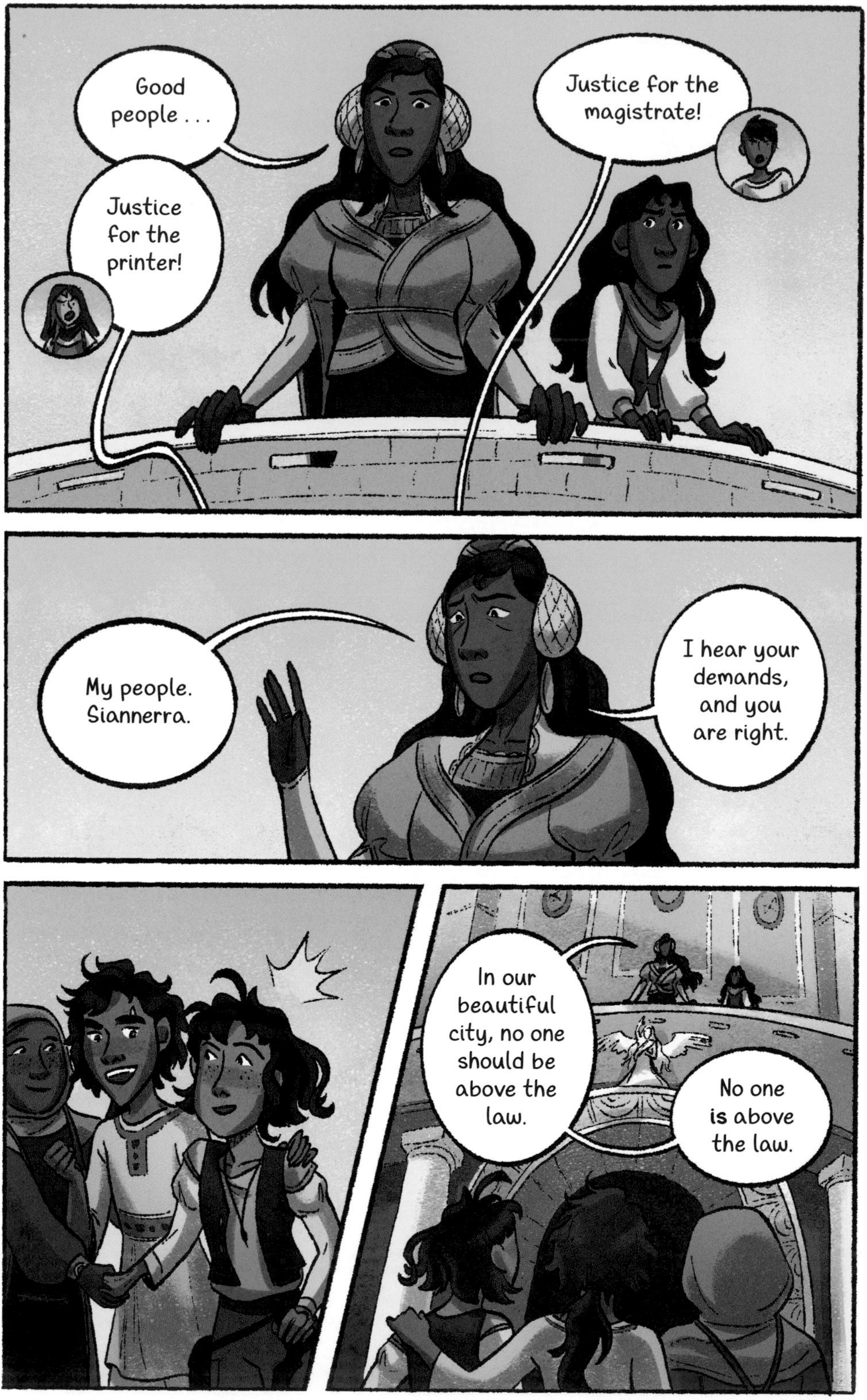
Good people . . .
Justice for the printer!
Justice for the magistrate!
My people. Siannerra.
I hear your demands, and you are right.
In our beautiful city, no one should be above the law.
No one **is** above the law.

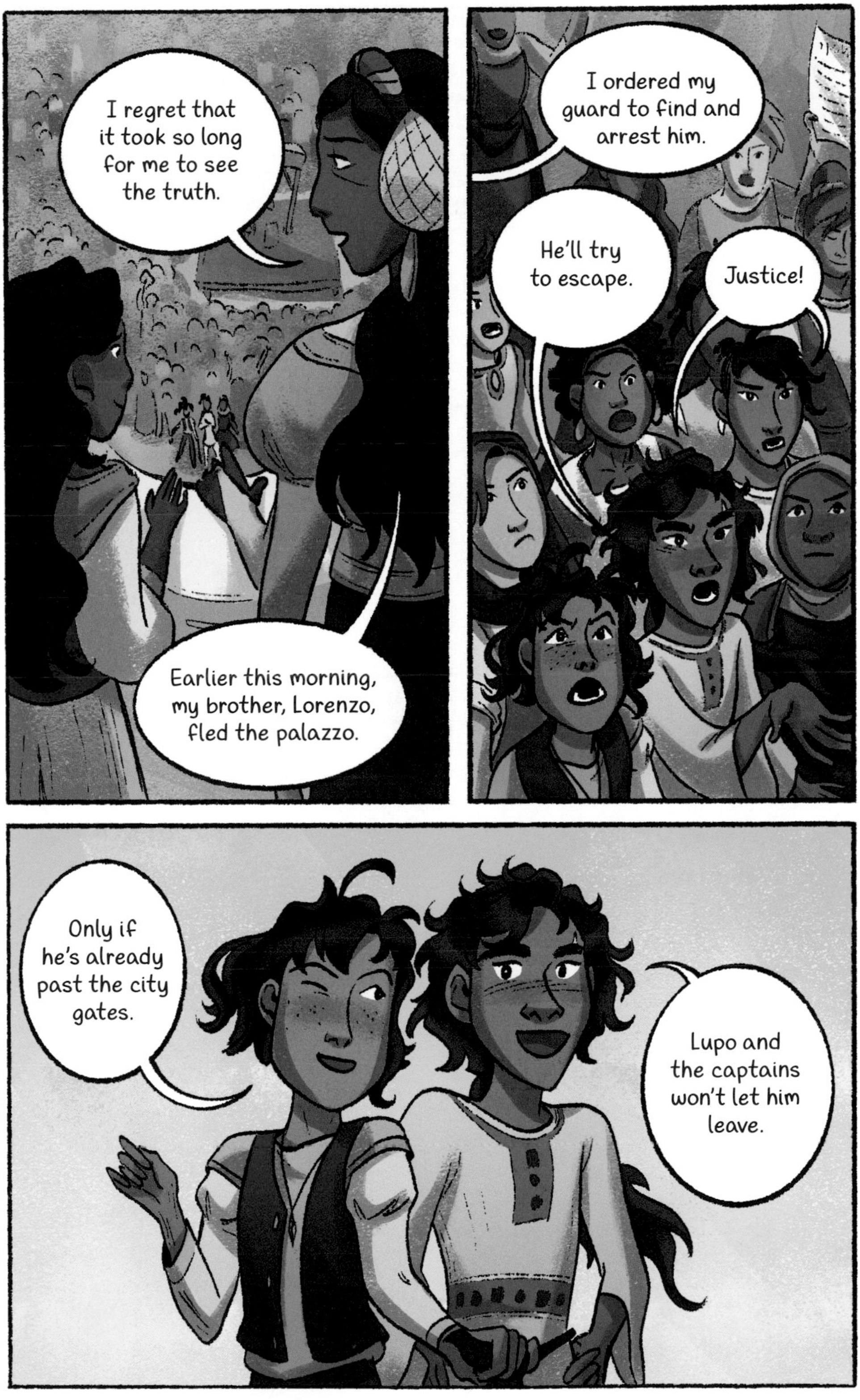
I regret that it took so long for me to see the truth.
Earlier this morning, my brother, Lorenzo, fled the palazzo.
I ordered my guard to find and arrest him.
He'll try to escape.
Justice!
Only if he's already past the city gates.
Lupo and the captains won't let him leave.

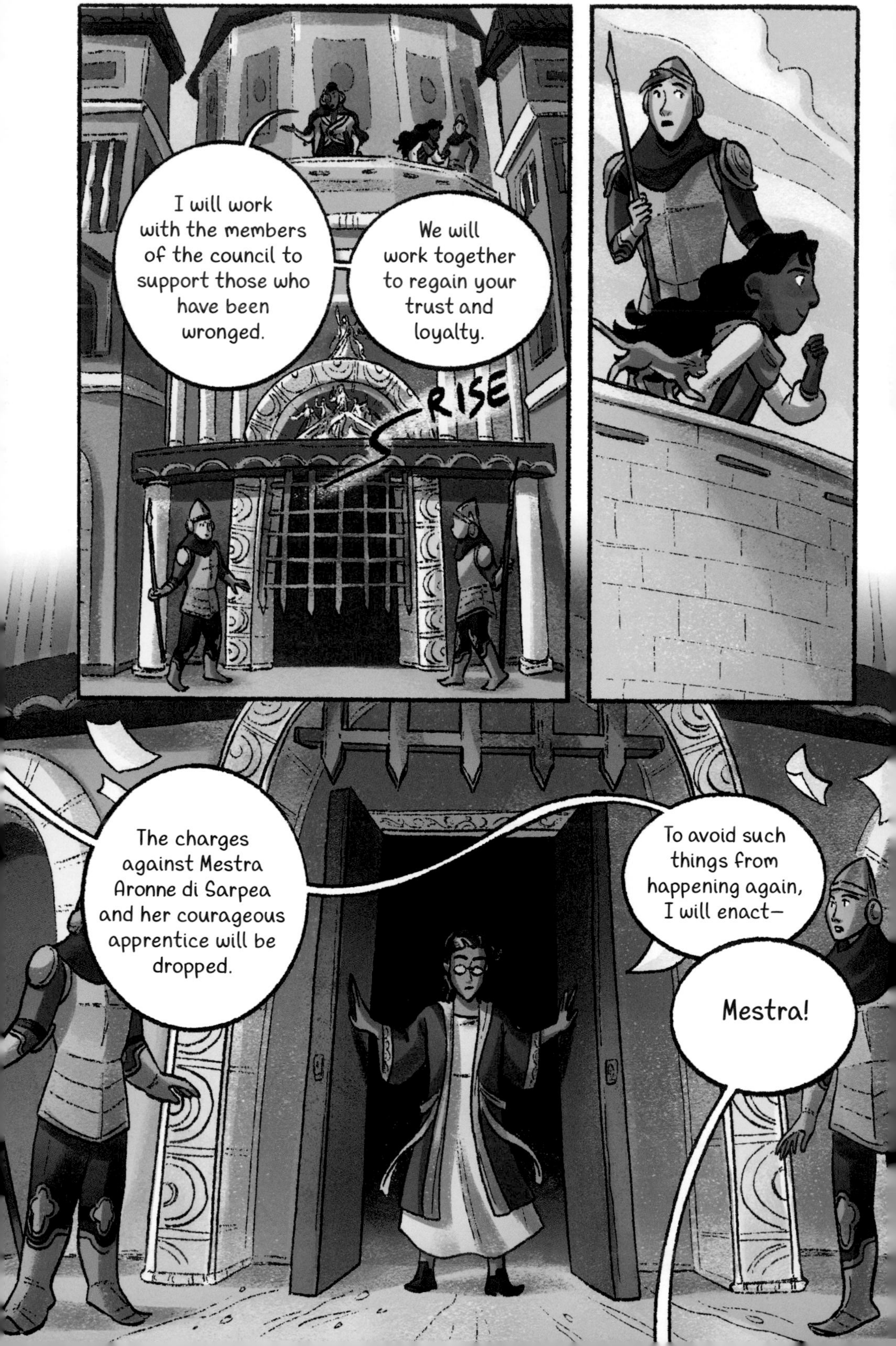

I will work with the members of the council to support those who have been wronged.
We will work together to regain your trust and loyalty.
RISE
The charges against Mestra Aronne di Sarpea and her courageous apprentice will be dropped.
To avoid such things from happening again, I will enact—
Mestra!

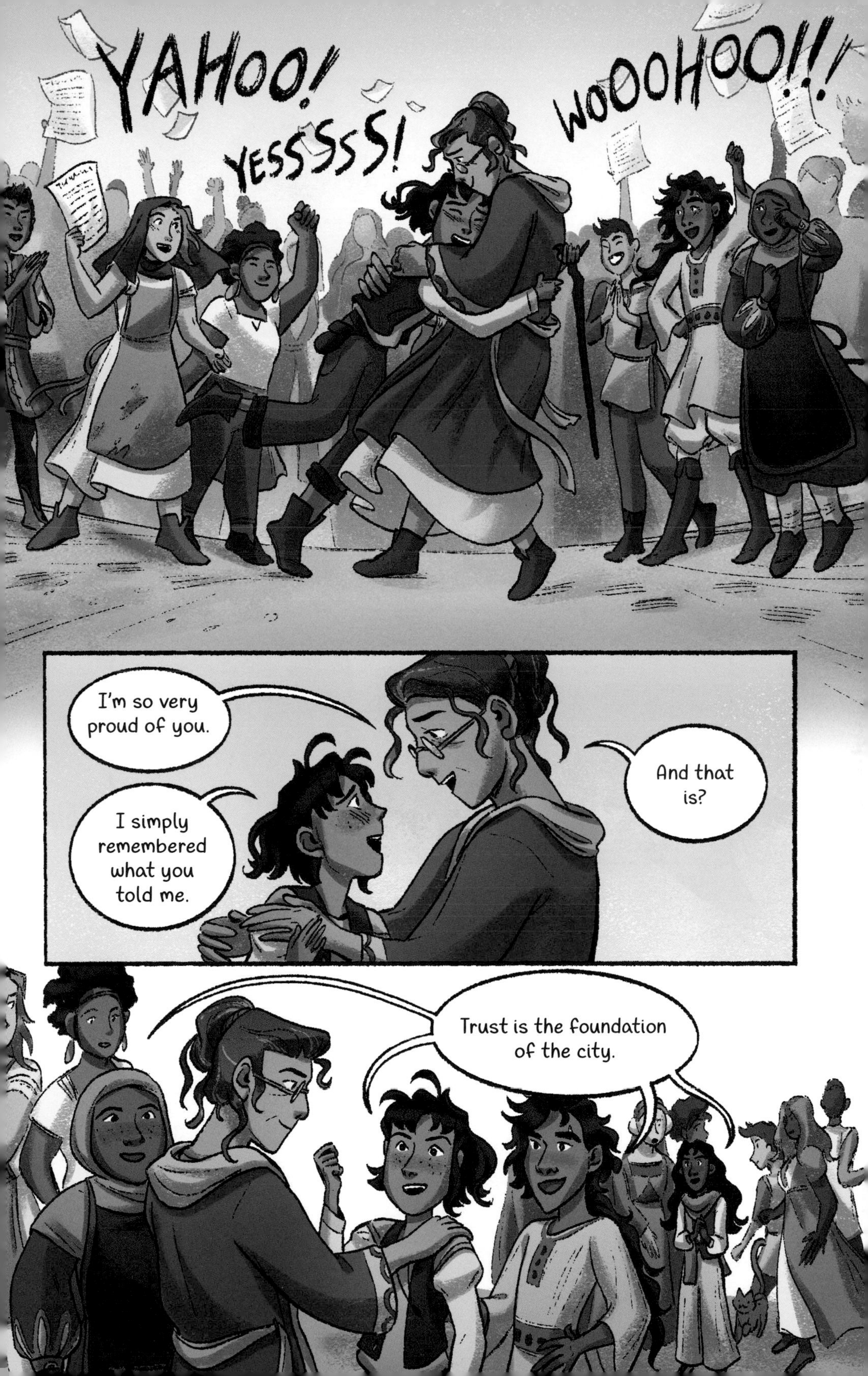
YAHOO!
YESSSsS!
WoOOHOO!!!
I'm so very proud of you.
I simply remembered what you told me.
And that is?
Trust is the foundation of the city.

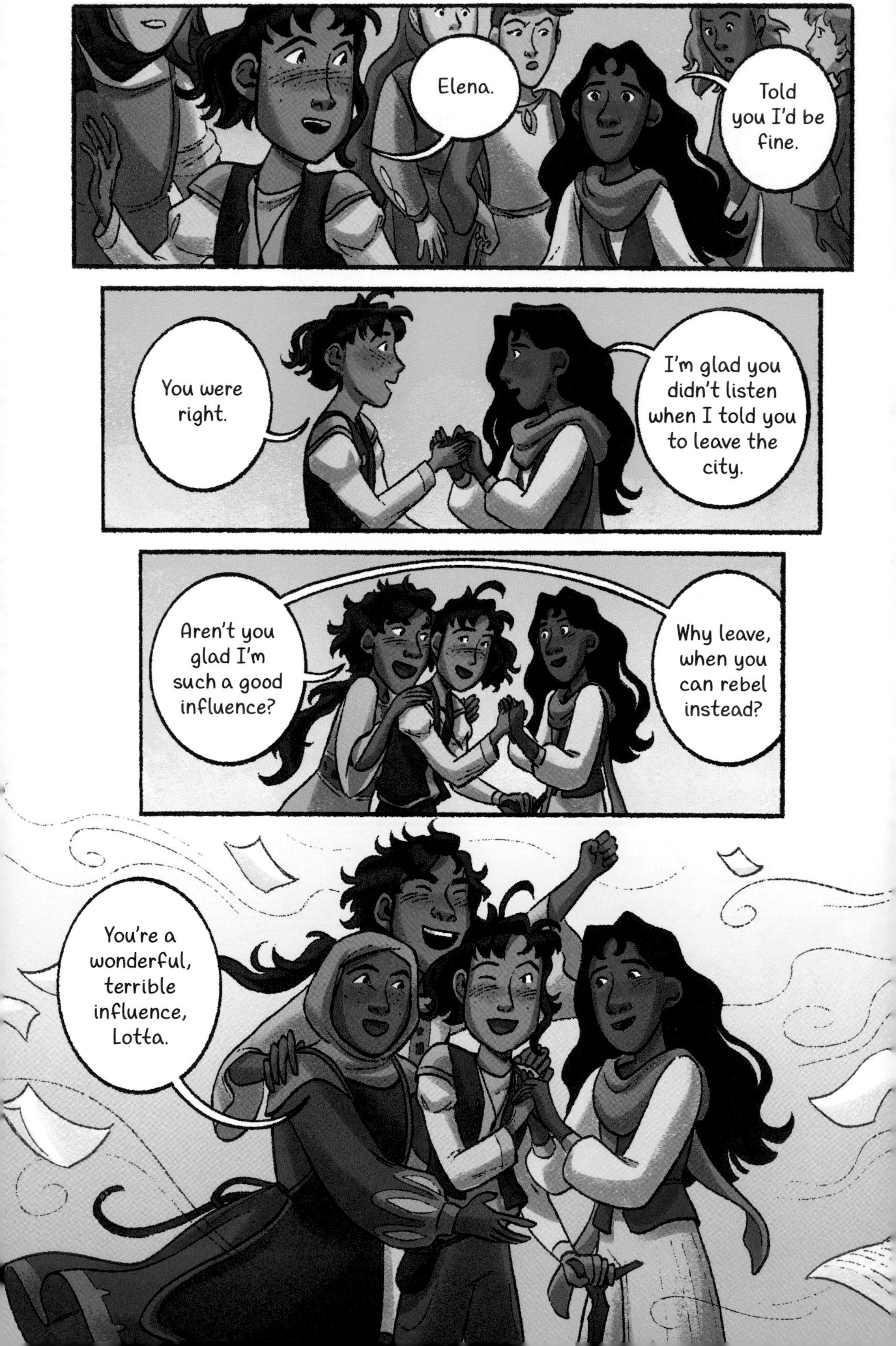
Elena.
Told you I'd be fine.
You were right.
I'm glad you didn't listen when I told you to leave the city.
Aren't you glad I'm such a good influence?
Why leave, when you can rebel instead?
You're a wonderful, terrible influence, Lotta.

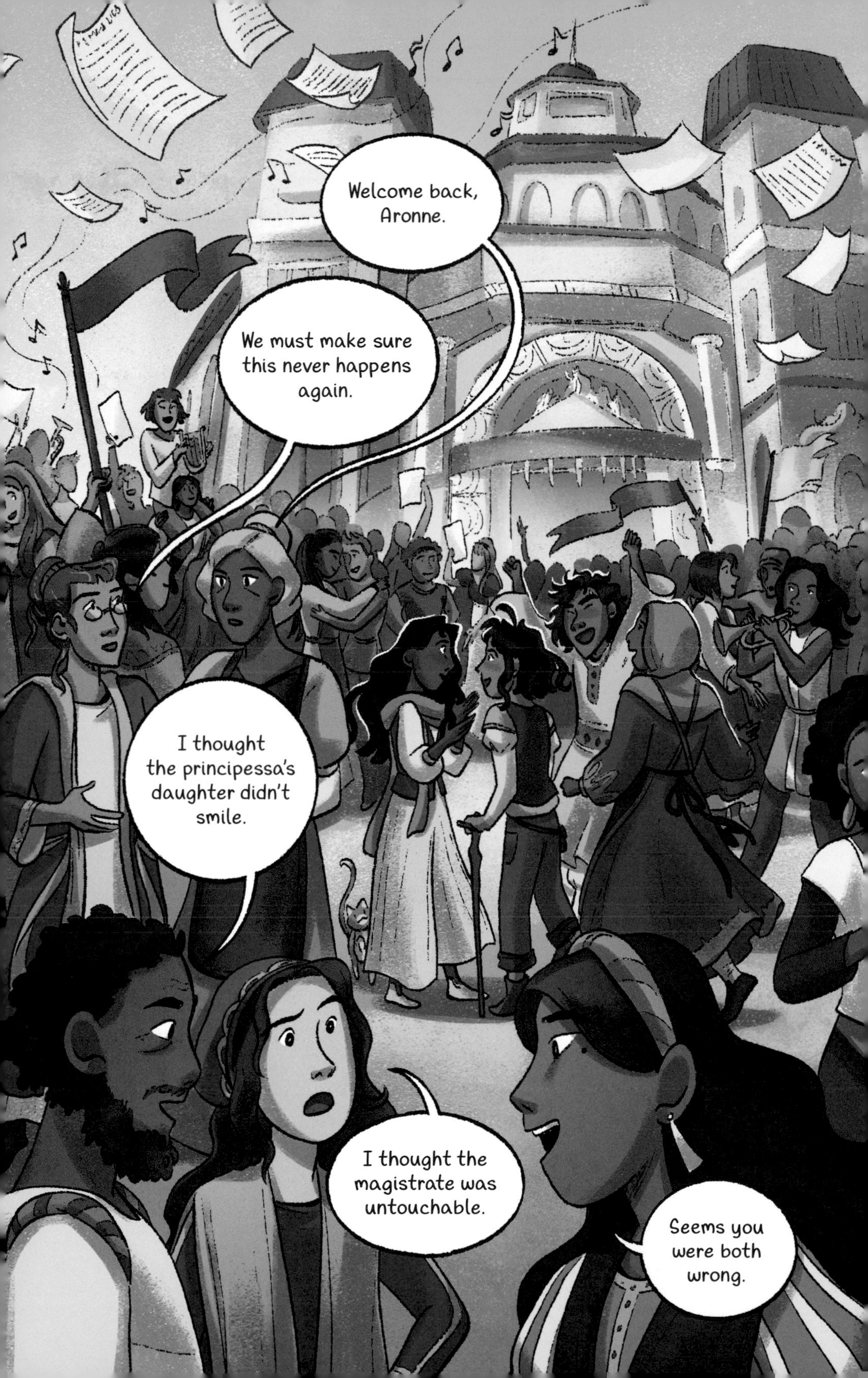
Welcome back, Aronne.
We must make sure this never happens again.
I thought the principessa's daughter didn't smile.
I thought the magistrate was untouchable.
Seems you were both wrong.

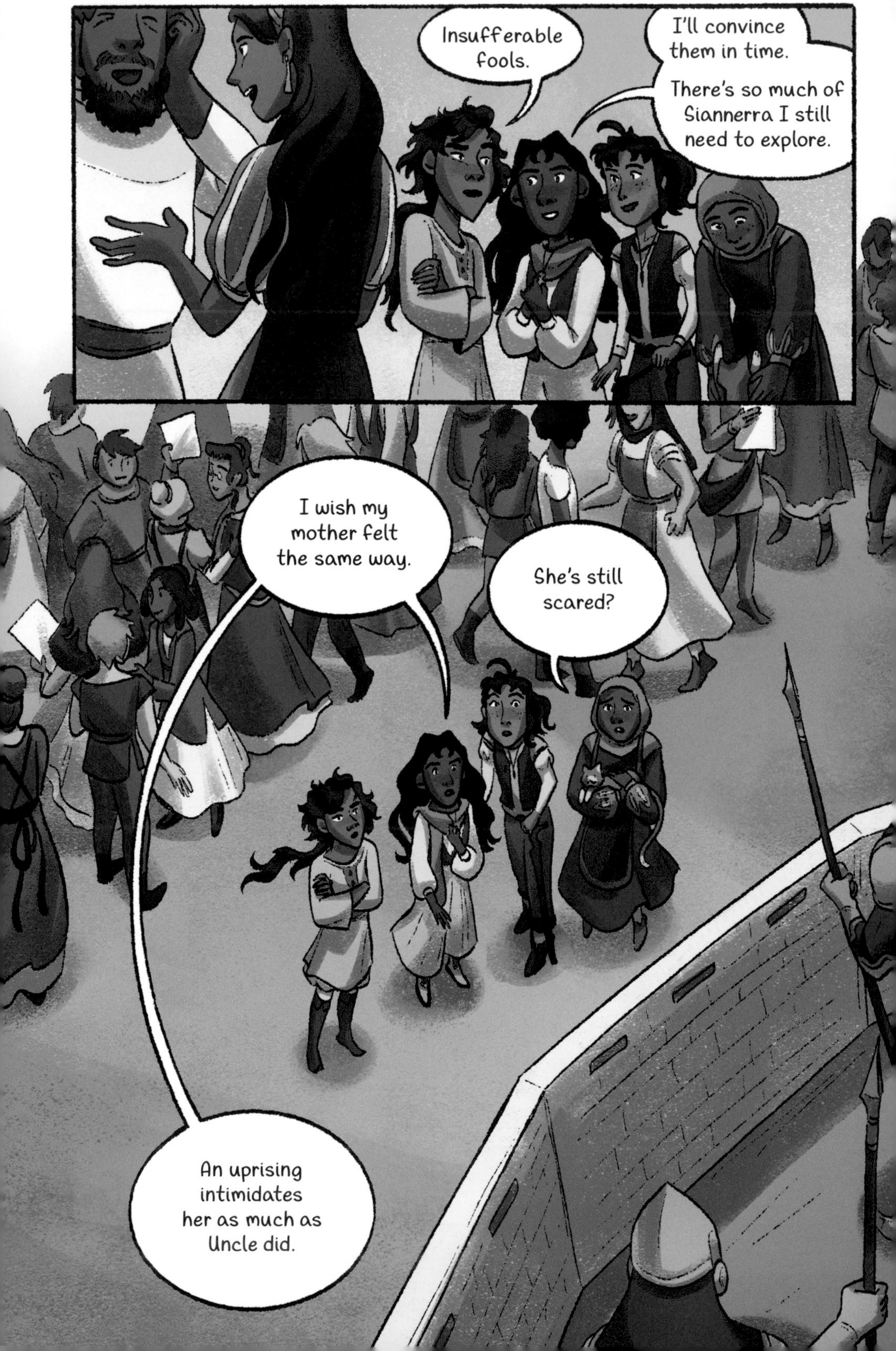
Insufferable fools.
I'll convince them in time.
There's so much of Siannerra I still need to explore.
I wish my mother felt the same way.
She's still scared?
An uprising intimidates her as much as Uncle did.

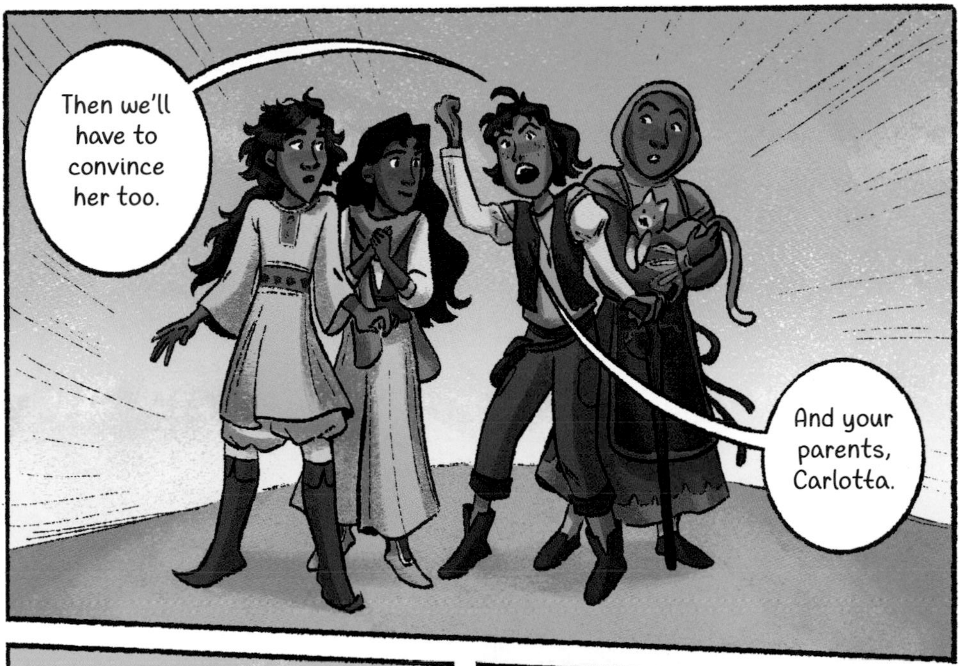
Then we'll have to convince her too.
And your parents, Carlotta.

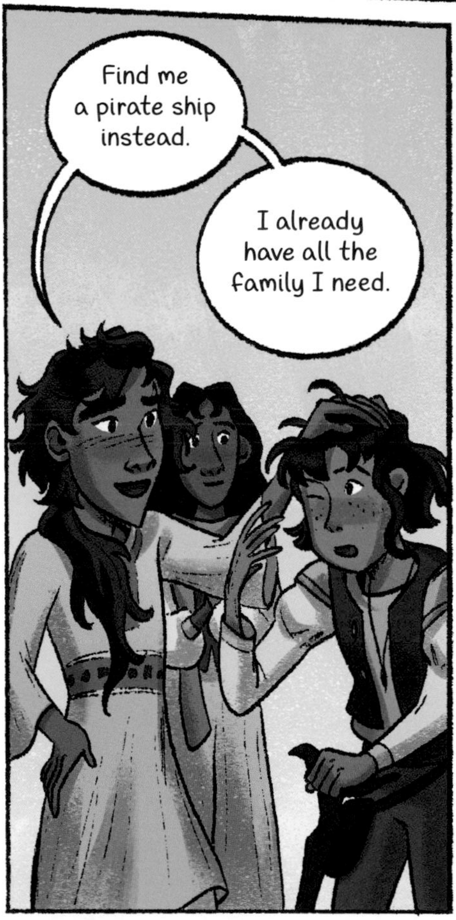
Find me a pirate ship instead.
I already have all the family I need.

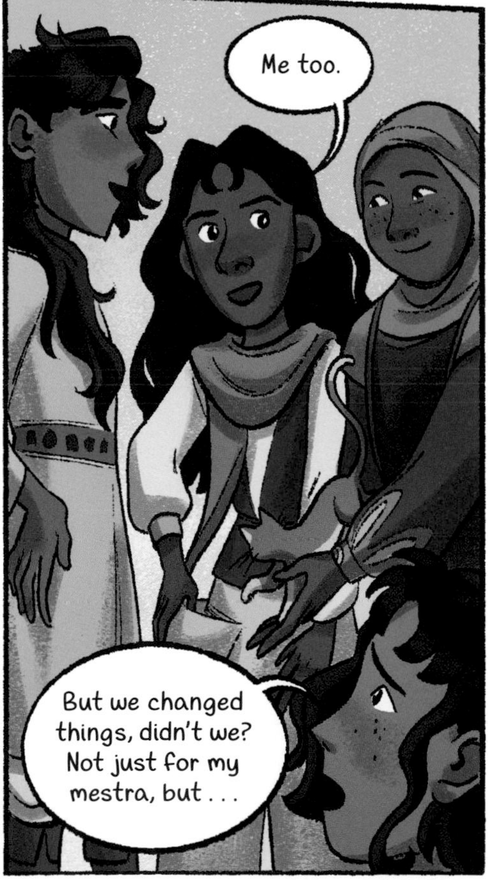
Me too.
But we changed things, didn't we? Not just for my mestra, but . . .

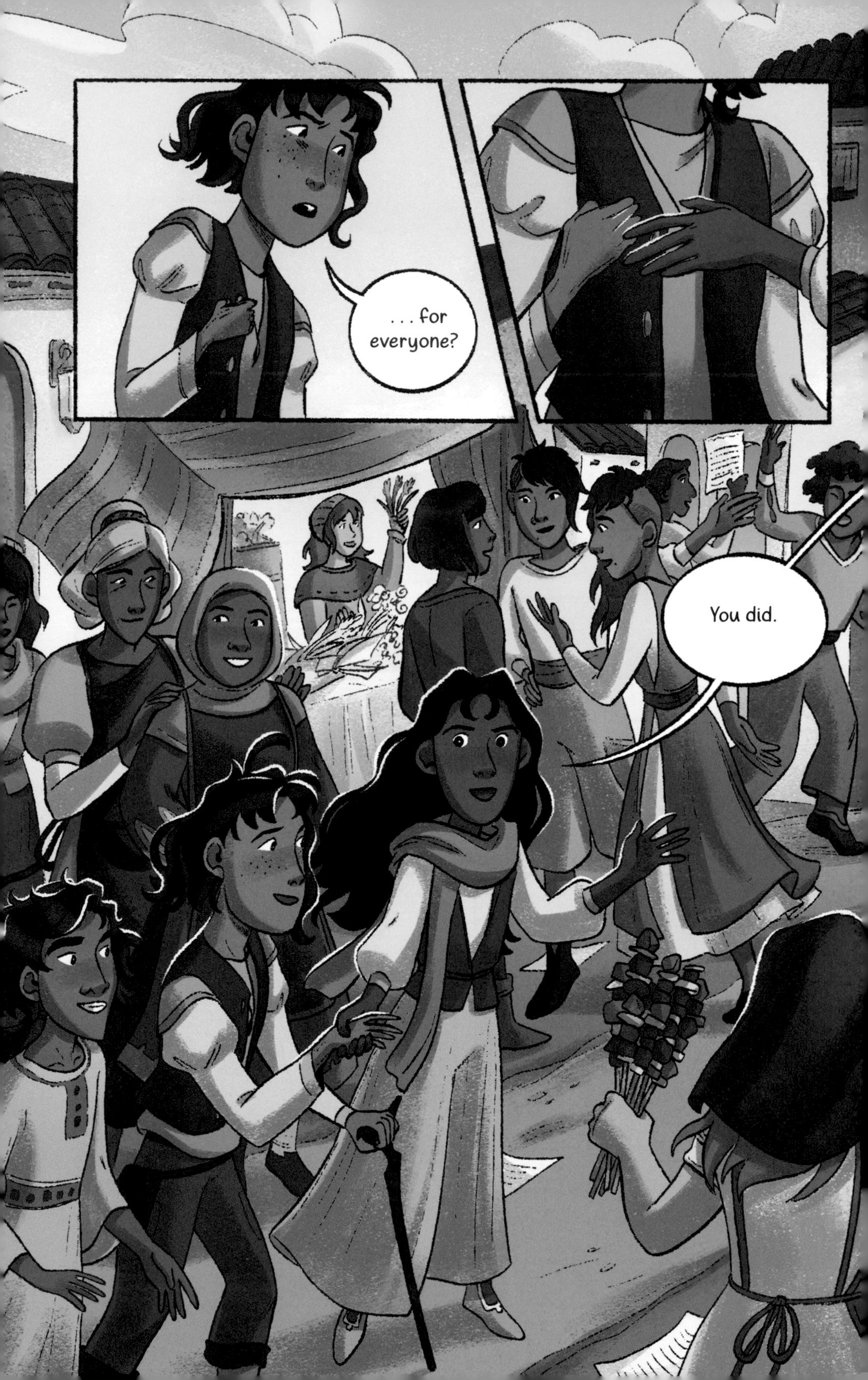
. . . for everyone?
You did.

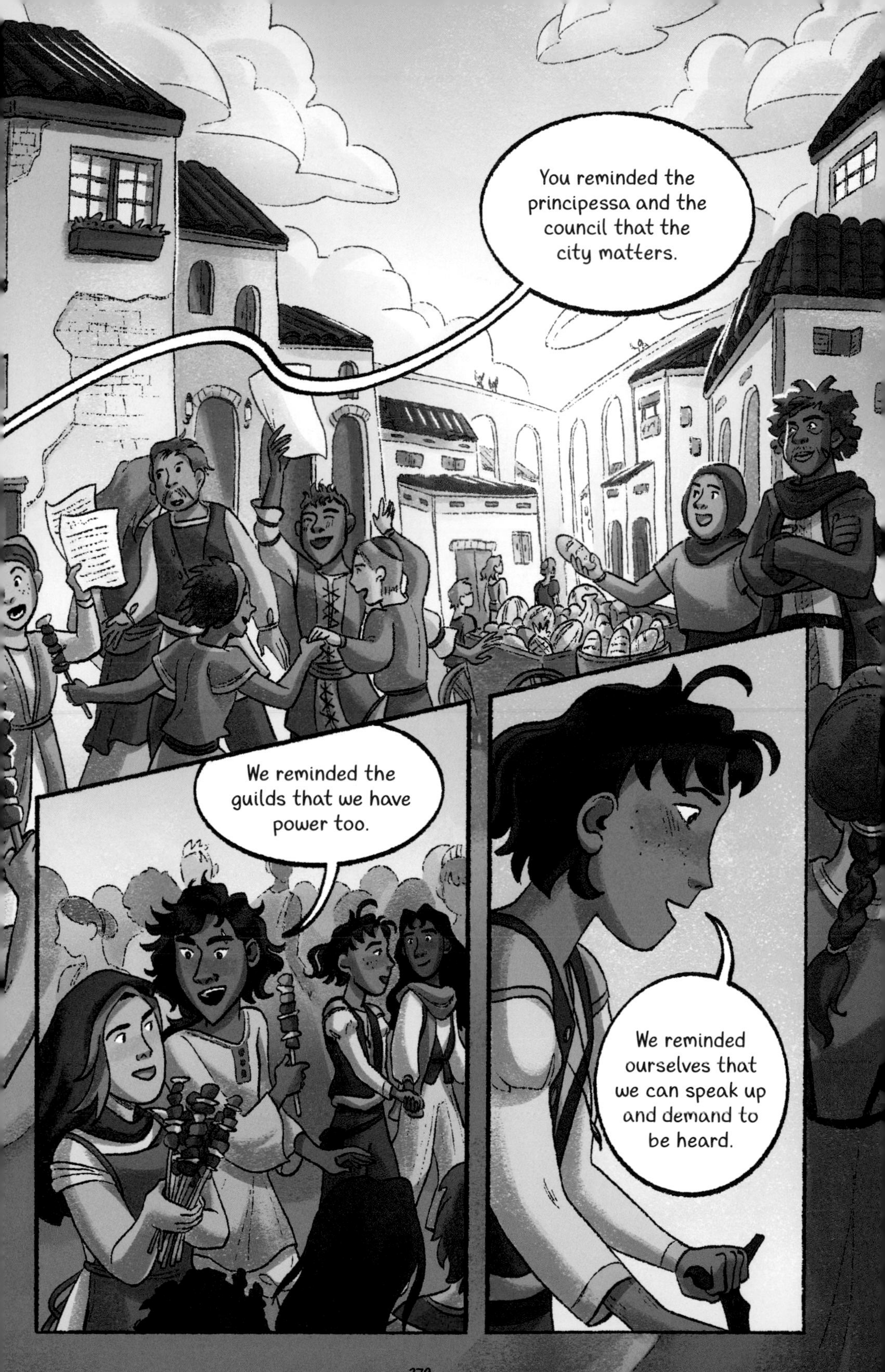
You reminded the principessa and the council that the city matters.
We reminded the guilds that we have power too.
We reminded ourselves that we can speak up and demand to be heard.

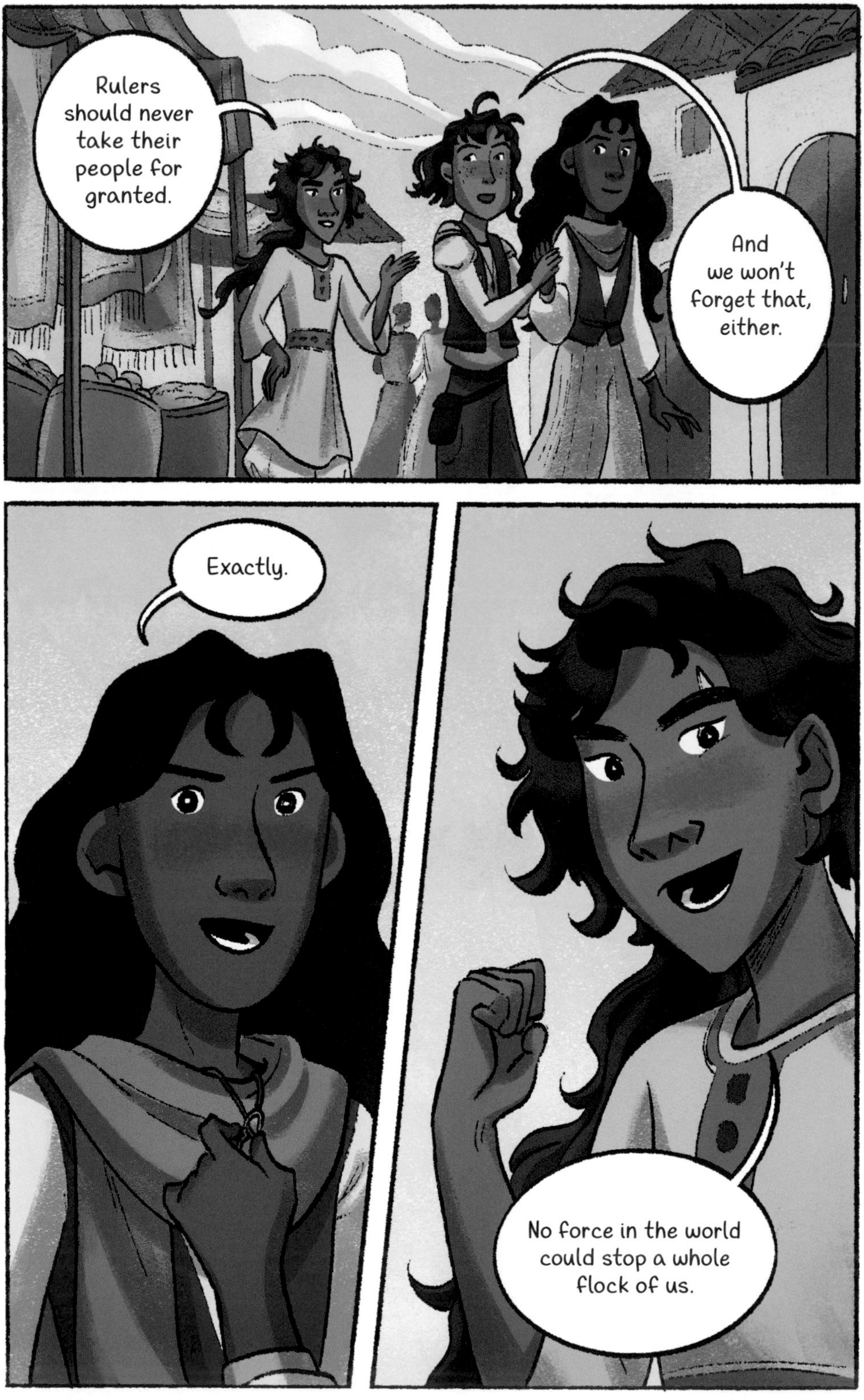
Rulers should never take their people for granted.
And we won't forget that, either.
Exactly.
No force in the world could stop a whole flock of us.

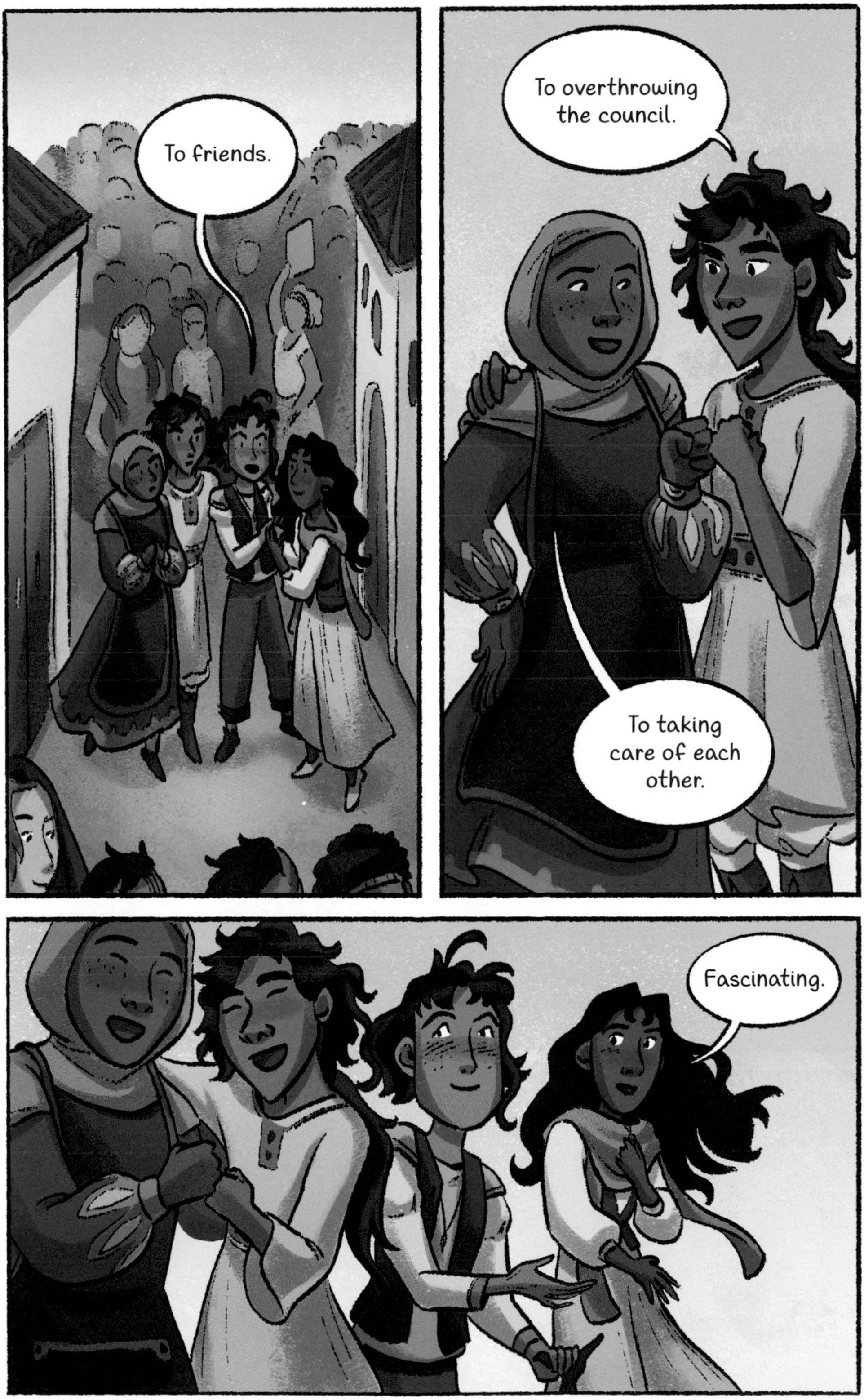
To friends.
To overthrowing the council.
To taking care of each other.
Fascinating.

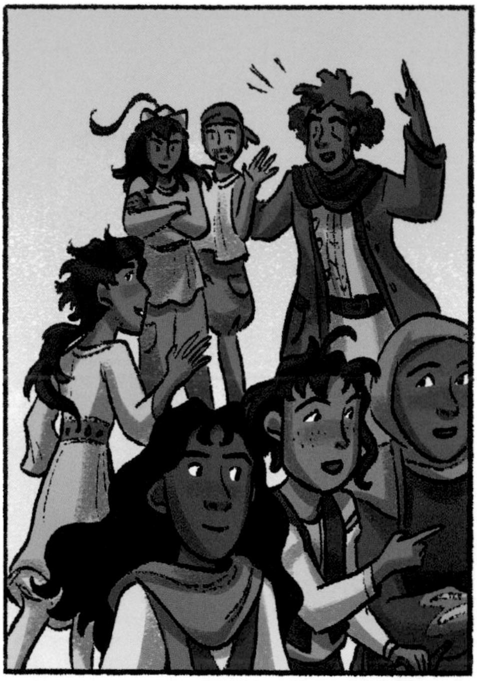

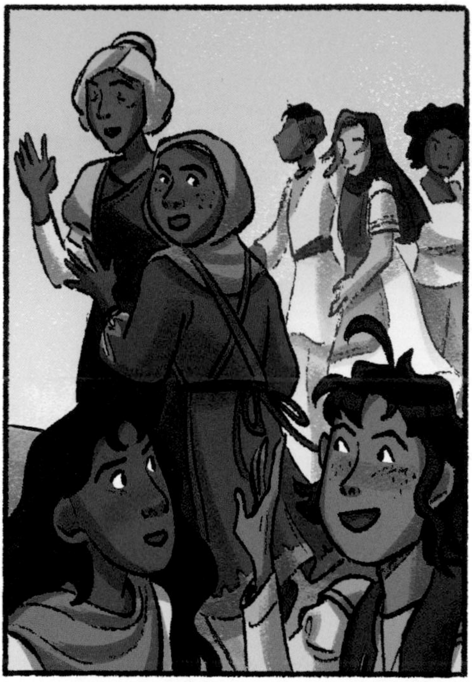

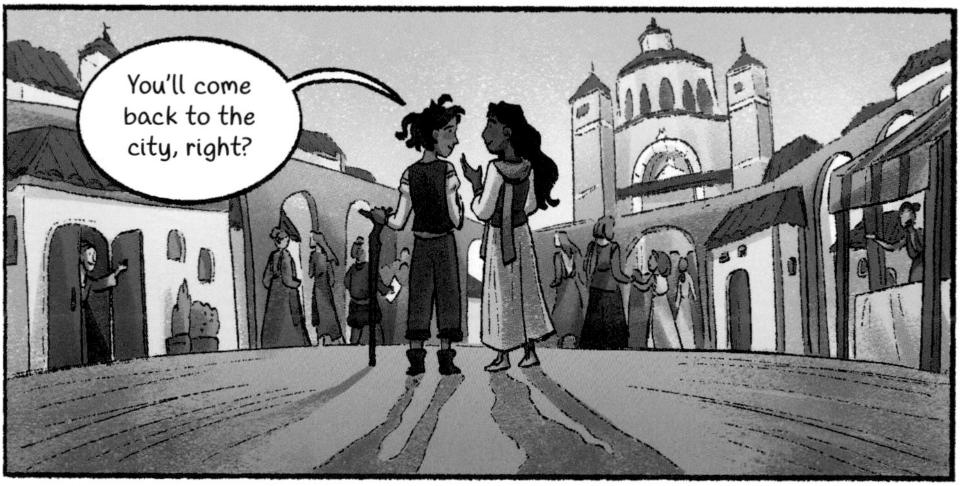
You'll come back to the city, right?

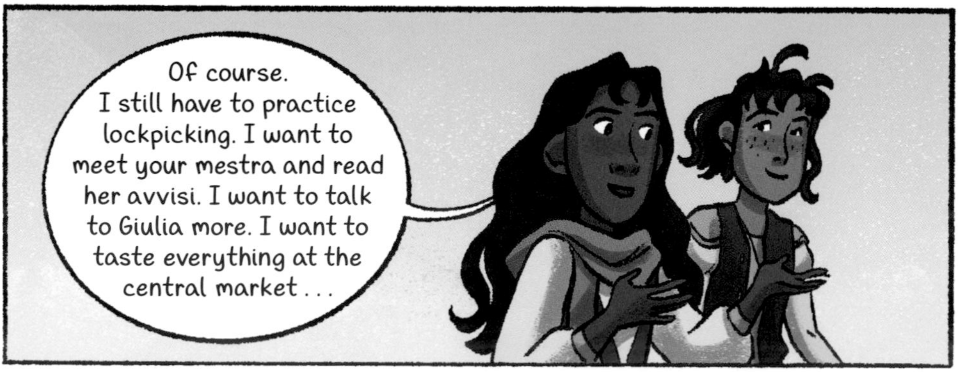
Of course. I still have to practice lockpicking. I want to meet your mestra and read her avvisi. I want to talk to Giulia more. I want to taste everything at the central market . . .

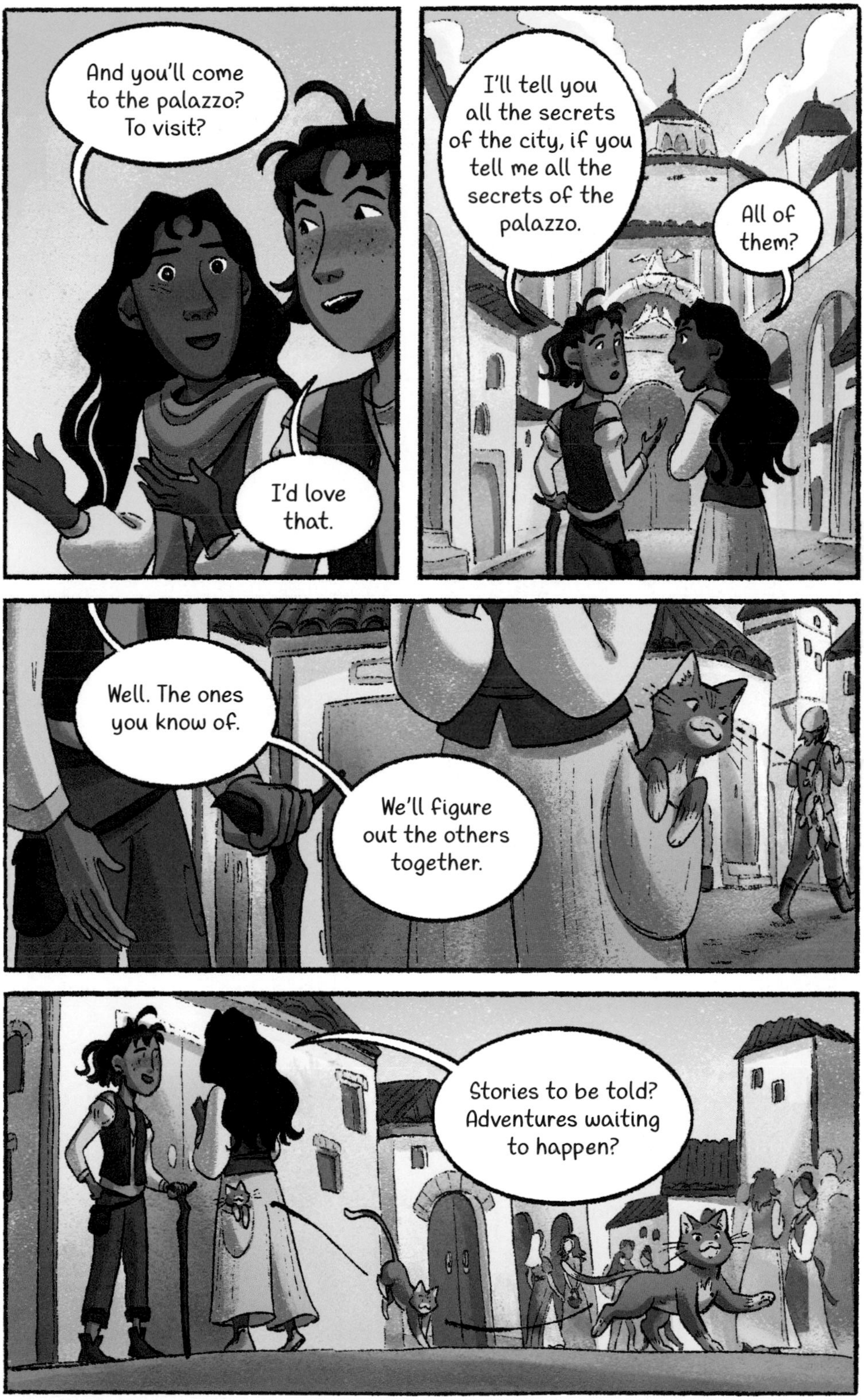
And you'll come to the palazzo? To visit?
I'd love that.
I'll tell you all the secrets of the city, if you tell me all the secrets of the palazzo.
All of them?
Well. The ones you know of.
We'll figure out the others together.
Stories to be told? Adventures waiting to happen?

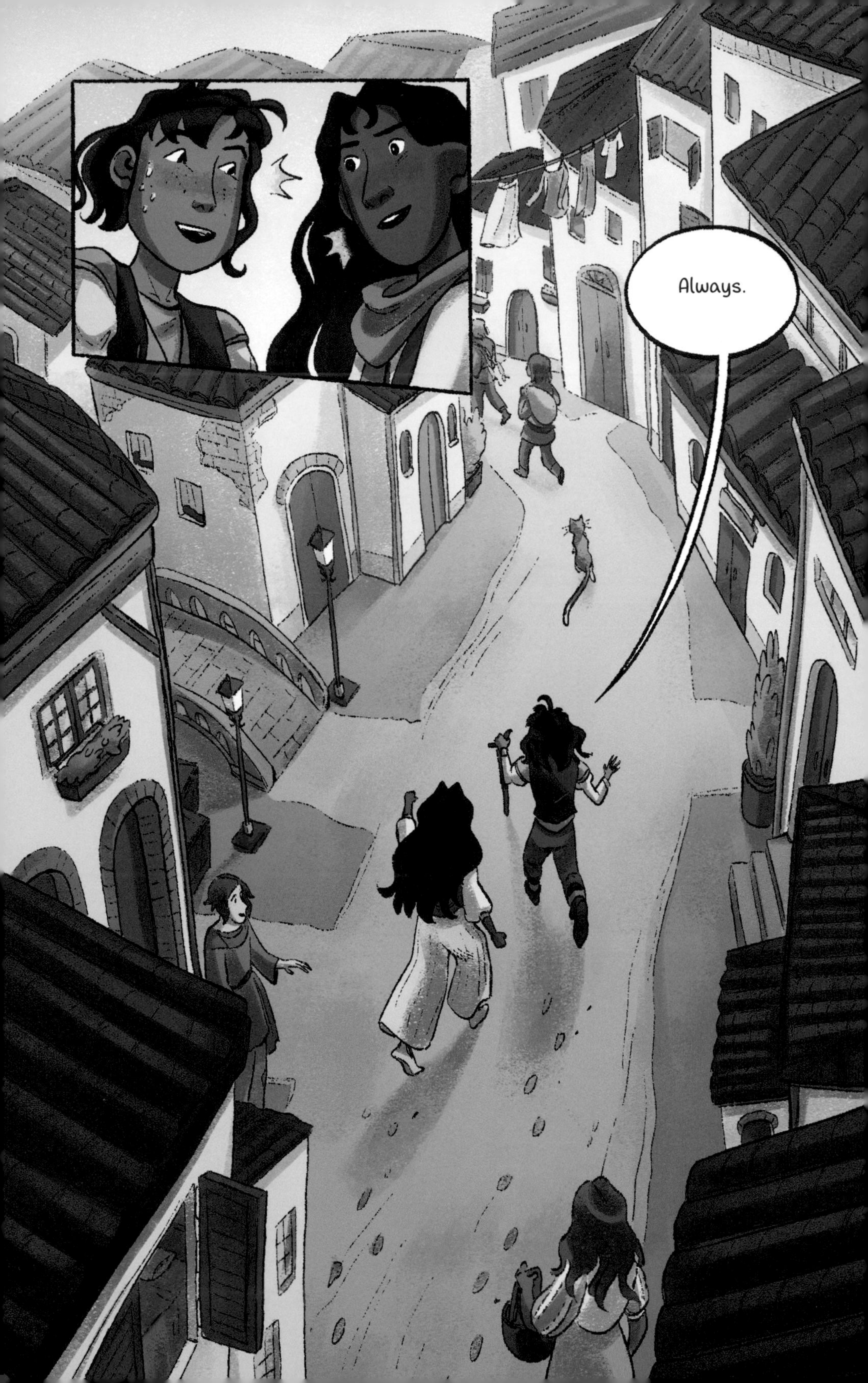
Always.